TER[illegible]ON

"The author's attention to detail and authenticity, coupled with his ability to spin a darned good yarn, makes it easy to see why Johnston is today's best-selling frontier novelist. He's one of a handful that truly knows the territory."
—*Chicago Tribune*

"Rich in historical lore and dramatic description, this is a first-rate addition to a solid series, a rousing tale of one man's search for independence in the unspoiled beauty of the Old West."
—*Publishers Weekly* on *Buffalo Palace*

"A first-class novel by a talented author."
—*Tulsa World* on *Dream Catcher*

"With meticulous research, vivid dialogue, memorable characters, and a voice uniquely his own, Johnston has once again written the finest of historical fiction, seamlessly blending together both time and place to bring to life a world as real as our own."
—*Roundup Magazine* on *Dance on the Wind*

TURN THE PAGE FOR MORE ACCLAIM . . .

Praise for *LAY THE MOUNTAINS LOW*

"Among novelists, Terry Johnston knows more about America's Indian wars than any other writer. From his first novel, *Carry the Wind*, in 1982, no writer has worked harder than Johnston to make a name for himself in the difficult and much-besieged field of Western fiction, and no other writer since Louis L'Amour has come close to Johnston's success. Read *Lay the Mountains Low* to see why."
—Dale Walker, *Rocky Mountain News*

"You are there, you are really there in Johnston's largest, most complex work: an apt hardcover debut in the series."
—*Booklist*

"Johnston is a skilled storyteller whose words ring with the desperation, confusion and utter horror of a fight to the death between mortal enemies. This is uncomfortable history, and it hits home like a blunt instrument."
—*Publishers Weekly*

"Compelling . . . Johnston offers memorable characters, a great deal of history and lore about the Indians and pioneers of the period, and a deep insight into human nature, Indian and white."

—*Booklist*

"A remarkably fine blend of arduous historical research and proficient use of language."

—*Colorado Springs Gazette Telegraph*

"Terry C. Johnston pierces the heart and soul of the 19th century men and women he writes about so well, capturing in unforgettable and gracious stories the joys and agonies of the great westward expansion of a young America . . . he will make your heart sing."

—Richard S. Wheeler, Spur Award–winning author of *Sierra*

"Excellent . . . very forceful and moving."

—Turner Kirkland, *Dixie Gun Works*

The Plainsmen series by Terry C. Johnston

Book I: Sioux Dawn
Book II: Red Cloud's Revenge
Book III: The Stalkers
Book IV: Black Sun
Book V: Devil's Backbone
Book VI: Shadow Riders
Book VII: Dying Thunder
Book VIII: Blood Song
Book IX: Reap the Whirlwind
Book X: Trumpet on the Land
Book XI: A Cold Day in Hell
Book XII: Wolf Mountain Moon
Book XIII: Ashes of Heaven
Book XIV: Cries from the Earth
Book XV: Lay the Mountains Low
Book XIV: Turn the Stars Upside Down

LAY THE MOUNTAINS LOW

THE FLIGHT OF THE NEZ PERCE FROM IDAHO AND THE BATTLE OF THE BIG HOLE, AUGUST 9–10, 1877

TERRY C. JOHNSTON

St. Martin's Paperbacks

LAY THE MOUNTAINS LOW

For information address St. Martin's Press, 175 Fifth Avenue, New York, NY 10010.

ISBN: 978-0-312-97310-0

Printed in the United States of America

St. Martin's Press hardcover edition / June 2000
St. Martin's Paperbacks edition / February 2001

St. Martin's Paperbacks are published by St. Martin's Press, 175 Fifth Avenue, New York, NY 10010.

10 9 8 7

Across the last fourteen years
as we collaborated on one
historically authentic and accurate
book cover after another,
we have forged a timeless and unbreakable bond
of friendship and camaraderie . . .
yet while I have been blessed to share his artwork
with my readers around the world,
I am even more honored this man
calls me friend—
I lovingly dedicate this heart-wrenching novel
of the turning point in the Nez Perce War to
that good ol' Virginia boy who is without peer:
my cover artist,
Lou Glanzman.

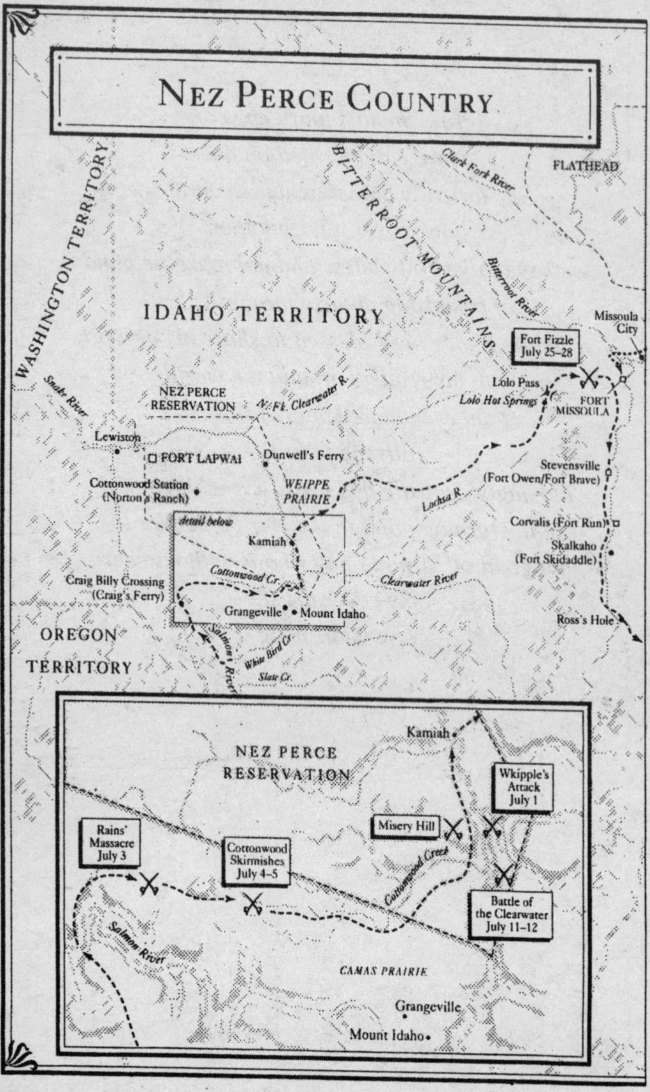
NEZ PERCE COUNTRY
WASHINGTON TERRITORY
BITTERROOT MOUNTAINS
Clark Fork River
FLATHEAD
Bitterroot River
IDAHO TERRITORY
Missoula City
Fort Fizzle July 25–28
Snake River
NEZ PERCE RESERVATION
N. Fk. Clearwater R.
Lolo Pass
Lolo Hot Springs
FORT MISSOULA
Lewiston
FORT LAPWAI
Dunwell's Ferry
Stevensville (Fort Owen/Fort Brave)
Cottonwood Station (Norton's Ranch)
WEIPPE PRAIRIE
Lochsa R.
detail below
Corvalis (Fort Run)
Kamiah
Skalkaho (Fort Skidaddle)
Cottonwood Cr.
Clearwater River
Craig Billy Crossing (Craig's Ferry)
Grangeville
Mount Idaho
Ross's Hole
OREGON TERRITORY
Salmon River
White Bird Cr.
Slate Cr.
Kamiah
NEZ PERCE RESERVATION
Wkipple's Attack July 1
Misery Hill
Rains' Massacre July 3
Cottonwood Skirmishes July 4–5
Cottonwood Creek
Battle of the Clearwater July 11–12
Salmon River
CAMAS PRAIRIE
Grangeville
Mount Idaho

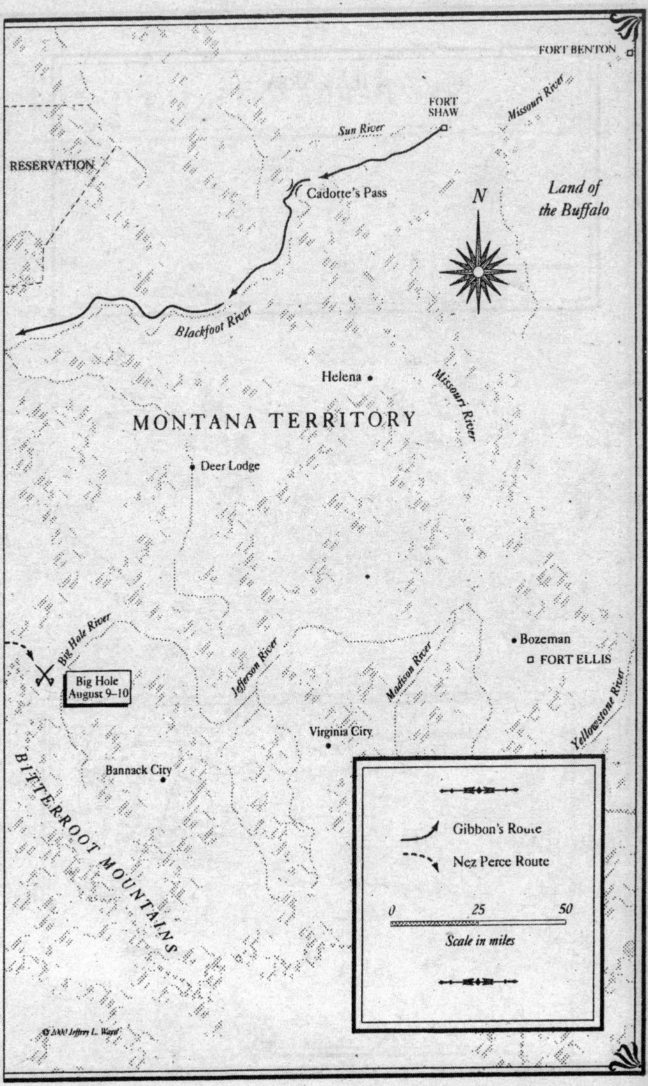
FORT BENTON
FORT SHAW
Missouri River
Sun River
RESERVATION
Cadotte's Pass
N
Land of the Buffalo
Blackfoot River
Helena
Missouri River
MONTANA TERRITORY
Deer Lodge
Big Hole River
Bozeman
FORT ELLIS
Big Hole August 9–10
Jefferson River
Madison River
Yellowstone River
Virginia City
Bannack City
BITTERROOT MOUNTAINS
Gibbon's Route
Nez Perce Route
0 25 50
Scale in miles
© 2000 Jeffrey L. Ward

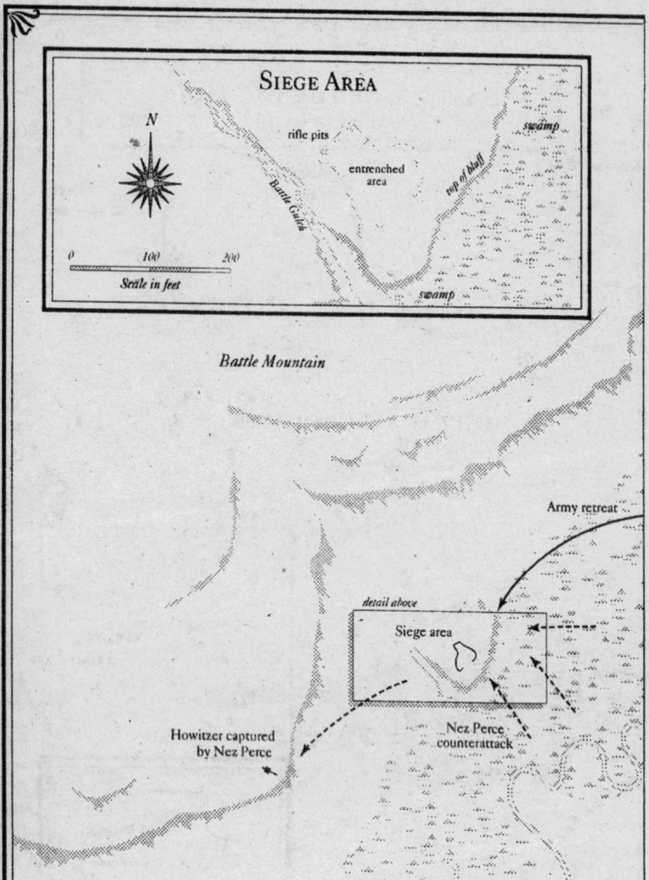

SIEGE AREA
N
rifle pits
entrenched area
Battle Gulch
top of bluff
swamp
swamp
0
100
200
Scale in feet
Battle Mountain
Army retreat
detail above
Siege area
Nez Perce counterattack
Howitzer captured by Nez Perce
boggy marsh
Trail Creek
Ruby Creek
© 2000 Jeffrey L. Ward

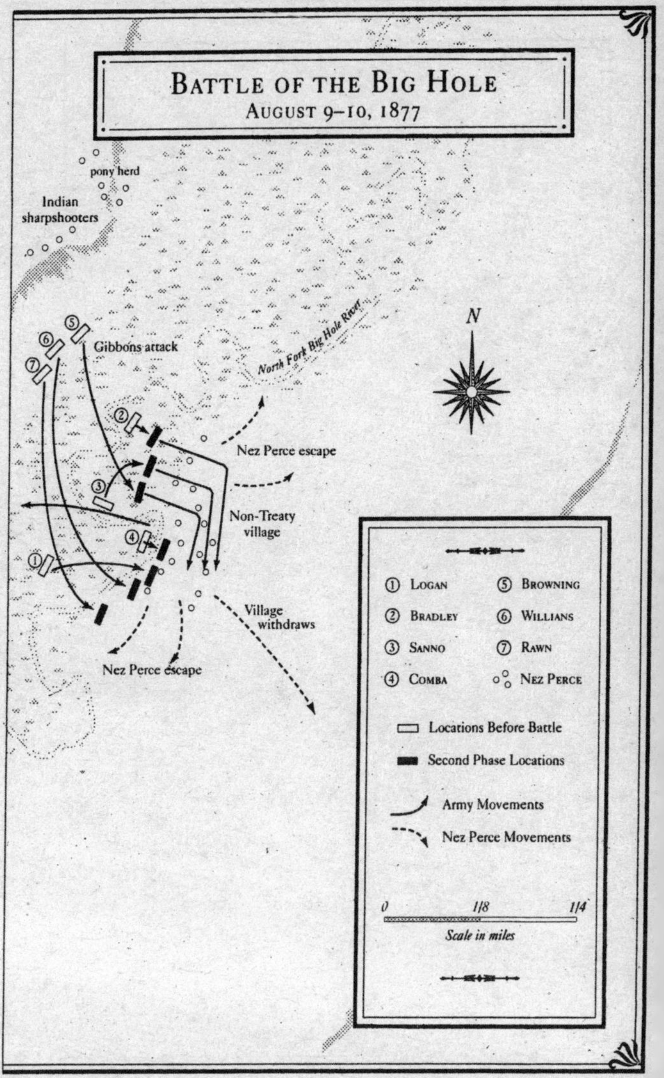

BATTLE OF THE BIG HOLE
AUGUST 9–10, 1877
pony herd
Indian sharpshooters
Gibbons attack
North Fork Big Hole River
N
Nez Perce escape
Non-Treaty village
Village withdraws
Nez Perce escape
① LOGAN
② BRADLEY
③ SANNO
④ COMBA
⑤ BROWNING
⑥ WILLIANS
⑦ RAWN
NEZ PERCE
Locations Before Battle
Second Phase Locations
Army Movements
Nez Perce Movements
0
1/8
1/4
Scale in miles

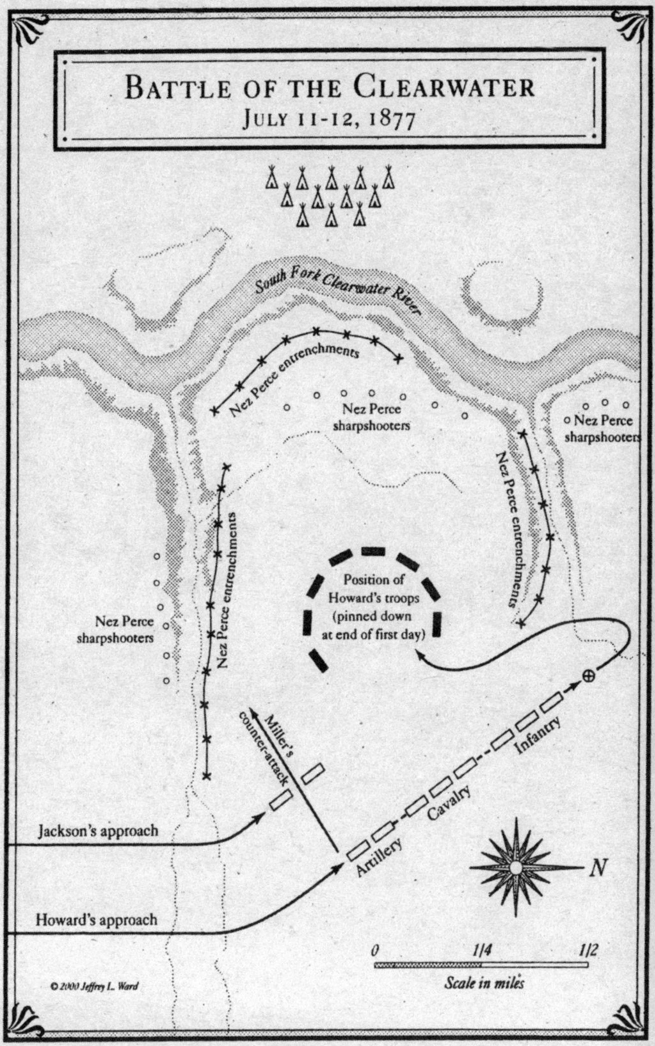

Battle of the Clearwater
July 11-12, 1877
South Fork Clearwater River
Nez Perce entrenchments
Nez Perce sharpshooters
Nez Perce entrenchments
Nez Perce sharpshooters
Nez Perce entrenchments
Nez Perce sharpshooters
Nez Perce entrenchments
Position of Howard's troops (pinned down at end of first day)
Miller's counter-attack
Infantry
Cavalry
Artillery
Jackson's approach
Howard's approach
N
0
1/4
1/2
Scale in miles
© 2000 Jeffrey L. Ward

Cast of Characters

CIVILIANS

Emily F. FitzGerald
Elizabeth FitzGerald
Bert FitzGerald
Jennie Norton
Elizabeth Osborn
Norman Gould
John B. Monteith
Erwin C. Watkins
"Captian" Tom Page
Benjamin F. Potts
Washington "Dutch" Holmes
Dave Ousterholt
Luther P. "Lew" Wilmot
"Captain" Benjamin F. Morris
Eugene Tallmadge Wilson
"Captain" James L. Cearly
P. C. Malin
Benjamin Penny
William Foster
Frank Parker
Jack Carleton
Chauncey Barbour
"Captain" John Humble
"Sergeant" Joseph Baker
Peter H. Ready
Frank A. Fenn
Henry C. Johnson
Cassius M. "Cash" Day
D. H. Howser
Alonzo B. Leland
F. Joseph "Joe" Moore
Charles Johnson
Henry W. Croasdaile
Williams George
George M. Shearer
Loyal P. (L.P.) Brown
H. C. "Hurdy Gurdy" Brown
John J. Manuel
Peter Matte
Thomas A. Sutherland
Benjamin Norton
Hill Norton
Lynn Bowers
Helen Walsh
George Greer
Peter Ronan
"Captain" William Hunter
"Captain" J. W. Elliott
William Watson
J. A. Miller
"Colonel" Edward McConville
John Atkinson
George Hunter
John McPherson
George Riggins
Elias Darr
"Laughing" Williams
James T. Silverwood
E. A. Kenney
W. J. Stephens
"Captain" Darius B. (D. B.) Randall
Frank D. Vansise
Ephraim J. Bunker
Pete Bremen
James Buchanan
Charley Case
Benjamin F. Evans
Mrs. Chamberlin
Peter Minturn
Paul Guiterman
Sarah Brown
Maggie Manuel
Albert Benson
John W. Crooks
"Captain" Orlando "Rube" Robbins
John Crooks, Jr.

William Silverthorne
Alexander Matte
Dr. John Morris
Charley Crooks
Dan Crooks
Arthur "Ad"/"Admiral" Chapman
Henry Buck
Fred Buck
Joe Pardee
"Captain" John B. Catlin
Wesley Little
H. S. Bostwick
Campbell Mitchell
William H. Edwards
Jerry Wallace
"Captain" John L. Humble
John Buckhouse
Reverend W. T. Flowers
Amos Buck
Jerry Fahy
Myron Lockwood
Father Anthony Ravalli
Joe Blodgett
Hugh Kirkendall
"Captain" William R. Logan
William Woodcock
Nelse McGilliam
John Miller
Alfred Cave
Wilson B. Harlan
Luther Johnson
Tom Sherrill
"Bunch" Sherrill
Mr. Bonny

MILITARY

Major General Irwin McDowell
Captain Birney Keeler
Brigadier General Oliver Otis Howard / "Cut-Off Arm" / "Never Going to Fight Until Tomorrow"

First U. S. Cavalry

Major George B. Sanford
Captain David Perry—F Troop
Captain Joel G. Trimble—H Troop
Captain Henry E. Winters—H Troop
Captain Stephen Gerard Whipple—L Troop
Captain James B. Jackson—B Troop
First Lieutenant Edwin H. Shelton—L Troop
First Lieutenant Albert G. Forse—E Troop
First Lieutenant George R. Bacon—K Troop
Second Lieutenant William Russell Parnell—H Troop
Second Lieutenant Sevier McClellan Rains—L Troop
Second Lieutenant William H. Miller—E Troop
Major John Wesley Green
First Sergeant Oliver Sutherland (Sean Dennis Geoghegan)—B Troop
Sergeant Bernard Simpson—L Troop

Sergeant Isidor Schneider—H Troop
Sergeant Charles Lampman—E Troop
Trumpeter Frank A. Marshall—H Troop
Farrier John Drugan—H Troop
Private David Carroll—L Troop
Private George H. Dinteman—L Troop
Private Otto H. Richter—L Troop
Private William Roche—E Troop
Private Franklin Moody—L Troop
Second Lieutenant Thomas T. Knox—H Troop
First Sergeant Michael McCarthy—H Troop
Private Patrick Quinn—E Troop
Private John Burk—E Troop
Private Charles E. Fowler—H Troop
Private Frederick Meyer—L Troop
Private Daniel Ryan—E Troop

Second U. S. Cavalry

Sergeant Edward Page—L Troop

Fourth U. S. Artillery

Captain Marcus P. Miller—commanding artillery battalion
Captain Eugene A. Bancroft—M Battery
Captain Charles B. Throckmorton—M Battery
Captain Harry C. Cushing—C Battery
Captian George B. Rodney—D Battery
Second Lieutenant Harrison G. Otis—E Battery

Seventh U. S. Infantry

Colonel John Gibbon—regiment commander
Captain Charles C. Rawn—I Company
Captain William Logan—A Company
Captain James M. W. Sanno—G Company
Captain Richard Comba—D Company
Captain George L. Browning—G Company
First Lieutenant Joshua W. Jacobs—regimental quartermaster
First Lieutenant William L. English—I Company
First Lieutenant Charles A. Coolidge—A Company
First Lieutenant James H. Bradley—B Company
First Lieutenant Charles A. Woodruff—K Company (aide-de-camp to Colonel Gibbon)
Second Lieutenant Francis Woodbridge—A Company

Lieutenant Tom Andrews—A Company
Lieutenant Levi F. Burnett—Gibbon's aide at Fort Shaw
First Sergeant Patrick Rogan—A Company
Sergeant John Raferty—A Company
Sergeant Michael Hogan—I Company
Sergeant John W. H. Frederick—G Company
Sergeant Patrick C. Daly—D Company
Sergeant Mildon H. Wilson—I Company
Corporal Charles N. Loynes—I Company
Corporal Robert E. Sale—G Company
Corporal Socrates Drummond
Private Charles Alberts—A Company
Private George Leher—A Company
Private Homer Coon—G Company
Private John O. Bennett—B Company
Private Malcolm McGregor—G Company
Private John H. Goale—G Company

Twenty-first Infantry

Major Edwin C. Mason—Department Inspector General, Howard's Chief of Staff
Captain Evan Miles—infantry battalion commander
Captain William F. Spurgin—commander, pioneer/engineer company
Captain William H. Boyle—G Company
Captain Robert Pollock—D Company
First Lieutenant Robert H. Fletcher—acting assistant adjutant general
First Lieutenant Fred H. E. Ebstein—regimental and column quartermaster
Lieutenant James A. Haughey—H Company
Lieutenant Harry Bailey—B Company
Private Francis Winters—B Company

Howard's Staff

Captain Lawrence S. Babbitt
First Lieutenant Melville C. Wilkinson
Second Lieutenant Guy Howard
Second Lieutenant Charles Erskine Scott Wood
Colonel John Gibbon—commanding, Seventh U. S. Infantry
Surgeon Jenkins A. ("John") FitzGerald—Fort Lapwai

Surgeon George M. Sternberg—Fort Walla Walla
Assistant Surgeon William R. Hall

TREATY NEZ PERCE

John Hill
Tom Hill
James Lawyer
Archie Lawyer
James Reuben
Luke Billy
Robinson Minthon
Yuwishakaikit
Joe Albert / Elaskolatat
John Levi / "Captain John" / Sheared Wolf
Abraham Brooks
Delaware Jim / Jim Simonds

NON-TREATY BANDS *Nee-Me-Poo*

Yellow Wolf / *Hemene Moxmox*
Old Yellow Wolf
Wemastahtus
Teminisiki
Horse Blanket / *Seekumses Kunnin*
Elm Limb / *Alahmoot*
Paktilek
Yiyik Wasumwah
Tomyunmene
Tommino
Going Across / *Wayakat*
Over the Point / *Teeweeyownah*
Three Feathers
Hair Combed Over Eyes / *Wottolen*
Weesculatat (Wounded Mouth / *Mimpow Owyeen*)
White Cloud / *Sewattis Hihhih*
Five Wounds / *Pahkatos Owyeen*
Rainbow / *Wahchumyus*
Kulkulsuitim
Poker Joe / Lean Elk / *Wa-wook-ke-ya Was Sauw* / Joe Hale
Joseph / *Heinmot* (White Thunder)
Ta-ma-al-we-non-my / Driven Before a Cold Storm
Sun Necklace ("Yellow Bull" / *Chuslum Moxmox*)
Wounded Head / *Husis Owyeen*
No Feet / *Seeskoomkee*
Black Raven / *Nennin Chekoostin*
Strong Eagle / *Tipyahlahnah Kapskaps*
Shot Leg / *Tahkoopen*
Eagle Robe / *Tipyahlanah Siskon*
Shore Crossing / *Wahlitits*
Smoker / *Dookiyoon*
Red Moccasin Tops / *Sarpsis Ilppil*
Burning Coals / *Semu*
Eagle-from-the-Light
Black Foot
Mean Man / *Howwallits*
White Bull
(Josiah) Red Wolf

Rattle on Blanket / *Lakochets Kunnin*
Red Heart / *Temme Ilppilp*
Chee-Nah
Dropping from a Cliff / *Tenahtahkal Weyun*
Stripes Turned Down / *Ketalkpoosmin*
Log / *Weweetsa*
Bighorn Bow / *Tahwis Takaitat*
No Heart / *Zya Timenna*
Grizzly Bear Youth / *Hohots Elotoht*
Ollokot / the Frog
Arrowhead / *Etemiere Aihits Palojami* / Fair Land
Red Elk
Toohoolhoolzote
Helping Another / *Penahwenonmi*
Pile of Clouds
Fire Body / *Otstotpoo*
Looking Glass / *Alalmiatakanin*
Bird Alighting / *Peopeo Tholekt*
White Bird
Red Spy / *Seeyakoon Ilppilp* / wife of *Wahlitits*—no recorded name
Swan Necklace / *Wetyetmas Wahyakt*
Grizzly Bear Blanket / *Yoomstis Kunnin*
Lone Bird / *Peopeo Ipsewahk*
Natalekin
About Asleep / *Eelahweeman*
Young White Bird
Dog / *Jeekunkun*
Suhm-Keen
Wahnistas Aswetesk
Sun Tied / *Weyatnahtoo Latat*
Calf of Leg / *Pitpillooheen*
Earth Blanket / *Wattes Kunnin*
Light in the Mountain / *Espowyes Quiloishkish*
Owhi (Yakima)
Horn Hide Dresser / *Tepsus*
Amos
Two Moons / *Lepeet Hessemdooks*
Going Out / *Otskai*
Kowtoliks
Five Fogs / *Pahka Pahtahank*

PALOUSE

Red Echo / *Hahtalekin*
Bald Head / Shorn Head / *Huishuishkute*

FLATHEAD

Charlot
Pierre

BANNOCK

Buffalo Horn

I would have given my own life I could have undone the killing of white men by my people. I blame young men and I blame the white men. I blame General Howard for not giving my people time to get their stock away from Wallowa. I do not acknowledge that he had the right to order me to leave Wallowa at any time. I deny that either my father or myself ever sold that land. It may never again be our home, but my father sleeps there, and I love it as I love my mother. I left there, hoping to avoid bloodshed.

—*JOSEPH*

The Rains encounter was a small but sweeping victory for the Nez Perces. Coming on the heels of their success over the army at White Bird Canyon, it had the effect of inspiring them to continue in their course. It impacted the army negatively, not only through the loss of Rains and his men, but it prevented Howard from attaining the upper hand in the war and ending it quickly, while simultaneously contributing to the building public skepticism about army capabilities.

—*JEROME A. GREENE*
The U. S. Army and the Nee-Mee-Poo Crisis of 1877

If Howard had been as bold [at the Clearwater] as General Gibbon [was at the Big Hole] we might have been all taken, although we intended to fight to the last.

—*WHITE BIRD*

The Battle of the Clearwater was indisputably a watershed in the army's campaign against the Nez Perces. By not pressing them in their retreat from the village, General Howard lost both the initiative and an opportunity to finally curb the non-treaty Nez Perces and end the war.

—*JEROME A. GREENE*

In retrospect, the Nez Perces' parochial perspective of the war, and their insensibility to comprehending the scale and span of the United States government's resistance to [their flight from their homes in Idaho Territory to the Big Hole in Montana Territory], became key ingredients in their ultimate tragedy.

—*JEROME A. GREENE*

[illegible]

[illegible]

[illegible]

[illegible]

[illegible]

[illegible]

[illegible]

[illegible]

[illegible]

AUTHOR'S FOREWORD

BEFORE YOU BEGIN READING THIS BOOK, I WANT YOU TO take a moment to consider that the story you hold in your hands is entirely true.

While I'm sure you realize that I have constructed dialogue from a myriad of historical documents to make this story leap off the page with a sense of immediacy, I have striven to capture each person's individual character in their manner of speech. Rest assured that I haven't fabricated a single one of the scenes that follow this introduction. Every incident happened when and where and how I have written it. Every one of the characters you will come to know actually lived, perhaps died, during these pivotal weeks during the Nez Perce War of 1877.

After my previous fourteen *Plainsmen* novels, millions of you already have an abiding faith in me, a belief that what you're going to read is accurate and truly authentic.

But for those of you thumbing through your first Terry C. Johnston book, let me make this one very crucial promise to you: If I show one of these fascinating historical characters in a particular scene, then you'd best believe that character was there—when it happened, where it happened. I promise you, despite the overwhelmingly popular and politically correct notions long held by most people, this is how the tragedy of the Nez Perce War did unfold.

Truth is, I could have written a book nearly twice as long as this if I had explored the complex historical background of the old treaties and how they were broken after gold was discovered deep in Nez Perce country, if I had begun reciting in chapter and verse all the intrusions by whites where they were not allowed by the early treaties, relating to you that seductive lure of alcohol and firearms on the young warriors; writing of the rapes and murders committed against those Nez Perce bands helplessly watching as their old way of life was trampled underfoot right before their eyes, not to mention the government's feeble efforts to keep a lid on each deplorable incident after the fact. . . .

But, for all that detailed background I didn't cram into these three novels I'm writing on the Nez Perce War, the reader can learn every detail he or she wants to know in the following books:

I Will Fight No More Forever, by Merrill D. Beal

The Flight of the Nez Perce, by Mark H. Brown

The Nez Perce Tribesmen of the Columbia Plateau, by Francis Haines

The Nez Perce Indians and the Opening of the Northwest, by Alvin M. Josephy, Jr.

As for my story—beginning with the outbreak of the war as I told it in *Cries from the Earth*—I dispensed with all that oft-confusing historical background because you can learn it far better elsewhere . . . and because I prefer to plop you right down into the middle of this tragic conflict.

As you are drawn back in time and reading the pages of my story, you may well wonder: What are these brief news articles that appear here and there at the beginning of certain chapters or scenes? Keep in mind that those clippings aren't the fruits of my creative imagination. Rather, they are ripped right from the front pages of the newspapers read by living, breathing people in that summer of 1877.

One more sidelight before you start what will surely be one of the most fascinating rides of your life—the letters that Emily FitzGerald, wife of surgeon John FitzGerald, writes home to her mother from Fort Lapwai are real, too. Transcribed verbatim for you, every last word of those letters make them simple, heartfelt messages from a woman who finds herself trapped squarely at ground zero, right in the middle of an Indian war.

I hope Emily's letters, along with those timely newspaper clippings, will lend an air of immediacy to this gripping tale that every other book on the Nez Perce War has not.

As you make your way through this story, page by page, many of you might start to worry when you find this tale missing our intrepid Irishman, Seamus Donegan. Be strong of heart! In the next volume—*The Broken Hoop*—Seamus; his wife, Samantha; and their son, Colin, will migrate from Fort Laramie in the spring of 1877, making their way north to Fort Robinson, where they will find themselves on center stage for the last months of Crazy Horse's life. When his old friend Colonel Nelson A. Miles marches his Fifth U. S. Infantry north from Tongue River in pursuit of the Nez Perce fleeing for Canada (that third and final act in this tragedy), the Irishman will be along . . . as a brutal winter storm and the army descend upon the Bears Paw Mountains—catching the Non-Treaty bands just forty miles short of the Old Woman's Country.

As you saddle up and begin this ride with me, I want to remind you that every scene you are about to read actually happened. Every one of these characters was real—and they were there to walk that hallowed ground . . . to live or die in what fading glory still belonged to the Nez Perce in a damned and dirty little war.

I couldn't have made up this remarkably intricate and tragic story if I'd tried. I simply don't consider myself that good a writer.

Prologue

20 June 1877

Cursing the rising sun under his breath, first sergeant Michael McCarthy ground the heels of both hands into his gummy, crusted eyes.

Already this morning the little settlement of Grangeville was slowly stirring—not just those soldiers and civilians who stood watch at the barricades for the approach of Joseph's Nez Perce warriors, but those men rekindling fires, women stirring up breakfast, and even the few children adding their cheery, innocent voices to the coming of this new day.

Squinting overhead, the Canadian-born McCarthy found a clearing sky. Far better than the low, leaden clouds that had hovered above them almost from the moment Captain David Perry had led them out of Fort Lapwai after the marauding Non-Treaty bands.

Perry. Just thinking about the man made McCarthy hawk up the night-gather clinging at the back of his throat. Now there was a coward weighed down beneath a captain's bars! There wasn't a goddamned reason they should have left more than a third of their command down in that valley of White Bird Canyon. A good officer, a brave commander, could have seized control of those wavering troopers, halted their wild retreat before it ever got started. . . .

The thirty-two-year-old soldier hung his head and took a deep breath as he clenched his eyes shut. McCarthy remembered—doubting he ever would forget—the sights he had left behind him on that battleground. Last man out that he was. The last to crawl up the 3,000 feet of White Bird Canyon . . . the valley floor behind him littered with dead and wounded comrades, swarming with Nez Perce horsemen like an attack of summer wasps boiling out of their nest.

Perry had gone and jabbed a big stick right into that nest. And when there was nothing left for any of them to do but turn about and high-tail it back up the canyon wall, Captain David Perry was powerless to control the panic. Damn, but Michael couldn't blame those poor enlisted weeds: Why would any of them want to stop, turn around, and start fighting anew for a commander like David Perry? Not when the captain had marched his bone-weary men down through the dark toward an enemy no one knew a god-blame-it thing about, every one of his hundred soldiers riding too-tired and ill-fed horses.

"They wasn't ready to fight," he grumbled under his breath now as he dragged over the first brown boot. For a moment he caressed the soft, saddle-soaped texture of the tall, mule-eared boot top. *God bless sutler Rudolph,* he thought. *Godbless'im, Lord.*

The afternoon after First Sergeant Michael McCarthy had been discovered and brought in by those two civilian volunteers from out near Johnson's ranch, near halfway between the White Bird divide and the settlement of Grangeville, Rudolph had graciously presented McCarthy with a pair of real leather boots to take the place of those ill-fitting rubber miner's boots the sergeant had discovered in an abandoned cabin on his way over the divide to the Camas Prairie. Once more, Michael knew how the Lord doth provide!

Left behind by the rest of those hardy old files bringing up the rear of the frantic retreat, McCarthy had lain there on the slope, playing dead until the screaming warriors thundered past. Only then did he quickly roll into the willow and wild rose lining the banks of White Bird Creek, slipping into the water so that only his head was showing there beneath the low-hanging brush. After waiting out the comings and going of the warriors searching for any wounded soldiers and looting the bodies of his poor dead comrades, it was no wonder the icy-cold water had soaked his regulation boots through and through. Soles falling away from lasts, stitches unraveling. Utterly worthless: just like near every other piece of equipment this god-blame-it army gave its soldiers to use. Boots that never would get him up that slope he had studied from between the leafy willow—only to find that he'd been discovered by a fat Indian squaw riding past on her pony.

How his heart had frozen when the fat one called over an old man—pointing to the clump of willow where McCarthy lay hidden. He had pulled out his service revolver and prepared to take as many of them with him as he could before he was killed. But . . . search as he did, the old man didn't spot him. He rode off with the woman.

In the quiet where he could hear his own heart surging in his ears, McCarthy quickly tore off his campaign hat, slipped out of his navy blue fatigue blouse with its telltale gold stripes. If he'd dared to tug off his light blue wool britches with their wide brassy stripe running down the outside . . . but he knew he would need them in his run for freedom. Wasn't no man going to make it to the settlements near naked!

Besides the gift of those knee-high boots, sutler Rudolph had presented the sergeant with a pair of leather gloves and a new felt hat—gray as the skies had been the last three days.

"You're a honest-to-God hero," Rudolph had announced to the crowd when he presented his gifts to the newly arrived McCarthy. "All you soldiers are heroes to us!"

And then the gathering of some forty men, women, and children huddled behind an upright stockade, which they had erected right around Grange Hall, huzzahed as if they had just been delivered from the hoary grip of death itself. Just the way Michael McCarthy had been scooped up by some angel and carried out of that valley of death, deposited at the top of White Bird divide, where he made three wrong turns and ended up wandering the heights for far longer than he should have.

When those two soldiers brought the ravenous McCarthy to the barricades, his nose caught the whiff of an enticing perfume. Someone had beans on the boil. "White dodgers!" he had exclaimed as he vaulted off the back end of that tired cavalry horse, lumbering across the breastworks for that seductive pot. First things first. He'd look for familiar faces from his H Company once his belly was full. Enough time to make reacquaintance with his weeds what made it out of that Injun fight with their hides intact.

"Sweet, sweet Joseph and Mary," he murmured again, clenching his eyes as he rocked onto his knees, preparing to roll up his blankets. Would he never forget the sight of Corporal Roman D. Lee being dragged from his horse, the entire front of his blue britches turned black with blood gushing from that bullet to the groin? Would he ever be able to blot out the nightmare of watching Lee stumble away from his handlers like a drunken sailor newly arrived on dry land, wandering off into that milling, confusing, maddening maze of confused men and frightened horses? Would he never be rid of watching the corporal unknowingly weave and lunge on down that emerald grassy slope—right for the enemy's lines?

At sundown each of the last two nights, Second Lieutenant William Russell Parnell had come whistling up the company, calling out men to post a rotation for night guard. Too much darkness, too much quiet, too damned much time each night on watch . . . time alone to think and remember.

He took a deep breath and pushed an unruly lock of his dark auburn hair from his eyes, telling himself such haunting was the lot of a soldier. Be he an Irishman like McCarthy or one of those pig-swilling Germans, a soldier was bound to lose friends. Maybeso, it wasn't a good thing for a sergeant to have him any friends. Only officers above him and enlisted boyos below. Maybe there was a damned good reason officers never talked to their weeds—communicating only through the noncoms like McCarthy. That way an officer didn't have to care who was thrown into the fray, who would never ride back with the company.

When McCarthy gave orders to H Company, it was with a voice still very thick with that Newfoundland Irish heritage of his. As soon as he was old enough to leave home and strike out on his own, McCarthy had wandered south from Canada, spending a short time in Vermont before migrating down to Boston. In that good Irish town he had knocked around a bit before he landed steady work as a printer's devil. A year later when the Civil War broke out, he was only fifteen—too young to enlist, having to content himself by following the war with every new edition or extra of the Boston paper.

By the time the Southern states had been defeated and herded back into the Union fold, McCarthy had wearied of the acrid stench of printer's ink etching every wrinkle and crevice of his hands, chuffing down the street to inscribe his mark on a five-year enlistment. Sending him west to Jefferson Barracks near St. Louis, the army trained him to be a horseman, then promptly shipped him off to a First Cavalry outfit down near the Mexican border to fight Apaches. Wasn't long before they transferred McCarthy, now wearing a corporal's stripes, along with some of his mates, all hustled north to Oregon country, where they ended up chasing half a hundred poor Modocs around and through the Lava Beds for the better part of a year.

Fact was, McCarthy had been in on the chase and capture of the Modoc leader, Captain Jack. A heart-wrenching tragedy that was, McCarthy thought many times since—how the chief's friends, advisers, and headmen had all turned on him. Sad, too, that most of those back-stabbing traitors went free while Jack swung at the end of a short rope.

He smelled tobacco all of a sudden. McCarthy glanced at the knot of men gathered on their haunches around a small fire, most of their number smoking their first bowl of the day. His heart seized with the sudden recollection of their blind descent into the valley of the White Bird behind Perry, ordered to halt and wait until it was light enough to make their advance on the village. Up and down the ranks of those two companies, five officers, and more than a dozen Nez Perce friendlies conscripted as trackers the order was given that no pipes be lit.

Later, as the horses snuffled and the men grumbled every time they were nudged to keep them awake in the cold, damp darkness, McCarthy spotted the bright, minute flare of the sulphur-headed lucifer. The sergeant had bounded over, ready to throttle and choke the stupid weed who was trying to light his goddamned pipe.

The match had flared for but the space of three heartbeats before McCarthy got it extinguished. Then thought nothing more of it until they all heard the off-key, muffled call of a coyote. Its eerie, echoing cry had raised the reddish hair on the back of his neck. A few of the old files had known right then what was in store for them come first light.

That weren't no coyote. Some Nez Perce sentry had seen the bloody burning match . . . and the bastards knew the soldiers had come for them—

"Sergeant! Sergeant!" called Trumpeter Frank A. Marshall as the soldier came trotting up the end of Grangeville's one long street, breathless.

As Marshall skidded to a halt right at McCarthy's toes, out of the trees to their left stepped the big German sergeant, Isidor Schneider. McCarthy liked the man—no matter that it was hard for McCarthy to understand his thick accent at times. Michael counted on the thick-hammed German to help him run H Company smoothly.

"Suck a breath, Private," the short, slim McCarthy reminded the trumpeter. "And tell me what orders you've got for us this fine morning."

McCarthy steeled himself, not sure he was ready for another of those assignments the officers always handed him alone—like picking a squad of steady men and holding off the screaming red heathens from that outcropping of rocks while the rest of Perry's command skeedaddled from the battlefield like banshees were nipping at their heels. Another god-blame-it suicide run—

"We're g-going b-back, Sergeant."

As a dozen or more of H Company's green-broke shavetail recruits inched closer, Farrier John Drugan lunged to a stop at Marshall's elbow. "Back? Whooo-eee! We're going back to our post?"

Marshall shook his head and swallowed, still struggling to catch his breath from his sprint over with the latest from Perry's headquarters.

"We're not going back to the fort?" McCarthy asked, sweeping one of the droopy, unkempt ends of his shaggy reddish-brown mustache away from his lips suddenly gone dry.

"No, Sergeant," the trumpeter confirmed steadily.

Michael was afraid to ask. He thought of friends and fellow soldiers already waiting for him at Fiddler's Green—the place in the great beyond where every good horse soldier went when his duty roster was up.

A drop of cold sweat slowly spilled down the course of McCarthy's spine, oozing into the crack of his ass. "Back where, Private?"

Pasty-faced, Marshall turned, pointed off to the southwest, toward the White Bird divide. "Going back . . . to the b-battlefield."

CHAPTER ONE

JUNE 21, 1877

BY TELEGRAPH

An Indian War in Idaho.

Twenty-Nine Settlers Killed—
The Troops Pursuing.

IDAHO.

Still Another Indian War.

WASHINGTON, June 20.—The following dispatch has been received by the commissioner of Indian affairs from the Nez Perces agency, Idaho: The non-treaty Indians commenced hostilities on the 14th inst. Up to date, the 16th, twenty-nine settlers are reported murdered, and four Indians killed. Gen. Howard is here in command. The hostiles are about one hundred strong. They are reported to have gone to the Solomon river country and are making for the Weiser Geysers, in southern Idaho. Troops are in pursuit twelve hours behind. The reservation Indians are true to the government. A company is formed under the head chief, and is protecting the settlement of Kamarah and employees.

[Signed] WATKINS, Inspector, and
Monteith, Indian Agent

HE HAD FOUGHT AGAINST THE CREAM OF THE CONFEDERACY and chased, then hung, the leaders of the Modoc insurrection in southern Oregon years ago. So why did he find himself dreading this ride down into the canyon of White Bird Creek the way a frightened schoolboy would fear a midnight trek to a cemetery?

Deep in the marrow of him, Captain David Perry knew that what awaited him on that abandoned battlefield was far worse than anything a schoolboy might encounter in some haunted graveyard. Not only would he be forced to view the bloated, contorted bodies of those men he had led into the valley at dawn on the seventeenth of June, but he was coming to believe that he just might confront the restless, disembodied spirits of those soldiers who would forever walk that bloody ground.

If Brigadier General Howard, even that damnable, self-serving coward Trimble, didn't utter a public charge about his debacle in the valley of the White Bird, then Perry was afraid his greatest fear would come to pass: The ghosts of those men sacrificed to the Nez Perce would shriek aloud their charges of incompetence and timidity . . . if not outright cowardice.

Oh, the hours and days he had brooded over every deployment of his forces, every action of his company commanders, each tiny reaction of his own during the short, fierce fight since that damp morning when he had been tested and somehow found wanting. Had he committed his one-hundred-man force to battle without trustworthy intelligence, taking only the word of the civilian volunteers that the Nez Perce wouldn't dare stand and fight?

David Perry, post commander at nearby Fort Lapwai, simply could not shake the unrelenting sleeplessness his doubts awakened within his most private soul, nor rid himself of the constant horror he saw behind his eyelids every time he shut his eyes and attempted to squeeze out the respite of a little rest from each endless night. He wondered if he would ever find a way to rid himself of this haunting.

Like an arrow a man would release into the air, aimed directly overhead—an arrow that might well fall back toward earth to wound or even kill that bowman—Perry understood his hasty, ill-considered journey into the White Bird Canyon would one day return to be his undoing. But the captain fervently prayed this would not be that day.

Before he led his men south from Grangeville that

Thursday morning, the twenty-first of June, Perry confided in those fellow officers who, with him, had survived their humiliating defeat on the White Bird.

"We'll make a reconnaissance as far as the top of the divide," he instructed them. "And stop where we began to descend into the valley on the seventeenth . . . halting where we can view the battlefield at a distance."

"We best keep our eyes skinned for them redskins," injected Arthur Chapman, a local rancher who was better known as Ad, bastardized from "Admiral," a name bestowed upon him for his uncanny ability to handle small craft on the region's swollen, raging rivers.

Perry turned to peer at that volunteer scout coming to a stop within the ring of officers. "You volunteering to lead us back across the ridge, Mr. Chapman?"

The tall civilian appeared to weigh that briefly, his eyes darting among the other soldiers who stood at Perry's elbows. Pushing some black hair out of his eyes, Chapman sighed. "I figger it's the decent thing to do, Colonel," he explained, using Perry's brevet, or honorary, rank earned during the Civil War. "But mind you, if them Injuns whupped us and drove your soldiers off once, they sure as hell can wipe you out now—they catch us in the open again."

Perry squinted his eyes, peering at that knot of horsemen who warily sat far off to the side of his column of blue-clad soldiers. "What of your recruitment efforts among the civilian populace, Mr. Chapman?"

"Maybe a dozen," the civilian replied. "No more'n that come along with me."

"That'll have to do—as many local citizens as you can muster." Perry did his best to sound upbeat. "Gentlemen, prepare your companies. We'll move out on our reconnaissance in thirty minutes."

Here at the top of the White Bird divide, the captain had halted his depleted, nervous command. Gathering both left and right at the front of Perry's column Chapman's civilians sat atop their horses, letting their animals blow. At their feet lay the steep slope Perry's doomed battalion had scrambled back up on the morning of 17 June. Only four short days ago.

His heart pounded in his chest. Surely the victorious Non-Treaty bands had abandoned the area.

"Don't see no smoke, Colonel," Chapman advised as he eased back to Perry's side.

Civilian George M. Shearer, a veteran of that all-too-brief White Bird battle, agreed, "Likely moved their village."

"Where?" Perry demanded.

With a shrug, Chapman answered, "Gone up or down the Salmon, I'd reckon. They whupped you already. Took what they wanted from your dead soldiers, then moved on."

"Surely Joseph has put out some war parties to roam this country, Colonel," Captain Joel G. Trimble asserted with an unmistakable air of superiority.

"At the least," added Second Lieutenant William Russell Parnell, "the chiefs assigned some spies to remain in the area to watch for us."

As some of the officers prattled on, Perry gazed into the canyon, not completely sure what he had spotted below. His eyes might be playing tricks on him the longer he stared. A dark clump here and there across that narrow ridgeline he had attempted to hold without a trumpet. More of them scattered back in this direction. Bodies. The unholy dead, their spirits raw and restless—

"Mr. Chapman." Perry suddenly turned on the civilian. "Select from your men a number of volunteers to accompany you for a brief reconnaissance."

The civilian cleared his throat, his eyes narrowing. "You ain't bringing these soldiers of yours down there with us?"

Perry straightened in the saddle, feeling every pair of eyes heatedly boring into him this warm midmorning. "No, Mr. Chapman. Make your search brief. Determine if there are any war parties left behind, then return to this position. We'll await your return."

For a moment Chapman glanced over the faces of the other citizens gathered from the nearby communities of

Grangeville and Mount Idaho. Shearer, the Confederate major who, so it was said, had served on General Robert E. Lee's staff, shook his head. Eventually, Chapman wagged his head, too, his eyes boring into Perry's. "You ain't goin' down there with us, ain't no reason for me and my friends to stick our necks out neither."

"You won't search the valley?" Perry asked, his voice rising an octave.

"No, Commander. Not without what few soldiers you got left coming along with us, what soldiers can still fight if them Injuns show up again."

With a sigh of finality, Perry said, "I can't chance that, gentlemen. My battalion is diminished in strength as it is. I dare not lose any more—"

Almost as one, the civilians turned away behind Ad Chapman without uttering another word, starting back down the slope for Grangeville and Mount Idaho. A few of them peered over their shoulders at those relieved officers and soldiers nervously sitting there with their cavalry commander. Overlooking what had become a field of death.

Perry shuddered with the frustration he swallowed down, reined his horse around, and signaled with his arm for his battered, beaten battalion to follow him back to the settlements.

BY TELEGRAPH

—

An Indian War in Idaho.

—

IDAHO.

—

Official from General Howard.

WASHINGTON, June 20.—The following telegrams in regard to the Indian troubles in Idaho were received at the war department: From Gen. McDowell, San Francisco, to Gen. Sherman, Washington.—The steamer California arrived at Fort Townsend this morning with all the troops from Alaska. I have ordered them to go to Lewiston Friday morning. Gen. Hully will go to Lewiston by that date.

[Signed] MCDOWELL, Major-Gen.

SAN FRANCISCO, June 19.—General Sherman, Washington—The following from General Howard at Laparoi to his staff officer at department headquarters is just received. There is rather gloomy news from the front by stragglers. Captain Perry overtook the enemy, about 2,000 strong, in a deep ravine well posted and was fighting there when the last messenger left. I am expecting every minute a messenger from him. The Indians are very active and gradually increasing in strength, drawing from other tribes. The movement indicates a combination uniting nearly all the disaffected Indians and they probably number 1,000 or 1,500 when united. Two companies of infantry and twenty-five cavalry were detached at Lewiston this morning and an order was issued to every available man in the department, except at Forts Harney and Boize, to start all the troops at Harney or Boize except a small guard. They may receive orders en route turning them.

Dear Merciful God in heaven—did he feel all of his forty-six years at this moment.

Commander of the Military Department of the Columbia, headquartered at Portland, this veteran Civil War brigade leader, this survivor of the Apache wars in Arizona Territory, Brigadier General Oliver Otis Howard stepped into the midday light and onto the wide front porch of the joint Perry-FitzGerald residence here at Fort Lapwai, slapping some dust from his pale blue field britches with the gauntlet of the one leather glove he wore at the end of that one arm left him after the Civil War.

The ground of the wide parade yawning before him teemed with activity this Friday, the twenty-second of June, as company commanders and noncoms hustled their men into this final formation before they would dress left and depart for the seat of the Indian troubles. As the officers and enlisted were falling into ranks here at midday, the incessant dinging of the bell-mare as her mule string was brought into line, a little of the old thrill of war surged through him anew.

If ever Otis had hoped to be given one last chance to redeem himself after the shame unduly laid at his feet with the scandals at the Freedmen's Bureau down south . . . then Otis, as he had been called ever since childhood, would seize this golden opportunity to bring a swift and decisive end to this Nez Perce trouble. A foursquare and devout believer in the trials and the testing the Lord God would put only before those men destined for greatness, Howard was all the more certain that this was to be his moment.

The days ahead would yank him back from the precipice of obscurity, redeem him before Philip H. Sheridan and especially William Tecumseh Sherman himself—commander of this army—and win for Oliver Otis Howard a secure niche in the pantheon of our nation's heroes. This was right where he should have remained since losing his right arm in battle during the Civil War. The winding, bumpy, unpredictable road that had seen him to this critical moment had been a journey that clearly prepared him for, and allowed him to recognize, this offered season of glory.

Born in the tiny farming village of Leeds along the Androscoggin River in the south of Maine on the eighth of November, 1830—the same day his maternal grandfather turned sixty-two—his mother dutifully named Oliver Otis for her father. His English ancestors had reached the shores of Massachusetts in 1643, migrating north to Leeds no more than a score of years before he was born.

After passing the most daunting entrance exams, he was admitted to the freshman class at Bowdoin College in September of 1846. Four years later found him beginning his career in the United States Army as a cadet underclassman at West Point. In the beginning he suffered some ostracism and ridicule because of his regular attendance of Bible classes, as well as his abolitionist views, being openly despised by no less than Custis Lee, the son of Colonel Robert E. Lee, who himself became superintendent of the academy in 1852. Nonetheless, one of Howard's fastest friends during his last two years at West Point proved to be Jeb Stuart, who would soon become the flower of the Confederate cavalry.

While Custis Lee was ranked first in their graduating class in June of '54, Howard was not far behind: proudly standing fourth in a field of forty-six. After those initial struggles, he was leaving the academy in success, a powerful esprit d'corps residing in his breast. Back when he had begun his term at the academy, Otis had little idea exactly what he wanted to become when he eventually graduated. But across those four intervening years, Oliver Otis Howard had become a soldier. It was the only profession he would ever know.

It had come as little surprise that the autumn of 1857 found him on the faculty of West Point, where he would remain until the outbreak of hostilities with the rebellious Southern states. Just prior to the bombardment and surrender of Fort Sumter, the spring of 1861 found Howard considering a leave of absence to attend the Bangor Theological Seminary. Until the opening of hostilities, the very notion that the North and South should ever go to war over their political squabbles was hardly worth entertaining.

But now it was war. Oliver Otis Howard had stepped forward to exercise his duty as a professional soldier. Rather than remaining as a lieutenant in the regular army, he instead lobbied for and won a colonelcy of the Third Maine Volunteers. Before that first year was out he had won his general's star, and scarcely a year later he became a major general.

Few men in the nation at that critical time had the training or experience to assume such lofty positions of leadership in either of those two great armies hurtling headlong into that long and bloody maelstrom. While Otis had indeed been an outstanding student during his time at the U. S. Military Academy, it was over the next four years that he, like many others, would struggle to learn his bloody profession on-the-job.

Ordered to lead his brigade of 3,000 toward the front in those opening days of war at the first Battle of Bull Run, on the way to the battlefield he and his men passed by the hundreds of General McDowell's wounded as they were hurried to the rear. The nearness of those whistling canisters of shot, the throaty reverberations of the cannon, the incessant rattle of small arms—not to mention the pitiful cries of the maimed, the sight of bloodied, limbless soldiers—suddenly gave even the zealous Howard pause.

He later wrote his dear Lizzie that there and then he put his fears in the hands of the Almighty, finding that in an instant his trepidation was lifted from him and the very real prospect of death no longer brought him any dread. From that moment on, Oliver Otis Howard would never again be anxious in battle.

Not long after George B. McClellan took over command of the Union Army, Howard was promoted to brigadier general of the Third Maine. In action during the Peninsula Campaign, his brigade found itself sharply engaged on the morning of the second day of the Battle of Fair Oaks as the Confederates launched a determined assault. Ordered to throw his remaining two regiments into the counterattack rather than holding them in reserve, Howard confidently stepped out in front of his men and gave the order to advance. Although Confederate minié balls were hissing through the brush and shredding the trees all around them, Howard continued to move among the front ranks of his men, conspicuous on horseback, leading his troops against the enemy's noisy advance.

When he was within thirty yards of that glittering line of bayonets and butternut gray uniforms, a lead .58-caliber bullet struck Otis in the right elbow. Somehow he remained oblivious to the pain as his men closed on the enemy. When they were just yards from engaging the Confederates in close-quarters combat, a bullet brought down his horse. As Howard was scrambling to his feet an instant later, a second ball shattered his right forearm just below the first wound.

With blood gushing from his flesh, Howard grew faint, stumbled, and collapsed, whereupon he turned over command of the brigade to another officer. Later that morning he was removed to a field hospital at the rear, where the surgeons explained the severity of his wounds, as well as the fact that there was little choice between gangrene—which would lead to a certain death—and amputation of the arm. By five o'clock that afternoon, the doctors went to work to save Howard's life.

Fair Oaks had been Otis's bravest hour.

Across these last few days, while panic spread like prairie fire across the countryside as word of the disaster at White Bird Canyon drifted in, townspeople, ranchers, and even the white missionaries from the nearby reservation had all streaked into Fort Lapwai, seeking the protection of its soldiers.

Now at last, five days after Perry's debacle on the White Bird, his army was ready to move into the fray. While he was leaving Captain William H. Boyle and his G Company of the Twenty-first U. S. Infantry to garrison this small post, Howard would now be at the head of two companies of the First U. S. Cavalry, one battery of the Fourth U. S. Artillery, and five companies of the Twenty-first—a total of 227 officers and men. One hundred of these were horse soldiers, and once Howard had reunited with Perry and his sixty-six survivors of White Bird Canyon, Otis would be leading a force of some three hundred after the Non-Treaty bands.

Oliver Otis Howard had a territory and civilians to protect and a bloody uprising to put down. To his way of thinking, he had just been handed what might well prove to be something far more than even his bravest hour had been at Fair Oaks.

This war with the Nez Perce could well be the defining moment of his entire life and military career.

Chapter Two

June 24, 1877

BY TELEGRAPH

—

Indian Outbreak in Idaho.

—

Desperate Engagement With
Serious Losses.

—

One Officer and Thirty-three
Men Killed.

—

The Salmon River Valley Desolated.

—

IDAHO.

—

Indian Outbreak.

SAN FRANCISCO, June 22.—A press dispatch from Boise City confirms the report of the Indian outbreak on the Salmon river. The Indians didn't kill women and children, but allowed them to be taken under an escort of friendly squaws to Slate creek, which has thus far been left undisturbed. At Slate creek the whites have fortified themselves in a stockade fort, into which has been received the wives and children of murdered men, with the families of men who escaped. A large number of families, women and children, are thus shut in in the midst of hostile Indians, without adequate means of defense and, without aid, they will certainly be overpowered and murdered. As the Indians declare the determination to take the fort and murder the men it can't be hoped that the Indians will again spare the women and children after losses they must sustain in capturing the fort, as the men will fight to the last one. Our informant says he is reliably informed that the Indians did not burn the buildings or destroy property but cleaned out the country of stock which they have driven to the south side of the Salmon river where they seem to hope they will ultimately be the undisturbed proprietors of all the property the whites are now compelled to abandon. They think, not without reason, that before the country can be regained from them the army must be created and a long and doubtful campaign passed through. The Indians have now their camp and headquarters on Salmon river, where the stock stolen from the whites is gathered and pastured in an extensive triangular-shaped region formed by the Snake and Salmon rivers and a high mountain range lying about the sources of Fayette and Weaver rivers. Here there is abundant pasturage for summer and winter, and there they will doubtless make a final stand. In contradiction to previous reports that troops behaved badly, our informant says that by citizens, who were in the fight, he was assured that the troops, although they allowed themselves to be decoyed into ambush, displayed, throughout the action, the utmost gallantry, and fought like tigers. About twenty-five or thirty soldiers were killed in about the same number of minutes. The situation in northern Idaho far exceeds in gravity any Indian outbreak of our day, and it will tax the best resources of the government and of the people immediately interested, to subdue the Indians and restore peace to the country. The Indians know that the army on this coast is but a skeleton, and the people helpless for want of arms. A special to the Portland Oregonian, just received from Lewiston, June 21st, 8 a.m., says: Sixty-five volunteers were to proceed from their defenses at Mount Idaho to reconnoiter the position of the Indians, who are supposed to be somewhere in the direction of the Salmon river. A steamer arrived this forenoon, having on board 107 troops. No extra arms came on the steamer. About fifty volunteers have arrived here. A few of them have no suitable arms, but are awaiting them from below.

"BESS!" EMILY FITZGERALD CRIED IN EXASPERATION, whirling on her seven-year-old daughter. "Take your little brother and go outside now while I am doing my best to finish this letter to your grandmother before the mail has to be posted."

"Yes, Mamma," responded young Elizabeth, immediately contrite at her mother's sharp tone. She turned to her younger brother. "Come on, Bertie. Let's find something to do outside with your toy horses until Mamma's done with her letter."

With a sigh not in the least born of relief, but more so the sound one makes when faced with an arduous task, Emily fixed her eyes on the small cabinet photo of her mother she cradled in her left hand. How she wished that dear Quaker were there to comfort her at that moment.

Ever since he had returned to the fort from Portland, her husband, Jenkins—but better known as John—FitzGerald, the man whom she more often called Doctor, had hardly experienced a moment's rest, what with all the campaign preparations, all those duties laid about his shoulders now that General Howard had departed with his column to find the Nez Perce.

As she gazed at that sepia-toned memento of a visit to a Philadelphia photographer's studio with her mother, Emily angrily scolded herself for being so selfish, then propped the photograph beside the letter she was crafting.

Why wasn't she able to just accept how much better it was that Howard had decided to leave her husband behind at Fort Lapwai to see to supply-train and organizational matters for the time being? Far better than watching him ride off with the others that might not return! Dr. Jenkins A. FitzGerald, army surgeon, First U. S. Cavalry. A man of duty and honor . . .

In all their years together since the Civil War, she hadn't

addressed him as Jenkins more than two, perhaps three, times. Instead, she called him John or—mostly—Doctor.

He had been away from the post, visiting Portland on army business, when news of the murders first reached Fort Lapwai. How glad she had been that her John hadn't been here when Colonel Perry marched off with his hundred men. There simply was no convincing Emily that John wouldn't have been among all those dead left to rot on the White Bird battlefield.

But when he did get back upriver, what a homecoming that had been! Even though they both knew it wasn't for long. General Howard was gathering 227 men, a complement of eight companies, from nearby posts and tiny garrisons: two troops of cavalry, five companies of infantry, along with a company of artillery who were armed with two Gatling guns and a mountain howitzer. My, but how they would go to work on Joseph's murderers now!

Fort Lapwa
June 24, 1877

Dear Mamma,

I have not been able to write or even to think for a week. Such a confusion as our quiet little Lapwai has been in. When I can, I will write the particulars. Since the battle, we have all had a great deal to occupy us. Mrs. Boyle and I have been with Mrs. Theller . . . Then all week there have been troops passing through and we have entertained the officers . . . The parade ground is full of horses, the porches are full of trunks and blankets, everybody is rushing about, and everything is in confusion. My brain is in as much confusion as anything else. The army is so reduced, and none of the companies are full, and all the troops that can possibly be gathered from all this region only amount to three hundred. Those are now in the field, and it is a little handful! Oh, the government, I hate it! Much it respects and cares for the soldier who, at a moment's notice, leaves his family and sacrifices his life for some mistaken Indian policy . . . I wish we were well out of it. The Nez Perce Indians are at war with the Whites. What a blow to the theories of Indian civilization. The whole tribe is wavering, and we don't know when it will all end—

"Excuse me, Mrs. FitzGerald."

Emily turned with a start, finding the slight woman framed by the open doorway leading onto the front porch, her pale hands clutched before her swollen belly like a pair of white doves that might take flight if she were not mindful of them. And those red, red eyes.

"Yes, Alice."

The very-much pregnant Alice Hurlburt cleared her throat, took one step closer to the surgeon's wife, then said, "If it's fine by you, ma'am . . . can my young'uns play with your li'l ones?"

"I just sent Bessie outside with Bert."

"Yes, I saw," Mrs. Hurlburt replied, half-turning her head out the door, then back again. "They all play so well together."

"It will be fine, Alice. Yes, quite fine."

Those red-rimmed, cried-out eyes did their best to smile at Emily as Alice Hurlburt turned back through the open doorway, stepping into the shade of the porch, little protection from the growing heat of that summer afternoon.

Emily FitzGerald swatted at a fly, dipped her pen into the inkwell, and continued writing.

I have a sad, sad story to tell about the family of one of those who did not come home after Joseph's murderers ambushed Colonel Perry's men. It appears that William Hurlburt made a fine mess of his life as a civilian. Problem was, he had a wife and two children. With nowhere else to turn, and no other way to feed his family, Mr. Hurlburt joined the army and soon found himself trans-

ferred to Nez Perce country. Only recently did his wife and children come west to join him at Lapwai. In such hardship cases with enlisted men, the government will pay the costs of transportation of a man's family to his duty station, but a little is deducted from every paycheck until those costs are paid off.

And now it's clear to see she is with child again, Mamma. Pitiful creature, poor Alice is, for she lost her husband to the Nez Perce last week on White Bird Creek. Now she finds herself without a husband, deeply in debt, and without any prospects on how to return east to her people. Not knowing what else to do, I performed on my Christian charity and took them in until their situation can be sorted through. She is a very nice little woman, and her children are as nice as I know. It does my heart good to have them under our roof instead of being left out in the cold now that the army will no longer provide for her, but comes demanding repayment on its transportation debt. The children play so well together.

She is left destitute. After her sickness, we will all help her. A purse will be raised to take her back to her friends. She is a helpless sort of a little woman, and I never saw such a look of distress in my life as has taken possession of her face.*

Outside, the children were shrieking with abandon and glee as they chased one another across the grass of the nearby parade. Emily went to the window, pushed aside the gauzy curtain, and peered into the unblemished June sunshine. *It is a blessing,* she thought, *a blessing the children can play as if they haven't a care in the world. As if one father isn't dead, mortifying in this harsh sun on an abandoned battlefield, and the other father soon to be marching off with those who will make the Nez Perce pay for their bloody crimes.*

---

*That peculiar nineteenth-century euphemism for pregnancy.

Search as she may out the window, Emily didn't catch a glimpse of the Doctor. So she returned to her letter, settling into the ladder-back chair at the small secretary once more, then dipped her pen into the inkwell.

Soon enough their parting would come. In a war the soldiers needed their surgeons. All too soon Howard would summon John to the battlefront. Like other officers, dutiful and honor-bound, he would kiss his family farewell, mount up, and ride off to join the others.

She dragged the back of her left hand across both damp cheeks and continued writing.

This last week has been the most dreadful I have ever passed through. John came home, and I felt a little relieved of the horrors that hung over me when I heard he was not to go out with the first detachment. I heard General Howard say, when arranging his orders, that someone must, for the present, be left here to arrange supplies, medicines, etc., and Doctor had better be left here, as he belongs to the post . . . You can't imagine how sad it all is here. Here are these nice fellows gathered around our table, all discussing the situation and all knowing they will never all come back.

One leaves his watch and little fixings and says, "If one of those bullets gets me, send this to my wife." Another gave me his boy's photograph to keep for him, as he could not take it. He kept his wife's with him, and twice he came back to look at the boy's before he started off. One officer left a sick child, very ill; another left a wife to be confined next month. What thanks do they all get for it? No pay, and abuse from the country that they risk their lives to protect . . .

Your loving daughter,
Emily F.

P. S. If John had been here, he would have gone with Colonel Perry and, in all probability, been killed. I am so thankful of that trip to Portland and hope and pray God will watch over the Doctor as wisely through all this horrible war. Even if he goes away from Lapwai, I shall be glad I am here, for we can hear from the troops in a few hours. We do hope this next fight will decide the matter forever.

Em.

CHAPTER THREE

JUNE 24, 1877

BY TELEGRAPH

—

The Idaho Indian Troubles.

—

Attempted General Combination of all the Tribes.

—

IDAHO.

—

Latest from the Scene of Indian Disturbances.

BOISE CITY, June 23.—Hon. T. E. Logan, mayor of Boise City, and Bonin Costin, member of the legislative council, who left here on Wednesday for the purpose of visiting the Indians encamped on Great Camas prairie, twenty-five miles southeast of this place, returned at noon, accompanied by fourteen of the chiefs of the Indians there assembled. There are now encamped in that locality about 1,500 Indians of both sexes and all ages, embracing members of Bannacks, Shoshones and Yellowstone tribes. Logan and Costin went to Willow creek, forty miles distant, where they found a party of Indians. They made known their object, to obtain the disposition of the Indians and their intentions. The Indians were asked to send forward their best riders to the main camp, and request the principal chief to meet the commission at Willow creek. The Indians complied and soon the chiefs made their appearance and an interview took place which revealed the fact that these Indians had been visited by emissaries from the Nez Perces and other hostiles in the north, and a portion of them had been considering whether to remain friendly to the whites or to join the hostiles . . .

SAN FRANCISCO, June 23.—A Portland press dispatch says General Howard telegraphs from Fort Laparoi, June 21st: Captain Miller with 300 men leaves for the front this evening. The Indian prisoners state that the soldiers left wounded on the field were killed but not mutilated. A steamer arrived at Lewiston this morning with 125 troops and a large quantity of arms, etc.

CAPTAIN DAVID PERRY WASN'T SURE IF HE READ DISAPproval in General Howard's eyes . . . or merely a deep, deep disappointment.

"Is that the extent of your report, Colonel?" Howard used Perry's brevet rank.

The captain cleared his throat nervously. "Not exactly, sir. With your permission—"

"There's more?"

"Not really any more to my report, General," then Perry felt angry with himself for hemming and hawing. "Yes, sir. I have something to say."

Howard shifted uneasily on the camp stool in front of his headquarters tent pitched near the base of one of the low hills here at the army's camp surrounding the Norton ranch on Cottonwood Creek.

Back in those early days of this dirty little outbreak, Benjamin Norton and his family had been flushed from their home by renegade warriors, chased onto the Camas Prairie, and run down miles from succor or aid. While Norton and others in the same party had died of their bullet wounds, his wife, son, and niece had survived their hellish ordeal. Now the road ranch stood in shambles: Warriors had ransacked the house as they rummaged through the white family's possessions, everything not taken or burned lay about in utter disorder, clothing cut or torn apart, drawers yanked out and dumped over, chairs chopped into kindling, sacks of sugar and salt strewn across the wood floors, an unrestrained victory riot gone completely mad.

The only signs that this had once been a peaceful setting

might well have been the upturned milking pails still resting on their corral fenceposts, a few unfed chickens scratching in the yard, and a lonely pup that cowered in the shadows beneath the porch.

Arriving here yesterday, the twenty-third, at noon after a forty-three-mile march from Lapwai, the general had put his men into bivouac, intending to use this spot as his base of operations against the Non-Treaty Nez Perce who were surely still ravaging the surrounding countryside. While Howard's eight companies established their perimeter, dug rifle pits, and organized a horse-guard, the general sent word to the nearby settlements of Grangeville and Mount Idaho with orders for Captain David Perry to report to his commanding officer at Cottonwood Station.

Taking the better part of two hours on the morning of the twenty-fourth, Perry had detailed every step of his march from Fort Lapwai, his approach to the seat of the troubles, along with a studied emphasis on the testimony of the local civilians that the Indians were sure to flee, certain to throw down their arms without a fight at the first sign of the soldiers, that Perry was convinced he must act quickly before the thieves escaped across the Salmon with their stolen horses and cattle.

At that point the captain explained his march across the White Bird divide, awaiting dawn when they could march down into the canyon for the attack.

"You had all your men deployed before they began falling back?" Howard had asked more than once.

"Yes, sir."

"With none of your elements held in reserve?"

"No, General."

Howard brooded at that. "But you chose to place the civilians on your far left, at a critical place along your line."

"Yes, I did."

"And that's where the Nez Perce rolled up your line, beginning with those untrained civilians."

The captain reluctantly nodded. "That appears to be exactly what happened."

It was a painful two hours—some of the hardest Perry had ever endured in the army. But these next few minutes, and what more he had to tell General O. O. Howard, might well be the most painful of all, or this might be just what saved his hash in this man's army.

"Well, Colonel," Howard said wearily as he tossed out the cold dregs from his tin coffee cup. "You said you had one thing more to report."

"I have a concern as to Major Trimble." He spoke in little above a harsh whisper, his heart thumping in his chest as he struggled to control his anger, an anger at the mere mention of the man's name.

Captain Joel G. Trimble, brevet major, commander of H Company, First U. S. Cavalry—and Perry's subordinate at Fort Lapwai—had ridden into the valley of the White Bird with David Perry . . . but had been the first to race back out in the retreat.

"Trimble failed to acknowledge your orders for him to halt and assist in your orderly retreat?" Howard asked, dumbfounded.

"Lieutenant Parnell will back me up, General," Perry asserted. "We both saw Major Trimble stop at the top of the divide, turn, and look back down at us as we closed the file. He had to have seen us calling for his assistance, seen us waving him back to cover our retreat."

"What did the major do?"

"We watched him turn away and disappear at the top," the captain explained. "I didn't see him again until I reached the Grangeville settlement—"

"Have you confronted Trimble with your accusations?"

Perry could no longer peer into Howard's eyes. He dropped his gaze to the thick grass beneath his boots. "More times than I care to count, sir—I've asked myself why I didn't upbraid him there and then."

Howard clinked down the empty coffee cup and asked, "You didn't state your charges against him?"

Still unable to look the general in the eye, Perry said, "No. The only reason I have been able to figure out for my failure to demand an explanation of him is that I found myself barely able to throttle back my anger whenever I'm around Trimble. I'm certain that if I ever got started on this topic in his presence, I might not be responsible for my actions—"

"Are you charging him with insubordination?"

It took a few moments before the captain finally raised his eyes to look at Howard's face, then nodded. "Yes, General."

"And dereliction of duty?"

"That too, yes, sir. In my opinion, the battle was lost when his left side of the line disintegrated. He could have held—even after the civilians were rolled up. But within minutes he had abandoned me. Major Trimble abandoned everyone who was behind him in the retreat."

"How many men was that, Colonel?"

Perry straightened and brought his shoulders out. "I doubt there was any more than a handful of soldiers in front of Trimble in their retreat out of the canyon."

Howard wagged his head and stared into the fire. "He was out ahead of all the rest?"

"Yes, sir."

"These . . . are serious charges." For a long time Howard continued to stare at the nearby fire. When he finally spoke, it was to call out to his dog-robber, who was perched on a canvas stool just out of earshot from that quiet discussion the two officers had been having. "Orderly, pour me some more coffee."

Perry watched the young private hurry over and drag the coffeepot off the coals with a greasy towel. These orderlies, who worked as servants for their superior officers, had been given that appellation commonly used by the army of that day: *dog-robber.* With the coffee poured and handed to the general, the private again retreated out of hearing.

"Colonel Perry," Howard sighed with finality. "We've got a war exploding around us at this moment."

"Sir?"

Howard took a long sip of the coffee, then continued

without looking across at the captain. "For the moment, I don't dare sacrifice a single one of my officers through disciplinary action."

That stunning admission caught Perry by surprise. "B-But, General. I wasn't considering bringing Major Trimble up on charges. No disciplinary action. Perhaps an official reprimand from you was all that I could expect. If his offense goes without notice, it serves to show a bad example to the enlisted men who all witnessed his dereliction—"

"Colonel," Howard interrupted him. "For me to take any action against the major would be to relieve him of duty, sending him back to Fort Lapwai under escort until an official inquiry is made, and I determine if a court should be called. I'd be taken up with having to prefer charges and you taken up along with me. We simply don't have the time for that right now. Instead, we've got a war to fight."

Perry kept staring at Howard's bearded face, wondering when the general would look up from his coffee tin, when Howard would take his eyes off that smoky fire. While he hadn't graduated near the top of his class, David Perry was nonetheless slowly realizing that he had this situation sorted out for what it was. There would be no arguing with the general's decision.

"Very good, sir," he said with a somber note of regret. "I understand this matter of preferring charges against Major Trimble will only be delayed for the time being?"

"Yes, by all means. Just for the time being."

He dragged his heels together, straightened, and saluted his commanding officer. "Very good, General. For the time being. . . . After all, we do have a war to fight."

Fort Lapwai
June 25, 1877

Dear Aunt Annie,

Your nice letter came this morning and decided me to write to you.

You ask about the Indians. They are devils, and I will not feel easy again until we are safely out of the country they claim as theirs. Joseph's Non-Treaty band was given thirty days to come onto the reservation. On the last day of the thirty, when everybody was comfortably settled and never dreaming of trouble, they began to murder the settlers.

Doctor was away in Portland. He came hurrying home horrified. He had heard this post was burned and all sorts of alarming rumors. I felt all my calmness and bravery departing when he came home, as he only came in the morning and expected to move out with the troops in the evening, but the General found it necessary to leave someone to forward supplies and look after the troops that are passing through here and left Dr. F. for the present. Dr. Alexander . . . is the chief medical officer in the field. Dr. Sternberg . . . was also with us last week and has moved on to the front. We have been busy entertaining the officers who are passing through, with our hearts aching, knowing they will never all come back, and fearing, too, all the time, an attack on the post.

We had one horrible false alarm of an Indian attack last week. The long roll was sounded, the men were all under arms, and the women and children all gathered into one house around which there are breastworks . . . Poor Mrs. Theller joined Mrs. Boyle and me. She had strapped on her dead husband's cartridge belt and was carrying his carbine and looked every bit as if she were ready to avenge her husband's brutal murder.

We fear there will be a horrible battle within the next few days. Everybody here is busy day and night. My poor John! I have not had five minutes to talk with him since he came home . . .

Doctor wanted to send us right home, but I can't leave him or leave here, even when he goes to join the troops that are in the front, as I can hear of him so often and so immediately here. If I should lose him (I hope and pray he will be spared to me) I would, of course, come right home to you all and expect you to take care of me, at least until I could think what I could do with my helpless little babies . . . Doctor says he thinks us safe here, or he would not let us stay. We are all well, only nearly worn out by the excitement and constant strain. I start at every unusual sound and feel the strength departing from my knees and elbows. John declares I have lost ten pounds. Everybody feels blue and anxious for the result. Another victory for Joseph would bring to his standard all the disaffected Indians in the Department, and the whole Nez Perces tribe is wavering.

After Lunch

The Nez Perce Agent lunched with us. He says he learns from friendly Indians that Joseph's command is not a large one, does not number much over a hundred, but that hundred is prepared to fight to the death. The Indians say they know they will be hung if taken, and they mean to kill as many soldiers as they can first and then die themselves. Our officers going through here think the campaign will be a short but severe one. I wish all the Indians in the country were at the bottom of the Red Sea. I suppose the country will have trouble until they are exterminated.

Your affectionate niece,
Emily FitzGerald

CHAPTER FOUR

JUNE 25, 1877

BY TELEGRAPH

—

Great Storm in the West.

—

Extending Over a Large Portion of the West.

—

OMAHA, June 25.—The storm, very general throughout the west, was first heard of at Cheyenne yesterday evening. Heavy hail and wind extended north of Sioux City, south of Kansas City, and over the state of Iowa.

FROM THE EDGE OF THE TREE LINE, FIRST SERGEANT Michael McCarthy turned in his saddle and looked back at the Camas Prairie laid out behind them like a soggy, rumpled bedcloth. Their bivouac on Cottonwood Creek was back there some fourteen miles or so through the sheets of sleety rain and wet snow.

H Company had followed Captain Joel G. Trimble and a Nez Perce tracker away from the Nortons' road ranch an hour after sunrise that morning, the twenty-fifth of June. While the general himself would be coming along at a much slower pace this Monday, Howard had ordered Trimble and his men to make a reconnaissance in force toward Slate Creek and relieve the citizens under seige at the settlement. In addition, Company H should be prepared to turn the Nez Perce when Howard's column flushed the enemy from their Salmon River hiding places.

With that last look over his shoulder, McCarthy still couldn't spot any signs of the general's column moving away from Cottonwood in the dance of those intermittent but heavy and wet snowflakes. Plans were that the rest of

Howard's men would march for Grangeville and Mount Idaho, halting briefly to reassure the frightened settlers taking refuge there. Then the column would push on over the divide for Perry's battlefield, where they would bury the dead before pursuing the Non-Treaty bands up the Salmon. That should give Trimble's H enough time to be in position at the Slate Creek barricades, where they could stem the red tide Howard's column was sure to stir into motion.

"Sounds to me we got the darty duty again, Major," McCarthy had growled to Second Lieutenant William R. Parnell earlier that morning as they were forming up their company, using the officer's brevet rank.

The tall and fleshy fellow Irishman's eyes darted over the ten new men who had arrived at Cottonwood two days before behind Second Lieutenant Thomas T. Knox, on detached duty from Fort Walla Walla. "Not all the luftenant's men are proper sojers, Sergeant dear," he replied guardedly.

"Must've picked up them recruits down at Walla Walla," McCarthy assessed the newcomers. "Them weeds look green as grass."

Parnell nodded. "But we'll take them shavetail boyos because you and me need 'em so bad. Ain't that right, Sergeant?"

True enough: Lieutenant Knox and his ten recruits bolstered the company roster at a most crucial time. Eleven men would go far to replacing the thirteen dead and one wounded ripped from the rolls of H Company on the seventeenth of June at White Bird. Their recent arrival brought Trimble's command up to some thirty men. Not a full company, but a damn sight better than a puny scouting patrol now that they were riding off against the red hellions who had butchered so many of McCarthy's friends eight days before.

Still, to get to Slate Creek, Trimble's men had to make sure they avoided any roving war parties and gave the Non-Treaty bands a wide berth. To accomplish that, H Company would take a circuitous route, following an abandoned and little-used trail through the high country to reach the mining camp of Florence. From there they would double back several miles, staying behind the ridges, angling down to reach the civilians who had gathered behind their barricades on the east side of the Salmon, at the mouth of Slate Creek.

There . . . in the distance, for a brief moment before he could no longer see the Camas Prairie laid out beneath the low-slung clouds, Sergeant McCarthy thought he saw the first dark figures snaking onto the grassy, rolling plains. Emerging from Cottonwood Station, as the locals called Norton's road ranch.

He turned around and settled himself miserably into that damp McClellan saddle again. It made him feel a little better diving into these forested hills and the unknown, realizing that Howard's column actually would be somewhere at their rear.

It was for sure that Colonel Perry was no fighting man. By the same token, neither was McCarthy's own company commander, Captain Trimble. He, even before the colonel, had turned tail and scampered away when things got warm. So it sure as hell didn't give a man a secure feeling to go traipsing off behind a man who had shown the white feather to those red heathens.

McCarthy quickly shot another glance at Knox's ten new recruits up from Walla Walla. Then his eyes continued down the column to those battle-weary survivors of the White Bird fray. And finally to the broad back of that fleshy Irishman, Parnell.

If the red buggers jumped H Company somewhere in these hills, at least the two of them would manage to hurl profane Irish curses at the red buggers until they got down to their last bullet. The one a man always saved for himself.

OLIVER Otis Howard was more than startled.

He had been shaken to his core to look over the men of Perry's command who had remained behind at the settlements while the captain rode to meet Howard at Cottonwood.

How different they are in numbers, different in their ap-

pearance, not the brisk and hearty troopers that left Fort Lapwai the week previous, he thought as his horse slowly moved toward the barricades.

Now the look on their faces, the studied horror in their eyes, reminded him of the war-weary, frightened soldiers he had seen every day, every campaign, in their war against the rebellious Southern states. Although those survivors of the White Bird fight cheered the general's arrival with the rest of the cavalry now placed under Perry's command, Howard realized those survivors had nonetheless been changed for all time.

At a parting of the roads on the outskirts of Grangeville, Howard had sent his infantry—B, D, E, H, and I Companies of the Twenty-first, as well as E Company of the Fourth Artillery—on ahead, with orders to make camp at Johnson's ranch near the base of the White Bird divide. The general would continue on with Captain David Perry, who was now leading a new battalion of horse soldiers: E and L Companies of the First U. S. Cavalry companies.

After an hour's layover in tiny Grangeville, during which time he gathered intelligence on the Non-Treaty bands from the locals and inspected those supplies, J. W. "John" Crooks was making available to the column, Howard resumed his march for Mount Idaho. With cheering, exuberant citizens swarming around him in that neighboring community, the general examined the hastily built fortress with former British officer H. W. Croasdaile before he walked down the main street to reach Loyal P. Brown's Mount Idaho House.

"Quiet! Quiet!" Brown shouted above the noisy throng of more than 250 settlers, ranchers, and soldiers, too. "I've prevailed upon General Howard to say a few words before he rejoins his column at Johnson's ranch. Ladies and gentlemen—I give you the man who will right the wrongs done us. The man who will recapture our stock and property from the red thieves. The man who will quickly put down this uprising and punish the Nez Perce. . . . I give you General Howard!"

He couldn't remember when he had been given such a splendid ovation. Surely not since those days of the Freedmen's Bureau, before the scandals, before he was forever tainted with the vicious slander that had almost ruined his career, almost ruined the work of a lifetime. How that raucous applause and hearty huzzahs thundered in his ears and refreshed his flagging spirit here as he set about snuffing out the first flames of a territory-wide war.

But as he self-consciously cleared his throat, Otis promised himself he would make it a short speech. Just the way he was going to make this a short war. "Ladies and gentlemen. Friends, and fellow countrymen. We have now taken the field in good earnest. More troops are on the way to join us."

That declaration elicited another noisy round of applause before he was allowed to continue.

"I propose to take prompt measures for the pursuit and punishment of the hostile Indians, and wish you—each and every one of you—to help me in that endeavor. Help me in the way of information and supplies, as much does lie in your power."

A quiet smattering of applause began what quickly exploded into a noisy response from the approving throng, more than two hundred heads bobbing in agreement with his proposal. Otis stood there, letting the praise wash over him a moment, sensing the strength it gave him, how it seeped into every muscle to give might to his own efforts in the coming struggle.

When the crowd settled, he said in a quieter tone, "I sympathize deeply with you in the loss of life, and in the outrages to which your families have been subjected. Rest assured that no stone will be left unturned to give you redress, to give you protection in the future."

An instant applause erupted again, and Otis stepped back, gesturing to L. P. Brown. The hotel owner came forward and said a few final words before the two of them turned to join Sarah Brown at the open doorway. As the general's party stopped just inside the Browns' hotel, a young man in his late twenties hurried forward, rolling a sleeve down over his bare forearm.

"General Howard," Brown began, "I'd like you to meet Dr. John Morris. Mount Idaho's physician."

They clumsily shook left hands and Otis said, "You're caring for the wounded, Doctor?"

The Missouri-born Morris nodded. "I was visiting Portland when news of the outbreak reached us. Boarded the next steamer for Lewiston and made my way over from there."

"How long have you been practicing in this area?"

"Came to Mount Idaho in seventy-five," the doctor explained. "Not long after I earned my license to practice from St. Louis Medical College."

Brown stepped up. "Dr. Morris returned home three days ago, the twenty-second. Poor fella hasn't had much sleep since."

"I catch a nap when and where I can, General," Morris explained.

Howard looked into the young man's warm eyes. "May I see, may I talk to the people, the civilians you are caring for?"

"Of course. By all means," Morris replied and started away.

In several of the small rooms on that floor, and on the second story as well, Morris led Howard and Brown to the bedside of every victim of the Nez Perce terror. Many sobbed quietly as the old one-armed soldier moved among their beds, cots, or simple pallets spread upon the floor.

Howard turned to the hotel owner. "Mr. Brown, what about the man you started for Fort Lapwai with news of the murders?"

Brown shook his head. "Lew Day? He isn't here anymore."

Howard turned to the physician, asking, "No longer under your care, Dr. Morris?"

"By the time I arrived here from Portland, his leg wound was in a dreadful condition," Morris declared. "I explained to Lew that it was his leg or his life. He agreed to the amputation." Then the physician sighed. "But I think he was so drained of all strength that he simply didn't survive for long after I took his leg."

"He died?"

Brown said, "We buried Lew Day up in the Masonic cemetery."

"Please, take me to the others," Howard stated, gesturing with his left arm. "I want to see all the others who suffered these attacks and outrages."

Joe Moore was barely able to speak, weakened so from a great loss of blood, critically wounded in the attack on the Norton wagon on the Camas Prairie.*

Both Herman Faxon and Theodore Swarts were still recovering from their terrible wounds suffered in the battle in White Bird Canyon. Jennie Norton lay in a small room, watched over and cared for by her son, Hill, and her younger sister, Lynn Bowers.

Next door lay the wounded Mrs. Chamberlin, who had watched the Nez Perce butcher her husband, murder one of her daughters, then suffered repeated assault by the members of the war party who had jumped the Norton party on the Camas Prairie road.

"She's suffered . . . unspeakable horror," Dr. Morris explained in a whisper at Howard's ear as the general stood gazing at the woman. "Every outrage they could have committed, the Indians perpetrated on her. Took her husband, one of her children, too. Then they repeatedly shamed her."

Howard's eyes drifted now to the youngster playing quietly on the floor with a tiny wooden horse, perfectly content near the end of the bed. "Whose child?"

"Mrs. Chamberlin's," Sarah Brown declared. "Unable to speak. The savages cut its poor tongue off."

"Never talk again?" Howard asked in a whisper as he started toward the side of the bed. There he bent slightly,

---

**Cries from the Earth*, vol. 14, the *Plainsmen* series.

laid his hand on Mrs. Chamberlin's, and closed his eyes in silent prayer.

When he concluded, Howard straightened and stared down a moment into the toddler's big brown eyes before he turned away with the doctor.

Besides Williams George, H. C. "Hurdy Gurdy" Brown, and Albert Benson, Morris was also tending the wounds of little Maggie Manuel.

"She tells us Joseph killed her mother and baby brother," L. P. Brown declared in a soft voice at the doorway to another room as Howard looked in on the child sleeping upon a pallet made of blankets folded upon the floor.

"How does she know it was Joseph?" Howard asked.

Brown shrugged. "Says she's seen him before."

"But Maggie's grandfather and an Irish miner never found the bodies, General," Morris asserted.

Howard asked, "She broke her arm?"

"The Irishman I mentioned—he set her arm before beginning their journey here," Morris said. "A good job of it, too. Didn't have to rebreak it at all. Farther up that same arm, she had suffered a penetrating injury—an arrow the miner managed to remove. We're watching that closely for infection. Keeping the wound open and treated with sulphur. She's been brave through it all—knowing as she does that she's lost both her parents to the Indians."

"Merciful God in Heaven," Howard whispered as he turned away, unable to look upon the child anymore. Feeling as if he could never gaze upon another wounded youngster as long as he lived. Beneath his full beard, the general felt the blood drain from his skin, his face blanch.

War was for men. Not for these women and their babies. War was a profession to be practiced by men, practiced on other men. Not on these innocent victims of such barbaric cruelty.

"I've seen enough, Doctor," he said in a soft voice, sensing the sweat bead on his brow as he replaced the hat upon his head, his flesh grown clammy. "I think . . . I've seen quite enough."

Chapter Five

June 25–26, 1877

"Who goes there?"

The instant that harsh voice challenged them out of the inky night, Sergeant Michael McCarthy snapped awake in the saddle.

Their company commander was the first to reply as the thirty-some soldiers of H Company and a handful of hangers-on from Mount Idaho clattered to a noisy halt in the dark, just after 2:00 A.M. on that Monday morning, 25 June. "Major Joel Trimble—First U. S. Cavalry!"

"Cavalry!" a second, different voice shouted now, less threatening and an octave higher with relief and celebration.

There came a sudden bustle of noise from the darkness in their front: sounds of shuffling, running feet, several more muffled voices mixed with a little unrestrained exuberance as the wooded river bottom came alive.

"Open this goddamned gate!" a new voice was raised. "Get it open for them soldiers!"

"By bloody damn," Lieutenant Parnell exclaimed with no small measure of exhaustion beside McCarthy, "appears we've found the settlers of Slate Creek!"

Just past two-thirty, early on the morning of 26 June, Company H had done just that.

It had been closing in on complete darkness the night before when they reached the tiny mining settlement of Florence, finally coaxing out a few of the Chinese and what few whites still remained in the town to report what they knew of the marauding Indians. It was useless attempting to pry any information from the Oriental laborers, but two of the white miners had a little news to relay on the movements of the Non-Treaty Bands. The Nez Perce were no longer encamped at the mouth of the White Bird. They had eased south, up the Salmon toward Horseshoe Bend.

"The savages appear to be acting as if we won't attack 'em again," Trimble had explained to the entire company just before he ordered them to remount.

Parnell had asked, "We still going on to Slate Creek, Major?"

"Get them saddled, Sergeant McCarthy," was Trimble's only reply as he ignored his lieutenant. "We're not sticking around here when we've got ground to cover."

Those weary, saddle-galled troopers had climbed back into their McClellans after no more than fifteen minutes with their boots on the ground and pushed on. Twelve miles later, as McCarthy's watch was nearing midnight, Trimble called for another halt in an open patch of meadow surrounded by stands of timber. The moon was just then tearing itself off the horizon to the east, somewhere behind the Bitterroot Mountains.

"Don't loosen your cinches, boyos," McCarthy warned his men. "You can eat your tacks if you got 'em, but no pipes. Remember what happened at the White Bird. No god-blame-it pipes in this country."

After something less than an hour Trimble gave the order to remount and they marched on, encountering some crusted snow just after leaving the small meadow and climbed ever higher. What with those snowfields reflecting the dim starlight, the whole countryside limned by a bright, silvery half-moon, the view was stunning. In awe at such breathtaking scenery, McCarthy knew it would take a pen much more eloquent than his to do justice to their cross-country ride.

The quiet of that mountain wilderness, the blackness of the night that surrounded them, the rhythmic plodding of the saddle horse beneath him—all of it proved more than McCarthy could fight. He drifted off and was dozing in the saddle when those voices called out from the dark.

After a brief celebration and a shaking of hands all around, the settlers helped Trimble's men find a corral for their weary horses, then led the soldiers within their log walls. Clutching their blankets about their shoulders, the troopers collapsed here or there, wherever a man might find enough room to stretch out, close his eyes, and sink immediately into a well-earned sleep.

By the gray light of false dawn McCarthy came awake, rolling out to join two civilians at the west wall where they had a low fire going, coffee warmed to see them through their watch.

"William Watson's the name," the older man introduced himself with a big hand.

The sergeant replied, "I heard you're the one knowed how to build this fort."

"That's right. Got all my learning during the war," Watson explained.

"Your education come in handy here," McCarthy said, admiring the sturdiness of the timbers the men had sunk into three-foot-deep trenches, then back-filled. "Can't see how the bloody h'athens could've broke in here on you."

Norman Gould said, "Bill here, he saw to it we'd get all the women and young'uns into the stone house back yonder if the bastards broke over the walls."

"We made the house our powder magazine," Watson explained, jabbing a thumb toward the structure. "Blow up everything—everyone, too—before the Nez Perce got their hands on 'em."

"Didn't know how long we'd have to hold out," George Greer said. "Word was that General Howard was somewhere in the field, but we didn't know just where you soldiers was, or when you'd get here to us."

"Wasn't the general moved out first," McCarthy explained dolefully. "Maybe it had been Howard what led us down into White Bird 'stead of Colonel Perry his cowardly self there'd be more of me friends alive to greet this very morning."

The coffee was good, but the sun that broke over the hills that morning felt even better. Trimble had McCarthy tell the men that H Company would be spending a day of rest at Slate Creek—recruiting their horses and gathering strength for the rest of their mission.

Later that Tuesday morning, some of the women and children ventured from the stone house, stepping outside the safety of the stockade walls for the first time in more than a week of dread. While the rest of the women were grateful for, and the children excited about, the arrival of the soldiers, not one of Trimble's cavalrymen got a peek at either Helen Walsh or Elizabeth Osborn.

"Rumor has it they was violated," Parnell explained in a whisper as he and McCarthy walked up the slope to relieve two men of their watch along the Salmon.

"Raped?"

"Shhh!" Parnell rasped angrily. "It's talk like that made them two women fear to show their faces."

"They was . . . shamed by the h'athens?"

The lieutenant nodded as they neared the improvised rifle pits. "Both of 'em, over and over again by the red bastards. 'Cause of it, neither of them women gonna ever be the same again."

It made his blood boil, to think of those painted-up, blood-splattered, stink-smeared warriors humiliating, dishonoring, shaming those two women.

The sergeant turned to stare a long moment down at the stone house, his heart breaking for both victims of such unspeakable horror. "No small wonder is it? Why them poor women can't hardly face their friends no more."

"They lost their husbands, too, I heard," Parnell said. "Come out of it only with their wee ones."

"Them's the ones we're fighting the Nez Perce for, Lieutenant Parnell," McCarthy growled. "Them women and children. They're the reason I wanna kill me ever' last Injun buck I can put in my sights, or get my hands around. They're less'n human, ever' last bloody one of 'em."

"WE should reach the scene before midmorning, General," declared Captain David Perry after he had saluted the campaign's commander in the misty damps of predawn that twenty-sixth day of June.

"You understand my purpose in going into that valley is not to engage the Nez Perce," Howard reminded.

"You explained that to me last night."

"I want only to find their location, then follow them with my trackers," the general continued. "But I won't come up on them and attack until I have been reinforced in the next few days. I'm afraid if your experience has taught me anything, it is that caution is the watchword."

Perry licked his lower lip. "I think we all have a newfound respect for their fighting abilities, sir."

"Besides discovering where the enemy is and where he is going, I also seek to honor those fallen men with a decent interment."

It made Perry's skin crawl to think of those bodies having lain in the open for the last nine days—bloating in the rising heat, blackening with decay. A fallen soldier deserved far better from his fellows.

AT six-thirty that Tuesday morning, barely an hour after sunrise, General Howard led his column of infantry, cavalry, and artillery out of that one-night bivouac at Johnson's ranch and started for the White Bird battlefield.

At the top of the hill, Howard had Arthur Chapman called over to the head of the march.

"Mr. Chapman, I'm putting you in charge of the Walla Walla volunteers."

"You got something in mind for us?" the dark-eyed civilian asked.

"A scouting mission," the general said. "To determine where the Nez Perce have gone."

"Very good, General," Chapman replied. He pointed off to the right of their line of march. "We'll push west till we reach the edge of the canyon, staying with the top of this ridge, where Colonel Perry and the rest of his men straggled out of the canyon the morning of the fight."

Perry asked, "Will that give you a good vantage point to look into the valley of the Salmon?"

But Chapman never looked at the captain. He merely nodded to Howard and answered, "None better. We'll have us a good look around for them red murderers for you, General."

Howard rocked back in the saddle, arching his back as if attempting to relieve a knotted muscle. "Very good. We'll be in the valley."

"Gonna bury them soldiers?" Chapman asked with a great deal of curiosity in his eyes.

"We're going to do what any God-fearing soldier would do for his fallen comrades."

Perry watched Chapman turn away without another word; then Howard spoke.

"Colonel, we'll leave Whipple's L Company and Captain Throckmorton's artillery unit in an advantageous spot at the top of White Bird Hill, perhaps over there."

"They'll cover our advance in the event of a surprise, sir?"

The general nodded. "Exactly." Then he turned to a knot of nearby officers. "Colonel Miller?"

The Massachusetts-born captain serving with the Fourth U. S. Artillery, Marcus P. Miller, urged his horse close to Howard's. "Sir?"

"You're assigned the advance as we enter the valley."

The captain saluted. "Yes, General. Captain Winters?"

Henry E. Winters wheeled his mount and approached. "Am I given the honor of supporting the colonel?" He used Miller's brevet rank.

"You are," Howard replied. "Colonel Perry and I will follow you down with the rest of the command. When we reach the battlefield, the colonel himself will organize the search for the bodies of his dead."

The first corpse they found startled the men in the advance with Miller and Winters. From a distance, the figure appeared to be an Indian hiding behind a bush, perhaps even pointing a weapon at the oncoming soldiers. While the rest of the column watched, Winters sent three men forward—their carbines held at ready, prepared to fire, all aimed at the rigid corpse. Up close they discovered that it wasn't an Indian at all, but a white man, his body standing, somehow attached to the spiny branches of a hawthorn bush—both arms outstretched as if he were clutching it.

"It's Sergeant Gunn," Perry grimly explained to Howard after they stopped near the remains of the gray-haired veteran. "F Company, sir."

"He sold his life dearly that day, Colonel."

Perry nodded, noticing the many copper cases in the grass near Gunn's feet. "Colonel Miller, assign three men to bury Sergeant Gunn."

The rest pushed on toward that distant ridge where Perry had deployed his battalion for their abbreviated battle against the screaming horsemen. After crossing another hundred yards, the captain realized he would never forget the grisly sight that greeted them this sunny Tuesday morning. While he was certain the terror of their frantic retreat would forever trouble his waking hours, Perry was just as certain the horror of what lay before him at this very moment would forever haunt his nights.

That and the unearthly stench.

Arms and legs frozen akimbo in death, twenty-some bodies lay scattered across the hillsides, every last one blackened by nine days of mortifying decay and a relentless summer sun, flesh grotesquely swollen with the gases of decomposition until most of the faces were totally unrecognizable in their horrid death grins.

Oh, the stench. When that morning's warm breeze suddenly died and the heavy air lay still upon that field of death, the pungent odor rose up to assault a man with a gagging ferocity.

Perry quickly dragged out his big bandanna and clamped it over his mouth and nose, remembering to breathe through his mouth. The next time the capricious breeze died, he felt his eyes beginning to water with the putrid stench of decaying flesh. His skin began to crawl as he pulled back on the reins and signaled a halt to Miller's and Winter's companies.

On both sides of Perry now the troopers came to a halt. He heard the quiet sounds as the men noisily swallowed, struggling to control their stomachs, while some audibly gagged. One man spilled off the side of his horse, collapsing to his knees as he retched himself free of his hearty breakfast of hardtack, sidemeat, and coffee. Most of it still undigested as it seeped into the grassy soil.

"Get that man back where the air is better," Perry ordered, his eyes streaming now with the very tangible sting of long-forgotten death, doing all that he could to keep from joining those who were gagging at the sight, at the stench, at the very sound of the big, bloated horseflies at work on the bloodied corpses.

Throbbing masses of insects blackened every dead soldier's eyes, waded their way around in his every wound, crawling in and out of the gaping nostrils, a'swim in every swollen, distorted mouth.

It almost appeared these dead were crying out, calling forth from the far side of eternity. . . .

He turned slightly, swallowed hard, and gave his orders. "C-Colonel Miller. Captain Winters. Bring up the infantry companies. Divide them and your men into three platoons each. One platoon from each company will be on burial detail at a time. The other two platoons from each company will remain in reserve, back where the breathing is a little better. Trowel bayonets. Is your mission understood?"

But Perry didn't really look at either of the officers for a response before he quietly, and quickly, concluded, "Do all that you can to give each man a decent burial, gentlemen."

Miller almost lost control as he nodded in answer. His tearing eyes held unabashed gratitude as he quickly turned aside and rode off to pass on the order to the infantry commanders.

Winters saluted, and swallowed hard. This Ohio-born officer had risen up through the ranks after enlisting in the First Cavalry in 1864. "Very good, Colonel. That way we can sp-spell the men."

One by one, the dismounted cavalrymen and foot soldiers located the bodies scattered in the tall, waving grass. It wasn't hard to find the dead.

Two or three soldiers sank to their knees beside a body and began scraping at the black soil with their trowel bayonets they pulled from the leather scabbards hanging from their 1876 pattern duty belts, which were fitted with fifty canvas cartridge loops. The three-man squads frequently spelled one another, as even the hardy were quickly forced to crawl away, retching, struggling to get upwind, to put some distance between them and the distorted remains until they could once again scratch at the ground, removing one small trowelful of soil at a time from what would be each fallen soldier's final resting place.

One small handful of dirt at a time. Scrape the ground with the trowel. Keep from heaving. Scoop the dirt out of the tiny hole. Gag a little. Scrape some more. Pull at the long roots of the tall, nutritious grasses. Scratch the loam from the shallow trench. Stop of a sudden and lunge away, gulping for air. Ashamed when your stomach won't obey and you gag on the burning contents of your breakfast as it hurtled on past your tonsils and over the back of your tongue.

Then you wiped your mouth on your sleeve and scraped some more, eyes burning, tearing spilling down your cheeks until you were almost blinded by the sting of the stench and could barely see.

How thankful Captain David Perry was that many of those men closest to the putrefying bodies had tears in their eyes, streams of them glistening down their cheeks. Right here no one would know exactly why he was crying among all these with tears in their eyes.

Merely looking at those bodies from F and H Companies. Men he might have recognized on the parade at Fort Lapwai had they lived through that fight on the White Bird. Nameless men who had died an ignoble death as the Nez Perce rolled up the left side of their line and hacked Perry's battalion to ribbons. Nameless, and now faceless, anonymous soldiers who had died here for their country . . . fighting an enemy that had surprised them all, rising up to show they were willing to die for their country.

One by one. By one. The hours crawled by with agonizing slowness because the burial details were often finding the swollen, mortifying bodies were unmanageable. As soon as the soldiers attempted to pull a corpse into a shallow grave, a leg or an arm tore free of the body already sticky, pasted to the grassy slope.

Because most of the dead had been stripped of outer clothing—boots, britches, and campaign blouse—every skull and every inch of bare flesh lying against the ground had begun to decay, so much so that when the burial parties dragged the corpses toward their final resting places, that flesh tore free. As hair was pulled free in the tangled, blood-crusted grass, it made many of the bodies appear as if they had been scalped or horribly mutilated by the victorious warriors.

Just the sight of those dismembered corpses, the blackened flesh ripped off and left clinging to the grass, was enough to cause men to begin retching anew.

From one group to another, Perry slowly rode among the burial parties, suggesting how the sergeants should proceed with their details.

"Dig the grave as close as you can to the body," he quietly told the noncoms from behind his bandanna. "Then do your best to roll the body into the hole."

"That way I won't pull off 'nother arm the way I just did," grumbled Sergeant Bernard Simpson, just before the First U. S. cavalryman had to swallow down a mouthful of bile. "S-sir."

"Do the best you can, Sergeant," Perry sympathized, feeling a touch of remorse for these men facing a horrid and daunting task. "Every man here understands we're all just doing for others what we'd want done for us."

CHAPTER SIX

JUNE 26, 1877

"THERE'S YOUR GODDAMNED MURDERIN' INJUNS FOR YOU!" bellowed Ad Chapman at the handful of "Captain" Tom Page's Walla Walla volunteers who had joined him in that ride due west along the high, bare ridge to reach this overlook where they could peer down into the valley of the Salmon.

"Those bastards are running south across the river!" exclaimed E. J. Bunker as they all squinted in the fading light as clouds rolled in to begin blotting out the sun.

Those half-naked horsemen the thirty-six-year-old Chapman had spotted across the Salmon could be no more than a small part of the village they had bumped into back on that bloody Sunday.

George Shearer rubbed an aching shoulder and growled, "I'll wager the squaws and nits've all crossed the river, fixin' to disappear in the mountains."

Chapman looked at his friend a moment, nodding. "Army never catch 'em once they get in that broke-up country other side of the Salmon."

"S'pose we oughtta get back to tell the general?" Bunker asked, his horse done blowing, starting to crop the short grasses on this nearly barren ridge top.

Chapman fished a plug of tobacco from his coat pocket. "If Howard's gonna have a ghost of a chance to get his hands on them Nez Perce, he'll have to quit his dawdling."

Bunker snorted, "That one-armed general still says he's gonna wait for more reinforcements before he'll attack that village again."

Chapman looked at each of their faces a moment, then said, "The way those red bastards fought us a few days back, might not be so bad an idea Howard has more men afore he jumps that camp. Let's get on down below—give that general the news he's been waiting to hear."

He rode tall in the saddle. Thin as a split rail and every bit as lean as a buggy whip. Chapman still had a full head of hair: black as the bottom of a tar spring did it spill across his shoulders. Born back east in Iowa, Chapman had been no more than seven years old when his family traipsed out to Oregon during that historic western migration along the Emigrant Road. His father would become one of the founders of Portland.

In this country rife with opportunity, nine-year-old Arthur had carried dispatches for the army between The Dalles and Fort Walla Walla during the Rogue River Indian War. Six years later, young Chapman had settled over east in Nez Perce country, sending down roots in a piece of ground beside White Bird Creek, at the mouth of a stream that would one day soon bear his name. There he began raising cattle and breeding horses, as well as operating his ferry across the Salmon River at the mouth of the White Bird.

Then almost three years back he had sold his ranch to John J. Manuel and moved north to a new homestead he built on Cottonwood Creek some eight miles from Mount Idaho, out on the Camas Prairie, where he continued to breed horses. Over the last two weeks of Indian troubles, Chapman had lost some four hundred head of prime stock to Nez Perce raiding parties.

He'd had himself a checkered history with the tribe, sometimes friendly, ofttimes not. On the balance, he'd admit, mostly not so friendly. With that short fuse he had to his temper, Chapman hadn't been all that good a neighbor to the Nez Perce, even though he had married an Umatilla squaw a few years back. Even though he spoke real good Nez Perce, too. A few years back the couple had a young boy, and now his wife was expecting another child come early fall.

Problem was, hard as he tried, for the longest time Ad couldn't seem to win with either side—not with most of the

Nez Perce, who distrusted him to one degree or another and not with most of the whites, who considered him a traitor because he had married an Indian woman and fathered a half-breed child.

Simple truth was, Chapman didn't endear himself to some folks simply because he called things as he saw them. To some white folks, that was downright heresy. A white man was supposed to stick up for a white man, no matter what.

But then, on top of that uneasiness, there was a story going the rounds that the Non-Treaty bands didn't trust him any farther than they could throw him because they claimed Chapman had stolen some of their cows and sold them off to Chinese miners up at Florence and Elk City in the mountains. Hell, if those Indians didn't take better care of their stock than to leave their cattle run through Chapman's upper pasture, they deserved to be missing a few cows!

Such was the delicate line he walked between the white world and red in this Salmon River country. For good or bad, there honestly wasn't a man who possessed more experience dealing with the Non-Treaty bands than Arthur Chapman. In fact, over the years, he had forged quite a bond with Chief Looking Glass and a few of his headmen. Ad figured when you got right down to it, his steadfast friendship with the old chief had to go a long way to showing the Nez Perce he wasn't so bad a white fella after all.

Why, on the Thursday before the White Bird massacre, two of his Nez Perce friends—Looking Glass and Yellow Bear—even rode over from the big traditional gathering the Non-Treaty bands were having at the head of Rocky Canyon on Camas Prairie to let Chapman know that some of the young bucks had gone on the warpath and had already killed seven white men by that time. Looking Glass said he was taking his people and moving back to their homes on the Clearwater, wanting to get away from the troublemakers. A damn honorable act by those two old Nez Perce friends to come warn him at a time like that, even going so far as to suggest that he clear out till things simmered down a bit. No sooner had he gotten his wife and son started away than the three of them spotted a war party headed for his ranch.

Chapman figured then and there he might well owe Looking Glass his life for that timely warning, since it turned out to be a horse race all the way to the outskirts of Mount Idaho. Sprinting into the tiny settlement barely ahead of those warriors screaming for his blood, Ad dropped out of the saddle in front of Loyal P. Brown's hotel and began spreading the alarm, shocking one and all with the first report of the Salmon River murders. By nightfall the folks flooding into town had formed their own militia company and elected Chapman as its captain.

In the predawn darkness of the following morning, June 15, Chapman had slipped out of town and back to his ranch to keep a planned rendezvous with Looking Glass and Yellow Bear. As the sky was graying just before five o'clock, he rode up to his friends, a bit surprised to find them accompanied by two other warriors. The chief grimly related the names of the settlers who had been killed up to that point in time on the Camas Prairie and along the Salmon, too. Good Indians they were, those Looking Glass people.

Ad was mightily relieved none of the Asotin band were involved with the murders or later on in the fight that left so many soldiers dead in the White Bird Canyon. Now if Looking Glass's people could manage to stay out of the way of Howard's army, the soldiers would quickly get the rest of those Non-Treaties mopped up and driven onto the reservation.

By the time Ad's civilians had backtracked along the high ridge, then picked their way down the west slope into the valley to reach the site of the army's White Bird debacle, the clouds were noticeably lowering. Distant thunder suddenly reverberated off the surrounding hills. Its long-dying rattle bouncing off the nearby slopes compelled many of the edgy soldiers to duck and scramble for their rifles, preparing for an attack by the Nez Perce.

An occasional finger of lightning starkly split the darkness with a brilliant display. As the civilians approached the first of the burial details, Ad noticed how the soldiers had tied bandannas over their faces, covering everything below their eyes as they tugged and rolled a bloated, distorted figure onto a gray army blanket, then dragged the corpse to the shallow trench they had scraped out of the rocky soil nearby. Hoisting up the four corners of the blanket, the four soldiers rolled the stinking remains into the hole.

One of the soldiers turned suddenly and fell to his knees, ripping off his bandanna as he violently puked into the grass.

Another soldier knelt over the sickened man, patting him on the back as the civilians rode up. He said to Chapman, "The critters been at this one."

"Critters?"

"Wolves, coyotes maybe?"

Chapman crossed his wrists over the saddlehorn and hunched forward. "Likely not wolves. Used to live right down yonder, mouth of that little creek. Maybeso it was a coyote got to that dead soldier—I've seen a mess of coyotes around here in my time. Still, I'd wager it was small critters ate on 'im. Raccoons, maybe a badger. Chewed the poor fella up, did they?"

The soldier nodded as the first of the big drops started to fall out of the lowering sky. Then he gestured across the slope. "Some of the rest been et on, too."

Giving the blackening heavens a sidelong glance, Chapman said, "Rain comin'—I figger your work for the day is 'bout over now."

Gasping, the soldier on his knees replied, "Thank Jesus in Heaven for small b-blessings."

The tall soldier patted the man on the shoulder, then looked again at Chapman as a roll of thunder faded on down the canyon. "Sounds just like God in Heaven is firing a burial volley to honor our dead."

Sensing the hair rise on his arm with more than the dramatic electrical charge in the clean, damp air, Chapman gently nudged his horse away from the three soldiers.

He didn't know if he believed in God anymore. Not when such terrible things were happening to women and children, even to some men—folks who had never given hurt to any person. Couldn't be a God to his way of thinking.

Finding Howard taking cover temporarily beneath some streamside trees about the time the general was giving orders to suspend the burial duties with only eighteen of the dead interred, telling his officers that he intended for his command to return to Johnson's ranch for the night, Chapman and the volunteers reined up nearby and dragged out their rubber ponchos as the underbelly of the low sky opened up on them. While the rain grew serious, the small band of civilians dismounted to report sighting the warriors upriver, across the Salmon.

"They've crossed already," Howard grumped.

"You can't spend much time here, General," Chapman advised.

That made Howard's face go stony, cold. "These men deserve a decent burial, Mr. Chapman."

"Meantime, your prey gonna waltz on outta sight."

"I'll just have to take that chance, won't I?" Howard replied testily. Then he turned and pointed on down the narrow valley. "Whose place was that?"

"Used to be mine, General," Chapman began. "Sold it to John Manuel."

"Was he one of the victims of the Nez Perce depredations?"

"Him, and his wife, their youngest, a baby—all gone. No hide, no hair. Had a daughter, Maggie, too—"

"No, I saw her yesterday in Mount Idaho," Howard stated sadly. "Claimed Joseph killed her mother and baby brother."

Chapman regarded the heap of ruins, all that was left of the nearby buildings he had hammered together of a time years ago. "You wanna ride along, we go take a look for ourselves, General?"

Howard and a handful of officers readily agreed as the

storm softened into a steady, soaking drizzle. For some time they inspected the blackened timbers that had caved in, digging around near the charred river stones of the chimney and fireplace that remained standing despite the destruction of the rest of the cabin.

"I found some bones, General," Chapman suddenly reported.

"The victims?"

"Naw." Ad shook his head as three of the civilians stepped over to expose more of the charred bones with the round toes of their tall boots. "Don't think so. These here bones ain't big enough to be human."

Howard sighed, arching his back in a stretch. "Look there. The Nez Perce raiders destroyed everything else . . . but that outhouse."

Chapman turned, chuckling to see his old single-seat outhouse still standing, sheltered back in the nearby timber. "Damn if that ain't the strangest thing. I'd figgered they'd at least tip it over on their way out, since they burned everything else to the ground."

"Maybeso them dumb Injuns don't know what a outhouse is for!" Bunker snorted.

"Let's go have us a look," Ad suggested.

Shearer and Bunker were already at the outhouse by the time Chapman and the officers had picked their way clear of the burned-out ruins of the Manuel house.

"Chapman!"

He jerked up to see Shearer frantically waving his good arm at the outhouse door they had flung open before them. As he watched, George and Bunker both bent to their knees in the open doorway, struggling with something.

"An Indian?" Howard asked.

"Ain't likely, General," Chapman replied as they both started trotting toward the nearby trees where the old structure stood all but surrounded by brush.

"Then that must surely be one of your men, a survivor, Colonel Perry," Howard said as the two civilians turned slowly, a third man suspended between them.

"My gawd!" Chapman said as he jerked to a halt before the trio, reaching out to raise the barely conscious man's chin. "It's John Manuel!"

"But his daughter said she saw him killed," David Perry declared. "Shot from his horse. She was wounded in the same attack."

"John. John," Chapman cooed, rubbing the man's skeletal cheeks with both of his damp hands.

The eyes fluttered, half-opening to stare at Chapman an instant before they snapped wide as twenty-dollar gold pieces.

"Ch-ch-ch—"

"Don't try to talk," Chapman reminded, still stroking the man's face.

"J-j-jen—"

"We don't know, John," Shearer admitted. "Ain't found Jennet's body."

"So she might still be alive," Ad said. "Maybeso your boy, too. Maggie's alive."

"M-Maggie?"

"She's waiting for you in Mount Idaho."

About that time Chapman noticed the wounds in Manuel's hips as the man's feet scuffed along the rain-soaked ground. Howard sent one of his aides to fetch a surgeon as the half-dead man's friends carried him toward a dry copse of trees where Shearer and Bunker eased Manuel to the ground. Over time that afternoon, with some hot coffee and a little salt pork fed him in small slivers, John J. Manuel told the story of his thirteen-day ordeal.

"Thirteen days?" Howard asked.

"This was one of the first places the bastards hit," Chapman growled.

With an arrow in the back of his neck, a bullet hole through both hips, Manuel had been hurtled off his horse into the brush where he lay still, feigning death as his wife and daughter attempted escape on foot. While he heard their screams and the war cries of the attackers, Manuel confessed there was nothing he could do. Unable to use his legs, he could only drag himself farther into the brush by pulling himself along with his arms.

By sundown on the second day he had managed to inch himself to the outhouse and crawl inside, where he listened to the comings and goings of horsemen for days on end. The sun rose, and the sun set. Over and over again. In the meantime, Manuel had managed to use his folding knife to dig at the four-inch iron arrow point embedded in the muscles of his neck, eventually working the barb free. It still lay on the plank floor of the outhouse, along with the blood-crusted knife Manuel had used in the surgery.

In the predawn darkness of the following morning, he had crawled from the tiny structure, back into the brush where he gathered horseradish leaves he stuffed inside his shirt before dragging himself back to the outhouse. There, Manuel explained, he had chewed the pungent, bitter leaves, crushing them into a poultice he then applied to his angry, infected wound. His frontier medicine had worked. Over the past eleven days the herbal poultice had eased the infection, and Howard's surgeon from Fort Walla Walla, George M. Sternberg, discovered that the once-ugly wound had begun to knit up nicely, without need for any sutures.

At night Manuel had ventured out, dragging himself through the darkness to the creek bank, where he slowly gathered wild berries, one at a time, and sipped at water he dipped from the White Bird in his cupped hand. With so little to sustain him through his ordeal, Manuel had progressively grown thinner and weaker, unable to venture from the outhouse these past five days.

Dr. Sternberg explained to the soldiers and civilians, "Chances are he would have died tomorrow, perhaps the next day, if we hadn't found him when we did."

"This is truly good news!" Howard exclaimed.

Chapman regarded the dimming light. "Too late now to start John back to the Johnson place. We'll take him on in to Mount Idaho come morning."

"He still won't be in any condition to ride," Sternberg declared.

"We'll make us a travois to pull him out of here," Chapman said as he stood. "George, you stay put with John. We'll do what we can to keep him dry for the night right here."

Howard cleared his throat authoritatively. "For the time being, Mr. Chapman, once you've seen to Mr. Manuel here, I suggest you use the rest of what light is left in the day to take your volunteers and search down to the mouth of the White Bird. See if you sight any more than those warriors you spotted from the ridge above."

As the drizzling rain sluiced from his wide-brimmed felt hat, Chapman nodded before he turned on his heel. Without a word he moved to his horse and rose to the saddle, setting off in the mist alone.

Even the sky was crying—either out of exultation at his finding an old friend still breathing . . . or out of some unimaginable grief for all those victims Chapman knew they never would find alive.

Chapter Seven

June 27–29, 1877

BY TELEGRAPH

—

More Details of the Great
Storm.

—

Causes of Idaho's Indian War.

—

Facts Regarding the Late Indian Outbreak.

SAN FRANCISCO, June 26.—A press dispatch from Boise City says that Rev. T. Mesplie, for thirty years a Catholic missionary among the Indian tribes of Oregon, Washington, and Idaho, and now stationed at Fort Boise as chaplain of the United States army, gives the following intelligence in regard to Indian matters: . . . In speaking of General Howard, Howlish Wampoo said the Indian laughed at the general and his fine speeches, saying he would never persuade them to give up Wallowa valley, which they were resolved to keep at every hazard. Father Mesplie says the chiefs and principal men who inaugurated this war are rich and influential, and that they will be able to draw to their support all the disaffected Indians belonging to the various tribes, and that these constitute a majority in every case. He is of the opinion that the war will be general and prolonged, as the Indians have been long deliberating and preparing for it, and have staked everything upon its issue. The father says the Nez Perces number in all about four thousand. Of this number about a hundred and fifty will remain friendly or inactive. He estimates the number of warriors which the Nez Perces can bring into the field at 1,000 . . . Besides these there are Flatheads and their confederates in Montana, with whom the Nez Perces are in close alliance . . . He obtains his data from accurate knowledge acquired by long residence among the Indians. He regards the liberty allowed the Indians to remain off the reservations and the unrestricted intercourse allowed between them and the whites as the principal causes of the present outbreak.

Fort Lapwai
June 27, 1877

Dear Mamma,

. . . Our little post is quiet today, but more troops will be here on Saturday. Major Boyle, Mr. Bomus, and Doctor, along with twenty men, are our entire garrison just now. All the rest are in the front. General Howard sent in dispatches last night hurrying up the troops. He wants to make an attack, and we all feel today that there may be a fierce fight raging and many poor fellows suffering not fifty miles from us. The Indians are in a horseshoe of the Salmon River, a place with the most natural fortifications, equal to the lava beds of the Modocs, and we know them to be well provisioned. They have at least five hundred head of cattle in there, and quantities of camus root, which they use a great deal. We hear this place has only one trail leading into it. So you see the advantages they have. Oh, how I hope our commanders will be cautious and not risk anything. I suppose General Howard has out there now about four hundred men and some artillery, which I don't suppose he will be able to use at all. Those four hundred men are nearly the entire body of troops from this Department. The army is so small at best, and the various companies are so small, that it takes five or six companies to make a hundred men. None of the companies, not even the cavalry, is full.*

**Devil's Backbone*, vol. 5, the *Plainsmen* series.

How glad I should be if I could pick up John and the babies and get out of this region. I feel that nothing else will let me feel calm and settled. My brain seems in a whirl, constantly seeing the distress of these poor women who have lost their husbands, and constantly expecting and fearing to hear from our friends in the front, and also sort of half afraid for ourselves here. I wonder if poor little Lapwai will ever seem peaceful and calm to me again.

Do write soon . . . We all join in love, and I am glad you are safe.

Your loving daughter,
Emily F.

MERCIFULLY, OVERNIGHT THE SOAKING RAIN HAD CLEANSED much of the stench from the air in that valley of death by the time Howard's troops returned early the next morning.

Second Lieutenant Sevier McClellan Rains had never been so happy to ride out of any place the way he had been happy to ride out of White Bird Canyon as the sun began to set yesterday. After a second night's bivouac at Johnson's ranch, the commanding general had everything packed up and ready to depart by 7:00 A.M. on the morning of the twenty-seventh. It continued to rain past dawn, a slow, steady weeping from a low gray sky. The young lieutenant dreaded ever returning to this valley of such unspeakable death.

As they had on Tuesday, the various cavalry and infantry companies again worked over the battlefield in platoons, searching the ravines and the thickets for the remains of fallen soldiers. While the rain kept down the revolting stench, the unrelenting showers soon soaked every man through to the skin, making them all as miserable as could be. So it was with no little eagerness that Rains looked forward to taking his nine men for a ride back up a sidewall of the canyon to search a narrow ravine for any of Perry's soldiers who might have fallen during their mad retreat back up White Bird Hill.

Born in Michigan, this young officer had graduated from West Point only the year before, a mere ten days before the Custer massacre in June of '76. Prior to graduation, Rains had applied for an appointment to the Fourth Cavalry, a move endorsed by the regimental commander, Colonel Ranald S. Mackenzie. Instead, Rains was assigned to the First Cavalry, disappointed that he would have to serve in the Northwest instead of on the Great Plains fighting the Sioux and Cheyenne. A cavalry officer by schooling, who now found himself thrust into a dirty little Indian war out here in Nez Perce country, vigorous and energetic, Rains was itching to show his superiors just what he was made of—

His horse snorted. Almost immediately his nose had found them. Even before any of the men spotted the bodies.

"How many of 'em are there?" one of the soldiers asked the other enlisted men arrayed behind Rains as they all scratched into their pockets for bandannas and handkerchiefs.

"I count eight, soldier," the lieutenant answered. "Eight of them."

The bloated corpses were strewn at the head of a short dead-end ravine. Six of them clustered together in a bunch. One of them lay by itself out by the mouth of the ravine. And the last man sat up alone against the end of the ravine, propped with his back to the grassy wall. The end of the line.

"Look there, sir!" exclaimed Private Franklin Moody, a member of Rains's own L Company, First U. S. Cavalry. "He's a lieutenant. Just like you."

"Hard to tell, but that's Theller, soldier," Rains replied quietly, looking down on his fellow officer, staring transfixed at the bullet hole between the eyes. "Lieutenant Edward R. Theller."

"I don't 'member him, sir. He First Cavalry, was he?" asked Private David Carroll as he inched up to stop at Rains's elbow.

"No, soldier. Theller was detached from the Twenty-first Infantry to go along with Colonel Perry's battalion when it marched away from Fort Lapwai."

Nearby, Private Otto H. Richter whistled in amazement. "*Mein Herr*—lookit the cawtridges."

"Das right, Otto. Dese fellas dun't give up easy," said Private George H. Dinteman in his stilted English. "Did dey, sir?"

Rains shook his head, continuing to stare at Theller's face, then at those copper cases scattered around him and the others, but always, always returning to that bullet hole in the middle of the lieutenant's forehead where the flies had busily laid their eggs. Another day, two at the most, these bodies would be crawling with wormy maggots. Again, as always, he came back to staring at that single bullet hole.

"We bury dem hare, zir?" asked Private Frederick Meyer in troubled English dripping with a thick German accent.

The steady rain overnight had made the ground soft. Rains tore his eyes from that bullet hole for a moment while he screwed his boot heel into the soil. "Yes," the young lieutenant told them. "Maybe one common grave is the best idea. Let's do that—over there at the mouth of the ravine. Those two with their fatigue britches still on—check their pockets for personal effects that the surviving families might wish to receive from Colonel Perry. We'll work in squads of three, spell each other like yesterday."

He went on to have the three Germans start: Richter, Dinteman, and Meyer. Good, solid men. Not particularly fast with any mental wizardry, but good, dependable soldiers. Not given to any complaining about this nasty work with the decomposing, stinking bodies. Once the three had started work on the mass grave for all eight men and the rest either started digging through the pockets of those two who still had some clothing on their bodies or simply plopped down in the wet grass to wait their turn at the trowel bayonets, the young lieutenant turned around once again to stare at the face of that other young lieutenant in this narrow ravine.

And that single bullet hole between the eyes.

Yes, indeed, soldiers, he thought in silence. *Look at all those cartridge cases around them. These eight men sold their lives dearly that bloody Sunday morning. Retreating from the battlefield, they must have ducked up this short, narrow ravine to take some cover from the bare naked hill-side—only to discover they were trapped in a box.*

"Private Carroll!" he called out, turning to speak over his shoulder. "I want you and Moody to begin gathering some stones."

"Stones, Lieutenant?" Franklin Moody asked.

"Rocks. Anything small enough for you to pull out of the ground and carry over here."

David Carroll asked, "You gonna lay 'em on the grave, sir?"

"Yes. Maybe they will keep the predators from digging up the remains once we're gone," Rains explained. "Once they're left here . . . to lie alone for all eternity."

The two privates shuffled off murmuring between themselves.

How would it be, Rains wondered, to have been Theller in his final moments? To find himself trapped with his small squad of men, surrounded and outnumbered, with no way out but to make the Nez Perce warriors pay dearly . . . pay very, very dearly for each soldier they would kill that day?

By the time the mist turned into a steady rain, falling harder, the men had begun to drag the first of the bodies into the long, shallow trench made big enough for eight bloated corpses. As all nine men in his burial detail began to quickly scoop the rich, damp soil back over the distorted remains, young Lieutenant Sevier M. Rains pulled off his soggy hat and stood above them on the side of that ravine—just over his nine muddy, soaked soldiers as they struggled with those eight dead, bloated victims—quietly murmuring his Presbyterian prayers, words he had learned by heart while still a boy in rural Michigan.

As the strong-backed Germans and the wiry Irishmen stood, one by one, stretching the kinks out of their muscles there beside the bare, muddy ground, having placed a layer of rocks over the common grave, Rains began the prayer he hoped they all would join him in reciting.

". . . Forgive us of our trespasses . . . as we forgive those who trespass against us . . ."

BY TELEGRAPH

—

MONTANA.

—

Reports in Regard to the Flat Head Indians.

DEER LODGE, Montana, June 27.—To Governor Potts, Helena: I am in receipt of the following from Postmaster Dickinson, of Missoula, Montana: Monday, June 26.—Rev. John Summers and Mr. Wilkins, who have just arrived from Corvallis, report that a Nez Perces, who talks good English, came from Lewiston, and says the Indians are coming into Bitter Root, and will come into the head of the valley and clear it out, and if the Flat Heads don't join them they will clear them out too. The Flat Heads have driven all their horses out of the valley, and the squaws and children are going up Lolo fork. A Nez Perces chief told Major Whaley that the Nez Perces were going to clear out the Bitter Root valley, and that the Flat Heads would join them on the 1st, as near as I can remember . . .

Fort Lapwai
June 29, 1877

My Dear Mamma,

I would give the world and all to see you, but I guess we will have to wait until the Doctor takes us in. I hope and pray the time will pass quickly until our time here is over, and that we will all be spared to meet again.

This horrible Indian war hangs over me like a gun. I

can't shake it off and am daily expecting the Doctor will be ordered to join the troops in the field. We are all very anxious here. The dispatches that came in last night told us the troops were in sight of the Indian stronghold. I shall hope and pray that I shan't have to come home to you, after all, without my dear husband. Poor Mrs. Theller is still waiting here. She won't leave until she can get her husband's body. This losing one's husband in this way seems too horrible to think about. I can't help feeling how awfully hard it would be to lose my dear John any way, but that way would be hardest of all.

Your loving daughter,
Emily F.

Chapter Eight

June 27–July 1, 1877

BY TELEGRAPH

—

Daring Postoffice Robbery at
Manhattan, Kansas.

—

IDAHO.

—

The Indian Situation—Telegram from Gen. Howard.

SAN FRANCISCO, June 29.—A Portland press dispatch says Colonel Wood has just received the following dispatch from General Howard, dated at the front, June 27, 8:45 A.M.: We have overtaken Joseph, who is well posted at the mouth of White Bird creek. Chief White Bird has been in charge of the entire united bands of Joseph and is the fighting chief. The Indians are bold and waiting for us to engage them. Lieutenant Trumbull and volunteers are at Slate creek. Our headquarters tonight will be at the mouth of White Bird creek. The rains are very troublesome; roads and trails bad; troops in best of spirits and ready for decisive work.

AFTER SPENDING THEIR SECOND DAY ON THE WHITE BIRD battlefield, General Oliver O. Howard ordered his column on down White Bird Creek to its mouth, where they turned left and marched south, up the Salmon River, approximately two miles before finding enough open ground to bivouac the command. Late that afternoon as the first pickets were being established on his perimeter, A, D, G, and M batteries of the Fourth Artillery and C Company of the Twenty-first Infantry rumbled in to join the command.

"In memory of the slain officer, this will be recorded as

Camp Theller," Otis told his united officer corps that evening after supper as the rain continued to pour down upon his column. "It's from here that we will begin our chase of the fleeing hostiles."

While the constant rain continued to batter the oiled canvas awning lashed over their heads, Howard went on to explain that, come morning, he was dispatching Captain David Perry back to Fort Lapwai for more ammunition and rations.

"This has more and more the appearance of a long campaign," he said regretfully, "longer than I would have anticipated on the day we departed Lapwai. But, with the additional reinforcements, we now have more than five hundred and thirty men, which include some sixty-five volunteers. In fact, 'Captain' William Hunter and his band of volunteers just arrived from Dayton, in Washington Territory. Accompanying them down from Lapwai, I'm most pleased to welcome Lieutenant Wood to my staff. Lieutenant, please take a step forward so all the men can get a look at you."

The slight, good-looking Wood eased into the center of that half-circle of cavalry and infantry officers. Nodding several times to the others, he then stepped over to stand near the commanding general.

"Mr. Wood will serve as my aide-de-camp for the remainder of the campaign."

SECOND Lieutenant Charles Erskine Scott Wood found it very difficult to sleep that night. Not that it was too cold or too damp for his tastes. Just that he constantly reminded himself to sleep light for fear of a surprise attack from the Nez Perce rumored to be right across the river from Camp Theller.

He finally gave up and crawled out of his bedroll after midnight. From the sounds of his snoring, General Howard was sleeping soundly in his tent nearby, so Wood lit a small candle and unbuckled the straps on his haversack. Reaching inside, he pulled out the spanking new leather-bound ledger book he had recently purchased in Lewiston on his way to the front. Positioning it across his thighs, Charles pulled a long pencil from the breast pocket he had had sewn inside his field blouse, then made the first entry on that very first page of his field diary.

> Overtook the main column, gentlemanly officers looking like herders, rough aspect of everyone, business not holiday costumes—
>
> Camp—singing, story telling and swearing, profanity—carelessness, accepting things—horrible at other times—as a matter of course. . . . Again there is the necessary leaving of last messages for sweet hearts, mothers, and wives, telling of jokes about being killed, about not looking for "my body" &c firing expected tomorrow. . . .
>
> Rain—eternal rain—veal & no veal—supper in camp. Visiting the different messes, youngsters with neither bedding nor shelter, rough it jokingly—night duty, posting the pickets—rough times all night standing in the rain—no fire—no talking, no bedding—no sleeping.

When next he tried to sleep, Wood had eventually drifted off, nonetheless kept restless at first by the distant howl of coyotes in the nearby hills. Most of the officers and most of the soldiers had long ago learned that just such a howl had been heard by many of Perry's men as they sat in the dark, waiting out the coming of dawn and their disastrous attack. To most every man in Howard's command, those calls from the hills in the dark on that rainy night could come from only Nez Perce scouts keeping an eye on the camp . . . perhaps even signaling everything in readiness for their attack.

Finally able to sleep deeply, the young lieutenant was abruptly awakened by a gunshot just past midnight. That single report was followed by lots of loud noises from men angry and frightened at being caught off-guard in the middle of the night with what they thought was a wholesale attack by Nez Perce warriors.

As it turned out, in the melee and confusion, the camp was not under assault. Instead, a picket returning to his company had been mistaken for an enemy by a groggy, half-sleepy lieutenant jostled into that frightening reaction. The wounded soldier lingered in great pain until morning. Just past daybreak, he was buried nearby before the command prepared to move upriver.

Lieutenant Wood found another moment to scratch at his diary beside his breakfast fire.

> The alarm sounded at midnight—one of our own pickets shot by one of our men.* Up at 2 o'clock for fear of Indian habits of attack—roll call at 6.

That Thursday morning, the twenty-eighth of June, Howard moved his column up the Salmon to Horseshoe Bend, where his troops began preparations to cross the river, following the trail of the fleeing Non-Treaty bands. Wood and others studied the swift, deep current and secretly wondered if the general would get his command across without incident utilizing the cable ferry Howard planned to employ after sending a pair of Nez Perce scouts across the river, dragging the ropes behind them.

But before they could even send the friendlies into the river, more than eighty-five warriors appeared on the hills across the Salmon, racing their horses down to the west bank, shouting, screaming, and firing their rifles. In another explosion of pandemonium, the soldiers dived this way and that for their weapons, precipitating another long-distance shooting match. Within minutes the noisy skirmish was over and the enemy horsemen were on their way, turning downriver to disappear beyond a nearby slope, with no apparent casualties on either side.

"The general has decided it was only a ruse, a diversion,"

---

*Most Indian Wars historians now agree that the lieutenant who was startled in his sleep and shot the returning picket was, in fact, Charles E. S. Wood himself.

Wood reported to the companies spread out along the east bank of the Salmon. "They only want to keep us from crossing, to give their village more time to disappear into the heights on the other side. We must keep working as quickly as possible to get the command across!"

As hard as the men worked against the confines of those steep canyon walls, against the boiling current of the Salmon now in its full strength with spring runoff, it was not until the next morning, 29 June, when the column began its crossing.

But it would take them the whole of three long summer days to force their way across the mighty Salmon before they could even think about slogging into the wild and rugged hills on the other side.

HE was not your young, excitable sort. Not this Stephen Gerard Whipple. Forty years old, repeatedly described as "reliable" in reports written by his superiors, this captain had been the officer selected to march two companies of cavalry into the Wallowa valley earlier in the spring while Joseph and Ollokot were attending a peace parley with General O. O. Howard at Fort Lapwai. It was from his cantonment located at the western approaches to the Wallowa country that he had brought in his battalion, along with "Captain" Tom Page and his twenty-one volunteers from the town of Walla Walla.

Of moderate height and strongly built, Whipple had a presence about him, stemming mostly from his dark-browed, steely gaze. Born in upstate Vermont, the captain had been living on the West Coast when the Civil War erupted. He had served out the war with the California infantry, where he rose to the rank of lieutenant colonel, saw extensive duty on the frontier, and held a brevet for "faithful and meritorious service." About a year and a half after Appomattox, Whipple received a commission as captain in the Thirty-second Infantry, but in December of 1870 he requested, and was awarded, a transfer to the First U. S. Cavalry.

Whipple was again the man Howard would now choose for another lonely, dangerous, and ultimately fateful mission.

"I want you to take two companies of cavalry and arrest Looking Glass," the general stated not long after sunset the night before.

"A-arrest him, General?"

For a moment, Howard ground his teeth as if in exasperation at searching for an explanation, then declared, "For some weeks it has appeared that Looking Glass and his band of Alpowai were going to be peaceful. But now intelligence has been brought to me from our friendlies, reports showing that the chief and his headmen are leaning toward joining the hostiles."

Whipple wagged his head. "But . . . don't we have a reliable report that Looking Glass left the other bands after the murders began?"

"Yes," and Howard nodded, watching the light fade behind the tall mountains on the other side of the Salmon. "We were told he and his band wanted nothing of the war Joseph, White Bird, and the rest were starting."

"So—with all due respect, General—why am I to arrest Looking Glass now?"

The general's eyes narrowed; he was clearly not a man comfortable with having his decisions questioned. "Because some of the friendlies say he and his people are turning toward the hostiles. I've just received news that Looking Glass may have supplied at least twenty warriors to those who butchered Perry's command on the White Bird. There's a credible report that he's become a turncoat now, intending to join the hostiles himself at the first favorable opportunity."*

—

*Howard and history do not clearly indicate how he reached these conclusions about Looking Glass's band, with the exception of the rampant rumors being circulated by Lewiston *Teller* editor Alonzo Leland, who repeatedly alleged in those days following the White Bird debacle: "Indian runners and Chinamen say the Looking Glass band has been increased in

More reports from four Mount Idaho citizens reached Howard that there was substantial evidence to show that warriors from Looking Glass's band had sacked two other homesteads: one belonging to Idaho County Commissioner George Dempster, and the other to James T. Silverwood. In addition, warriors had driven off stock. When the four whites attempted to approach the Looking Glass camp on Clear Creek, they were motioned to stay away in a hostile manner. In the minds of most white citizens, the Alpowai were clearly up to no good.

Even Inspector Erwin C. Watkins of the Indian Bureau wrote Howard that Looking Glass was "running a recruiting station for Joseph."

As history turns out, Howard's "friendlies" were actually two Mount Idaho civilians, Ezra Baird and Robert Nugent, who rode to Lewiston to excite the populace and local newspaperman with their tales that the Looking Glass people had declared war on the whites, intending to start hostilities in a few days!

Whipple gestured across the river at the west bank of the Salmon. "So we can't afford to have him and his warriors join up with the rest who are running loose over there in the Clearwater country."

It was evening on the twenty-ninth, the first day of those three it would take Howard to get his column across the turbulent current.

"Exactly, Captain. Looking Glass's people live and tend their gardens, graze their cattle, and breed their horses on their traditional grounds somewhere along the Clearwater."

"Yes, sir—I know the place."

"Technically, the Alpowai reside inside the reservation boundaries . . . but they've never signed any of the treaties."

"Are some of the Christian bands nervous about the

---

numbers, that they have plundered Jerome's place at the Clearwater bridge, that their whole movements indicate hostile intention though they pretend to yet be friends to the whites."

sympathies of the Looking Glass people, now that hostilities have broken out?"

"That's a mild way of putting it, Captain," Howard declared. "I've decided to arrest the chief and contain his people long enough to turn them over to the Mount Idaho volunteers."

"You really want to put them in the care of the citizens, General?" Whipple challenged. "Isn't that like turning over a canary to the care of the house cat?"

Howard appeared to bristle at this unvarnished questioning of moral sensibility of his planned arrest. "It will only be for a short time, Captain Whipple," he grumbled assuredly. "They will be in the care of the volunteers only until I can bring in the rest of these Non-Treaty troublemakers."

"You figure to catch up to them and drive them back across in this direction, General?"

"With you having the Looking Glass band under control on the east, and I herding Joseph from the west—we'll have them all onto the reservation within a week's time."

"As your order, sir. I'll draw four days' rations and sufficient ammunition for my march tonight, then depart in the morning."

"I would prefer that you leave before dawn, Captain."

Whipple nodded, sensing even more the importance of this mission. "We don't want to give Looking Glass or his henchmen any more time for making trouble."

"You might remember that I'm sending Colonel Perry back to Lapwai in the morning. He'll be covering part of the same trail up to Camas Prairie, where you'll turn off."

"To bring up more reinforcements from his post, General?"

"No," Howard answered. "He's taking the pack train with him to pick up more supplies and ammunition . . . on the outside chance that this campaign to drive the hostiles back across the Salmon takes longer than a week. In the final analysis, Looking Glass's band inhabits the country near my supply lines. So no matter what way you look at it,

Captain—I must take care of him before I subdue the others."

Whipple's cavalry battalion moved out beneath a leaden sky before first light on the morning of 30 June, marching back down the Salmon to the mouth of the White Bird, then groping their way along the creek, moving east to the divide and over to Mount Idaho, where, during a short stop that afternoon that allowed the men time to eat and rest their horses, twenty civilians under "Captain" D. B. "Darius" Randall enthusiastically volunteered their services in helping to arrest Looking Glass. It was as plain as the brass on his buttons that these volunteers were itching to get a little revenge on the Nez Perce who had murdered so many friends of theirs. But Whipple was certain he could control them, and if the unthinkable happened . . . all the better to have more rifles along. One of the older volunteers, J. A. Miller, offered his services as an interpreter.

With the addition of these civilians, the captain felt nothing but confidence that he and his officers could handle what might be thrown their way. Accompanying Whipple's L Company was Captain Henry E. Winters in command of E Company. Serving with Winters were First Lieutenant Albert G. Forse—an 1865 graduate of the U. S. Military Academy, who had spent the last ten years serving with the First Cavalry in the Northwest—and Second Lieutenant William H. Winter, who graduated in 1872 and was promptly thrown into the Modoc War in southern Oregon.

In order to be on Looking Glass's doorstep at dawn on the first of July, Whipple ordered his detail men back into the saddle as the sun began to set that thirtieth day of June. Leaving behind their two .45-caliber Gatling guns and a detail of four men to operate those weapons in Mount Idaho so they could travel all the faster without the encumbrance of those prairie carriages, the eighty-seven men set off north, their objective some twenty-five miles away. Angling across the extreme southeastern corner of the Camas Prairie as the light faded, they struck the South Fork of the Clearwater, fully intending to make quick, efficient work of their warrant from Howard to prevent more of Looking Glass's warriors from joining up with those hostiles to whom Howard was preparing to give chase.

No matter the black of that moonless night, despite the ruggedness of the hills as they picked their way down one grade, then up a long, difficult slope to reach the high ground that rose abruptly along the east side of the Clearwater, Captain Steven Whipple pushed on, fully intending to catch the sleeping village unawares and completely unprepared at the peep of day.

Chapter Nine

Khoy-Tsahl, 1877

BY TELEGRAPH

—

The President Once More in Washington.

—

Harvard Wins the Boat Race.

—

Latest From the Idaho Indian War.

—

OREGON.

—

Latest from the Scene of Indian Hostilities.

SAN FRANCISCO, June 30.—A Portland press dispatch gives the latest reports from the scene of the Indian outbreak . . . It is reported that the Clear Water Indians, under Looking-glass, had turned loose and plundered George Dempster's place, between the middle and south forks of the Clear Water, and driven off all the stock of the settlers between these forks, and had it at their camp about six miles above Kamiah. They confirm Jim Sawyer's statement made in the Indian council yesterday at Lapwai as to the purposes of Looking-glass and his forty men. These Indians told two Chinamen on Clear Water that they had declared war against the whites, and would commence their raids upon the inhabitants within ten days. When this news reached Mount Idaho a force of twenty volunteers started immediately for Clear Water, but no news has come from them yet. General Howard was notified and said that he would send a detachment of regulars to scour the country in that direction this morning. The volunteers who were in the fight on White Bird saw the Indian who went out as

> one of the friendly Indians with Col. Perry from Lapwai beckon the hostiles forward to the fight, and saw other movements of some friendly Indians evincing their privity with the hostiles. During the fight a report, which lacks confirmation, was received that General Howard had attacked Joseph and dislodged him from Horse Shoe Ridge . . .

BIRD ALIGHTING, CALLED *PEOPEO THOLEKT* BY HIS PEOPLE, sucked on the stringy beef Looking Glass's sister had boiled her brother for an early breakfast that morning. In a matter of days the women would have more of the camas roots and *kouse* dried so that they could cook those roots in the boiling pots, along with the beef and what game the men brought back to their people at this traditional camp they called *Kamnaha** on the east bank of Clear Creek.** It wasn't a large camp, this village of Looking Glass.

After about a dozen young hot-bloods rode away to join the war against the wishes of their chief, the only men left numbered no more than four-times-ten. The women and children counted up to three times that. They were a small, yet prosperous, band.

Even though their traditional camping grounds lay within the boundaries of the shrunken reservation the Shadows had marked off for his *Nee-Me-Poo* people, these Alpowai had refused to sign what they called the Thieves' Treaty of 1855 and agreed to the subsequent land steal of 1863. Unlike the Christians who lived close to the whites up at Lapwai with Lawyer's many friends, Looking Glass's people were traditional. They were Dreamers, not Christians. Since this was the white man's special religious day, many of Looking Glass's Dreamers were away from camp, having gone downriver to Kamiah to attend a traditional Dreamer service. Which meant that no more than half of

*A Nez Perce term that cannot be translated.

**Approximately six miles above present-day Kooskia, Idaho.

their men, only two-times-ten, remained in camp this quiet morning.

One big difference between those Lawyer Christians and the Looking Glass Dreamers—the traditional people felt compelled by their ancestors to hold onto what had never been theirs to give away, much less theirs to sell.

This was their land. And they meant no white man any harm as they went about living their lives in the old way.

Eh-heh, there was no question that some of the younger men had slipped away despite Looking Glass's scolding of those war-making chiefs at *Tepahlewam*, despite his repeated warnings not to foment trouble for the camp in those first heady days after killing so many soldiers at *Lahmotta.**

Bird Alighting, like Looking Glass and other leaders, knew that some of their young men had raided one, perhaps two, of the Shadow homesteads in the valley of the Clearwater. But the warriors claimed no Shadows were harmed in their fun. Truth was, no white people were still around. They had already fled south to Mount Idaho or Kamiah to the north or farther still—running all the way to Fort Lapwai or Lewiston.

No white men hurt in that first frantic burst of young men raids. Only houses and barns burned. Horses and cattle stolen, then driven back to this camp on Clear Creek. When matters had quieted down, Looking Glass and men like Bird Alighting vowed they would return what cattle and horses they could to their rightful, white owners. Until then, the *Nee-Me-Poo* would graze the animals and care for them. They had every reason to believe that by the middle of the summer moon all things would have returned to normal. Chances were good the Salmon River murderers would be caught and punished by the Shadows and Looking Glass's people would go back to living their lives in the same old way.

Which meant going to the *Moosmoos Illahe*—the buf-

*A Nez Perce term for White Bird Canyon.

falo country—every year or so to visit their friends the *E-sue-gha.** Some of the *Nee-Me-Poo* referred to that tribe by the name of *Tsaplishtake*, or "Pasted On" people, because of their practice of making their hair longer by gluing on longer strands. Perhaps that meant they would help these friends fight the bellicose Lakota again, as they had in summers past, returning home to Idaho with their horses and travois sway-backed under the weight of buffalo hides scraped for lodge covers or tanned into hair-on robes for winter sleeping.

Looking Glass had become a hero in the faraway buffalo country. Once he had helped his old allies the *E-sue-gha* in a fight against the Lakota. That was a good country, Bird Alighting thought. That *E-sue-gha* land was good country. At the least a good second choice to this one. If the *Nee-Me-Poo* had to journey another place to find the buffalo, then that country beyond the high mountains was a good one—

"Soldiers are here!"

At that warning cry ringing outside the lodge, Bird Alighting spit out the long piece of meat he was chewing and bolted to his feet beside Looking Glass. They both shot out the doorway to stand among the many frightened people come to hear this news.

"Where?" someone shouted to those women on the creek bank who had given the warning and were pointing.

"Across!" a woman yelled, motioning to the far side of Clear Creek.

Bird Alighting saw them creeping down the steep hillside, sure enough. Perhaps ten times all his fingers. Not every one of them dressed in soldier clothes, so some of these Shadows—the white men who had no soul—were settlers, wagon men, or miners who scratched in the ground for the yellow rocks. Come to help the *suapies* or merely come to watch—either way . . . the arrival of all these white men bode no good for Looking Glass's peaceful camp. But *Peopeo Tholekt* tried to squeeze that fear out of his mind.

—

*The Crow, or Absaroka, tribe of Montana.

After all, Looking Glass was known to those Mount Idaho Shadows—for just last year before he left for the buffalo country, the chief had delivered a speech in which he pledged friendship to the whites.

Seizing his friend by the shoulder, Looking Glass suddenly spun Bird Alighting aside. Leaning his face close, the chief instructed, "Go to these *suapies.* Find the soldier chief and say to him, 'Leave us alone. We are living here peacefully and want no trouble.' Tell him my hands are clean of white man's blood and I want him to know they will remain clean. The other chiefs have acted like fools in murdering white men. Tell him I will have no part in such things and I will have nothing to do with such chiefs.' "

Bird Alighting nodded, saying, "I'll go fetch my horse, Looking Glass."

The chief wagged his head adamantly, squeezing Bird Alighting's arm. "No time! Take mine," and he bent to untie the long lead rope attached to his prize horse picketed to one of the lodge stakes.

"I will go tell them to leave us be."

Bird Alighting felt his stomach flutter and his heart pound mightily beneath his breastbone as he eased Looking Glass's horse across the creek and onto the grassy bank on the far side, continuing to the slope of the hill where the soldiers and Shadows waited. Which one was leader—

One of the soldiers immediately urged his horse forward. Three more of the *suapies* joined him, as well as two of the plain-dressed Shadows. Settlement or wagon men, for sure, Bird Alighting thought.

To his surprise, one of those wagon men spoke the *Nee-Me-Poo* tongue reasonably well. "Hello!" he called in a friendly tone that belied the misgivings *Peopeo Tholekt* felt to his marrow.

Bird Alighting turned to that left end of the small group where the two settlement men sat astride their horses. He began telling the Shadow what his chief wanted him to say: "Leave us alone. We are living here peacefully and want no trouble—"

He was interrupted as the second wagon man suddenly raised his rifle and shoved its muzzle right into Bird Alighting's ribs, pressed just below his left nipple so hard that it made the warrior wince.

At the same time, the Shadow angrily growled something Bird Alighting did not understand, but it nonetheless looked and sounded like a squint-eyed demand. Still, he did not know exactly what this man wanted. Maybe nothing more than to pull the trigger on his gun and blow a hole through Bird Alighting's heart—and he was afraid because he smelled the heavy stench of the white man's whiskey on the Shadow's every word.

Before Bird Alighting could protest or twist himself away from the gun's muzzle and the strong whiskey breath, that first settler—the *Nee-Me-Poo* talker—shoved the barrel downward, shouting at the bad-talker in some Shadow words Bird Alighting did not completely understand.

"This is not Looking Glass. Only a messenger, goddammit."

That's when the soldier chief asked something and the *Nee-Me-Poo* talker explained to Bird Alighting, "Go back to your camp and tell Looking Glass we want to talk to *him*. Talk only to him. Not a messenger like you. Talk to Looking Glass."

By the time Bird Alighting had turned Looking Glass's horse around and it was scrambling back up the east bank of Clear Creek, he could see how excited the men and women in the village had become. They had witnessed how the gun was shoved into his ribs. Maybe even heard the bad, loud talk from the Shadow. If they could not understand the words, then it wasn't at all difficult to understand the meaning—from both the tone and the strident volume of such angry talk.

As he reined the war pony among those eleven lodges, Bird Alighting saw that one of the older men was propping a new lodgepole against Looking Glass's lodge. But this pole had a big white cloth attached to it: well known as the

Shadow signal for making peace, for talking truce—a signal for not making a fight.

"Peopeo Tholekt!" Looking Glass shouted, shuffling forward on foot. He held his bare hands aloft, imploring his friend, "Why aren't they leaving our country? Why are the *suapies* still here?"

"The soldier chief wants to speak only to you."

Looking Glass's face instantly went gray with worry. "This cannot be good. Go back now, and tell them my words again. Maybe they did not understand you good enough. Tell them once more that I want no trouble and to go away. We hurt no one, and want no one to bother us."

Back across the creek among the five Shadows, Bird Alighting was desperate for his words to take effect this time. "Looking Glass is my chief. I bring you *his* words. He does not want a war! He came back here to our country to get away from the other chiefs who would do wrong, come back here to escape war. He says: Do not cross to our side of the little river. We do not want any trouble with you! So go and leave us live in peace."

Grown even more red-faced than before, the angry civilian jabbed his rifle muzzle all the harder into Bird Alighting's ribs this second time. And once more that mean-eyed Shadow growled foul-sounding words the messenger could not understand. Again the friendly talker interceded, shoving the loud-talker's rifle aside, urging his horse forward, putting himself between the bad-talker and Bird Alighting for some modest protection. While Bird Alighting kept his eyes on the bad-talker, the good Shadow spoke in their foreign tongue to the soldier chief.

Finally, the Indian talker said in *Nee-Me-Poo*, "The rest of the soldiers will come with us when we come across the little river to speak—"

"No, Looking Glass says for the soldiers to stay on this side. Do not come across. Leave us alone—"

"The soldier chief wants to talk with Looking Glass," he interrupted sharply, as if losing patience. "If it makes it better, you tell him just the five of us will come across to talk. No more."

"All right," Bird Alighting replied with a little relief, turning the chief's horse around for the swollen creek.

He looked over his shoulder as the angry Shadow started to harangue all the others left behind on the bank. More loud voices joined his, primarily those of the other wagon and settlement men. None of the soldiers joined in the red-faced yelling. The next time Bird Alighting glanced over his shoulder, the angry one was shaking his rifle at the soldier chief and Shadows in the creek—but especially he shook it menacingly at Bird Alighting.

It took only minutes for them to cross, and their horses were scrambling onto the bank, dripping as they carried their riders into the village. Warriors and women and many, many curious, frightened children appeared among the few lodges. Ruff-necked, several dogs slinked close to growl at these strange-smelling horses and men—

A single gunshot rang out.

Bird Alighting whirled about on the bare back of that war-horse. In that instant he could not find the warrior who had fired the shot. Nor could he see a one of the soldiers or that Shadow-talker as they fell from their horses.

Then he turned the Looking Glass pony some more and peered across the little river in horror, shocked to find the rest of the Shadows and soldiers speeding their horses down to the water. A gray tendril of gunsmoke was still curling away from the barrel of that bad-talker's rifle!

Chapter Ten

July 1, 1877

Captain Stephen G. Whipple jerked around in his saddle at the loud boom of the gun, watching as that red-faced, loudmouthed civilian named Washington "Dutch" Holmes entered the stream and slowly lowered the needle-gun from his shoulder, gray smoke snaking from its muzzle.

How in Jupiter had things gotten so out of hand?

For starters, Whipple's detail hadn't been where he had hoped they could be at first light. Because of both the rugged terrain and the miscalculations of Randall's volunteers, the Looking Glass village turned out to be more than ten miles farther than they had assumed when they first embarked from Mount Idaho. After riding through the dark, in broken country, they had ended up on the hillside opposite the village close to 7:00 A.M., well after daybreak.

By then it had become clear some of Randall's men had kept themselves warm, or worked up some bravado, by sipping at a little of the whiskey they passed around in some pewter flasks. Just before Whipple had started into the stream, prepared to parley with Looking Glass, Dutch Holmes's companion Dave Ousterholt had hollered out with a slur, "Tell that red son of a bitch we'll move 'im to Mount Idaho by bullets or bayonets—don't make us no mind!"

The whiskey in their bellies was doing all the talking now, and . . . Katy bar the door!

Just as suddenly as he had jerked around in the saddle to peer at the cursing civilians—Ousterholt and Holmes—the captain now whipped back around to look at the village where most of the Nez Perce stood frozen in place, stunned. Except for that one hapless warrior who had been standing closest on the creek bank. He was clutching both hands around one of his thighs, a dark ooze seeping between his fingers.

Right on the heels of that breathless moment when everything around him seemed to be suspended in time . . . the Indians let out a concerted yell: men with their angry war cries, women with their anguished wails of disbelief, and the children with their fearful, bewildered sobbing. Of a sudden everything was in motion once more, but in a blur now. Women scooped up their children as they dashed behind lodges, seeking safety. Old men stood haranguing the men of fighting age. Warriors sprinted here and there in the bedlam, dashing into their lodges for weapons, reemerging with bows or a few old rifles in hand. Even some young boys leaped bareback atop those horses kept in the village—shrieking as they raced for the herd on the outskirts of camp.

There could be no delay now!

"Retreat!" the captain called to his three fellow soldiers and that single civilian interpreter whom he had brought with him across the creek. "Pull back! Pull back!"

As one the four of them wheeled their horses about, kicking the animals savagely as they leaped off the grassy bank, landing with a spray in the creek running at its full strength with mountain snowmelt. All five riders leaned low across their horses' withers as they raced for the opposite bank where the rest of Whipple's detachment were milling about as they came out of the creek. The first arrows were reaching the far side by the time he and the four were scrambling up the bank to join those two companies of soldiers scattering without orders, seeking cover of any sort.

And in the midst of it all sat those two damned civilians!

"Just what in the name of Jupiter did you think you were doing?" Whipple shouted at the man as he reined up between Dutch Holmes and the rifleman.

"They wasn't gonna do what you wanted 'em to do anyway, Captain," snorted the red-faced, whiskeyed-up Dave Ousterholt. "Lot of useless talk while that Looking Glass and his red bastards have time to get ready to fight."

In fury, Whipple snapped, "We didn't come here to fight!"

The volunteer sneered as he said, "Blood. That's all the red-bellies understand, Captain. Time we give back what they give our friends on the Salmon. For what they done out on the Camas Prairie, too!"

"Damn you! There was no call—"

"You're already in the soup now, Captain," interrupted Dutch Holmes.

"That's right!" Ousterholt said with an evil grin. "Let's take this goddamned village: grab ol' Looking Glass and his boys afore they can put up a fight. You're wasting time jawing with me when there's killing to be done!"

Whipple's horse suddenly sidestepped, fighting the bit, the instant an arrow quivered in its rear flank.

"Fire!" the captain bellowed in frustration—at these two hotheaded civilians and those Indians across the way. "Lay down a covering fire!"

It was only a matter of heartbeats before the men of his battalion began doing just that. Kneeling behind some brush, standing behind trees, crouching behind some low rocks, or sprawled on their bellies—the cavalrymen poured a devastating fire into those warriors streaming toward the creek bank to defend their village. With the fury of their fire, it took no more than the space of four minutes for the Nez Perce to be driven back from the water—back, back toward their lodges.

Behind those few warriors, women and old ones were herding the children over a low hill to the east, scattering out of range from those bullets landing among the buffalo-hide lodges like a spring hailstorm. Every now and again a pony would cry out in pain as a wayward bullet found one of the huge targets.

"Shoot that one getting away!"

Whipple turned, finding Dutch Holmes pointing upstream at a figure wrapped in the hide of a wolf slipping out of the bushes. Several of the civilians instantly trained their weapons on the Indian and fired, forcing the figure to whirl about and retreat into the brush.

As Whipple lunged up on foot, Dave Ousterholt growled at his companions, "Was that a buck or a squaw?"

"Don't fire on the women! That's an order of the U. S. Army!" the captain snarled his answer to the question.

"Them bitches can kill you just as quick as a buck, Captain!" D. B. Randall bellowed in defense of his volunteers. "As for my outfit, we'll shoot anything that moves over there."

"Captain Whipple!"

He turned to find Henry E. Winters racing up, still in the saddle. "We need to get into the village *now!*"

"Agreed, Captain! Deploy your E Troop on a skirmishers' front, right flank. My men will take the left flank—"

Randall interrupted, "What about my volunteers?"

For an instant he considered telling Randall exactly what he could do with his liquored-up, unruly bar brawlers . . . but he reluctantly said, "Spread out behind us and act as reserves." Then Whipple turned quickly so that he wouldn't have to take any more guff from these damnable trouble-making civilians.

Scanning over his L Company, Whipple located First Lieutenant Edwin H. Shelton shaping up the line for their charge. "Mr. Shelton! I want you to pick ten of our men. Get Lieutenant Forse from E Troop to divide off ten of his. Your squad will go after the horse herd. Above everything else, you must surround that herd, prevent it from running off, and capture it."

Shelton snapped a salute. "Capital idea, sir!"

"There must be no failure in your task," Whipple emphasized. "You must get your hands on that herd!"

Wheeling about, Shelton hollered for Lieutenant Albert G. Forse.

It took a few minutes to get the men up and out from behind what cover they had taken, a distressing development to Whipple's way of thinking, since his men weren't suffering any real resistance from the opposite bank at all. Nearly every one of the warriors had taken shelter among the lodges now, making only potshots at best. No concerted defense, nothing of any real danger posed to Whipple's battalion.

The captain was just starting his men off the west bank of the stream—

"I hit the bitch! Whooo-damn! I know I hit her!"

Right by Whipple's elbow, Dave Ousterholt was shouting with unbridled glee, dancing about and pointing as Holmes and Randall pounded him on the back with their congratulations. Just downstream a woman had pitched off her pony, loosing her grip on her infant as she tumbled into the swift water. At the same moment, the frightened horse wheeled around on the uneven, stony stream bottom, the woman and child imprisoned between its flailing legs and slashing hooves. As the pony stumbled, then regained its balance, the woman's head popped to the surface of the swift-flowing stream.

She screamed, slapping the water with her arms, attempting to fight the current, struggling to reach the spot where her child had disappeared beneath the surface. As the pony lurched and lunged across the creek bottom, the woman was tossed about, hurtled downstream away from Whipple's attackers, her faint screams interrupted each time she was bowled over and submerged by the roiling current.

Dutch Holmes cheered his friend, "That's one scalp you can't get your hands on, Dave!"

"Shit!" Ousterholt replied with a wolfish grin. "I brung down two for one bullet! Not bad hunting, I'll wager!"

Whipple finally tore his eyes off the struggling woman as her body was swept around a gentle bend in the creek, carried out of view. He swallowed hard as he whirled around on his heel and roared, "You volunteers—get in and secure the village!"

ALMOST as soon as the mean-talker's bullet struck one of the older little chiefs, a man named Shot Leg—who had just returned from the buffalo country only two days before—the soldiers were retreating and Bird Alighting was sucking in another breath. Now all those uniformed *suapies* were diving for cover, where they started to lay down a deadly fire among the eleven poor lodges and those few willow shelters for the young, unmarried warriors.

With a grunt, Shot Leg crumpled to the ground nearby, both hands clamped around his bloody wound. He stared up at Bird Alighting in disbelief. "Can you understand this?" he asked, dazed. "My name is *Tahkoopen*, from a wounding many summers ago—and now I am shot in the same leg again!"

Bird Alighting was just about to cut off a strip of his breechclout when his ears brought him the hammer of hoofbeats. Wheeling about, he saw the two warriors riding up in a blur. Leaping out of the way just in time, he watched as the pair leaned off their mounts and seized hold of the wounded Shot Leg, dragging the warrior away in a blur of color. With him hoisted between them, the horsemen dragged the man toward the eastern hills, where he would be out of danger.

Spinning around, Bird Alighting found himself alone and looking for a pony, any horse that might get him out of the village. Across the creek, the Shadow voices grew louder and more strident. He glanced their way again. They were moving out of cover, advancing on the bank—preparing to cross. Around him the bullets slapped the thick buffalo hides now, chipped splinters off the lodgepoles. Whined like angry wasps as the air grew deadly around him and the frightened, wandering cattle bawled helplessly, stirring dust as if in a buffalo surround. The odor of fresh manure and urine from the ponies and beeves stung his nostrils—

There—he saw a pony!

It was struggling against its long halter rope, lashed to a stake at the side of a lodge. Forgotten and forsaken by its owner already run into the hills.

Imene kaizi yeu yeu, Hunyewat! he mouthed his thankful

praise to the Creator as he burst into a sprint, racing for the pony bucking and rearing near the middle of the small camp.

Seizing hold of the long halter, Bird Alighting was nearly yanked off his feet by the powerful animal before he looped the rope around one wrist and freed the knot with his other hand. Wild-eyed with terror, the pony watched as the man lunged past its neck and leaped onto the narrow back.

Drawing up the excess rope, Bird Alighting suddenly realized something was wrong. The horse stood perfectly still, as if turned into stone.

"*Amtiz! Ueye!*" he shouted into the horse's ear, slapping its front and rear flank with that coil of rope. "Let's go! Run!"

It was as if the ground exploded beneath him when the pony started bucking. Interlacing his fingers within its mane, locking his toes beneath its belly, gripping that rope with all his strength, Bird Alighting bounced into the air, landing on the horse's bare back with a brutal thud each time the animal struck the ground.

As the pony whipped itself into a whirling dance, Bird Alighting spotted the *suapies* and the other Shadows reaching the middle of the stream, their horses threading through the strong current, all but having reached the near bank.

His horse landed again with a teeth-jarring thud, then trembled and stood still once more—

A burning ribbon of fire licked through his thigh.

Bird Alighting jerked from the pain, his eyes finding the soldiers on the near bank and beginning to urge their dripping horses in among the lodges. The muzzles of their weapons were smoking. And he knew he had been hit by one of their bullets.

"*Mimillu!*" he screeched at the horse, knowing this was his only chance to flee. "You stupid creature!"

In his gut, Bird Alighting realized he would never stand a chance on foot, not with that wounded leg burning. He'd never manage to put any weight on that side of his body in a run to escape.

Whipping the pony with the coil of rope on one side, flailing his one good foot against the other side, the warrior finally got the horse started away through the lodges. But slowly. The animal took a few tentative steps, paused and whipped its head around, then set off again at a little faster pace.

Not far ahead Bird Alighting saw another man running in the same direction, for the base of the hill where the women and children had disappeared. One bullet, then a handful more, snarled past him and the horse as the warrior on foot peered over his shoulder and spotted Bird Alighting coming.

With those oncoming *suapies* and the Shadows, Bird Alighting realized death would not be long in finding the man left to flee on foot. He would be run down—shot from behind or clubbed with a rifle before he was finished off at close range.

"Come up behind me!" he shouted to the warrior as he drew near.

Without a word, the breathless warrior lurched to a halt and held up his hand. Grabbing it in his, Bird Alighting swung the man up behind him on the slow horse.

That exertion suddenly seemed to fill the morning sky with shooting stars. He found it hard to focus, could not see much of anything at all around him as he began to wobble on the back of the pony.

"Hold on! Hold on!" the warrior behind him yelled in his ear.

But Bird Alighting was having trouble staying upright. He wanted to tell the man about his leg wound, that he must be losing too much blood, that his head was not working right anymore and he could not see. . . .

Then all color, all light, went out of his body—

RACING out of the north and east sides of the village, more than a hundred of the Nez Perce were streaming away from Captain Whipple's troops and D. B. Randall's Mount Idaho volunteers.

They reminded Lieutenant Sevier M. Rains of rats streaming from the tall piles of grain sacks rising from the wharves in Lewiston. Why, if Whipple ordered these eighty-some men after the Indians, it would be like trying to contain mercury under their fingers. A worse than useless proposition. Little more than a fool's errand.

"Mr. Rains!"

He wheeled his horse at Whipple's call, found the officer approaching on horseback. "Captain?"

"You're to be commended, Lieutenant," Whipple began, a bit breathless.

"Commended, Captain?"

"Racing ahead of the skirmish line the way you did—alone."

"Truth is, sir . . . I was hoping to catch Looking Glass myself. I figured he was the biggest prize of all. But I think he got away with the rest."

"Next to that chief, their horses are the next biggest prize we could hope to corral," Whipple advised. "With two of my lieutenants gone after the herd, I need you to take charge of the destruction of the camp."

"Burn the lodges, sir?"

"Yes. See how the volunteers are already going through every one— looting all that is worth a pittance."

"Firearms, powder, that sort of thing, Captain?"

"Save it from the fires, but torch the rest."

Rains touched his fingertips to his brow in salute. "Very good, Captain!"

As it turned out, the lieutenant's detail could get no more than two of the lodges burning. The hides were either too damp with the morning dew to burn or simply too thick to do more than smolder. For the better part of an hour it was like a celebration for Randall's civilians as they whooped and hollered each time one of them dragged something of value from the captured lodges. Small buckskin pouches of black powder, satchels of vermillion paint, and finely tanned buffalo robes, not to mention cooking utensils, blankets, china dishes, and some clayware. Anything that could not be set ablaze was stomped on or busted with the butts of their rifles, broken in pieces so small no one would waste time retrieving them from the damp ground.

"Hey, Lieutenant!" D. B. Randall called out to Rains as the officer came to a halt by a lodge standing at the edge of camp. "You see how my friend Minturn proved himself the best shot of this whole bunch, didn'cha?"

"Can't say as I had an eye on any of your men in particular, Mr. Randall."

"Shit, Lieutenant!" Randall exclaimed, waving over one of his fellow civilians. "Here, this is Peter Minturn—best shot in this here territory, I'll wager."

Rains glanced quickly at the young volunteer's face, saw the bemused pride in Minturn's eyes. He asked the volunteer, "So you accounted for some enemy dead, did you?"

Instead of Minturn answering for himself, Randall snorted, "Hell, Lieutenant—this here friend of mine was hungry for Injun meat, I'll tell you. The man damn well proved himself to be a dead shot each time he pulled the trigger!"

"H-hungry for Indian meat?" Rains repeated, bewildered by the crude expression.

Minturn finally spoke: "Just like I'm off hunting to make meat for the stew pot, Lieutenant. This here jump on Looking Glass's village was no different than shooting into a bunch of scampering jackrabbits!"

Chapter Eleven

Khoy-Tsahl, 1877

SLOWLY, GROGGILY, BIRD ALIGHTING CAME ALIVE AGAIN.

He looked around. Felt the arms locked about him. Stared down at those two hands wrapped in the horse's mane and wondered whose they were.

Then all color and light returned to his mind—and he remembered the warrior he had stopped to pick up in his flight from the village.

Sensing the labored, uneven lope of the overburdened horse, Bird Alighting gazed down at his legging, finding half of it entirely soaked with his blood. Even though he was still light-headed, the warrior realized he had suffered a severe loss of blood and hadn't fallen for only one reason—the man behind him.

"See our friend?" the warrior behind him yelled in his ear. "She's coming out to us!"

Bewildered, Bird Alighting looked in the direction of the approaching hoofbeats—his eyes finding *Etemiere* coming off the hillside at a gallop. This woman, called Arrowhead among his *Nee-Me-Poo*, was racing toward them at a slant out of the skimpy timber. She had a large gray-black wolfskin tied around her neck, its head positioned atop hers, held in place by a cord knotted under her chin. With the speed of her pony, that drape fluttered behind her as she slowed to a lope, coming alongside them and matching the pace of their pony.

"I tried to find a place in the brush at the creek's edge where I could make some shots at the *suapies*," she said breathlessly. "Make some kills across the water—" but Arrowhead suddenly interrupted her words when her eyes saw Bird Alighting's wound. "You are bleeding—badly! Stop—stop your horse now!"

The warrior behind him pulled with one hand in the

pony's mane, the other tugging on that long coil of rope Bird Alighting still gripped in one palm, convincing the frightened pony to stop. Immediately vaulting from her horse, Arrowhead leaned over, pulling up the bottom of her cloth dress with one hand as she yanked a knife from its belt scabbard with her other and quickly hacked off two long strips of the wool cloth.

Standing at Bird Alighting's knee, Arrowhead quickly folded one piece over the seeping wound, then flung the other, wider strip around the leg itself. She pulled her makeshift bandage as tight as she could before looping the ends into a knot, then secured it with a second knot. "Perhaps this will stop the bleeding now."

"Yes," the warrior behind him agreed quietly. "Then his mind won't go to sleep again from losing any more blood. But we will need to get him some raw liver to eat soon."

All Bird Alighting could do was nod. Eating raw liver was the best thing for the weakness caused from a great loss of blood.

"I saw a young herder boy killed," Arrowhead told them as she inspected the bandage she had just tied around the leg. "He was trying to drive off the horses when the Shadows came charging up to steal the herd from us."

"You saw him fall?"

"Yes. He pitched off the back of his pony and did not move," she explained. "I wanted to go see to him, if there was any breath left in his mouth—but the herding ground was too crowded with soldiers by that time. They were shooting at me, so I hurried to the hills to catch up with the rest of our village."

"What will we do now?" the warrior asked as Arrowhead turned away to leap atop her pony.

She said, "We should find the rest of our people."

A crackle of sporadic gunfire sounded dangerously close as they gave heels to their ponies and started toward the top of the hill.

With desperation in his voice, the warrior declared, "No,

I mean to ask: What will Looking Glass's people do now that we have lost all our horses, left our lodges and homes and gardens behind . . . abandoned everything we own?"

"What law of warfare says an enemy has the right to shoot you when you are surrendering?" Bird Alighting asked, surprising them both that he was talking after so long a silence.

"It is evil treachery," the warrior growled. "To shoot at innocents."

"There is only one thing we can do," Bird Alighting added, the colors in his mind more crisp and certain than they ever had been. "Blood will always follow blood."

"Is your head right, Bird Alighting? Or is your thinking gone far away?" asked Arrowhead. "What do you mean—blood will always follow blood?"

In a stronger voice, he said, "Now is the time we must join the rest of Looking Glass's people and go in search of the others who are fighting these Shadows and soldiers."

SECOND Lieutenant Sevier M. Rains had done an admirable job plundering the village . . . even if he did say so himself. His father had ransacked Seminole villages in Florida, Mexican towns far south of the border, then struggled in a lost cause against Federal troops during the Civil War. He would approve of the way the lieutenant and his men left nothing of any value for the Nez Perce.

"Lieutenant!" Captain Whipple called out as he approached with Captain Winters.

"Sir!" and Rains snapped a salute as the officers' eyes raked over the destruction he had made of Looking Glass's camp.

Whipple asked, "Are you far from completing your assignment?"

"We are all but finished, Captain."

"Good," Winters said. "We're about to move out."

"Where to, sirs?" Rains inquired.

"Back toward Mount Idaho," Whipple explained. "We're

going to give more than six hundred horses to the volunteers, hoping to keep them out of the hands of the hostiles. Then we'll rejoin our column across the Salmon."

Winters added, "General Howard should have the command across the river by now."

"So we're going to join in the pursuit?" Rains asked after he had given the command for his detail to mount up.

"This bunch won't cause any more trouble, I'd wager," Winters snorted.

Whipple agreed as he gestured for them to move out, starting upstream. "With what little we're leaving behind for his band, we've taken Looking Glass entirely out of the equation for the rest of the war, gentlemen."

Rains still felt the hot giddiness that had come from the brief fight forcing their way into the enemy camp. "I sure hope we're *not* done, sirs."

"What do you mean, Mr. Rains?" Whipple asked.

"I only hope the general will leave some warriors for us," Rains admitted. "I pray we're not too late to get in on a little more fighting before this shabby, second-rate war is over."

AFTER sending a courier upriver to remind Captain Joel G. Trimble to hurry across the Salmon and rejoin the column, General O. O. Howard could now begin his tortuous pursuit of the Non-Treaty bands as the warriors and their families slipped away into the wrinkles of that rugged terrain rising steeply between the Salmon and Snake Rivers.

Back on their first night in Camp Theller at Horseshoe Bend in the Salmon, William Hunter and more than forty of his volunteers had arrived in camp. They had announced they were from Dayton, in Washington Territory—a small town midway between Lewiston and Walla Walla—come to help the general put down the uprising in any fashion they could. Howard had put them to work early the next morning, 29 June. Hunter himself and a pair of his civilians willingly stripped off their clothes, dragged the saddles from their horses, then braved the icy-cold, roiling torrent of the

Salmon as they dragged two lengths of thick rope and their pulleys to the west bank. Reaching the far side, they dismounted to the raucous cheers of Howard's hundreds. With three rowboats acquired from settlers living upstream, the long column could now begin its crossing and its pursuit of Joseph's Non-Treaty bands, one boatload of soldiers at a time.

The goal was to attach a boat to the main cable by means of a loop sling, muscling each small load back and forth with the muscles of their backs pitted against the strength of the Salmon. But the ropes Hunter's men lashed to a trio of stout, stately cottonwoods did not last out the day's battering and buffeting as Howard started his command across. What with the strength of a snow-swollen current, the hemp lines finally gave out early in the afternoon, and one of the hastily constructed rafts started spinning downriver with its terrified crew. Almost a mile down the Salmon, they managed to beach their unwieldy craft and step onto solid ground.

The following day, 30 June, the soldiers attempted something stronger in the way of a wire cable, hoping it would prove stronger than the rope . . . but it, too, ultimately failed against the racing current. With less than half the men having reached the west bank, most still on the east side with the general, this second day ended in even more frustration for Howard.

Contrary to those who would eventually claim that he was overpious and refused to march on Sundays, O. O. Howard himself crossed the Salmon on the afternoon of 1 July after holding a small prayer service for his officers and what enlisted men chose to attend. It was a miserable day, raining and snowing alternately, as the general followed William Hunter and four of his men into the Salmon River breaks—where they nonetheless did find half a thousand Nez Perce ponies they managed to herd back to the crossing and forced across the river. Those animals that did not drown in the turbulent waters were turned over to Lieutenant James A. Haughey and his H Company of the

Twenty-first Infantry, called up from Fort Vancouver. While the rest of the command had boated to the west side of the river, Haughey's detail remained on the east bank to guard Howard's supply depot.

It was no small victory, therefore, that by sundown of 1 July the general had removed 500 ponies from his enemy and his entire column was finally across the frothy Salmon—in addition to their pack train, ammunition and supplies, artillery pieces, and other assorted impedimenta. An intermittent rain continued to fall, swelling the river at their backs, turning the green hills around them into a slick, soggy quagmire.

With no time to celebrate their victory over the Salmon, Howard's column now had to face another, and perhaps even more daunting, ordeal.

For the three days before he had reached Horseshoe Bend with his command, it had rained off and on. But once they were in Camp Theller beside the Salmon, the skies were gutted and it began to pour almost nonstop, a storm that lasted three more days and nights while the soldiers struggled to get their animals and matériel across the Salmon. What part of the trail hadn't been turned into a sticky morass had become so slick that even the surefooted mules were having difficulty maintaining their grip on the mushy hillsides.

The packers who handled those mules hadn't hired on to accept army scrip or paper greenbacks in exchange for their ordeal. Instead, the civilians were to be paid the going rate of one dollar per animal, per day, in "coin," or what those grizzled frontiersmen called hard money. But that was just for the use, and steady abuse, of their animals. The packers themselves were paid even more. Howard had engaged ten of the best mule-skinners in the country at eighty-five dollars in coin per month and another forty-eight packers for sixty-five dollars in hard money.

But securing enough money for their pay was the least of Howard's problems. He had other, niggling details that bellowed for his attention. For one thing, his quartermasters had assured themselves that all their supply wagons had the proper number of wheels before setting out from Fort Lapwai. A shipment of dead-axle (or springless) wagons was brought upriver from Portland by the Oregon Steam Navigation Company. Problem was, the riverboat company hadn't brought wagons up with two *front* wheels and two *rear* wheels! Then, too, much of the harness supplied Howard's teamsters was already dried and rotten as unscrupulous traders attempted to make their quick money off this brief action against the Nez Perce.

But when he got a wagon with the correct complement of wheels and hitched up the teams with usable, field-worthy harness . . . Howard found he still wasn't able to hire enough teamsters from the surrounding countryside. Most of the low-end laboring classes in the Idaho towns were already attached to the column to help as road-building crews, who were paid a skimpy daily wage and found. Still, many of the teamsters he was able to hire out of the towns ended up quitting once the army crossed the Salmon and the going toughened far beyond what any of them had bargained for.

Most of the hangers-on, those so-called volunteers, with their leaders brandishing honorary titles, had already become an inconstant irritation to the general as well. The first bunch, twenty-one citizens from Walla Walla under Tom Page who had accompanied Howard to the battlefield days ago, ended up quitting and turning around for home, citing "pressing business," before Howard even had his column across the Salmon! Fortunate for the general and his campaign, that very same day William Hunter and his forty men had showed up from Dayton.

But a third cadre of some twenty-five citizens under "Captain" J. W. Elliott were a different color of horse altogether. They had reported in, then promptly rode off, creating more of a nuisance of themselves in the area than they were assisting the army in putting down this rebellion. That band of volunteers from Pomeroy, a small community some twenty-five miles east of Dayton in Washington Territory, had disgusted Howard in that they were far more interested in rustling any local settler's loose stock than in pursuing the Non-Treaty Nez Perce.

And it wasn't only the civilians in this area who seemed to be securely resting at the bottom of the proverbial barrel. Major General Irwin McDowell, commander of the Division of the Pacific and Howard's superior, was scraping the bottom of his own barrel when he ordered C Company of the Twelfth Infantry up from Fort Yuma in Arizona, including its own junior officer, Second Lieutenant Guy Howard—the general's oldest son. Upon his arrival, Otis would make Guy one of his aides for the duration of the Nez Perce conflict. In addition, McDowell ordered up the Eighth Infantry's H Company, then in California. By the time those two outfits reached San Francisco by train, McDowell had added companies C and L from the Fourth Artillery. Altogether, that was a complement of ninety-six unproven, untested soldiers and ten officers. Together with thirty-two green recruits fresh from their enlistment depots back east, all were loaded onto a steamer and sent north to Portland. They reached Lewiston on 19 June, the quickest deployment for any troop shipment then under way.

All the delays and those men pouring in from around the country reminded O. O. Howard of that most unholy of holdovers from their days fighting the Civil War when the highest echelons of the Union command refused to budge, much less engage the Confederates, until they were assured of superior numbers and thereby certain of victory even before they marched into battle.

In order to track the Non-Treaty bands, Howard realized he needed a complement of trustworthy scouts. While it was not near the number Howard had requested, McDowell nonetheless authorized the hiring of twenty-five Indian trackers. Later, on the fifth of July, Howard would be instructed that he could hire a total of eighty in all—some of which came from Fort Hall on the Bannock-Shoshone Reservation, a number of those having seen service in the previous year's campaign against the Sioux and Cheyenne on the Northern Plains. With his supply line assured, his manpower being hustled to the front, and competent guides mustered to keep him on the Nez Perce's trail, Howard felt assured of putting an early end to this outbreak.

Still, the delays and lack of rapid progress had been frustrating to the old soldier.

The fleeing bands had chosen well when they crossed into this forbidding landscape of a rugged and lofty terrain squeezed up between the two deep, precipitous, and all-but-inaccessible canyons of the Salmon and Snake Rivers, just south of the point where the Salmon angled west in its quest to join the Snake. Atop the ridges lay a broken undulating prairie, while the only route to that plateau forced a horseman up the steep walls of the Salmon River gorge. Those slopes were a mixture of grassy prairie dotted with patches of evergreen timber.*

Because the column was taxed in its climb to ever-higher altitudes, the excruciating exertion on man and animal began to show. While every soldier had his own complaints, the artillerymen grumbled the loudest. After Captain Charles B. Throckmorton, commander of the artillery battalion, had shown himself to be a laggard by the time they reached the Salmon, Howard had replaced him with Captain Marcus P. Miller. After only two days the fact that the artillerymen were unused to Indian campaigning was painfully apparent. Miller's four gun crews let it be known what a toll it was taking on them as they struggled to keep up with the cavalry and infantry companies.

It wasn't that Howard's scouts had trouble finding and following the Non-Treaty bands—what with Joseph's people cutting a wide, telltale swath as more than seven hundred people drove along more than two thousand horses, many dragging travois. But at times the command reached a short stretch of that well-marked trail where the passage proved so slippery, the footing so treacherous, that a few of

---

*Much of this area crossed by both the Nez Perce and Howard's army in 1877 is today known as the Joseph Plains.

the pack animals slid right over the edge, tumbling down and down until some trees or jagged rocks put an end to their descent hundreds of yards below. By the time packers scrambled back down to see what they could salvage, there wasn't much left of either the loose-footed mules or what supplies the animals had been carrying.

Able to advance rarely more than ten, perhaps as much as twelve, miles per day, Howard cajoled, begged, and snapped at his column to keep them after their prey. Meanwhile, his scouts could only prod the soldiers with the distressing news that the Non-Treaty bands were staying far, far in the lead.

No surprise, it continued to rain as they struggled toward the summit of Brown's Mountain. But as they made that grueling 3,500-foot ascent, the rain turned to snow. Just below the summit, the entire command had to halt and hunker down as the wind came up, the clouds pressed down, and they were battered by a freezing sleet that soaked every man, caked every animal, in layers of bone-chilling ice. During the storm that night, the cooks attempted to prepare a dish made from abandoned and broken-down Nez Perce horses, which, among the officers, was laughingly called *fricandeau de cheval*. Most claimed it tasted like a stringy beef, so the majority opted for their ration of salt pork as they hunkered around their blazing fires, the wind howling through what some now labeled Camp Misery.

By the time Howard reached the summit, he had convinced himself that Joseph's people had split into two bands. To meet the threat posed by the one group he was certain was inching its way south to unite with the dissident Shoshone and Bannock tribes along the Weiser River, the general had already ordered that troops under Major John Wesley Green march north from Fort Boise to the seat of the Indian war—thereby trapping the Nez Perce between them.

But what of the other, larger group?

Otis believed they still marched in front of him—that he could follow them until he caught them in camp, immediately surround them, and force a surrender. He became even more certain of this scenario when his Nez Perce scouts located one cache after another, each containing some of what the Non-Treaty warriors had stolen from the homes of the Salmon River and Camas Prairie settlers: cigars and clothing, flour and meerschaum pipes, along with other sundry supplies. The afternoon of their third day west of the Salmon, the advance even ran onto more than five hundred horses that had evidently strayed off from the Nez Perce herd.

Destroying the cached supplies and ordering the horses driven back across the river, Howard convinced himself that all this circumstantial evidence indicated that Joseph was leading his people back toward the Wallowa and Imnaha valleys—the chief's traditional camping grounds.

While his officers grumbled among themselves, while the bone-weary, soaked-clear-through soldiers glared at their commander, Oliver Otis Howard steadfastly assured himself that he was about to bring the war to an end. Joseph was taking his bands back to their ancestral homes, where they would be trapped between two converging armies. It was only a matter of time now, Howard vowed. A few more days and a few more miles.

This damnable little war was almost over.

Chapter Twelve

July 2, 1877

"I can't order you to stay on this side of the river, Mr. Hunter," General O. O. Howard had told the civilian leader from Dayton back on that first day the soldiers were attempting their perilous crossing. "Nor can I guarantee your safety if you go wandering off alone on the other side of the Salmon."

"You still have your mind set against sending any of your friendlies out to find the war camp, General?" asked William Hunter.

"Not until I have enough of my men across should we have any more displays from the warriors like we had here day before yesterday."

"Mind you, me and my men don't aim to get ourselves in any trouble, General Howard," the civilian had assured him. "Just want to see where those Nez Perce have run off to. We figure to be back before this time tomorrow."

He and two of his best friends from Dayton—a tiny community in eastern Washington Territory—swam their horses over to the west bank of the Salmon, then started north into the broken country. They hadn't been moving more than two hours when they were rewarded with sighting a half-dozen figures on foot in the distance.

"*Enfant de garce!*" one of the six men sobbed as they lunged up among the trio of horsemen.

"Shit, any of you Americans?" Hunter asked, perplexed. "Speak English?"

"A little some," confessed another of the bedraggled half-dozen.

"You look a sight, fellas," Hunter said. "Where's your horses? Your guns?"

The good-talker shook his head as if searching for the

right words, perhaps any words, to use in telling the story as Hunter and his companions dropped to the ground and let their horses blow. Slowly, painstakingly, the story unfolded.

When the outbreak first began, the six Frenchmen had been on this west side of the Salmon, farther to the south. In fact, they claimed they had yelled a warning across the river to some American friends. Once hundreds of the Nez Perce showed up near the mouth of the White Bird, the Frenchmen fled deep into the hills on the other side of the Salmon. But not so far they hadn't heard all the gunfire the day of the battle.

Keeping to their side of the river, they had trained a keen eye on the migrations of the Non-Treaty bands as the Indians moved south to Horseshoe Bend, then crossed and started back north to where Larry Ott had been homesteading on Deer Creek then started to climb into the formidable terrain. Three days ago they had run across a trio of Chinese miners who warned them that war parties were prowling the countryside, horsemen who had allowed the Chinese to pass unharmed.

Two days back, the Frenchmen had taken refuge, hiding in a tiny abandoned cabin when they heard horses approaching outside, and were suddenly confronted with five warriors armed with rifles. The frightened Frenchmen quickly surrendered their three old shotguns. Before they rode off, the Nez Perce took more than one hundred dollars in gold and coin from the six miners—then told the Frenchmen to get away as far and as fast as they could from the country where no white man would be safe.

William Hunter dragged the short stub of his fat stogie from his teeth and thoughtfully inspected the moist, much-chewed end of the cigar. Then he said, "Lost your bird guns to them red bastards, and all your money, too."

"They say they give us our lives in trade," the French miner repeated.

"Tell you what, fellas," Hunter declared. "You talk it over together, because I'll guarantee you boys one thing: If you throw in with us and Howard's soldiers . . . you won't just get back what guns and money is owed you, but a whole heap of revenge, too."

WHILE the *suapies* of Cut-Off Arm were struggling to maintain any momentum at all, the Non-Treaty bands were already more than twenty miles downstream, north along the Salmon at a traditional fording site known as Craig Billy Crossing. Joseph realized they had chosen well when they decided to follow the suggestions of Rainbow and Five Wounds, just returned from the buffalo country the afternoon of the fight at *Lahmotta*.

"We cross the Salmon, wait for the soldiers to follow, then lose them on the other side," Rainbow had advised.

"And when we have lured the Shadows across, getting them snarled and lost in that rugged country, we will recross," Five Wounds proposed. "That's when we'll be free to roam as we always have."

Days ago, the scouts watched two smaller groups of soldiers leave Cut-Off Arm's massed army. One band took its empty pack animals and marched north for Fort Lapwai, clearly intending to bring back more supplies—which meant a longer effort on their part. An army so large surely needed a great deal of food. But that second band of *suapies* had marched directly for the settlements of Grangeville and Mount Idaho with a wagon gun, and from there they moved at night into the twisting canyon of the Clearwater, where the scouts lost track of the soldiers. None of the *Nee-Me-Poo* warrior chiefs could figure out where the *suapies* were bound or why.

After three days of struggle, Cut-Off Arm's foolish soldiers made it across the river—which meant it was finally time for the village to break camp where they had been waiting just north of the crossing, near the Deer Creek homestead of Larry Ott,* where there was a little level ground on which to pitch their lodges against the rainy sky.

**Cries from the Earth*, vol. 14, the *Plainsmen* series.

Now they must forge their way across the muddy, broken landscape, climbing toward the Doumecq Plain above that evil Shadow's abandoned farm.

But to make time and to assure that they would stay far enough ahead of the soldiers, they would not be able to take everything from this point. As the chief in charge of the women and children, overseeing the camp itself, Joseph ordered that every unnecessary item of food and clothing be buried in numerous caches dug near rocks they would mark for their return when the present troubles were over.

And then he had turned to the young men not yet old enough to have fought against the soldiers at *Lahmotta,* youngsters nonetheless old enough to experience an eager enthusiasm. Their orders were to cull the old and the lame horses from their combined herds. These animals would be separated out from the stronger horses, then driven down their back trail where they would likely encounter the slowly advancing soldiers at some point in the next few days. It was a maneuver that might not necessarily retard the progress of the *suapies* but most assuredly would accelerate the progress of the camp in its march.

In the two weeks since his brother had defeated the horse soldiers at *Lahmotta,* there had been much said about Joseph behind the chief's back. None of it was good. Nearly all the talk was about his not taking up a weapon to fight off the soldiers, how he had not ventured out of camp to do battle even though Ollokot's warriors were outnumbered two-to-one. For some time now the talk whispered and often laughed about behind the hands had not been good.

But it was in these last few days that Joseph began to establish the reputation that would withstand the test yet to come. A legacy that would endure those terrible trials the *Nee-Me-Poo* could not even imagine at that moment. It was in this time that Joseph began to make decisions not having anything whatsoever to do with making war on some group of Shadow civilians or on that band of soldiers. No, without the showy fanfare of the war chiefs, Joseph had already begun to quietly reach decisions that—months from now and many, many miles away—would ultimately assure the survival of his people.

There was no country better suited to ducking and dodging than this between the Snake and Salmon Rivers. And while Cut-Off Arm got bogged down in the mire of crags and rain-slickened trails, the *Nee-Me-Poo* would leap back across the Salmon, across the Camas Prairie, and on to the deep canyon of the Cottonwood that would lead the bands all the way to the Clearwater. Because this hard country lay in an arduous maze, few of the individual family groups or clans wandered away on their own. Fear of what followed them bound the many together and kept them moving north.

At one point they came across a large herd of cattle that Joseph's *Wallamwatkins* had been forced to abandon weeks ago when they crossed the Salmon at Rocky Canyon to join the last ever of the celebrations at *Tepahlewam*—just before the first settlers were murdered. After stopping here for most of a day, just long enough to butcher a few of the cattle, the village pushed on, leaving the lion's share of the beeves behind in the hills to graze until a better day when Joseph's people hoped to return here, when they could gather up their herd to take it back to their beloved Wallowa valley. But at this point in their flight they could ill afford the snail's pace burden of the white man's beef.

"*Eeh!* Look below!" one of the riders near the front of the march hollered out in unbounded joy.

Joseph smiled at his wife, then put heels to his pony as he sped along the column. Reining up beside Ollokot and Yellow Wolf, he gazed down the steep slope of the canyon.

"Our ford across the *Tahmonah,** Brother," Ollokot an-

---

*The Salmon River.

**While the white men would come to know this as Craig Billy Crossing, to the *Nee-Me-Poo* this was "Luke's Place," named after *Pahka Yatwekin*, one of their people who was called Luke Billy by the Shadows, a man who had a poor cabin standing on the south bank of the Salmon River.

nounced as they paused to gaze down at their traditional crossing.**

"Now that we've left Cut-Off Arm behind to struggle through these mountains," Joseph said quietly, "we can start across the prairie, where we'll rejoin Looking Glass's people."

> "Once we reach that valley of the Clearwater," Ollokot agreed, "the soldiers won't know where to find us. And if they do come looking for our camps, the dark canyons east of *Kamisnim Takin** are good places for our people to hide. Cut-Off Arm will never find us there."

As for his own wound, Bird Alighting counted himself fortunate.

It could have been far, far worse for the rest of Looking Glass's band. Good that the Shadows were such poor shots when they became excited or angry or frightened. All those soldiers and the Shadows had managed to shoot only one *Nee-Me-Poo*, the young pony herder—named *Nennin Chekoostin*, called Black Raven—who had been caught in some cross fire before he could escape as their horse herd was captured. The other two deaths the enemy had caused only because of the terror the Shadows had created when they opened fire, without warning, on the sleepy morning camp. That young woman and her little infant—both of them drowned in Clear Creek—their bodies unclaimed until the white men left and the Looking Glass people could slip back into their devastated camp to look for what they could salvage.

A few of the women and one old man burned their hands putting out the smoldering fires of those two lodges the *suapies* had managed to destroy, hoping to save anything that hadn't yet burned. Oh, there were a few scrapes and cuts from running through the brush or stumbling among the rocks as the men, women, and children scrambled out of camp, fleeing beyond the hill just behind the village.

---

*The Camas Prairie.

While the sun went down and the stars came out that day, Looking Glass and what warriors hadn't already gone off to join White Bird's and *Toohoolhoolzote*'s fighting men gathered in the descending darkness and talked of what to do and where to go now that Cut-Off Arm had made war on them. It had served no purpose for their chief to stay neutral, many argued. The white man had attacked them. Even a neighboring chief camped nearby, the Palouse *Hatalekin*, was as homeless as they. Now they must choose.

"Even though we are already on the reservation," Looking Glass protested, "our feet must take one path or another from this moment on."

"We must drive the *suapies* from our country!" shouted Arrowhead, the warrior woman.

"The enemy will keep looking for our camps, which means the women and children will continue to suffer," argued *Hatalekin*, the Palouse chief. "See how the soldiers came looking to attack White Bird."

Shot Leg laughed and said, "But see what good it did those soldiers!"

"Yet other soldiers came looking for another village to attack, and this time it was ours!" Black Foot continued the lament.

"There really is little choice," Looking Glass interrupted the heated discussion minutes later. "Do we want to become Christian Indians like Lawyer's or Reuben's people?"

"No!" Arrowhead growled throatily. "*Tananisa!* Damn them! Let the Kamiah people believe in the white man's god. We are Dreamers!"

"Or," Looking Glass continued, "do we join the fight to hold onto this land of ours?"

"As for me," Black Foot said, "there is no choice in what options the Shadows have handed us."

Slowly the chief looked over that suddenly hushed gathering. A small child whimpered from the dark. Then it was quiet, so deathly quiet, again. The summer night held its breath around them.

When he finally spoke again, Looking Glass said, "We

will leave as soon as our women have everything packed on what horses we managed to save from the enemy."

"Where is it you would have us go?" *Hatalekin* asked as the black of night seemed to swallow all their hopes of staying neutral in the struggle.

"We will go in search of the fighting bands," the chief answered. "Our only strength now lies in fighting the white man together."

The moon had just made its appearance at the horizon, its creamy yellow color illuminating the underbellies of some scattered clouds by the time Looking Glass and two old men started the village downstream for the Clearwater. From there they would strike upstream for the mouth of the Cottonwood. It was that creek and its canyon they would follow up and onto the Camas Prairie in the dark of this night.

How noiseless they made that march. The children who had been wrapped in arms or carried on backs had surely fallen asleep. No one talked but some headmen who spoke in low voices of hearing reports of the few warriors who rode both flanks, out there in the dark. From time to time Bird Alighting and the other young men came in to report their news on what lay ahead upon the route Looking Glass had chosen for them all.

In the first, early light of the sun's coming Bird Alighting saw the smudge along the western horizon of the prairie. He rubbed his eyes again, blinked, and stared. He had never been one of those far-seeing men who had the ability to find distant objects without the far-seeing glasses of the Shadows. So he did his best to determine what the smudge meant.

"Is that dust?" Arrowhead asked in almost a whisper as she rode up and came to a halt beside Bird Alighting.

"I cannot tell if it is dust . . . or maybe smoke."

The warrior woman asked, "Where is it? Can you tell that?"

"Far up Cottonwood Creek," Bird Alighting said. "Perhaps as far away as that Shadow settlement on the road to the soldier fort."

"I think it is dust," Arrowhead asserted. "That much dust . . . cannot be Cut-Off Arm's *suapies*. He has his army far to the south of here. No, Bird Alighting, that can only be some of our own people."

How he wanted to smile, his heart wanted to hope. But his head would not let him. "Let's hope your eyes are right, *Etemiere*. I pray those are not soldiers barring our way."

Chapter Thirteen

July 3, 1877

It hadn't taken very long for First Sergeant Michael McCarthy to figure out that Trimble's H Company should have stayed at Slate Creek with the civilians huddled there. Far, far better than what they had been forced to endure as they slogged along after those damned fleeing Indians.

From downriver at the crossing General Howard sent orders by "Colonel" Edward McConville and his Mount Idaho volunteers that Captain Trimble's outfit was to rejoin him on the west side of the Salmon. In company with that band of volunteers, they had made their own crossing right there at the mouth of Slate Creek in a driving rain, then marched down the west bank until they reached a house said to belong to a Mr. Rhett. While Trimble's horse soldiers began to take cover out of the soggy weather, Rhett showed up and angrily ordered the men out of his cozy cabin. McConville's men shared their meager canvas shelters with the cavalrymen that stormy night of 1 July.

"Not a good goddamned reception from one of our own citizens!" McCarthy grumbled, wishing he could pry the wet boots off his feet.

"Sorry that son of a bitch ain't got a touch of hospitality in his soul," McConville apologized. "Some folks don't give a damn what the army's here to do for 'em."

Ascending Deer Creek the next morning, Captain Trimble had started them into the rugged hills, following the route taken by the fleeing Nez Perce.

A perfect sea of mountains, gullies, ravines, and canyons.

Each day's march of ten miles seemed more like a march three times as far made on level ground. What had been merely difficult terrain before the incessant rains had now become treacherous as the slopes turned into rivers of mud. With the cavalry assigned to lead the way, that first afternoon they had reached the top of a small plateau just at dusk, turning in their saddles to peer back at that long line slowly snaking its way up the precipitous mountainside. Trimble ordered a bivouac made near some stunted pines, and the men did what they could to make it a cheerful camp. Still, most everything, tents and rations included, was back with the pack train and infantry, neither of which would likely catch up to the advance until midday tomorrow. So all these troopers had was what little coffee, hardbread, and bacon remained in their saddlebags.

To add to the misery of their bivouac at the summit of Brown's Mountain on the evening of 2 July, a cheerless camp made in the open without much in the way of supper, just after dark a hard and icy rain began lancing out of the sky. Most of the officers ended up crowding into the general's headquarters tent, leaving the noncoms and enlisted to fend for themselves around those sputtering fires whipped by the stormy gales that tortured the top of this high, barren plateau. Howard's aide, First Lieutenant Melville C. Wilkinson, graciously named this spot "Camp Misery" in his daily report.

The following morning, 3 July, the advance command awoke to find that a dense fog had descended upon the mountaintop. While they remained in camp, recuperating and waiting for the pack train and infantry to catch up, the general dispatched Trimble's company and McConville's volunteers to search the trail ahead as far as they could march and still return by dusk. Late in the morning the patrol found the Nez Perce trail had split into two, the troopers following one branch, the civilians following the other. By late in the afternoon Trimble's patrol bivouacked where those two fresh trails rejoined—a place where Canoe Encampment and Rocky Canyon trails intersected. From all the sign, it appeared the last Nez Perce camp was at least three days old.

This meant that here late on the afternoon of 3 July

Howard's column was now something on the order of four or more days behind the hostiles.

With little food and not a swallow of coffee to speak of—but with all the rain, fog, and wind an Irishman from Nova Scotia could ever hope for—on top of everything else now they knew just how far ahead the enemy was. McCarthy was afeared the hostiles never would stop and give an accounting of themselves—so he could get in his licks for all those comrades who had fallen at White Bird.

Blessed Mary and Joseph! Oh, how Sergeant Michael McCarthy prayed those goddamned heathens would stop running away and give this army a fight to decide the matter, once and for all.

"CAPTAIN Whipple!" Lieutenant Sevier M. Rains called out as he stepped up to his company commander. "I brought those two civilians you asked for."

Whipple turned on his stool, positioned behind his field desk standing just outside his tent, and gave his second lieutenant a salute that early chill morning. "Very good, Mr. Rains. Please stay. I want you in on this."

Rains nodded. "Very good, sir." He pointed to the closest of the two Mount Idaho volunteers. "This is Foster, and this is Blewett."

"Your nominal leader, Captain D. B. Randall, said I could depend on you to get me some intelligence."

"Intelligence, Captain?" William Foster repeated.

"We need to know what we're facing here," Whipple explained. "What bands are in the area. If there are war parties prowling the nearby Camas Prairie. That sort of thing. Captain Randall claimed you two know this area better than the others."

"We know it," Charles Blewett affirmed. "Been on this prairie a few years. So we know the ground, and we know the Injuns, too. Never would've figgered Looking Glass's people for turning bad on us the way they did up on Clear Creek."

"I want you volunteers to find out what's become of

those Indians," Whipple said. "They've had plenty of time to make it onto the prairie since yesterday morning. With Colonel Perry's supply train due along here from Fort Lapwai any day now, I don't want any war parties slipping up and surprising us."

"Better to know what the bastards are up to and where they're going," Blewett agreed.

Foster asked, "You gonna send some soldiers along with us, Captain?"

"No, more men would just make you a bigger target, easier to spot. With just the two of you, I figure any roving war parties won't spot you so easy." Then, in afterthought, Whipple added, "I don't figure you'll be all that far from this road station that you can't make a fast dash back here if you confront any ticklish situation."

"Awright, Captain," Foster replied. "We'll get us some rations and ride out."

Whipple nodded. "Can you make it over to the country by Craig's Landing, see if the hostiles are on the river, and get back by supper to make your report?"

"Back before dark," Blewett assured.

Whipple had established his camp a day ago among the deserted, ransacked buildings then known as the Norton ranch. The captain had brought his battalion here early yesterday, 2 July, after returning to Mount Idaho at midnight on the first, the day his command had destroyed Looking Glass's village. Captain Lawrence S. Babbitt, a member of General O. O. Howard's staff, was waiting for them there with written orders for Whipple to establish this presence at the Cottonwood road station. There he was to await Perry and his supply train, as well as intercepting, if possible, the Nez Perce if they should happen along his way after recrossing the Salmon.

"The general commanding orders that if Perry does not arrive with his supply train in a timely manner," Whipple had told his handful of battalion officers before they put Mount Idaho behind them yesterday, "I am to leave no stone unturned to ascertain where the Indians are heading.

We are to report to the general by courier as often as we can." Then, the captain read another sentence from the note brought by Babbitt: " 'I expect of the cavalry tremendous vigor and activity even if it should kill a few horses.' "

Have no doubt about it: Howard wanted Joseph caught, corralled, and defeated.

When they had put Mount Idaho behind them yesterday, Lieutenant Rains wasn't sure how any of them should feel about that. This small battalion augmented by a few undisciplined civilians wasn't meant to confront and give battle to the hostile Nez Perce who had demolished Perry's command at the White Bird. Laying into Looking Glass's small village was one thing, but ordered to stand in the middle of this open prairie and bar the way of that band of heathen cutthroats, murderers, and rapists was altogether different. If Howard figured the hostiles were coming this way, then why the hell wasn't he here with reinforcements?

So Rains wholeheartedly agreed with the tactical decision Captain Whipple made regarding gathering intelligence on the wandering, dispossessed people of Looking Glass. Better to know what your enemy was doing than for anything to hit you as a total surprise. In the meantime, Colonel Perry would be coming down from Lapwai with supplies and ammunition, and maybe the advance of Howard's cavalry would make it in, too. In another day or so there would be enough soldiers here to put an end to the great Nez Perce war with a dying whimper.

Norton's road ranch was the only structural complex of any consequence on the whole of the Camas Prairie. Originally laid out in a wide brush- and tree-lined gulch along the south side of Cottonwood Creek some twenty miles west of its junction with the Clearwater, the house, barns, stables, and corrals overlapped the Mount Idaho–Lewiston Road. The house itself, where Jennie Norton had run her hotel business, sat on the south side of the creek.

Fifteen years before, a settler named Allen had built the original way station, consisting of a store, a saloon, a few hotel rooms, and a stage stop. The next year it sold to a pair of enterprising men, but within a year they had sold it to another man. John Byrom operated the place until Joseph Moore and Peter H. Ready of Mount Idaho bought the station. When they sold it to Benjamin and Jennie Norton, Moore stayed on to work for the new owners and Ready started hauling freight up and down the road to Lewiston,* which ran northwest from the ranch through a rolling countryside broken by some deep ravines carved by the tiny streams and rivulets feeding Cottonwood Creek.

Hearing stories told at Mount Idaho about the war party's raid conducted against the civilians and Ben Norton's death back on 14 June, when the Nez Perce outbreak was just getting under way, Rains was completely surprised to discover that the hostiles hadn't put a torch to any of the buildings. Upon the battalion's arrival here at this peaceful place, the lieutenant had taken a deep breath of air and looked about, finding it hard to believe there was an Indian war breaking out—and that it had started here.

"You two going to search from along the hillside?" he asked as he came to a stop near the two civilians and their horses. Foster was rising to the saddle.

Blewett swept his arm across the slope of nearby Craig's Mountain. "It makes sense to. There's plenty of timber for cover while we have us a look over the other side to see them Injuns come over the Craig Billy Crossing."

Foster reined his horse in a half-circle and tapped it with his heels as both civilians started away. He said, "Yonder side of that ridge, Lieutenant . . . that be where we figger we'll find us some Injuns."

"JESUS God!" William Foster hissed under his breath as he yanked back on the horse's reins, his heart suddenly a lump in his throat.

Beside him, Charles Blewett spotted the large herd of horses at the same moment. Together their animals dug in their hooves and slid to a stop on the bare slope.

**Cries from the Earth*, vol. 14, the *Plainsmen* series.

That herd of Indian ponies had suddenly appeared around the brow of a nearby hill barren of timber, north of the Cottonwood near the road to Fort Lapwai and Lewiston.

"That ain't no loose stock," Blewett said as they both quickly glanced this way and that for possible cover.

"They'll have herders with 'em," Foster grumbled the moment before he spotted the riders arrayed on the flanks of the large herd.

At this distance, he could tell those outriders wore feathers and carried weapons. No youngsters these. A war party for damned sure.

Foster started to wheel his pony around, saying, "Let's get afore they—"

But he was interrupted by the first pop of a far-off rifle.

As the sun had come out and their damp clothing began to steam that morning following days of hard, intermittent rain, the two civilians had traveled northwest on the Lewiston stage road to the point where it crossed Boardhouse Creek, then angled off to the left on the Salmon River Trail in the direction of Lawyer's Canyon. It had been a trail that took them over a long, rolling ridge before it descended into a little open saddle, then climbed once more up the shallow slope at the southwest side of Craig's Mountain.

That's where the broad, open terrain butted up against some light timber on this east side of the mountain rising more than a thousand feet above the Cottonwood. They were two ridges away from the soldier camp when they spotted the herd . . . and those warriors.

Jerking his head around to look over his shoulder at the distant gunshot, Foster saw the puff of smoke drifting on the cool wind, finding more than a handful of the warriors already galloping full-tilt in their direction.

"You don't need to ask me to get more'n once!" Blewett screamed as he flailed the side of his horse with the long reins.

Foster pointed as his horse shot him past Blewett's. "We make that brush, maybe we can lose 'em!"

The pair of civilians had covered no more than a hundred yards when Foster heard his friend call out with the sort of cry that instantly brought a chill to a man's spine.

"Bill!"

It took a moment for Foster to yank back on the reins and get his hell-bent-for-leather horse to slow to a halt. By the time he could turn the animal around in place, he watched Blewett finish his brief flight through the air, hitting the ground, hard, on his hip—his horse rearing back on its hind legs and pawing the air before it came down on all fours and tore off, riderless.

"Goddammit, Bill!"

"I'll go catch that damned horse for you!"

Before he got very far, Foster heard the first snarl of a bullet passing by his head, watching first one, then another, of the Indian guns spew gunsmoke in the distance as the half-dozen warriors approached at a gallop. That's when he realized he wasn't going to reach Blewett's horse in time to pick him up and ride on out of there with his friend. The horse was tearing off hell-for-leather toward Lawyer's Canyon, too damned close to those warriors.

"Get hid!" Foster screamed loud as he could while he sawed back the reins, shoving down on the stirrups, wrenching his horse around in mid-stride. "I'm goin' for help."

"*No!*" Blewett pleaded in dismay from the distance, hands up and imploring. "Come back an' get me yourself! We kin ride double—"

"I'll bring some soldiers!" Foster promised. "Get hid in the brush, Charlie! Get hid!"

Then he was pummelling the horse's ribs again, no longer able to look at that frightened, pasty blur of Blewett's face. The dismay, the terror, written there as he had to hear the pounding hooves straining ever closer.

William Foster had just made his best friend a promise. And a man never broke a promise to a friend.

He'd get some of the captain's soldiers and they'd hurry back to drive off the small war party. It wouldn't take long for him to reach Cottonwood Station from here, Foster told himself as another bullet whined past his ear. It wouldn't take him long to bring back some help.

After all, William Foster never broke his promise.

Chapter Fourteen

Khoy-Tsahl, 1877

"See how the two of them run!" shore crossing roared to his cousin as the two riders in the distance wheeled and bolted away.

Red Moccasin Tops, the one called *Sarpsis Ilppilp* by their people, laughed. "I haven't seen men run so afraid since we chased the *suapies* and their Shadow friends from the valley of *Lahmotta!*"

Already Rainbow and Five Wounds, another pair of inseparable warrior friends, were yelping, too, waving their rifles as their ponies shot away from the herd they were guiding back to their camp on the upper Cottonwood. It was a bright and beautiful morning after many days of intermittent rain and wind. Nothing more than a light breeze had blown in their faces as they started some captured Shadow horses back for the village. The sun felt good on the bare skin stretched across Shore Crossing's tawny, sinewy limbs.

"Come ride after the Shadows with us, Swan Necklace!" Shore Crossing cried to his younger nephew.

"*Eeh!*" the one called *Wetyetmas Wahyakt* cried back in youthful glee. He wasn't nearly as old as his two companions, no more than twenty summers old now. "We haven't shot our guns at any Shadows since we fired them at Cut-Off Arm's soldiers when he started to cross the river *Tahmonah!*"

In a broad line the warriors were streaming away from the herd now, right behind Rainbow and Five Wounds, the two daring warriors who had rejoined the bands the very day of the fight that had brought a resounding defeat for the soldiers. Two Moons, called *Lepeet Hessemdooks*, rode on the far right flank. And the strong and powerful *Otskai*, known as Going Out, brought up the left.

Shore Crossing, this young man called *Wahlitits*, had been the catalyst of this war. What had started out as his hunger to prove himself a man before a pretty young woman in those days of *Hillal* at their traditional gathering ground of *Tepahlewam*, had soon blown itself into a general uprising. So much the better! For now all the People had fallen in behind Shore Crossing's daring act to finally avenge the wrongful death of his father many winters ago.

Eagle Robe, known as *Tipyalhlanah Siskon*, had consented to loan a conniving Shadow named Larry Ott some of his land to graze a few cattle and horses while the *Nee-Me-Poo* rode east into the buffalo country. But when White Bird's band returned and Eagle Robe went to ask the Shadow to leave his land near the mouth of Deer Creek, Ott had pulled his gun and shot Shore Crossing's father.

When Eagle Robe did not return for the longest time, *Wahlitits* went looking for him, only to find his father dying against Larry Ott's fence.

"Please," Eagle Robe begged. "Promise me . . . promise me you will not take vengeance—"

"I cannot!" his son had shrieked.

For the longest time Eagle Robe had tried to speak, but no sound came from his tongue; none crossed his bloodied lips. He was about to die . . . and Shore Crossing knew he could not let his father die without hearing the words he so wanted to hear his son speak.

Eventually, Shore Crossing spoke softly, very reluctantly, and most sadly.

"I promise you, Father."

Eagle Robe had closed his eyes at last. *Wahlitits* heard that last breath gush up in a ball from his father's punctured lungs as his head gently sagged to the side.

Anguished, Shore Crossing had sobbed, pressing his head against his father's bloody breast, "I promise . . . promise not to kill this man who has killed you!"

But . . . that had been back when he considered himself a boy.

In the last three winters since his father's murder, *Wahlitits* had grown to manhood and taken a wife. Just this last spring she had announced she was carrying their first child.

"Maybe you want another woman because your first wife is growing bigger, eh?" Red Moccasin Tops had asked him that first day of their search for Larry Ott. Shore Crossing had been making soft eyes at a young woman in Joseph's band.

Bringing Swan Necklace along as their horse holder, the trio hadn't found the murderer, so they went in search of another man who had mistreated the *Nee-Me-Poo* before, even setting his dogs on them. After Richard Divine was killed, they remembered Jurden Elfers had many fine horses and were sure that he had some guns, too. They shot the horse breeder and three* more men before starting back for *Tepahlewam* to the village—where the whole camp came alive with war fever. Sun Necklace,** the father of Red Moccasin Tops, led out the first band of warriors who were hot to spill some more blood of the Salmon River settlers who had done them so much wrong for many seasons.

Now they had defeated the *suapies* in the canyon of *Lahmotta*, then led Cut-Off Arm's soldiers on a merry chase through the Salmon River breaks while the village had recrossed to camp at *Aipadass*, a sagebrush flat just north of Craig Billy Crossing, where the village had rested for a day before starting across the Camas Prairie for the Clearwater this morning.

Whooping and shrieking in glee this warm summer day, the exuberant warriors sped after the two fleeing Shadows. Like those raids of burning, raping, and murder, this chase, too, was nothing less than great fun. Too bad there were

---

*Shore Crossing and Red Moccasin Tops killed only four of five men they shot in their first spasm of revenge; Samuel Benedict was only wounded and feigned death until the war starters rode away.

**This is the historical figure who, after the Nez Perce War, changed his name to Yellow Bull (*Chuslum Moxmox*)—as recorded by most of the war's historians.

only two of the Boston men—a term the *Nee-Me-Poo* had long, long used to indicate the pale-skinned traders who had come among them bringing goods from afar, carried on ships that plied the far oceans.

Wahlitits and *Sarpsis Ilppilp* had grown up together, more like brothers than cousins. Much more than cousins, they were best friends in everything. Red Moccasin Tops was an excitable young man, part Cayuse in blood, in fact a grandson of *Tomahas*, one of the murderers of missionaries Marcus and Narcissa Whitman many years before.

"He's mine!" Rainbow shouted the moment the Shadow was pitched off his rearing horse less than two hundred yards away.

"No!" protested Five Wounds, Rainbow's best friend since childhood. "It was my shot made him fall!"

"You two argue all you want over the one who is put on foot!" Strong Eagle bellowed. This capable warrior called *Tipyahlahnah Kapskaps*, like Shore Crossing and Red Moccasin Tops, had tied a red blanket at his neck as they rode into battle against the *suapies* at the White Bird. From that morning the three were known as the "Red Coats."

Strong Eagle brought his rifle to his shoulder, preparing to fire. "I want the other Shadow who thinks he is getting away!"

"You will not be so lucky today, Strong Eagle!" screamed Shore Crossing. "That foolish Shadow is mine!"

The other Red Coat snorted with a wide grin, "Only if that poor horse of yours is faster than mine!"

"Farewell, *Wahlitits!*" cried Red Moccasin Tops as he pulled his pony aside for the Shadow put afoot. "I am going after the one hiding in the brush like a scared rabbit!"

"There is no sport in that!" Shore Crossing chided his cousin. "No bravery running down some poor, frightened ground squirrel who has soiled himself in fear of us!"

They laughed as they parted company, some of them streaming right after the Shadow scampering into the timber and brush on foot, while the others galloped after the fleeing rider. *Wahlitits,* Strong Eagle, Five Wounds, and

Rainbow were closing the gap on the big horse that had grown weary of the long run. Shadow horses may look pretty, but they simply did not have the mighty lungs the *Nee-Me-Poo* bred into their ponies. And that dramatic difference was showing as they dashed up this long, gradual slope, tearing through the green grass growing tall here in midsummer radiance. The Shadow disappeared momentarily over the top of the grassy knoll.

"Now we will catch him!" Shore Crossing shouted as he brought the long rawhide strands of his quirt down against his pony's rear flanks. "It will be a race between him and me to the Cottonwood!"

The last word was barely off his tongue when the four of them reached the top of that bare hill and started down the long slope after the Shadow—gazing far beyond the single rider to that gulch where stood all the buildings of the white family . . . suddenly finding more *suapies* encamped there than Shore Crossing could count. Tiny, dark figures only—but, there must be at least ten-times-ten of them!

Where had they come from?

"Ho! Ho!" Rainbow called, throwing up his hand as he yanked back on the horsehair rein wrapped around his horse's lower jaw.

Why were these soldiers camped here on the upper reaches of the Cottonwood? Did they intend to attack the Non-Treaty camp? Perhaps they were planning to march all the way down the creek so they could prevent the warrior bands from forming a junction with Looking Glass's people on the Clearwater?

"Let him go, *Wahlitits!*" Five Wounds ordered gruffly.

Shore Crossing was the last to stop his horse, finally halting farther down the slope than the others. His pony was lathered and excited, having just caught its second wind, raring to finish the race its rider had started it on. The animal pranced round and round, tossing its head in protest.

"I know; I know," he told it, bringing the horse under control, patting its damp neck. "Angry disappointment sours in my stomach, too. I could almost feel that Shadow's hot blood on my hands!"

"RIDER coming!"

Second Lieutenant Sevier M. Rains turned at that strident cry from one of the outlying pickets. In fact, there wasn't a man in Whipple's battalion who didn't immediately stop what he was doing and turn to watch that lone civilian streaking down the long slope toward the wide gulch where their bivouac stood among the abandoned buildings of Cottonwood Station.

Just as he was shading his eyes with a hand, Rains watched at least four horsemen break the skyline right behind the lone rider. From the looks of things, they had been gaining on the civilian and—had not the soldiers' bivouac been where it was—those Nez Perce warriors would have clearly turned the scout into a victim.

"Where's the other'n, sir?" asked Private Franklin Moody.

Private David Carroll replied before the rest, "I s'pose he ain't coming back at all."

"We don't know that!" Whipple snapped as he lumbered out of his tent, yanking on his blue blouse with its two rows of small brass buttons sewn down the front. He stopped at Rains's elbow.

"Captain, he can't be bringing us good news," the young lieutenant said quietly, hoping that most of the enlisted would not hear.

For a long moment, Whipple gazed at his second lieutenant. Then he said, "Mr. Rains, you're my most trusted second. As adjutant of this command, I want you to select five men from our L Company, and call out five more from Captain Winters's E."

"Rescue detail, sir?"

"Exactly," Whipple answered, roughly shoving the last button through its hole, every man around him watching one warrior slowly turn his horse around and rejoin the others at the brow of the hill, where they eventually disappeared from view. "You'll go in the advance and I will come on your rear with a larger force in your support. A word of caution: don't extend yourself too far, keep on the high ground, and report back to my command at the first sign of the Indians."

"Fifty rounds for our carbines?" Rains asked.

"Yes—and your service revolvers will require another twenty-four."

Rains wheeled on Moody, excitement hot in his veins. "Private, now you and Carroll have the chance to ride with me."

"Sir, respectin' your authority an' all," Moody replied, "but them red bastards is just gonna run when they see us riding out after 'em."

Rains's eyes crinkled with a smile as he replied, "Then we'll all just get a chance to see a little more of the country as we chase the buggers off. Now you and Carroll go draw three hundred rounds of carbine ammo and one hundred and fifty cartridges for our Colts. I'm going to call out the rest of the detail."

Captain Henry E. Winters was returning from the trench latrine dug in a dry wash downwind of camp, his shirttails flying as Rains met him in the middle of the company street. The lieutenant quickly explained Whipple's orders, at which Winters began calling out the first five men of E Company he spotted nearby. From nothing more than their names, the young lieutenant immediately figured they all had to be Irishmen. Seven Irishmen in all now, along with his three Germans.

It was Foster who galloped into camp gripping that half-crazed, snorting horse on the verge of lathering. The civilian was swinging out of the saddle and lunging to the ground even before the animal had completed its bouncing, four-legged skid to a halt.

"Captain Whipple!" he gasped as more than half a hundred soldiers pressed close to listen.

"You are?"

"William F-Foster." He breathed it hard. Not so much from any exertion as from the hot flush of adrenaline that must be shooting through his veins.

"Where's the other one? I sent two of you out. What happened to—"

"His horse bucked him off," Foster interrupted. "Too far back for me to get him, too close to the Injuns for me to pull 'im up to ride double with me—"

"You left the man?" Rains interrupted now accusingly, taking a step right up to the civilian's knee.

Foster glared at the lieutenant, jaw jutting. "I'll take you back, any of you man enough to go," he rasped. "Get me a fresh horse and we'll go back for Blewett."

Whipple put his hand on Rains's shoulder. "The lieutenant here is preparing to do just that, Mr. Foster. Sergeant! Get this civilian a fresh horse, immediately!"

In less than ten minutes the lieutenant's detail was armed and mounted, moving out as a trumpeter played "Boots and Saddles" in that bivouac they put at their backs. Rains and his men followed William Foster, who had climbed atop a fresh army horse. The civilian rocked forward, then backward, trying to get comfortable in the McClellan saddle already cinched around the belly of the animal given him to ride.

"Wish I'd swapped for my own saddle, Lieutenant."

"Don't you fret, Mr. Foster." Rains kept his eyes on the brow of that hill where the half-naked horsemen had disappeared as soon as they spotted the soldier camp. "I don't believe we'll be in the saddle all that long. Just enough time to collect your friend, perhaps learn what we can as to the location of that war party jumped you, then return to our camp."

"Location?" Foster repeated. "You mean you're going to follow them warriors to find out where the sonsabitches are camped?"

"No," Rains replied, tugging at that leather glove he

wore on his left hand, the one he had pulled over his West Point class ring. "But if we happen to see the direction they ride off in . . . that will be a good indication of where their village lies. All the better for us to protect that pack train due down from Fort Lapwai any time now."

Chapter Fifteen

Khoy-Tsahl, 1877

Cottonwood, 4 P.M. (Tuesday)

One of our scouts just in reports seeing twelve or more Indians from here toward Salmon River. On returning he was fired upon by a single Indian and he and the other scout returned the shots. In some way one scout was dismounted and took to the brush and the other was obliged to leave him. These Indians were coming from the direction of the Salmon river on the trail leading toward Kamai and crossing the road passing the place about eight miles from here. The whole command starts in a few moments and may bag the outfit unless the whole of Joseph's force is present.

Babbitt, commanding.

"Look behind you, *Wahlitits!*"

He twisted half-way around on the bare back of his pony when Red Moccasin Tops shouted and pointed. A long way back, they were coming. A short, wriggling worm of *suapies* riding out from that soldier camp down in the Cottonwood gulch. Already, *Seeyakoon Ilppilp*, the young warrior called Red Spy, had killed the lone Shadow who had taken refuge in the brush, and came riding back to show off the dead man's guns.

"Five Wounds! We must find a place where we can greet these Shadows!" *Wahlitits* cried in anticipation. Shore Crossing could feel the excitement flushing away the disappointment that had surged through him when he had to give up the chase minutes ago.

"Yes!" Five Wounds cried with similar enthusiasm. "Up there in those trees. We'll wait for the others. Red Moccasin Tops—go get them. Tell Two Moons we have some good quarry coming and we want them to help us close the trap."

Shore Crossing asked, "We'll put the Shadows between us?"

This time Rainbow smiled. "Yes. We'll wait to ride out of the timber until they are past us."

"Then they will be caught between you and Two Moons's men!" Red Moccasin Tops whooped, taking off like a shot, shrieking in glee.

It was a long time to wait, those heartbeats while they kept an eye pinned on the approaching Shadows. At times none of the warriors could see the soldiers for the broken hillsides, then the short line of *suapies* would reappear from behind a slope, still coming on and on. As they got closer and closer, finally passing just below the copse of dark timber where the warriors waited in the shadows, Shore Crossing could see how the white men kept turning their heads this way and that. Not only did they appear to be keeping their eyes open for an ambush, but they seemed to be looking down for something in the tall grass—

Then *Wahlitits* remembered. "The other rider!" he whispered to Five Wounds beside him. "They're searching the grass, looking for the other dead man!"

Close enough, they could hear the persistent cough of one of the soldiers who slowly passed by them just down the slope. He was not a well man—his cough sounding full of noisy water. Then the *suapies* had moved on by. And Shore Crossing found himself all but squirming on the back of his pony, anxious to get about the killing.

Rainbow inched his pony forward one length, then turned it so he could face the others. "When we ride out of the trees, we must race down the slope *behind* the soldiers. That way we will keep them up the hill from us."

"And that way the Shadows can't get out of our trap by racing downhill," Shore Crossing said, anticipation squirting through his veins. "We must go now! Hurry before the others kill them all!"

"These are not unarmed Shadows asleep in their beds, *Wahlitits*," Rainbow scolded. "These are soldiers."

"I fought soldiers at *Lahmotta!*" Shore Crossing snapped

angrily, wounded by the criticism. "I wore my red coat for the enemy to see me! And I rode right past their lines, time after time!"

"Which is why we don't want any of these soldiers to escape us today the way some soldiers escaped from *Lahmotta*," Five Wounds emphasized. "Let them get a little farther on the hillside before we ride down on them. There—you see that low brush on the slope ahead of them?"

"Yes," Rainbow answered. "Near those low rocks?"

"Yes—we will have Strong Eagle stay in sight by that dead pine tree while we turn back to the timber uphill. *Tipyahlahnah Kapskaps* will be the decoy to bring those soldiers on and on," Five Wounds explained his plan. "When they have gone past those rocks, the rest of us will ride out and show ourselves, then chase them into the ground."

"LIEUTE*NANT!*"

Rains heard the war whoops and those hoofbeats at the same moment the rest of them realized the Nez Perce were swooping up behind them.

"They want to get between us and our relief!" the lieutenant shouted. "Shut off our escape! But they don't realize Captain Whipple is coming!"

"There ain't that many of 'em," Private William Roche said.

Private Patrick Quinn agreed. "We can knock 'em all down, Lieutenant!"

Yanking back on his reins, Rains spun his horse around in a half-circle, staring farther up the slope at the barren hilltop. In an instant he realized he had been a little too eager, too anxious to distinguish himself—and had outrun his support. In too much of a hurry the lieutenant had followed Foster along the ridge that angled away from the valley of the Cottonwood toward Craig's Mountain. After loping two quick miles to the northwest of Norton's ranch, the scout led them down into a broad swale before they began their gentle ascent of the mountain slope. At their rear now, cutting south from the saddle, extended a shallow coulee, but . . . Whipple and his support were nowhere in sight.

"We better get onto the high ground, men," Rains ordered the instant he caught sight of those warriors. He knew they could hold out until Whipple's outfit arrived in a matter of minutes. "C'mon!"

They had just kicked their horses into motion, these dozen men no longer clustered in formation—no more than thirty yards from the top of that rise when the patch of skyline that had been their destination suddenly bristled with at least eighteen warriors.

"Shit!" Private John Burk cried as they all sawed backward on their reins, horses colliding with one another, bumping their riders as they milled and wheeled about.

"I'll take my chances against them others behind us!" Sergeant Charles Lampman roared. "Ain't as many!"

"We can ride right through 'em!" Private Daniel Ryan proposed, pointing.

Private Frederick Meyer bobbed his head. "Ride through 'em. We can do that, can't we, Lieutenant?"

His eyes scanned the distance, quickly trying to calculate how far back it would be to make their run, to figure just how long before Whipple would show up on the next hilltop. Foster had done it. The civilian had made it back in one piece. Maybe they could ride downhill right through that smaller band of warriors and be at a full gallop before the rest could be on their tails—

"Them rocks, Lieutenant!" Lampman shouted, pointing along the slope. "We can hold out in them rocks!"*

At that moment those boulders seemed to be a far smarter idea. Far more inviting than a long, ten-mile horse race back to Cottonwood. Rains hollered, "To the rocks!"

Private Otto H. Richter was the first to start at an angle for the boulders, William Roche right behind him. Rains

---

*These rocks, still visible today on private property, are actually some 750 feet south of the old Lewiston–Mount Idaho Road.

twisted around in the saddle as the others broke past him. "C'mon, Dinteman! Ride, goddammit, man!"

The private was having trouble with his mount. The animal sidestepped as George H. Dinteman kicked and flailed it, trying to goad it into motion. Just as it started to rear onto its hind legs, the horse suddenly twisted aright and flung itself into motion. The private was suddenly ahead of him, less than a full length . . . making them the last two riding for the rocks—

That sound was like no other on earth. He immediately remembered what his father—that great Confederate hero—had repeatedly said: A man always heard the bullet that got him.

But by the time Second Lieutenant Sevier M. Rains turtled his head into his shoulders, the bullet had already passed and struck the private in the back less than three yards ahead of him. Dinteman screwed off his horse, his arms flailing, hung momentarily in the off-hand stirrup, then was flung free to tumble through the grass like a sock doll.

Rains shot past the private before he could react, yanking back and sawing the reins to the side at the same time. For a moment he could not locate Dinteman in the tall grass; then he saw the private's knee sticking up. Just the one knee. Unmoving. And coming on at a full gallop was not just one bunch of bare-chested, feathered, screeching horsemen but a second: streaming out of the broad coulee behind them!

Dinteman was dead already. If he still breathed, Rains told himself, it wouldn't be for long. Since he wasn't moving, then he couldn't help in his own rescue—and the lieutenant realized he didn't have enough time to make that rescue on his own. Step out of the saddle, kneel and lift the deadweight, hurl it onto the back of his horse, then remount . . . none of that was possible now.

There went Foster, the son of a bitch, racing off to the south on his own. Rains hated him: a man who could run away from his friend minutes ago, and now the civilian was scampering away from this fight. The lieutenant almost felt good a moment later when he watched a bullet knock Foster off his horse and a pair of warriors ride up to fire down at the body sprawled in the tall grass—

"Lieutenant!"

One of Winters's men was shouting, standing exposed there in the smaller of the two rings of low boulders. Patrick Quinn, good Irishman that he was. The private was waving Rains in, urging him on.

As Rains wheeled his horse and goaded it with those small brass knobs at the back of his spurs, he gradually sensed something not quite right. Quinn's face suddenly began to swim, growing more and more watery as the horse carried him closer and closer to the boulders. The lieutenant looked down, saw the black molasses stain of blood spreading across his belly, seeping into his crotch.

"Hep! Hep!" he growled at the horse, angry at himself for getting shot, then yanked at the bottom of his blue blouse, pulling it up to have a close look at the wound.

A small finger of intestine was already protruding from the exit wound. As he watched, more of the gut squirted from that ragged hole with every rugged lunge of his exhausted horse. By the time Quinn and Moody grabbed hold of the bridle and were dragging him down out of the saddle, Rains had his forearm filled with his own sticky gut.

"Set me down! Set me down where I can shoot!" he shouted at them through gritted, bloody teeth. Bright crimson gushed up at the back of his throat, hot and thick. He struggled to swallow his gorge back down. Better that than to puke it up in front of his men.

Lord Almighty, Rains thought as they positioned him against the rocks and knelt around him, *a gut wound is a slow way to die. A damned slow way to die.*

"Make every shot count!" Quinn was reminding the others for him. "Shoot low for the horses first!"

Sergeant Lampman whined, "And ours run off with the ammo!"

"Hol' . . . hold 'em back till Whipple hears the gunfire.

He can't be far now," Rains told his men, wanting to inspire more hope in them than he felt for himself.

Out there in the grass, the warriors were swarming over the first of the six wounded men who hadn't made it into these rocks, each of those soldiers shrieking in terror and pain, their high voices more shrill and grating than the war cries—

A Nez Perce bullet spun John Burk around. He landed across the lieutenant's legs. Ryan dragged the body off Rains, knelt again, and continued to fire with his carbine.

Rains continued to speak in a practiced, even tone. *Gotta keep their spirits up.* "We can do this. We can do this, men. One of you, give me Burk's carbine. Load it and put it in my hands."

Lampman had just handed Rains the dead man's carbine as more than ten of the warriors dismounted and spread out in a broad front to fire their weapons when Lampman himself was hit, low in the back of his head. Blood and brain matter splattered over Rains's face as the private fell atop Burk, knocking the lieutenant's carbine aside.

With a great exertion of conscious thought, Rains picked the carbine up, his gloves gummy with blood. So much blood.

Just how in Hades did you go through the whole of two goddamned wars and never get a scratch, Father dear?

A brigadier goddamned general—that's how, he thought as he brought the sticky carbine to his cheek and gazed down the barrel at the warriors popping up out there in the grass.

Someone groaned and fell into the grass out there to his right. Dying noisily. Rains prayed the man would die quick. Sounded like Roche. *Godblesshim.*

How did my own father command a guard of soldiers that protected the Walla Walla councils back in 1855, out here in this northwest territory, and not suffer one damned wound? How had my father played a role in the multitribal wars that followed those councils . . . and not once have a bullet blow a hole through his belly?

"Goddamned lucky, weren't you?"

"What did you say, Lieutenant?" Quinn asked.

"Nothing," Rains said, his tongue thick with blood. "Just . . . we've got to keep them from getting any closer in that grass. They can hide. So, shoot low up that hill, men. Shoot low and conserve your cartridges until Whipple gets here with relief."

Richter was next out there in the grass. Then Moody right behind him. The bullets that hit them shoved both soldiers back into the grass as they were crabbing toward the rocks. Not a good thing. The red bastards could see how few of them were still alive.

Ryan whimpered when a bullet slammed into the side of his head. But he didn't make noise for long. Almost immediately, Quinn was bending over his bunkie, laying the dying soldier down before he bent over to pick up his friend's carbine—when the private was hit twice and his own body flopped over Ryan in a leg-twitching sprawl.

The next time Rains threw back the trapdoor on his carbine, he found a cartridge already shoved into the breech. For a moment he thought the extractor wasn't working, that the empty cartridge had been fused into the chamber with heat and verdigris—but he was able to extract the copper case from the weapon, finding it hadn't been fired.

"You stupid son of a bitch," he cursed himself as he shoved the cartridge back into the action and snapped the trapdoor closed over it.

He had been so intent on watching the warriors crawl up through the grass, watching as those six men were picked off and whittled down one by one, that he had forgotten to fire the damned carbine after reloading it.

The forestock was gummier as he brought it up to his cheek, aimed at a figure in the grass, then pulled the trigger.

While he was reloading with his sticky, bloody gloves, pulling a shell from Ryan's pocket, he willed his eyes to make a count. All the rest were down.

Getting so weak, barely able to lift the weapon . . . by the time he could get the carbine back into position, Rains found David Carroll lying in a heap out there twenty yards away, curled up like a cat on an autumn day, groaning and pawing at the bubbling wound low in his chest.

Who in Hades is going to hold off the red bastards till Whipple arrives? Everyone else gone already. I'm the only one for them to save now.

For a moment he stared at two of them lying here, close enough for him to touch: Quinn had been driven backward by the impact of the bullet that had killed him, hurtled against the low rock where he had been kneeling, then slid down to crumple across Richter.

Irish and German, Rains thought as he stared at their death masks. *Only one of us for Whipple to save now. All the Irish and German dead. Wasn't for the Irish and German . . . there'd be no goddamned frontier army.*

Gradually he became aware of the quiet. So very, very quiet as he fumbled in Ryan's pocket for another cartridge. Empty. Maybe Burk there had some. Where was the man in this jumble of arms and legs and blood and brain . . . and his own gut?

Grown so quiet out there now that he could hear the red bastards whispering, even hear the rustle of the tall grass as they moved closer.

Carefully, slowly—a few heads rose in the grass, dark eyes staring at him.

More than a dozen of them—

His fingers located a cartridge in Burk's pocket. Frantically he shoved it into the action as the warriors started to slink toward him in a half-crouch. The copper case pasted to the blood-crusted fingers of his gloves.

Maybe Whipple will hear now . . . now that things have gone so damned quiet up here.

Snapping the trapdoor down, he dragged the hammer back but found he didn't have the strength to raise the carbine to his shoulder. Rains could only position the butt against his lower chest. The instant he fired he realized his shot went wild, but the warriors nonetheless flung themselves into the grass momentarily.

With an ear-numbing shriek, in unison they rose as one and rushed him in a blur.

He watched the first, then a second and third gun explode, each muzzle spewing fire from close range. He felt the dull racket in his head; an instant later his chest was on fire.

Too late to call for Whipple. Too late.

But it was time to call for his father. *A brigadier goddamned general would know what to do now. Just call for the general.*

"Father . . . General . . . tell me, what am I to do now, s-sir? Help me. . . . Sh-show me now how a good officer dies."

Chapter Sixteen

Khoy-Tsahl, 1877

This was but his twenty-first summer, but he had himself killed four of the *suapies* who had come to attack their *Lahmotta* camp. Young though he might be, Yellow Wolf stood second in warrior rank only to *Ollokot*, Joseph's young brother.

Yellow Wolf had been the one who made the most noise out there in the grass below the boulders, jumping up to show himself here, then there. Never the same place twice as the others crept in, slowly, silently. This young warrior called *He-mene Mox Mox* made the noise in the grass, shouting and calling out to draw the horse soldiers' attention as Five Wounds led the others in for the kill.

Six of the *suapies* had fallen from their horses before the fight even began, hit during the last mad scramble. The other half barely made it to those low rocks before Yellow Wolf's friends got started on the serious killing. When the rest made the last rush, there was but one last shot fired from the white man. As their bullets struck that last Shadow, his rifle slowly spilled from his hands covered with those bloody gloves.

Yellow Wolf knelt before him, looking into the man's face, seeing how it was drenched with blood from that bullet hole almost directly between the soldier's eyes. Blinking repeatedly, the white man seemed to stare right through Yellow Wolf, his lips starting to move, sticky with the blood that drenched the Shadow. Yet all that came out of the soldier's mouth was a chicken sound . . . *cluck. Cluck. Cluck. Cluck—*

"Do you know what he is saying in the Shadow tongue?" asked Five Wounds as the older warrior knelt beside the inquisitive Yellow Wolf.

"No. I never learned any of the white man talk," Yellow

Wolf replied. Then he looked deep into the man's eyes, saw the eyelashes coated thickly with blood that seeped from that bullet wound between the eyes. Noticed the way the soldier looked right on through him as if he weren't there. "Maybe," he said to Five Wounds and the others who were starting to pilfer through the pockets of the other five soldiers, "this one is asking me to help him die quicker."

"Perhaps that's true, that he cannot live," *Wahlitits* said. "His body is too badly hurt."

Red Moccasin Tops added, "But he still lives. He is a strong warrior, refusing to die. He is like *Nee-Me-Poo*."

Five Wounds shook his head. "No Shadow is like us. But, this one is strong enough to live if he wants to. But he has to want to live."

Old *Dookiyoon*, known as Smoker, took his ancient flintlock horse pistol from his belt and wagged the muzzle near the soldier's left ear. That gun had belonged to his family for three generations—handed down from the early days of contact with the Boston Men.

"We cannot leave him like this," Smoker said with a hint of sadness to his voice. "He will be too long in dying."

"And he was a brave fighter," Yellow Wolf asserted with a measure of respect. "He deserves to die quickly, this brave fighter."

Suddenly Smoker said, "Yes. Die quickly, brave fighter." And he immediately shoved the muzzle of his old pistol against the Shadow's chest, pulling the trigger.

The force of the big lead ball caused the white man to topple to the side, where he lay quietly, no longer clucking like a chicken scratching feed on the ground between lodges.

Yellow Wolf was just beginning to feel better about it when the body stirred and the soldier slowly, painfully, raised himself back to a sitting position there against the rocks splattered with some of the man's brain. Once the Shadow was upright, he began to quietly cluck again: his lips moving ever so slightly, the tip of his blood-thickened tongue appearing as he made his strange talking sound. Yellow Wolf wished he knew the white man's language. Then the eyes rolled slowly around, as if looking over the half-dozen or so warriors gathered closest to him. Those eyes studied Yellow Wolf's friends as blood continued to ooze from the head wound, dripping over the eyelids and lashes.

"Ho, ho, Smoker!" Red Moccasin Tops snorted with laughter. "Your old gun—it is weak as a young foal's penis! It did not kill this strong, strong Boston Man, even up close!"

Just as Smoker was about to argue, wrenching up his pouch to begin reloading the old flintlock pistol, Two Moons stepped up, clutching his *kopluts* in his hand. Without a word, he swung it against the side of the soldier's head with a hard crack that knocked the dying man over again.

"Stop!" Yellow Wolf yelled, waving his arms at the old warrior. "Get back, Two Moons! Get back from him!"

Five Wounds grabbed the young warrior by the elbow. "Yellow Wolf—it is all right what Two Moons does. He is doing what is best for this soldier now."

For a moment, Yellow Wolf looked at Two Moons's face, then reluctantly nodded as he looked down at the soldier, watching how the man struggled to breathe. "Yes. I see. We have no healer with us. Poor, poor Shadow—he is suffering." Then he drew in a long sigh. "All right. Maybe we should put him out of his trouble now."

"You, Yellow Wolf?" asked Two Moons.

"Yes."

The old man handed the young warrior his short-handled war club. Yellow Wolf gripped it securely, raised it over his shoulder, then drove it down into the top of the white man's head. The *suapie* grunted. Then he hit the soldier a second time. And the enemy made no more sound.

Bending on his knee, Yellow Wolf put his face down close to the soldier's, looking into those unblinking eyes, watching those bloody lips and tongue for any movement. There was none. And now he closed the eyes. They were no longer staring up at him, gazing into Yellow Wolf's soul and asking for assistance.

"You have helped him?" Five Wounds asked.

Rocking back on his haunches, Yellow Wolf handed the *kopluts* back to Two Moons. "Yes. The last one is dead now."

"CAN you believe that?" asked Captain Henry Winters. "They're pulling off!"

Stephen G. Whipple nodded in disbelief. "Even though they outnumber us, we've driven them off."

Minutes ago as he had listened to the faint, distant booming of the Springfield carbines, Whipple had been advancing with more than seventy of his enlisted, leaving their Cottonwood camp in the care of fewer than thirty soldiers and volunteers. Instead of riding to the sound of those guns, Whipple grew confused by the echo of that gunfire—halting his command on the eastern side of that low saddle while he studied the slope and timber above him.

Wondering why Rains had ridden out of sight. With that gunfire so near, Whipple surely expected to see the lieutenant and his detail come galloping right over the top of that ridge any moment now. He waited, waited . . . then the gunfire died off—

When suddenly a broad band of warriors arrayed themselves before his men at the top of the hill.

"Rains must have driven them off!" Whipple cheered to Winters. "He's driven them into us!"

Whipple dismounted the entire body and ordered horse holders to the rear, instantly reducing his tactical force by one-fourth. The rest he spread out on a wide front, double distances between each of the soldiers as more warriors appeared on the hillside, making bold and provocative movements along his skirmishers' front. Now there were more than a hundred of the enemy facing them, horsemen who occasionally fired their rifles and shouted at the soldiers.

It became painfully clear to the captain that Lieutenant Rains and his ten-man detail were not going to reappear, full of life, herding a small war party toward Whipple's seventy-man battalion. They were lost, swallowed up by these

Nez Perce who slowly advanced as Whipple prepared his men to withstand the charge . . . but that assault never came. Not in the two hours his battalion held their ground on the side of that hill. For some reason that Whipple and Winters could not fathom, the warriors—who clearly outnumbered their soldiers—never pressed their advantage.

He shook his head as the Nez Perce mounted up and pulled back late that afternoon. "Should we withdraw, Captain?" Winters asked.

"We should continue our search for Lieutenant Rains," the captain replied. "But the enemy outnumbers us. I'm certain they will prevent us from advancing."

Winters regarded the lowering sun. "Might I suggest that we countermarch to Cottonwood?"

Whipple sighed, "We'll search for the bodies come morning."

Just before dusk, Whipple formed his battalion into a square around their horses, then slowly marched back to Cottonwood without having seen another Nez Perce throughout their retreat. As his battalion rode down into the wide gulch of the Cottonwood, he grew uneasy about their position, the fading light, and the close proximity of the enemy.

As night fell, he had his men establish a small defensive perimeter at the top of an adjacent hill where Whipple felt safer than down in the bottom with those gutted, abandoned, ghostly ranch buildings. Here at least they could command the high ground, able to see greater distances across the rolling Camas Prairie, too.

Not long after moonrise, the captain dispatched two couriers to carry word of the Rains affair to General Howard—the second leaving a half hour after the first.

Cottonwood, 10:30 P.M.

(Tuesday)

Joseph with his entire force is in our front. We moved out at 6 P.M. to look after the Indians reported. Rains, with ten men moved on ahead about two miles. We heard firing at the foot of the long hill back of Cottonwood, and mounting a slight elevation saw a large force of Indians occupying a strong position in the timber covering the road. Nothing could be seen of Rains and his party and we fear they have been slaughtered. We moved up close enough to see we were greatly outnumbered by enemies strongly posted. Night was approaching and after a consultation of all the officers it was decided to return to this place and hold it until Perry . . . should arrive. There was no diversity of opinion in this case, and there is no doubt that the entire command would have been sacrificed in an attack. We shall make every effort to communicate with Perry to-night and keep him out of any trap . . .

Whipple, Cmd'g
Cottonwood Station

That done, Whipple had just begun to fitfully doze a little after midnight when a lone Christian tracker rode in, slipping down from the north.

"I'm amazed you got through from that direction!" the captain exclaimed as the friendly handed Whipple a folded letter. "That country was swarming with warriors earlier today."

In his dispatch, Captain David Perry informed whomever the courier would find in command of the closest outpost that he would be setting off from Fort Lapwai before first light with his supply train, moving south under a twenty-man escort.

"With the Nez Perce crawling across the countryside, we desperately need those supplies and especially that ammunition," Whipple told his officers he had called together in the starry darkness.

Lieutenant Shelton said, "I feel a bit uneasy about Colonel Perry, sir."

"To tell the truth, so do I," Whipple admitted. "Captain Winters, our entire battalion will depart at first light and march north to meet up with, and provide protection for,

Colonel Perry's supply train."

"I'll see the men are awakened at five."

After his two army couriers returned after becoming lost in the darkened and unfamiliar terrain, Whipple himself spent the rest of that sleepless night waiting out the coming of the time when his noncoms would move among the enlisted, jarring them awake. No fires and no pipes. Which meant no coffee or fried bacon. Just a few crumbly bites of the inedible hardbread washed down with water from the Cottonwood before they moved out in the waning darkness of that morning, the anniversary of the nation's independence.

After crawling little more than two miles in the gray dawn, they stumbled across the remains of yesterday's massacre—at least, they found twelve of the thirteen bodies.

From their positions it was clear to see how the brief, hot fight had progressed. One body—of the civilian named Foster—was found in the tall grass, far out from the others. Then five more, soldiers all, scattered between the scout and those rocks where they located the last five, men who had attempted to sell their lives dearly. Empty copper cases glittered around them. But the weapons, gun belts, and their clothing were gone. And though the bodies had been stripped, none were mutilated or scalped.

"That's the lieutenant there, Captain," announced First Lieutenant Edwin H. Shelton. He would know. He and Rains were officers together in Whipple's L Company, First U. S. Cavalry.

Nonetheless, it was hard for the captain to believe that the disfigured body was that of young Rains.

"Appears the lieutenant really made the bastards angry," Whipple said quietly. "Look how many times they shot him before they finally caved in his skull."

"Shall we bury them here, sir?" Shelton asked.

Whipple regarded the climbing sun a moment, then answered, "No, Lieutenant. We can't help them now—but we must see what we can do to help Colonel Perry's escort. We'll push on."

Marching beyond the hillside where the Rains dead had taken refuge among those low boulders, Whipple's men spotted a solitary horse silhouetted atop a knoll, off to their right. Even with his field glasses, the captain was unable to determine if it was an Indian pony or one of the army horses claimed by those warriors who had committed the butchery on Lieutenant Rains.

"It could be one of ours, sir," Shelton reminded.

"I don't want to take the chance that it's a decoy," Whipple argued. "We won't be lured into an ambush as easily as others might."

Some six miles later the column he had deployed in double skirmish lines spotted Perry's seventy-five-mule supply train in the distance, its escort of twenty men from Company F, First U. S. Cavalry, just coming over the divide formed by nearby Craig's Mountain.

Perry patiently listened to Whipple's extensive report on the Rains affair, then put the captain at ease when he announced, "I'm assuming command of your entire outfit. We'll continue on in the direction of Cottonwood Station and reestablish our base there. On the way, we'll stop and bury your dead."

But upon retracing their steps to the boulders by midmorning, the Perry-Whipple command soon discovered the Nez Perce had returned in aggravating numbers. Enough marksmen began firing from the rocks and timber on the slope of Craig's Mountain that the burial details proved impossible. After close to an hour of long-distance sniping at the warriors, Perry ordered the efforts abandoned and they withdrew to Cottonwood.

Reaching the Norton ranch about noon, the combined battalion now boasted 113 men under arms. For the rest of that Fourth of July morning Perry, along with Whipple and Winters, supervised the digging of four long rifle pits, one arranged in a semicircle on a large hill immediately southeast of the Norton house, another in a semicircle on the height southwest of the house, along with barricades erected near the house and barn, constructed using the split rails taken from the fences they tore down, in addition to some native brown stone found in several piles around the ranch. One of the rifle pits that enjoyed the most commanding view of prairie for miles was backed up with one of Whipple's two Gatling guns.

The temperature continued to climb through the long summer morning, baking the men unmercifully as they toiled. The sun had reached midsky when the first picket hollered the alarm.

"Injuns! Injuns!"

Hurrying to the barricades at the northern side of their perimeter, Whipple was the first to watch the detail he had engaged to bury Lieutenant Rains turning back for the lines as several warriors approached the group from the upper reaches of Cottonwood Creek. As the soldiers watched from their rifle pits, more and more warriors arrayed themselves on the brow of the nearby hill, not far from where they had watched scout William Foster return at a gallop just yesterday. Some more gathered on another hill to the east and even more on the knoll just to the west, until the bivouac was completely surrounded by horsemen.

"How many of 'em?" some soldier asked.

"What the hell does it really matter, son?" growled civilian George M. Shearer. "There's more'n 'nough of the red niggers up there for all of us put together."

THE Yankee soldier who had lost them their fight in White Bird Canyon had assigned Shearer to supervise the construction of their fortifications at Norton's ranch. George was good at that. Lots of experience in that recent war against Yankee aggression.

But it seemed strange that he would be put in charge of so important a task when Colonel Perry had officers in his command who might have just as much experience building such defenses. But, George thought with a wry grin, while he and the poor enlisted men were up here on the heights digging the rifle pits, most every one of Perry's officers were down there in the gulch near the station buildings, idle as could be, not occupied with a damned thing.

Shearer had come in from Mount Idaho late that morning with three friends, having received word that there were soldiers at Cottonwood who might be in need of reinforcements. Four men weren't much, but every man with a gun could well mean several more dead Indians by the end of a skirmish. Besides, if there was any chance of cutting down some more of those redskins, George was the first to mount up and ride into the fray.

Back when the outbreak was just getting under way, Shearer had put together a posse of twenty volunteers to go in search of any additional survivors after the raid on the Norton party. He had rallied them into action, reminding his group of the pitiful sight of that Chamberlin woman as she scrambled away from her rescuers like a terrified animal, reminding them, too, of the wounded, inhuman cries that had escaped her throat.

"Ain't none of us ever gonna forget the sight of that poor Mrs. Chamberlin, fellers," he had drawled in that distinctive Southern manner of his, something unique that set him apart from most others here in the Northwest, "knowing full well what them red Neegras done to her again and again: a fate that's nigh wuss'n death."

Such treatment of women and children was enough to lather a gentleman something fierce.

"So let's go see 'bout catching us some red bucks and chopping off their balls afore we kill 'em real slow!" Shearer had goaded his band of twenty, shaking his double-barreled Parker shotgun over his head.

Little wonder he was worked up by the time they got the jump on a trio of Nez Perce bucks out at Ab Smith's place. That set George to whooping with something akin to the Rebel yell, partly growling like that big black-haired mastiff one of the shopkeepers kept chained up outside his trading tent in the mining camp of Florence. Why, he sounded just like a snarling dog ready to lunge and latch onto your leg, take a hunk of meat right out of your arm . . . maybe even clamp its jaws down on your throat—if you were a Nez Perce.

While two of the trio had leaped their horses over a fence, the third dismounted and started to hobble away. The posse shot the warrior several times before George halted over the Indian's body and unloaded one of the two barrels into his back, so close the black powder started the Indian's shirt to smoldering. But when he discovered the buck's hand still twitching, Shearer had dismounted and inverted his shotgun, slamming the buttstock down into the warrior's head. With a second blow, George shattered the stock.

"Goddamn, if that didn't feel good!" Shearer roared triumphantly, shaking his blood-splattered double-barreled shotgun in glee.

"Bet this son of a bitch was one of them what got to Chamberlin's woman!" one of the posse had cheered.

"This'un prob'ly killed that li'l girl, too," another voice chimed in.

A third man had growled, "Likely this bastard chopped off the other girl's tongue!"

The killing of that lone warrior had in no way cooled the unmitigated fury Shearer felt at the Nez Perce for what they'd done to those women and children they had attacked out on the Camas Road. And the army's defeat at the White Bird only added more heat to his bloodlust for those less-than-human warriors who could commit such savage acts against the innocent.

Maybe now, here at Cottonwood—he brooded—they could finally pit themselves against these red sonsabitches in a stand-up, man-to-man fight.

Chapter Seventeen

Khoy-Tsahl, 1877

THE DAY WE CELEBRATE.

> The nation will celebrate to-day the one hundred and first anniversary of the declaration of independence. The first century with its record of heroic achievement and splendid growth has closed, and we stand inside the threshold of the second. The war of the revolution, the second conflict with England, the conquest of Mexico, the determined struggle for the union, the social, industrial, moral, commercial and political progress of the first hundred years of national existence, with all their proud memories and patriotic reminiscences, are now matters of a past century,—to be recalled on each recurring anniversary, to impress their lessons of duty and patriotism upon every citizen of the republic . . .
>
> —editorial
> *Rocky Mountain News*
> July 4, 1877

SHORE CROSSING COULD SEE THAT THE SOLDIER CHIEF WAS content to fight nothing more than a defensive skirmish through the rest of that long, hot afternoon. Evidently, the *suapie* saw no need to order his men out of their deep holes and charge off in pursuit of all those warriors who had them surrounded. In their hollows,* those soldiers were far safer than the soldiers had been at *Lahmotta.*

For the most part, the *Nee-Me-Poo* also seemed content to harass the *suapies*, staying on their ponies, just out of

*The term the Nez Perce veterans historically used to describe the rifle pits in their testimony on the Cottonwood skirmishes after the war.

range of the Shadow guns, riding this way and that around the entire circle of the soldier camp while a long-distance duel was waged throughout the long summer afternoon. But a few men dismounted from time to time, creeping up through the grass, often slipping as close as two arrow flights to the hollows, hidden by the brush choking the ravines, until they were discovered—when they were either driven back by soldier bullets or forced to keep their heads down, stalled in their skulking.

Just before dusk Rainbow called for an attack on the southwestern edge of the *suapie* lines. But before the mounted charge could get very close, the soldiers turned their wagon gun* on the horsemen, hitting four of the ponies and turning back their daring assault. At times through the day, one or more of the horses were hit, here or there around the huge circle, but no man was ever struck by a bullet. There were no wounded or killed in that hot, noisy fight.

Those soldiers had no idea that the *Nee-Me-Poo* weren't fighting to dislodge the white men dug in like frightened gophers. No, this skirmishing with a lot of noise and yelling but no killing was only a diversion being conducted to keep the *suapies* busy while the camp inched across the naked, barren prairie just behind the northern hills. The men were buying time for their families, women, and children to escape down the Cottonwood to the Clearwater, where they could join up with the Looking Glass people.

They kept up their shooting until it grew dark; then Rainbow and Five Wounds had their warriors mount up. They rode off to rejoin the village.

And when the sun rose tomorrow, there might be some more long-distance skirmishing to keep the soldiers in their holes while the village finished its journey across the rolling prairie. This diversionary tactic had been decided by the Non-Treaty bands at a council held all the way back on the west side of the *Tahmonah* two days ago.

---

*Whipple's Gatling gun.

Finding that Cut-Off Arm was indeed determined to follow them into that high, rugged, muddy country, the chiefs hurried the people north until they reached the familiar crossing at Luke Billy's place.* But before ordering their people into their bullboats once again, the chiefs met in a hastily called council to decide where they would be going once they had crossed the river. North, east, or south? To the north lay the friendly Cayuse but also the Flathead, who might prove troublesome to the Non-Treaty bands because they were so closely allied with the Shadows. Over to the east lay the buffalo country that Looking Glass knew so well—but to reach it they would need Looking Glass's help. And to the south lay a route that, Joseph explained, would take his *Wallamwatkin* people back in the direction of their ancestral hunting grounds.

"I wish to stay close to my homeland," the Wallowa chief told the assembly. "If we need to fight, my heart tells me to fight the war in our own country. To fight *for* our own country."

Listening to the other chiefs, Shore Crossing was thankful White Bird and *Toohoolhoolzote* spoke on behalf of turning east and fighting their way across the Camas Prairie. A good thing the fighting chiefs outnumbered the Wallowa leader in the arguments made in that council. Joseph was silenced when White Bird announced that they would cross the river and march in search of Looking Glass on the Clearwater.

Over the past two days of fighting the *suapies*, first in the rocks and later from their dug-out hollows, Shore Crossing had been reminded how most of the warriors really felt about Joseph. That soft-spoken orator had taken no part in the fight at *Lahmotta*. Instead, his brother, *Ollokot*—called the Frog in his childhood—had dashed out to join in humiliating and routing the soldiers.

Every one of the fighting men who had listened in on that fateful council among the chiefs before crossing the

---

*Craig Billy Crossing.

river believed that Joseph should leave the fighting decisions up to the war leaders. His words and wishes shunned on the west bank of the Salmon, Joseph had been relegated to an even more subordinate role.

It made Shore Crossing grin to think how this Wallowa who had spoken so strongly against the struggle at its start, was now helplessly swept up in that war, overshadowed by real fighting men. *Eeh! Let Joseph take care of the women and children and sick ones! Leave to this camp chief only those decisions no more important than those made by a herder!*

Yet one thing remained a constant: The *suapies* would follow the village. They always followed. Which meant that the real fighting was yet to come.

Shore Crossing didn't think he could wait for the blooding.

"COUNT me in, Cap'n Randall!" cheered thirty-eight-year-old Luther P. Wilmot as he scrambled up to join the small group gathered around D. B. Randall in front of Loyal P. Brown's Mount Idaho House hotel.

"I'm proud to have you ride with us, Lew!" answered Darius B. Randall, the popular leader of the civilian militia recently banded together, what with the Nez Perce uprising. He himself had a long-standing dispute with the peaceful Treaty bands, who claimed Randall was illegally squatting on their reservation.

"I ain't got no horse, 'cept that wagon puller brung me in when Pete and me was jumped on the Cottonwood Road," Wilmot apologized in his soft voice, brushing some of the dirty blond hair out of an eye.

"One of you boys fetch Lieutenant Wilmot a saddle," Randall asked the crowd, then looked at Lew again.

"L-lieutenant?" Wilmot echoed the rank.

Randall nodded. "You're a steady hand, Lew. We're gonna get in a fight with these redskins soon enough. Something happens to the captain of this outfit, they're gonna need a lieutenant—a steady hand—to keep 'em together. Besides Jim Cearly over there—you fit the bill nicely, Lieutenant."

"T-thanks, D. B.," he answered quietly, a little self-conscious in front of the other men.

"Now go get that big horse you rode in here," Randall suggested. "That wagon puller of yours was strong enough to get you to Mount Idaho just in front of them Injuns. It'll be strong enough to carry you on that scout I want you to lead over west to Lawyer's Canyon."

This first morning after Independence Day, a Thursday, Randall was calling for volunteers to join him in going to relief of the army entrenched on Cottonwood Creek.

For the last two or three days news had been drifting in that the hostiles had recrossed the Salmon River and were slowly marching for the Clearwater, with the likely intention of joining up with the survivors of Whipple's botched attack on Looking Glass's village.

Wilmot and his handful of scouts hadn't gotten but a couple of miles out of town, making for Lawyer's Canyon on the far side of Craig's Divide, when they met a Camas Prairie settler, who told them the hostiles had in fact reached the east side of the Salmon and were crossing behind Craig's Mountain.

"I was up to the soldier camp at Ben Norton's ranch last couple of days," Dan Crooks explained. "Told them the news, too. To see for themselves, the officers sent out a scouting party two days back, with near twice as many men as you got with you, Lew."

"Them soldiers see the Nez Perce camp like you done?"

Crooks wagged his head dolefully. "All of 'em got wiped out."

Of a sudden, Lew remembered how the body of John Chamberlin had looked when they found him on the prairie. "Massacred?"

"Soldiers went right out that evening to bring back them butchered bodies, but on the way back to Cottonwood they was jumped by an even bigger war party and was drove back to Norton's about nightfall," Crooks declared.

Lew studied the face of this youngest son of John W. Crooks, a wealthy landowner in these parts. "Them Injuns move on?"

Crooks wagged his head. "They come right back yesterday for a long fight with the soldiers; noon till moonrise, it was. So last evening I decided I was gonna light out for Mount Idaho at sunrise this here morning—gonna bring word to my pa and everybody that them soldiers need a hand."

"C'mon," said the lean and lanky Wilmot as he reined his horse around. "We're going back to tell Captain Randall your bad news. I figger he'll want us all to light out for Cottonwood Station to give the army some help."

If anything was going to be done about stopping that Nez Perce village marching east from Craig's Mountain, then they would need every man—soldier *and* civilian—to get the job done.

Lew Wilmot and his twenty-eight-year-old freighting partner, Peter H. Ready, had had their own run-in with some murderous Nez Perce out on the Cottonwood Road just twenty days before, the same night the Nortons and Chamberlins were jumped and most in the escaping party killed. But the pair of teamsters had managed to cut free a couple of their big harness horses and lumber off bareback while most of the warriors slowed and halted to rummage through all those supplies destined for the Vollmer and Scott store in Mount Idaho that the white men had been hauling in their two wagons. Up to that moment, neither of them had heard a thing of what trouble was then afoot. An outright Indian uprising.

So this morning when Randall issued his call for volunteers, Wilmot could think of nothing more than his Louisa and their four young children. Brooding not only about the aging and infirm father he was caring for, as well as his wife, Louisa, and their three daughters . . . Lew's thoughts were also all wrapped up in that two-day-old son Louisa had just given him. What sort of place would this be if the Nez Perce weren't driven back onto their reservation? How would life on the Camas Prairie go on if this bloody uprising wasn't put down and the murderers hung? Lew Wilmot had to do what he could to make this country safe for women and children.

He had come here from Illinois when he was but a lad himself—his father marching the family to Oregon on that long Emigrant Road. Not once in all those years growing up in this very country had Lew ever done one goddamned thing against these Cayuse or Palouse or the Nez Perce. But . . . the way they had screamed for his blood during that dark night's horse race across the prairie sure convinced Lew those warriors had some score to settle with somebody.

Lew and Pete had lost just about everything when they lost their freight, those two big wagons, and the rest of their draft animals to the war party.

"But we got our hair, Pete," Lew had reminded his younger partner as they reached the barricades at Mount Idaho in the inky blackness. "Just remember that: We still got our goddamn hair."

When Wilmot carried the news of the skirmishing at Cottonwood back to Randall, the captain announced he would be leaving for Norton's ranch within the hour.

"Lew! Lew!"

Wilmot turned as he finished tying off the horse to the hitching post outside Loyal P. Brown's hotel. It was a red-faced Benjamin F. Evans, a local.

"You coming along, Ben?"

"I'd like to go, but don't have no horse."

Turning slightly, Wilmot patted the rump of his horse and said, "Listen here—I've got a friend who owns one of the best horses on Camas Prairie, and he told me any time I went out for some scouting I could have his horse to ride. You can ride this'un here, and I'll go fetch that other'un for myself."

Although twenty-five men had offered to ride with Randall earlier that morning, only fourteen others answered D. B.'s call, joining Wilmot and Evans when they rose to the saddle a half hour later, all seventeen starting out of Mount Idaho for Cottonwood. Lew looked around him at the others. At least ten were joking and slapping at one another, acting like this was going to be some Fourth of July church picnic.

At the same time all Lew could think about were those three girls of his, Louisa, and that two-day-old baby boy—the five of them taking cover back there in Loyal P.'s hotel.

Cottonwood lay some sixteen miles off across the gently rolling Camas Prairie. A lot of bare, goddamned open ground to his way of thinking.

"CAPTAIN Whipple!"

He turned on his heel at the cry.

"Two riders coming in—at a gallop!"

Stephen Whipple could see how those men licked it down the road from Mount Idaho. Clearly soldiers, the yellow cavalry stripes on their britches aglitter in the summer sunlight that late morning, their stirrups bobbing with every heaving lunge the horses made, hooves kicking up scuffs of dust as they tore down the aching green of the Camas Prairie.

"They're gonna have trouble now, Captain!" announced Second Lieutenant William H. Miller, pointing off to the east, where a war party of some twenty warriors suddenly popped over a low rise. A half-dozen of them immediately reined aside and started angling in a lope toward the two couriers while the rest came to a halt to watch the attack.

As soon as this news was reported to Captain David Perry, the commander ordered half of L Company to saddle their mounts and prepare to go to the aid of that endangered pair of riders.

"How far off do you take them to be, Lieutenant?" Whipple asked Miller, who had his field glasses pressed against his nose.

"Two miles, Captain. No more than that."

Whipple turned at the rumble of hooves as those mounted cavalrymen rattled past at a walk, then broke into a lope as soon as they cleared the outer rifle pits. A quarter of a mile away the detail halted and shifted into a broad front, removing their carbines from the short slings worn over their shoulders. As the soldiers at Cottonwood watched, puffs of dirty gray smoke appeared above the detail. Then, two seconds later, the loud reports reached the bivouac. Volley by volley, the rescue detail was shooting over the heads of the couriers, laying their fire down at those six pursuing warriors.

"It worked, Captain!" Miller cried. "By damn, it worked, sir!"

Whipple only nodded, his attention suddenly snagged on something else. "Let me see those glasses, Lieutenant."

Miller handed the binoculars to him. Putting them to his eyes, Whipple slowly twisted the adjustment wheel, bringing the distant figures into focus.

The lieutenant asked, "More Indians, Captain?"

"I'm not really sure," Whipple replied. "They don't look to be riding like Indians. And they're coming across the Prairie from Mount Idaho."

"How many? Can you tell, sir?"

"Less than two dozen," the captain said. "No more than twenty at the most."

"With news from us about the Rains defeat," Miller began, "would General Howard be sending us any reinforcements from his column?"

"No—I think that's a band of civilians, Lieutenant."

Then Whipple slowly dragged his field of vision to the right, scanning the Camas Prairie just west of the Cottonwood–Mount Idaho Road. But he stopped, held, took a breath as he twisted the adjustment wheel.

"The village is on the move, gentlemen."

Out in the lead of the distant mass were the horses, two—maybe as many as three—thousand of them. As he watched, Whipple's heart sank.

Sixty, seventy, shit—more than a hundred horsemen began peeling away from both sides of the column now, feathers and bows and rifles bristling atop their painted, racing ponies. More than a hundred-twenty of them now made their appearance from the back side of Craig's Mountain. And instead of coming for Perry's bivouac at Cottonwood, they were angling off for that small group of horsemen coming out from Mount Idaho.

Whipple moved his view back to the south, finding those civilians once more, as the massive war party put their ponies into a gallop.

"Something tells me those riders aren't soldiers," the captain declared. "I figure them for a band of hapless civilians whose luck has just run out."

CHAPTER EIGHTEEN

KHOY-TSAHL, 1877

FOR THE *NEE-ME-POO* THESE WERE THE FIRST DAYS OF THE season when the blue-backed salmon made its mating run in Wallowa Lake. The meat of those strong fighting fish was red and sweet. Every bit as sweet as were these days now that they had the *suapies* on the run.

After they had ambushed the two Shadows and fought the rest of the soldiers all the way back to their burrows on Cottonwood Creek, Yellow Wolf proudly rode into the village singing an echo of his medicine song. This echo, as his people called it, was a peculiarly intoned melody that announced to the camp that the singer had met and killed an enemy. Oh, how the young women looked at him then! It had been a good night of dancing, singing, and celebrating with those soft-eyed ones who peered at him from beneath thick lashes in the firelight.

Early this morning, the older women and men were up before dawn, preparing for another day's march across the Camas Prairie. This time they were packing for the short journey that would bring them to *Piswah Ilppilp Pah*, or the Place of Red Rocks, a good campsite in the canyon that would take them down to the Clearwater.

As Yellow Wolf crawled on hands and knees from his brush shelter into the bright light, gazing around at the bustle of activity, *Weesculatat* rode up, calling out, "You, young fighter—come with me this morning!"

He ground his knuckles into his red eyes sleepily. "I was awake too long last night."

"I have a ride for you," offered this warrior, who was also called *Mimpow Owyeen*, or Wounded Mouth. "If you want to come with me."

Running his tongue around inside his mouth, Yellow Wolf did not think his belly was particularly hungry for breakfast. He squinted up at the older man, a father whose son was a Christian living on the reservation. "All right. Where do you want to ride this morning?"

"We will call out some other young men," *Weesculatat* replied. "No older fighters—just young men like you. And we will go ride over to see who we might find along the Shadow road out on the prairie. There might be some horses, or rifles, maybe some fighting, too, if we catch anyone out."

By the time *Weesculatat* and Yellow Wolf had moved through camp, calling out to other young men still a little groggy from their long night's celebration, two-times-ten riders were strung out in a crude V that passed right on by the soldier camp.

"See down the road!" *Weesculatat* shouted, waving the arm that he pointed south across the prairie. The older man announced, "We have two in the hand!"

Yipping like playful coyote pups setting off to chase and harass a jackrabbit across a grassy meadow, a handful of the young warriors kicked their ponies into a gallop, reining for the pair of *suapies*.

"You aren't going, Yellow Wolf?" *Weesculatat* asked.

"No," and he shook his head as the pair of distant horsemen spurred their horses into a terrified sprint, both men lying low in the saddle and whipping their animals without mercy. "There are already enough to see to those unlucky soldiers. I killed two of my own yesterday."

"This will be great fun to watch," *Weesculatat* said as Yellow Wolf turned on the back of his pony to peer across the great heaving expanse of the prairie.

Surely there had to be a better game than this. What with all those Shadows holed up in the two settlements nearby, with so many *suapies* hunkered down in their gopher burrows on the Cottonwood, there had to be better sport for a real fighting man than wiping out two lonely mail carriers caught unawares and in the open.

It wasn't long before the soldier chief sent out some men who halted their horses, aimed their rifles toward the six warriors closing the gap on the two horsemen, and fired three volleys.

It was easy to see how the soldiers aimed over the heads of those two oncoming riders so their bullets would land in front of the charging warriors. *Weesculatat* and the five others were just breaking off their chase when the breath caught in Yellow Wolf's chest.

"Now that's what I call a challenge for a fighting man!" he suddenly announced with a shrill cry, every muscle in his body tensing with anticipation. "See who is coming now!"

At the far sweep of grassy prairie, more riders just made their appearance, advancing from the southeast.

"Are they more *suapies?*" asked *Weesculatat.*

"I don't think so," Yellow Wolf replied, one hand tensing on the reins, the other gripping the hardwood carbine he had captured at the White Bird fight. "None of them are dressed the same, and they are coming from the Shadow settlements."

"*Hi-yiii!*" the older warrior shrieked exuberantly. "Yes, this is far better for a fighting man!"

Two Moons reined up beside *Ollokot* in a cloud of dust their horses kicked up with their hooves. "String out!" Two Moons ordered loudly to the rest, all five-times-ten of the young men arrayed along the white man's road. "String out and make a broad line!"

Yellow Wolf agreed, "Yes—we will charge into them and break them up!"

By the time Two Moons and *Ollokot* got their fifty-plus warriors started off the road and onto the long sweep of rolling grassland, Yellow Wolf began to quickly tally the enemy. There were three fingers less than two-times-ten. It would be interesting to see when the Shadows reined up in a hurry as they spotted the warriors, turned around, and fled back for their settlement barricades. But . . . the horsemen kept coming! Instead of halting and wheeling about on their heels, the white men began to spread out, just as *Ollokot*'s warriors were doing in a wide front.

"What trick do you think they are up to?" *Weesculatat* asked.

Yellow Wolf quickly looked over his shoulder, seeing how the mail carriers were just then reaching the soldiers sent out to rescue them and all were retreating to the rifle pits dug around the white man's buildings raised at Cottonwood. Still, there weren't any soldiers coming out to show themselves and lay down a cover fire to protect this bigger group of Shadows.

"I don't think they have a trick to play on us at all," Yellow Wolf said as he saw how the horseman in the center was waving and wildly gesturing while the entire line of white men suddenly kicked their horses into a frenzied sprint. "They are going to try to beat us to the soldiers' gopher burrows."

Weesculatat flicked a look over his shoulder as their ponies lunged into a low, grassy swale. "It is a long way to race us to safety!"

Yellow Wolf quickly glanced at the distance. Many, many bullet flights to the hollows. If the soldiers did not come out to lay down some cover, *Ollokot*'s war party could stop the outnumbered Shadows and cut them up one at a time.

Faint sounds erupted from the throats of those white horsemen as they raced closer and closer, heading on a collision course with the wide band of warriors. Then the first of their guns popped, a puff of smoke appearing at the muzzle of a belt gun, a gray mist whipped away behind the rider. Others fired, and Yellow Wolf heard the first snarl of a bullet as it sang past him. On either side of him, those who had firearms put them to use—more for noise and bluster than to do any good atop a racing horse.

Yellow Wolf hoped the others would not use up too much of their hard-won ammunition in such frivolous sport. They would need those bullets when the tough killing began. Better to save their cartridges until they were sure of hitting a target—

Yelling at the top of his lungs, Yellow Wolf swung his

kopluts, that short hardwood war club, at the closest Shadow the moment both lines converged on the slope leading out of that low, grassy swale. In an instant the white men were beyond them, through the warriors and on their way to the soldier hollows.

Immediately all the warriors swung their ponies around in broad, sweeping curves, each rider leaning hard to the inside as he brought his horse tearing in an arch that nearly toppled a handful of the Nez Perce as they barely avoided colliding with one another. With yips and howls and screeches, too, they were after the galloping Shadows in a heartbeat, racing after the rumps of those fleeing horses, making as much noise as they could.

Yellow Wolf's throat was a little sore by the time he saw the first of the white men's horses stumble and pitch its rider into the grass. Another horseman quickly reined aside and took the dismounted Shadow up behind him.

"Yes!" *Weesculatat* cried. "Aim for their horses! Aim for their horses!"

"Put them on foot!" came the order from Two Moons.

Almost immediately another Shadow horse stumbled; then it kicked and bucked, throwing its rider clear before it settled onto the ground.

Up ahead of the white men, one of them had reached the top of a low hill where he threw himself out of the saddle and was waving with an arm that brandished a repeater. Yellow Wolf had a lever-action carbine like that in his mother's lodge. But she was with Looking Glass's people. How he wished he had that repeater now instead of this single-shot *suapie* gun.

One by one the rest of the white men were leaping off their horses around that first man, two of them lunging up on foot, their horses already down in the swale behind them.

"*Yi-yi-yiiii!*" Yellow Wolf yipped, his blood running hot.

Hot because they had the Shadows stopped on the brow of that low hill and the white men were going no farther. If those few horsemen had kept on riding, chances were very good most of them could have made it on into the soldier burrows.

But, as it was, *Ollokot*'s warriors could now take their time and have some fun wiping out these foolish whites.

SINCE putting Mount Idaho behind them, Lieutenant Lew Wilmot and the other volunteers who rode with Captain D. B. Randall had done their best to save the strength of their horses. While he knew every man around him wanted nothing less than to gallop full-out for that soldier camp at Cottonwood Station, they nonetheless reined in their mounts as they descended to the rolling prairie. No more than a fast walk. Save the horses' strength for when it was really needed.

But the endurance of the animals beneath them wasn't the only worry troubling Wilmot. As he looked around him, Lew quickly tallied the odds against this band of civilians if they did have to make a running fight of it. He himself had been up against it with the Indians more than once, but . . . besides Randall and three more, none of the other twelve had ever found themselves in an Indian fight.

As he looked around at the group tightly bunched behind their leaders, Lew realized there wasn't a good shot among them. Make no mistake, he thought: The odds were in favor of the Nez Perce who had cleaned up every command sent against them so far.

"You see the smoke, D. B.?" Wilmot asked. He had just spotted the signal fires burning atop Cottonwood Butte, which straddled the divide.

"Seen it a minute ago," Randall said. "Likely that's them Injuns talking about those soldiers down below 'em."

Lew was still brooding on the uncertain odds stacked against them if they ran into trouble after covering some two-thirds of the distance to Norton's ranch—when Wilmot's eyes caught some distant movement on the sweep of prairie far off in their advance, a little to their right.

"D. B., you look at all that ahead of us; I think we need

to hold up a minute," Lew suggested to the man riding just ahead of him.

"All right," Randall agreed. "Give us a minute to figger out what all this is."

"Lookit all them horses!" Ben Evans cried behind him.

The herd slowly undulating off the last slope of the divide and pouring onto the prairie was impressive in size, to say the least. But it wasn't those Nez Perce horses that held Lew Wilmot's attention. It was those fighting men who suddenly popped up, right out of the low swale about halfway between Randall's volunteers and their village on the move.

"Here, Lew! Look for your own self."

Turning, Wilmot found James Cearly handing him a small looking glass. Lew quickly twisted the outer section until the distant figures slipped into focus. Then he twisted it back, taking the advancing horsemen out of focus as he concentrated on the distant forms among the structures that were Cottonwood Station. The house, barn, and outbuildings appeared clearly, and all those soldiers rising out of their rifle pits, too, at least a hundred of them, watching, what was about to happen. Watching, and waiting.

"Have a look, D. B." Wilmot jabbed the spyglass at Randall. "We don't stand a chance of getting to Cottonwood now."

As their leader was studying the distance, most of the untried men behind Wilmot were shifting nervously in their saddles, an uneasy banter and hollow bravado coming over them as they stared at the distant line of more than a hundred-fifty warriors just then stringing itself into a wide but uneven V, its long side adhering to the Mount Idaho Road, the other angling across the pitch and heave of the Camas Prairie itself.

"While we still got time, we oughtta turn around for the barricades," Lew proposed.

"No!" James Cearly screeched like a bull calf with its bangers tangled in some cat claw.

"I ain't never been yeller!" cried Frank A. Fenn,* elected sergeant of their volunteer company just that morning.

"If we ride back to our families now, nobody's gonna say we was yellow," Wilmot protested, refusing to listen to their angry protests. "Besides, that village is headed in the direction of our towns. Don't you boys figger we oughtta protect our families?"

"G'won back now if you don't wanna get in on the fighting, Lew," Cearly snapped, edging his horse up on the other side of Randall's.

Even young Alonzo B. Leland, the Lewiston *Teller* editor's son, refused to consider retreat while they still had the chance. "Captain Randall, you can lead the rest of us through to the soldiers. I know you can."

"That's right, Captain!" Cearly agreed boldly. "If anybody can get us through, you can."

Lew pleaded one more time, "We've all got families to protect—"

But Randall sternly interrupted, "Helping them soldiers stop those Injuns is the best way I know of protecting our families back at Mount Idaho."

His eyes darting across the rolling sea of tall grass, Wilmot grabbed Randall's elbow with one hand, pointing with his right arm. "Lookit that hill way off there to the left. We got time to make it there. That's the kind of place where we can make a stand, D. B. Just tall enough, let the Indians attack us there, we can wait for the soldiers to come out and drive 'em off—"

"No," Randall growled, his eyes squinting testily. "I'll get everyone through to Cottonwood like I promised." Then he turned away from Lew, looking at James Cearly. "Jim—I think it's time you took over for Lew. I need someone I can count on behind me, so you're lieutenant of this outfit now."

Most of the group hooted and hollered like schoolboys on a summer's lark down to the fishing hole. Wilmot

---

***Cries from the Earth*, vol. 14, the *Plainsmen* series.

quickly glanced around at them—looking into those eager faces, realizing there wasn't a single one of them who knew what they were about to plunge themselves into.

Suddenly he scolded himself for even caring about these men whom he had known—well, *thought* he knew—friends who were turning their backs on him and the loved ones all of them had left behind in Mount Idaho to wait and wonder.

The wide formation of distant warriors disappeared down the slope as the Nez Perce dropped into the low swale of Shebang Creek. They were getting closer and closer yet still approaching at an easy pace. So there had to be enough time to get to the top of that low hill nearby—

Right now it didn't matter who the hell was lieutenant or sergeant . . . or even the goddamned captain. Gulping, Wilmot vowed to try to convince them all one last time.

"D. B., it's better we have us some high ground 'stead of getting caught out—"

"Lew," Randall interrupted, flinging Wilmot's hand off his arm, "if you wanna go back, I said you can go. Me and the rest of the boys have started for Cottonwood and we are going."

Wilmot's horse seemed to sense the tension and side-stepped. Lew leaned over, grabbing for Randall's wrist again. Nearly breathless, he pleaded, "D. B., you know I ain't going back 'less the rest of you go. These here fellas brung near all the guns in Mount Idaho with 'em when we rode out. And now there's enough Injuns between us and Norton's place to have us outnumbered ten-to-one."

"C'mon, Captain!" Fenn shouted. "Let's ride right through those sonsabitches!"

Emboldened by the confidence in the others, Randall shook off Wilmot's hand again. Smiling like it was all a joke, he said, "Well now, Lew—if you're afraid of all them Injuns, why don't you climb up here behind me on my horse?"

The instant laughter was cruel and metallic, sharp-edged, as it fell about Wilmot. There were muted murmurs from some of the others who suddenly voiced criticism against him and Ready for running to Grangeville when the Nortons and Chamberlins were fighting off a brutal attack. Their laughter, even at his expense, showed just how little they understood what they were confronting as the warriors reappeared out of another low swale, closer still.

"D. B.," Wilmot said with a sigh and rocked back in his saddle, fighting down the frustration threatening to overwhelm him, "this is too goddamned serious a situation for you to be making a joke of. I can stand to ride with you if the rest are going. But lookit them warriors now—I still think the best thing is for us to get back to the barricades before it's too late."

Instead of answering, Randall jabbed his heels into his horse and reined away. Caught by surprise, the rest quickly put their mounts into motion, yipping and cheering as they lumbered past Wilmot. Lew quickly sawed the reins around and kicked his horse into a lope to catch up with the other fifteen men who were riding at the rear of D. B. Randall's mount. They had their noses bravely pointed for Cottonwood Station.

Trouble was, a hundred or more warriors stood between them and there.

The half-naked horsemen had emerged out of the swale and put Shebang Creek behind them when they stopped, arrayed in a half-mile-long line that stretched across the road, covering the movement of their women and children and that huge herd of horses. Some of them still sat atop their ponies, while a number of them dismounted and stood alongside their animals, all of them waiting as the small band of white men drew closer and closer.

By now Wilmot could hear a little of the distant yelps and songs from those warriors. Some of them were anxiously shaking their weapons. *Hell, yes,* he thought. They'd be worked up for a fight. *There's enough of the red bastards right out there to chew us up and spit us out in the time a man takes to piss.*

But . . . still . . . those Indians were just sitting there on their ponies.

After weeks of unseasonably cool and rainy weather, the summer sun felt very, very hot on the back of Lew Wilmot's neck. Cold sweat dribbled down his backbone.

Those goddamned Injuns weren't making a move.

Just . . . waiting.

Chapter Nineteen

July 5, 1877

Lew Wilmot couldn't take the silence anymore. Not the way they just kept riding, riding, riding toward that broad V of the Nez Perce that surely outnumbered them by more than ten-to-one . . . none of Randall's men saying one goddamned word.

"D. B.!" Lew shouted into the dry, hot breeze of that midsummer day. "What the hell you propose to do? Just keep on aiming straight for them warriors?"

"Shuddup, Wilmot!" James L. Cearly growled like a half-sick yard dog.

"I'm fixing to charge the Indians!" Randall announced suddenly before anyone else had a chance to speak. He turned slightly in his saddle, flinging his voice behind him so that all could hear. "We'll charge the Indians!"

They whooped and hollered with that news.

But in the midst of the noise, Lew prodded their leader. "We gotta have some idea what every one of us is gonna do, Captain. What are your orders if someone's shot, or a horse goes down under one of the boys?"

Randall's eyes glared at Wilmot a moment, angry at being questioned. Then their leader said, "Any one of us is shot, or killed, or if their horse goes down—it's every other man's job to stop and pick up that man!"

That edgy bravado of his caused a wild cheer to erupt from the fourteen who were bunched behind Wilmot, Randall, and Cearly.

Moments had passed, mere heartbeats and yards gobbled up and gone, when D. B. Randall bellowed a raspy cry that was immediately answered from all their throats. Something wild and feral that swelled around their tiny group as they kicked their horses into an uneven gallop down the long, low slope of the rumpled prairie.

By then they were so close to that line of warriors that Lew could almost make out the eyes of the enemy—maybe even close enough to read some of the confusion on the faces of those Nez Perce who had no earthly idea why such a pitifully small bunch of white men would be riding straight-out for an overwhelming number of warriors.

"We got 'em!" Cearly shrieked, almost in glee. "By God, D. B.—we got 'em!"

Wilmot was screeching and hollering with the rest as the seventeen charged across that last hundred yards.

The nervous Indian ponies fought their handlers. A few of the Nez Perce rifles popped, but from where Lew sat, he didn't see anyone get hit or their horses falter with the enemy gunfire.

Ten more yards—

Some of the warrior ponies bolted away from the line as the white men slammed against the wide array of Nez Perce.

Jerking his head around, Wilmot peered over his shoulder at the Indians suddenly behind them, realizing he hadn't taken a breath in the last few moments. He dragged the hot morning's air into his lungs and hurrahed right along with the rest of them. They had made it through the enemy and were on their way for the rifle pits at Cottonwood! A little more than three miles to go. That was all!

Then the bullet snarled past his left elbow.

Wilmot twisted with a jerk and looked over his shoulder again. They were coming now. Make no mistake about that. Those warriors had whipped around, regrouped, and were on their way. Not a one of them left standing on foot any longer. Had to be more than a hundred-twenty of them all told. Not just full of false bluster now—but every last one of them angry as spit-on hens as they swarmed like summer wasps after the fleeing white men.

Off to his left, just ahead, Frank D. Vansise's horse crumpled clumsily, pitching its rider ahead into the tall grass. Vansise rolled off his shoulder, hunched over as he frantically searched the grass for his rifle.

"Henry!" Lew hollered at his friend who was coming up behind him. He reined up, levered a shell into the chamber of his saddle carbine, and brought it to his shoulder. "Get Frank! Pull 'im up behind you!"

He fired at the closest warrior, watching the rider immediately drop to the side of his pony, out of sight.

As Vansise's horse keeled over onto its side, neck thrusting as it tried to rise one last time, Henry C. Johnson, who lived close to the White Bird divide, reined up in a whirl, holding down a hand and kicking his boot out of a stirrup. Vansise grabbed the offered hand, hurtling off the ground to plop behind Johnson as Henry wrenched his horse around and both men kicked the animal into an ungainly, lumbering gallop.

Wilmot levered another cartridge into the chamber, expelling the hot copper cylinder, its shiny glitter spinning into the tall green grass beside his horse.

By now more and more of the civilians were strung out to the left of Wilmot, following Randall and Cearly into a wide depression between three low hills after Wilmot stopped to cover the rescue of Vansise. At the moment Lew yanked the reins aside to turn around and light out, more warriors burst over the edge of the prairie; tall grass split in waves as their ponies heaved in the race. But instead of following Randall as the others were, Wilmot turned slightly to the right, away from the distant rifle pits at Cottonwood.

There was no way they were going to make it to the soldiers anyway, Lew reflected. Randall and the other followers—now they were making directly for the ranch. But that would take them over ground where they wouldn't have a single advantage against the warriors . . . especially if the Indians kept picking off a horse here, dropping a rider there.

"Cearly!"

Wilmot heard Randall's anguished cry just before he fired the next shot, holding on a Nez Perce pony. He jerked aside without waiting to see if the pony fell, finding D. B. Randall was rolling onto his knees, hollering for James Cearly, who was hauling back on his reins that very moment. Randall vaulted onto his feet and scrambled for his downed horse. It lay thrashing in the grass at the bottom of that low swale, legs beginning to slow the moment he reached the animal and yanked his carbine from the saddle boot.

Spinning on his heel, Randall started hollering into the dry, hot air.

"Boys! Don't run! Don't run! Let's fight 'em! We can fight 'em here!"

Lew Wilmot turned his back on Randall, reining his horse around savagely, kicking its flanks with his boot heels, pushing it up the easy slope to the crest of that low hill. It wasn't much, save for being the highest thing in this part of the prairie now. The only knob where they could take refuge, maybe make a stand. Everything else was out of the range of possibility now, like those hills Lew had wanted them to light out for minutes ago. No way to reach them or those soldier rifle pits, either. Just this bare, grassy knob still some two miles from Cottonwood.*

Right where he felt like an inflamed boil sticking up on the rounded ass of the world. Up here where they could be easily seen by the enemy, at least the remains of Randall's brave volunteers could command a good field of fire—

"D. B.!" Wilmot shouted as loud as his raw throat would allow while he kicked his right foot free of the stirrup and spun out of the saddle to land on that leg.

Lew fired three rapid shots with his repeater, hot copper cartridges spinning, spinning, spinning out of the weapon in a jagged arc as they tumbled through shafts of bright, brilliant sunshine.

"Eph! Cash! All of you—get over here! C'mon! C'mon, now!"

Ephraim J. Brunker was the first to join Lew on the low rise. Then Cassius M. Day. Charley Case and Pete Bremen

*One and one-half miles southeast of the present-day community of Cottonwood, Idaho, and one-third of a mile east of the memorial and sign located off U. S. 95.

rode up together, as lathered as their horses. Lew was among them immediately, darting here and there as he shouted for them to dismount, grab their weapons and cartridges loose, then free the horses.

"Let 'em go!" Cash Day agreed. "Maybeso the Injuns chase off after 'em!"

D. H. Howser lumbered up, wobbling in the saddle, clutching his side. "I been hit."

"Git 'im down!" Brunker bawled.

They dragged Howser to the ground. Someone slapped the frightened horse on the rump and sent it clattering off, stirrups flapping crazily.

"George!" Lew hollered at Riggins the moment the man hit the ground on his feet. "Grab up D. H. there and get him over to that rail fence yonder. Stay with 'im and you watch that right flank!"

Riggins glanced over his shoulder to a spot at the side of the rise where Wilmot was pointing, nodded, then sank to one knee beside Howser. "Let's go, D. H. We got a li'l walking to do."

"Cash Day!" Wilmot called out. Day fired a shot and turned before Lew continued, "Get on over to our left! You cover that side!"

Day wagged with his rifle in agreement and rose to a crouch, all hunched over as he shuffled through the tall grass in the direction opposite to that taken by Riggins and Howser.

"Where you want me, Lew?" Ben Evans shouted as he leaped off the wide back of the wagon horse a few yards down the slope from Wilmot.

Lew watched the draft animal lumber away, racing for the end of the Indian line as the warriors fully encircled their knoll. "Stay down there at the bottom, Ben!" he hollered. "You'll be out of sight where you can pick 'em off when they come by you 'cross the bottom!"

Evans shook his carbine and scurried down the slope, where he plopped to his belly, disappearing in the tall grass.

"Where's D. B.?" Bremen asked.

Quickly looking around, Lew spotted Randall hunkered down between the legs of his horse. Nearby sat James Buchanan, slowly firing his carbine as he squatted in the grass, his legs crossed and drawn up under his elbows for a proper shooting rest.

The two of them might do well enough, Wilmot thought. *Well enough to hold the bastards back for as long as it will take for the soldiers to come out and drive them off us.*

But the next time Lew Wilmot turned to gaze over his shoulder at Cottonwood Station some two miles distant, he was baffled why there weren't any figures clambering out of their rifle pits, much less mounted up and riding out on horseback.

A few minutes later Charley Case grumbled, "How long you figger we're gonna be till them soldiers come get us, Lew?"

Wilmot shook his head. "Don't know, Charley. From the looks of things, we may damn well be on our own out here."

FOR the last two days George Shearer had put up with these goddamned Yankee soldiers hunkering down at Cottonwood Station, refusing to lay into the red bastards. But being forced to sit here and watch while his friends were jumped as they were riding to Norton's ranch was simply more than the Southern fighting man could take.

Besides the hundred-and-twenty-some soldiers Captain David Perry commanded, there was a bevy of civilian packers and a handful of volunteers who had shown up to add their weapons to the fight by the time those two couriers had raced into Norton's ranch earlier that morning. In something less than thirty hours, the men Captain Whipple had dispatched made it over to Howard's command across the Salmon River and back again.

To Shearer's way of thinking, there was more than enough men to take on those warriors in a stand-up, head-to-head fight. The odds were all but even!

So why hadn't Perry sent out some men to rescue the

civilians when he had ordered Captain Winters's detachment to rescue those two couriers?

The first answer Perry gave the astonished volunteer was, "I'm not all that sure those are civilians. The warriors could be clever enough to wear some clothing taken from a settler's farm—arranging a ruse or decoy to lure some of my men to their deaths."

But when the shooting got closer and the civilians hunkered down on that slight rise with more than a hundred-fifty horsemen swirling around them, it was all the proof anyone needed that those weren't warriors dressed up like white men!

Yet did that blue-belly Perry send help out then? Hell no!

To Shearer the only excuse could be that those men weren't soldiers.

On top of everything else, George knew Perry had to be dwelling on that trouncing he had suffered at White Bird Canyon three weeks ago, able to think of little else!

That wasn't to say all the officers were duplicitous cowards to Shearer's way of thinking. Why, Lieutenant Edwin H. Shelton had even stepped right up to Perry and volunteered to lead a detail that he would take across that narrow strip of ground left open by the hostiles. But the commander was having nothing of it.

"It's too late to do any good," Perry equivocated by the time he got around to giving Shelton an answer. "They cannot last much longer—those men should have known better than to travel that road, as dangerous as it is."

"We owe it to them to try, Colonel," Shelton begged.

"If I did send any relief," Perry refused, "it might well sacrifice our position here."

"Here?" Shearer echoed, a heavy dose of sarcasm mixing with his Southern accent.

Perry wheeled on the civilian near his elbow. "We have a great store of arms and ammunition here. I fear that the moment I would start a detail to help the civilians on that hill, the enemy would rush in here and overrun what men I would leave behind. And all those weapons would fall into the hands of the Nez Perce. Supplies meant for General Howard's column—"

"Bullshit, Colonel," Shearer drawled. "It's a goddamned shame and an outrage to allow those men—those brave men—to remain out there and perish without you making an effort to save them!"

Perry was clearly growing red, about ready to burst, when one of his officers stepped in front of Shearer to plead their case.

"Let me ask for volunteers, Colonel," Henry Winters begged, having finally worked up the nerve to question the battalion commander. "I won't take so many men that you'll be in danger of being overwhelmed. Give me the chance to show that I can force the Indians to break off their attack simply by us starting out of here—"

"No, Captain," Perry snapped, clearly irritated with this proposal by a fellow of the same rank.

To George's way of thinking, Perry was already frustrated and angry by all those pulling and prodding him to put together a rescue.

"It's simply too late," Perry continued.

In exasperation, Shearer was turning away from the group as some of the bystanders grumbled. One of the men in the ranks grabbed the civilian's arm and spoke up, none too quietly.

"Shearer," growled Sergeant Bernard Simpson a little too loudly to be under his breath, "you civilians damn well don't need to come to the First Cavalry for any assistance—since you won't be getting any!"

"Who said that?" Perry demanded.

Not one of those officers and enlisted who stood nearby dared admit a thing or betray their compatriot from L Company.

When no one answered, Perry snapped, "I'll court-martial the next man who questions my authority or my decisions!"

"I'm volunteering to take any of your soldiers with me,"

Shearer spoke as he stepped up. "After all, they're my friends. Those civilians are our own home guards—"

"Request denied," Perry shot back. "I'm not letting go of a man to a lost cause."

"Goddamn it, you puffed up blue-belly martinet!" Shearer roared, wagging a finger in Perry's face for a moment, then flinging his arm out in the direction of the skirmish. "You hear that gunfire? See that gunsmoke? That fight ain't over!"

"I'll ride with you," Sergeant Simpson volunteered, stepping forward now. This soldier from L Company, First U. S. Cavalry, turned to Perry. "With all due respect, Colonel—I was the one who made the comment 'bout the civilians not getting any help from the First Cavalry."

Perry's eyes narrowed menacingly. "Sergeant?"

"Yes, sir, I own up to it."

Perry fumed a moment as if searching for what to say, then turned to Whipple. "Captain, place this man under arrest for insubordination!"

"Colonel?" Simpson grumbled. "Let us go and fight. I joined the army to fight our enemies . . . not each other!"

"Colonel Perry," Stephen Whipple pleaded as he pushed Simpson aside, "I wish you would reconsider about the sergeant."

"The man will stay under arrest," Perry shot back. "Nor will I have you questioning my authority either!"

"Not about the sergeant, sir," Whipple said, stepping up to stand directly in front of Perry. "I'm asking you to reconsider sending a relief party while there's still men to save."

Shearer watched as Perry chewed on his lower lip for a long, breathless moment. Then it all came at a gush.

"Very well. Captain Winters!"

"Sir?"

"You'll accompany Captain Whipple and his gun crew—prepare a relief party." Whipple saluted. "How many men, sir?"

"Two companies," Perry ordered.

"I request to go along," Lieutenant Shelton offered.

Winters waved him on as both captains turned away from Perry. Shearer was lunging right in front of Whipple after a few steps, causing the officer to draw up short.

"I'm going, too," George volunteered. "I'll bring some friends with me."

"The more the merrier, as they say, Mr. Shearer," Whipple growled as he brushed by the civilian. "The more the merrier."

Chapter Twenty

July 5, 1877

When George Shearer turned around to fetch his horse, he ran right into a friend, Paul Guiterman, who already had the reins to their animals in his hands.

"I figger they're 'bout out of cartridges, George," the stocky civilian declared. "And it's gonna take some before these soldiers are saddled up to ride out."

Shearer studied the look on his friend's face a moment before saying, "Maybeso we ought'n give it a try on our own?"

"I was hoping you was thinking same as me," Guiterman admitted. "I stuffed ever' bullet I could in our saddlebags."

Shearer grinned at the man as he grabbed his reins and stuffed a boot into the stirrup. "Sure you was a Yankee during the war, Paul?"

"I was Union down to my soles, you ol' Reb." Guiterman swung up. "But I can still give one hell of a Rebel yell."

As Shearer jabbed his heels into the horse's ribs, he said, "Better unlimber your tongue—'cause them Injuns just opened up a nice li'l road for us to sashay right on through!"

Lew Wilmot wasn't sure if his eyes or his ears were deceiving him. But—gloree! It looked as if two riders were sprinting their horses right through a narrow gap the warriors had left open between the soldiers' camp at Cottonwood and the knoll where D. B. Randall's "Brave Seventeen" were fighting for their lives.

"Lew! By God, here we come!"

Wilmot blinked, and blinked again, not sure what was happening when dim, distant figures emerged from Norton's ranch and started wriggling their way. The way his eyes were swimming with moisture and the sting of sweat, the man wasn't sure just what he saw. All through the fight, Lew couldn't get the image of that pink, wrinkled, bawling baby boy of his out of his mind. Now as he dragged the back of a hand under his runny nose, Wilmot realized he just might see Louisa and the girls again. Just might get himself a chance to watch that boy rise up to manhood, too.

It was George Shearer hollering at him as the pair of riders approached—that slow-talking, hard-drinking Southern-born transplant who claimed he had served on the staff of no less than Robert E. Lee himself—and Paul Guiterman, both of them yanking back on their reins, horse hooves skidding, stirring dust into the golden air, sweat slinging off the animals and men alike as a few of Randall's men came lumbering out of the grass the moment Shearer and Guiterman stuffed their hands into those saddlebags and started tossing out boxes of ammunition.

".45-70?" a man asked.

"Here you go," Shearer replied, tossing him a carton of twenty as the Nez Perce bullets sang around them.

"Any .44?"

"I brung some," Guiterman declared.

"Where's ever'one else?" Shearer asked as he knelt beside Wilmot.

Lew was concentrating on holding the warriors back a good distance, where he knew the Indians weren't all that sharp with their rifles. "You're looking at us."

"How many was comin'?"

"Seventeen."

"Shit," Shearer murmured. "Hope like hell we can hold 'em a li'l longer, Lew. Them blue-bellies sure do know how to dillydally when it suits 'em."

"Dillydally?"

"We finally shamed that Colonel Perry into sending you some relief."

Wilmot felt the smile grow from within. "You mean you ain't the only relief that's coming, George?"

"Lookee there now, you side-talking cuss you," Shearer

said, slapping Wilmot on the shoulder and pointing. "There come your soldiers now!"

"Wh-where you going?" Lew asked as George Shearer leaped to his feet and lunged toward his ground-hobbled horse.

"Them Yankee blues gonna be all day getting here," Shearer grumbled as he flung himself up onto the horse's back. "I'm fixin' to go nudge 'em to come a li'l faster, is all. Gimme some cover fire whilst I ride outta here, will you, Lew?"

Wilmot levered and fired, levered and fired again, over and over, then flicked a glance at that narrow gauntlet Shearer was racing through for a second time.

Beyond the lone rider, the soldiers were throwing out an overly wide, skimpy line of skirmishers as they began their two-mile advance on that low knoll east of the road ranch. As the wide advance of fifteen foot soldiers emerged from the mouth of the ravine known as Cottonwood Canyon, Randall's survivors could next spot about twice that many soldiers marching behind them in a much tighter formation. With his small looking glass Lew was able to see that they were accompanied by a Gatling gun. As this unit began to make its crossing behind the fifteen skirmishers, about twenty more soldiers, all mounted, shuffled into view and began to cut obliquely across the skirmishers' path—

Of a sudden, the hiss of one last bullet from the Nez Perce quickly reminded Lew Wilmot that the enemy still had them all but encircled. But as he turtled his head into his shoulders and peered around at the naked horsemen, he found the warriors drawing back. While the skirmishers plodded on at an angle that would eventually put them in the Indians' front some distance from the knoll, the larger unit of foot soldiers and those eighteen horse soldiers kept on for the besieged civilians.

In the mid-distance Wilmot could make out a few shouts and screams from the hostiles as they pranced about, shaking their bows and carbines at the soldiers. But the fighting was over.

"What you figger they're telling us?" Henry Johnson asked.

Lew sighed. "Saying there's gonna be another day, another fight, and a lot more killing before this war's ever settled."

"Lew!"

Wilmot whirled at the cry of his name. "George!" he cried, his throat sore and raspy from overuse. "By damn—you hurried them Yankee soldiers, you ol' Reb you!"

Shading his eyes in the bright afternoon sun as he peered up at Shearer as the man came skidding to a halt again on the sweeping slope of their knoll, Lew suddenly realized just how many hours they had managed to hold off those one hundred fifty warriors. "Get down off that horse!" he yelled at Shearer, starting toward his friend, his thoughts thickened with hope—

He was surprised when he heard a rifleshot from close by, watched the bullet wing Shearer's horse across the withers. The animal began to buck and dance as the civilian struggled to bring the mount under control. Blood seeped down its neck.

"George, by God—get down outta that saddle!"

Vaulting from the back of the wounded horse, Shearer lunged toward Wilmot as a squad of soldiers started loping for the Indian sniper's position. The two friends shook and pounded backs; then Shearer stepped back as a few of the other survivors stomped up at the same moment the first of the cavalry were reaching the hilltop.

His eyes darting about, Shearer asked, "Where's D. B.?"

Wilmot turned on his heel. Pointing, he exclaimed, "Randall was down there, last I saw of him. There! That's his horse on the ground!"

The two were off in a sprint, down the slope to the grassy swale where Lew had watched D. B. Randall's horse crumple to the ground early in the seige. As he raced closer and closer, Wilmot spotted the back of Randall's head resting against the animal's motionless front flank. D. B. was reclining back in the tangle of the horse's legs as Wilmot leaped around the rear hooves and slid to a stop. His breath caught when he saw the dark, shiny smear that covered the whole of his friend's chest, like he'd spilled an entire bowl of blackberry preserves on himself at breakfast that morning—

"D. B.!"

The eyes fluttered slightly, eventually opening halfway. "That you? That Lew Wilmot?"

He held his face down close. "It's over, D. B. Gonna get you to some help now." And laid his palm against the wet, sticky, black stain on that shirt.

"I'm mortal hurt, Lew"—then he coughed, wet and long. "I ain't goin' nowhere now. This gonna be where I die." The eyes seemed to widen perceptibly as Lew moved over Randall, making some shade for the wounded man's face. "Got any water?"

He quickly glanced up at Shearer. "George? You get a canteen for D. B.?"

When the water came, Randall drank a little, then coughed some more, bringing up gouts of blood, almost like he was heaving from a terrible stomach wound as well. When he finally caught his breath and had licked some blood from his bottom lip, D. B. Randall looked up at the two civilians.

His eyes fluttered as he asked, "Tell . . . tell my wife—"

Then the eyelids didn't tremble anymore. They simply stopped moving. For a long time Wilmot and Shearer squatted there by their forty-four-year-old friend. Probably to be sure before Wilmot gently eased the eyelids back down and rose to his feet, watching the approach of an empty lumber wagon rattling toward the bottom of the slope.

James Cearly came up. "D. B.?"

Lew nodded. "He's dead."

"Ben, too."

"Where?" Shearer asked.

Cearly pointed. "No more'n three other boys wounded."*

"That's all?" George Shearer asked, his voice rising a pitch in amazement.

Wilmot looked around them, counting five dead horses, their big carcasses scattered from the long depression to the top of the low rise where he had started their stand.

"We held 'em off, by Jupiter!" Cash Day exclaimed. "Can't believe it's over."

"It ain't over for none of us," Lew declared sourly. "This is far from over—"

"You civilians get your dead and wounded loaded up in that wagon!" announced one of the mounted soldiers Wilmot recognized as the officer called Winters. "I'm moving my forces back to Camp Rains."

"Camp Rains?" Lew repeated, looking at Shearer.

The civilian nodded. "They named their bivouac at Norton's place after the dead officer what led his scouting party into an ambush couple days back. Ain't that just like a Yankee soldier's way of things? Givin' honor to that dead Lieutenant Rains who got hisself killed and ever'body else with him?"

DURING all that fighting, Yellow Wolf wondered why the soldiers refused to budge from their squirrel holes they had dug. Instead of coming out to save all the Shadows, for the longest time they instead chose to merely watch the skirmishing from long distance. No matter; it was a glorious fight while it lasted. Lots of riding past the Shadow guns at a gallop, some of the men crawling on their bellies through the tall grass to get close enough to the white men to see faces clearly.

That's when Yellow Wolf and his friend *Wemastahtus* recognized one of the young Shadows.

---

*Charles Johnson, Alonzo B. Leland, and D. H. Howser (who subsequently died of his wounds).

"He is Charley Crooks?" asked *Wemastahtus* in a whisper after they had all stared in amazement.

"No," Yellow Wolf replied. "That Charley was at the fight in *Lahmotta.* This is another Charley, son of a settler who raises his horses at the bottom of the hills, this side of the White Bird Hill."

"John-son?" *Wemastahtus* asked.

With a nod, Yellow Wolf said, "I think it is John-son's boy, the one called Charley." He held his head up slightly and yelled at the others his announcement: "John-son's boy, Charley . . . he is here with the other Shadows. He's a friend, so do not hurt him! We should do him no harm!"

"Who is this?" shouted *Weesculatat*, that older warrior who had urged Yellow Wolf to come along for the fight. His pony pranced up, boldly making a target of its rider.

"A Shadow friend of ours!" Yellow Wolf shouted, waving his arm emphatically for *Weesculatat* to dismount. "Get down! This Shadow who was a friend is shooting right at us!"

A bullet suddenly sang through the grass between the pair hiding in the grass, a bullet from John-son's location. *Weesculatat* dropped to the ground, kneeling as he held onto the long single rein knotted around his pony's lower jaw.

"See, *Weesculatat*? This Charley John-son is shooting at us now!" *Wemastahtus* cried.

"I cannot see this friend of yours," *Weesculatat* said as he turned, studying the white men scattered across the slope. "Which one is he?"

A bullet from one of the white man guns struck the older man's horse, causing the frightened animal to rear and hop in pain and fear. *Weesculatat* bolted to his feet, yanking on the long rein, doing what he could to gain control of the frightened animal as Shadow bullets snarled around them.

"Get down!" Yellow Wolf shouted as he started to reach up an arm to pull *Weesculatat* down.

But the older warrior was twisted away by the spooked pony—

Yellow Wolf flinched the instant he heard the slap of lead against flesh. *Weesculatat* let out a little groan as he collapsed forward into the grass, clutching at his knee. Blood was seeping between the fingers of both hands, but he was an older man, a proven warrior who had control of his voice, so he did not cry out when he was hit by Charley John-son's bullet.

Instead, he looked up at the other two and said, "Time for us to go from here."

"I can help you," Yellow Wolf offered.

"I think I can make it on my own, brother," *Weesculatat* explained, using that familial term to honor a friend.

The moment Yellow Wolf turned his head to look back at the young white man who was shooting at them, the older warrior pushed himself up from the grass. A puff of smoke immediately spurted from the muzzle of John-son's gun and another bullet hit *Weesculatat*, this time in the back, throwing him face-down into the grass but not blowing out a hole in his bare chest.

"This Charley John-son," Yellow Wolf yelped in confusion. "I thought he and his father were our friends!"

As *Wemastahtus* started to crawl toward *Weesculatat*, more bullets snarled into the grass and he stopped where he lay. He and Yellow Wolf could both hear the older man's loud breathing, coming hard and wet.

"I will come get you!" Yellow Wolf said. "Wait for me to come!"

"N-no," *Weesculatat* replied, his voice no longer strong as it had been only moments ago. "I can still get away on my own. The bullet did not come out . . ."

Weesculatat slowly rose to his hands and knees in the grass, his head slung loosely between his shoulders like that of a weary dog as he wobbled, eventually pulling himself up to a squatting position, where he looked down at his chest again.

Then he turned to peer back at the two warriors nearby. "See, the bullet that hit me in the back did not come out—"

Another shot from John-son's gun slammed into *Wees-*

culatat from the side, driving him off his knees, where he skidded in the grass a foot, then lay still, gasping louder and louder, his fingers clawing up a handful of the green shafts.

He was barely breathing when Yellow Wolf reached him. Three bullets. The first would have made him lame, if only he had stayed low. It made Yellow Wolf angry in his belly, very mad to think that an old friend of theirs had done this to *Weesculatat*. Yellow Wolf knew most of the other young men had refrained from shooting at this Charley John-son because his family were old friends of the Non-Treaty bands. But—hard as it was for Yellow Wolf to consider—maybe no white man would ever be a friend to the *Nee-Me-Poo* again.

Not long after Yellow Wolf reached the older warrior, many of Two Moons's warriors started to drift back toward their herd and migrating village, breaking off the surround in favor of putting themselves between the white men and their families once more. He could not blame the others—none of them had any idea when the soldiers would emerge from their hollows or what they would do when they got brave enough to make a fight of it while the camp was in the open and vulnerable.

The other warriors under *Ollokot* did what they could to keep lots of pressure on the outnumbered Shadows with their loud guns—repeating weapons the warriors respected, like the rifle Yellow Wolf himself owned, a lever-action carbine his mother held in safekeeping for him back in Looking Glass's village. More than the single-shot soldier guns, these warriors had a healthy respect for the Shadows' rapid-firing repeaters.

Into the afternoon *Ollokot*'s men wondered if the *suapies* would ever emerge from their hollows. That did not happen until the sun was halfway down in the sky toward its evening set. And then they came out in that opening made when Two Moon's fighters drifted away, soldiers advancing with a big, many-noises gun that rumbled right in the front of some walking soldiers.

"Let us quit for a while!" *Ollokot* shouted as he raced

past on his horse, the fringes sewn at the heels of his moccasins flying in the hot breeze like the mane and tail of his pony.

His first horse had been shot out from under him in the early stages of the fight, but his youngest wife, known as *Aihits Palojami*, known as Fair Land, had been watching from a nearby hilltop and quickly brought him another good fighting horse as the bullets landed around them both.

Two others came to join Yellow Wolf and *Wemastahtus*, helping to drag *Weesculatat* back from danger. In a grassy depression they laid the older man over the back of a horse and started with him to the village that would be making camp this afternoon in the canyon of the Cottonwood at *Piswah Ilppilp Pah*, the Place of Red Rocks. Another man had been wounded, but not nearly as bad. *Sewattis Hihhih*, the warrior known as White Cloud, was a half brother of Two Moons. A man of short stature, White Cloud was nonetheless a very brave fighter, shot from his pony during a daring charge on the Shadows.

Despite the rescue of those white men by the *suapies*, the fighting chiefs had accomplished what they had set out to do. If that small war party of Shadows had reached the soldier camp that afternoon, the chances were good the white men would have believed themselves strong enough to leave their camp and venture onto the prairie, where they would have attacked the village then migrating to Cottonwood Creek. The women and children would have been threatened, havoc caused by the Shadows.

As it was, the young men had prevented any interruption in the camp's march. The white survivors of the fight limped back with the soldiers to their hollows, and the village was able to reach *Piswah Ilppilp Pah* without any trouble. Now the mouth of the Cottonwood at the Clearwater was no more than a matter of two marches, three at the most, away. They were not running. No, they were in full control now. Cut-Off Arm and his big army were many days and far, far away across a turbulent river. The warriors had neutralized the only possible threat from the burrow soldiers and now were in the clear.

Over there in the canyons of the Clearwater, the Non-Treaty bands would take refuge with Looking Glass's people—themselves fleeing a band of soldiers. The night they had crossed the Salmon and were camped at *Aipadass*, word had come that the *suapies* had attacked the old peace talker, Looking Glass! Now even he was ready to join the other war chiefs and drive the Shadows from the land of the *Nee-Me-Poo* for all time.

Yellow Wolf felt strong in his heart.

Because of what the fighting men had accomplished that day, those *suapies* entrenched far up the Cottonwood would not dare leave their burrows to follow the village. And Cut-Off Arm was still far, far away on the other side of the Salmon, mired down in mud with his "day-after-tomorrow army."

CHAPTER TWENTY-ONE

JULY 5–7, 1877

BY TELEGRAPH

—

General Grant Leaves England for the Continent.

—

Later Dispatches from the
Oregon Indian War.

—

OREGON.

—

Latest from the Indian War.

PORTLAND, July 5.— A courier arrived at Lewiston, July 2d, from Kamia, says Colonel Whipple and his command had an engagement with the Looking-glass band on Clear Water, to-day. Four Indians were killed and left on the field dead. Many others were wounded. The squaws and children took to the river and several were drowned. The fighting was still going on when the courier left. Looking-glass's band is estimated by scouts to number about 400. At three o'clock this morning a courier arrived, having left General Howard's camp on the night of the 29th. The troops had made a crossing that day, and scouts who had been out on the hills found stock but no Indians The latter are believed to have gone down toward the mouth of the Salmon, and to be making for Gray's crossing on the Salmon, thence crossing on Snake river at the mouth of the Grande Ronde. Dispatches were forwarded to Walla Walla, to be telegraphed, so as to apprise persons in Grande Ronde and Wallowapays.

HIS FIRST LOOK AT A NEZ PERCE HAD BEEN FROM SOMEwhat of a distance: across the Salmon River that is, back three days and many, many miles ago, just before General Oliver Otis Howard had somehow willed his army column to this western side of the furious and foamy Salmon River.

An Easterner by birth and Harvard graduate by way of laurels, Thomas A. Sutherland had done a bit of traveling in Europe and the Middle East through the aid of some family money before he ended up in Portland, Oregon, working as an ill-paid stringer for the *Standard*. The very afternoon the newsroom was first abuzz with reports of the Nez Perce outbreak, the twenty-seven-year-old had abandoned everything else and marched into his editor's office, applying for this opportunity to march into the field when the army set off on its campaign to punish the hostiles, just as the army always had.

"Newsmen have always been along with the principal officer," he had declared boldly.

"And who would that be now?" he was asked.

"Why, I suppose it would be Howard himself. A general, one-armed, lost it in the Civil War, you see. I've looked up what I can on him. General Oliver Otis Howard—I shall attach myself to him."

"Just the way Mark Kellogg attached himself to Custer, will you?"

Sutherland had immediately reacted to the reference. He felt his face drain of blood as he remembered how Kellogg had gone in with Custer at the death. Two days later they had found the civilian's body among the butchered and mutilated dead.

"I don't think that has any way of happening," he retorted, tugging at his collar in the editor's steamy third-floor office. "Those were the mighty Sioux, after all. Crazy Horse, Sitting Bull—those Sioux. But these . . . these are the . . . well, they're just Nez Perce, sir."

"Very well," his editor had agreed. "I'll grant you a month's leave with the same rate of pay. Send in your dispatches by courier or telegraph if you can, but I'm not going to pay for anything extravagant from you, young man."

His heart leaped in his chest. "No, sir. Nothing extravagant at all!"

Thomas Sutherland wasn't dull-witted, either. He promptly sprinted down to the telegraph office and fired off several telegrams he sent speeding all the way across the continent, paying for the lofty charges out of his own pocket on the speculation that one of the newspapers would bite. Three days later, as he was making his final preparations to embark for Lewiston, Idaho, that very afternoon, Sutherland had received word from not only the San Francisco *Chronicle* but no less than the New York *Herald* itself! Why, he'd have eyes from coast to coast reading his copy written at the front.

He reached Lewiston the following evening, finding the town patrolled by eighty armed men under torchlight, ever watchful of any dark-skinned intruder. In the saddle before dawn the following morning, pulling his packhorse, Sutherland was bound for Fort Lapwai and points south where he could track down Howard's column.

While he soon found out he wasn't the only correspondent hurrying to the front, he alone enjoyed the élan and prestige of arriving with credentials from two of the most prestigious papers in the entire country.

"My editors wanted to assure themselves of a firsthand account for their readers on both coasts," he had explained when first introduced to the general commanding.

Clearly, such status was not lost on the famous one-armed Union general and survivor of the scandals in the Freedmen's Bureau. Since that first day, the twenty-ninth of June, Sutherland had been messing with Howard and the general's staff.

"Extend young Sutherland here every courtesy," Howard had told his headquarters staff and the officer corps that night before they made their first attempt to cross the Salmon after the Nez Perce. "See that he is not wanting for the details that will tell his readers just what a noble effort this army and its campaign is all about."

Not that there weren't times when Sutherland didn't

wonder just what he had bitten off, slogging up the narrow trail toward the Seven Devils area, high into a country where nothing but grass grew and even the mules had trouble staying upright. The soldiers lost a few of the overburdened ones careening down the side of the Salmon River canyon, tumbling some two thousand feet to a rocky death below. Cold and wet nights, when it alternated between rain and snow, followed by foggy, drizzly days. And when the sun came out the men became even more miserable when their dampened clothing gave each one of them a steam bath in the saddle!

But there were small victories as well, like the discovery two days ago of those caches left behind by the fleeing hostiles at Canoe Encampment some eight miles below Pittsburgh Landing on the Snake River—proof, so the officers claimed, that Joseph's Indians had grown desperate and were fully on the run now.

Still, it had been many days now since the army had struggled across the Salmon into this unforgiving wilderness, and the best scouting reports said the enemy was miles ahead of them. Then as the correspondent rode with Howard's advance on the afternoon of the fifth, word sent with friendly trackers from Captain Whipple at Cottonwood relayed how Joseph's hostiles had recrossed the river up ahead at a place called Craig Billy Crossing, putting not only distance but also days between them and the army in striking across the Camas Prairie.

Sutherland could read the utter frustration and seething anger on the general's face as they descended to the mouth of Billy Creek—a canyon so narrow the command had to work their way down single-file—and these officers, proven veterans of the Civil War, all studied the snow-swollen torrent that was the Salmon River . . . wondering how the Nez Perce had gotten their horse herd across, how they had managed to negotiate their women and children and camp equipage across that river racing more than seven miles per hour, foaming and tumbling like a caldron. Wondering,

Sutherland knew, how they themselves were now going to effect this army's crossing, too.

That's when Christian tracker James Reuben demonstrated how Joseph's people had reached the far side by swimming his horse into the frothy current to the north bank, then returning in due fashion. But when one of the white scouts, Frank Parker, bravely attempted the same feat, he got no farther than a few yards from the shore before the mighty current made him think retreat was a far better choice. Then Reuben instructed Howard in the old craft of constructing bull boats—but this column had few buffalo hides!

After sending two volunteers, Jack Carleton and "Laughing" Williams, upstream to commandeer some boats the command could use in ferrying men and supplies across the Salmon, Howard learned that the pair of scouts had located a boat—but in coming downstream to Billy Creek they had encountered a series of turbulent rapids, capsized, and barely escaped the river with their lives.

That's when Second Lieutenant Harrison G. Otis, artilleryman, was bold enough to point out the poor cabin standing nearby and asked one of the interpreters to see if any of the friendlies along knew what the white owner's name was.

"Why is that of any import to our crossing?" asked the general's young aide, Lieutenant C. E. S. Wood.

"Because," Otis suggested, "we could ask of the owner to disassemble it and construct a raft."

"Capital idea, sir!" Howard roared, slapping his one glove against that left thigh in exuberance.

As it turned out, the poor hovel didn't belong to a white homesteader at all.

"His name is Luke Billy?" Howard repeated as Sutherland wet the end of his pencil on the tip of his tongue and scratched down the pertinent details in his small leather-bound field ledger.

"That's what the white men call him," Ad Chapman said,

waving up one of the trackers from Lapwai. "He's a friendly himself."

"This one?" Howard asked. When the interpreter nodded, he continued, "Ask him if we can dismantle his cabin—use it for a raft to cross the river here and pursue the Joseph bands."

Without delay, Luke Billy readily agreed and even helped the young Otis and his soldiers tear down the roof and walls of his poor house here at the mouth of Billy Creek. At the same time, the cavalry was collecting all their lariats, those three-fifths-inch ropes each man was assigned to picket his mount each night, used in erecting company rows in bivouac. The logs proved to be no skimpy planks. Instead, they were at least a foot thick, measuring a foot wide by some forty feet in length. The sweating, bare-backed enlisted men hauled the rain-soaked timbers down to the bank of the Salmon, where the engineers and artillery officers took over, supervising the assembly of that huge raft on which General Oliver Otis Howard's fortunes would soon sail some two hundred yards across the white-capped, wind-whipped surface of the Salmon, so he could continue his dogged pursuit of Joseph and his bloodstained henchmen.

God knows Howard had the manpower and the resources coming to crush the upstart rebels . . . if only the army could only get the hostiles to stop and fight. It seemed that not only the division commander, McDowell, but also the leaders of the army itself in Washington wanted to snuff out this little fire, and as quickly as possible.

To Sutherland's way of thinking, despite the general's numerous setbacks, Howard simply refused to regard the Nez Perce as a serious threat. What he was fearful of more than anything else was the possibility that Joseph's hostiles would form a junction with the Indians south in the valley of the Weiser River, or with the noisy renegades along the Columbia River, even the small bands of Spokanes and other inconsequential tribes to the north and northwest who, while they were no danger of and by themselves, could make for a lot of trouble when confederated under Chief Joseph's bloody outlaw banner.

"You do realize there are some twelve thousand Indians residing in the Northwest, Mr. Sutherland," the general declared. "If Joseph is able to score a decisive victory over our forces, why, the disaffected among those tribes would likely swell the ranks of Joseph's fighting men. Instead of us having to fight hundreds, my army would be pitted against thousands! I simply must stop them and stamp out this fire in the next few days."

So as his troops sweated and groused constructing their huge raft of hewn timbers that fifth day of July, Howard disclosed to Sutherland the details of just what plans he had put into operation to counter such threats of a full-scale territorial outbreak.

"Counting what I presently have in this column, and what is already on its way to me," Howard explained, "I'll soon have ten companies of cavalry—six hundred and seventeen men. In addition, Mr. Sutherland, I'll lead six companies of infantry, one hundred and seventy-seven men. Add to that five companies of artillery, more than one hundred and sixty-six men, and your final tally shows that I'll presently be leading an army of more than nine hundred and sixty soldiers drawn from two departments of the army. Once we catch up to the Non-Treaty bands, you can plainly see why this war will be brought to a swift and dramatic conclusion."

"How long do you believe that will take, General?" he had asked while the raft took shape.

"No more than a matter of days," Howard proposed. "Tell your readers, east and west, that we'll have this outbreak over within a matter of days."

Taking what ropes they hadn't used in constructing the bulky raft, the soldiers tied the lariats end-to-end, fastening one end to the rivercraft, the other wrapped around a stout tree so that a gang of some two dozen soldiers could belay the raft into the river—hoping the men on the craft could get drift close enough to the opposite shore that a soldier could plunge into the current with a section of rope over his shoulder and make it to the north bank, where he would secure the line to another tree. Whereupon Howard would have his ferryboat!

Despite their best efforts to construct that raft, Howard's men were stymied by the full fury of the Salmon on the morning of the sixth.

While Lieutenant Otis's crew prepared to launch their raft, Lieutenant Parnell of the First U. S. Cavalry and fifteen selected men stripped naked, mounted bareback, and attempted to force the horse herd across the river. After losing more than a dozen to the Salmon, the sixteen soldiers admitted defeat and turned back to the south bank. Then came the most stinging disappointment of all.

The unimaginable power of that river was simply too much for that raft the soldiers constructed on the south bank. It came apart in the torrential current, ropes splitting and hewn timbers creaking as they were ground into nothing more than children's jackstraws by this mighty western river. Otis, his men, and matériel were all tossed into the frothy current and hurtled downstream more than four miles until they could struggle to one shore or the other. The tossing timbers of Luke Billy's dismantled cabin tumbled on, making for a junction with the Snake . . . and Lieutenant Otis fondly went down in campaign legend as "Crusoe."

Indeed, some of the young man's fellow officers quickly made up a campaign ditty, sung to the tune of "Turn Back the Pharaoh's Army":

"The raft went down the river, hal-le-lu!"

Despite those grand attempts at good humor, Sutherland watched how that string of defeats registered on Howard's bearded face. Hell, he felt the frustration take root in himself—realizing how these unschooled warrior bands had outwitted West Point's finest graduates and methodologies at every turn!

Perhaps most depressing to the general was the news brought to him here at Craig Billy Crossing by those two Christian trackers James Reuben and Captain John Levi, a report that the hostiles were in the neighborhood of Norton's ranch, where Captain David Perry had established a base of operations on the Camas Prairie. What few depressing details Sutherland overheard quickly proved that Perry's soldiers were not up to the task of stopping Joseph's devils as the Non-Treaty bands pressed on east for the Clearwater, where they would likely join forces with the Looking Glass village Captain Whipple had failed to neutralize.

After watching his cavalry's failure in their attempt to swim their horses across on the afternoon of the sixth, followed by the disintegration of Lieutenant Otis's raft on the seventh, Howard had had himself enough of this northern crossing. The shortest line that would carry him to the seat of the conflicts was to turn back upstream.

Ordering the destruction of some twenty ponies the Non-Treaties had abandoned on the south bank before their crossing, the general gave the command for a countermarch. Noisy, none-too-quiet grumbling reigned as soldiers who had just spent the last five days in this Salmon River wilderness were now told to retrace their steps back through those same hills to that crossing opposite the mouth of White Bird Creek . . . where they had first attempted to tackle this river back on the twenty-ninth of June!

"The Non-Treaties have no intention of surrendering anytime soon, Mr. Sutherland," explained young Lieutenant Wood in confidence the following evening, 7 July, when they were camped nearly opposite Rocky Canyon, close by the traditional Nez Perce gathering ground.

Having left orders for his infantry to come on with all possible speed, Howard had pushed ahead with his cavalry—accomplishing that retrograde march in something less than two days! Sutherland asked, "The general doesn't believe Joseph and his outlaws are running?"

Wood shook his head. "First came word of the defeat of

Lieutenant Rains and his scouting detail, and now friendlies have brought us news of Colonel Perry's skirmishes with the hostiles around his Cottonwood bivouac. General Howard isn't waiting until first light to dispatch help: He's sending McConville's and Hunter's volunteer companies across the river here at Rocky Canyon to make their way to Colonel Perry's troops at Camp Rains."

"The general shouldn't be angry with himself," Sutherland observed.

Wood asked, "Why shouldn't he be upset with these setbacks? We're still more than a day from reaching our crossing at White Bird Creek and Joseph's henchmen are roaming at will!"

"But Howard's demonstration on this side of the Salmon has had a great effect on the hostiles, Lieutenant," Thomas argued. "By getting this great army over here and keeping them in motion, he prevented Joseph from leading his hostiles south and west back to the naturally fortified country of his Wallowa homeland. Now he can't reach those impregnable valleys with his herds of cattle and horses to hold out against five or six times his number of fighting men. Don't you see?"

Wood's brow knit in consternation. "See what?"

Thomas had warmed to his argument. "Now Joseph and the other renegade chiefs have been forced out onto the open ground of the Camas Prairie—where they have no cover. In sending those volunteer companies across the river, General Howard is executing a bold maneuver. If all the civilians now holed up at Grangeville and Mount Idaho can be united with Colonel Perry, surely they can stop the enemy village and turn it back on General Howard . . . if not annihilate the renegades outright by themselves."

Chapter Twenty-Two

July 8, 1877

BY TELEGRAPH

—

Several Stores and Contents Burned at Pueblo.

—

General Grant Quietly Arrives at Brussels.

—

OREGON.

—

Later from the Indian War.

SAN FRANCISCO, July 6.—A dispatch to the Portland News from General Howard's camp, on the Salmon River, up to June 30th, says: Five Indians passed along Bald Mountain, opposite camp on the 29th, in full view of the soldiers. General Howard is hurrying with all possible dispatch in order to pursue or find the direction taken by the Indians. If the trail indicates that Joseph intends escaping to the buffalo country, General Howard will immediately retrace his steps to Lewiston, and endeavor to head him off by way of Harmon's creek. Captain Conneville, of the Lewiston volunteers, starts to-day to skirmish the country in the vicinity of Slate creek to find the direction Joseph has taken. The Malbar Indians, in Baker county, Oregon, are restless, and fears are entertained that they will effect a junction with the hostiles. The squaw men say that Joseph has gone toward Spokane river mill, and taken up his position in impassable gulches and canons, intending to stay and fight it out in Walowa valley. The opinion at headquarters is that he will strike for the buffalo country. Joseph has now a day and a half start on the troops. General Howard has telegraphed for a regiment of regulars, which it is understood can get here in ten days from Omaha, Nebraska. He has now about 500 men, three howitzers, and two Gatling guns.

THE LAST THREE DAYS SINCE THAT FIGHT ON THE KNOLL and the army's shilly-shallying in sending out a rescue from Cottonwood had been little more than an angry blur for Lew Wilmot.

A little while after the survivors reached Norton's ranch with their dead and wounded packed in that lumber wagon, D. H. Howser died from his injuries.

Fires were refed near twilight, not long before more than sixty civilians galloped in from the southwest, just after 6:00 P.M. It was a happy reunion for both groups: Perry's soldiers were relieved for the reinforcements who had just managed to reach them after leaving Howard's column on the far side of the Salmon, and the citizens were gratified to reach the security of the army bivouac after a narrow escape with an Indian ambush in Rocky Canyon.

Finding that the leader of the Idaho volunteers was an acquaintance from Lewiston, Edward McConville—a Civil War veteran and a steady hand who ofttimes put Wilmot up when he and Pete Ready came north to pick up supplies at that Snake riverport town, it turned out to be a happy, and intriguing, reunion.

"Tell me what happened out there today," Ed had asked that evening of the fifth as he settled onto his haunches beside Wilmot's fire.

"Ain't so much what happened out there on the prairie," Lew disclosed, "as it was what *didn't* happen right here in the soldier camp."

Then Wilmot let fly with the whole story, not dismissing a single detail about the fight that had done nothing to improve the strained, prickly relations between the army and the local civilians. Even George Shearer showed up to fill in some gaps in the story by divulging those arguments he had heard between officers, the temporary arrest of Sergeant

Simpson for disorderly conduct, and Shearer's own dash to reach the volunteers ahead of the wary soldiers.

"That war party was already pulling off when the soldiers decided to come rescue us," Wilmot sneered. "Wasn't any fight left in the Injuns by then—so it was safe for them soldiers to come out to help us."

"I'll bet some of the same bunch pulled off you came to lay an ambush for us," McConville disclosed. "You 'member which way they rode away from your hill?"

Wilmot shook his head. "Can't say as I do. Just glad to see 'em go! Why, you figger your outfit was jumped by the same Injuns killed Randall and Ben Evans?"

"Had to be the same li'l red bastards," George Shearer declared bitterly. Earlier that evening he had been elected as "major" of McConville's militia.

"I'd lay a month's wages they was the same redskins," McConville asserted, then went on to tell how General Howard had ordered his bunch and William Hunter's civilians to go to Whipple's aid.

To reach the army's camp at Cottonwood, the volunteers had stripped naked to swim their horses across the Salmon just above the mouth of Rocky Canyon. But that was only the beginning of their adventurous ride. Because that route offered the fastest journey out of the Salmon River breaks, all sixty-seven riders hurriedly redressed in their clothes and started into the narrowing canyon, repeatedly peering up at those walls towering some two thousand feet over their heads. Every man was understandably on edge, wary of ambush and knowing just how vulnerable they were. . . . The whole bunch nearly jumped out of their skins when they spotted a dozen warriors when they popped into sight about two hundred yards up the trail.

"Some of the fellas were more'n ready for a fight by then," McConville confessed. "No matter it was only a handful of the redskins."

But cooler heads prevailed and both leaders decided they had to get themselves out of that canyon. After all, their argument went, those had to be decoys, nothing less than tempting bait a larger war party was dangling out to draw the white men farther and farther into the ever-narrowing canyon.

"So we backtracked a ways and somehow managed to scramble up the side on a deer trail to reach the prairie," McConville declared. "Once we were all together on top, we lit out east for Johnson's ranch, then come round the head of the canyon, making for Cottonwood on the run."

"You see anything more of them Injuns as you come in?" Shearer asked.

The leader wagged his head. "Nothing but some smoke signals on Craig's Mountain, and a big dust cloud off the far side of Camas Prairie."

"Over toward the South Fork?" Wilmot asked.

McConville nodded. "Yep—there's no doubt that village is making for the Clearwater."

Shearer proposed, "Don't you fellas think the army would appreciate knowing where the Injuns are camped once the red bastards make theirselves to home on the South Fork?"

"Damn fine idea, George," McConville said, a twinkle coming to his eye. "What say we head back to Mount Idaho? That's where we can rest up a day or so, while we remount our outfit on some fresh horses. We can cull what we need outta that herd you run off from Looking Glass's camp."

"Once we got horses, then what?" Wilmot asked.

McConville grinned. "We have ourselves a little look-see over toward the Clearwater."

The next morning, 6 July, McConville's volunteers had escorted Randall's dead and wounded, along with most of the survivors, out of Cottonwood Station, bound for Mount Idaho. About the same time, Captain Whipple's men mounted up to ride west with Assistant Surgeon William R. Hall, assigned to retrieve the bodies of Lieutenant Rains's doomed detail. This burial detail had Perry's orders to inter the remains of the ten soldiers, which had been lying out in the hot sun for several days where they had fallen near the boulders. The officer's body would be placed in a crudely fashioned coffin and brought back to Norton's ranch for a decent Christian burial, complete with military honors.

For his part, over the last three days Lew Wilmot had stewed in his own juices, growing all the angrier, and resolved to confront General Oliver Otis Howard with the cowardice and dereliction of duty perpetrated by his subordinate Captain David Perry. Especially after Lew and his friends had laid poor Ben Evans in the ground, then held a burial for D. B. Randall with full Masonic rites in Mount Idaho's little cemetery—a quiet, shady place tucked back among some peaceful pines. Just the sort of place where Lew could get to brooding on his dead friends, all the while nursing his loathing for the man who had delayed and deliberated before sending the civilians any assistance.

As for David Perry, the captain went on with his prosecution of the war: loading up those supplies he had transported down from Fort Lapwai, then led his entire command out of their Cottonwood bivouac on the night of 8 July, after a courier brought word that Howard's advance was approaching Grangeville, exactly where the army had started out on their merry chase thirteen days before!

Earlier that Sunday, McConville had come looking for Lew at Wilmot's tiny home in Mount Idaho. "We're leaving, Lew. Give the family your farewell."

After warmly embracing Louisa and his four children, Wilmot followed his friend into the shadows between some ramshackle buildings.

"There's much afoot, Lew," Ed McConville said as they stood watching three soldiers slowly walk past the nearby barricades. "I've been doing a lot of thinking and talking with some of the men while you been to see your family, Lew."

"What's this got to do with?"

McConville took a deep breath. "I don't figger the army means to do much fighting."

Wilmot snorted, his gall rising again just to think about how the soldiers were far, far better at sitting on their hands than they ever were at fighting. "Howard or Perry, they're the same when it comes to catching the Nez Perce: always a day late and a dollar short."

McConville nodded. "These officers can bumfuggle all they want, but they're never gonna catch up to the Injuns. Why, Frank Fenn and I went to talk with Howard himself when he was sitting on his thumbs at Craig Billy Crossing."

"What'd you tell him?"

"It's what I showed him," McConville explained. "That's a narrow ford, Lew. A few of his men could've defended that crossing if he'd sent some cavalry ahead—or sent word to Whipple for him to get soldiers over from Cottonwood to block the road."

"I don't figger Howard listened to you."

"Oh, he listened to our suggestions politely enough," McConville replied. "Then told us that he believed himself fully competent to manage his own campaign!"

"So what you figure to do now on your own?"

"We've rode down to the mouth of the White Bird late yesterday, where Howard gave our battalion some ammunition since I told him we was going to find out where them hostiles are for him. You wanna come on a little ride with me?"

"Ride? Where?"

"We're gonna cover some ground before nightfall and maybe do a little fighting on our own by morning. It's for certain this army doesn't wanna rub up against the Injuns." Then McConville reached out to grab Wilmot's forearm. "That's why I wanted you to get said what needed saying to Louisa and the young'uns now."

"Just you and me going on this ride?"

"The whole outfit," McConville declared. "Now we got seventy-five ready to ride out tonight, my boys from Lewiston, your bunch from Mount Idaho, along with Hunter's men from over at Dayton—they throwed in with us at Rocky Canyon for the rest of the war. Hunter and Jim Cearly just come back in. From the sounds of things,

Joseph's can muster more'n three hundred fighting men. We gotta go find that camp."

"Where you figger on looking?"

McConville said, "Forks of the Clearwater. Wanna get that far north before first light."

Wilmot grinned in the shadows. "Sounds like a fine plan, Captain McConville."

"That's another thing, Lieutenant Wilmot." McConville cleared his throat self-consciously. "I ain't a captain no more."

"Shit—don't tell me someone else is boss of this outfit now!" Wilmot groaned, his belly turning a flop with disappointment. "Not that goddamned Cearly who wanted to take over Randall's bunch when D. B. was killed?"

"Naw," and McConville shook his head. "Way things turned out when we was planning our scout this afternoon, the whole bunch elected Hunter as their lieutenant colonel, and voted me to serve as their colonel."

"*C-colonel* are you now?" Wilmot shrieked with joy, slapping McConville on the back as they turned and stomped away, past the tangle of barricades erected at the end of the street, approaching that large cluster of horsemen gathered back near the shadows cast by a grove of pines.

As they stopped among the others and George Shearer handed them both the reins to their horses, Lew looked over the more than seventy men who stood at the ready beside their fresh mounts selected from that herd taken from Looking Glass's band seven days before, every grim-faced volunteer bristling with weapons and eager for this scout to find the enemy village.

Wilmot smiled in the morning light as he turned to their leader just then swinging into the saddle and said, "All right, *Colonel* McConville. Let's go put our noses on the scent and scare us up some Nez Perce."

As they had crossed the Camas Prairie, war parties from the Non-Treaty bands fanned out to search each settler's homestead. Knowing full well that every Shadow family had already scurried toward the towns where they had erected their barricades, the warriors tore through every room in every building, looking for anything of value to them or in trade with the white men for ammunition. The rest they destroyed or burned. Shore Crossing's party left each structure they came across no more than a smoking ruin when they mounted up and rode on to find the next farm dotting the lonely prairie.

If the Shadows had attempted to force the *Nee-Me-Poo* off their ancestral lands, then his warriors were going to see that those Shadows had little to return to once the Non-Treaty bands had cut a swath of destruction through central Idaho. Maybe then, their leaders hoped, the white men would clear out and allow the *Nee-Me-Poo* to live unmolested and in peace once more.

Following the narrow canyon of the Cottonwood east to its junction with the South Fork of the Clearwater—at the traditional camping place called *Pitayiwahwih**—the fighting bands were reunited with Looking Glass's Alpowai, who had at first refused to join with White Bird and *Toohoolhoolzote* at *Tepahlewam.* Now two days** after the fighting bands' skirmish with the Shadows on a low hill, the Non-Treaties set up a large camp erected for the most part on a wide plot of flat ground stretching down the west bank of the narrow river, just upstream from the mouth of the Cottonwood. A handful of families chose to erect their lodges on the narrow strip of ground between the east bank of the Clearwater and the high, steep bluffs that protected the valley. The village numbered a minimum of 750 women and children and boasted of more than two hundred fighting men.

That night, a furious and resentful Looking Glass called a gathering of the leaders so that he could speak to those

---

*Literally meaning "mouth of the canyon," a few miles above the present-day town of Stites, Idaho. In the historic literature, this Nez Perce term is sometimes rendered *Peeta Auuwa.*

**July 7, 1877.

men he had disdained and rebuked the last time they gathered.

"Six days ago my camp was attacked by soldiers," he told those faces lit by leaping flames. "I tried to surrender in every way I could. My horses, lodges, and everything I had was taken away from me by the soldiers we have done so much for. But I know better."

Looking Glass waited for the grunts of approval to fade, then continued, "Now, my people, as long as I live I will never make peace with the treacherous Shadows. I did everything I knew to preserve their friendship and be friends with the white man. What more could I have done?"

Again he waited while the approval became noisier. His eyes narrowing with menace, Looking Glass said, "It was because I was a good friend of theirs that I was attacked. The soldier chief who came to my camp may say it was a mistake what he did. But that is a lie. He is a dog, and I have been treated worse than a dog by him! He lies if he says he did not know it was *my* camp. I stand before you tonight to say I am ready for war!"

Every war chief and fighting man was suddenly on his feet, for this was a great reunion of the warrior bands who had never buckled under to the treaty.

His strong voice becoming a powerful roar, Looking Glass harangued the crowd, "Come on and let us attack the soldiers at Cottonwood. Many a man dies for his dear native land and we might as well die in battle as any other way!"

The clamor raised from all the war cries and wolf yelping made the hair bristle on Shore Crossing's forearms. Now they had the strength of a man's fist, with all five fingers tightly united into action: White Bird, *Toohoolhoolzote*, Joseph, along with *Huishuishkute*, known as Bald or Shorn Head, the Palouse leader . . . and finally Looking Glass.

Three of these other chiefs came forward one-by-one to call for an all-out fight against the treacherous Shadows.

Only Joseph did not step into the firelight and add his voice to the call for total resistance.

The following day was one of nothing but relaxation for the warriors who lay about in camp while many of the Non-Treaty people journeyed north to Kamiah to attend Dreamer services that Christian morning.* From this camp a few raiding parties came and went, striking the nearby farms of Lawyer's reservation Indians—driving off their stock of horses and cattle. Scouts, too, rode in and out of camp, slipping onto Camas Prairie to watch for movements of the *suapies* and the civilians venturing out from their fortified settlements. The chiefs needed to know if Cut-Off Arm would come traipsing after them again after they had embarrassed him across the Salmon.

They didn't have long to wait for an answer.

But this time the *Nee-Me-Poo* were completely surprised that it wasn't soldiers who came looking for them.

---

*Sunday, July 8, 1877.

CHAPTER TWENTY-THREE

JULY 9, 1877

BY TELEGRAPH

—

Incoherent Accounts of the Indian War.

—

Hard to Tell What the Hostiles are Doing.

—

OREGON.

—

Latest from the Indian War.

SAN FRANCISCO, July 7.—A special dispatch from Lewiston, July 4, via Walla the 6th, says Colonel Whipple's command, with volunteers under N. B. Randall, came across Looking Glass' band at Clear Creek at 7 a.m. The Indians told the colonel that they were prepared to fight, and opened the ball by the first shot. When the order was given to commence firing the Indians soon broke for the hills and places of shelter. It is not known how many were killed or wounded, as they scampered in all directions. The command captured the Indian camp, burned all their provisions and plunder, and took about a thousand Indian horses, which they brought here. No citizens or soldiers were killed or wounded. The command returned last night . . .

News received at department headquarters from Gen. Sully, commanding at Lewiston, says Col. Perry with thirty men, on his way to Cottonwood, was attacked by hostiles. Lieut. Rainez and ten soldiers and two civilians were killed. Col. Whipple joined Col. Perry, and drove the Indians off. The fight is still going on. Maj. Jackson's company of first cavalry, which left Fort Vancouver yesterday morning, will arrive at Lewiston tomorrow at noon. The following dispatch comes from Walluwa. It was probably received by the steamer Tennie, which arrived at headquarters Thursday night. They say that Joseph decoyed Gen. Howard across the Salmon river, and then Joseph recrossed the river and got on the Cottonwood between Howard and Lapwai, within thirty miles of Lewiston . . .

Fort Lapwai
July 9, 1877

Dear Mamma,

I must send you a note this morning or you will be anxious about us. We are all alive and well, though all very anxious and in confusion. If you were not so far away, I would come home at once, but I can't bear to think of leaving John and going so far from him. I am thinking seriously of going down to Portland on the next boat and waiting there until things are settled. This post is in such confusion and excitement continually that I feel my strength departing, though I do so want to be a strong woman and able for whatever happens.

There have been so many alarms of Indian attacks, and so many horrible stories are continually being brought in that John says he wants to send us away. This matter may be settled in a few days, and I will not make up my mind what I will do until we hear further.

Our trouble is not enough troops. Another regiment is expected here in this Department at once, but what is a regiment these days? The companies are so small that it only means a hundred or so men after all. Joseph has had strong reinforcements and he has managed so wonderfully that he has been successful everywhere. Another fine young officer, such a nice fellow, has been killed, and we have lost about fifty men. It is time the tide turned!

. . . I will write a longer and more connected letter next mail. We are all right here. Don't be alarmed about us. It is only the worry and anxiety that Doctor wants to save me by sending me away. I don't think I will leave Lapwai, not unless the troubles increase. We all join in love.

Your loving daughter,
Emily F.

THE LOUD REPORT OF THAT SINGLE GUNSHOT SNAPPED Lew Wilmot awake.

"Shit," someone nearby whimpered in the dark. "I-I didn't mean to—"

In a blur, McConville loomed over John Atkinson, wrenching the volunteer's .50-caliber Springfield rifle from his hands. "Keep your eyes open now, boys," the leader growled. "I expect some company to show up real soon."

Wilmot swallowed hard as he swiveled the lever down and opened the action on his big needle-gun. He had a reputation as being the best shot on the Camas Prairie. And now that this poor daisy from Hunter's bunch had just announced to the whole canyon that they were there . . . Lew Wilmot was going to have to prove just how good a shot he was, all over again.

By midday on the eighth, McConville's seventy-five volunteers had crossed the open, rolling land to reach the canyon of the Cottonwood, following the creek until dark, when they decided they could go no farther and went into a cold camp. McConville's subordinate "Captain" Benjamin F. Morris divided the men into two watches, then put out the first round of pickets while the others tried to catch a little sleep right where they had landed when they came out of the saddles. Lew tried but could not do anything but listen to the sounds of the night, thinking about his three daughters and that brand-new baby boy.

Them and poor George Hunter—who lay back in Loyal P. Brown's hotel turned hospital after he had been shot in the shoulder by another volunteer from Dayton in Washington Territory, Eugene Talmadge Wilson, climaxing a quick, hot argument reaching the boiling point after a long-simmering feud the two had carried with them into the Nez Perce War. Wilson was under arrest back in Mount Idaho.

Wilmot wondered why a man like Wilson had failed to realize there were more than enough warriors to go around when he got mad enough he had to shoot George Hunter. A few of Hunter's friends had been understandably edgy as they lit out on their scout, and Wilson's friends were even standoffish by the time they made camp night before last.

Just as Wilmot was dozing off in the dark, one of the pickets from the first watch clambered back into camp to announce that he had discovered that they were less than a mile from the Nez Perce village located at the mouth of the Cottonwood. McConville picked John McPherson to carry word back to Howard that night, since the general was expected in Grangeville before morning.

"You might figger to send another rider or two off with the same news," Lew suggested in the dark as the anxious men settled down to await the dawn.

"Think McPherson might get jumped?"

Wilmot nodded in the starshine. "They're bound to have scouts and outriders sniffing around."

"Then why the hell haven't they found us?" James Cearly goaded in a whisper.

Before Wilmot could snap, McConville said, "Unless you two figger out a way to get along, I'm gonna order you both back to Mount Idaho."

Wilmot was just waiting for McConville to take a breath. "Colonel—"

"Your arguing likely gonna cost the lives of some of these men," McConville interrupted. "Either you get along, or you get out."

Lew looked at Cearly's face, waiting for the other man to make the first move . . . then said, "All right, Colonel. I can get along with any man if I'm given half a chance."

"Me, too," Cearly replied, holding his hand out. "Besides, we're gonna need to have the best shot on Camas Prairie with us if we run into trouble tomorrow."

"All right," McConville said as he settled on his haunches. "I'm gonna send out two more men with orders to get word to Howard."

After George Riggins and P. C. Malin were on their way, each taking a different route back to Mount Idaho, McConville dispatched E. J. Bunker and nine other men toward a high hill figured to be halfway between their bivouac and the enemy camp.

"Bunker, you and your men are under orders to hold that hill at all hazards. Be sure you give the alarm at the first approach of Indians."

Hours later, McConville crawled back to where Wilmot was resting, propped against a tree. He signaled Lew to follow him and together they crabbed over to where James Cearly was dozing.

"We got about an hour or so left till first light," McConville whispered. "I want the both of you to have a look at that camp. Close as you can. Count the lodges; see the strength of those Injuns. Then get back here afore sunup."

The two of them had gotten well within a half-mile of the village before they decided they had little time to beat a retreat back to the bivouac.

Wilmot had reported upon their return, "We counted seventy-two tepees, Colonel. From what we could see in the dark, we counted more than one hundred and fifty of their ponies staked right in camp."

"It look to you that all the bands were there?"

Cearly nodded. "We waited till the first light started to show across the Clearwater—just to be sure we had counted everything we could see."

"We headed back when the herder boys crossed the river toward a few other lodges and their ponies," Lew explained.

McConville called the rest of the men together that dawn, and they discussed their options. Couriers were already on their way to the soldiers, although a significant number of the volunteers doubted Howard and Perry would ever have the will to prosecute this war the way it should have been fought from the very beginning. In fact, many of the volunteers from Mount Idaho even feared the murdering redskins would either get away with their crimes completely or come slinking back to Howard for a compromise and protection from the outraged citizens. To their way of thinking, General O. O. Howard had proven he would make a better missionary than an Indian fighter. At the end of their long, angry discussions, however, they decided to wait and see what the soldiers would do, what word might come back from Howard.

"We'll wait out the day right here," their leader told them. "If we haven't heard from the general by nightfall, I'll send out another dispatch with news on the strength of the camp. When Howard gets here, we'll join in the attack."

They had waited out the morning, then midday as the sun rose higher and hotter, making Lew all the sleepier as the insects buzzed and droned around their faces. He had just been drifting off when that gun belonging to one of Hunter's men tumbled from its stand against a tree and discharged.

They were in the soup now!

"Bring the water!" Wilmot was yelling as he clambered to his feet.

"Where we going?" one of the Dayton volunteers demanded.

Lew pointed at the hill.* "There—where the colonel sent Bunker and his men."

"T-that's *toward* the Injuns!" another Dayton man whined.

"But it's the highest hill we can reach in this country before the Injuns get to us," McConville snarled. "Now do what Wilmot told you: get your canteens filled at the creek and push on for that hill—on the double!"

---

*"Misery Hill" (sometimes called Camp Misery) is located on present-day Doty Ridge.

Those who had brass kettles along filled them with water, making the sprint for that hill an interesting one as they attempted to keep as much water from sloshing out of the vessels as possible as they covered that broken ground and deadfall. By the time the first of them reached Bunker's position, they found those ten guards already prying stones out of the ground with their belt knives and dragging up downed trees to throw up some sort of breastworks.

Lew nodded as he rode up and spun to the ground, pitching his two canteens into the pile McConville was supervising at the center of the scene. It was a good spot; that much was for sure. Nearly flat on top, the crest was as good as anyplace to make a last stand.

"A damn sight better'n that grassy rise on the Camas Prairie," Lew muttered under his breath as he turned his horse among the others and started toward the breastworks, where all of McConville's volunteers were feverishly scratching at the ground, digging rifle pits with their belt knives or tin cups. Anything that could move some dirt.

It wasn't many minutes before some two dozen horsemen appeared, the first to come investigate. Lew had to give the Nez Perce credit for being smart bastards. They could see the white men had a decided advantage on top of their hill. The warriors didn't make a charge or press an attack. Instead, they seemed content with surrounding the knoll with more than a hundred fighting men, occasionally firing an ill-placed shot and constantly hurling oaths at the volunteers. Into that long, hot afternoon and evening, it was a long-distance scrap, if anything.

Then darkness fell and they were all reminded to be extra cautious about making any noise. Their ears were going to have to warn them if any warriors were sneaking up on their fortifications. Besides, there weren't many of them even trying at some sleep, not the way the volunteers shivered with the cold in their sweat-dampened clothes, none of them having blankets along.

A little after 11:00 P.M., while the second watch was on

duty, the hillside below them fell quiet for the longest time . . . until the clatter of hooves shattered the starlight.

"They charging?" some man shrieked in terror.

"No, goddammit!" came a growl from the other side of the hilltop as the hammer of hoofbeats faded. "The red pricks just run off our horses!"

"We're staying put for sure now!" Cearly grumbled.

Wilmot nodded. "I wasn't planning on going nowhere anyway."

Not long after midnight the warriors burst forth with a litany of unearthly war cries and screeches, accompanied by the calls of wild birds, the howl of a prairie wolf, and the scream of the mountain panther. It had lasted for the better part of an hour when, from all sides, the warriors opened up a sudden and frightening gunfire. Tongues of yellow and red jetted from the muzzles of their rifles, many of which had been stolen from the dead in White Bird Canyon.

"Just stay down!" McConville hollered.

"You heard the colonel!" Wilmot shouted. "Keep your heads down and they won't have nothing to hit!"

After listening to some steady, sustained fire coming from one of the rifle pits, Wilmot crawled over to find a volunteer firing into the black of night.

"Elias," Lew whispered, "just what the blazes you shooting at?"

Nonplussed, Elias Darr looked over his shoulder and replied, "I-I don't know, Lew. It's so goddamned dark I can't see a blamed thing . . . but I thought it was a good idea to keep the ark a-moving."

With a smile, Wilmot put his hand on his friend's shoulder. "Elias, I figger an even better idea is to save your ammunition for morning, when we might need to move the ark even more."

Some sporadic harassing fire from the enemy was kept up on into the blackening of night as the moon fell. Then as first light started to bloom, the firing died away and the hillside fell quiet again. Afraid of drawing a bullet, the volunteers maintained an uneasy silence.

"Hey, you fellas!" a voice cried from down the hillside, heavy with Nez Perce accent.

The volunteers fell silent, watchful and wary of some trick.

Finally one of them hollered, "What you want, you red nigger?"

"We going to breakfast allee same Hotel de France!" the voice called out, referring to one of the best hotels in Lewiston. "You fellas come over and eat with us!"

Wilmot couldn't help it. He started snorting with laughter at the image that created in his head—this band of grubby civilian horsemen setting down for breakfast in the dining room of that fancy hotel with some painted, half-naked Non-Treaty savages.

As a lark, Lew sang out, "No—I got a better idea, fellas. You boys come on in here and have breakfast with us! C'mon now."

For a moment it was deathly quiet; then the voice came again from the timber, "I no think so, fellas. You ain't got nothing to eat much!"

McConville chuckled, grinning at Wilmot. "Leastways they got that right, Lew. We don't have much at all in the way of hold-out food!"

An hour later, as his pocket watch was nearing 7:00 A.M., several of the men on the other side of the breastworks called out a warning.

"They're coming at us now, for God's sake!"

Bunker was pointing as Wilmot came loping over. Down near the base of the hill in the summer sunlight they could see at least a hundred of the warriors lining up in a broad front, as if preparing to make a massed charge on foot.

"Hold your fire until you see the color of the paint on their faces!" Wilmot ordered.

"That's right," McConville agreed. "Make every bullet count!"

Then as the volunteers were hunkering down behind the

rocks and deadfall, preparing to sell their lives dearly in those shallow rifle pits, a pair of Nez Perce rode up to the warrior lines, waving and gesturing. In seconds that line of chargers dispersed, turning away to fetch up their ponies lazily grazing in the grassy swales below the hill. One by one and in pairs the warriors mounted up and started away, heading back in the direction of their camp.

Finally, McConville asked, "Hey, Lew—you think they pulled off for good? Or is this a trick?"

He wagged his head. "I dunno, Colonel. Just when a fella thinks he's got these Nez Perce figgered out, that's when they'll up and surprise him—catch 'im in a trap . . . and kill 'im."

Chapter Twenty-Four

July 9–10, 1877

BY TELEGRAPH

—

More Dispatches From the Front— Serious State of Affairs.

WASHINGTON, July 7.—The following telegram from Gen. McDowell, commanding the military department of the Pacific, was received at the war department this morning:

SAN FRANCISCO, July 5.—*Adjutant General, Washington.*—The following telegrams, both from Lewiston, have just been received from my aide-de-camp I had sent up to Gen. Howard's command. The first telegram, July 4th, says: No news direct from Gen. Howard since the first. The Klamath company is expected to-morrow. Shall go with it. Captain Whipple's detachment struck a band of Nez Perces, under Looking Glass, at Kawais, Sunday, and inflicted severe punishment, capturing a large amount of stock. Indian Inspector Watkins, who has recently been with Gen. Howard, writes from Lapwai this afternoon, to Gen. Sully here, that this success, and Gen. Howard's vigorous action are producing marked results. Looking Glass wishes to come in with his band. Watkins states that Joseph has crossed the Salmon and is making east for the Bitter Rock country, with General Howard at his heels and Whipple barring the way, but Joseph thus harassed is on the point of breaking up. There are no signs of the other Indians taking a hand.

The second dispatch is dated the 5th, and says the following was received from Captain Perry, dated 9 a.m., and that the Cottonwood Indians have been around us all day in force and very demonstrative. It is unsafe to send anything to him until the Klamath company arrives. He urges that it be sent to his command with all dispatch. Information just up by boat postpones the arrival of that company a day or two. Still no news from Howard. It is probable his courier has been intercepted. A citizen from Colville just in represents the situation on the Spokanes as most threatening. General Sully, who is here, shares in his apprehensions. It seems there is ample ground for General Howard's application for more troops.

Signed
KEELER,
Aide de Camp.

Instead of sending the infantry as directed I have determined to send it as General Howard desired, that is by rail to San Francisco and by steamer to Portland, thence by boats to Lewiston. The troops en route to Boize City, Idaho, will be sufficient, I believe, for that district, which can be more readily reinforced than that of Columbia. I have ordered all the troops from Fort Yuma, two companies to Boize, and have broken up Camp Independence and sent the company to the same destination.

MCDOWELL,
Major General.

"HAVE YOURSELF A LOOK, COLONEL."

Wilmot handed his looking glass to Ed McConville. It was no more than a heartbeat before the civilian commander took the long brass tube from his eye. "That for sure looks like a band of volunteers coming our way, Lew."

"And that war party headed for them?"

McConville half-grinned. "You think you can come up with some way to help those fellas afore that war party rides 'em down?"

Wilmot stood at the edge of the breastworks. "Can you spare twenty men?"

"Surely. That'll even up the odds something nicely," Mc-

Conville declared, then called for volunteers to accompany Lew Wilmot as he went to spoil the war party's ambush of those horsemen headed for their hilltop fortress.

What with the Nez Perce running off all their good horses just before midnight, those twenty-one men had nothing more than a dozen poor and played-out horses the Nez Perce considered unfit to ride. Instead, Lew and the others vaulted over their low rock-and-log walls and started down the southern slope on foot, ever watchful that they themselves weren't being lured into a trap by the wily Nez Perce who had disappeared into a ravine that would eventually carry them onto the prairie near the oncoming white riders.

By the time those civilian horsemen were a half-mile away from Wilmot's volunteers, the Indians put in a show just off to the riders' left. . . . But it was only a matter of heartbeats until Lew had his twenty spread out five feet apart and kneeling down to take steady aim at the enemy advancing on the horsemen, thereby springing a surprise on those who had hoped to spring a surprise of their own.

Beneath an intermittent shower of bullets and epithets from the chagrined warriors, the riders continued on their advance until they approached Wilmot's footmen.

"By the glory of ol' Jupiter hisself!" roared George Shearer. "If that ain't Lew Wilmot!"

He loped up close to his friend as the horsemen swirled around those twenty men on foot, every one of them huzzahing and congratulating one another on their rescue.

"Seeing your face here must mean the soldiers are right behind you!" Wilmot bellowed as they shook.

Shearer stopped pumping his friend's arm, his face draining of joy. "No, Lew. There ain't no soldiers comin' behind us."

"N-no soldiers? Didn't Howard get to Grangeville after we left on the eighth?"

The Southerner nodded. "Says he ain't marchin' till he gets all his men up from their mess gettin' across the Salmon."

It wasn't good news, not good news at all, they carried back to those breastworks. Instead of learning they had only to wait a matter of hours for the arrival of Howard's column, McConville's volunteers could come to no other conclusion but that they had been abandoned by the army.

For some of those men, like Lew Wilmot, it felt as if they had been discarded and left to the Nez Perce all over again.

"Lew, I want you and Penny to pick the two best horses George's men rode in here," McConville ordered.

"You best be sending me with a message for Howard," Wilmot said. "And your dispatch better say something about soldiers sitting on their asses while civilians are fighting this goddamned war for 'em."

McConville shrugged it off. "The two of you will carry word to Howard all right," he told them both, "but rather than infuriate that pompous ol' Bible-thumper, I'll inform him of our dire situation and only *request* reinforcements."

After darkness had fully swallowed the valley of the Clearwater, Lew Wilmot and Benjamin Penny led those two strong horses out of the breastworks and down the bare slope, making for the closest patch of timber. There they would wait for a few minutes, listening to every night sound, before they finally mounted up and dared to ride into the open beneath that blackened banner of starry sky.

Heart thumping, Wilmot finally nudged Ben Penny with a tap on the shoulder, and they both mounted up. Without a word exchanged between them, the horsemen quickly shook hands, reined about, and put their heels to their mounts, leaping out of the timber onto the barren ground where a few hours earlier a swarm of warriors had been waving blankets and hollering for white blood.

Lew couldn't recall if he had remembered to breathe that first mile or not. But by the time he figured they had come a half-dozen miles on the backs of those racing horses, Lew Wilmot had indeed begun to breathe easier and finally started thinking about Louisa and those children as the animal rocked beneath him in the dark. Closer and closer, with every lunge of those powerful legs. With every mile, he was leaving that enemy village and those miserable breastworks farther and farther behind.

"You see that?" Penny asked more than five harrowing hours later. It might be the dim flicker of a fire. And from the outline of the stars to the south it appeared that was the heights rising above Mount Idaho just ahead . . . but the fire lay to the southeast instead of the south. Unless he'd gotten turned around. Another glow appeared now as they rounded the brow of a low hill. Then within another mile and a broad sweep of prairie more than a hundred watch fires lay in the distance.

"That can't be Grangeville!" Wilmot cried, his voice raspy with disuse.

Benjamin Penny exclaimed, "What the hell are them fires?"

"That has to be Howard's camp. And those are his soldiers."

His eyes stung, too. They had made their escape.

The sky was graying in the east by the time the two horsemen guided their lathered animals across the South Fork of the Clearwater on the Jackson Bridge and reined into that great encampment spread near the gutted, looted ruin of the Walls ranch.*

"Who goes there!" a cry came out of the dawn's murky light.

"We're looking for General Howard!"

The guards and curious soldiers formed a cordon, refusing to allow the civilians through.

"Who's asking?"

"We need to speak with the general," Wilmot said, trying hard to keep his anger from boiling. He shook an arm to the north. "There's more'n eighty men fighting for their lives off yonder! We've found the goddamned village for you! Why don't you soldiers get up off your rumps and come fight the redskins with us?"

---

*Just outside the present-day community of Harpster, Idaho.

"I'll take you to General Howard," a voice announced as a young officer pushed his way through the older enlisted men.

The officer asked the civilians to dismount and turn over their horses to a saddler sergeant before the three set off down a row of company tents where morning fires were being coaxed back into life and sleepy, trail-weary men were slowly getting onto their feet, rubbing knuckles into gritty eyes.

"I should be ready to move on the morrow," General Oliver Otis Howard told the civilians after he had listened to their story and told them he was aware of McConville's plight from an earlier messenger. "Until then, I can't advise engaging the Nez Perce."

"Right now, right here," Wilmot said with no little exasperation, "you've got twice as many soldiers as they got warriors!"

"Good sir, I will not be dissuaded by you from my campaign," Howard snipped. "I think it goes without question that I know more about such things than either of you, or Captain McConville."

"He's a colonel now," Lew said.

"A . . . *colonel* you say," Howard replied with the hint of a grin as two of his aides turned aside with contemptuous smiles on their faces. "Please tell Colonel McConville that he and his battalion are in this kettle of fish because he did not seek out my advice or attempt to work in concert with me."

"I think the entire battalion volunteered to go on our mission because your officers and this damned army haven't done anything but eat tack soup for more'n two weeks!" Wilmot exploded, watching a sudden look of shock cross Howard's face. Instantly he figured he was better off not shaming this soldier. "The Nez Perce are making fools of your officers, General."

"I got here as quickly as I could, sir," a voice announced as it came up behind Wilmot and Penny.

Lew turned to see Captain David Perry stepping up beside Howard.

"Are you gentlemen acquainted with Colonel Perry, commander of my cavalry battalion?"

"Yeah, I know him," Wilmot answered. "Last run onto him at Cottonwood."

Howard turned slightly, speaking to Perry. "These men have just come in from McConville's volunteers, with another request for us to go to their assistance."

The captain said, "You explained to them that we'll be waiting until we have our entire infantry and artillery wings reunited with us, General?"

"I can see the color of this horse!" Wilmot roared. "You fellas are just like all them Union generals was in the war: waiting till you got more soldiers than the enemy before you'll think of budging—"

As two of the general's aides stepped forward, Howard said, "This interview is over."

"Over?" Wilmot snapped. "I was figuring I might be able to talk sense to you, General Howard. But I can see how this Cottonwood coward has poisoned your mind!"

"Coward?" Perry growled.

"That's what you are when you didn't come to the aid of our civilians last Thursday."

"You're accusing me of cowardice?"

"I haven't seen a goddamned thing to make me change my opinion of you."

"You're nothing less than a low-class liar, mister!" Perry snapped. "Fabrications and nothing but half-truths, General."

Wilmot snorted, "What lies, Perry?"

"You just told the general I never came to your aid," Perry retorted. "I did send out the cavalry and infantry both, and a fieldpiece under Lieutenant Shelton, too!"

"Not till you were shamed into it!" Wilmot said forcefully, but to Howard instead of speaking to Perry. "Then George Shearer led your men out to our position on his own—alone!"

"I have no control over the actions of civilians," Perry snarled, whirling on Howard. "I had an entire train of supplies and ammunition destined for you, which I had to protect, General. I could not chance that train falling into enemy hands because of their diversionary tactic—"

"The only reason you sent help was you were shamed by your own officers into sending us some relief!" Wilmot's voice rose a notch higher.

"Get out of here now!" Perry shouted, his face flushing. "Your very presence in this army camp fills me with contempt!"

"C-contempt?" Wilmot echoed loudly with a snort. "You ain't got one-half the contempt for me that I hold for you—so I will leave your goddamned camp!"

Twisting around on his heel, Wilmot was brushing past Penny when Howard bellowed, "Stop where you are! Arrest that man!"

Flicking a glance over his shoulder, Lew saw several of the general's staff lunge for him. On instinct he bolted into a run, but he got no more than three long steps before he found himself in the arms of a pair of armed guards. And both men were a lot beefier than rail-thin Lew Wilmot. They manhandled him back to Howard, his toes barely dragging the ground.

"Perry—when you die, you're gonna be turned away from the gates of both Heaven and Hell!" Lew growled as the soldiers clamped down all the harder on his arms and removed his pistol from its holster. "When you die and your body's gonna be laying out on the prairie . . . the coyote's gonna tuck his tail between his legs and sneak off. The buzzard will fly away from your stinking carcass, and even the little worm that would delight to worry the carcass of a lowly dog will crawl away from yours in disgust—"

"Mr. Wilmot!" the general shouted, red-faced. "It makes my blood boil to hear a civilian blaspheme an officer!"

Struggling between the two large men who imprisoned him, Wilmot said, "Not half as much as it makes my blood boil for this coward to tell me right to my face that I lied!"

The general took a deep breath, staring at the graying sky for a long moment as if attempting to regain his composure. "Why don't you calm yourself, and we'll put this entire affair behind us. I would rather you serve as a guide for us, to show my column where that Indian camp is, instead of placing you under arrest."

Wilmot stared hard at Perry, then turned his withering gaze on Howard. "No, because you're both cut of the same cloth. I ain't gonna guide for either one of you. Hell, I prefer fighting alongside the Indians now to fighting for your officers!"

Howard jutted his bearded chin angrily. "Take this civilian to the officer of the day and tell him I've placed him under arrest."

"What for?" Wilmot snarled as the guards uprooted him off his feet once more.

"I don't have to have a reason right now, Mr. Wilmot," Howard said. Then, looking at one of the guards, he added, "Have the officer of the day put him in shackles until tomorrow when we're ready to march. That should give you enough time to cool down and reconsider your contempt for the officers who are here prosecuting this campaign . . . so you civilians can live in peace on what was once Nez Perce land."

"Is that it, General?" Wilmot shouted over his shoulder. "You and your soldiers don't wanna fight no war to protect your own goddamned citizens?"

Howard took two steps following the guards who had a firm grip on their prisoner and said, "Sometimes, Mr. Wilmot, in this dirty little war, I wonder who really needs protecting from whom. If it isn't the Nez Perce who need our protection from the likes of you!"

Chapter Twenty-Five

July 11, 1877

BY TELEGRAPH

—

More of the Mexican Border
Troubles.

—

The Administration Strongly
Favoring Invasion.

—

No Satisfactory News From
General Howard.

—

OREGON.

—

Latest from the Indian War.

SAN FRANCISCO, July 9.—A press dispatch from Portland has the following from Lewiston, under date of the 6th, via Walla Walla, 9th: Left Horse-shoe bend and came down Salmon river near its junction with the Snake, leaving Howard in force up the river. A courier express is just in from Colonel Perry who was en route for Howard with a pack train, and an escort of thirty men, says he was attacked on the 4th and ten soldiers and two citizens killed. Captain Whipple, in command at Cottonwood, came to the rescue and repulsed the Indians. The latter are in force around Colonel Perry and Captain Whipple who have only force enough for defence. The route is unsafe to Cottonwood. It is a bold stroke of Joseph and his band, and it is reported by signal to the Indians north and east, and stirs them up to the offensive . . . The Indians have destroyed some fields and gardens and rifled some dwellings. News here this morning indicates a purpose to meet or act with those on the Spokane and such a move will imperil all the upper settlements on the Palouse. It is evident that a volunteer cavalry in large force ought to be put in the field to reinforce General Howard and stop this uprising before it assumes larger and more definite proportions.

Fort Lapwai
July 11, 1877

Dear Mamma,

. . . Everything here has been in such confusion that I believe my mind is in the same condition. I can't tell you, or expect you to imagine, what a horrible time we have had and the unsettled state of everything for the last few weeks. I shall be so thankful when it is all over and we can go to sleep at night without imagining that we will be awakened by hearing Indian yells before morning.

You probably see by the papers what Mr. Joseph is doing. He is the smartest Indian I ever heard of, and does the most daring and impudent things. The command under General Howard in the field is so small that scarcely anything more can be done than to protect settlements. The country all about this region is so particularly adapted to Indian fighting that Joseph has every advantage and would have, even if the soldiers outnumbered him three to one. We know that Joseph's force numbers over two hundred, and we think it may be much more, as it is thought that there are a great many Indians who have joined him lately. No one has any doubts but that a few more successes for his band will bring to him all the Non-Treaty Indians in this Department, and there are hundreds and hundreds of them, different tribes all scattered along the Columbia River. Another regiment of infantry will be here within three weeks, but what Joseph and White Bird will do in those three weeks, no one knows. At first the idea was that Joseph (Indian like) was getting out of the road and making for the buffalo coun-

try. There was great fear that he would get off, but it was soon discovered that he had no idea of getting away, and that he was quietly doing all the mischief he could, and reinforcing his band, and preparing for a fight with the soldiers. He says he can whip them. I do hope there won't be a chance for him to try until more troops get here.

Companies of volunteers are gathering from all around, and they will help to swell the number. Colonel Perry was here for three or four days last week. He came in to escort a packtrain for supplies.

. . . Some of the stories of the poor people who have suffered so much make your blood run cold. There was something dreadfully touching to me in the defense that the Norton family made. They were among the first of the settlers molested . . .*

We are uneasy today about a packtrain of arms and ammunition that left here yesterday with an escort of one company of cavalry (50 men) and about 20 Indian scouts. They feared an attack, as the Indians know of the train, and we heard they were going to jump it.

Your loving daughter,
Emily F.

HIS CHRISTIAN NAME WAS JOE ALBERT.

Painful as it was for his traditional parents, in recent years young Joe had moved his own family onto the reservation and become one of the peaceful Treaty Indians who lived and farmed near Lapwai.

When trouble broke out with the Non-Treaty bands of White Bird, *Toohoolhoolzote*, and Joseph's *Wallowa*, Joe Albert answered the one-armed soldier chief's call for scouts to lead the *suapies* to find those bad warriors who had murdered many Shadow settlers and burned their farms. Joe led the soldiers into the valley of *Lahmotta,*

**Cries from the Earth*, vol. 14, the *Plainsmen* series.

where a few of *Ollokot*'s warriors turned the frightened, spooked soldiers around and sent them fleeing.

Rather than kill them—as they had done with any *suapie* they found alive on the battlefield—*Ollokot*'s warriors captured three of those Christian trackers scouting for the army. Although many of the young men had screamed for their blood and the women heaped scorn upon the trio, the chiefs decided they would release the three, once the prisoners had vowed to never again raise arms against the Non-Treaty bands or help the soldiers in what everyone believed would be a quick little war.

"If we catch you again, then we will whip you with hazel switches."

Which was a punishment much worse than death itself.

After Robinson Minthon declared he wanted to stay with the White Bird band, the other two vowed they would return home to wives and children, even though both had relations among the Non-Treaties. And since the pair had their soldier horses taken from them, the young warrior Yellow Wolf gave *Yuwishakaikt* a pony to ride, while a kind woman took pity upon Joe Albert. She gave him one of her old travois horses for his ride north.

Still nursing the invisible wounds his pride had suffered by the time he reached Lapwai, Albert eagerly enlisted to work for Cut-Off Arm when he went to punish the warring *Nee-Me-Poo*—despite his promise to the Non-Treaty chiefs . . . even though the white men were often slow on the back trail and sometimes, to Joe's way of thinking, might even be a little frightened of confronting the warriors again. Yet he stayed with the *suapies*, even when they were turned back by the river and forced to return to the mouth of White Bird Creek.

As they plodded slowly up the steep canyon, it was immediately apparent how the heavy rains had been suffered upon the land while Cut-Off Arm's soldiers were on the west side of the Salmon: washing away what skimpy soil the soldiers had scraped over the battle dead. But Cut-Off Arm did not stop to rebury his dead. It was nearing sundown and they still had many miles to go before the advance soldiers reached the settlement called Grangeville. The first of the officers and soldiers did not drop from their horses until the great darkness at the middle of night.

Then Cut-Off Arm had them on the march again at dawn . . . halting and going into camp after crossing the old mining bridge that spanned the South Fork of the Clearwater. From the many charred and splintered timbers it was plain the warrior bands had attempted—but failed—to destroy the bridge. To Joe, it was a sure sign the Non-Treaties were planning to stay in this part of the country.

The soldiers had lain in camp through the next day,* waiting for more troops, which did not reach them until late in the afternoon. At long last, in this camp scattered below the bluffs on the east side of the South Fork, Cut-Off Arm now had all his *suapies* ready to go in search of battle.

Joe Albert had been ready for some time. Now, after so long a wait, the soldiers would strike the offending warriors, punish them and their women, too; then everything would return to normal once more. When that end to the troubles came, Joe could again visit his father and mother—both Dreamers—without being shamed by so many in the Non-Treaty camp that he had chosen to become a Christian. It should not take long—just one good fight.

After all, Cut-Off Arm had enough soldiers now. One of the scouts who talked the Shadow tongue made marks on the ground for those scouts who did not know the white man's talk. Each mark counted for ten *suapies*, mule packers, or the civilians who traipsed along with the soldiers. One mark after another, after another, until there were fifty scratches on the ground to signify all the white men who would attack the warrior bands. White Bird, *Toohoolhoolzote*, Joseph, and even Looking Glass did not stand any chance of getting away now.

They would hang in the white man way of retribution for having a hand in killing all those Shadow women and chil-

*Tuesday, July 10, 1877.

dren. War was not supposed to be fought against the wives and little ones. But the bad warriors had mixed whiskey and gunpowder, then done very, very bad things, sometimes terrible things, to the women and children. As it was explained in the white man's Book of Heaven, the time had come that these evil ones should pay for their sins.

At dawn the following morning, Cut-Off Arm started north along the South Fork, his long, long column strung out on the broken pine-dotted ridge that rose more than eight hundred feet above the river below. Many steep ravines and coulees made it impossible for the column to travel anywhere near the edge of the bluff. Instead, the soldiers had to make ever-widening detours to skirt around the heads of the deep ravines. The sun rose high and hot that morning as the *Nee-Me-Poo* scouts made fewer and fewer trips to the very edge of the ridge to look down at the river searching for the Non-Treaty village.

Since no one among the Shadows knew for sure where the camp lay, Cut-Off Arm was depending upon his trackers to find it for him while the bluffs rose higher and higher on that east side of the river, eventually more than a thousand feet above the South Fork. And the ravines grew steeper, deeper, and darker too, each one requiring a longer detour for the grumbling soldiers. The sun was nearing its zenith, burning in the sky after so many, many days of cold, rainy weather. Joe was sweating heavily in his wool soldier jacket and broad-brimmed black cavalry hat. He wondered when Cut-Off Arm would allow the column a midday halt to rest the horses and catch a nap under a little shade—

Suddenly the white men were shouting, cheering, excitedly forming up, shuffling this way and that. So much noise—

"They found the camp!" came the cry in the middle of all that pandemonium. One of the other two Treaty scouts was shouting as the pair came galloping back from the front of the march.

"Narrow-Eye Chapman found the camp!" announced the other, shaking his soldier rifle in the air. "It is back upstream a ways! Just above the mouth of the Cottonwood!"

Racing their ponies through the shifting masses of white men, sprinting across the bluff, Joe and the others stopped at the pine-covered edge of the ridge and gazed down into the narrow valley of the Clearwater. There, off to their left a long ways, lay the camp of the Non-Treaty bands.

"The soldiers almost missed them!" Captain John said. "Nearly passed them by!"

Then Joe observed, "They are still a long way back—too far to attack from here."

"I think the *suapies* will have to find a way down to the valley to make their fight," James Reuben said.

"If they don't, then the Non-Treaties will get away before the soldiers can capture the village," Albert declared.

"They're not going to wait to find a way down!" Captain John said. "Look!"

When they turned, looking through the trees, the scouts watched some of the *suapies* hustling one of the two wagon guns through the patchy evergreens and right up to the edge of the bluff, where they were hollering at one another. Farther away at the edge of the ridge, Cut-Off Arm and his soldier chiefs stopped their horses at the edge and peered down as the wagon gun belched its first charge. It made a lot of noise, but no damage, as the shot landed in the river far short of its mark—for the village stood a long, long way upstream.

The *suapies* around the wagon gun shouted at one another again and went about their crazy business with the weapon, swabbing and reloading it for a second charge. Which landed a little closer this time. A little better with the third shot . . . but it was soon clear to Joe Albert that the wagon gun would never come close to those Non-Treaty lodges.

But as he peered down into the valley, through the drifting shreds of dirty cannon smoke, Albert could see that—even while the huge black balls had failed to reach the camp—the noise of the gun and the explosion of those charges was not lost on the warrior bands. The camp was a swirl of motion: men and women racing about on horses and on foot, bathers leaping out of the river, children darting among the lodges, arms flailing in terror.

Riders bristling with weapons appeared at the edges of camp, near the Cottonwood and on the bank of the Clearwater. It appeared they were prepared to fight . . . if they could only find their invisible enemy.

Of a sudden, in the midst of all that blur and dust and panic gripping the village down below, Joe was struck with an instant horror—wondering just where his father was.

Chapter Twenty-Six

Khoy-Tsahl, 1877

Yellow Wolf had not been this happy in a long, long time. Two days ago Looking Glass's Alpowai band had rejoined the Non-Treaties, and for the first time since this war began, Yellow Wolf was reunited with his mother, *Yiyik Wasumwah*.

Her cheeks were wet as she held her son's face between her hands, chattering like a happy, happy jay. Then she would lay her cheek against his bare chest and hug him, sighing all the while. After a moment, she would again hold his face in her hands and stare up at her son, telling him how tall he looked, young warrior that he was now.

"He killed four *suapies* at *Lahmotta!*" Five Wounds had announced as he came riding by in that happy rejoining of the people.

"Yes," agreed Rainbow. "Yellow Wolf is a true guardian of the *Nee-Me-Poo!*"

Staring into his mother's eyes, he asked, "Where is *Tommimo*?"

Yellow Wolf's stepfather was three-quarters French and had been raised a member of Joseph's *Wallowa*, but for the past few winters they had lived with Yellow Wolf's mother's people, the Alpowai who farmed on the Clearwater.

She looked at the ground a minute, her face gone tense. He knew his mother was fighting some angry tears.

So he had dared to ask, "He . . . he wasn't killed by the soldiers?"

"No," she replied. "He was not here. *Tommimo* had gone to the Shadow town by the Snake River,* to trade some horses. Others have brought news that my husband has

---

*Lewiston, Idaho.

been arrested and won't be coming back until this war is over."

Then she had turned away and scurried back to that bundle of what few belongings she had managed to carry away from the village when the soldiers and Shadows struck Looking Glass. She pulled out a long scrap of blanket and laid it across her arms as if presenting it to him. Yellow Wolf's fingers had gripped the blanket wrap, the hot blood pounding in his ears blotting out the noisy celebration swirling around them.

It was his repeater!

"You have not needed to shoot it, Mother?"

She shook her head. "No, but I protected it for you, knowing one day you would come back and—if I saved anything from the soldiers—I wanted to protect this rifle for you, Son."

Quickly Yellow Wolf wrapped her close in one arm. His mother knew how to use the gun if she needed to against any soldiers or band of Shadows—a good shooter, she was. And his mother was a strong woman, too, capable of riding any wild pony. In the *Illahe*, the buffalo country near the *E-sue-gha* far to the east, he had watched her bring down buffalo with a big rifle. This woman would not tremble even at the sudden appearance of a grizzly bear.

Yellow Wolf knew he was his mother's son!

And now he had a sixteen-shot carbine for the war—no more would he have to use the one-shot soldier gun, condemned to searching out soldier bullets for it.

That night they had camped near the Middle Fork, farther north and close to Kamiah where many of the Non-Treaties went on Sunday morning for their special services. It was the next morning when riders came galloping back to report that they were being watched by some Shadows.

"*Suapies*?"

"No, not soldiers. But a lot of Shadows."

By the time the young men under *Ollokot*, Five Wounds, and Rainbow had returned with their weapons and their red blankets, the whites had scurried to the top of a large hill

Yellow Wolf's people called *Possossona.* At this place known as Water Passing, the Shadows were throwing up rock barricades they could hide behind. But the white men were unable to hold onto their horses that night after it grew very dark.

It was a good thing, too, this taking of the horses, because they had found that most of them belonged to Looking Glass's people.

"These were taken by those Shadows when they came with the soldiers to drive us from our camp!"

"Good," *Ollokot* had said to the Alpowai. "Now we've taken them back and the Shadows can walk on their sore feet if they want to return to their hollows or towns."

They kept four-times-ten of the ponies they had run off from Shadows, then led the rest—those they did not want—onto the Camas Prairie and scattered them far from the Shadow strongholds.

For another day they kept up a little sporadic fire at the whites, just enough to force the Shadows down behind their rock and tree barricades. Even though there had been a lot of shooting, only one warrior was injured: his right trigger finger shot off while he was leading away a pair of Looking Glass's horses the Shadows stole. In all the excitement, *Paktilek* had not realized he was hit until he noticed that the mane of the horse he was riding was wet and sticky with blood. A big ring on another finger was badly dented. It had saved the rest of his hand!

That next morning the chiefs decided it would be better to march upstream a ways.

Toohoolhoolzote said, "If the Shadows have found us here, then the soldiers will be the next to come."

"Yes," agreed White Bird. "We should take our families and lodges away from this place and deeper into the canyon of the Clearwater."

Looking Glass suggested, "We will be safe at *Pitayiwahwih*; there is room enough for us all to camp there."

Away they marched from those Shadows hunkered down in their hollows, just the way the soldiers had been kept in their holes at the far side of the Camas Prairie for many days. Why wouldn't the Shadows and *suapies* learn that whenever they attempted to attack the Non-Treaty bands they were always struck back with an even stronger blow?

Now this morning in that new camp the sun had been long in creeping over the lip of the tall, rocky bluffs just east of the river. Many of the young men slept in after singing, dancing, and courting late into the night. And when they did arise, there was nothing much to do. Already they had lost interest in keeping a close guard on those hill-bound Shadows downstream, and the *suapies* were still far away at the settlements. . . . So this would be a day to relax, here in this most beautiful of settings.

Through this narrow canyon the South Fork of the Clearwater flowed strong and clean, braced on the east by sheer cliffs rising more than a thousand feet in height, while to the west rose irregular bluffs. Both walls were inscribed with deep ravines climbing up to grassy rolling plateau. For much of the morning the canyon remained in shadow. Here summer days reigned.

For Yellow Wolf, it seemed as if the war was holding its breath. Camp would not be moved this day, the sun would be hot, so now had come the time to celebrate—even though there was no more whiskey in the camps. They would hold horse races and games of chance. There would be time for bathing in the cold river, or trying to talk to that young woman in White Bird's band, the pretty one Yellow Wolf had had his eye on for weeks now. At dusk, some of the older men would put out the call when it came time for the *timei*—a special race held but once every summer—when each contestant announced to the whole village the name of the young woman whose hand he would be racing for.

Perhaps she would see in him something worthy, although he was hawk-nosed and snake-eyed, his skin the color of an old saddle many times sweated on. No, Yellow Wolf had not the beautiful burnished copper skin of most *Wallowa*. He was not a handsome man like Shore Crossing or *Ollokot*, but in the last few weeks he had won a reputation as a fighter and man of integrity—one who would provide for and protect a woman and the children to come of their union.

Yellow Wolf had been sitting on his pony, watching some of the horse races on the long flat above the village, when his friend *Wemastahtus* came up and said with much excitement, "Yesterday a soldier was killed below here. I found him this morning."

"I want to see him."

Wemastahtus led Yellow Wolf several miles to the spot on down the Clearwater toward Kamiah. The body was lying in some brush by the side of the river trail, almost as if the man were asleep, except that a cloud of flies tormented his eyes, nostrils, and his slack mouth, too, with their black, buzzing fury. The man had a lot of bushy hair on his upper lip that ran down to the bottom of his chin.

"Maybe he ran away from the army," *Wemastahtus* suggested.

"No," Yellow Wolf said, "I think he ran away from the Shadows pinned down at *Possossona*."

His curiosity sated, Yellow Wolf now wanted to find the young woman with the big eyes. He loped back, reaching the lower end of the village, knowing the chances were good she would take her younger sisters and a brother down to the river to watch the children while they bathed and splashed in the water, now that the sun was high overhead. The best place to tell her his soft words would be in the cool shade of those big cottonwoods here in the quiet of this midday heat, with nothing but the gurgle of the Clearwater—

That loud boom echoed off the canyon wall, then died as the shattering noise was swallowed by the low hills west of the river.

At first, every motion stopped, every voice stilled—the air itself suspended in stunned and stupefied silence. Then, as the loud roar faded, Yellow Wolf heard again the buzz of the flies and other wingeds here along the shady bank. A heartbeat later, the first woman's scream split the dry, hot air.

Her cry was quickly taken up by a hundred more—women and children all, scrambling out of the water as a second dull *whoosh* whistled down the canyon and ended with a terrifying blast that shook the birds out of the nearby trees. Such a *whoosh-boom* could be nothing but a two-shoots wagon gun: roaring once when it was fired, roaring a second time when its round charge exploded on the far bank, well short of camp.

Men were shouting now, war leaders exhorting others to grab up their weapons. A young man was riding down the opposite side of the river, waving a blanket back and forth, back and forth over his head in warning.

Yellow Wolf gazed into the young woman's frightened eyes a moment as she held out her hand. Yellow Wolf touched it for but a moment, feeling her long, slim, cool fingers—

"Yellow Wolf!"

He whirled around, finding *Wemastahtus* on the low bluff just above him. Then he turned for one last look at the young woman, her eyes full of fury and fight, eyes telling him what her lips did not need to say.

"I am coming!" he yelled at *Wemastahtus*, not taking his eyes off her just yet. "We have an enemy to fight today!"

Her face softened for him but a moment before he turned away, scrambling up the slope.

"*Toohoolhoolzote* is already rushing to the bank with a few of his men," *Wemastahtus* announced as they raced their ponies through the camp, heading for the lodge of Yellow Wolf's mother. "I think that old war man wants to be the first to sneak up behind the soldiers!"

Stripped to nothing but his breechclout like the other warriors rushing past them, Yellow Wolf ducked back out of the lodge with one cartridge belt buckled around his waist, slipping a second belt over his left shoulder. Now with his sixteen-shot repeater in hand as he went into battle for the first time in many weeks, Yellow Wolf snatched the long lead rope from his friend, then leaped onto the pony's narrow back. Together they raced to the closest ford just upstream from camp, finding *Toohoolhoolzote* and a few others had already reached the far side—more than twenty, these first to answer the old warrior's call to action, all of them pitching across the river, racing to throw their bodies between their families and the attacking soldiers.

Behind them on the west bank the chiefs were shouting their orders to the rest—by this date in their war with the soldiers and Shadows numbering close to three hundred men of fighting age. Quickly they split all those remaining warriors in two groups, both of which would remain behind to protect the camp. One started to stream toward the north, the direction from which the cannon fire had come, where that group of Shadows might still be pinned down on their hilltop. The other group raced to the south, the direction where they had believed Cut-Off Arm was still camped with his soldiers. And those boys too young to fight drove more than two thousand ponies up the gentle slope west of the village, reaching the top of the plateau, where the herd would be safe from the army's loud guns.

"*Koklinikse!*" *Toohoolhoolzote* bellowed his scolding command at those who swarmed onto the east bank behind him. "Move faster! Faster!"

Slinging water as they came out of the Clearwater, the first of these most eager of the young men reined their horses into the timber dotting the sharp side of the bluff. Yellow Wolf's strong pony quickly vaulted him into the lead, clawing its way into one of the two jagged ravines* that carried the defenders in an ascent to the top of the ridge some nine hundred to a thousand feet above the river. Both hearts beat fast, lungs gasping hungrily for air, as man and horse lunged to the top—a leap at a time—the hoofbeats and war cries of the others right on their tail.

Slipping from the mouth of the rugged right-hand ravine, Yellow Wolf yanked back on the reins of his heaving

---

*The two ravines taken by *Toohoolhoolzote*'s warriors extend east away from the river on either side of a geographical feature that today is called Dizzy Head.

pony. To his left a dark swarm of soldiers covered the ridge top and prairie to the north of him. They were scurrying around, some headed this way and others headed that way, not seeing him or the first warriors to bristle up on his sides. *Suapies* running in all directions, forming up then breaking apart as they moved here and there—a strange preparation for a fight.

As his pony caught its wind, Yellow Wolf watched a stream of soldiers break off and start down another wide ravine leading to the river below. "Can't you see the soldiers!" he screamed at those who had rushed to the top right behind him. "They're going to attack our camp! Come on now—we must get up close and do some shooting at them!"

Without waiting for a word or sign of agreement from the others, Yellow Wolf jabbed his bare heels into the ribs of the animal and shot away, sprinting across that broad flat south of the massing soldiers. A wide canyon suddenly separated the young men from those white enemies. Leaning far back on his horse's spine, Yellow Wolf urged the horse down the steep wall of the ravine, then rocked forward as the pony clawed its way up the far side, until he found himself in rifle range of the *suapies*. Now these first warriors had placed their bodies between the soldiers and the spring. The white men would have no water today!

"Tie your horses here!" growled the deep bullfrog bass of old *Toohoolhoolzote* as his exhausted pony lunged out of the wide cleft in the ridge and hoof-slid into a thick stand of trees.

As one the two dozen followed the war chief into a small copse of tall pines, leaped to the ground, and tied off their horses, out of danger from soldier bullets. At the edge of those trees the old chief's young fighters could see how Cut-Off Arm's soldiers would soon be making for the edge of the bluff . . . and from there they could descend into the valley and attack their village.

"Come, all you young men!" *Toohoolhoolzote* cheered.

"*Eeh-heh!* We have to stop those soldiers from reaching our camp!"

"*Amtiz!*" Yellow Wolf yelled. "Let's go! We must throw our bodies between the end of this ridge and those soldier guns!"

"BLESSED Mary and Joseph!" he growled as the firing grew hotter and the Indians stopped their advance dead in its tracks.

First Sergeant Michael McCarthy wasn't sure just how many of those redskins they were confronting at the edge of the bluff, but he was sure it had to be at least a hundred!

At least, that's how many warriors Perry's cavalry battalion believed had stopped them cold in the valley of the White Bird last month, a little less than the size of the attacking force that flung itself at Perry's Cottonwood bivouac and somewhere close to the same number of horsemen who had jumped the seventeen civilians racing for Norton's ranch. So it made perfect sense a hundred or more of the Nez Perce fighting men must have rushed up the draws to reach this ridge-top prairie, where they managed to stall Howard's advance in a matter of minutes.

Surely the general and his officers could repulse this handful of troublesome snipers, having some 450 men at their command after Howard had waited to gather all his troops and all those supplies before setting off across the corner of the Camas Prairie after the hostiles!

On the eighth of July Howard's advance had recrossed the Salmon at the mouth of the White Bird. Pushing on with H and I Companies of the First U. S. Cavalry, the general's men passed by those shallow graves, a few of which were marked by hats suspended at the tops of short sticks, most of the skimpy dirt having settled into the depressions, what with the heavy rains. By midnight they rendezvoused with Perry's battalion in Grangeville, learning that the Nez Perce were camped on the South Fork of the Clearwater. On the outskirts of town, Howard established what he christened

Camp Randall, in honor of the civilian who gave his life in this struggle back on the fifth of July.

Just after dawn that Monday morning, Perry pushed on for the Clearwater with his four companies of cavalry, crossing to the east side of the South Fork on the Jackson Bridge, which some Nez Perce raiding party had attempted to torch in recent days. The horse soldiers went into camp on the long slope behind the burned-out buildings of Thelbert Walls's ranch.

Meanwhile, it took part of the eighth and most of the ninth of the month for Miles's infantry and Miller's artillery batteries to ferry themselves across the mighty Salmon—having virtually run out of supplies by the time they established their wretched bivouac at the mouth of the White Bird: without food or tents or dry blankets. Finally, early on the morning of the tenth, Captain Miles of the Twenty-first Infantry led in his battalion of eight footsore companies. Every man jack of them bailed out of the wagons Howard had sent down to the Salmon for them, collapsing into the grass at Camp Randall, where they promptly fell asleep, knowing it wouldn't be long before they would be ordered back on the road to catch up to the cavalry once more.

Over on the South Fork at Walls's ranch, in those first dim shadows at daylight on the tenth, one of the cavalry pickets opened fire on another guard, making for a brief but lively exchange until the camp discovered they were shooting at themselves and things quieted down once again while they waited out the day and those wagons filled with foot soldiers. They finally rumbled across the bridge and into the midst of the burned-out ranch just before 8:00 P.M. Told to quickly build their fires, choke down their supper, then climb into their blankets, Howard's command learned they would be marching on the enemy at first light.

By 7:30 A.M. on the eleventh, Howard gave the honor of the lead for the day to Trimble's H Company, this time behind a local guide, James T. Silverwood, and a contingent of Nez Perce scouts under Ad Chapman. Behind the rest of Perry's cavalry battalion came the infantry, then the pack train, along with a few horses detached from the main body, while the artillery brought up the rear. A few miles out of Walls's place, the advance ran across a small bunch of mares and their foals, horses that Chapman identified as having been stolen from his ranch. To the army's way of thinking, that was a clue they might be closing on the enemy. Trimble put out skirmishers and they resumed their march.

In short order, they were climbing a thousand or more feet to reach the high ground between the South and Middle Forks along a well-used mining road, forced to inch back farther and farther from the edge of the bluff where they had hoped to keep an eye trained along the Clearwater for signs of the enemy village or war parties. Hour after hour that clear, breezy morning, the ravines grew deeper, scarring the landscape of the plateau, each one more choked with brush and boulders than the last.

As the sun rose higher, and hotter, too, talk was Howard had designs on trapping the enemy between their column and McConville's gutsy volunteers who had gone out days ago to locate the village and were known to be under seige somewhere north of the advancing soldiers.

Captain Joel G. Trimble's H Company was about a half-mile in the vanguard, just emerging from a forested area onto more open prairie, where clumps of brush and small stands of trees made for a thick fringe on either side of the rolling grassland. Three of the civilian scouts in the lead came racing past, on their way to Howard with a report that they had just spotted some Nez Perce herders driving stock over the edge of the bluffs toward the Clearwater below.

Within minutes Howard ordered the artillery to the edge of the bluff and his vanguard to about-face. Far in the lead, McCarthy's H Company was marching slowly, deliberately watchful, when they heard that first distant cannonshot off to the south. Trimble halted his skirmishers and sent a courier back to headquarters to learn what had developed. In minutes the order came racing back that they were to turn about and support the pack train. After all, it contained the many thousands of rounds of ammunition—just what the Nez Perce would covet most.

Dashing up on the double, McCarthy's men found Captain George B. Rodney's D Battery of the Fourth U. S. Artillery—assigned that morning to protect the pack train—taking some harassing fire. Already one of the packers had been killed. As McCarthy's H Company came to their assistance, another packer was struck in the head, dead before he flopped to the ground. There followed a sudden rush of motion on the far side of the frightened packers and their bawling mules when the pack train suddenly split in the middle and a handful of mounted warriors belched through the widening gap, waving blankets at the terrified mules.

Through the heroic efforts of both companies, only one of the mules galloped off behind the raiders. But that mule was carrying two large crates filled with ammunition for the twelve-pounder, a mountain howitzer.

One thing was for certain, McCarthy thought. These sure as hell weren't reservation Injuns!

In a moment more both Rodney and Trimble were shouting orders for their officers to prevent a repeat of that sudden, frightening rush by the red horsemen on their small ponies, warriors who seemed to appear one minute and be gone the next. Dismounting their cavalrymen, Rodney formed his troopers into a column of fours on the prairie side of the bawling, braying, anxious mules, while Trimble likewise formed him men up on the bluff side of the pack train before they started the mules back to the south, carrying that valuable ammunition to the rest of the command.

McCarthy hadn't really noticed the terrain as they marched north, figuring he had been half-dozing there with the rocking of the saddle, the heat and intensity of the sun at its midday strongest. Now as they steered the pack train around the head of a deep ravine, the sergeant saw how this patch of ridge-top prairie was cordoned off north and south by a pair of rugged ravines less than a mile apart. Thick brush not only lined both gulches, but tall trees shaded the sides of those ravines—which meant the enemy had ample cover on three sides of this field where Howard was just now setting up an extensive perimeter: north and south, as well as to the west, along the edge of the ridge itself.

Escorting the pack train around the head of a deep ravine and into a slight depression at the center of that crude semicircle some seven hundred yards across, which the deploying troops had established on the grassy flat, Trimble and Rodney brought the balky mules to a halt near the head of that ravine, where Howard and his staff were just then establishing their headquarters. It was plain to see that their delay in getting the pack train and their companies around that wide ravine had allowed the Nez Perce those critical minutes they needed to establish themselves in the shady timber on both sides of the draw.

Trimble must have realized the threat those snipers represented to the mule train, for he gave the order for his men to leave their horses with holders and follow him to the edge of the timber, where they were suffering the hottest battering at the hands of an unknown number of Nez Perce snipers. They dodged around a number of small boulders and a few sparse trees, grinding to a halt in the tall grass just then going to seed and turning brown with the first real heat of the summer.

And realized there were even more warriors popping onto the grassy plateau from a second ravine. Now Trimble's H Company was pinned down, taking a deadly cross fire.

It was enough to send a shiver down his spine and cause goose bumps to sprout on McCarthy's arms—the war cries of those savages, the braying of the frightened mules Rodney's men were fighting behind them, the yells and cheers of his fellow soldiers, the harsh orders shouted by the officers, all of it mixed with the unsteady racket of Springfield and carbine fire as well as the unfamiliar *clack-clack* of the two Gatlings as they were brought into the fray.

For a moment he considered hurrying in a crouch to the right so he might reach the edge of the bluff and have himself a look down at the enemy camp, maybe even watch for McConville's civilians when they made their appearance. That would throw the village into an uproar, McCarthy thought. To find themselves between the soldiers on one side and that citizen battalion on the other! Any time now, McConville's volunteers would be riding into this fray from the north.

McCarthy quickly turned and gazed over his shoulder at the sky, feeling just how hot the sun was that seared its heat through his wool jacket and gray undershirt. He inched his head up but a moment, looking around the prairie—a mile in any direction now was commanded by General Howard's army.

Already McCarthy's throat was parched, his tongue pasty against the roof of his mouth.

The sergeant wondered if there was any water within the sound of his voice. Hell, if they had any water within the army's perimeter.

Chapter Twenty-Seven

July 11, 1877

BY TELEGRAPH

—

Particulars of the Indian War in Oregon.

—

Russians Abandoning the Seige of Kars.

—

OREGON.

—

The Indian War—Details of the Late Fight, and List of the Killed and Wounded.

SAN FRANCISCO, July 10.—Dispatches from Lewiston, via Portland, give the details of encounters with the Indians on the 3d, 4th, and 5th inst., near the Cottonwood. Tuesday, Colonel Whipple sent out Foster and Blewett scouting for Indians in the direction of General Howard's camp on Salmon river. They had not gone far when they met three or four Indians, who ran them back toward camp. Foster reached camp, and Whipple ordered the command in readiness to move. Meantime, Lieutenant Raines and his men rode over the first rise this side of the Cottonwood and down into the ravine where the road crosses before the ascent of Craig's mountain, and were attacked before Whipple could get to them, after he heard the firing. Raines and his whole party were killed, including Foster. Whipple's command came forward and formed in line of battle on the east side of the ravine, and the Indians on the west, all on open ground, about one thousand yards apart, and only the ravine between them. Here they remained menacing each other for about two hours, till darkness came.

Whipple retired to his camp, and the Indians passed over to a point on the Cottonwood trail to Craig's crossing. No more was done that night. Next Morning Whipple with his men started this way to meet Colonel Perry, who was expected with a supply train from Lopway, and kept out his skirmish lines along the route. They met Colonel Perry with his train near Board house and escorted him to camp. Baird and two men arrived from Mount Idaho soon after, and about 5 p.m. the rifle-pits were placed in position. The Indians made several attempts to storm the rifle-pits, but were kept at a distance. About 9 p.m. the firing ceased for the night. On the morning of the 5th two couriers arrived from General Howard, chased into camp by the Indians. Soon after they moved their camp, with about sixteen hundred head of stock, across the prairie in the direction of the Cottonwood. No move was made to intercept them. Soon after, Captain Randall and sixteen volunteers from Mount Idaho approached. About one hundred Indians intercepted them at the junction of the Elk City trail with the stage road. At this crisis, being seen from Perry's position on the hill at the rifle-pits, the Colonel was urged to go with troops to their rescue, to which he replied it was no use, they were gone, and he would not order a rescue. The volunteers say that their captain, seeing his position, ordered them to charge and break the line of Indians, dash over toward the creek bottom, dismount, and return the fire, and hold their position, partly under cover of a small hill, until the force at Cottonwood could reach them. The command was no sooner given than Captain Randall and his sixteen men made a charge, broke through the Indian line, reached the position named, dismounted, and returned the fire. In the charge Captain Randall was mortally wounded, Benjamin Evans killed, and three others wounded. They fought there for nearly an hour, and kept the Indians at bay. In about half an hour after, it was known that the Indians had the volunteers in a tight place. Colonel Perry gave orders for fifty men to go to their relief. It was quickly obeyed, and they were relieved in about an hour after the charge. No pursuit of the Indians was ordered, but a retreat was made to camp and no pursuit had been made since, up to the time of Morrill's leaving on the night of the 6th. The volunteers say they know they killed several Indians and wounded many others, as they saw the Indians packing off their dead and wounded the same night. McConville, with a volunteer force, has arrived at Cottonwood from Howard's command. On the 6th a detachment of seventy-five men, under McConville, was sent as an escort to a wagon carrying the killed and wounded to Fort Idaho. Morrill says that Randall, after he was mortally wounded, had got into position, sat up on the ground, and fired many shots at the Indians, the last not more than five minutes before he fell back dead. Not one of the seventeen faltered in the least, or showed the white feather, though hard pressed by 100 Indians, nor did one of them seek to run for Cottonwood after they had broken the Indian lines, but strictly obeyed orders to hold their ground . . .

When Baird and Morrill left, the Indians were in full possession of Comas Prairie except for Mount Idaho, Grangeville and the camp at Cottonwood. Yesterday several fires were seen in different directions, some about three miles from the creek, and appearance was that houses, barns and hay stacks were burning. From Lapwai it is reported that the Indians crossed Clearwater yesterday at 11 a.m. near Komia, with their stock. Settlers are being plundered and robbed on Cow creek, on the Colville and Walla Walla road. Forty to sixty volunteers have gone from Walla Walla to the scene of the difficulty.

"YOU'RE A DAMN FOOL TO THINK YOU'RE GONNA WALK all the way back to Mount Idaho on foot!" Edward McConville growled.

George Shearer finished tucking his pants into the tops of his tall boots, then straightened before he spoke.

"Colonel McConville. It's past noon and I don't figger we're gonna see a sign of any relief party sent out by that goddamned one-armed Yankee general. Anyone wants to walk out of here is more'n welcome to join me."

They had waited for the better part of a day and a half after Lew Wilmot and Benjamin Penny rode off with a second plea to Howard. As the hours passed, day becoming night, then night seeping into day once again, more and more it appeared that there was only one thing to think: Wilmot and Penny had been jumped and butchered by some roving war party haunting this rim of the Camas Prairie. Over time, George grew angrier and angrier, brooding how he had lost another friend. Lew Wilmot—lying dead and flyblown out there on the rolling prairie.

By noon of this eleventh day of July, Shearer had decided he had had enough.

"You're like to g-get picked off out there!" warned Ben Morris.

"Better'n dying in here from hunger or thirst," Shearer had snapped.

McConville wondered, "What of the Injuns?"

George shrugged and asked, "What Injuns? We ain't seen nary a one since early yestiddy, Ed. I'm gonna take the chance I can make it on shank's mare all the way in to Mount Idaho."

He was the first to clamber over the low rock wall they had piled up for breastworks. A half-dozen of the men were right on his heels when he stopped and looked back at the rest.

"Well, you boys comin' or ain'cha?"

That did it for most of the eighty-some men who stood arrayed across the flat top of that hill. They immediately bolted over the rock and timber barricades, gaping with grins as wide as if they were embarking on a spring social.

Shearer started down the slope at the head of the bunch. After less than fifteen yards, he stopped and went to his knee, scooping up a handful of empty cartridges left by the warriors who had kept them under seige. His eyes slowly climbed back up the hill to their breastworks for a moment, as he realized just how close the enemy had come to overrunning them. Then he spotted Ed McConville standing stoic and unmoving behind their low barricades.

Getting to his feet with a sigh, Shearer turned away and continued down the hill. In less than a minute Bunker loped up to his elbow.

"E. J., g'won an' sneak a look back—tell me if the colonel's coming," George whispered. Bunker turned his head and glanced back while he kept scooting on down the hill with George at the point of that arrow-shaped formation of white footmen. "Ed's coming. He's all the way back there . . . but he's coming."

"Good," Shearer whispered with a deep sigh, picking up the pace a little now. They had a long, long way to walk if they were going to make it to the settlements by morning. "I was afraid to go off an' leave the man all on his lonesome, standing back there on principle an' nothin' else if them red savages was to come back for us."

NOT long after *Toohoolhoolzote*'s small band of warriors had stopped the soldiers and forced them to take cover in the tall grass on that dusty plateau,* *Ollokot*, Rainbow, and Five Wounds came bounding up the north ravine and burst into the middle of the white man's pack train—waving blankets, firing pistols, and yelling like demons.

It was a pretty charge, Yellow Wolf had to admit. A rush into and on through the soldiers that he wished he himself had been part of. As it was, the fighting men around him had their hands full once the *suapies* stopped, turned around, then spread out in a great circle with their baggage and animals protected at its center. The few guns carried by those first warriors had forced more than ten times their number to hunker down in the grass without giving a fight!

It was the old war chief, *Toohoolhoolzote*, who had

*This battle site, located on private land, stands on what is today called Battle Ridge, just above the present-day community of Stites, Idaho.

killed the first soldier with his ancient muzzleloader. Then he quickly reloaded as the rest of his war starters crawled up behind him in the timber, and the chief killed a second soldier. The swelling puff of muzzle smoke from his old gun betrayed his position and brought a shower of bullets his way . . . but none found *Toohoolhoolzote*.

"Come, young ones; come!" he cried again and again, goading his warriors into daring to pit themselves against unimaginable odds. "Let's show these soldiers how to fight: rock-to-rock, tree-to-tree! If they gain any ground on us, let them leave blood on every step!"

Eeh-heh! The old fighter's *wyakin* was mighty strong that day!

As the soldiers began to fire wildly at the shadows in the timber, random bullets began to fall among their ponies. The horses grew scared, making noise and stomping around where they were tied, drawing even more soldier bullets.

"Four of you, go back to the ponies and take them to a safer place," *Toohoolhoolzote* ordered, then named the four young men he selected for this task. "I am afraid they will break loose; then we will not have them when we need them in the fight."

Right after this, their old leader and the two-times-ten set up a hot fire into the soldier lines. Then from two directions, more soldiers came in at a run, diving into the tall grass once they found themselves within range of the *Nee-Me-Poo* rifles. As Yellow Wolf watched and the sun started to slowly slip off midsky, the *suapies* massed, beginning a gradual movement against the timber from which the young riflemen had poured the first fire at the white men.

Back, back, back the soldiers pushed, slowly gaining ground . . . but only one hand span at a time. Although they now outnumbered the young warriors some twenty-to-one, the *suapies* paid for that ground with some blood and plenty of sweat under the broiling sun. Although *Toohoolhoolzote* and the other fighters rallied one another with cheers of encouragement, the pressure finally became too much and the old chief gave the order to leave the timber and slip down into the edge of the ravine. The instant the soldiers found the warriors were no longer keeping them pinned down, their fighting chiefs ordered them to make a charge.

On they plunged toward the timber. *Toohoolhoolzote* stopped and whirled around in a fury, kneeling as he aimed his old one-shoot muzzleloader. It hissed and the round lead ball found its mark, driving a soldier backward off his feet at the same moment the squat warrior scrambled to his feet and joined the others in running from that timber where the bullets buzzed like angry bees, smacking the trunks of trees, zinging through branches—

Suddenly Yellow Wolf slammed his bare feet to a halt. He had forgotten his horse! All of them had forgotten their ponies!

Wheeling about, he squatted and peered off to where the horse holders had taken their animals. The four were nowhere to be seen! They had abandoned the ponies as soon as the firing grew too intense even for *Toohoolhoolzote*. And the rest of the fighters were scampering behind the old chief toward another patch of timber west of the *suapies*.

Yellow Wolf felt the anger rising in him like a fever. The holders had abandoned their horses, and the others had abandoned him. That was a good horse and he wanted it back, even though the soldiers approached the edge of that narrow patch of timber. It was a disgrace for a fighting man to lose his horse to the enemy in battle.

Death while recapturing one's horse would be preferable to leaving the fight without the animal!

At first he started to creep through the trees; then he realized he wasn't going to get there in time to rescue the pony if he did not run. The young warrior took off at a sprint, jumping low rocks and dodging around the pines until he reached the animal, yanked its lead rope loose, and hurled himself onto its back—no matter the whine and whiz of bullets coming into that stand of trees.

Yelling at the top of his lungs, Yellow Wolf did his best to drive off the other horses, sweeping those that would be herded before him as he pressed low against his pony's neck and followed the route taken by *Toohoolhoolzote*. Bullets sang past, striking the ground and singing off the rocks, smacking trees, as the horse carried him down one side of the wide ravine and desperately clawed its way up the steep side onto the plateau once more. He recalled the words of his uncle, Old Yellow Wolf: "If you go to war and get shot, do not cry!"

Just remembering that admonition helped him be brave. Better to die with his horse than to turn away from the fight without it.

In heartbeats the snarling of the bullets was fading behind him. The crack of rifles no more thundered about his ears. He had reached the timber on the south side of the saddle. Dismounting, he tied off his strong brown horse, letting it regain its wind and graze while he started toward the sound of firing on that south side of the fight. Near a copse of trees he came upon a stand of large boulders where many men—mostly older—had gathered to talk about the fighting, make plans, and catch their wind, too. To the *Nee-Me-Poo* this was a "smoking lodge," where older warriors whose day had come and gone now passed their pipes around while discussing the fight others were making against the soldiers.

The sting of the tobacco smoke stung his nose and made his eyes water as he hurried past. Yellow Wolf never had smoked. He did not like it, and it made his head sick when he smelled others burning tobacco. Moving into a lope, the young warrior hurried to the east where the sound of gunfire was the heaviest.

At the edge of the timber he noticed how many of the finest warriors were flat on their bellies behind low boulders they had pushed before them, right out of the timber and into the tall grass, sneaking up on the soldier lines. They had good guns to use against the *suapies* this day! In little time they had captured more than three times the number of his fingers in new firearms from those soldiers dead or frightened and fleeing from White Bird Canyon. And the warriors took a dozen more from the men they ambushed some distance away from the soldier burrow holes at Cottonwood. This meant that now a good deal more than half of the *Nee-Me-Poo* warriors had guns to carry into this hot fight with Cut-Off Arm's men.

Many of those guns had been used most effectively against four, even five times their number, stopping the soldiers in their tracks and forcing them into that protective square while the rest of the warriors rushed out of the valley—once everyone realized the village would not be threatened—and climbed to the plateau to join the fight. Cut-Off Arm must surely be hiding somewhere in the middle of his *suapies*, concealed among the horses and mules at the center of the square in a low depression where he would be safe.

There was no manhood in having others do your fighting for you like that!

The young warrior spotted his uncle, Old Yellow Wolf, lying in the middle of those veteran fighters where the noise was the loudest and the shooting the hottest, firing his soldier gun at the enemy. Beside him lay another old fighter who refused to go to the smoking lodge. Fire Body, called *Otstotpoo*, had killed the first soldier at the White Bird Canyon fight—his bullet hitting a man who blew on a brass horn.* *Tomyunmene* was on Yellow Wolf's uncle's left side. The faces of all three were flecked with bloody scratches caused by flying rock chips as soldier bullets careened off the boulders they lay behind to take their shots.

This had to be the most exposed part of the entire line of these patriots fighting for their country!

Yellow Wolf plopped on his belly as the bullets hissed around him. There were no trees or shade here to hide within. Only these low boulders.

"I see that hat again!" Fire Body announced in a raspy whisper.

"Can you hit it?"

—

**Cries from the Earth*, vol. 14, the *Plainsmen* series.

"I did twice before!" the veteran warrior answered Old Yellow Wolf.

He took careful aim through the long sight attached to the top of the rifle barrel and squeezed the trigger.

Tomyunmene shouted, "You took off that Shadow's hat!"

"Three times now!" Old Yellow Wolf cried, slapping his bare thigh in joy as his nephew crawled up beside him and took a place behind the low boulders.

"Welcome, young one!" cried *Howwallits*, the one called Mean Man, sometimes referred to as Mean Person. "I see you brought your rifle today. You will see lots of game to hunt out there in the grass. Look carefully and you won't fail to find yourself a target—"

A bullet smacked the edge of the rock to Yellow Wolf's left, knocking off a large chunk, then ricochetting off to strike his uncle just above the eye, driving the older man's head backward. Old Yellow Wolf grunted as he flopped onto his side . . . then lay still.

"Uncle! Uncle!" Yellow Wolf shouted far too loudly as he brushed the bright, gleaming blood from the older man's face.

Bullets immediately followed the noise, forcing the warriors to hug the ground for a few moments.

When the soldier fire lessened, Mean Person suggested, "See if breath comes from his mouth, or the nose."

Yellow Wolf laid his ear against his uncle's face, trying to hear the movement of air. But with so much yelling coming from both sides of the fight, he could not tell.

"Lay your head over his heart," Fire Body ordered. "Press your ear tightly and feel for the life."

After what felt like a long, long time, his uncle's chest moved a little, and Yellow Wolf believed he heard a little flutter of the old man's heart.

With great joy, he shouted, "I think my uncle will live again!"

Chapter Twenty-Eight

July 11, 1877

They had been fighting these redskins for more than three hours by the time Howard ordered Captain Evan Miles to take some of his infantry in a charge on the ravine lying at the northern extreme of the battlefield—a patch of grassy prairie that extended a scant mile and a half wide north to south and a couple of miles long east to west—where the troops, both foot and horse, were forced to fight in the open, their only protection the tall grass just starting to turn with these last few days of searing heat.

While the first few weeks of this campaign, indeed the beginning of summer itself, had been cool and rainy at best, the past handful of days had turned unmercifully hot as storm clouds disappeared from the sky and the sun reemerged with a vengeance—seeming to burn like fire right through an enlisted man's flannel and wool.

First Sergeant Michael McCarthy had first unbuttoned his tunic, praying to the Virgin Mary for a breath of air to stir; just a little breeze it could be. Then he had pulled off the tunic completely, stripped down to his sweat-drenched gray undershirt like most of the other men in Trimble's H Company.

He and the rest, too, were all beginning to dwell more and more on the subject of water. Was there a pond of it back in that center of their perimeter with the supplies? Or would there be a cool spring or gurgling creek somewhere in those trees currently held by the enemy? Where in blazes would his next drink of water come from?

Miles's attack on the northern ravine had been so successful that by 3:30 P.M. Howard had ordered Captain Marcus P. Miller to take his artillerymen and launch the same offensive against the timber west of their enclosure. Breveted a colonel during the Civil War, Miller was an 1858 graduate of the U. S. Military Academy and a workhorse who had spent his entire career in the Fourth U. S. Artillery. Having fought at Antietam, Fredericksburg, and Chancellorsville, he came west to battle Captain Jack's Modocs. It was Miller's leadership of an artillery battery that rescued the survivors of Canby's peace commission after the general was brutally assassinated.*

But today Miller's charge bogged down when the resistance proved fierce and the warriors would not be moved. The rest of that afternoon and into the long summer evening, the battle settled into a sniping match between the two sides as both the Nez Perce and the soldiers devoted time between shots to scratching at the hot dirt, attempting to hollow out a shallow rifle pit—the infantry using their trowel bayonets, the cavalry having to plow with their belt knives and scrape with tin cups.

With the sun having slid off midsky, the hottest part of the day had come as it slowly sank to the west, baking this plateau of drying grass and parched soldiers.

The hottest fighting of the battle was yet to begin.

FROM time to time the *suapies* turned their big-throated gun on the timber where so many of the warriors had taken up positions after they rode up from the valley floor. Most of the time the noisy charges overshot the horsemen who had followed *Ollokot* out of the village, but every now and then an explosion showered the men with dirt and tree branches or wounded some horses.

"We must take that big gun!" *Ollokot* exhorted the men from the many bands who had shown up to fight on this west side of the ridge.

Their first three charges at the gun emplacement and those soldiers hunkered down there were as unsuccessful as the quick dash they had made among the pack train earlier that afternoon. Each time *Ollokot*'s warriors were driven back . . . but each time his men managed to get a little

—

**Devil's Backbone*, vol. 5, the *Plainsmen* series.

closer, a little closer to the big-throated gun. Withdrawing with his warriors, *Ollokot* vowed with the failure of each charge that their next attempt would bring them success. But a fourth and fifth assault only got them to within two long horse lengths of the weapon.

A final attempt might just force the soldiers back enough that *Ollokot*'s warriors could seize the powerful weapon, when they could turn and use it upon the soldier lines.

As he dashed back and forth along his wavering lines of naked warriors, *Ollokot* watched a soldier crawl out through the tall, dry grass until he lay directly beneath the cannon. From that position the *suapie* could load the weapon without exposing himself any more than he had to. As the white man started to slide backward in the grass, *Ollokot* realized the soldier was about to fire the gun. And had to be stopped before he touched fire to the back of the long weapon.

"Come on, all you men who would rather die than give up your country!" *Ollokot* cried, streaming out in front. "Do this for the graves of your ancestors! Do this for the weak and the small ones! Do this so your children will live free!"

In a screeching red wave they broke from the shadows, swarming across the tall grass as the soldiers immediately began to fall back. Of a sudden there was a soldier chief among the *suapies*, then a second, both of them yelling their orders, mingled perhaps with their own encouragement. The fleeing soldiers stopped, turned, and started back toward the gun. On either side of it they were thick as summer wasps now.

Closer and closer both sides advanced, the bullets like clouds of noisome flies, the gunsmoke gagging the fighters. Three arm lengths, no more, *Ollokot*'s warriors got away from the gun and those soldiers protecting it with their bodies. Three arm lengths: close enough to stare into the sweating faces of those frightened soldiers. Three arm lengths and both lines were preparing to fight by hand . . .

Then the first of the warriors fell and two of his companions started pulling him back.

A soldier collapsed, close enough that *Ollokot* recognized some of the Shadow words the man shouted in pain. Others dragged him back from the fighting.

Too many of the warriors were backing up instead of following their leader into the breach.

The soldier guns were too intense that final charge. Three arm lengths . . . close enough for this war chief, brother of the *Wallamwatkin* leader Joseph, to see that the soldiers would not prevail. Yes, they would fight to protect their little square of ground—but they would not succeed in attacking the village of women and children.

The warriors had stopped Cut-Off Arm in his tracks.

EVEN before the Non-Treaty bands migrated upriver to this camp at the mouth of the Cottonwood, every day saw a great number of Treaty people coming in from Lapwai, especially from Kamiah, to join the disaffected ones. With that string of successes in those early weeks of their war against the Shadows and *suapies*, many of the once-steadfast Christians and old Chief Lawyer's Treaty supporters had begun to waver in their loyalties.

Indeed, over the last few days the desertions had become so apparent that the government agent named Monteith had threatened banishment and exile to *Eeikish Pah*, the Hot Place,* for all those he caught supporting the hostiles. Why was it still so hard for the white men to see that things were not black or white, that you stood squarely on one side of this agony or the other?

And why did the Shadows fail to realize that many of the Treaty people had family among those bands now taking a stand against the government?

In this distinction, Joe Albert was not alone.

This young warrior named *Elaskolatat* was only one of many who had answered Chief James Reuben's call for volunteers to scout for and guide the soldiers in their chase af-

---

*Indian Territory.

ter the Non-Treaty bands. . . . Although Joe Albert had family among those fleeing camps.

To his way of thinking, this reality was nothing of great note, because there had always been, and always would be, a great measure of tribal pride, if not outright solidarity—no matter if a man were Christian or Dreamer, no matter if his heart came down on the side of the struggling soldiers or those victorious warriors. It was the white man—his ways, his words, and those land-stealing treaties—who had caused the fractures in ages-old loyalties. The Shadows and their soldiers were to blame for chipping away at the cohesiveness of Albert's people.

And now that these Non-Treaty bands were steadily giving back to the Shadows a small dose of the pain that had been inflicted upon all of the *Nee-Me-Poo* over many years, even those who made their home near Lapwai or over at Kamiah could take some degree of satisfaction. Perhaps Albert, like others, hoped the old ways of their people would not be crushed by the white man. Hoped that now, in this season of *Khoy-Tsahl*, these Non-Treaty bands would somehow hold the strong white culture at bay . . . if only for a few more winters, a few more joyous summers.

As the summer had warmed, Joe Albert gradually found himself losing what hope he still clung to that his people could be healed. The fractures went deep—especially in his own family—for his own parents were with these Non-Treaty bands camped below on the Clearwater. His father, *Weesculatat*, was a veteran warrior, who had steadfastly refused to give himself over to the white man. Father and son had argued many times, but in the end Joe had walked his own road and converted to the Christian faith, while *Weesculatat* had stayed with the Dreamers.

When Cut-Off Arm first ordered his soldiers to bombard the Non-Treaty village down below in the valley of the South Fork, Albert felt his heart rise to his throat in fear. Not for himself, but for his relations. His parents surely had to be among those scurrying among the lodges at this moment, herding ponies out of the camp, streaming off toward the western plateau. But it wasn't long before he found himself able to think of little else but this dirty fight, what with the Non-Treaty snipers firing from the timber, shouting encouragement to one another as the few pinned down the many—

Of a sudden the hot air caught in his chest, burnt gunpowder stinging his nostrils as he listened intently. It was a *Nee-Me-Poo* voice he thought he recognized as it cheered the others each time a *suapie* was hit or encouraged the Non-Treaties to inch a little closer to the soldier corral.

"*Pahkatos Owyeen!*" Albert cried out from behind the low shelter he had constructed of thin rock slabs like the soldiers around him.

Of a sudden, most of the Non-Treaty voices fell silent, and their guns ceased roaring, too.

"Five Wounds! Answer me! It is your friend!"

"Who calls me?" came the loud demand from the timber. "Who dares call me a friend when he lies among the soldiers come to kill my people?"

"*Elaskolatat* is my name!" Joe shouted.

From the timber a new voice asked, "The son of *Weesculatat?*"

Albert recognized that throat, too. It was Rainbow, the best friend of Five Wounds. "Is that *Wahchumyus?*"

"Yes—you are really *Elaskolatat?*"

Just then a bearded soldier crawled up and tugged roughly on Joe Albert's elbow. "Tell them redskins now's their chance to give up peaceable, or we'll chew 'em up with lead the way we're gonna do to their village and their relations. You tell 'em that now!" Albert's eyes narrowed at the harsh look crusted on the soldier's face. He had no intention of saying anything of the kind. Instead, he turned back to face the timber and shouted in his native tongue, "I am *Elaskolatat!* Son of *Weesculatat!*"

"Why have you have brought these soldiers to attack our camp?" Five Wounds asked.

"They would have come anyway, even if I did not bring them here," Joe Albert explained what he knew to be the truth, listening to the rustle of talk and unconnected words drifting in from the timber where the snipers lay.

"*Elaskolatat*, your father—"

"My father?" Albert interrupted. "Is he with you? Father? Father, talk to me yourself!"

Rainbow spoke now. "*Weesculatat* is not here."

"Then it's as I feared," Joe said. "He is down in the village, protecting my mother?"

"Your father is no longer with us."

His heart leaped to his throat. Joe struggled to holler, "N-no longer with you? He has given up your fight and taken my mother into Lapwai . . . or even Kamiah?"

"No," Five Wounds said with much sadness from the shadowy timber.

His next words were even more disembodied than before. Almost as if each one were a ghost by itself, drifting out of the shadowed place into the bright sunlight where it refused to take form, dissipating slowly as Joe Albert attempted to wrap his mind around it. "*Weesculatat* was killed by the white men a few days ago. Near Cottonwood Creek."

"D-dead?"

Now a new voice shouted from the trees. *Ollokot* said, "*Uataska*, it is true. He is the first warrior killed in this war against the Shadows. A brave man. Be proud of your father, *Elaskolatat!* In all our fights, he is the only man to die, and he died a courageous warrior—"

"My father was killed by soldiers?"

"No!" Five Wounds cried. "By a band of white men—"

"He's dead?" Joe croaked, disbelieving. "Really dead?"

"Your mother is grieving in the old way, the *timnenekt*," Rainbow explained. "Days ago, over the place where they buried him at *Piswah Ilppilp Pah*, the *tewats* said their prayers over him—"

Leaping to his feet, unmindful that he wore a soldier coat, Albert roared with an unspeakable pain shooting through his heart, pounding his breast in anguish. "Ahhhh-hgh!"

"Get down! Get down, you stupid Injun!"

The soldiers around him tried to pull Joe Albert down as a few of the Non-Treaty guns instantly opened fire again . . . but *Ollokot*, Rainbow, and Five Wounds shouted to all the rest, screaming that they must not fire at this old friend of theirs who had lost his father to the Shadows.

Joe was standing exposed in the bright afternoon light, the *suapies* sprawled in the grass behind their skimpy breastworks, three of them dragging at him with their hands, shouting at him to get down, get down. "Get down or you'll be killed!"

"In the name of *Hunyewat*, our Creator!"

With half a breath caught in the back of his throat, *Elaskolatat* leaped over one of those clawing for him and took off at a dead run . . . leaving Joe Albert behind—racing headlong to reclaim himself. To reclaim *Elaskolatat*.

Son of *Weesculatat*—the first hero of the Non-Treaty war against the Shadows.

Of a sudden his chest was filled by the hot afternoon air buzzing with shouts and bullets. He was screaming in horror, shrieking in pain, shouting in fury, his heart pounding as he sprinted for the timber.

"Don't shoot him!" Rainbow cried, lunging to the very edge of the trees. "He is one of ours!"

With one hand still clutching his soldier rifle, *Elaskolatat* flapped the sleeve of his soldier blouse from his free arm, then slapped the rifle into the other hand and struggled to shed himself of the white man's dark blue coat from that last arm. A few soldiers were getting to their feet back at their lines now, more of them kneeling behind their rocks, too—all of them growling and shrieking, shooting not at the snipers in the trees, but shooting at the runaway tracker.

He could hear the bullets whistle past him as he raced ahead for the trees. And there at the edge of the tree line some of the warrior faces suddenly took shape as the bravest of the brave stepped into the light, showing themselves to the enemy, and began to lay down a murderous cover fire for this returning son of *Weesculatat*.

Midway between the two lines of shouting, shooting enemies, *Elaskolatat* finally flung the soldier blouse from his wrist and sent it pinwheeling into the air.

He left it settling behind him in the tall grass and dust. Left those soldiers and his Treaty friends behind.

"*Imene kaizi yeu yeu, Hunyewat!*" he roared as he neared the Non-Treaty warriors. "Thank thee, O my Creator!"

The moment he reached the timber, *Elaskolatat* sprinted into the welcoming arms of the war leaders. So many hands pounding him on the back, tongues wagging, until he stopped in front of *Ollokot*.

"Your tears tell me you never really left your father's people," the *Wallowa* war chief said.

Elaskolatat raised a finger and touched his cheek, finding it wet with his tears. "My eyes bleed for my father's spirit," he told the warriors in that copse of timber. "And my heart tells me I must now lead you against those *suapies* who killed him!"

Without waiting for any of them to join him, the young warrior whirled on his heel and let out a shriek.

"*Kiuala piyakasiusa!*" he raised his voice to the hot summer sky, his *simiakia*, his personal warrior spirit, on fire. "It is time to fight!"

Shaking his rifle, *Elaskolatat* burst into a sprint, heading back for the soldier lines across the hot, grassy no-man's-land.

But this time, he was firing at the *suapies*, leading more than ten of the others in a sudden, surprising charge against the enemies who had murdered his father at Cottonwood.

Elaskolatat had come home to his father's people.

IN the last, lingering light of that long, hot day, Lieutenant C. E. S. Wood took out the narrow ledger and dug the pencil from his pocket. Lying on his stomach in the grass there at the edge of headquarters, the young officer scratched at the page, making nothing more than notes really, impressions perhaps—on that day's fierce fighting:

> July 11 Advance on Indians Engage them at about 11:30 A.M., we occupy a rolling broken plateau they the rocks and wooded ravines. Howitzers open fire. Skirmishing, sharpshooting, Famous Hat knocked off three times. The sergt & Mcanuly shot. Charge by line in front of me. Firing until after dark. Indians in ravines after horses. Caring for the wounded. No food no drink no clothing. All day without water. Night in the trenches preparing for an attack at dawn. Anxious times. Sound of Indian dancing and wailing. Williams and Bancroft wounded. I, lost on the picket line.

The lieutenant put the pencil between his teeth and bit down hard, feeling the wood give way. He did not want to break it, only stifle his scream. Frustration, anger, disappointment . . . and maybe a little fear. That, too.

He wrote a bit more:

> Warriors continually pressed upon us, their brown naked bodies flying from shelter to shelter. Their yells were incessant as they cheered each other on or signalled a successful shot. Some even wore tufts of grass tied to their heads as they crawled about for a better position, would shoot, then move on to another likely spot.

For a moment the lieutenant remembered how he had seen the war chief he was convinced was none other than Joseph himself.

> Saw him everywhere along the line; running from point to point, he directed the flanking movements and the charges. It was his long fierce calls which sometimes we heard loudly in front of us, and sometimes faintly resounding from the distant rocks.

On all sides of him in the dark he could make out the men grumbling about their thirst and talking incessantly about water, some thanking God for the evening breeze and a little respite from the heat, others saying it was going to get downright cold and they'd all be freezing by morning.

And the wounded. How they groaned and cried out piteously, begging for water, pleading for the surgeon to see to them next, one man asking his fellows to kill him so he would be out of all the ache and pain he could no longer stand it was so monstrous—

Wood clenched his teeth together to keep from screaming himself. If this was Indian fighting, he wasn't sure this army had anything to be proud of.

And he didn't know if he wanted anything more of Indian fighting.

Chapter Twenty-Nine

July 11, 1877

Correspondent Thomas Sutherland found it impossible to sleep that night as the temperature sank and the wind came up atop that barren plateau where the men huddled in the cold, cursing their sweat-dampened clothing that now had them chilled to the bone. As the cold, humid air settled to the ground around their rifle pits, the dew soaked their uniforms, making the men even more miserable.

A few of the wounded men whimpered, and some screamed as the surgeons continued to work over them with the probes and the saws, despite the dark that smothered everything but the sounds of suffering. One of them cried out for his mother just before he died. Sutherland had never heard of such a thing before. Then an old gray-bearded infantryman told him it happened all the time.

"Hundreds of times, fact be," the soldier said beneath the dim starshine. "Back to the war, heard more men beg for their mammas than I ever wanna hear again."

The thought made Sutherland even colder, so chilled to the marrow that he wondered if he would ever be warm again.

Off and on he wrote in his journal, long handwritten pages covered by his tight scrawl, from which he would compose his newspaper dispatches:

> Although we outnumbered the Indians . . . we fought to a great disadvantage. The redskins were in a fortified canyon, shooting from the brow of a hill, through the grass, and from behind trees and rocks, while our men were obliged to approach them along an open and treeless prairie. At times a redskin would show his head, or jump up and down, throwing his arms about wildly, and

> then pitch himself like a dead man flat upon the grass, and these were the only chances our men had to fire . . .
>
> During the early part of the fight an Indian with a telescopic rifle was picking off our men at long range with unpleasant rapidity (evidently mistaking me for an officer the way his shots fell around me), when one of Lieutenant Humphrey's men "drew a bead" on the rascal . . .
>
> Desultory shooting is kept up, with intervals of sharp firing, for seven hours . . . Wishing to enjoy all the experiences of a soldier, I took a rifle and crept out to the front line of pickets prepared to take notes and scalps. My solicitude in the former direction was nearly nipped in the bud, for the moment I inquisitively popped up my head, a whine and thud of bullets in my proximity and a very peremptory order to "lie down, you d——d fool," taught me that hugging mother earth with my teeth in the dirt was the only attitude to assume while in that vicinity.

He sighed, vividly recalling just how deadly the enemy fire had become as the temperature rose and the sun slowly sank for the west. That experience was something Sutherland knew he never would forget:

> At one point of the line, one man, raising his head too high, was shot through the brain; another soldier, lying on his back and trying to get the last few drops of warm water from his canteen, was robbed of the water by a bullet taking off the canteen's neck while it was at his lips.

Sutherland brooded on how Private Francis Winters, serving with Captain S. P. Jocelyn's B Company of the Twenty-first, had his black felt hat shot off three times; then spare minutes later a fourth bullet clipped his ammunition belt as if it had been cut with a knife. The same bullet severely wounded him in the hip.

For some seven hours the battle never cooled as the Nez Perce pinned down Howard's army on three sides, despite how the Gatling guns and two howitzers raked the Indian positions.

Crawling up to the west side of the line late in the afternoon, the correspondent had watched Captain Eugene A. Bancroft, M Battery of the Fourth U. S. Artillery, leap to his feet for but an instant—saying he intended to survey that part of the battlefield where the Nez Perce were putting pressure on his howitzer emplacement—and instantly be struck in the left side of the chest.

At another place in the line Sutherland had watched Lieutenant C. A. Williams take a bullet in the hip. As the young officer calmly began to dress his own wound by himself, he accidentally raised one arm too high in the grass and took another bullet, this one shattering his wrist.

Late in the day, Lieutenant Harry Bailey—serving with Jocelyn's B Company of the Twenty-first U. S. Infantry—had come into headquarters, where he blew off a little steam with Sutherland before meeting with Howard's staff among those stacks of pack saddles and apishamores, ammunition and ration cases Trimble's and Rodney's men had piled up at the center of the battlefield, constructing a network of head-high barricades.

"I had a helluva time of it, keeping my men on the firing line this afternoon," Bailey admitted. "As soon as I got some placed at proper intervals and I moved on down the line to instruct others, as many men would run back to their holes or trenches in the rear!"

Grinding a fist in an open palm, Bailey continued, this time telling a story of two officers.

"They were lying behind small head shelters with dusty sweat streaks down their faces, dodging bullets. They yelled at me to get down as I was drawing fire. When two bullets tipped the earth between their heads and my ankles, I dove for cover! After a few minutes of that dangerous give-and-take, I began to realize that a nearby company and my own had mistaken one another for the enemy, Mr. Sutherland! Friendly fire, I'd say!"

"You were drawing fire from another outfit?"

Bailey nodded. "Those damned warriors! They were shooting and whooping so much at us, my company and an artillery battery were distracted enough to start jumping around, bobbing up and down, firing at each other at a lively rate."

"How'd you get it stopped?"

"At first I tried yelling, but the racket of the guns was too much for me, so I ran out between the two lines yelling for all parties to cease fire! 'You're firing into your own men!' "

"You're lucky you weren't hit!" Sutherland snorted.

"Little chance of that," the lieutenant grumbled. "I suppose I'm fortunate that the army can only afford to give each man three cartridges a month for rifle practice."

"Was anyone hurt in that exchange?" the correspondent inquired.

Bailey shrugged. "None of us can ever be certain, and I'm sure no one will ever say a thing about it, but Private Winters claims nothing will ever convince him otherwise but that his dreadful hip wound was caused by a bullet from that artillery battery."

Thinking now about Bailey's powder-blackened, sweat-smeared face, Sutherland shaved a little more off the end of his pencil, sharpening the lead with his small penknife, then licked it and went back to writing, remembering how some companies right at the farthest extent of the firing line had reported they were running low on ammunition earlier that afternoon. When none of the soldiers or officers volunteered to resupply those units,

> Ad Chapman jumped on his spirited horse and with a heavy box of cartridges on his back hip, started at full run amid a shower of balls for the front, where he safely landed his precious burden. Surely this citizen soldier and guide is one of the most intelligent and bravest men in the command.

Then Sutherland's mood darkened a bit again, and he recalled:

> Not long ago Surgeon Sternberg was called at night to go to the fighting line . . . where he found a man who was a packer, badly wounded and bleeding profusely. Sternberg feared he could not remove him any distance without danger of great loss of blood. Surgeon instructed his assistant to light a candle and screen it with a blanket, in order to form a shield behind which he could tie the artery. No sooner had the candle been lighted than the bullets came thick and fast at this little mark, and it had to be quickly extinguished.

At times this night could be excruciatingly quiet, eerily so. They could hear the warriors moving about in the timber and brush nearby, scraping rocks atop one another as they fortified their breastworks. At times the sounds of drumming, the shrieks of war dances, and the wails of mourning women drifted up from the river valley encampment somewhere below the bluff.

In such a morose, gothic atmosphere, Sutherland could not help but remember his brief friendship with Sergeant James Workman of the Fourth Artillery and how it had come to such a tragic end in the brilliant glare of a sunny afternoon:

> He was a very intelligent young man, being one of the best Shakespearean scholars and readiest quoters from standard English poets I've ever met. But I think him quite depressed these last few days, weighed down with unspoken troubles and bitter recollections from his past.
>
> During the battle I was shocked, startled when Workman suddenly stood up and charged alone toward the Indians. Almost instantly he fell flat on his face, pierced by Nez Perce bullets on every side. How tragic is his death, but the man seemed fixed upon it, determined to die—

Suddenly in that murky silence of summer night Sutherland was interrupted in his writing when one of the sergeants gruffly reminded his men to get back to work deepening their rifle pits there in the dark beneath the cold pinprick stars, scratching shallow trenches in the barren, rocky soil. Although none of them had eaten since breakfast, come night there wasn't a complaint about food. Only the lack of water.

Thirst had created its own exquisite brand of incomparable torture.

YELLOW Wolf lay with his cheek against the earth, listening to the sporadic gunfire as the hot afternoon waned, and closed his eyes. So tired was he that the young warrior did not realize he had fallen asleep until he awoke with a start and furtively looked about. The sun was lower, and no one else was around anymore.

He remembered his wounded uncle crawling off earlier, saying he wanted *koos*, so would attempt to reach the spring for a drink. But he had not come back, and the others had crawled away, too. Yellow Wolf could not see another fighting man, only hear the soldiers on their line, dangerously close behind the tall grass. As he was lying there, thinking what to do now that he was alone with the enemy, a voice barked from behind him.

"Why is he lying there? Yellow Wolf must be wounded!"

Then another voice came from a closer point off to his left: "Who are you, lying flat like you are? Soldiers are coming close! Don't you see them?"

Keeping his head low, Yellow Wolf tried to see who had spoken but could not for the grass. In a moment, the same voice whipped his ears again.

"Yellow Wolf! Are you wounded? Why aren't you shooting? Go ahead and kill some soldiers! They are coming close to kill you if you don't defend yourself!"

This time the young warrior raised his head up a little, far enough to see that it was *Wottolen*, the older warrior known as Hair Combed Over Eyes. He was one of the war leaders who commanded some young men at the edge of that bluff. And he was right.

When Yellow Wolf looked, he saw how the soldiers were crawling toward him in the grass, no more than thirty steps from him already, slipping up cautiously like a snake you could not see until it struck.

It made the young man very angry to be left by so many to the soldiers. He did not care if he died; he was going to fight these *suapies* like a man. He had a reputation earned in the White Bird Canyon fight, and he would not lose it here.

Unafraid of the soldiers, Yellow Wolf crawled against two boulders and placed his carbine between them. Quickly levering shells, he fired six shots, stopping most of the soldiers where they were.

As the crack of that last shot faded, he heard heavy breathing behind him and immediately turned. Fire Body was grunting as he dragged his old limbs out of the brush in Yellow Wolf's direction.

"I just heard your bullets, so I realized you were alone, Nephew," Fire Body said while he crawled up on his belly. "We are going to die right here! But remember: Do not shoot the common soldier. Shoot the commander!"*

He understood exactly what the older man said. Fire Body had killed the trumpet soldier at the *Lahmotta* fight and stopped the soldiers from advancing any farther. Now Yellow Wolf looked at the nearby enemy and spotted the commander who knelt behind his soldiers.

Yellow Wolf took aim, and his bullet struck that officer, knocking him back into the grass where others quickly dragged him out of sight. But it was not long before another commander took his place and hollered at the soldiers.

Yellow Wolf shot at him, too. As soon as their second

---

*"This characteristic of the Nez Perce's combat methodology was to singularize their performance in subsequent engagements with the army." Jerome A. Greene, *The U. S. Army and the Nee-Me-Poo Crisis of 1877*.

commander was hit, the soldiers promptly began to scoot backward, retreating. He wanted to cheer, for his bravery alone had caused that retreat.

Wottolen pounded a hand on his shoulder. "That was good shooting, Nephew. I think the soldiers know to stay where they are for the rest of the day."

As twilight arrived and it grew darker, the heat escaped the earth and the air grew cold and damp. As the stars came out, only an occasional gunshot was heard.

Through that evening, Yellow Wolf had stayed right where he had been when he shot the two soldier commanders. Even though he began shivering. Dressed only in his breechclout, those two cartridge belts, and that pair of moccasins he had brought with him from the lodge, his body trembled. The night was clear and still. The earth's warmth quickly sucked into the sky. Finally, after moonset, he could not stand the cold any longer and crawled back toward the timber and rocks.

Back at the smoking lodge where the no-fighters had gathered during the afternoon's battle to talk about the fight and other serious matters, Yellow Wolf found no one awake. At least ten men lay asleep, curled up on the ground of the smoking lodge, clutching their legs for warmth. He found that Looking Glass was not among them. Earlier in the day, talk was that the chief made repeated trips down to the village rather than staying put on the fighting lines with his warriors.

Yellow Wolf did not tarry at this place of the no-fighters but crept on for the place where many of the ponies were tethered. He remembered how when the sun was high *Teeweeyownah*, the old warrior called Over the Point, came among the ponies tied in the trees, clearly angry. Here and there this member of White Bird's band had selectively turned some of the horses loose. When those young men finally emerged from the safety of the smoking lodge, they were furious to find their ponies gone.

"Where is my horse!" *Alahmoot* growled. He was called Elm Limb.

Over the Point admitted, "I let them go."

"You have no right to turn our horses loose!" Elm Limb blustered.

"You go too often to camp," the older man explained as more warriors gathered to watch the argument. "We are here to fight."

"I came to fight!"

"No, Elm Limb—you came to smoke and make others think you were fighting," Over the Point protested. "All you young cowards,* I will die soon. But you—you will soon see hardships in bondage to the Shadows. Your freedom will be gone, liberty robbed from you. Our people will be slaves for all days to come. Now, go fight and die for your families!"

Yellow Wolf crabbed into the grove, finding a few ponies still tied there, thinking hard on the old man's strong words. It was hard not to feel deep rage for those who did not help in that first day's fighting, leaving it to the few who did put their bodies on the line. Even Joseph, the village chief, climbed up to the bluffs to take part in the struggle. Shame was, only half of the men of fighting age showed their faces in the ravines or the snipers' grove: ten-times-ten against four, maybe five, times as many soldiers! *Eeh*, he thought, no matter that the warriors were outnumbered—they still managed to keep all of Cut-Off Arm's *suapies* pinned down without any water!

Suddenly spotting a man lying on the ground, curled up against some brush, Yellow Wolf asked the stranger, "May I sleep with you, on account of the cold?"

"Yes," the man answered. "We can share our heat." As Yellow Wolf knelt beside the man the stranger said, "Yellow Wolf, it is you!"

"Cousin!" Yellow Wolf said with no small joy. His heart was very glad to see *Teminisiki* again. They had known each

*In Nez Perce culture, cowards or laggards in battle were rarely, if ever, shamed or ostracized.

other from the time when they were both small children just learning to walk.

"There aren't many here now."

"I know," Yellow Wolf replied. "Where did they go?"

"*Ollokot* tried to stop them, telling all the fighters that they should stay and keep the soldiers away from the water."

"Someone told them different?"

Teminisiki nodded in the dark. "Looking Glass. He did not like *Ollokot*'s plan to keep the soldiers from the spring, so most everyone else left for the camp with Looking Glass."

"I am glad you stayed," Yellow Wolf said as he eased himself down to the earth. "It is good to know my cousin is a fighting man."

Just as he was lying down with his back against *Teminisiki*'s, they heard soft footsteps and a woman's voice whispered from the darkness.

"May I stay the rest of the night with you? I have no blanket and I am cold."

Without any hesitation *Teminisiki* said, "Come on! Get in here between us! You will keep warm that way!"

The woman quickly did as he suggested, scooting down between the two young men. As they lay there those first few minutes, Yellow Wolf felt her quivering between them, and it made him all the colder for it. He thought how good a woman felt, with her many curves and soft places. . . . Then he thought of the young woman who had touched his hand as this fight had started that afternoon. How he wanted to find her now—

But suddenly Yellow Wolf remembered what was taught him by the old ones, people who were no longer alive now—the wise warriors who had gone to the buffalo country many times, fighting the Lakota and others in that faraway land.

They had always said: In wartime a man cannot sleep with woman. He might get killed if he does.

"Where are you going, Yellow Wolf?" *Teminisiki* asked as his cousin stiffly got to his feet.

"I will go somewhere else to sleep. You two keep each other warm for tonight."

He went off a little ways and found a low boulder where he could get out of the blustery wind that was growing cold. Whenever the breeze died, he could hear his cousin and the woman talking low. Despite the cold, Yellow Wolf was sure the two of them would couple that night.

But he did not want to take the chance. He wanted instead to believe in the ways of the old ones he had been taught summers ago.

Yellow Wolf shivered all night long, until it grew light enough for the fighting to start again.

Chapter Thirty

July 12, 1877

Thursday, July 12, 1877

Mamma,

I wish I could talk to you this morning instead of writing. One of the things I meant to tell you yesterday was the active part the Indian squaws take in these fights our soldiers have had. They follow along after the men, holding fresh horses and bringing water right into the midst of all the commotion. Colonel Perry says that in that fight of White Bird Canyon, he saw one Indian (one buck, as they speak of them here) have as many as three changes of horses brought him by his squaw. See what an advantage that is to them. As soon as their horses are a little blown, they take a fresh one, and our poor soldiers have perhaps ridden theirs fifty or sixty miles before the fight begins. In their efforts to get at the Indians, they do their fighting on their tired animals. Then, in the fight, the soldiers fall scattered in all directions and the bucks can't stop to plunder in the midst of the fight. So, wherever a man falls, they set a squaw to watch him. I do hope their successes are at an end.

We are waiting anxiously for news from General Howard who is about 50 miles away from Lapwai. A young man named Rains was killed last week. It was his first fight. He was a lovely boy. Mrs. Theller felt dreadfully about his death. He was the officer in charge of the party that found and buried Mr. Theller's body. Rains had so marked Theller's grave that he would have no difficulty finding it again, and now we don't know that it can be found. Mrs. Theller is so anxious to have the body. Poor woman . . . it was two weeks after the fight before they were able (from the small number of men and the large number of Indians) to go out to bury the men killed in that first fight, and Mrs. Theller used to say, "If he was only buried. Oh my poor Ned, lying there with his face blackening in the sun."

. . . Last Sunday night, an Indian (friendly) came in and told that he had seen Joseph's men and they were coming to "clean out" the post that night. "Maybe in the night. Maybe in the morning," they said. "Only little bit of soldiers here. Is good time. Plenty muck-a-muck (food) and plenty gun." The Indian is a reliable one, as the good ones go, so every precaution was taken to guard against the surprise. Everybody at the post slept in one house, and the men slept in the breastworks . . . They did not come, but we have many such alarms . . . I am so tired of all this excitement, but the children seem to thrive on it. They look neglected but happy as clams at high tide.

Your loving daughter,
Emily F.

THROUGH THE LONG, COLD, BLACK HOURS OF THAT NIGHT, First Sergeant Michael McCarthy listened to the groans of the wounded gathered at the hospital behind the lines in the dark—their cries fading time and again into eerie echoes that stole through the awful suffocating stillness.

At least the wounded were lucky—they had been picked up off the battlefield and hauled back to the hospital in the wagons, where they lay under awnings erected for shade and waited their turn under the surgeon's knife and saw. The dead, all those dead, still lay where they had fallen.

Those cries of the wounded mingled with the harangues of the enemy chiefs as they exhorted their warriors in the still, gray hours hovering just before first light, while the clear, starry sky gradually faded far to the east.

Yet what nettled him most were the soft, sad whimpers of the women as they keened and mourned for their fallen warriors. Ghostly tatters of their pitiful wails drifted up from the valley below. Enough to make a man give up even the thought of a belly-warming drink . . . if he'd been lucky enough to have himself a flask here on the line this bloody black night.

Hell, to have anything to drink would have been a boon through that first, long day.

When the soldiers went in search of water around midday on the eleventh, a few got close to a spring* tucked up in the head of a timbered draw. But close was all they got. Every time some daring trooper attempted to cross from the cover of trees to the brushy spring, swaybacked under a clattering load of wool-covered canteens, Nez Perce sharpshooters drove him back. It was here that Private Edward Wykoff was killed and another infantryman was wounded. As the hours dragged on and on, their horses and mules suffered every bit as much as the men hunkered down on that thin crescent moon of a battle line.

From time to time the enemy's leaders had signaled an attack or change in strategy to their warriors by emerging on some prominent point where one of them came out, jumping around as he waved a red blanket or circled a pony in some significant manner. At times, McCarthy even spotted blinding flickers of mirrored light and realized some war chief was sending a secret code to his men. Within minutes of every signal, a small group of four, perhaps five, warriors suddenly burst from hiding to make a noisy charge on a weak spot along the line, singing, chanting, screeching all the while. When they tore past his end of the line, it was enough to make even a brave man pucker. After all, Sergeant Michael McCarthy had been left for dead on the White Bird Battlefield. He knew firsthand what fear could do to a man.

And when the momentary terror had passed and the rush was over, it came to the sergeant that the Nez Perce had not dared press their case against the center of Howard's big

---

*Located in the ravine currently called Anderson Creek.

square. That's when it came to him: how the general had posted his artillery and infantry, with their long-range rifles, at the center of this broad square, positioning the cavalry with their shorter carbines on the two flanks. The goddamned warriors had less respect for the horse soldiers' guns.*

That afternoon as the sun reigned supreme in its sky, McCarthy had stripped out of his dark navy blue fatigue blouse trimmed with tarnished brass buttons, he was sweating so. But now, in the coldest part of the day, he was shivering, his teeth threatening to rattle like ivory dice in a bone cup. He struggled to keep them under control, lest any man mistake the cold for fear.

When darkness fell, orders came round for them to hold their position on the line, the men spaced more than five yards apart, with instructions to improve their defenses by making their breastworks taller where they could find rocks or digging their rifle pits deeper on that part of the line where there were no stones to hunker behind. And McCarthy had his men bunkie-up so one man might try to catch a little shut-eye while the other kept watch.

Twice during the night, H Company had been resupplied with ammunition from the quartermaster's stores. But there was no food for those on the firing line. Didn't matter after awhile: It would've been damned near impossible to swallow the crumbly hardbread and salted beef without some water to wash it down anyway. Earlier in the afternoon as the temperature soared, McCarthy heard of an officer who had been driven so mad from thirst that he had lapped at the muddy water in a grassy mire where the mules and horses had been trampling the ground. By moonrise the man was taken sick, doubled over with terrible cramps at the field hospital back among the pack saddles and apishamores.

—

*At the end of the Nez Perce War, Captain George H. Burton reported: "It is explained by the Indians themselves, who acknowledge freely that they have but little fear of the short gun, in consequence of the short range of the carbine and the difficulty of aiming a piece so light and short with accuracy. . . ."

Hours of darkness, during which the sergeant and others listened to the sounds of the Nez Perce working on their barricades—rocks scraping together as one was piled on top of the other for the fight they knew was to come with the rising sun. That night General Howard approved a few sorties against the enemy, small squads of soldiers sent out to probe the edges of the timber, hoping to outflank the Nez Perce snipers. Wasn't long before each bunch came crawling back. What with the darkness and getting strung out far from their lines, the soldiers needed very little excuse to turn back after encountering the first stiff resistance.

A time or two even McCarthy had heard noises from the night that caused him to think the Indians were attempting to penetrate what they hoped would be a weak part of the army's lines through the night.

"Cap'n Trimble says these here Nez Perce are no despicable foe," Lieutenant William Parnell repeated quietly as he eased down beside his sergeant in the cold.

"They've fit us good this second time," McCarthy groaned. He was so thirsty, it even hurt his tongue to wag. "Leastways, we didn't have to run this time, Major."

Parnell nodded. One of the few survivors of the British army's "Charge of the Six Hundred" at Balaklava during the Crimean War, this large man sighed, "The cap'n and me was talking about how these Nez Perce were such pacifists—couldn't be goaded into a fight—before a few of 'em started murdering . . . and now we've seen 'em put a courageous defense of their homeland. This shaped up to be a beautiful battle, didn't it, Sergeant: all of Joseph's reds against all of Howard's soldiers."

"I ain't never heard of no Injuns digging in and holing up the way this bunch has," the Irishman commented. "Always figured they'd be running off once their women and children was safe."

"For a second time, it strikes me these warriors aren't the running kind."

McCarthy studied the big lieutenant in the dark. "You givin' these redskins their due?"

Grudgingly Parnell said, "I told the cap'n there never was a tribe more worthy of my respect, Sergeant."

A rustle of grass and an angry grumble from men disturbed in their sleep caused them both to look over their shoulders. Out of the darkness came the soft clatter of those wool-covered canteens slung around the neck of a young hospital steward.

"Hold up there, bucko." Parnell put out his beefy hand. "Where you think you're off to in the dark?"

With a gulp, the young soldier said, "Surgeon Sternberg sent me, sir. Crawl over to get some water at the spring yonder. The wounded are begging for it something awful."

"The spring's yonder," McCarthy said, pointing with his outstretched arm into the gray light at that ground halfway between the lines.

"T-that far?"

"And them Injuns gonna see you comin' every step of the way," McCarthy advised.

With a rapid, anxious shake of his head, the steward shrank to the ground and groaned, face in his hands. Finally slipping the canteen straps over his head, the soldier turned to his left, finding an open spot behind a low pile of rocks, then crabbed over to join some of McCarthy's men behind the breastworks.

After a few minutes of staring at the foolhardy steward, the sergeant finally asked, "Them wounded the surgeon's working on . . . you say they're really wanting some water in a bad way, are they, soldier?"

With a reluctant nod, the soft-cheeked steward said, "They was begging for water like it was life itself, sir."

Glancing for a moment at the rear of their lines, where Surgeon Sternberg had erected his hospital, McCarthy eventually raised his voice to announce, "I'm asking you weeds for volunteers. Any man of you to crawl to the spring with these here canteens for the wounded?"

He waited a minute more, glancing left and right along the line. "Any one of you—"

"I'll go with you, Sarge."

McCarthy turned back to the left, finding Private Fowler rocking up onto his knees, carbine in hand. For a long moment he measured the young fair-haired soldier, discovering no recklessness, no bravado, about him. The sergeant nodded in appreciation to the blue-eyed youth.

"Awright, you weed. Leave your carbine right there if you want, for you'll need to fill your hands with these goddamned canteens."

"I-I'd just as soon take my rifle with me, Sarge," Charles E. Fowler replied.

"Have it any way you want." McCarthy sighed. "Let's do this."

As they started over the barricade and away from the rifle pits, Parnell's voice boomed behind them.

"Give them brave boys some cover! Any of them bleeming bastards open up on them two, let 'em have it! Watch for the muzzle fire and let the redskins have it!"

Zigging and zagging across the grassy field, McCarthy and Fowler reached the brush-choked spring with a gasp of surprise that they hadn't been hit by those few random shots igniting the waning darkness from the Indian lines. Both collapsed to their bellies and immediately cupped their hands into the cool water, lapping at what little they managed to bring to their lips. One by one they filled the canteens, holding them under the surface of the shallow spring as the air gurgled past the necks.

"We had it easy getting here, you know," the private said softly. "Gonna be weighed down with all this water now getting back out."

McCarthy worried the top back onto the last of his canteens. "I figger we ain't got much a choice, soldier. We stay here—or we run best we can back to the lines."

"I'm f-for running, sir."

"Lead off, soldier. I'll cover your back door."

They hadn't trudged under the weight of those canteens more than twenty yards when the first bullet whistled past, cutting the strap on a canteen Fowler carried. It spun to the grass. The instant the private stopped and stooped to retrieve it, McCarthy lumbered to a halt over him. "G'won! G'won, goddammit! Leave the damn thing!"

As they rocked into a lumbering gait once more, McCarthy could see how Parnell was just getting to his feet above his riflemen, directing fire toward the trees where the Nez Perce marksmen lay hidden. At times in that sprint, the sergeant turned, bringing the carbine to his shoulder, more than relieved he hadn't left his weapon behind. Quickly snapping off a shot at a puff of smoke just then appearing in the distant brush, the sergeant raked open the trapdoor. As the copper cartridge came spinning from the breech, he shoved in a new round.

Whirling around again, he started running, the heavy canteens swinging rhythmically in great arcs from both shoulders. And noticed for the first time how Parnell was still standing, fully exposed as he directed the cover fire. The huge, fleshy lieutenant was waving the two of them on toward the barricades.

With each lunging step, the canteens swung front, then back in opposing arcs that threatened to pull McCarthy off-balance at every stride. An enemy bullet whimpered past just as he reached the breastworks and was dragged down by Parnell and another man. Two others already had Fowler on the ground, patting him over as they searched for wounds, yanking those blessed canteens from his shoulders.

McCarthy clambered to his hands and knees. "Back off, you goddamned weeds!" he roared, kicking at a man who had pulled at a stopper without even taking the canteen from Fowler's neck.

Every one of them froze. Then one of the soldiers said, "Sarge, we just covered your retreat, so I was thinking we all was due a li'l drink of this here water—"

"No, you ain't due no drink till them wounded get theirs," he growled back. "Not till they've had their fill." He knelt beside Fowler. "You think you can get your canteens and mine over to the hospital from here?"

Fowler grinned hugely, his blue eyes sparkling. "Damn right I can, Sergeant."

McCarthy watched the soldier start away, mindful of the uneasy silence that surrounded him. He suddenly called to Fowler, "Say, Private! I'll see to it Cap'n Trimble hears of this."

Fowler stopped, looking back over his shoulder at his first sergeant.

"Fact is, I'll see the cap'n makes you a cawpril for this, soldier. Any private sticks his neck out to make that run you just done for the sake of our wounded . . . least he deserves is a goddamn cawpril's stripes!"

Chapter Thirty-One

July 12, 1877

As the darkness had deepened around his lines, General Oliver Otis Howard had learned more and more of the many wild rumors circulating among the men at the front regarding the extent of their casualties. Some were reporting that as many as one in four men had been killed or dragged back to the surgeon's hospital.

That sort of thing was like a smoldering fire to a unit's fighting morale: If you didn't stomp it out right at the start, it could flare up when and where you least expected it. He had seen enough of that sort of reckless, groundless rumor during the recent War of Rebellion.

Howard brushed aside offers to carry word out to the front lines from his aides. Instead, he had announced he was himself going to reassure the troops their casualties were minor in number.

"Besides," he told his staff, "this will give me a chance to reconnoiter our position in relation to the Nez Perçe lines."

For more than an hour he had walked the barricades and rifle pits, calmly buoying the men, contradicting the wildfire rumors, and assessing the strengths of his own fortifications while measuring the weaknesses of the enemy. By 4:30 A.M. as the sky grayed, he was back at headquarters among those stacks of pack saddles and crates, blowing on a cup of scalding coffee.

"The men appear exhausted, General," declared First Lieutenant Melville C. Wilkinson.

"Exhausted perhaps, but not discouraged," Howard corrected. Then he glanced at the hospital a moment before continuing, "Our torn and bleeding comrades give us cheer by their brave words spoken, by their silent suffering."

He drank his coffee in silence as this new day came aborning, privately brooding on the failures that had turned what should have been nothing more than a brief flare-up by a few renegades into a full-scale war threatening to spill over the borders of his department.

Perry's singular defeat at the White Bird had convinced Howard that, man for man, these Non-Treaty bands were at the very least the equal of his best soldiers. Since that debacle, he had learned that what the Nez Perce lacked in precision drill and unit discipline they more than made up for in their fighting zeal and the accuracy of their aim. Especially on horseback—something he had never expected to see from mounted warriors. If he were to be successful against such a band of zealots, Otis realized he must be very, very cautious in not overplaying his hand. Another defeat like Perry's at White Bird would likely bring other disaffected tribes in the Northwest to Joseph's banner.

And that would likely mean the end of Howard's military career, the end of everything he had ever cherished as a fighting man.

Just after dawn Howard made his play for the spring—a force of his men under Captains Miller and Perry finally managing to rout the Nez Perce snipers from the spring and secure the area for his command. Which meant the firing at that end of the battlefield quieted down somewhat and the men could begin taking the first of the horses and mules to the spring in rotation. In the general's most private thoughts, this was the first tangible sign that the tide of this battle might well be turning in his favor. The end might be in sight. He thanked God for that glimmer of hope on the horizon, then ordered that coffee and freshly baked bread be taken out to all the men on the front line.

"They haven't had a meal since their breakfast yesterday," he told aide-de-camp Wilkinson. "Let's feed the men before we see what deviltry this day brings."

But despite all those hopes given birth with that dawn, the firing from both lines steadily increased in tempo and intensity as the air grew hotter. Determined that this would not be his Waterloo, Howard put every available man on the line, ordered to dig in and hold out. Late that second morning, a few Nez Perce horsemen even drove several hundred ponies through the soldier lines in an attempt to cause confusion and disrupt the effectiveness of their fire, perhaps even hoping to stampede the pack animals.

Although the warriors' valiant effort failed and they had already been forced back from the spring where they had caused so many soldier casualties the day before, for some reason the Nez Perce steadfastly persisted on the fringes of the battlefield. Here, then there, they made a rude, noisy appearance on his front. Small groups of them would ride up behind some low elevation in the rolling prairie, leap off their ponies, then quickly fire a few rounds at a weak spot in the soldier line before flinging themselves back atop their horses and racing out of sight. More of them crept forward on their bellies, snaking through the tall grass until within rifle range, whereupon they put their weapons to deadly use—proving just what marksmen they were with those Springfields taken from the White Bird and Rains massacre dead. Some of the more resourceful ones even tied clumps of grass to their heads to better conceal themselves as they made their approach.

And so that morning and early afternoon passed while each side sought desperately to make the jump on the other, wheedling at every little advantage, but with neither the enemy nor Howard's men making any real progress beyond where the lines had remained for the last eight hours.

That was the end of Howard's patience.

Just before two o'clock, the general called Captain Marcus Miller back to headquarters, where he detailed orders for a daring charge. "Colonel, I'm withdrawing your artillerymen from the line and filling that gap with some thinly spread cavalry and infantry," Howard explained.

From his lips the captain tore the short-stemmed pipe he always had clamped between his teeth. "Where are you sending us, sir?"

"You will move your line directly toward the bluff. Your objective will be that shallow ravine I believe is holding most of the warriors. One of the howitzers will be in support."

"Support, General?"

"Lieutenant Otis will be in charge of laying down a harassing fire with the twelve-pounder, to loosen things up in there before your advance; then your men will sweep around the left end of the Nez Perce to take them in the rear."

"Very good, sir," Miller replied, enthused. "With your permission, I'll go begin my withdrawal from the line so we can prepare for our attack."

Howard was squinting into the bright sunlight, watching the right of his line where Rodney's and Trimble's men were deployed, when Lieutenant Wilkinson came huffing up on foot.

"General!" the young officer gasped. "Look there—in the distance, sir!"

Otis quickly put the field glasses to his eyes and adjusted the focus. Beneath that low dust cloud clinging to the ridgeline far to their south he could begin to make out the approach of a blue column.

"Who are they, General?" asked Lieutenant C. E. S. Wood as he came to Howard's elbow.

"That can only be Jackson's cavalrymen," he answered, dread filling him, "bringing in the pack train from Lapwai—"

At the very moment he was about to drop the field glasses from his eyes, something off to the right hooked his attention. His heart sank with the sight.

The enemy had spotted Jackson's company. Howard knew B Troop, First U. S. Cavalry, likely had a complement of no more than forty men along to guard that 120-mule pack train that had been expected to reach his column days ago. The Nez Perce would scatter Jackson's mules and create havoc among the troopers at best. At worst, the warriors would tear through the pack train as they butchered Jackson's undermanned escort.

"Colonel Miller!" he roared, using the officer's brevet rank.

The officer jerked to a halt and turned on his heel as Howard realized just how unusual it was that any of his officers ever heard him raise his voice, much less bellow like that.

Leading his horse, Miller returned. "Sir?"

"Your orders have changed, Colonel," Howard said, shoving the field glasses toward the officer. "Have yourself a look."

As Miller studied that distant detachment advancing beneath the dust cloud, able to see how the warriors were growing agitated with the escort's approach, Howard said, "Your battalion has my orders to do all that's necessary to keep the enemy off that pack train. See that Captain Jackson's men reach the safety of our lines."

"Yes, sir!"

Within minutes Miller was extending his forces to the left of the line, by company-front formation, moving A, D, E, and G Batteries of his Fourth Artillery toward the ridge a mile from Howard's compound—then two miles—continually keeping themselves between the warriors and the heading that oncoming pack train was taking. The Nez Perce horsemen made a few showy, but ineffectual, charges along Miller's flanks but never got close enough to actually engage the foot soldiers pressing ever on to rendezvous with Jackson's escort.

Howard promptly ordered Rodney's cavalrymen toward the left side of their line, to be in position to act as reserves, should Miller require assistance.

It was nearing 3:00 P.M. by the time the pack train neared Howard's lines, with Miller's battalion arrayed entirely on Jackson's left flank. When he had his batteries opposite the end of the jagged ravine along the southern side of the battlefield, the captain gave his order.

"Men!" he roared above the cries of the oncoming warriors and their horses. "Get up and go for them! If we don't do something now, they'll likely kill us all!"

With startling speed, Miller wheeled his artillerymen by the left flank and, as a whole, they bolted into a ragged sprint, racing impetuously for the surprised warriors in the ravine.

As the pack mules and their escort rattled inside Howard's lines, the general immediately threw Captain Rodney's reserves into motion, ordered against the left flank of what would momentarily be a noisy collision.

Just as Howard had gambled, Nez Perce horsemen burst from the ravine, streaming along Miller's front, racing for the soldiers' left, where it was plain they intended to flank those four batteries of artillerymen. But the instant they swept around the back of Miller's artillerymen, the warriors ran right into Rodney's horse soldiers! As the general watched, all but breathless for those few desperate minutes, it seemed the Nez Perce flung every one of their men against that end of his line, attempting to roll it up just as they had done to Perry's battalion at the White Bird.

A fierce, swirling skirmish raised a boiling dust cloud that swallowed both soldier and Indian in the stinging heat of that midafternoon. Moment by moment, the Nez Perce made a most valiant resistance to check Miller's charge, attempting to angle back on Miller's rear when they were caught by surprise between the two forces. Rodney's men had outflanked the flankers and were just beginning to roll up the end of the Nez Perce line when . . . when—the enemy broke!

Only a few horsemen at first. Soon more. Eventually the rest as their entire line gave way, with both Miller's and Rodney's outfits advancing into the onslaught, right on the warriors' tails. Those few who held to the bitter end waited until the soldiers were no farther than twenty yards before they wheeled about and fled.

"To the river!" began the cry from those soldiers experiencing their first success. "To the river!"

Otis knew he must not let Joseph and his warriors escape.

"Captain Winters!" Howard bawled, knowing he had but

moments to capitalize on this fracture just opening in the enemy's defenses. "Take two companies of infantry and your dismounted cavalrymen and reinforce Miller! On the double, man! On the double now!"

With Winters on his way toward the retreating tribesmen, Howard next ordered up Jackson's dismounted B Company—weary from its escort duty—to join Trimble's H and advance in double time to support one of the Gatling guns and both howitzers to the edge of the bluff, where the gun crews were to open up a hot fire on the fleeing warriors.

By Jupiter! If this didn't feel a great deal better than had that news of Perry's defeat on the White Bird, than the mucking around back and forth across the Salmon, not to mention those Cottonwood fiascos!

With Joseph on the run now—maybe . . . just maybe, he could end this war in the next two days, three at the most!

Arghghgh!

Yellow Wolf hadn't felt anything like the pain piercing his left wrist!

The instant that soldier bullet had smacked him earlier that morning, he had flopped onto the ground, slowly swallowing down the waves of pain, gripping the bloody wound tightly in his right hand. For a long time he lay there, unmoving. When he finally did attempt to raise himself so he could lean back against part of the stone barricades, another soldier bullet slapped the boulder near his cheek. A rock chip gouged the flesh just below his left eye.

Temporarily blinded, he collapsed back into the grass, listening to the increased fury of the *suapie* volleys sent hurling into the timber at the ravine. His cheek felt damp, warm. Yellow Wolf touched it. Blood, streaming down his face from the flesh wound. Closing his right eye momentarily, he realized he couldn't see from the left. He closed them both and worried how this fight would end now.

At dawn, there hadn't been enough warriors to blunt the soldiers' daring charge on the spring. No more than five-times-ten stayed with *Ollokot* now. The rest had long ago retreated back to the village for the night or still slept safely in the smokers' lodge where they held long discussions on what path this struggle should take. Some of the chiefs and older warriors had wanted this to be the last fight against the *suapies*—either defeating the white men in a decisive and pitched battle or being destroyed by Cut-Off Arm. But others still argued for retreat and flight. Looking Glass talked ever stronger about a new life for their people across the mountains.

It turned Yellow Wolf's sour stomach into knots when he thought of so many of fighting age electing not to put their bodies in the struggle . . . while a young man like *Eelah-weeman*, called About Asleep—just in his fourteenth summer—bravely carried water up to the hot, thirsty warriors fighting on the ridge top all that first afternoon and again into this second.

Red Thunder was the only brave fighter killed yesterday, shot from his horse during that fierce charge against the mule train as the battle was opened. But it was in that brushy ravine around the spring early this morning that the *Nee-Me-Poo* suffered their heaviest losses. Two veteran warriors gave their lives. *Wayakat*, called Going Across, was killed instantly, and *Yoomstis Kunnin*, known as Grizzly Bear Blanket, received a mortal wound. In addition, *Howwallits*, the one called Mean Man, suffered a slight wound before the warriors were driven back from the water hole.

With things turning out badly as that second day of fighting progressed, the chiefs were already arguing among themselves. *Ollokot* and *Toohoolhoolzote*, Rainbow and Five Wounds, Two Moons and Sun Necklace—too many of their fighting men had refused to add their bodies to this fight. Some had hung back in the village to guard the women and children, but more had simply not advanced to the front to join the fighters. They had tarried at the smoking lodge, safe from the sting of soldier bullets. By the time some of those men on the far right of their defenses spotted the approaching dust cloud, they had been fighting for much of two days. *Ollokot* called for volunteers to follow him as he cut off the arriving Shadows and their long pack train, then rode off to make his noisy charge.

That's when everything went into a blur for Yellow Wolf. Both sides were shooting more furiously as they collided far to the right along the edge of the ridge. In minutes the dust cloud over that part of the fight started rolling in Yellow Wolf's direction. It didn't take him long before he realized why the soldiers were coming on so quickly. There were few warriors to oppose them!

Looking this way and that, he found himself all but alone on this far side of the ravine, where the fighting men were suddenly scrambling to their ponies, pitching them on down the draw for the river below—the *suapies* right on their heels. Glancing a moment into the valley, Yellow Wolf worried about his mother, wondering if she were among those now streaming up the Cottonwood, leaving behind most of their lodgepoles and camp equipment.

Enimkinikai!

Curses to the war chiefs for denying Joseph the opportunity to dismantle the village yesterday! A thousand curses for not allowing the *Wallowa* leader time to have the women prepare to move the village in an orderly retreat rather than this sudden, shocking, and uncoordinated flight—like that of a half-thousand mud sparrows before the night owls' warning screech. Instead of taking all that they owned and slipping away while the warriors had done battle with Cut-Off Arm's soldiers . . . now the families were forced to scramble for their lives, able to take only part of what they owned as they drove their huge pony herds up the steep hillsides west of the South Fork and onto the Camas Prairie once more.

"Nobody here!"

Yellow Wolf heard the voice cry out in his tongue. "Who is that?" he asked.

"*Wottolen,*" the disembodied voice replied. "Is that Yellow Wolf?"

"Yes—I thought I was alone!"

"We are. There are but a few of us left now!" *Wottolen* bellowed as he burst into view, leading his pony through the trees. He leaped onto its back and wrenched the animal toward the head of the ravine. "Come, Yellow Wolf! It is time to *quit!*"

He started running on foot, following the older warrior—then suddenly remembered his pony, where he had tied it. Yellow Wolf raced for the tree, relieved to find the animal, and lunged onto its back, doing his best to clutch the reins and his rifle both with his right hand. Down, down, down he put it in motion, flying faster and faster down the ravine toward the river. Cutting left as he reached the valley, the young warrior dashed for the ford. Into the river, each lunging step took him closer and closer to the abandoned village. Up the far bank and into the empty camp.

The first boom of the cannon echoed overhead. Then the shrill whistle of the ball, closer and closer. That shell crashed through an abandoned lodge and exploded in a fury of dirt, flying lodgepoles, and smoke.

As the deafening roar faded, his ears caught the pitiful sound of a woman's cries. The whinny of a frightened horse.

Another boom rattled the valley. He whirled to look at the ridge top, mesmerized by the whining hiss of the oncoming cannonball. It whistled overhead into a patch of ground just beyond the lodges, tearing into their race ground with a loud, dusty explosion that hurtled clods of earth in a hundred directions.

As he kicked his pony into motion again, the woman and her crying horse suddenly appeared between the lodges to his right. She fought the pony as it reared, pawed the air, and landed with a bone-jarring jolt, then pranced and reared again, eyes mooning with terror. It was Joseph's wife, *Ta-ma-al-we-non-my*, the one known as Driven Before a Cold Storm. Her eyes were just as big as the horse's when he chattered to a halt beside her. There was no one else left but the two of them.

"*Heinmot!*" she shrieked his familial name, White Thunder. "My baby! I am worried about my baby!"

"Where?"

"Behind you!"

He whirled his horse to look, but his attention was immediately riveted on the ravine across the river, seeing how the soldiers had begun their descent right on his heels. Tearing his eyes away, Yellow Wolf spotted Joseph's newborn in a *tekash*, its cradle board, propped against a set of bare lodgepoles—where the buffalo-hide cover had been torn away from the graceful spiral of poles. Laying his rifle across the crook of his left elbow and stuffing the reins between his teeth, Yellow Wolf leaned over and seized the top of the *tekash* in his strong hand.

By the time he was bringing the pony around, the woman's horse had settled. She laughed with such unbounded joy as he handed her that bawling child lashed in its cradle board, a daughter, who had been born just as this war ignited against the Shadows.

He ripped the reins from his teeth. "Where is your husband?"

She looked up from the baby's face, saying, "He went ahead, leading the village away to safety as he has done since we left that last happy camp at *Tepahlewam*. I am sure he did not know I would be the last one here with his daughter," her words came breathlessly. "He could not have left us here if he had known. Joseph must think I am the head of the march with the other women and children—"

"Your husband has done what only a great chief would do, woman," Yellow Wolf reminded her. "His duty was to see all the rest of our camp to safety, before seeing only to his own family."

As they brought their ponies around and started away, she dropped her eyes a moment, saying, "For many days now, since the war on us started, my heart wanted Joseph to be something more than a camp chief. Sometimes . . . I secretly hoped he would become one of the fighting chiefs—"

She was interrupted by another loud roar as rocks

rained down upon them, limbs from the trees spinning out of the sky.

Yellow Wolf sighed, looking down at the face of Joseph's daughter in that *tekash*. Then he said, "Your husband, our leader, he has always done what he thought best to protect his people—taking charge of the old men, the women and little ones, a sacred duty. I am proud to be part of his family," Yellow Wolf admitted.

She looked at him kindly as their ponies began to clamber into the Cottonwood canyon. "And Joseph is proud of you."

"Your husband, our chief, I have come to think of him as a better warrior than those loud-talkers in the smoking lodge, or those like Looking Glass who slip back to the village." Quickly glancing over his shoulder at the ruins of the village they were leaving behind, Yellow Wolf added, "Joseph is a man who always puts the needs of his people before his own. The same way our warrior chiefs put themselves between our camps and the enemy."

Chapter Thirty-Two

July 12, 1877

"*Boots and Saddles!*" THE SERGEANT BAWLED AT HIS MEN. "*Boots and Saddles*, you godblessit weeds!"

First Sergeant Michael McCarthy hurled his slim frame atop his horse without using the stirrup and yanked back on the reins, immediately bringing the frightened sidestepping horse under control.

Parnell was among them an instant later, Captain Trimble seated on his mount, waiting off to the side as H Troop shuffled into ranks with the other cavalry troops. The mustachioed veteran of the Crimean War bellowed, "On the double, Sergeant! For-r-r-rad!"

With a yelp of his own, McCarthy flung his arm forward, leading them out in a lope after those fleeing warriors skidding, slipping, sailing ass over teakettle down the ravine hundreds of yards ahead of them. But almost as suddenly Parnell hurled his arm upward, halting the column as McCarthy bolted up beside him. He came to a halt beside the large officer, staring down in amazement at the body of a dead Indian—nothing less than gigantic in stature.

"Take a good look at that, you Irishman," declared the lieutenant with the growl of a dog suddenly released from its chain.

The sergeant's eyes poured over the stone breastworks. "Easy to see why we wasn't turning many of 'em into good Injuns this day," McCarthy lamented.

He quickly regarded the tall stacks of rock piled up by the Indians, most of the formations high enough for a man to stand behind as he sniped at the army lines. Many of the stacks even had willow branches poking from their tops—put there so the warriors and their weapons would be concealed from the soldiers.

Of a sudden, behind H Troop arose the noise of a broad

front of approaching horsemen. Parnell kicked his horse, ordering, "Let's get this company down to the river!"

At the east bank of the South Fork both Trimble's company and Whipple's men held up, waiting momentarily until Captain David Perry, commander of the cavalry battalion, raced up to the advance and gave the order for those two companies to ford the stream then and there. Like so many of the men milling on the bank, McCarthy, heart pounding, was barely able to wait before crossing in pursuit of the fleeing village, at long last wiping away the stain of the White Bird debacle. Revenge was within reach—

"Cross and hold the village!" Perry declared, his horse backing slightly under the anxiety of its rider.

"*H-hold* the village, Colonel?" Trimble asked.

Perry glared at the captain, his nemesis from the White Bird Canyon debacle. "Yes. *Hold* the village."

"Beggin' your pardon, Colonel," Parnell pleaded. "We ain't never gonna get another chance like this'un to follow up them buggers and tear apart their retreat!"

Perry's withering gaze suddenly pinned Parnell to his saddle. "Your captain has his orders to cross and hold against possible attack, Lieutenant."

Good soldier that he was, Parnell snapped a salute. "Very good, Colonel!"

As Perry ordered, both cavalry companies crossed right there, plunging into the deep, cold water without going in search of a shallow ford. As McCarthy brought his shuddering horse under control, lunging onto the far bank as it flung water from its hide, he glanced up and spotted the last two riders escaping to the top of the far hill just beyond the village. One of the pair carried something bulky in his arms while the other turned to glance over his shoulder before disappearing from sight—

"There's some of 'em still in that creek bottom!" a trooper cried.

McCarthy wheeled his horse, catching the blur of motion as a dozen or more of the warriors took up positions in the trees along Cottonwood Creek, northwest of the village.

With the warning, Perry quickly ordered three companies forward at a walk, slowly advancing on the creek, driving the Nez Perce back into the timber. But his charge was so cautious and dilatory that it was plain, even to General Howard, who was crossing the Clearwater at that moment, David Perry never again had any intention of pitching into an enemy so close at hand.

With Jackson's B Troop recalled to the riverbank, Trimble and Whipple deployed their troopers, spreading them on a wide skirmishers' front before they cautiously entered the camp on horseback after warning their men of snipers. The fragrance of cooking meat made McCarthy's mouth water. For more than thirty-six hours Howard's army hadn't eaten anything but bread and spring water. But here, on one fire after another, kettles simmered or meal broiled over low flames—supper already started for the fighting men.

On the far side of the village where both companies were halted and dismounted—with horse holders sent to the rear—the troopers established a skirmish line in the event the enemy decided to double back and make an attack. McCarthy's H Troop discovered a network of extensive log barricades the Nez Perce had constructed. It clearly showed how the war chiefs believed attack would come from that western side of their camp facing the Camas Prairie.

Within minutes the first of the infantry were reaching the far bank, where Jackson's troop was assigned to transport the foot soldiers across the river, riding double on the backs of their horses, then turning around to take up another soldier, one after another.

Already several of the civilians from Mount Idaho and Grangeville and some of the packers were leaping from their horses among the lodges. While some of the men ducked inside to determine what valuables might have been left behind, others yanked the cleaning rods from their rifles and began to probe any likely spot of freshly turned soil.

"What the hell you poking for?" McCarthy asked one dark-faced citizen.

"Caches. Where these red niggers buried the stuff they couldn't take with 'em."

Another volunteer came to a stop nearby, his arms loaded with a blanket and brass kettle, along with an assortment of other goods. "Looks to me them Nez Perce figger to come back for their plunder soon."

"Soon as they get shet of you army boys," the first man commented with a snort, "they'll double round and be back here to dig all this up."

One at a time, or by the handfuls, the treasures emerged from those lodges abandoned beside the South Fork of the Clearwater. A beautiful blue silk dress, which, by tying up the sleeves in the right manner, a woman had cleverly fashioned into a bag to hold her camas roots. An old-fashioned hoopskirt had been adorned with beads and feathers, reflecting the new owner's tastes. Knives and forks, china plates, much more clothing, all the white man's goods now intermingled with dressed furs, moccasins, feathered headdresses, and more of their dried meat and berries. Some of the packers roared with delight when they ran across jewelry, fine silver tableware, and even small bags filled with gold dust or coins. Ammunition discovered in the lodges indicated many of the warriors were using Henry and Winchester carbines, along with some cartridges for some unknown model of a long-range target or buffalo gun.

But what caught McCarthy's attention was a pair of beaded moccasins sewn for a very small child he spotted near the base of a lodge. Right next to them lay some little white girl's rag doll. At a glance it was easy to see that this was not a Nez Perce toy. Side by side these discarded items lay, Indian and white together—

"The general wants it all burned!" Perry shouted as he rode onto the flat, leading some of Howard's headquarters group as more and more infantrymen were "ferried" across the river all around them.

"Give us a little time to get through all this goddamned plunder!" one of the citizens pleaded as he dragged a blanket out of a lodge. On it lay a collection of valuables he was determined to save from the fires.

"Captain Whipple!" Perry shouted. "Give these civilians five more minutes, then put your men to work setting the tepees on fire!"

On all sides of McCarthy the civilians scrambled like ants on a hill a playful child has stirred with his stick—frantic to pull out everything of any value, claiming it for themselves . . . or reclaiming that which it was plain had been stolen from the farms along the Salmon or the ranches dotting the Camas Prairie. *The spoils of war*, Michael thought. *The spoils of a mean, dirty little war.*

In reality, most of what he saw was the few earthly possessions left behind by some dead man or woman now mercifully torn from this veil of tears in that first flurry of brutal and senseless murders.

The sergeant listened as Captain Trimble rode up to Perry, saluted, and asked, "Colonel, when can the men fall out and prepare supper? They haven't eaten much but coffee and a few bites of bread in more than a day and a half now."

"As soon as we have a defensive perimeter established and these lodges burned—just as General Howard ordered," he replied, watching the east bank as more and more of the command streamed down to the riverside from the plateau above.

McCarthy's mouth was already watering, as he thought of the potatoes and bacon back on those pack animals, hot food they could fry up while the coffee was boiling. The first decent meal in days now that they had a firm victory in hand.

His stomach growled in protest. They'd eat till they could eat no more tonight, then set off in the morning, running those fleeing warrior bands into the ground somewhere on the Camas Prairie.

Joseph and Mary—with them Injuns on the run, this war damn near has to be over now!

HE was disgusted with the warrior chiefs. Disgusted with the other so-called fighting men, too. Still, Shore Crossing understood why they had decided to leave the soldiers behind and flee the camping place they called *Pitayiwahwih*. After two days of fighting, when no victory was in sight, it was better to leave so that a man could fight another day, in another place.

As the white man's big-throated guns sent the fiery balls into the camp, the women mounted up on their saddle horses and the young boys shooed the herds over the western hills, out of danger. At the edge of the timber west of the camp, Shore Crossing joined one of the knots of warriors waiting in the shadows for the first soldiers to come in pursuit of more than 450 fleeing women and children. But the *suapies* did not come racing in pursuit. It was easy to see how little the soldiers knew about crossing the river. The fast water would delay the white men long enough that the fighting men would not have to keep them busy while the camp escaped up the Cottonwood canyon.

With a struggle the soldiers reached the village, where some of them spotted *Ollokot*'s fighting men in the timber. After making a few shots at the *suapies*, the chiefs gave signals with the wave of an arm. Most of the warriors slipped away through the hills to rejoin the rest of the people already on their way. By the time Shore Crossing and the others caught up to the frantic retreat, White Bird, Looking Glass, and Joseph had restored some sense of order to the line of march. No longer were they in mad retreat. Once more the warriors were positioned along the sides of the column as it emerged onto the edge of the Camas Prairie. As their hearts began to slow and their thoughts were collected, the chiefs, headmen, and warriors began to deliberate their options.

Shore Crossing and the other Red Coats wanted all the young men to follow them and make one last, grand attack on Cut-Off Arm's soldiers. Whoever was whipped, it would be the last fight. But most of the chiefs and warriors said that events did not warrant one last, suicidal fight.

"Why all this war up here? Our camp is not attacked! All can escape without fighting. Why die without cause?"

Which meant that if the chiefs of the Non-Treaty bands were not going to risk their women and children in one last deadly battle, then their only course was to fully commit themselves to a war of retreat and evasion. And that decision left but two options for the leaders.

That night Joseph again proposed, "I want to return my people to the *Wallowa*. That is where we will make our stand, where we can die if we are to be wiped out."

But Looking Glass sneered, arguing, "To march back to that rugged country between the Salmon and the Snake would expose our families to danger on the open ground of the Camas Prairie. The *suapie* fort is on one side, and the Shadow towns are on the other. No. We must stay close by the Clearwater, for here the canyons are deep enough that Cut-Off Arm's men become entangled as they cross back and forth. We can stay out of reach of the white men until we decide what to do, and where to go."

Shore Crossing did not like this Looking Glass. At first the Alpowai chief had turned his back on the warrior bands, calling the fighting men fools for making war and shedding the blood of white men. Then last night, Shore Crossing had seen Looking Glass for what he was. After the darkness deepened and the shooting stopped, the Clearwater chief had slinked back down to camp to eat and sleep—as if no fight was going on above them! To *Wahlitits*, what Looking Glass had done was nothing short of cowardice. The chief was running away from the war.

In the end, the headmen elected to follow Looking Glass's proposal. But this time when they took refuge, they would send out scouts to prowl the surrounding countryside.

"Never again must we allow the white man to slip up on us undetected," Shore Crossing told that large group of chiefs and fighting men.

With a triumphant grin, Looking Glass said, "Perhaps we can leave this war behind here in the Idaho . . . and slip away to the buffalo country, where we will never have to worry again that we will be attacked while our village is sleeping."

There were many, many murmurs of agreement. Shore Crossing had to admit that it sounded seductive, safe, and luring. Could there really be a place where they would no longer be concerned with a blood-hungry army and Shadows crying for vengeance? But . . . was such a choice of running away from the enemy really the sort of decision a fighting man would make?

There on the Cottonwood the head of the march came back around on its tracks, starting east once again, looping for the Clearwater once more. As the sun began to settle atop the far mountains, those in the lead angled north, following the river bluffs downstream. Those warriors riding far out on the flanks stopped on the heights where they could once more look down on what had once been their camp of celebration and joy. The ground of *Pitayiwahwih* crawled with soldiers like a nest of spiders while spires of oily black smoke rose in the hot afternoon air. In huge bonfires the *suapies* were destroying everything the People had left behind. Sadly, the Non-Treaty bands dropped behind the bluffs, continuing downriver for Kamiah, where the Dreamers sometimes visited the Christian Indians who tended their fields there.

If little else was clear, Shore Crossing knew that Cut-Off Arm's soldiers had no intention of chasing them this night. The white men believed they had won a great battle. Even though the *suapies* had managed to kill only four warriors* while three times as many whites were dead, the soldiers

---

*Going Across or *Wayakat*, Grizzly Bear Blanket or *Yoomtis Kuunin*, Red Thunder or *Heinmot Ilppilp*, and Whittling or *Lelooskin*. Both *Wayakat* and *Lelooskin* fell so close to the soldier lines they had to be left where they lay in the retreat from Battle Ridge.

would think they had won! Even though the village had escaped, even though the *Nee-Me-Poo* still had their great herds of horses and cattle . . . the white man would make much of that fight on the Clearwater.

From experience, the chiefs knew Cut-Off Arm would make much of a few tired, old horses they had abandoned to the *suapies*. He would make even more of all the lodges the women had been forced to leave behind—even though the women could eventually cut more lodgepoles and the men could hunt more hides, once they were gone to the buffalo country.

So how was it that the white men could turn an ignominious defeat for them into such a glorious victory over the *Nee-Me-Poo*?

"How the hell old do you think she is, Lieutenant?" Thomas Sutherland asked the general's aide just after sunset.

It was nearing 7:00 P.M. Melville Wilkinson shrugged as General O. O. Howard came up to a stop in that narrow gauntlet made by the Treaty Nez Perce who served as his trackers. The lieutenant whispered to the newsman, "From the looks of her, my guess is she's close to a hundred!"

Sutherland figured that wasn't far off. The old woman had to be no less than ninety, frail and wrinkled and so slow to move that she had been waiting for the soldiers to find her propped against this tree on the outskirts of the abandoned village. While soldiers and civilians alike were gallivanting around camp, showing off their buckskin clothing and moccasins they had saved from the burning lodges, the correspondent had trotted over as soon as he heard the call for some of the Christian Indians to help interpret the gap-toothed woman's garbled talk.

Now that Howard was here, the trackers began to string together broken words in English, a few phrases, for the white men, explaining what she had told them in their native tongue.

"Where is the camp going now?"

She didn't know for sure. Just getting away from the soldiers. They wanted to be left alone, and the chiefs were arguing about how best to leave all the trouble in Idaho behind.

Howard inquired, "What will it take for Joseph to surrender his people and come on the reservation?"

She gazed up at the one-armed general long and steady with her rheumy, watery eyes, then informed the translator that Joseph was not the chief of that village. There were five bands. Five chiefs. And Joseph was too young to be a chief over them all. Older men had the wisdom to assume that sort of leadership in emergencies such as this. Men like *Toohoolhoolzote*, White Bird, and especially Looking Glass.

"*Toohoolhoolzote*," Howard echoed with an angry growl. "I put that old man in jail months ago. Should have kept him there."

"No, he will never lead the camps," she replied, folding her arthritic hands across her lap. *Toohoolhoolzote* was too unstable, too fiery, too harsh to reign as chief over all the bands together.

"White Bird? If Joseph isn't leading them, is White Bird?"

Again she stared the general in the eye and told the Christian trackers that the only one who seemed to have enough power to hold all five bands in his hand was her chief.

Howard looked quickly at the trackers. "Who the blazes is her chief?"

"Looking Glass."

Sutherland watched Howard wag his head, realizing the general must suddenly be considering how Whipple had botched his mission to arrest the chief and hold him for the duration of the hostilities. Had that sad little debacle been handled better, Howard might well have deprived the warriors' bands of that one chief they were now rallying behind.

"General, sir?"

Howard turned with the rest of them as Lieutenant Parnell rode up on horseback, accompanied by another of the Christian trackers.

"This one just came back from seeing things to the north, General," Parnell explained.

Howard studied him a moment. "Reuben. That's your Christian name?"

"James Reuben," the man said in passable English. "News for you."

"Out with it," Parnell nudged.

"Kamiah," Reuben began. "Warriors go to Kamiah—"

"Seems the hostiles aren't fleeing onto the Camas Prairie like we figured they would when we spotted 'em running west," Parnell declared impatiently. "They're scampering north instead, downriver."

With a lunge, Howard came up to Reuben's knee, staring up at him in the evening twilight. "That's a Christian settlement, isn't it?"

Reuben nodded. "I come back with word of the burning and stealing."

"Joseph's warriors are already destroying Kamiah?" Howard asked.

"They come to cross the river at the Kamiah ford," the tracker explained, his eyes shifting anxiously. "They cross the river there to burn houses of James Lawyer people, or . . . or—"

"Or what?" Howard snapped impatiently.

"Kamiah is the end of the road."

Now Howard grabbed Reuben's reins. "End of what road?"

"End of the Lolo. Kamiah begin the road to the buffalo country."

Chapter Thirty-Three

—

July 13, 1877

BY TELEGRAPH

—

OREGON

—

Joseph Apparently Getting Away.

SAN FRANCISCO, July 12.—A Portland press dispatch telegram received to-day at military headquarters, dated Cottonwood, July 8, says that all of Joseph's band have crossed the Clear Water, supposed to be heading for the Bitter Root country. Should this be true, the fight will prove a running one. The infantry will prove comparatively non-effective. Decisive work will have to be done by the cavalry.

Fort Lapwai
July 13, 1877

Dear Mamma,

I hurriedly finished up a letter this morning, as John came in and told me a mail would leave in five minutes. I did not say half I wanted to, and I will begin this and write a page a day.

. . . The news we were all expecting from General Howard came. There has been a fight, a very severe one. Our loss was 11 killed and 26 wounded. Two of the officers, Captain Bancroft and Mr. Williams, are wounded. We know both of them well. The Indians must have lost heavily. They make desperate efforts to carry off their dead, and 13 dead Indians were left on the field . . . This is our first good news and we all feel thankful. I hope the end of the war is near, but John and other officers think

that after more troops come the Indians will get out of the road, and there will have to be a winter campaign organized to finish them up . . . Two of the medical officers now in the field are not in good health, and I am dreading daily that they will give out and be sent back here to look after the hospital and supplies, and John will be sent out in their place. In case he should go, he would not like me to stay here, as his movements for the entire campaign would be uncertain . . .

Before I forget it, the jack straws came. The children have had two or three nice plays with them. I meant to speak of these things long ago, but indeed I have forgotten everything I ought to remember for the last month.

Your loving daughter,
Emily F.

IT HAD ALMOST BEEN A MONTH SINCE CAPTAIN CHARLES C. Rawn and his small infantry detachment put Fort Shaw and the Sun River behind them on 9 June. His own I Company, along with Captain William Logan's A Company—a total of forty-five men—had come here to this valley of the five rivers with orders to purchase supplies and hire quartermaster employees, who would help construct a small post* some four miles southwest of Missoula City, Montana Territory. Back in May, Lieutenant General Philip Sheridan requested an allocation of $20,000 from the secretary of war for this post that would police intertribal conflicts over hunting grounds. The citizens on this side of the Bitterroot, on the other hand, wanted Colonel John Gibbon's Seventh U. S. Infantry to make a firm show of protecting the settlements.

After all, from here the Nez Perce War was no more than a mountain range away.

Back in April a large band of Looking Glass's people—returning from a successful buffalo hunt on the northern

---

*This post, officially established on June 25, 1877, was not named a fort until November of that year.

plains—camped with Chief Charlot's* Flathead, still residing south of their reservation and Missoula City in the Bitterroot valley. For generations it had been a common practice for the Non-Treaty bands to spend a little time with their acquaintances in Montana Territory, both Flathead and white. Later, in mid-June, an additional thirty-some lodges of Nez Perce stopped in the Bitterroot on their way home to Idaho Territory, just about the time the wires began to hum with news that war had broken out. Because a growing number of his citizens were becoming nervous that trouble could boil over into Montana Territory, Governor Benjamin F. Potts began raising hell with the army and officials back in Washington City, asking permission to raise a state militia. He was turned down at the highest levels.

Instead, the army said they had already dispatched this detachment of two companies west to Missoula City, there to establish a presence in the Bitterroot valley, where the Nez Perce were often seen coming and going, as well as trading, during the hunting season.

A Civil War veteran, with sixteen years in the regiment, Captain Rawn didn't know what more he could do to quiet the inflamed passions of the settlers in this country. Upon his arrival, valley locals recommended he place an outpost somewhere up the Lolo Trail because of the threat and the Nez Perce tradition of traveling to and from their home through the Lolo corridor. Rawn agreed, *if* the citizens would provide his detachment with horses. None of the civilians would, so things quieted down somewhat when the locals went back home, grumbling and disgruntled at the army's inaction.

Which gave Rawn the opportunity to pay a call on Peter Ronan, newly appointed agent to the Flathead. Together they had gone to see Chief Charlot, securing his promise that, should the hostiles spill over into Montana, the Flathead would remain neutral but nonetheless provide intelli-

---

*In Flathead, Charlot means "Little Claw of the Grizzly."

gence of Nez Perce movements to the white man.

"You feel like you can trust this Charlot?" Rawn had asked as they rode back toward the agency.

"I'd like to think I could," Ronan admitted. "But something tells me we'd better keep an eye on him."

"That's exactly what I was thinking," Rawn replied. "There are simply too many of these Flatheads for a right-thinking man not to be wary and mistrustful of them catching this contagion if it spread from Idaho. Something in my gut is telling me I better not be too trusting of that Indian. His eyes shift a little too much."

Maybe it was nothing at all to worry about, but some time back a small band of eleven Nez Perce lodges under Eagle-from-the-Light had already joined Charlot's Flathead, more or less permanently, erecting their camp circle just south of the exit from the Lolo Trail, declaring they wished to stay in Montana despite the fact that Howard and agent John B. Monteith had ordered them back to Idaho and a life on the reservation.

Just last week Eagle-from-the-Light had come to Ronan requesting permission to camp right on the reservation just north of Missoula City itself, in his people's attempt to stay out of trouble should the hostile bands invade Montana Territory. But the Flathead agent refused, saying he did not want to provide a haven for Indians illegally off their reservation. In the end, those eleven lodges stayed where they were near the terminus of the Lolo Trail in the Bitterroot valley.

Even though Governor Potts made his second request of the army to form a citizen militia this very day, the thirteenth of July, for the time being Captain Rawn felt like everything was under control. Word was, General Oliver Otis Howard had a column of some six hundred men, both soldier and civilian, about to crush the upstart Nez Perce. It was an Idaho war. Bred, born, and fanned to a white-hot heat over there in Idaho.

So the kettle would have to boil with a mighty tempest

for those troubles to erupt across these mountains.

Despite the constant rains that early summer, Rawn kept on chopping, hauling, and stacking logs as the walls of a few sheds were completed and he surveyed the site for the larger buildings. So much for the unbounded excitement and romance of a frontier officer's life.

AFTER Captain Robert Pollock's men buried the blackened bodies of their twelve* dead comrades in temporary graves at dawn on the battlefield plateau where the soldiers had given their lives, full military honors given over a mass grave dug just behind the field hospital, and Captain Henry Winters's E Troop of the First U. S. Cavalry started Surgeon Sternberg and twenty-seven wounded** for Fort Lapwai in dead-axle wagons and crude travois at 9:00 A.M. that Friday, the thirteenth of July, General O. O. Howard's command set off on that trail leading them down the Clearwater after the retreating Nez Perce.

Marching across the northeastern corner of the Camas Prairie, the column passed by McConville's now-abandoned Misery Hill. By midafternoon they had covered nine miles on the trail to the subagency at Kamiah, located on the north bank of the Middle Fork of the Clearwater. At 3:30 P.M. atop a low rise on the south bank of the river, the general's staff halted to pass around two pair of field glasses, gazing at the well-manicured gardens and the culti-

---

*At this date, one of Howard's men was officially MIA, eventually raising the number to a total of thirteen dead. Almost twenty years after the battle, settlers in the area discovered the remains of a soldier "back of one of the hills near Stites," along with four canteens, some army buttons, and a few silver coins. Could this have been that one soldier listed as missing in action?

**An interesting footnote to this battle's history is the fact that nearly one-half of the casualties, both dead and wounded, were officers, noncoms, and trumpeters—clearly exhibiting the Nez Perce understanding of the army's command structure, which plainly shows they aimed their weapons accordingly.

vated fields. What drew their attention even more magnetically some three miles away was that sight of the last of the Non-Treaty bands fording the river in their crude buffalo-hide boats shaped like overturned china teacups.*

While he had been congratulating himself for more than a day on the success of the battle, Howard wondered how he was going to follow Joseph and that village across the Clearwater.

When the Kamiah Christians under the leadership of James Lawyer, son of the noted Treaty chief, learned the warrior camp was coming their way, they had the foresight to remove their boats normally kept at the crossing. In addition, they had disabled the cable ferry used with those boats at this crossing. With those actions taken, most of the Lawyer Indians retreated into the hills, unwilling to openly oppose the Non-Treaties. Denied those boats, the warrior bands had resorted to the ancient bullboat, using what few buffalo hides they had managed to take with them in their precipitous retreat from the Clearwater encampment.

Just beyond those last stragglers clambering onto the north bank stood the subagency's buildings, surrounded for the moment by the massive horse herd. A little farther up the hill many of the warriors were already busy erecting some crude breastworks of stone and downed timber.

Howard's belly burned in frustration. Barely late again! One step behind. Always one step behind Joseph!

"Get Colonel Perry up here on the double!" he ordered C. E. S. Wood, then watched the lieutenant salute and rein about.

In moments, Perry's horse was sliding to a halt before the general.

"Bring Whipple's company and take your cavalry battalion on the double to the right. Stop those Indians from getting away!" the general ordered grimly. "I'll send

---

*The crossing place used July 13, 1877 was adjacent to the geologic feature and cultural artifact called Heart of the Monster, which figures into *Nee-Me-Poo* origin folklore.

Wilkinson with a Gatling and limber to support you, then lead the rest myself."

He did not wait for Perry to get his battalion pulled out of column and on its way, content to watch those distant figures finish their crossing, slowly winding away from the east side of the Clearwater. Instead, the general ordered Jackson's B Troop, in the vanguard, to advance on the river crossing as they bore left of Perry's and Whipple's men. Behind Jackson came Miles with his infantry battalion, then Miller's artillery, followed by the rest of the cavalry and pack train. Trimble's H Troop served as rear guard while the column began its descent to the ford.

At the moment Perry's battalion reached the river and wheeled left to return to the main column—which was no more than four hundred yards away—the Nez Perce opened a brisk and concentrated fire on his troopers. It appeared his cavalry had walked right into a well-conceived ambush.

"Order the gallop!" Perry shouted, waving an arm and whipping his horse around as the mounted men began to shoot past him.

But as the bullets sailed around them in the confusion and panic, some of the horses became unmanageable, even wild—rearing and wheeling. Three of the men in the captain's company flung themselves out of their saddles and abandoned their horses, while others dismounted and hung onto their frightened horses, all of them sprinting through a grainfield to the left of their formation, racing back for the main column.

By the time Perry's entire battalion reached Wilkinson's artillerymen at the ford, they had withdrawn from the effective range of those enemy carbines. Already the Gatling guns had been wheeled into position and set up their first distinctive chatter.

"General, sir," said Major Edwin C. Mason as he came to a stop at Howard's elbow, "if I may be so bold as to express my disgust at the lack of . . . of courage shown by Colonel Perry and his cavalry."

"Colonel Mason?" Howard said, his eyebrows narrowing at his newly appointed chief of staff. "What's your complaint?"

"It's clear the Nez Perce hold the colonel's cavalry in profound contempt after the White Bird fiasco. Which is as it should be, General," Mason continued, warmed to his criticism. "The truth is, the First Cavalry is almost useless to you. They cannot fight on horseback, and they *will* not fight on foot!"

Howard seethed, wanting to rebuke Perry then and there for the embarrassing display—but held his tongue, for they had a hot skirmish just getting under way. He had to admit: He was growing disgusted with the captain who had failed him not only at White Bird but again at Cottonwood Station, too, then only the day before when he failed to follow up the fleeing warriors once his men were across the Clearwater.

For some time the warriors kept up their brisk fire, pinning down the soldiers and returning the long-range Gatling and rifle fire from the Springfields. When the noise began to taper off, Howard finally figured out that the warriors were only covering the escape of their families while the Nez Perce streamed out of sight and into the timbered hills, climbing north-northeast.

"Report on casualties, Lieutenant," the general ordered his aide, C. E. S. Wood.

In a matter of minutes, as Howard sat impatient in the saddle, Wood was back.

"No dead. Two men wounded. One in bad shape with a head wound, sir."

Just down the slope from him, Wilkinson's artillery continued to pound those slopes across the river without any effect. After an hour, a disappointed Howard ordered the shelling stopped. With the warriors and their families retreating, it was time for him to begin a crossing. But to do that would require the nonexistent boats of the Lawyer Indians. Complicating matters, the heavy wire cable had been freed from one end of the crossing.

As he was forced to watch the dark figures disappear

among the green hillsides, Howard continued to seethe with the failure of his troops. It felt as if he was foiled at every step, kept no more than a narrow river from catching his quarry.

Sending details out to scare up the Christian Indians in hopes of securing their boats and repairing the ferry cable, the general ordered the rest of the command to withdraw a few hundred yards and go into camp for the night.*

That night he would begin laying plans on how he could catch those escaping hostiles between two pincers of his command.

---

*The troops encamped where the Kamiah airport is today.

Chapter Thirty-Four

Khoy-Tsahl, 1877

In the middle of the night Joseph and his people had reached the crossing in darkness, finding that Lawyer's people had hidden the boats traditionally kept at the ferry, along with dismantling the ferry's wire cable. Cruel acts to commit against one's people, but Joseph was beginning to understand how those Christians wanted more than anything to stay out of the war. Perhaps more than everything to be seen as not helping their blood relations the Non-Treaties.

Now with the way the warrior bands had been driven away after two days of fighting on the Clearwater and with Lawyer's people doing what they could to blunt the efforts of the Non-Treaty bands to escape, it was clear the tides were shifting in favor of Cut-Off Arm and his soldiers.

No matter they didn't have those boats. As the five camps came to a halt just above the Kamiah settlement, some fell to the side, intending to get a little sleep while the rest started cutting willow or dragging out what they had left in the way of buffalo lodgeskins. But this was not a camp of mourners resigned to running away from a fight with the army. Instead, Joseph saw around him a people enjoying a rising euphoria. For two days they had held off far greater numbers than they were ever able to put into their fight with Cut-Off Arm. And though they had to retreat, they were not fleeing for their lives.

Here, once again, they had the river between them and Cut-Off Arm.

Before marching away from the crossing, the warriors managed to leave the *suapies* with one final indignity as they popped up from cover and fired into the soldiers. As the white men scrambled off their horses and sprinted into the fields, the *Nee-Me-Poo* fighting men hooted and jeered.

On this north side of the Clearwater, maybe they could even choose a place to turn around on their heels and snap back at the army again—if only to show the general that there was clearly enough fight left in the Non-Treaty bands that he had little choice but to offer them favorable terms for their surrender. But . . . Joseph was not leading this camp. For more than a moon now the war chiefs had held the highest favor. Still, after those two long days on the Clearwater, the fighting men were clearly fighting among themselves on what to do, which way to go. There was even growling among the fighting chiefs as Looking Glass snapped at *Toohoolhoolzote*, White Bird sniped at *Huishuishkute*.

Over the last two days he had proposed a dramatic, if not risky, plan.

"I want to take my followers across the Camas Prairie," he had told the gathered chiefs. "From there we will cross the Salmon River, where the *Wallamwatkin* can make our final stand in our homeland of the *Wallowa* Valley. In a man's own country should he die defending the bones of his relatives. Only in a man's own country can he die with honor defending home and family."

But Looking Glass scorned his heartfelt proposal. "You say you are thinking only of the women and children? To march across the naked extent of the Camas Prairie would put them at great peril, Joseph. On one side stands the *suapie* fort at Lapwai, and on the other side stand the Shadow towns. No, you cannot throw those innocent lives against the very real possibility of death!"

"Then what would you have us do now that we are here at Kamiah," Joseph prodded, "where we get no help from Lawyer's people?"

With a grand smile, Looking Glass told the group, "Because of all those possessions and supplies we had to leave at the Clearwater and because these Kamiah people have run off and won't help us . . . we have but one choice."

"What is that?" White Bird demanded.

"We must go across the mountains to trade with the Shadows who have been our friends for many, many summers." Then he turned his self-assured smirk on Joseph. "Better to go among friends, Joseph—than to risk your people's lives making a suicidal retreat, eh?"

After that rebuke, Joseph thought it best to stay in the background and follow the movements ordered by the others who were swayed by the power of Looking Glass's impassioned oratory. For now—with the army nipping at their heels—he reluctantly decided he could best protect his *Wallamwatkin* band by staying among the other Non-Treaties as they climbed toward the ancient root-digging meadows at *Weippe* Prairie.*

As he pointed his pony toward the tail end of the retreating families, Joseph longed for an end to this fighting, when he could return to his beloved *Wallowa* valley with his people—there to live out the rest of his days with his wife and newborn daughter. But . . . would the child ever know anything but fighting and running, running and fighting?

BY TELEGRAPH

—

The Indian War—Reported Defeat of Joseph.

—

Just in Time to Prevent General Howard's Removal.

—

Move Against General Howard.

CHICAGO, July 14.—The Times' Washington special says the cabinet yesterday secretly but seriously considered the propriety of displacing Howard and putting Crook in his place. Howard, who has made such a bad mess of the campaign, was sent to that remote country as a sort of punishment after the failure to convict on the court martial for his share in the freedmen's bureau frauds. It is quite possible that he will be removed to-

—

*Where the Lewis and Clark Corps of Discovery first came across the people they called the Choppunish.

day, as Secretary McCrary, who was absent at yesterday's (Friday's) cabinet meeting returned last night.

"The hostiles aren't moving?" Howard asked James Reuben, one of his most trusted trackers, that evening of the fourteenth.

Howard's command had been resting in their camp beside the Clearwater all day, most of the men taking advantage of the river to bathe and wash their ragged campaign clothing, besides digging some entrenchments in the event the warrior bands revisited the crossing.

The Christian scout shook his head. "Four miles. Maybe five. They stay in camp. No sign they move off."

For a moment Howard studied the tracker's dark eyes. Over time and many muddy miles across the Salmon, he had come to trust this Christian. Reuben was an educated Nez Perce, schooled here on the reservation. But because he was Indian, he was distrusted by the volunteers and settlers. The fact that Reuben carried a better gun than those the army was providing to the civilian militia was just another reason the scout ofttimes appeared haughty to McConville's volunteers. One more thing to hang their hatred on.

Balling his left hand into a fist as he turned from Reuben, the general told his staff, "Now we'll put in motion my plan to lull the hostiles into making a mistake, to catch them between the arms of two forces, compelling them to surrender, or fight to the death."

"But as soon as we set off, General," argued David Perry, "the Nez Perce will just up and run off."

"Not if they believe I'm headed back to Lapwai."

He went on to explain how, come the following morning, he would leave the artillery and infantry at the crossing when he departed with the cavalry, marching downriver on the well-traveled road to Fort Lapwai.

"So they'll believe you've headed back to the post!" Captain Marcus Miller exclaimed.

"After we've put enough distance between that cavalry battalion and this crossing, I will abandon the road, ford the river at a suitable spot James Reuben tells me exists at Dunwell's Ferry,* then move into that broken country, where we'll push ahead with our cavalry on the mining road takes us up the Orofino Creek to Pierce. In that way I can take the hostiles in the rear while Colonel Miller crosses here at Kamiah and pursues the camp, herding the unsuspecting hostiles right into the front ranks of my cavalry near the junction of the Orofino and Lolo Trails."

At six o'clock that rainy morning of the fifteenth Howard rode at the head of four troops—B, F, H, and L—of the First U. S. Cavalry, along with forty volunteers who had arrived the afternoon before under command of Colonel Edward McConville. To disguise his real purpose, the general climbed up the steep Lapwai–Kamiah Trail,** as if retreating to the army post to gather more supplies—for the benefit of those spies Joseph was sure to have posted. Once out of sight beyond those heights behind his bivouac, Howard cut back cross-country, striking north. They had some twenty miles to wind along the snaking course of the Clearwater before they would reach Dunwell's Ferry but had covered no more than six when Christian scout James Lawyer came dashing up to the column to report that the fighting bands had broken camp in the hills on the far side of the Clearwater and were this morning climbing to the traditional camping ground at *Weippe* Prairie.

"That's at the western end of the Lolo Trail, General," Captain James B. Jackson advised.

"Which makes it good news, gentlemen," Howard enthused. "That means Joseph's warriors are on the way toward us already."

While his officers were making plans to cross then and there, a second Christian courier rode up with even more astounding news for the general.

"Reports from Joseph!" the breathless James Reuben told him. "He wants to talk to you."

---

*Near present-day Greer, Idaho.

**Today's Idaho State Highway 62.

"J-joseph . . . wants to parley with me?"

"He sends me to ask what terms for his surrender."

"S-surrender?" Howard echoed, his voice rising noticeably.

"That's the finest news we've had in weeks!" Captain Joel Trimble roared.

Howard took a step closer to Reuben, almost afraid to hope. "Where does Joseph want to talk to me?"

"Kamiah," the tracker explained. "At the crossing."

Without another word.to the Indian, the general wheeled on his aides, flush with the excitement of a schoolboy. For a moment his tongue would not work, and he was terrified he would act as if he were a stuttering idiot . . . stammering, if not utterly speechless, now that he had the end of this war in his grasp. A half-dozen miles back up the Clearwater waited Joseph, the architect of the Non-Treaty resistance, the brilliant tactical mastermind behind their victories at White Bird and Cottonwood, the driving force behind the Nez Perce escape from their battle on the South Fork!

Joseph, the leader of the Dreamer resistance, was asking to come before the one-armed general, hat in hand! What would Sherman and all the rest who had cried for his removal think then!

"This war," he began, not at all surprised to find a lump of unbridled anticipation clogging his throat, "it's all but over, gentlemen. Let's hurry on our back trail to the crossing so that I can accept Joseph's surrender at the Kamiah agency—just as Grant accepted Lee's at McLean's farmhouse!"

While he and Perry's F Company turned around for the crossing, Howard ordered the rest of the cavalry and civilians to continue downriver under Jackson's command to Dunwell's Ferry, where they hoped to get their hands on a boat or two for use in breaching the Clearwater. Although his heart could take wing with hope, his head still told him that he must prepare for the eventuality that this peace overture would dribble through his fingers. As hard as he might pray to the Almighty, Oliver Otis Howard was nonetheless a practical man who realized the Lord most assuredly helped the man who helped himself.

"His name is *Kulkulsuitim*,"* James Reuben announced later at the crossing, when the nervous-eyed messenger brought his pony onto the south bank of the Clearwater beneath that strip of white cloth he had fluttering at the end of a yard-long stick.

The Indian turned his eyes this way and that as the general gestured Major Edwin C. Mason forward with him and Reuben, signaling the rest of his aides to remain behind at a distance that would not intimidate this nervous courier.

"Be watchful of any false moves on his part, sir," Mason warned as the trio walked on foot to the crossing. "There may be sharpshooters on the far bank waiting for a signal from that Indian soon as he finds out it's you."

"The path to peace is never an easy one, Colonel."

Even before the general, Mason, and their Christian translator came to a halt several yards away, the horseman began talking.

"Says he knows who you are," James Reuben explained, pointing to the general's empty sleeve. "They all know you're the one they call the Cut-Off Arm chief. So he wants to tell you the camps have two white men, captives. Caught them going to Lewiston on business with horses."**

"Forget them for the moment!" Howard snapped, impatient now that the moment was at hand. "This messenger knows why I'm here. When will Joseph come in to talk to me himself?"

"Young Joseph wants to surrender, all right," Reuben said after some brief conversation with *Kulkulsuitim*.

---

*Even the identity of this messenger is in dispute among the records of that day. Some scholars claim it was a man named Tamim Tsiya, while still more say it was definitely a young warrior named No Heart, called Zya Timenna.

**William Silverthorne and half-breed Peter Matte, who would claim they were captured on their way to Lewiston to buy horses. Within a week, they would escape and carry some vital news to the soldiers who will be waiting at the eastern end of the Lolo Trail.

With a quick glance at the heights across the river, the general said, "I suppose the bands are camped somewhere nearby in the hills, but not close enough to make it down here before it grows dark. So, tell this messenger that Joseph can come in with his people tomorrow morning to surrender."

After a moment of translation, Reuben said, "Joseph will try hard to break away from White Bird and Looking Glass. His people have little ammunition and food now. They left much upriver when they made a two-day fight on your soldiers. Says Joseph wanted to surrender to you on last two days, but he was always forced to move with the others."

"Tell him to remind Joseph that I never lied to him. I always spoke the truth."

Then Reuben translated, "How hard will you be?"

"Do you mean what terms I am giving Joseph and his men?" Howard corrected. "Tell him there are no conditions. Explain that to him—unconditional surrender. They give up their weapons and their ponies to me."

"Then what? What of the chiefs?" the translator posed. "What of the fighting men who made war against your soldiers?"

"The war chiefs are the ones I will arrest," Howard said. "Explain that to him. The bad leaders I want—not the warriors who took their bad advice. Once they have surrendered, I will appoint a court of officers who will try them according to military law—"

From across the Clearwater rang the report of a rifle, its sound magnified as it reverberated from the hills hemming in this gentle crossing. The bullet itself whined past and struck a nearby boulder with a splatter of lead and fractured rock chips.*

"What the devil!" Howard growled, his heart racing.

---

*There is even some broad disagreement on which side of the river this shot was fired and who might have fired it— the Nez Perce on the north side of the Clearwater or one of McConville's citizens on the south side (just as they had started the fight at Looking Glass's camp).

As he lunged forward, Mason ordered, "Hold that Injun!"

Although the messenger hadn't attempted to flee, Reuben seized the warrior's reins and held the frightened horse. The courier's eyes darted anxiously over those soldiers scurrying about, up and down the bank, responding to that single gunshot. He was jabbering at the translator in a high-pitched voice.

"Says Joseph want to surrender now!" Reuben cried in an excited tone as he tried to keep the horse and rider between himself and that other side of the river, where at least one sniper was hidden. "His people are getting so hungry. Had to leave so much at the Clearwater. The only thing for them to do is to take the women to *Weippe*—"

"They're already on their way to *Weippe*?" Howard shrieked in dismay.

"Yes," Reuben confirmed, "where they wanted to dig some camas to feed the hungry people before they surrender. But even though they are going to *Weippe*, White Bird, *Toohoolhoolzote*, and Looking Glass will not allow him to surrender. They want to make for the buffalo country and do not like Joseph talking peace with you."

"Tell him to remind Joseph that I will be here tomorrow morning to receive him," Howard repeated nervously, "right here in the morning—waiting for him to come down out of the hills. He has my word that he will not be harmed. Have him tell Joseph he will have a fair trial, an army trial. A white man's trial."

As soon as Reuben finished his translation, the messenger turned without another word, tearing his rein from Reuben's grip, and splashed into the river. Howard watched the water flow over the man's thighs, on over the pony's back, and up to the courier's waist as the animal struggled against the current that carried it downstream a quarter of a mile before they clambered onto the north bank, where the man pulled aside his breechclout and slapped a buttock before kicking his animal in its flanks. They quickly disappeared into the timbered hillside.

Choosing not to incite himself with that parting vulgarity on the part of the young messenger, Howard turned on his heel, his insides a jumble of excitement and apprehension mixed, troubled by a hint of skepticism. From the bank he hollered up to those officers arrayed on the side of the knoll.

"Colonel Miller! We need to send a courier downriver to Captain Jackson," Howard bellowed. He was clearly fearful of losing the momentum he had just won at the Clearwater with a resounding defeat at *Weippe* Prairie. "The hostiles are marching into the hills for *Weippe*, which will put them in position to wipe out our cavalry battalion. We must recall Jackson before he makes contact."

"I'll start a courier immediately!" Miller shouted as he started to turn away, but was stopped with Howard's next announcement.

Ever the optimist, Howard said, "Colonel, once that rider is on his way to Jackson's battalion I want you to prepare your men to receive the surrender of Joseph and his Nez Perce when they reach us at dawn!"

THAT morning the Non-Treaty bands had awakened in their last camp before reaching the camas grounds of *Weippe* Prairie, a beautiful, extensive meadow where the blue camas flowers extended for as far as the eye could see with a color so vivid it made Yellow Wolf believe he was seeing the sky itself reflected in huge ponds of trapped rainwater. On nearly all sides they were surrounded by timber-blanketed hills, those hills themselves surmounted on the east by snow-mantled mountain peaks.

In the first misty light of dawn Yellow Wolf had watched the older woman lead a pony out of the camp circle. There the mother of *Wayakat* climbed on the animal's back before the woman noticed that he was watching from his mother's blanket shelter.

"Yellow Wolf," she whispered as he approached, his moccasins growing soaked with the heavy dew.

"Where are you going so early?" he asked, looking up at her red, bloodshot, and puffy eyes.

"Now that the *suapies* have left the battlefield on the plateau, I am going to claim the body of my son."

"He was a brave fighter," Yellow Wolf said with admiration. "Your son fell too close to the soldier lines for any of us to get his body for you."

"I do not hold bad feelings for any of you fighting men because my son was left behind when we fled our camp," Going Across explained as she reached down and touched the back of his hand. "But, I need to go bury him now."

"When will you return?"

"By nightfall if I can," she said. "If not, and the camp moves on up the trail to *Weippe*—I will find you."

"Yes," Yellow Wolf said quietly as he took a step back and held his arm up in parting. "I am sure you can find your way."

Late that afternoon just after the Non-Treaties reached the extensive camas digging grounds, a small band of people emerged from the trees at the end of the trail over those mountains. Even from a distance it was easy for Yellow Wolf to recognize that they were *Nee-Me-Poo*—their horse trappings, dressed as they were. Five-times-ten of them, women and children traveling with seventeen warriors under their leader, *Temme Ilppilp*, called Red Heart.

"You have just come from the buffalo country?" asked Looking Glass as the hundreds crowded around the new arrivals, tongues trilling in welcome.

Red Heart's eyes and smile grew big with this unexpected reception here in the meadows of *Weippe*. He gestured toward their numerous travois pulled by trail-weary packhorses. "We have many buffalo robes, yes."

"See?" Looking Glass roared at the crowd pressing in on the newcomers. "What did I tell you? All things are good in the buffalo country!"

Red Heart took the older man's elbow in his hand and said, "Over there in the valley of the Bitterroot River, we have heard talk of your struggles against the army. But—looking at you now—I don't see a people who are at war!"

Looking Glass let his head fall back as he laughed loudly

before saying, "We are at war. The *suapies* just can't keep up with our village of women and children!"

But the laughter quickly died as those close around the chiefs realized that Red Heart was not laughing. Yellow Wolf shouldered his way closer to hear all the words.

"The army is chasing you now?" Red Heart asked, his tone heavy with concern.

"Yes!" Looking Glass answered enthusiastically. "But they will never catch us now."

"Then it is as the Shadows in the Bitterroot were saying," Red Heart explained. "They were afraid of us when we marched past their homes and stores this time. Never before were they afraid of *Nee-Me-Poo*, but now these people did not want us to stay long in their country."

"Those settlers in the Bitterroot have nothing to worry about," White Bird vowed.

Red Heart asked the older chief, "If the army is chasing you, where will you go?"

"I told them we should go to the buffalo country, where the animals are fat and we will camp next to our friends, the *E-sue-gha!*" Looking Glass cheered. "Come back with us on the trail over the mountains. It is no longer safe here in the Idaho country for our people."

As he stared at the ground a long moment, it appeared Red Heart already had his mind made up. When he looked at White Bird and the other leaders, he said, "We have already decided: If what we were told was true, we will not join in your fighting. We want to be left alone."

"The soldiers will not leave you alone!" Looking Glass roared angrily.

"Then we will surrender to them and give them our guns," Red Heart countered. "That way they will know we are not part of this war."

"G-give them your guns?" White Bird blustered.

Red Heart wheeled on the old war bird. "Better that than to give them the lives of all these women and children!"

"You are not a man!" Looking Glass bawled with fury. "A man would fight and die for his women and children—"

"I will go surrender with you, Red Heart," a voice suddenly interrupted Looking Glass's tirade.

Yellow Wolf and the rest of the crowd watched a minor leader in the Non-Treaty bands step forward.

"You will abandon this fight?" Looking Glass demanded.

"Yes," Three Feathers answered.

"Don't you remember what Wright did to the Yakima and Cayuse leaders when they surrendered after making a war with the army?"* Looking Glass scoffed.

"Yes," Three Feathers sighed. "Those chiefs were hanged."

"Do you want the same to happen to you?" White Bird chided.

It took a moment before Three Feathers answered, "It is one thing to go east and hunt the buffalo in the land of the *E-sue-gha*. It is another thing entirely to leave our fair land behind for all time."

Toohoolhoolzote asked, "You are not afraid of the white man's ropes?"

"Yes, I am afraid of hanging," Three Feathers replied, "but I will go with Red Heart and surrender my guns so that my families don't have to run anymore. And if I have to die . . . then I prefer to die in my own country. Not in a faraway land of strangers."

---

*Thirty Nez Perce scouts had served with Wright's campaign in 1858 and witnessed the hangings of those Indian leaders. Later, in 1873, Captain Jack and other Modoc leaders had suffered the same fate at the hand of a vengeful government.

Chapter Thirty-Five

July 15–16, 1877

Fort Lapwai
July 15, 1877

Dearest Mamma,

This is such a bright Sunday morning. The children look so nicely in their best blue stockings and little brown linens, and they are playing on the porch. This is the first day this summer I have felt like fixing them up from top to toe. Even now I am afraid we will hear something horrible before the day is over and spoil all my pleasant feelings. The Indians (friendly ones) who were in that last fight say that one officer had his leg cut off by the officers in the field, and they describe it so plainly, it must be so. Then from the fact that General Howard named the Camp "Williams," we fear poor Mr. Williams has lost his leg. He is only a young fellow and very fine one . . . Dispatches came in from General Howard yesterday saying the Indians had recrossed the Clearwater River and were making for the mountains with the troops in pursuit. The trail over the mountains, which the Indians are supposed to be making for, leads over into Montana into what they talk about here as the buffalo country, but from a great many things, nearly everybody thinks Joseph doesn't want to get out of the country around here, but is only withdrawing in that direction to prepare for another fight. You never heard of such daring Indians in your life. In this last fight, they charged to within ten feet of the soldiers, and charged up to the artillery and tried to take the guns from the men . . .

My head is full of Indians. It was very warm yesterday, and I baked a cake and churned my butter on a table on my back porch, and I kept one eye and one ear up the ravine watching for Indians all the time. It is a horrible feeling . . .

Everybody here seems to feel a little more cheerful since the last fight . . . It is like the old cry of "Wolf! Wolf!" and when we don't look for it, the wolf comes.

We all join in love and hope to hear soon.

Your affectionate daughter,
Emily FitzGerald

BY TELEGRAPH

—

A Run on the Savings Banks of St. Louis.

—

WASHINGTON.

—

Dismissal from the Indian Bureau

WASHINGTON, July 14.—L. S. Hayden clerk in the Indian bureau, was to-day dismissed by the secretary of the interior as the first public result of the pending investigation of the allegation of irregularities and fraudulent practices in the Indian service . . . Hayden, according to his own evidence, has accepted money and other things of value from contractors . . .

—

Better News.

WALLA WALLA, July 14.—*To Gen. McDowell, San Francisco*: Have been with Gen. Howard in the battle of to-day, which he reports in detail. I consider this the most important success. Joseph is in full flight westward. Nothing can surpass the vigor of Gen. Howard's movements.

(Signed) KEELER, A.D.C.

Gen. McDowell says that he thinks this defeat will tend to cause the other Indians to remain peaceable, and may make it unnecessary to act under the president's authority to call out volunteers for temporary service. He will at least defer action till he gets Howard's report.

LATE LAST NIGHT AFTER AGENT JOHN MONTEITH AND INDIAN inspector Erwin C. Watkins arrived from Lapwai, General Oliver Otis Howard dashed off a short dispatch to be wired to his commander, McDowell, in San Francisco:

CLEARWATER, July 15th

Joseph may make a complete surrender to-morrow morning. My troops will meet him at the ferry. He and his people will be treated with justice. Their conduct to be completely investigated by a court composed of nine of my army, selected by myself. Col. Miller is designated to receive Joseph and his arms.

[signed] O. O. Howard
Brig. Gen. U. S. A.

The following morning, a Monday, the general was up before dawn, composing the congratulatory address one of his aides would read before his troops following their battle on the South Fork of the Clearwater River:

Headquarters Department of the
Columbia,
In the Field, Camp McBeth,
Kamiah, I.T., July 16, 1877.

GENERAL FIELD ORDERS NO. 2

The General Commanding has not had time since the battle of the 11th and 12th instants, on the South Fork of the Clearwater, on account of the constancy of the pursuit, to express to the troops engaged his entire satisfaction with the tireless energy of officers and men, that enabled them to concentrate at the right time and place with the promptitude of the first assault; the following up of the first advantage for a mile and a half with incon-

ceivable speed; with the quickness to obey orders; sometimes to anticipate them, which prevented the first flanking charge of the Indians from being successful; then with the persistency of uncovering their barricades and other obstacles, and clearing ravines, both by open charge and gradual approaches under constant fire, thereby making an engagement of unusual obstinacy of seven hours hard fighting; also his satisfaction with the remaining in difficult position and entrenching a long line at night while fatigued, and almost without food and water, till the afternoon of the second day, when the Infantry and Cavalry of the command cheerfully thinned out their lines so as to cover two miles and a half of extent, and to allow the Artillery battalion to turn the enemy's right and enable an approaching train with its escort to come in with safety; then turning briskly upon the foe, the Artillery battalion, by a vigorous assault, sent him in confusion from his works, and commenced the pursuit in which all the troops, including the new arrivals, immediately engaged—through the ravines and rocks and down the most impassible [sic] mountain side to the river; after this crossing, the taking possession of the Indian camp, abandoned and filled with their supplies, and surrounded by their "caches," causing the Indians to fly over the hills in great disorder.

The battle, with its incidents, is one that will enter into history; its results, immediate and remote, will surely bring permanent peace to the Northwest, so that it is with great satisfaction the General can say that not one officer or soldier that came under his eye on that field failed to do his duty, and more gallant conduct he never witnessed in battle. The General feels deeply the loss of the killed, and sympathizes heartily with the wounded, and unites with their friends in their anxiety and sorrow. He mentions no one by name in this order, hoping to do justice to individuals after reports shall be received. The command is indebted to the officers of the staff for their indefatigable work previous to and during the engagement.

WITH that bit of officiousness put behind him, the general gathered with his headquarters staff on the south bank of the Clearwater, waiting for Joseph to bring his people in to surrender.

"This surrender means nothing short of the end to the war," Howard enthused outwardly, while inside he remained full of doubt.

"We've heard reports from a few Christians that White Bird is driving all those who hoped to surrender before him with the lash," Monteith admitted. "There's some room for error in these rumors, but . . . I feel that if Joseph attempts to surrender, it will lead to an open clash between the Non-Treaty bands."

That's when Watkins declared, "And Agent Monteith doesn't think Joseph will risk such a clash within the Dreamers."

The hours slowly dragged past that morning. The Nez Perce did not show.

His hopes crushed, Howard sensed his anger simmering—figuring that he had been played a fool by Joseph. Not only was the chief a superb military tactician in outmaneuvering Oliver's West Point–trained officers, but Joseph was an unequalled diplomatic strategist in outplaying Howard himself in this ruse* at surrender.

"It was nothing more than a well-manufactured lie de-

*As the years passed, ample evidence came to light to show that Joseph may have indeed been very interested in surrendering to Howard. Years after the war, Lieutenant C. E. S. Wood wrote that he had been told by an unnamed Nez Perce informant, "Joseph wished to surrender rather than leave the country or bring further misery on his people, that, in council, he was overruled by the older chiefs . . . and would not desert the common cause." As late as 1963 Josiah Red Wolf stated, ". . . not only was Joseph hard to persuade to stay in the fight, but he tried to drop out after the [Clearwater battle]."

signed to hold me in check while he had time to take his hostiles and their livestock toward the terminus of the Lolo Trail," Howard admitted to his staff later that morning as they gathered for officers' call in the shade of some trees.

"Joseph wants to play cat and mouse again with us," Captain David Perry said, "we'll show him the cat can catch that mouse—"

"General Howard! General Howard! Pickets report Indians coming down to the crossing!"

Was it too much to hope?

Howard busted through the circle of officers who barely had time to step aside for him. The moment he had a clear view of the distant hillside, the general stopped in his tracks, staring. A thin column of Indians both on horseback and foot angled down the grassy north slope toward the Kamiah crossing. Not quite a hundred, but close enough from what he could tell. While it was nowhere near all the souls in that hostile camp, it was nonetheless a start. So with Joseph at the head of this first group to surrender, the others would soon see the rightness in giving up and eventually follow their leader in to turn over their weapons and horses.

But by the time the first leaders had their ponies halfway across the Clearwater, Howard was standing at the edge of the river, shifting from foot to foot, bewildered that he did not see Joseph among those riders.

"Where is Joseph?" he demanded of his translator as James Reuben came up at a lope and dismounted on both feet.

"Joseph isn't with them," Reuben said after he had spoken to the first arrivals. "He is with the others camped back in the hills."

"Joseph is coming down later?"

"No, General. These are the only people surrendering today," Reuben explained. "Their names are Red Heart and Three Feathers. They brought their families in to give up their guns and horses. Don't want to fight the soldiers. No war, so they come in to you."

Bitterly, with more disappointment than he wanted to admit was boiling in his belly, Howard grumbled at his aides, "Take their guns and dismount them. They are my prisoners of war."

He whirled on his heel.

"General," Reuben said, lunging in front of Howard, "these are no fighters. Never fight the army. You can't make them prisoners of war."

He glared at Reuben as he snapped, "I can make any Nez Perce a prisoner of war when I know they've been with the hostiles in their camp. Who's to say they're not spies? Or that they don't mean to kill me if they had the chance? You tell them they are my prisoners!"

Later that morning Second Lieutenant Charles Wood came up to report that Red Heart's people had only two old guns to turn over.

"Were they completely searched?" Howard inquired.

"Yes, General. The translator told me they said more of their people would be coming in later today or tomorrow."

"Joseph?"

Wood shook his head. "The one called Three Feathers said Joseph has been compelled to take his people to the buffalo country with White Bird and Looking Glass. He also claimed he lived on the reservation and has never been—"

"A reservation Indian, is he?" Howard sniffed. "I want them all arrested and taken off to Lapwai under armed escort. They shall remain my prisoners of war until this war is over."*

"I'll see that escort is arranged, sir," Wood replied. "It seems to me that these people showing up to surrender to you is a good sign."

---

*Which is just what happened. These men in chains, along with their women and children, were herded on foot through scorching heat and choking dust to Fort Lapwai, more than sixty miles away, then on to Lewiston, from there by steamer to Fort Vancouver, where they remained incarcerated behind walls and bars until the end of the Nez Perce War that winter.

"A good sign?"

"Yes, sir. To me it shows that there is dissension in those warrior bands. I think it bodes well that the war is close to an end, General."

He allowed himself to enjoy a little self-congratulation, at least until midafternoon, when a courier arrived from Fort Lapwai with a leather envelope filled with letters and even a dispatch from division headquarters in Portland. Included was a terse wire from General Irwin McDowell's aide, which read in total:

> See Associated Press dispatches which state General Howard's removal under consideration by cabinet.

That flimsy was attached to several clippings from recent newspapers, all dealing with stories picked up off the wire from Washington City.

His long string of failures, blunders, and misplaced optimism had gotten him nothing but a blackguard's treatment in the press. All at once, the awful specter of those scandals at the Freedmen's Bureau loomed over him once more like a sword suspended on a very thin thread. Everyone, it seemed, had been calling for his removal, and those cries had found ears all the way to Washington itself.

But, as General McDowell himself wrote in a wire to Howard, with that news of his success in the Clearwater fight Howard himself had reversed all that ill will with one fell swoop:

> To army heads sorely perturbed over Nez Perce successes, your telegrams were welcome news when they reached headquarters a day ago.

Instead of being the one who would have had to remove Howard by order from Washington, General McDowell now relayed his unbounded elation at Howard's turnaround, writing, in part:

> Your dispatch and that of Captain Keeler of your engagement on the eleventh (11th) and twelfth (12) gave us all great pleasure. I immediately repeated them to Washington, to be laid before the Secretary of War and the President. These dispatches came most opportunely, for your enemies had raised a great clamor against you, which, the press reported, had not been without its effect in Washington. They have been silenced, but I think they (like Joseph's band) have been scotched—not killed—and will rise again if they have a chance . . .

"This is great news, General!" Thomas Sutherland exclaimed as he came up to join the headquarters group. "Those wags with their asses plopped down in some comfortable horsehair sofa back in Washington—what do they know of Indian fighting?"

The other officers cheered that approbation.

"It's for sure they haven't been reading any of my dispatches!" Sutherland continued. "If they had, those myopic narrow-sighted imbeciles would know better than to criticize a fighting man in the middle of a fight!"

Howard nodded. "I appreciate your help and understanding, Mr. Sutherland."

"No need to thank me at all, General," the correspondent replied. "Only a blind man couldn't have seen that those two days on the Clearwater were the only fight Joseph's had where his ambition was victory . . . and its plain to see that, ever after, his highest aim will be simply to escape your army."

CHAPTER THIRTY-SIX

KHOY-TSAHL, 1877

"I AM NOT AFRAID TO SAY THIS!" WHITE BIRD EXCLAIMED AS the twilight deepened, accenting his many wrinkles as the firelight played off his face. "There were too many cowards in our last fight with the *suapies!*"

Toohoolhoolzote grunted his agreement just an arm's length from Yellow Wolf. "There was no convincing them to rejoin us in our fight. Cowards who fled to the smoking lodge. Some cowards slipped back down to the village while the rest of us held the soldiers away from our families!"

Looking Glass bolted to his feet, furious. "Because I came down from the ridge to see that my people were safe, does that make me a coward in your eyes?"

"Did you stay and fight through the cold night?"

Shaking his head, Looking Glass answered White Bird, "You do not understand. My people had been attacked and run off by the soldiers. More than any of you, I did not want to be chased away again, carrying only what we had on our backs." He whirled on the *Wallowa* chief, pointing accusingly. "Joseph should have had the camp packed and ready to go before we were forced to fall back the second day. Joseph should have made more women tear down their lodges and pack their goods so that we would be ready."

Yellow Wolf glanced over at his chief. It was true he had not played a major role in any of the fights against the *suapies* thus far. But Joseph had fought as a warrior with the other fighting men, returning to the camp only when it appeared the soldiers were about to roll over the entrenched warriors. There had been little time for the women to tear down the lodges and pack the travois before the warriors came boiling down to the river.

The sun had finally come out that morning, warming the

lush, grassy meadows where the thousands of ponies grazed after the last two days of intermittent rain that made for a muddy, slippery trail ascending from the Kamiah crossing. After breakfast the women scattered to dig what camas the Shadows' hogs hadn't already rooted out of the damp soil. The white men who had settled in the area had always been that way—turning those disgusting animals loose on the *Nee-Me-Poo* digging grounds. Many days ago the settlers fled the *Weippe*, so this morning the young men rode off to torch all the white man's buildings they could find in the area, shooting and butchering what cattle they did not want to steal but refusing to touch one of the white man's hogs. Instead, the warriors killed every one.

Now with the sun's setting, this momentous, solemn council had begun to air all the grievances among the chiefs and to determine the future of the Non-Treaty peoples.

"But instead of talking about what is behind us in the past," Looking Glass growled, "I think we should be talking about what should be for the days ahead."

"I agree," said *Hahtalekin*, known as Red Echo or Red Owl. Earlier that afternoon the Palouse chief had come in with sixteen warriors. "Yesterday is behind us. Now we must think about what to do tomorrow. Where to go."

"Why do you and Looking Glass say we have to go anywhere?" Joseph argued, having been silent for a long time. "Why can't we stay and fight, die if we must, in our own country?"

"Some of our leaders are giving us bad advice," Shore Crossing said as he leaped to his feet near White Bird. "I think we should listen to Looking Glass and go to the buffalo country!"

White Bird shook his head, pointing at the young "Red Coat" warrior from his own band, one of three who had worn their famous red blankets tied at their necks while making the daring charges at *Lahmotta*. "Is this what you want to do now that we are gathered to fight the soldiers? You sons of evil started this war for all the rest of us. No, you are not running away. You will stay with me and Joseph and fight till we kill all the white men, or die like *Nee-Me-Poo* warriors!"

"No, this cannot be so," argued Looking Glass. "Don't we have enough friends and brothers dead already? And still the *suapies* and Shadows come after our trail. They seem like the sands in the riverbed. No matter how bravely we fight them, the more we kill, the more will invade our country."

"Can't we make the best peace we can with Cut-Off Arm?" Joseph pleaded. "Think of our women and children—they will be left widows and orphans if we keep on fighting."

"Surrender?" Looking Glass snorted. "Those of our fighting men the soldiers do not kill in battle Cut-Off Arm will hang."

"This is true," White Bird agreed begrudgingly. "I remember what the *suapies* did to Captain Jack and his Modocs when he surrendered to the Shadows. They died at the end of a rope!"

"If our men are either killed by the soldiers in battle or hanged," Looking Glass argued, "then who will care for our women and children, Joseph? How can you say we should stay when our brothers from Lapwai and Kamiah have turned their backs on us and are helping the Shadows like snakes?"

Joseph turned to White Bird, saying, "Perhaps some of the Shadows' wrongs against us have made a few of our young men do bad things. Because of that you are saying we must now give up the land of our fathers and follow Looking Glass into the land of the buffalo far away from the place of our birth?"

"Yes!" Looking Glass cheered. "The white men there are not like the Shadows in this Idaho country. They trade with us. We leave our lodges and poles and many horses with the Shadows and the Flathead every hunting season when we visit them on our way home from the buffalo country. Rainbow and Five Wounds are just back, so they will tell you: The *E-sue-gha* say they are willing to go on the warpath against the white man with us!"

"But what of Cut-Off Arm?" White Bird wondered.

Rainbow stepped forward to say, "If we follow Looking Glass, we will put the Idaho soldiers behind us. Cut-Off Arm will not follow us with his army over the mountains."

"Joseph," White Bird persuaded, apparently won over, "perhaps we can leave the war here. The Shadows will not remain angry with us for long. If some of your people want to come back, they can return to their old homes in a few summers; maybe even by next spring everything will be back to the way it was before."

But the tall chief of the *Wallamwatkin* band prodded the other leaders by saying, "What are we fighting for? Is it for our lives? No. It is for this land where the bones of our fathers lie buried. I do not want to take my women among strangers. I do not want to die in a faraway land. Some of you tried to say once that I was afraid of the whites. You evil-talkers stay here with me now and you will have plenty of fighting at my side! We will put our women behind us in these mountains and die on our own fighting for them. I would rather do that than run I know not where."

Toohoolhoolzote, that stocky firebrand, now said in a calming tone, "Joseph, I know you think only of the families, those who do no fighting. Now it is time for you to think of the good we will do for them by no longer fighting, by going over the mountains away from the soldiers."

"Joseph?" Looking Glass prodded impatiently.

He wagged his head. "I don't know—"

Suddenly the canny Looking Glass was moving around the circle, gesturing grandly. "The rest of you? Do you want your families to die here like Joseph does? Tell me how many more of your young warriors do you want to bury before you will see we can make a new life for ourselves on the plains of the buffalo country?"

White Bird laid a hand on Joseph's shoulder. In a soft, fatherly voice, he said, "Joseph, we must take our bands across the mountains." Then he promptly turned to the crowd and loudly proclaimed, "I vote with Looking Glass! We take our people east from this trouble."

Looking Glass literally bounded around the fire with youthful exuberance, shouting out a song of victory as he whirled and stomped in the dancing firelight. "To the buffalo country!"

Then more than seven hundred voices—warriors, women, and children, too—were raised to that summer sky, to the very stars hung over that ancient camping ground of *Weippe*.

"To the buffalo country! To the buffalo country! To the buffalo country!"

Fort Lapwai
July 16, 1877

Mamma Dear,

. . . Dispatches from the front have just come in. They say Joseph wants a talk with General Howard. He says he is tired of fighting. He was drawn into it by White Bird and other chiefs, and he wants to stop. We hear there is great dissatisfaction among the hostiles themselves. The squaws are wanting to know who it was among their men that took the responsibility upon themselves of getting into this war with the Whites. They have lost their homes, their food, their stock, etc. . . .

The artillery companies we were with in Sitka are on their way up here. I will be glad to see our old friends again . . . I shall feel so sorry to see them move on to the front.

They talk of making Lapwai a big four company post with the headquarters of a regiment here, and there is no knowing, even if the war is soon ended, where we will all turn up next spring. Poor Mrs. Boyle says she hopes she won't be left here. She shall have a horror of Lapwai all her life. The Boyles had not been here a week until this trouble began.

Your loving daughter,
Emily FitzGerald

AD Chapman was ready to ride.

The last four days of sitting around on his thumbs with these soldiers who dillydallied in this direction, then hem-hawed in the other had just about driven him crazy! But late last evening Major Edwin C. Mason, Howard's former inspector general, came round to the bivouac of McConville's volunteers, whistling Chapman up to ride out this morning so he could lead and sometimes translate for the half-dozen Nez Perce trackers the major was taking along under James Reuben.

They weren't all Presbyterians or Catholics, Ad knew. At least one of them, a fella called Horse Blanket, claimed he had no religion of any kind. He hadn't cut his hair like his Christian companions. Chapman knew Horse Blanket kept his hair tucked up under his white man hat.

Chapman was up by three-thirty on the morning of the seventeenth. Mason had the scouting detail moving out less than an hour later when it grew light enough to see the trail as it wound into the hills away from the Kamiah crossing. What with Mason being an infantry commander, Chapman thought it a mite strange that Howard had assigned his newly appointed chief of staff to command a battalion of five companies, both cavalry and a detachment of artillerymen, including their mountain howitzer, along with more than twenty of McConville's citizens, to reconnoiter beyond the junction of the Lolo and Orofino Trails to the *Weippe* Prairie. It had taken the command all of yesterday, the sixteenth, to get itself across the Clearwater—no more than ten soldiers at a time in that single boat they could find and put in service.

Then, too, Chapman thought it strange that General Howard had picked the major to lead this scouting detail, because in the last few weeks Mason hadn't lost an opportunity to show just how much disdain he held for horse soldiers. In fact, it was plain to everyone who had ever listened to the man talk that Mason viewed the fighting abilities of the First Cavalry with nothing less than an undisguised distrust, if not an outright contempt.

Just above the crossing, they entered the timber and began climbing toward *Weippe*. This wasn't like crossing the Camas Prairie, Chapman brooded. Now the column slowed to an agonizing crawl as the trackers up ahead tried to thread their way up a rocky, muddy trail, through the thick stands of windblown trees, over and around centuries of deadfall that lay like stacks of jackstraws a child might toss carelessly upon a thick green carpet where the new day's sun streamed through in broken shafts as it would slash through the slats of a garden fence. After a brief, hard downpour, storm clouds were beginning to break up.

After some twenty miles of tough going, they had stopped for an afternoon halt to blow the horses right after crossing the open meadows at the *Weippe* Prairie. Before thirty minutes had passed, the anxious major had the men hurry through their skimpy lunches of hardtack and bacon, then saddle up once again. On the far side of the soggy meadows they reentered the timber, and less than three hours later they reached a low summit that overlooked Lolo Creek. Here the wind-downed timber became even more of a nuisance to the civilians and soldiers, but ever more so for the artillerymen struggling to keep up with their howitzer.

Less than a hundred yards below them along the Lolo Trail, another stretch of open meadow beckoned. Beyond it the hoof-pocked path the Nez Perce village had taken now angled into narrow defile, thickly wooded.

At the tree line where they halted on the edge of the meadow, Reuben told Chapman and McConville, "Some scouts watching up there."

"You hear 'em?" Chapman asked. "See 'em maybe?"

The Christian tracker shook his head. "Just feel they're close now."

Anxiety stretched across McConville's features when he told Chapman, "While we wait here for Mason's soldiers to come up, why don't you send the six trackers ahead?"

Ad gave his order to Reuben, then watched the trackers cross the open ground and into the trees. It was becoming clear the soldiers coming up behind them were advancing slower than ever.

"Ain't no way in hell that major gonna get us back to Kamiah by nightfall," McConville grumped as they watched the trackers reach the far side of the open meadow,* where they began to penetrate the shadowy timber penetrated by irregular shafts of afternoon sunlight. Chapman wagged his head. "I don't think he figgers to have us back to the crossing at all until he's got some idea how far ahead the war bands got on Howard."

"Hell, it's easy enough to see where the red bastards've been—just lookit the ground!" McConville declared, pointing at the forest floor disturbed by thousands of hooves.

"But Joseph and the rest are moving faster'n this outfit," Chapman said as Mason and the cavalry came up behind them. He nudged his mount into motion. "From the looks of things they ain't packing many travois poles now to slow 'em up—"

He jerked back on the horse's reins at the shocking nearness of the gunshot, causing the animal beneath him to spin about and fight the bit until he quickly brought it under control. Two more shots rang out, then at least a dozen in quick succession—intermingled with cries and yelps from the timber just beyond the meadow . . . right where the six trackers had just disappeared into the shadows.

First one, then suddenly three, of the scouts burst from the timber, dismounted and without their army carbines, leading their horses with one hand and frantically motioning the white men back, back, back toward the cover of the far trees.

"God-*damn!*" McConville bellowed as he wrenched his horse around, making a dash back for the tree line.

---

*This incident on the western end of the Lolo Trail took place near Musselshell Creek, about three miles from Orofino Creek—where the Idaho gold rush began in 1860.

Two other volunteers shot back with McConville, pounding the devil out of their horses for the cloaking shadows and the timber, but Chapman waited a heartbeat longer than the others—watching a horseman bolt away from the trees on the far side of the meadow. There should have been three of them, he thought. As the tracker got halfway across the opening, Chapman could see the rider was wounded, pressing a hand against a shoulder wound, his face as white as riverbank clay as he raced away as another quick rattle of gunfire rocked the woods behind him.

"Chapman!" McConville's cry stabbed out from the shadows. "Get your ass back here!"

Wheeling his horse, he flicked one more look over his shoulder, watching the line of trees for the Christian trackers called Abraham Brooks and John Levi, then jabbed his heels into the horse and raced for the timber. He was reining up beside McConville just as Captain Henry E. Winters was coming forward through the dappled light shafts streaking the forest.

"McConville!" the officer called out. "Colonel Mason sent his order for your volunteers to accompany my men to the front."

"We was *at* the front, Cap'n," McConville snapped. "So we already got us a pretty good idea them trackers run onto some rear guard. You see how they was shot up?"

Winters shook his head. "I only saw one of them wounded—"

"Two of 'em's missing," Chapman interrupted as his horse came to a halt.

Straightening his spine, Winters said, "Be that as it may, we are under the colonel's orders to discover what we're facing. I'll expect you to obey those orders—"

A final gunshot rang out from the trees, its echo swallowed by the hills.

Without waiting for an acknowledgment from McConville, Winters turned in the saddle and hollered, "By fours—horse holders to the rear and remain at the ready! The rest, form a skirmish formation here at the edge of the trees. Five feet apart, five feet and no more!"

Behind Chapman the soldiers were squeaking out of their saddles, attaching the throat latches and passing off three horses to every fourth man, who turned and started them back into the timber away from the attack formation.

"Keep your eyes open, men," Winters reminded. "Don't let us get surprised . . . forward, E Troop. Forward!"

Chapman was willing to let the captain ride across that meadow and into the woods, but he himself left his horse tied at the edge of the trees still dripping with the remnants of the morning's thunderstorm and walked at the middle of that long line of dismounted skirmishers. They had made it no deeper than sixty or seventy yards into the forest cluttered with downfall when a soldier cried out to their right.

"Captain! Captain Winters! Come quick!"

Ordering everyone to halt and hold their positions, Winters turned in the direction of the voice. In twenty-five yards he and Chapman spotted the trio of soldiers clustered together, one of them kneeling over a body.

"You know him?" asked the captain, turning to Chapman.

"Name's Sheared Wolf," Ad replied. "Took the Christian name John Levi."

Winters asked, "He dead?"

"He's done for. Bullet in the head."

At that moment Chapman and the others heard a groan from some nearby shadows.

"Careful, civilian!" Winters advised as Chapman turned aside and bounded off for the sound.

He could hear the others, their feet pounding through the forest behind him, as he approached the body. At least this one was still alive. Chapman dropped to a knee beside the scout.

The eyes fluttered a bit in the dark face gone pale and pasty. He had both hands interlaced over a messy gut wound.

"This one dead?" asked the first soldier to join him.

"No," Ad replied softly, his eyes scanning the forest

ahead of them, then glanced over his shoulder to see how Winters was bringing his skirmishers forward through the dense cover. "He may live a little longer."

"Chapman," Abraham Brooks said softly, blood glistening on his lips. "Don't let me die here alone."

"No, I won't let you die here alone, Abraham."

Winters was growling orders at his men, inching his horse this way and that through the tangle of trees and deadfall, the clutter of stumps and the maze of brush, as he fought to keep his men in position to withstand a sudden attack. He came over to Chapman.

"How far before we get out of this tangle and back onto the Lolo Trail?"

Chapman stared up at him, dumbfounded at the question. "This is the Lolo Trail, Cap'n."

For a long moment Winters blinked at Chapman, then gazed around him at the thick timber in which a man could easily lose his direction. "You're telling me the general intends to follow these Indians through this?"

Chapman shrugged and waved two of McConville's civilians over from the line of skirmishers. "There's a dead one back yonder a ways. Go find his horse and tie him over it. This'un—he's called Abraham—we'll make him a travois and get him back to the rest of the soldiers."

"He gonna last long?" one of the civilians asked.

Chapman waited until the tracker's eyes clenched shut with another wave of agony. Then he wagged his head without uttering a sound.

Chapter Thirty-Seven

Khoy-Tsahl, 1877

THE VOICE THROUGH THE DARKENED TIMBER AHEAD OF them spoke with the *Nee-Me-Poo* tongue.

It said, "There are fresh tracks—tracks made this morning!"

"Christians?" Yellow Wolf whispered to the man beside him.

The older warrior nodded, his eyes never leaving the trees ahead where the disembodied voices emerged. Here they waited a short distance from the Bent Horn Trail.* These two were among the seventeen who had come down their backtrail, scouting for soldiers and Treaty trackers, stopping only briefly to eat their lunch of dried meat butchered from the white man's cows the warriors had killed on the *Weippe* Prairie two days ago.

Earlier that morning as camp was breaking, Two Moons had come among some of the young men saying, "We cannot remain here, idle. We must meet the soldiers and engage in another battle! They will not stop chasing us. Hear my words! Let our families travel on while the warriors go back to find a suitable place where we can lay for our enemies."

A second voice talked in their language about the pony tracks. Then it advised the other that they should go tell the *suapies* their finding.

That's when the leader of this scouting party spoke loudly enough to be heard by those Christians.

"We are your relations," *Wahchumyus* said. "This war leader called Rainbow declared, 'Your skin, your hair, your

---

*Perhaps it's named this for the many switchbacks climbing up from Lolo Creek?

bodies—everything you have about you is the same as ours.' "

"Who is that who speaks to us from the shadows?" one of the trackers demanded.

"I am *Wahchumyus*," he answered. "One who knows you by name, Sheared Wolf."

"Show yourself."

Rainbow gestured for his men to advance to the edge of the tiny clearing. It was there they surrounded the five surprised Christians.

"Hello, my brother," Yellow Wolf said to *Seekumses Kunnin*.

"This is your brother?" Rainbow asked.

"Horse Blanket is my half brother," Yellow Wolf explained, never taking his eyes off the older man who stood with the rest of the Christians. "We had the same father."

"Give us your guns and cartridge belts," Two Moons demanded of the trackers as he stomped up to them.

As the five dropped their soldier guns and unbuckled their belts, Rainbow said, "Do you remember that we caught three of you Treaty men at *Lahmotta*, then set them free with a warning not to lead the soldiers? I see you are not afraid of our warning, Sheared Wolf."

"I broke no promise—"

"The soldiers!" a Christian's voice warned. "They are close on our heels!"

"You brought the soldiers with you?" Rainbow demanded of the Christians. "Your friends, the Americans, have chopped up our native land, spilling on it the blood of your relations! But still you help them against us. Every word you speak and every deed you do is a lie. But I will keep my word to you: the next *Nee-Me-Poo* we capture, we will kill at once. You, Reuben and Sheared Wolf, you are the two we really want—"

"He's running!" someone warned.

The instant Rainbow whirled with the noise of voices and feet pounding on the thick bed of pine needles, Sheared

Wolf and Reuben took off at a sprint in a different direction—all five of the Treaty captives were scattering.

Yellow Wolf did not wait for any order from his leader. The Christians were guilty of bringing soldiers down upon their own people. Sheared Wolf could have saved himself if he had agreed to go back to the soldiers and turn them around.

But instead . . .

Yellow Wolf shot the coward in the back as he was fleeing. They all watched Sheared Wolf hurtle forward, flopping to the ground between some mossy deadfall. Another man's bullet hit Reuben as the Christian was vaulting into his saddle and hammering away.

Rainbow stepped deliberately to the wounded tracker rolling onto his back, his eyes flicking over his kinsmen as he coughed up blood from the hole in his chest. Sheared Wolf gazed up at the war party leader with a different look come over his face. Yellow Wolf saw how haunted and afraid was the light behind the eyes.

"S-spare my life, Rainbow," the tracker begged, then coughed up a ball of blood again. "I am badly wounded and have . . . have some news for you."

"I am not interested in your news, Sheared Wolf," he said, stepping up to the tracker's shoulder. "But my news for you and the rest of your kind is that we have spared your lives too often already." He pressed the muzzle of his Henry rifle against the Christian's head. "Now you can go to Heaven to tell your news to all your dead relations."

Sheared Wolf's head barely moved as the bullet crashed into the man's brain. The eyes stayed open, still and lifeless, as Rainbow turned and walked toward the other Treaty men.

"Go on back to the Shadows now," Rainbow said. "If you ever help the soldiers against your people again, you will have a bad end like Sheared Wolf."

"We can keep our horses?" James Reuben asked.

"Go now," Rainbow ordered. "Take your horses and go!"

"What about the other one we shot?" Yellow Wolf asked when the Christians were hurrying away on foot, leading their ponies.

"We will let him go tell the Shadows about us and what we do to those who betray us," Rainbow said.

Two Moons grumbled, "We may as well go on back to our camp and take our families to the buffalo country. No use in staying here any longer now."

"We must get farther back into the trees," Rainbow warned. "The soldiers are close enough I can smell them already."

BY TELEGRAPH

—

WASHINGTON.

—

Sitting Bull will Remain North.

WASHINGTON, July 14.—Major Walsh, of the Canada mounted police, visited Sitting Bull near the headwaters of French creek. Sitting Bull said he desired to remain with the Canadians during the summer; that he would do nothing against the law; he came there because he was tired of fighting, and if he could not make a living in Canada he would return to the United States. Spotted Eagle, Rain-in-the-Face, Medicine Bear, and a number of other chiefs of the hostile Sioux, were present, together with two hundred lodges. It is believed there must be some four or five hundred lodges of hostile Sioux now north of the boundary line, numbering at least 1,500 fighting men.

With Lieutenant Albert G. Forse of E Company guarding the rear of their withdrawal, Major Mason stopped his battalion every now and then on their retrograde march for the Clearwater that afternoon of the seventeenth, allowing Ad Chapman a chance to rest his two wounded trackers. While James Reuben welcomed every opportunity to get out of the saddle with his wrist injury, if only for a few minutes before they pushed on, Abraham Brooks's shoulder wound prevented him from moving off his travois.*

At their first stop, after posting some pickets, Mason assigned a few artillerymen to scrape out a shallow hole beside the trail. Here they laid the body of Captain John Levi, then dragged dirt back over the corpse before the battalion moved on into the late-afternoon light.

"Having accomplished all I desired in making this scout," Mason had explained to his officers while the grave was being dug, "I have determined we won't pursue the Indians with my cavalry over a trail plainly impossible to handle a mounted force on."

To Chapman's way of thinking, a double handful of Non-Treaty backtrail scouts had just succeeded in turning back Howard's army of half-a-goddamned-thousand!

As it fell progressively darker that evening, the going got slower and slower. They did not reach Lolo Creek until close to eleven o'clock. The volunteers led them across the stream to a small clearing on a gentle hillside, and Mason's command went into a cold bivouac.

Chapman himself didn't mind in the least. As soon as their wounded guides were made comfortable under a thin blanket, Ad curled up, the reins wrapped around his wrist, while his weary horse cropped at the nearby grass. Chapman figured the animal had to be more hungry than tired—while he himself was more weary than worried about his belly's gnawing emptiness.

Ad drifted off to sleep, thinking how lucky they'd been to lose only one in the ambush. If those warriors who had jumped their trackers had only waited, been patient a little while longer, letting Mason's battalion continue on up the trail into that dense maze of a forest where cavalry simply could not maneuver . . . why, he might well not be curled up here right now, missing the warmth of his wife's body

---

*Horse Blanket claimed the white men, soldiers and civilians both, abandoned their Nez Perce scouts and he was compelled to carry Brooks with him on his horse, getting soaked with blood during the long ride.

lying next to him in their bed, the coolness of his son's hand clutched in his as the boy learned to ride and to hold a carbine.

A nervous Mason had them up at first light and moving out as soon as it was clear enough to see the trail ahead, moving steadily down the slick, muddy slopes toward the Clearwater crossing. Chapman and his scouts brought the battalion to Howard's camp on the east bank of the river just after the main column had finished taking its breakfast and was preparing to recross to the south bank of the Clearwater in preparation for a march downriver to Lewiston.

As soon as he had turned over both wounded trackers to the army surgeons, Chapman walked into headquarters camp, tied off his horse, then settled on his haunches by the general's low fire. Within moments Howard had his cooks pouring coffee for Major Mason and the civilian, along with starting some bacon and hardtack frying in the grease already hardening on the bottom of the cast-iron skillets.

It had been more than twenty-eight hours since he had eaten last, so that breakfast beside the Clearwater in the shadow of the immense Bitterroot Mountains was just about the best Ad Chapman could remember eating in a long, long time.

Fort Lapwai
July 18, 1877

Dear Sallie,

Mamma said she had sent a letter of mine to you, so I need not explain what a commotion we have been in. This morning our first warriors arrived, the first officers that have come in since the battle of the 11th and 12th, and they brought such good news. We have had, at least I can answer for myself, a very thankful day. Several officers came in early this morning and brought news that the Indians in bands have been giving themselves up for the last two days. Quite a number of Joseph's band came in, and they say Joseph himself wants to come in, but White Bird won't let him. The cavalry are out after those that are still hostile, but our officers think the war is practically over and that there will be no more fighting. They say that the fighting up to now has been horrible. They never saw such desperate fighting as these Indians did.

We are all pretty well but tired, and even though the war may be over, the fuss for this little post will not be. Eleven companies are on their way here from California, will be here this week, and will go into camp until things are settled. A whole regiment of infantry is also on the way. As soon as matters are a little more settled out in the front, General Howard intends leaving the cavalry to follow up the scattered bands out there, and bring the rest of [the] command in here . . .

One of the officers, a nice fellow, walks in his sleep. He was unfortunate enough to get up in the night in camp and shoot the picket outside of his tent (one of his own men) and killed him instantly.

. . . Mrs. Perry and Mrs. General Howard are coming to Lapwai tomorrow . . . In a few days all the wounded are to be brought in here, nearly thirty poor fellows. They say there are some awful wounds.

Affectionately,
Emily F.

"You understand your orders, Lieutenant?" Charles Rawn asked the youngest officer in the Seventh Infantry, who stood stiffly beside his horse.

At attention a few yards in front of the four members of his small scouting party, who were already mounted, Second Lieutenant Francis Woodbridge said, "Yes sir, Captain. I'm to look over the trail ascending into the mountains, get up to a point where I can look six or eight miles into Idaho, and determine if the Indians have passed or if they are coming up the far side."

"Very good," Rawn replied. "You have rations for four days, but I am expecting you back on the twenty-first."

"Three days from now."

"That's right, Lieutenant," Rawn emphasized. "It's no more than thirty miles from our end of the trail up to the pass itself. See what you can of the far side—looking for those Nez Perce said to be fleeing from Idaho—then get on back here to help us finish building this post."

Woodbridge saluted and without a word he mounted. Taking up the slack in his reins, the bright-eyed lieutenant, fresh out of West Point, said his farewell: "We'll be back by supper on the twenty-first, Captain."

Rawn watched those five backs disappear through the trees, riding south up the Bitterroot valley where they would reach the end of the Lolo Trail. He sighed, hoping the young lieutenant would not put his small scouting detail in harm's way. He really needed the muscle of those five men if he was going to get these quarters and storehouses finished and sealed off before another Montana winter blew in.

Chapter Thirty-Eight

July 19–20, 1877

Now that he knew where the Non-Treaties were headed, Oliver O. Howard felt more uncomfortable sitting on the horns of this dilemma than he did sitting in one of those damnable instruments of torture the army called a McClellan saddle!

Once Joseph's warrior bands crossed from Idaho into Montana, they would no longer be Howard's Indians to chase and pacify. Then they would belong to Brigadier General Alfred H. Terry and his Department of Dakota. With the Nez Perce already well started on the Lolo Trail across the Bitterroot, Howard had begun to think it didn't make any sense for him to go traipsing along in their wake—although he had received orders from McDowell that he need not be mindful of division boundaries in pursuit of the Non-Treaty bands.

Through division headquarters in San Francisco, Howard had received General William T. Sherman's instructions to ignore such geographic boundaries on 26 June, and McDowell had again reminded him of Sherman's orders three days ago on 16 July when it appeared Howard was putting an end to his direct pursuit of the hostiles. What gave Oliver pause was the fact that according to settlers in the area and reports from Christian trackers, the terrain of the Lolo Trail was even more rugged than what his men had encountered on the far side of the Salmon River back in June.

At this point, 19 July, Howard was staring at an exhausted command, weary of almost a solid month of campaigning: breaking trail and fighting Indians both. Hacking their way through another two hundred miles of even rougher terrain was far from appealing.

Then there was his guarded concern that if he did follow

the retreating Indians, that would leave this region of Idaho devoid of enough soldiers to handle the eventuality of neighboring tribes rising up in revolt. Made bold by the Nez Perce successes, the other tribes in the Northwest had white settlers uneasy for hundreds of square miles. But Howard had more troops on the way: Colonel Frank Wheaton was on his way from Atlanta with infantry, and Major John Green was marching north from Fort Boise with more horse soldiers. They would reach Lapwai within the week. Then, Howard convinced himself, he would feel a lot more secure about pursuing the Nez Perce out of Idaho.

At that point, it didn't take long for him to devise a plan that should carry him over the next several weeks and on to putting an end to this outbreak. He would push downriver for Lapwai, on to Lewiston for resupply. Then he would march his column north for the Mullan Road. Although this route would be more than double the distance of the one-hundred-fifty-mile Lolo Trail, the fact that this freight route extending between Missoula and Spokane Falls was no more than a narrow wagon road did not deter his thinking. The Mullan was undeniably the best means for his command to reach western Montana.

His plan was as ambitious as it was daring—hoping to be in position south of Missoula when the Nez Perce finally debouched from the trail in the Bitterroot valley. Over the last few days Oliver Otis had come to realize he could not afford to rest on the laurels of what he had won at the Battle of the Clearwater. That faint praise sent his way in the Western papers was already beginning to fade. He needed to keep the pressure on if he was going to blunt the criticism coming from both the civilian press and the highest echelons of the army.

In the last month the Nez Perce had killed nearly ninety people and done close to a quarter-million dollars in damage, a monstrous sum in a day and time when the average laborer made no more than seventy-five cents at the end of his dawn-to-dusk workday. To put the very public humiliation of the scandal at the Freedmen's Bureau behind him, to blunt the unseemly reputation he suffered among his army colleagues, Howard had to press forward with his plan without delay.

But, right from the start, the general's hopes began to suffer one wounding after another.

Just yesterday, on the morning of the eighteenth, his men had discovered three Non-Treaty warriors hiding among the ruins of the agency buildings on the east side of the Clearwater. Two of them were wounded, in all likelihood left behind when the rest of the village fled toward *Weippe* Prairie.

After stationing a token force—Throckmorton's battery of artillery, Jocelyn's company of infantry, and Trimble's troop of cavalry—at the Kamiah crossing on the nineteenth and directing McConville's volunteers back upriver to finish destroying the last of the caches at the enemy's Clearwater camp, Howard set off with the rest of his command for Lewiston. He got no farther than the halfway point when a courier reached him with the news that hostiles had doubled back, slipping out of the hills, and had the soldiers pinned down at Kamiah—stealing more than four hundred of the Christian Indians' horses, killing what cattle they could not drive off, and diligently burning houses of Lawyer's Indians.

Leaving his infantry and artillerymen there at Cold Springs, Howard ordered his cavalry back to Kamiah before he and a small headquarters group rode on to Fort Lapwai with Captain David Perry's escort. At the post he intended to make arrangements for the supplies required by the next phase of the war.

When they were finished with their destruction on the Clearwater, McConville's militia was under orders to drive several hundred head of captured ponies past Mount Idaho and Grangeville, into the head of Rocky Canyon, where they were to be slaughtered, in hopes of eliminating any reason the warrior bands might have for returning to central Idaho. That done, McConville and his men were to station themselves in the area, protecting the settlements should

Joseph and his henchmen slip back out of the mountains and make a wide sweep for the Salmon River.

Oliver knew it would be a tiring ride for his old bones, pushing those long hours in the saddle, but three days ago he had received word that his wife would be arriving by steamboat in Lewiston that very night. Oliver managed to make it in time, but when the steamboat was moored at 10:00 P.M. his sweet Lizzie was not on board. However, Mrs. Perry was on board. And upon spotting her husband among those welcomers on the dock, she went into a fit of theatrical hysterics, a display that totally disgusted Howard.

In town for the night, he picked up the first newspapers he had seen in weeks—finding he was under personal assault from the normally conservative San Francisco *Chronicle* to the New York *Herald*. But the sharpest attacks were those of the local papers like the Lewiston *Teller*, whose editor, Alonzo Leland, lost no opportunity to write about how poorly Howard had done with the campaign so far. His brutal words cut Oliver to the marrow.

"The sheep is a very pleasant and amiable animal and has none but sterling qualities," Leland had written in the most recent editorial, perhaps still furious over his own son's reports on the poor showing the army made at Cottonwood, "but we do not expect him to chase wolves and coyotes; we assign the task to the dog—also an amiable brute, but better adapted to the purpose."

Leland broadcast that General Crook was a better man to send against the wolves and coyotes: "He sticks his breeches in his boots, keeps his powder dry, eats hardtack, and goes for 'em. . . . But Howard regards the army as a kind of missionary society for the Indians and holds himself as the head of a kind of red freedman's bureau."

While Crook was a first-class Indian fighter, as proved down in Arizona and during the Sioux campaign, if Howard continued to lead the chase of the Nez Perce, the war would be a six months' campaign, hunting the enemy in the mountains.

Summoning up from inside him his reservoir of fairness

in the face of brutal assault, Oliver sighed and folded the paper before handing it off to Lieutenant Charles Wood, his aide-de-camp.

"How wonderfully news can be spread," he began with a cool, even detached, air so unlike what he had boiling inside. "It is like the cloud no bigger than a man's hand, when it leaves us, it is magnified several times before the journals at Lewiston and Walla Walla have put it into type, and by the time it has reached Portland and San Francisco it has become a heavy cloud, overspreading the whole heaven."

"It's those civilian volunteers, General," Major Edwin Mason grumbled. "They play at citizen militia when they're nothing more than a worthless set of trifling rascals! Utterly worthless, a cowardly pack of whelps, sir!"

Captain Birney Keeler jumped in, saying, "Many times I myself have explained to General McDowell how he should not give a grain of credence to any of the civilian accounts of our campaign, sir. Time and again I've informed the division commander that such news reports and editorials are nothing more than wanton, systematic lies. I've even told him that to continue employing civilians of such low character would be worse than useless in ending this war."

"Yes, well," Howard replied to McDowell's aide, sent by the department commander to have a look at the campaign for himself. He cleared his throat of the ball of fury just then rising. "I'd like to put a few of these dishonest enemies attacking me far from their warmth and safety of the rear out on those mountain trails of the Salmon, or march them dawn to dusk and order them to fight under a broiling July sun."

By the following morning, Oliver Otis Howard had changed his mind. It was to be one of the most crucial decisions he made in his life. Turning his back on his initial plan to loop north to the Mullan Road, then sweep down on the Non-Treaty bands emerging from the Lolo Trail just south of Missoula, the general had now committed his men to pursuing the fleeing camp across the Lolo itself. While awaiting his reinforcements in Lewiston, he polished the details of his three-column strategy.

Upon his arrival at Lewiston with his ten companies of the Second Infantry, Colonel Frank Wheaton would start north to the Mullan Road, accompanied by F and H Companies, First Cavalry, along with two companies of mounted volunteers mustered from the eastern regions of Washington Territory. Inspector Erwin Watkins of the Indian Bureau, on the scene with Agent Monteith, had proposed this march of thirty-six officers and 440 enlisted men through the Coeur d'Alene country to blunt any rising zeal the disaffected tribes in the area had for joining up with Joseph's Nez Perce.*

Major John Green, of the First Cavalry, would position his Fort Boise column and some Bannock scouts at Henry Croasdaile's ranch,** located ten miles from Mount Idaho on Cottonwood Creek. With D, E, G, and L Troops of the First Cavalry, along with B and F Companies of the Twelfth Infantry, in addition to those thirty-five Warm Springs trackers, the entire force of twenty-two officers, and 245 enlisted men, Green would be deployed in a central location allowing his men to protect the Camas Prairie settlements and the Kamiah subagency, too, where the major would position an artillery battery and two fieldpieces. From his base of operations Green would dispatch reconnaissance parties to the region of the Salmon and Snake, with orders to capture and arrest any Nez Perce who might possibly be allied with the Non-Treaty bands.

---

*Wheaton would not reach the theater of operations until July 29, having traveled from Atlanta to Oakland, California, by rail, boarded a steamer to Portland, and traveled by riverboat up the Columbia to Lewiston.

**In August 1877, an officer with the campaign wrote: ". . . The [Non-Treaty] Indians entered the house first and destroyed most of the furniture &c and were followed by the soldiers & volunteers who completed the destruction." From the home of this retired British army officer the Non-Treaty warriors removed many high-powered and explosive bullets, some of which later saw use by the Nez Perce at the Battle of the Big Hole and eventually at the Battle of the Bear's Paw Mountains.

But O. O. Howard had saved the right column for himself. Accompanying him on Joseph's trail would be a battalion of the Fourth Artillery A, C, D, E, G, and L Batteries, commanded by Captain Marcus P. Miller. Under Captain Evan Miles would serve a battalion of foot soldiers: Company H, Eighth Infantry, Company C, Twelfth Infantry—both of which had recently arrived from Fort Yuma along the Mexican border in Arizona Territory—in addition to C, D, E, H, and I Companies of the Twenty-first Infantry, who had already been seeing a lot of service with Howard in the first weeks of this outbreak. Major George B. Sanford was coming up to command the general's horse soldiers: B, C, I, and K Troops of the First Cavalry—all of them fresh companies that had not seen any service so far in the campaign.

Howard wired McDowell: "Will start with the rest of my command through the impenetrable Lolo Pass, and follow Joseph to the very death."

This one-armed general was about to lead forty-seven officers, 540 enlisted men, seventy-four civilian and Indian scouts, as well as some seventy packers for his 350-mule pack train into one of the most far-reaching and inhospitable tracts of wilderness in the United States.

Chapter Thirty-Nine

July 20–21, 1877

BY TELEGRAPH

—

The St. Louis Bank Panic Subsiding.

—

The Great Strike on the Baltimore and Ohio road.

—

OREGON.

—

Latest From the Indian War.

SAN FRANCISCO, July 18.—A Walla Walla dispatch says the Indians have killed three men and one girl on Cow creek. Old Salty, a Spokane chief, believes fifty of his warriors have gone to join Joseph. They are beyond his control. Col. Green with his column has reached Little Salmon river from the South. A messenger from Smookhalls and Spokane Jerry, non-treaty Spokane chiefs, announces that they desire to remain friendly and go upon a reservation, provided one is set apart for them and food furnished for the winter.

Fort Lapwai
Friday, July 20, 1877

Dear Mamma,

All our troubles are upon us again and worse than ever. I feel even more upset, as John is ordered into the field and I will have to be here alone. He was to have gone with the troop that leaves tonight, but since morning he has been ordered to wait and assist Dr. Sternberg to get the wounded comfortable and then follow with the next detachment. The wounded are being hurried in here.

Some will arrive this afternoon, and it is so hot. I never in my life felt such weather. The thermometer in my shady sitting room (the coolest room in the house) stood yesterday at 98 degrees, and that was much less than it was at the hospital and on the porches.

The Indians have gone in full retreat towards the buffalo country. The cavalry went after them nearly a hundred miles and reported them all gone and impossible to follow, from the condition of the country. So General Howard started his command back here, leaving three companies up there to watch the place the Indians ford the river, the ford that leads to the mountains. We knew yesterday that General Howard's command was near Lapwai. In the evening, an officer, who had been sent on in advance, came in and said there were signal fires burning in the mountains. By and by, General Howard himself and some other officer came in, and in a great hurry. A messenger had just reached them from the three companies left to watch the ford saying the Indians were all back. So, of course, everything is in confusion again. General Howard did not wait to rest but started right back, and those poor, tired soldiers have to turn and do it all over . . . I don't know what we will do after John goes. I wish it was over! The confusion, outside of everything else, which is even worse, will set me crazy!

. . . They are going to leave all the Indian prisoners here and double this garrison. With the wounded here, and the Indian prisoners here, and Doctor gone, I think I would like to go, too, but I suppose I had better stay, as I have no friends near I could go to. To board somewhere would be lonely and worse than here . . .

Lots of love to all, and write to me.

Yours affectionately,
Emily FitzGerald

CHARLES RAWN WATCHED THE YOUNG FIRST LIEUTENANT stride across the dry, dusty ground, leading his horse. Just steps behind him followed an enlisted man and a handful of civilians, all of them dismounted, their animals in tow.

"We're ready to ride, Captain."

Rawn sighed. "It shouldn't be hard to find Lieutenant Woodbridge . . . if his men stayed on the trail. I've never been over it myself, but from what these settlers in the valley tell me, it's hard as hell to make a mistake and get off the Lolo."

"We'll find them for you, Captain," promised First Lieutenant Charles A. Coolidge, jabbing his thumb at that small band of civilians who had volunteered to guide the two soldiers up the mountain trail. "We have rations for three days, just as you ordered."

"Scout the trail as far as is prudent. I want you back here by the twenty-fourth, if you've found Woodbridge's party or not. Between his group and yours being gone from the post, I'm feeling a little whittled down—should any of those Nez Perces pop up nearby."

"From everything these civilians have told me about that trail, sir," Coolidge declared, "Joseph's Injuns are going to take a long time getting over the mountains on the Lolo—what with all their women, children, baggage, not to mention that pony herd, too. They aren't going to be making good time up there in those mountains."

Taking a step back, Rawn saluted the lieutenant. "Let's pray those warriors are crawling over the pass real slow. And while we're at it, maybe we should pray young Woodbridge hasn't stumbled into any of them, too."

BY TELEGRAPH

—

The Railway Strike Spreading
Over the Country.

—

Trains Moving Under Military
Protection.

—

Great Activity of Black Hills
Road Agents.

—

Late War News and General
Intelligence.

—

CHEYENNE.

—

The Ready Road-Agents Robbing Left and Right.

CHEYENNE, July 19.—The coach from Deadwood was stopped, last night, near Cheyenne river, by road agents, who robbed the passengers of about $50. Twelve miles further they were stopped again by four robbers, who took the passengers' arms and part of their blankets. The treasure box was opened but contained no valuables . . .

While Cut-Off Arm attempted to sneak off downriver from the Kamiah crossing so he could slip up behind them, the *Nee-Me-Poo* had decided to follow Looking Glass toward *Moosmoos Illahe*, the buffalo country. For fighting men like Shore Crossing, it was less a matter of possessing any real enthusiasm for this flight over the mountains than it was a matter of there simply being nothing better to do . . . at least for the present.

Indeed, there were many more who felt the frustration he did: warriors who believed that those who wanted to fight the *suapies* should be allowed to stay behind in their own country, there to attack and harass the small groups of soldiers, there to run off horses, mules, and cattle belonging to the Christian Indians at Lapwai and Kamiah, staying behind to slow the army's pursuit to a standstill.

As fierce a fighter as *Ollokot* had been in those early days of the war, at the councils held on the *Weippe* Prairie he had nonetheless joined his older brother, Joseph, in arguing that once the bands had crossed the Lolo and headed south, up the Bitterroot valley, they should recross the mountains into Idaho, circling back to their beloved Salmon and Snake River country.* With every day now, the Frog was sounding more and more like his non-fighting brother, chief of the *Wallowa*.

Since their battle against Cut-Off Arm on the Clearwater, White Bird had begun to advance the possibility of turning north once they had reached the end of the Lolo Trail. There the bands could pass through the country of the friendly Flathead and march for the Old Woman's Country, perhaps even rendezvous with the Lakota expatriates of Chief Buffalo Bull Who Rests on the Ground.**

But in the end, Looking Glass was more persuasive than the others. Why go north when they had friends in the buffalo country, land where they had hunted for many generations with their longtime friends the *E-sue-gha*? Hadn't several of the leading men—like Looking Glass, Rainbow, and Five Wounds—fought against the Lakota time and again? In fact, at this present time weren't a few of their own young men gone east to the buffalo plains to help the army round up the Lakota?

No, Looking Glass orated, the Old Woman's Country was strange to them; no one he knew had ever been there. Besides, once they had put the Idaho country at their backs, put its soldiers and Shadows behind them, there would be no need to run away to join the Lakota north of the Medicine Line. The *Nee-Me-Poo* would be leaving their war far behind, back there beyond the Bitterroot.

In the end Looking Glass won the day. While *Wottolen* and Two Moons vigorously opposed any alliance with the *E-sue-gha* and Joseph said nothing because he favored returning his people to the *Wallowa* valley, White Bird, *Toohoolhoolzote*, and *Hahtalekin* were unanimous. "All right, Looking Glass—take us to the buffalo country."

—

*Via what is known as the Southern Nez Perce Trail, over Nez Perce Pass, southwest of present-day Darby, Montana.

**Sitting Bull, the spiritual leader of the Hunkpapa Lakota.

The morning of their second day on the Lolo, Rainbow went down their back trail, accompanied by more than three hands of warriors. They were to watch for soldiers. Five of their number had been selected by the chiefs to remain behind near the *Weippe* for three suns. Red Moccasin Tops, White Cloud, and three others were to watch for Cut-Off Arm's men coming up the trail. If, after those three days, they hadn't seen any soldiers following, they were to come on with their good news and reunite with their families. If, however, enemies were sighted, two of their number were to race up the trail with the report so the warriors would have time to prepare a fight to hold the *suapies* on the trail while the families escaped. The last three were to stay and keep watch, staying just ahead of any white or Christian scouts in the process as they fell back.

Riding off in a different direction, Shore Crossing joined Looking Glass's raiding party that swept down on the Kamiah Christians—running off their horses and cattle, burning a few small buildings, and doing their best to frighten Lawyer's Indians. The warriors were able to scatter and harry those Treaty people just they way they had driven the horses and a few head of cattle* back into the hills while exchanging a few long-range shots with those *suapies* left behind when Cut-Off Arm marched north for Lapwai.

By the time the raiders returned to the Lolo late that afternoon, it amazed Shore Crossing how much ground all those people, a few hundred dogs, and more than two thou-

---

*Several white ranchers and their hired hands took advantage of the war and its confusion to run off some neighbors' stock for themselves, along with the cattle and horses belonging to the Christian Indians, hoping the blame would fall on the Non-Treaty bands. Nervous settlers raised a protest when Howard prepared to march away from the Camas and Clearwater country—crying that they would be left to the mercy of the savages. Their clamor would cause the general to remain in the area another ten days before Howard was convinced the warrior bands had indeed abandoned Idaho.

sand horses had covered in a day. Forced by necessity to stretch itself out for several miles while on the march, the column inched its way deeper and deeper into the wilderness along that tenuous strand of timber-clogged trail taking them ever higher, into ever thicker, mazelike forests. How they were able to accomplish this feat mile after mile, day after day, with women and children, the old and the very young, along with their sick and wounded, too, was nothing short of miraculous to the young warrior.

These Non-Treaty bands were able to march with energy and precision through such impossibly rugged terrain and the clutter of downfall forests because they had two cultural characteristics working for them. The first was that Shore Crossing's people had, for generations beyond count, developed and refined a system of moving people and property, whereby each family unit was responsible to the band by seeing to its own organizing and packing, along with transporting its own members in harmony with the needs of the camp as a whole, day in and day out. The second feature of their success derived from decades of learning to travel through steep mountains and across barren plateaus.

What other people would dare face the terrible ordeal of this trail burdened with their wounded and sick on travois, all those women and children and belongings, not to mention all those thousands of horses? With or without an enemy snarling at your tail, this would be a feat unmatched by any other people. Only the *Nee-Me-Poo* would pit themselves against the Lolo the way they had pitted themselves against the U. S. Army.

Still, for young fighting men like Shore Crossing, the best part of each day's journey was that with Cut-Off Arm sitting on his haunches somewhere near Fort Lapwai, every march put that much more distance between the *Nee-Me-Poo* and the army Looking Glass vowed could never touch them again.

"They are so far behind," Shore Crossing announced when the war party reunited with the village as it was going into camp at the end of that second day on the trail, "we will never have to worry about those soldiers again!"

"Your eyes are half-closed if you think Cut-Off Arm's are the only *suapies*, Shore Crossing," old *Toohoolhoolzote* warned. "We have seen the soldiers over in buffalo country."

"No," he snorted at the old *tewat*, refusing to be cowed by worry. "We won't have to worry about any of those soldiers or Shadows over there. The Montana people have known us for a long, long time."

"JESUS Christ! You fellas scared the piss out of me!" one of the pickets hollered from that dark ring of night surrounding their bivouac.

Second Lieutenant Francis Woodbridge nearly leaped out of his skin when that picket suddenly shrieked his high-pitched alarm. The other picket lunged into the dim light thrown off by the low, flickering flames, joining Woodbridge and the other two privates who were scheduled to take their second watch later that night, the twenty-second of July.

"I'll be go to hell!" exclaimed one of those soldiers beside Woodbridge as the picket materialized out of the dark, right behind two young civilians. "They're white fellas!"

"Who the devil was you expecting to come walkin' into your camp, soldier?" one of the strangers growled, his eyes shimmery with relief. "We'd been Looking Glass's red devils sneaking down this trail, you'd never see'd us come up on you the way we done!"

The picket snapped, "I'd shot you in the gut afore you'd got 'nother step—"

"Hold it!" Woodbridge interrupted, then waved the two strangers closer to the light. "C'mon over here and sit yourselves down. Where's your horses?"

"W-we ain't got none," said the sullen, darker-skinned of the two.

"What's your name?"

He looked at the lieutenant, then stared down at the fire and rubbed his hands over it as he said, "Peter Matte."*

"And you?" Woodbridge asked the other stranger, who had been the first to speak to the picket.

"William . . . Bill Silverthorne."

The second picket asked, "You fellas from the Bitterroot?"

Silverthorne flicked a glance his way, saying, "By a damned long way around."

That sounded really odd to the suspicious lieutenant. "What are you two doing out at night on the Lolo Trail, without horses, and you're all the way up here from the Bitterroot to boot?"

"Wasn't my idea to take no trip back over the pass to Montana on foot," Silverthorne snorted. "But we was forced to come with the Injuns."

"Injuns!" one of the privates echoed in a high-pitched whine.

Silverthorne stood up and turned his buttocks to the low fire, rubbing them with his palms as he explained, "Nez Percey, they was. Seven days ago—no, eight days—me and Pete, we was heading to Lewiston to buy us some horses more'n a week back, when a war party of them Nez Percey bucks jumped us on the way to the Clearwater and brung us right on in to their camp. Hundreds of 'em was up to the *Weippe* Prairie, camped there digging the roots and hunting. Didn't ever hurt us none—"

"But back at home at Stevensville in the Bitterroot, we both heard how they butchered a lot of white folks over in Idaho not long ago," Matte said.

Woodbridge wagged his head in wonder. "So why'd they let you two go now?"

Silverthorne gazed over at the young lieutenant with undisguised disdain. "The red sonsabitches didn't let us go, for Chrissakes! We slipped away and come on down the trail, making for Missoula City fast as we could."

---

*Recently released from prison after serving a sentence for horse theft.

"How far's we from there now?" Matte asked, the low flames flickering off his dark face.

The lieutenant figured the man for a half-breed, must have some Indian blood in him. "Twenty, maybe twenty-five miles. The pass is only thirty in all—"

"You fellas headed on up the trail tomorrow?" Silverthorne interrupted.

"No, we're on our way back to the post we're building south of Missoula City," Woodbridge explained.

"Awright we go on in with you come morning?"

Woodbridge nodded to Silverthorne. "Sure. We'll ride double or swap off horses. See you get to town."

"We better skeedaddle come morning," Matte said as he glanced around at the dark.

"They find we're missing," Silverthorne said, "they'll come looking, I'll bet. 'Sides, them reds up near the pass anyways."

Woodbridge swallowed. They had covered a lot of ground, crossing over the pass, something on the order of sixty-five miles from Missoula City. "We hadn't seen any sign of the Indians when we stopped up at the top and looked down the west approach."

"Didn't see all of them?" Matte cried, his voice rising two octaves in disbelief.

The lieutenant wagged his head, ready to speak, when Silverthorne blurted out, "Shit, soldier! That bunch of Nez Percey strings out on the trail for better'n two miles, likely more! And that horse herd of theirs! I'll lay a bet there's more'n two thousand, twenty-five hundred of 'em . . . and you say you didn't see anything of 'em when they had us climbing up the other side of the goddamned mountain?"

With a shrug, Woodbridge admitted, "Not a thing. So how far back from here you get away from the Nez Perce? They still on the other side of the pass?"

"*Other* side of the pass?" Silverthorne snorted, waving an arm off into the darkness. "Those red devils is already coming down this side fast as you please, soldier."

Woodbridge stared into the night as if trying hard to listen, hearing nothing more than the crackle of the fire and the pulse of his own blood in his ears. "How far up the trail are they from us here?"

"Six, maybe seven, miles," Silverthorne said. "It's goddamned hard to tell stumbling down the trail on foot in the dark, y'know."

Turning on his heel, the lieutenant waved his two pickets in. "Finish out your last two hours, then come wake me to take over. That way you can get a little sleep in before we ride out soon as it's light."

"Awright we use their blankets?" Matte inquired with a grin.

"Yeah—but don't get too comfortable," Woodbridge advised. "Soon as we can see far enough in front of the horses' noses that we don't stumble over down timber, we're making a run down the trail for Missoula City."

CHAPTER FORTY

KHOY-TSAHL, 1877

BY TELEGRAPH

—

Late War News and General Intelligence.

—

OREGON.

—

Captain Perry and His Men Defended.

SAN FRANCISCO, July 10.—The following has been received here: General McDowell, San Francisco:—Your dispatch of the 10th just received . . . The difficulties of communication have been great. The country from front to rear has until now been infested with hostiles, and couriers and supplies in many instances have failed to get through, though none have been lost. I am not aware of the exact tenor of the reports to which you refer, but I infer that they are principally those reflecting upon General Howard and Captain Perry. I have investigated the most important ones, and find them to be false. The statement in the local papers of the affair at Cottonwood on the 5th, to the effect that seventeen citizens were surrounded by Indians and the troops under Perry refused to go to their relief for an hour and a half, is a wicked falsification. The troops, 113 in number, were themselves outnumbered, environed and attacked by Indians, but nevertheless were sent instantly a mile away to the rescue, which was accomplished within twenty minutes, and not only the life of every man in the command was risked, but the safety of a most important position and a large amount of ammunition and other stores. The accounts as published originated with one Orrin Morrill, of Lewiston, who was at Cottonwood at the time, but who, although armed, remained ensconced in a little fortification there, instead of going with the soldiers to the aid of his imperilled fellow citizens. The other citizens who were present agree with the officers in this statement of facts. The conduct of officers and men has, under the most trying circumstances, been particularly good. They have justified all reasonable expectations. The campaign has been successful. The hostiles have operated skillfully and fought desperately, but they have been defeated and driven from this section with great loss of numbers and supplies. Gen. Howard reports by this courier the events of the last two days and the present situation. The number of killed and wounded on both sides in the action of the 11th and 12th turns out to be larger than at first believed.

KEELER, A.D.C.

NOT ONLY DID THE WOMEN HAVE TO COAX THE HORSES over, around, and through a maze of deadfall, but every day that village on the move discovered even more trees blown down by high winds or uprooted by heavy, wet snows the higher they climbed toward the summit of Lolo Pass.

Because of the many outcroppings of sharp rocks, not to mention the neck-wrenching switchbacks as they inched from ridge to ridge, the *Nee-Me-Poo* were unable to use their travois in this flight from war. Instead, the strong young men stumbled along, carrying the litters with their war wounded, carrying those too old and weak. Besides, they simply hadn't dragged that many poles along with them anyway. Those they had managed to dismantle before escaping the Clearwater fight they ended up having to abandon one camp out of *Weippe*, at a place the People named Dead Horse Meadow. It was nothing but a small, elongated patch of meadow ringed by a windbreak of timber. Stacked into the forks of every tree available went the hundreds upon hundreds of peeled, dried lodgepoles the women were leaving behind against the prayers they could one day return to everything they had ever known.

Here in the middle of summer they found the trail little more than a muddy ribbon disappearing through the impenetrable timber that, even at this late season, still shaded deep drifts of soggy, slow-melting snow. Each step upon the saturated ground soon became an ordeal of its own: muddy water gushing into every footprint and hoof hole as the grim, silent procession continued, this march away from everything that had ever been.

Day by day, they were forced to abandon more and more of the poorer horses on the trail—those animals who had stumbled off the rocky path and broken a leg, those with severe, gaping lacerations from shoving through the narrow gaps between boulders and thick timber, along with those growing progressively weaker from what poor forage was available at the infrequent forest glades. The *Nee-Me-Poo* did not have time to stop and tend to their horses now. They pushed on.

Instead of following one ridge all the way to the top, this long-used, traditional trail snaked up and down ever-ascending slopes, a physical necessity that made the journey more taxing than the mere distances on a map would ever indicate. From first light until late afternoon, they put one foot in front of the other and climbed a little more with every step—waiting for that day they would stand at the top and look down on the land of Montana, the buffalo country.

Because of the difficulty of finding one site big enough for all the families, a site that possessed enough grazing for the huge herd and enough water, too, the *Nee-Me-Poo* chiefs usually ordered a string of camps made along the trail rather than the hundreds congregating in one site. These stops were usually at what they called *woutokinwes tahtakkin*, or meadow camps, when they could find them for the night. If not, the column leaders pushed on until they eventually came across a place big enough for their weary people and their exhausted animals. Some of these spots were beautiful, unexpected interludes in the harsh severity of the trail—lush marshlands dotted with shallow ponds of bone-chilling ice melt, their placid surfaces blanketed by pond lilies, each of these tiny meadows ringed by a verdant, chest-high brush, the leaves of which were boiled into a delicious tea.

But many times the People could find nothing better than cramped, waterless sites where the poor horses had nothing more to feed on but the wire grass and dwarf lupine, where the men, women, and children wearily collapsed and slept until it was time to awaken and start out all over again.

It was not an entirely joyful exodus. The People simply made forced marches, went without, and endured in the cause of freedom.

Nonetheless, a couple of days ago when they finally reached the top and everyone paused a few minutes to take in the breathtaking view both ahead of and behind them, there was much cause to celebrate. Many of the women trilled their tongues in joy and the children laughed with unfettered happiness while most of the older men sang their victory songs.

Yes, this, too, had been a battle. But now the long side of the trail lay behind them. From here it would be a quick journey down to the Bitterroot valley. Not only had they won a victory over the Lolo Trail, but this flight meant they had secured a victory over Cut-Off Arm and his soldiers. A victory over the Shadows in Idaho country. A victory that meant they had escaped without any more loss to those who wanted to steal away their long-held way of life.

That was the day, too, when Red Moccasin Tops and his four companions had caught up with the retreating column. This five-man rear guard reported that Cut-Off Arm had given up, marching away from the Kamiah crossing, leaving only a few *suapies* to protect Lawyer's Christians from raiding warriors. What soldiers they hadn't defeated outright they had managed to hold off long enough to exhaust the resolve of Cut-Off Arm. The war was behind them!

So at the top there was much singing, keening, chanting, and prayer giving before they passed over into the Montana buffalo country. Much, much thanksgiving to *Hunyewat*, their Creator, because they had reached a land of plenty and of peace. Truly Cut-Off Arm's war and his angry soldiers were far, far behind them now.

Still, there was another, although less important, reason to celebrate. Just below the pass they would find the lush meadows surrounding those pools of hot water said to possess a magical power to heal and refresh the weary traveler. And here was the first good grass and clear water for their horses encountered since leaving the *Weippe* six camps ago. The People had arrived.

For summers without count, many women returning from the buffalo country had left their lodgepoles here at the hot springs* so they would not have to drag the travois over the roughest part of the crossing from here into Idaho. As the first, eager *Nee-Me-Poo* rushed into these meadows surrounding the steamy pools, those peeled and dried poles stacked in the forks of so many trees stood like a warm and welcoming gesture.

As one of the young warriors riding advance for the village, Yellow Wolf quickly tore off his shirt, moccasins, and breechclout, then eased himself into the hot waters. As more and more of the *Nee-Me-Poo* arrived, singing out with joy as they reached the meadow and selected a camping spot, the men and women, children, too, all stripped off their dusty, trail-sweated clothing and plunged into the life-affirming springs. Yellow Wolf could not remember a finer day since this war had begun.

In fact, Sun Necklace and his son, Red Moccasin Tops, were so relaxed and jovial that they invited their two white captives to strip off their clothes and join them in the pools. The ropes were freed from the prisoners' wrists and ankles, but the pair hesitated to tear off their clothing and sink into the springs like the rest of the *Nee-Me-Poo* were doing all around them—coming and going, yelling, joking, laughing, a raucous cacophony of sounds and a blur of long-denied

---

*The Lolo Hot Springs made famous by Lewis and Clark on their journey west in 1805.

happiness. Why the Shadow was a man to keep so much of his body covered with clothing in spite of the summer's heat was something Yellow Wolf doubted he would ever sort out. The white man simply thought with a different brain than did his own people! The Shadow looked at things with a different eye, heard with a different set of ears, too, perhaps even tasted life with a foreign tongue as well.

Here in the riding steam of the pools with the sun going down and the sky behind them turning to a brilliant rose, drinking in the fragrance of those many fires where strips of meat sizzled, hearing the soft tinkle of women's laughter and the playful giggles of the many children—Yellow Wolf wondered if he ever would go back to Idaho country now. After all they had gone through, life seemed far better over here on this side of the mountains.

On this eastern slope of the Bitterroot, the *Nee-Me-Poo* would no longer have to worry about Cut-Off Arm and his soldiers, would not have to concern themselves with the angry Shadows who many winters ago had started the conflict by stealing, raping, abusing, and killing their people. Perhaps one day the Idaho men would get over being mad and the *Nee-Me-Poo* could go back home. But for now, this was a good country . . . where they could hunt buffalo, court young women, and sleep till midday if they wanted, because they would not have to look back over their shoulders ever again.

They had left the Idaho country behind. They had put the angry Shadows at their backs, and now they were in a new land—

There arose a sudden commotion as three older warriors raced into the meadow from the east, returning from a scout made on down the trail toward the Bitterroot valley. Yellow Wolf could tell they brought word of something important, something very grave, from the way the trio of riders gestured, pointed, held up their hands to indicate numbers of strangers—and from the way the chiefs and old headmen quickly gathered around those scouts, drawing up close around the three who had arrived with some terrible news like a piece of rawhide shriveling beneath the midsummer sun.

"Where are those two Shadows of yours, Sun Necklace?" someone called out in the middle of the hubbub.

The older man, and his son, too, turned this way and that as they searched the trees on three sides of them.

"Ha!" another man laughed at them. "Did your prisoners get away from you while you were getting your manhood soaked?"

Red Moccasin Tops angrily slapped the surface of the steamy pool as the clamor continued to grow down in the meadow around those three horsemen.

But it was Shore Crossing, his older cousin, who snarled like a dog restrained too long on a short rope, "We will find them for you, Sun Necklace. Your son and I are good at finding runaway Shadows—"

A loud yell arose from many throats in the meadow as more than two hundred men and women cried out in unison—a sound that raised the hair on the back of Yellow Wolf's neck as he stood, the hot water sluicing off his sinewy muscles, down his bony shoulders and boyish hips. Through the midst of the cries and keening, he heard *Ollokot* calling his name as the war chief loped toward him on foot.

"Yellow Wolf!"

"I am ready, *Ollokot*!"

With an impish grin the *Wallamwatkin* war chief skidded to a halt and peered at this naked young warrior. "You better put on your clothes before you cause a stir among the young women in the camp! I want you to come with me."

"Come? Where?"

"Even though we have left Cut-Off Arm's *suapies* behind," *Ollokot* began as a serious expression came over the *Wallowa* war chief's face. He pointed to the east, in the direction the Lolo Trail took into the Bitterroot valley, then finished, "it seems there are some Montana soldiers waiting down below to make new trouble for us now."

* * *

REINFORCEMENTS were coming, but—at best—they were more than a hundred-fifty miles and a week away. Back when the captain in charge of building the army's newest post four miles southwest of Missoula City came asking for volunteers to ride up the Lolo Trail with one of his lieutenants in a search for an overdue reconnaissance party, Chauncey Barbour volunteered right there and then. Even though he was editor of the *Weekly Missoulian*, putting out a newspaper would have to wait, and folks might just have to miss an issue for the first time in many years—because settling these Indian troubles was that much more important.

Besides, those oncoming Nez Perce had made themselves the biggest news of this summer.

Along with a handful of other local citizens, Barbour had climbed toward the pass with Lieutenant Charles Coolidge of A Company, Seventh U. S. Infantry, hoping to run across another officer named Woodbridge. They ended up finding the lieutenant's party coming down the trail, at which point Coolidge's detail turned back for town themselves. Woodbridge's men would spend one more day taking a more leisurely pace down to the valley.

But Woodbridge had hurried back to the unfinished post by midday with two hard-used Bitterroot civilians, both of them reporting to Captain Rawn—along with every one of his quartermaster employees helping in the fort's construction—that the Nez Perce had reached the hot springs!

The warrior bands who had chopped up Perry's First Cavalry at White Bird Canyon, the butchers who had wiped out Rains's eleven-man scouting detail, then went on to play cat and mouse with Randall's seventeen civilians before killing two of them . . . the very same bunch of Joseph's henchmen who had stood off more than half a thousand of General Howard's finest troops were now thundering down the east slope of the Lolo Trail and heading right for the Bitterroot valley!

"I need your help, more than ever," Charles Rawn had

proposed to his eager civilians. "I don't think I can stare down seven hundred and fifty Nez Perce with only the thirty-five soldiers I can muster in my command." His intense eyes started to rake over the civilians slowly.

"Count me in, Captain," Chauncey Barbour was the first to declare.

"If any of you volunteer," Rawn offered the rest, "I'll do my best to provide you with ammunition and rations."

"Sounds fair 'nough to me," responded E. A. Kenney.

"I'll go, too," W. J. Stephens said.

Barbour turned around and looked over the group. "Enough of us thrown in with Captain Rawn here, we just might have what we need to keep Joseph's warriors out of the Bitterroot."

More of the civilians started to volunteer then.

Finally, Barbour suggested, "Captain, I figure we ought to ride into town and spread the word. I know we'll enlist more volunteers soon as the folks know what's coming our way."

On 25 July, after only one day of preparation, Rawn left behind a skeleton force of ten men and started his command of twenty-five regulars away from the unfinished walls of his new post, accompanied by more than twenty heavily armed Montana citizens, all of whom had volunteered to stop the Nez Perce from bringing that Idaho war into their valley.

At the mouth of the Lolo they ran into thirty-five civilians from Fort Owens, near Stevensville in the Bitterroot valley. It was here that the nominal commander of that volunteer militia told Rawn he doubted they had enough manpower to turn back the Nez Perce. Refusing to be cowed by civilian naysayers, Rawn told the valley men to go back to their homes and he forged ahead. The thirty-five reluctantly followed.

Sixteen miles from Missoula, only five short miles up Lolo Creek from the mouth of the canyon, the mountainsides narrowed to less than two hundred yards, with a rugged, precipitous wall closing in on the south—both sides of the trail bordered by thick stands of timber, the forest floor cluttered with deadfall.

It was here that the cautious captain's slow-moving skirmish formation took its first fire from a few Nez Perce outriders. Both soldiers and civilians quickly scurried for cover and had themselves a short, ineffectual exchange with those Indian riflemen seen only from the puffs of gunsmoke dotting the canyon vegetation.

"My intentions are to compel the Indians to surrender their arms and ammunition, and to dispute their passage, by force of arms, into the Bitterroot valley," Rawn explained as the Nez Perce fire noticeably trickled off, then—for some reason—disappeared entirely.

"This is the place," Rawn determined as he peered from side to side, studying the site he had chosen; which occupied a bench north of Lolo Creek. "Steep as that slope is, they can't get around us to the south. Even though that north side isn't near so treacherous, I don't think even a mountain goat could pass, much less a tribe of Indians with all their impedimenta. So unless they disarm and dismount, we'll give them a fight right here. Let's dig in."

He now put some his soldiers and volunteers to work scratching out a line of rifle pits in a lazy L shape, one leg stretching to the north from the bench, the other roughly to the west. The rest of his command Rawn ordered to drag up deadfall and to cut down more, all of it to be laid horizontally atop the dirt excavated from those trenches at the rear of the log barricades. To top off their fortifications, the men dropped what is called a head log on top of the walls, shoving a short limb under it at intervals, which opened a space large enough to get the muzzles of their rifles through.

While he got these labors under way, the captain sent local E. A. Kenney to ride on up the trail and attempt some contact with the Nez Perce camp. Early that evening of the twenty-fifth, the scout, who had been elected as "captain" of the Missoula volunteers, returned with an Indian he declared had the Christian name of John Hill.

"This one's been sent to you by Joseph hisself, Captain," Kenney explained.

"Those warriors we skirmished with got back and told him we're here?"

"The whole camp knows," Kenney said. "Four scouts was left behind to keep an eye on us when three of 'em headed back with the news. This fella Hill was one of 'em waiting along the trail to keep an eye on us. When he spotted me coming up the road on my lonesome, he come out of hiding. He led me to their camp this side of the hot springs."

"How far's that?"

"Less'n a handful of miles from here," Kenney answered.

"How many? Two or three?" and Rawn's eyes narrowed, the skin between his eyes wrinkling with worry.

"No more'n that," Kenney said with a shrug, chewing on the side of his lower lip. "Lemme tell you—them chiefs and all their bucks was painted up and ready to wrassle when they surrounded me! I figger they mean to strut and crow up a storm in front of us so we'll just step aside for 'em when they come on down the trail."

The captain asked, "You get a chance to tell the chiefs we're here to turn them back from entering the valley?"

"I told 'em that's why you're digging in here," the civilian sighed. "Explained how folks here in Montana didn't want 'em bringing their Idaho war over here."

"So what'd Joseph have to say for himself?"

"He sent this Injun back with me to ask the soldier chief if you're gonna let his people leave the pass, let them go on by way of Missoula City for the buffalo country."

"That almost sounds like a man who doesn't figure on making trouble," Barbour piped up scornfully.

"How the hell we gonna trust that red son of a bitch after he's been killing men and ruining white women over there in Idaho?" Amos Buck shrieked.

His brother Fred Buck chimed in, "I say we hold this here redskin as our hostage while we explain to the rest of them savages what's gonna happen to 'em if they come on down the trail!"

"Hold on," Rawn soothed, then turned back to Kenney. "Does Joseph sound to be peaceable to you?"

The scout nodded. "The chiefs said they would go their way peacefully if you let 'em pass."

Rawn sighed, studying his boot toes a long time before he looked up at the civilian to say, "All right, Mr. Kenney. We'll hold this Indian here with us for safekeeping while you go back up the road."

"Go back up the road, Captain?"

"I'm sending you to tell Joseph I want to talk with him myself tomorrow," Rawn explained for the hearing of them all. "Tell him to come to our camp in the morning and we'll have a talk about where his people can go now."

Chapter Forty-One

July 26, 1877

"WHICH ONE OF THESE IS WHITE BIRD?" CAPTAIN CHARLES C. Rawn quietly asked of volunteer leader E. A. Kenney as the white men brought their horses to a halt a few yards from the two Nez Perce.

"The oldest one there on your left," indicated the civilian as the two chiefs looked over the line of white men.

"Looking Glass is the other," Rawn surmised with much disappointment, glancing at the decorated mirror hanging from the chief's neck. "Which means that Joseph didn't come."

"Right." Kenney pointed beyond the pair. "I figger he's back with the rest of their chiefs—in that group you see waiting at them trees."

"If he's the leader of the whole band of hostiles, do you suppose he sent these two other chiefs out simply to toy with me?"

Kenney didn't speak immediately. Instead, he looked over that group waiting well behind the two delegates, searching for Joseph. Finally he shrugged and said, "Maybe he's over there. Hell, I don't have no idea why Joseph ain't here."

It was late Thursday afternoon, 26 July, when Rawn, accompanied by Captain William Logan, Chief Charlot, and the newly arrived Montana governor, Benjamin F. Potts, along with more than a hundred soldiers and "irregulars," moved out from behind their log-and-pit barricades under a white handkerchief tied to the barrel of a Long-Tom Springfield rifle and rode up the Lolo Trail toward Woodman's Prairie, where Joseph's village was now camped. Upon spotting the big gathering of warriors drawn up on a ridge and displaying themselves in an intimidating manner, the white delegation had stopped just beyond the range of the Nez Perce rifles.

"Let's begin with the point you need to impress upon them about disarming, Captain," prodded Potts, ever the politician.

Over the last few days the governor of Montana Territory had hustled down from Helena by stage. Leading a group of some fifty volunteers from the territorial capital, Potts and his civilians had reached Missoula City a little past three o'clock that very morning. As soon as he had acquired three horses at a livery, Potts and two of his staff immediately led their volunteer brigade south for the Lolo Trail, reaching the barricades just before noon.

Sizing up the situation as only an elected official could, the governor told Rawn, "It would be madness for us to attack their camp with an inadequate force. The only thing that can be done is to hold these Indians in check until such a force arrives that will compel their surrender."

Hell, that was the same damn thing the army itself was asking the captain to do with his two forlorn, outgunned companies! Hold these savages who had butchered or eluded the best Howard's department could throw at them—and Rawn was expected to nail their moccasins to the ground until help arrived? Even though a hundred more Bitterroot volunteers had drifted in throughout the previous afternoon and that very morning, the captain fretted that he wouldn't have enough men to actually block the Nez Perce if it came to a showdown.

Shit, this was just the sort of assignment that could make a man a hero . . . or a goddamned martyr.

Yesterday afternoon he had written a dispatch to Fort Shaw on the Sun River, addressing it to Colonel Gibbon's aide, Lieutenant Levi F. Burnett.

Up the Lou-Lou Pass
July 25th, 1877
3:00 o'clock P.M.

Am entrenching twenty-five regulars and about fifty volunteers in Lou-Lou canyon. Have promises of more vol-

unteers but am not certain of them. Please send me along more troops. Will go up and see them tomorrow and inform them that unless they disarm and dismount, will give them a fight. White Bird says he will go through peaceably if he can, but will go through. This news is entirely reliable.

The captain was so certain of this development simply because a half-breed named Delaware Jim had brought him word only minutes before he sat down to write out his dispatch.

Having just gotten back from the Nez Perce camp, this mixed-blood Salish, given the right proper and Christian name Jim Simonds, lived with a Nez Perce woman as part of Eagle-from-the-Light's band, who themselves had moved in with Charlot's Flathead people and adopted the Bitterroot south of Missoula City as their own.*

When Chief Charlot had led more than twenty of his fighting men up to the barricades earlier that morning of the twenty-sixth, volunteering to help the soldiers against the Nez Perce, Delaware Jim promptly offered to ride on to the hostiles' camp because he could speak a passable Nez Perce. He had had himself an audience with the venerable old White Bird.

And now Rawn was standing before the chief himself.

"Don't forget what I told you," Potts whispered out of the side of his mouth as the Nez Perce held out their hands and there was a lot of shaking all around. "You must stand fast. Don't budge a single inch on your demands—the safety of our communities depends upon it."

"That's right, Cap'n," Kenney reminded at Rawn's other elbow. "You can't let these here Injuns buffalo you and walk right over the U. S. Army."

---

*Delaware Jim reportedly had scouted for explorer John C. Frémont in the 1840s and had worked in this local area as early as the 1850s as a hunter, guide, and interpreter.

"Not like they've done in Idaho," Potts hissed assuredly.

Once the introductory preliminaries were out of the way, Rawn began explaining his demands to the two chiefs, attempting to make his voice strong enough, loud enough, that it would reach the clutter of warriors embraced by the trees in the mid-distance. Chances were the ringleader himself, Joseph, was among them. If not him, then at the very least every other renegade Nez Perce warrior who wore the blood of innocent white people on his hands.

"By order of the Indian Bureau of the United States of America," Rawn began, pausing for the first time to allow for Delaware Jim's halting translation, "you and your people are hereby ordered to halt, and cease your approach into Montana Territory.

"With the authority of the U. S. Army," he continued, "I order you to surrender your weapons and ammunition immediately. Then your warriors will have to dismount and turn over your horses to me.

"When that is done, then your people can turn around and return to Idaho, where you have been ordered upon your reservation."

"Chiefs says the reservation is not theirs," Delaware Jim interpreted. "That it belongs to Lawyer's people."

"If they have a grievance about their reservation, they should take it up with their agent and the Indian Bureau," Rawn said firmly. "I am a soldier, so I'm here to stop them entering Montana Territory."

The translator did his best to listen to the talk going back and forth between the two chiefs until he finally could tell Rawn, "White Bird says they'll give you their cartridges, but they won't let go none of their guns."

Rawn wagged his head emphatically, uneasiness swelling in him like a hot, festering boil. The tension in the other white men around him had suddenly grown palpable as well. He knew both sides were watching for any sign of treachery. "Tell the chiefs that's not good enough."

"They say what you ask is not something they can decide for themselves," Simonds interpreted. "To give up their guns and horses—that is something every man must decide for himself."

"That means this will take more time?" Rawn asked, a dim flicker of hope warming his breast. "Perhaps a day or two so they can deliberate?"

"Maybe so," Delaware Jim admitted, then listened to more of White Bird's talk.

Rawn drew himself up, feeling a bit more confident that he was not about to be bullied and shoved aside by these Indians. "Tell them they must make their decision no later than midnight."

"The middle of the night?" Potts echoed with disbelief.

Rawn turned slightly and flashed the governor a knowing wink. "And, interpreter—be sure to tell these two chiefs that I'm making them responsible for the actions of their warriors. I don't want any of their young men roaming about or attempting to sneak around our fortified barricades."

The white men waited while those two prickly topics of contention were relayed to the Nez Perce, then for Delaware Jim to absorb what he was told in response to Rawn's stern ultimatums.

"Chiefs vow not to fight the valley settlers, if the white men with you don't shoot at them. The Nez Perce are friends with those white men, and do not wish to have trouble with the settlers in the Bitterroot valley since they have been friends for many years."

Rawn glanced over the faces of those volunteer leaders, studying the effect the chiefs' word had on men like Potts, Kenney, and newspaperman Barbour, too. Then he asked, "What about my soldiers?"

The Salish interpreter said, "White Bird says if your soldiers force them to fight, they will ride over you to get to the buffalo country."

Just then a figure on horseback appeared through the center of those warriors waiting back among the trees. But he did not stop there. The closer he came, the more Rawn found the man remarkably handsome. His approach toward the parley was causing quite a stir among the warriors and headmen.

"Captain Rawn?" whispered William Logan, captain of A Company. "Do you recall how Captain Jack's Modocs ambushed General Canby at the Lava Beds?"*

Rawn tore his attention from that solitary horseman to study the rest of those eighty-some warriors plainly growing more restless, if not belligerent. "I remember, Captain. Send one of the men back to pass word to the noncoms that the units should be ready to advance at once should anything untoward happen up here with us."

Logan turned and whispered to Lieutenant Coolidge, directing the young officer to turn about for the rear.

That's when Rawn peered again at that handsome horseman and asked, "So who is this coming to our conference?"

"He's the one you been waiting to meet," Kenney said before Delaware Jim could get the words out. "That's Joseph hisself."

When the chief came up to dismount among the others, Looking Glass and White Bird began relating to him what they had discussed with Rawn. In a matter of moments, Joseph made only a simple gesture with his hand to show his token assent to the plans of those other chiefs, but he did not utter a word.

That gave the captain a sudden overwhelming sense of relief: to think that he might be able to stall the hostiles and thereby delay the inevitable clash until either General Howard made it over the Lolo Trail or Colonel Gibbon got down from Fort Shaw with reinforcements. Even with the growing number of civilian riflemen and Charlot's Flatheads augmenting his paltry twenty-five foot soldiers, the captain was not at all eager to plunge headlong into a scrap with some two hundred resolute warriors fresh from Idaho and their stunning battlefield victories scored against numbers far stronger than his.

—

Devil's Backbone, vol. 5, the *Plainsmen* series.

"So," Rawn sighed, trying to appear as if he were disgruntled with the news, "these leaders are telling me they can't make a decision on their own right now?"

"Yes," Delaware Jim replied with some visible measure of his own relief as the three chiefs began to turn away for the trees.

"So they'll let me know by midnight?"

"No," the interpreter admitted as they watched the backs of those three leaders returning to their lines. "But Looking Glass claims they will come back to talk with you again sometime tomorrow morning."

BY TELEGRAPH

—

The Strike Subsiding—Bummers Still Rioting.

—

More Indian Massacres in the Black Hills.

—

BLACK HILLS.

—

Indians Murdering Near Deadwood—A General War.

CHEYENNE, July 26.—A dispatch from Deadwood, dated yesterday, says: James Ryan, a resident of Spearfish City, just in, states Lieutenant Lemly, with his company of soldiers augmented by a dozen civilians, left this point Sunday morning with two days' rations, and have not been heard from since . . . Two large bodies of Indians were seen yesterday morning on Red Water, about five miles from Spearfish . . . Intense excitement prevails throughout Deadwood. At short intervals since yesterday morning, horsemen have been arriving from the different towns and hay fields in this vicinity, bringing details of fresh murders and outrages by the savages, who seem to have broken loose from the agencies in large numbers and are infesting the country in all directions . . .

Chauncey Barbour wondered if he should slip Captain Rawn's courier a little hard money to have the man stop by the newspaper office this Saturday morning, where the soldier could pick up some writing tablets to bring back to the barricades the next time one of those privates was sent down the trail to Missoula City with some bit of news or a dispatch for those army commands known to be both west and east of the Bitterroot valley.

For now the newspaperman thought he had enough paper to last him until tomorrow. But if he kept on writing as much as he had put down on paper already, Barbour would run out before morning. There had been more to tell about than there had been Indians to shoot at during these last couple of inconclusive days of this stalemate. With all those hours of nervous waiting, Chauncey had more than enough time to reflect, to interview other volunteers, time enough for all of them—civilian and enlisted man—to argue over just what course they should take.

It was downright intriguing for the newspaperman to watch human nature at work. Despite their extensive fortifications, many of the valley volunteers continued to believe that if the warriors showed up for a fight, it would turn out to be another Custer massacre. John L. Humble, "captain" of volunteers from Corvallis, was clearly the leader of that school of thought.

"Captain Rawn," he said, presenting himself and a delegation before the officer, "it's clear to me there's too many of them for us. Clear, too, it's useless to try fighting them."

"Useless?" Rawn echoed. "But I'm an officer of the U. S. Army. My job is to fight the enemies of my government—"

"You do not have to get yourself killed needlessly," Humble interrupted.

Rawn wagged his head, rain sluicing off the brim of his soggy hat. "I've been sent here with a job to do."

Then Humble said, "I have soldiered, too, Captain. Served in many dirty battles in the Civil War. Union, I was. So I want to remind you—most times it's too damned easy to get into trouble . . . but damned hard to get yourself out once you're in."

"Just what in the blazes are you trying to tell me?" Rawn snapped.

Humble flinched. "I want to tell you that if you are going to fight those Indians, I will take my men and go home."

"If I'm going to f-fight them?" Rawn repeated as if not believing what he had heard. "If you're going to turn tail for home at the sign of a fight . . . then why in hell did you and your men ever come here in the first place?"

Humble wagged his head and turned away. "We're going back to our families."

"The best I can tell you men," Rawn announced, pausing while the Corvallis civilians stopped and turned around, "is that I won't fight them if I can help it."

However, there were many more of the civilians and some soldiers, too, who figured that the simple fact that the Nez Perce hadn't charged down the trail signified that Rawn was striking some sort of deal with the chiefs that would allow them to pass on by without a fight.

Yesterday morning, Territorial Governor Potts had once again come out from Missoula City to visit Rawn's rifle pits after he had issued a general alarm to all the papers in the area, putting out a call to all area citizens to reinforce his local militia.

When the Nez Perce chiefs had refused to put in an appearance by midafternoon yesterday—after telling Delaware Jim they would show up in the morning—Rawn decided to press the issue and called for a hundred mounted men to march out with him again. Some of the Flathead warriors rode along under Charlot. With skirmishers posted on both flanks, the column pushed up the canyon until reaching a knoll less than a half-mile below the Indian camp. Here Rawn halted his irregulars and, this time, sent forward one of the Flathead, a man named Pierre.

"Looking Glass come alone," Pierre had explained in his halting English before the hushed crowd of white men after he had returned a half hour later. "Say you, too, come alone. No guns. No guns on him. No guns for soldier."

That was the longest five-minute round-trip Barbour could remember watching in his life. Maybe not even a full five minutes at that—every second of it spent staring at the backs of Rawn and Pierre, seeing Chief Looking Glass emerge from a group of his warriors at the edge of their village. The three men did not sit atop their horses for long and talk things over. The captain and his interpreter turned around and were back among the irregulars within the span of those same five minutes.

"Well?" Chauncey demanded.

"Yes, Captain," Potts huffed. "Is the fact you've returned so quickly a good sign? Or a portent of trouble?"

With the makings of a shrug, Rawn disclosed, "I don't know for sure. A voice inside is warning me that the Nez Perce are planning an attack. But on the other hand, Looking Glass offered to surrender all the ammunition in his camp, as a guarantee his Indians intend to go through this country peaceably."

"I sure as the devil pray you set that godless red bastard on the right path!" Potts grumbled.

"I think for want of ammunition, or Charlot's threat to fight alongside with us, the Nez Perce are wavering," Rawn declared.

Potts enthused, "Now's the time to hold fast, Captain!"

With a nod of affirmation, the captain continued, "I repeated that nothing short of their unconditional surrender would be accepted by the army. I could tell he didn't like that a whit, gentlemen. Not at all. But, in turn, he could see I was not about to bend like a reed in the wind. So that's when he asked me for another meeting tomorrow morning."

"Tomorrow?" Potts echoed in a higher pitch.

"Perhaps another day will find General Howard's column racing up behind the village," Rawn had asserted hopefully.

"Have you received some news from Idaho I don't know about?" the governor demanded.

"No," the captain admitted. "But, even allowing for the Nez Perce marching a little faster up the Lolo, with General Howard's column coming out of Idaho right behind these hostiles, they shouldn't be but a day, maybe two, behind this camp."

Potts puffed his chest out showily. "So we're going to have to come out here again and beg a goddamned audience with this vermin-infested redskin tomorrow morning?"

Rawn's face had suddenly beamed, as if he were the cat who had cornered the canary. "No, we won't be begging for another meeting, Governor. Before he turned to leave, I told the chief if he wanted to have any further communication with me . . . it would have to be under a flag of truce at our fortified barricades."

"So there's no definite plans to hold another parley?" Barbour inquired.

"Nothing definite," Rawn confessed. "But I did tell him that I had to see him at the rifle pits by noon tomorrow."

Later that Friday evening as a relentless drizzle began, the newspaperman crabbed through the log-and-rifle-pit barricades, making a firm count of the current manpower available to the captain. A day ago, at the height of the scare, Rawn could boast a strong garrison. Including officers and enlisted, civilians, and about eighteen Flathead warriors, Barbour had tallied 216 men ready to deny the Nez Perce passage if and when they pressed the issue a day ago.

But things sometimes have a way of unraveling on a man.

As more and more of the valley volunteers argued over the possibility of the Nez Perce remaining peaceable as they passed through the Bitterroot, small groups of civilians began to slip away just after darkness gripped the canyon. Rumors that Looking Glass had guaranteed not to harm any of the valley residents were good enough for more than half of them.

Throughout that soggy night of 27 July, volunteers continued to saddle up and ride away for their homes. Then, just before dawn, three unarmed Nez Perce approached the breastworks and were taken into custody.

"Tom Hill," one of them gave his name to E. A. Kenney.

Kenney in turn explained to Rawn, "He's kin to John Hill, Cap'n. Part of Poker Joe's band."

With Hill were a half-breed companion named George Amos and an elderly full-blood named *Kannah*.

"The old one's a squaw man," Kenney explained.

"He looks awful Indian to me," Rawn stated. "Where I come from a squaw man is a white fella who marries an Indian squaw."

"In this country, it means half-man, half-woman."*

All three had been visiting the Non-Treaty camp up the Lolo Trail but sneaked out to reach the soldier lines over the objections of their chiefs. Having spent years in the Bitterroot, they admitted not having much stomach for a fight with the white man.**

Still, Rawn's diminishing manpower wasn't the thorniest problem he had to tackle. Come morning, he was about to find out that Looking Glass and his people weren't going to play along with the captain's delaying game any longer.

At 8:00 A.M. on 28 July Pierre had come in from scouting close to the Nez Perce camp with the astounding news that the hostiles were tearing down their lodges and packing up for the trail.

"That could mean that the scouts they surely have posted on their back trail have brought news of Howard's approach!" Rawn cheered. "We'll have to delay them only a little while—until the general's cavalry can race up on their rear."

---

*A squaw man, as the Nez Perce would put it, is "one who does not have the dignity of a warrior." To their way of thinking, such a person was gender-neutral. In history contemporary to the Nez Perce War, there were two such persons. One had been killed in Lewiston by a miner during the gold rush, and the other died at Kamiah, one of Lawyer's Christians.

**Dawn placed the three under arrest and would take them back with him to the Missoula post where they would remain in custody for the remainder of the war.

"It might also mean that Looking Glass has decided not to enter Montana," Potts conjectured, tugging on his Van Dyke. "They might be pulling back to Idaho after all."

"Either way," Barbour declared aloud as he madly scribbled notes on that pad perched upon his knee, "you've won this bloodless little fray, Captain Rawn!"

Some of the giddy civilians set up a hurraw for the officer, for themselves, and for that day they sent the Nez Perce packing without firing a shot.

But at just past ten o'clock, Chauncey Barbour and the rest were brutally yanked out of their self-congratulatory reverie.

"Injuns! Injuns!"

"I see 'em!"

"Goddamn—lookit all of 'em!"

Barbour brought the looking glasses from his eyes and quietly exclaimed, "The red bastards are slipping right around us!"

Chapter Forty-Two

July 28, 1877

His Lakota enemies called him Limping Soldier. To the crow scouts who had served him during the Great Sioux War he was known as No Hip.

Since July of 1863 the man had walked with a decided limp, having suffered a debilitating pelvic wound at Gettysburg.

John Gibbon was his name, colonel of the Seventh U. S. Infantry, stationed in the District of Montana.

During the Civil War, General George McClellan, then commander of the Army of the Potomac, had lauded Gibbon's "Iron Brigade" as being the equal of any soldiers in the world. But after he was promoted to brevet major general and transferred to the command of a full division, Gibbon experienced a humiliating defeat at Fredericksburg, suffering 40 percent casualties, including his own severe hand wound. Just hours after the battle, Gibbon shook his bloody fist at the officers and enlisted of his failed command, roaring at them, "I'd rather have one regiment of my old brigade than to have this whole damned division!"

By the end of the war he had been wounded numerous times and was the recipient of no fewer than four brevet promotions. A shining example of the army's old school—dependable, straightforward, not at all full of inflated self-consciousness as were so many of his contemporaries—war hero Gibbon accepted the colonelcy of the Thirty-sixth Infantry, regular army. Five years later he took over the Seventh and moved onto the plains to fight a new enemy.

Sporting a gray-flecked Van Dyke, Gibbon was fifty years old this summer of 1877.

For the last few years his regiment had been headquartered at Fort Shaw, on the Sun River in north central Montana Territory. But Gibbon was also in charge of Fort Ellis at the head of the Gallatin Valley* along with Camp Baker in the valley of the Smith River just east of Helena, the territorial capital, and he also maintained a small detachment at the important steamship terminus of Fort Benton, on the high Missouri River. In addition, Gibbon was overseeing construction of Fort Custer on the Bighorn at the mouth of the Little Bighorn.

While he owed some small measure of allegiance to his departmental commander, General Alfred H. Terry, this Civil War hero of South Mountain, Antietam, Spotsylvania, and Petersburg had long ago given his loyalty to the brash, cocky, hot-tempered little lieutenant general who was not only in command of the entire Division of the Missouri but also the second highest ranking officer in the whole bloody army—Philip H. Sheridan.

Over the past two months this straight-talking hero of Gettysburg had been watching the Idaho situation brew itself into a foul-smelling broth. Knowing firsthand just how nervous a lot the Montana citizenry were, Gibbon was not at all surprised when Governor Benjamin Potts was able to persuade Secretary of War George W. McCrary into sending troops to the western part of the state, hoping to quiet things down a bit earlier that summer. The colonel wrote back to the secretary, in his own inimitable way, questioning that decision made by civilian bureaucrats all the way back in Washington City.

> Your dispatch of yesterday (19) received. Have but sixteen (16) privates for duty, a little better off at Ellis, and I will send all the men that can be spared from there. The force remaining in the District is so small that to scatter it any more than it is now is objectionable.

His polite disagreement with the War Department was barely gathering momentum when the wires buzzed with

---

*Near present-day Bozeman, Montana.

word from the west that the Nez Perce were indeed headed for Montana. No longer merely a rumor.

That very next day, the twenty-first of July, Sheridan ordered Gibbon into the field with what troops he could muster to stop the Nez Perce. That same afternoon, the colonel sent a wire to Charles Rawn, whom Gibbon had constructing a post near Missoula City, informing the captain that it would be up to him to hold the Nez Perce in check until Gibbon could bring up reinforcements.

On the twenty-second, Gibbon wired Sheridan in Chicago:

> Dispatch of yesterday received. Have ordered one company of infantry from Fort Ellis to Missoula direct. As soon as I can assemble troops here from Camp Baker and Fort Benton, I shall move via Cadotte Pass down the Blackfoot River towards Missoula. Shall probably be able to take nearly one hundred men. The troops being all infantry, these movements will necessarily be very slow and can do little but check the march of the Indians in the passes . . .

Departing Fort Shaw six days later to the music of Professor Mounts's barrel-organ harmonica pumping out "Ten Thousand Miles Away," Colonel John Gibbon had his hundred marching off to the Nez Perce War.

The same morning that dirty little war was spilling over into Montana Territory.

ON the twenty-second of July, General Oliver Otis Howard had returned to Cold Spring on the Camas Prairie from Lewiston, bringing with him those two batteries of artillery culled from the San Francisco area and two companies of infantry from Fort Yuma, Arizona—both commanded by Captain Harry C. Cushing.

Although it had been a crushing disappointment for Howard not to find his wife on that steamboat, there had been a joyous reunion on the docks of Lewiston nonetheless. Coming down the gangway was Cushing's junior officer, a dear and familiar face that brought joy to the old warhorse's heart. The general embraced his eldest son, Second Lieutenant Guy Howard, declaring he would serve out the campaign as one of Howard's aides.

Across the next four days settlers came out from Mount Idaho and Grangeville to visit the army camp at Cold Spring—registering lost cattle and stolen horses with the army, selling beef to Quartermaster Fred H. E. Ebstein, or simply to gawk, talk, and gab. During that time, the general, along with his newly appointed aide-de-camp, Guy Howard and correspondent Thomas Sutherland, reveled in the fishing at this popular resting spot for wayfarers traveling between Kamiah and Lapwai. Here, the correspondent detailed in his journal, the command settled into Camp Alexander near the mouth of Lawyer's Canyon and slowly went about the recuperation and preparation required of them if this army were to successfully pursue the Nez Perce fleeing Idaho.

"This stream would have made Izaak Walton himself brave all the Indians in Christendom for just one day's whipping at it," Sutherland opined.

Howard grinned as if the war were held at bay and far from his mind, happy perhaps just to watch how much his son enjoyed their daily excursions along the leafy banks.

"We've already caught enough fish to drive amateur fly flingers into a hospital with sheer envy!" Sutherland gushed.

Howard's face went grave. A sudden cold dash of realism seemed to mock the newsman's high spirits. The general declared, "I only wish Joseph and his hotbloods could be caught this easily."

Sutherland knew just how much Howard was suffering at the public criticism going the rounds in the national papers. It did not take a phrenologist to diagnose that this beating the general was taking at the hands of the press was the primary, if not the sole, reason for his decision to follow Joseph's war camp himself.

In a dispatch intended for all three of his newspapers, sent with a mail courier back to Lapwai and beyond, Sutherland wrote:

> General Howard rode into Lapwai that night on special business . . . and returned the next afternoon with the face of his proposed campaign somewhat changed. He had learned at Lapwai that on account of the hounding of several influential papers, the Cabinet at Washington had been considering the feasibility of removing him from his command and appointing Crook in his stead. Hearing that the cause of dissatisfaction was want of activity—which is not only baseless but almost ironical, as we have been constantly on the go ever since the troops have been in the field—General Howard resolved to . . . start with the rest of his command through the impenetrable Lolo Pass, and follow Joseph to the very death.

In private circles, Major Edwin Mason was telling others that the plan for the command to take up the chase over the Lolo was his idea, preëmpted by the general commanding.

"No matter," Mason grumbled to Sutherland, and in a letter to his wife as well, "my plan will tell in the end—if we keep after them we are bound to strike them sometime and somewhere."

On the morning of the twenty-sixth of July, Howard led the short march from Lawyer's Canyon to the subagency at Kamiah, where the command set about the laborious task of crossing the Clearwater with men and matériel, horses and mules, soldiers and packers, along with a contingent of Treaty scouts. The general paid a few of the Treaty men one dollar per head to swim the command's stock over.

Early the next morning, 27 July, Howard dispatched two of McConville's civilians, "Captain" James Cearly and "Sergeant" Joseph Baker—both Mount Idaho volunteers—each to carry a copy of his message for Captain Rawn. Should the pair run into trouble and have to split up, Howard was counting on one of them to make it through to

Missoula City. But instead of setting off on the Lolo route Howard had chosen for his column, Cearly and Baker decided they would take what was called the Old Nez Perce Trail. Following the Clearwater to its source in the mountains, they would make their crossing of the southern pass,* then drop into the head of the Bitterroot valley, where they would finally point their noses north for that new army post being raised near Missoula City.

In his dispatch, Howard informed Rawn that the Nez Perce were demoralized, so he believed it wouldn't take much to hold the Non-Treaty bands until the general could come up from the rear to take them in whole:

> If you simply bother them, and keep them back until I can come close in, their destruction or surrender will be sure. We must not let these hostile Indians escape.

On each of those three laborious days of crossing and seeing to a thousand final preparations, Howard received a telegram from General McDowell back in Portland, besides a flurry of frantic messages from Governor Potts in Montana Territory, all of them relating the most current revelations about the Indians' movement up the Lolo Trail, clearly intended to nudge the general into starting on his chase. At the bottom of every one of McDowell's wires, the division commander had hand-written the same succinct postscript: "I most strongly encourage your rapid movement up the Lolo Trail."

In the last few weeks Sutherland had come to know Howard as a man who held his emotions close to the vest, rarely allowing anyone to get a glimpse of who he was inside or what turmoil he was going through. All the correspondent could learn was that the general's dispatches back to McDowell remained steadfastly upbeat day after day, repeatedly explaining to his commander and their superiors

---

*Today's Lost Trail Pass in extreme southwestern Montana.

back east: "In another month I shall surely be able to make clean work of the whole field."

Then early on the morning of the twenty-eighth, just as they were honing the final preparations to depart Kamiah the following day, some fifty packers—who had charge of more than 350 mules for the campaign—went on strike for higher wages.

In a spasm of anger, many of Howard's officers threatened to commandeer the mules and assign their own men to duty as packers. But it did not take long for the general to realize what an impossible struggle greenhorn troops would have with the notoriously testy animals on that impossibly narrow and treacherous wilderness trail over Lolo Pass. Without making the slightest complaint or threatening the civilians with retaliation, Howard gave the Mexican head packer, Louis, and his civilians their due.

As the general walked away from that meeting with his mule skinners, Thomas Sutherland read the expressions of unvarnished satisfaction, happiness, and downright respect for this one-armed officer those half a hundred hard-cases wore on their faces. After those many muddy days tramping through the Seven Devils region of the Salmon River wilderness with this column, the correspondent was already impressed with this outfit of packers. When describing them in several of his dispatches, he referred to them as a splendid class of men physically, with just enough of an accent—since many possessed some degree of Mexican blood—to give proper pronunciation to the word *aparejos* or to swear in a most musical tone. Sutherland marveled how those crude, unlettered, and rough characters were always the first to build their campfires at night and the first to cook their meals. More important for what was yet to come, the packers had never faltered in battle or on long marches demanded of them.

Howard had not only done the just thing in giving those civilians their raise in pay—no matter that to some it seemed like a bold case of highway robbery since they were less than a day from embarking on their journey up the

Lolo—Sutherland knew the general had done the right thing.

Now all this column had to do, come dawn, was finally get on the trail of those hostiles once more . . . before the Nez Perce had a chance to scatter all across the buffalo plains of Montana Territory.

Wreaking havoc and murder in their wake.

"DON'T shoot! Don't shoot!" came the cry from that lone stationary horseman who continued to shout at his fighting men as the warriors turned aside, starting up that ridge less than a half-mile from the white man's breastworks.

Captain Charles Rawn focused the field glasses on the Nez Perce riders as Pierre, the Flathead interpreter, quickly translated the horseman's commands for every man, soldier or volunteer, who could easily hear the chief's loud bellow, admonishing his warriors to protectively flank the column of women, children, and old ones.

" 'Don't shoot,' Looking Glass tells them," Pierre explained. " 'Let those white men shoot first!' "

The vanguard of the fighting men had escorted their families and horses laden with baggage to within some eight hundred yards of the fortress before angling away to their left, starting up the ridge rising at the north side of the narrow canyon. For the longest time the white men did nothing but stare, dumbfounded at how they had been caught so flat-footed.

"White Bird told you he didn't wanna fight if he didn't have to," reminded scout E. A. Kenney, breaking the uneasy silence. "I s'pose you can take 'em at their word about it now."

Frustrated to the point of taking a bite out of his soggy slouch hat, Rawn stomped around the rifle pits, angrily keeping his soldiers and what few civilians were left at the barricades ready for an assault, watchful for anything that might prove this to be a ruse meant to conceal an attack by more of their warriors.

The captain hadn't gotten much sleep the night before—

what with all the clatter and chatter as more than a hundred of the brave Bitterroot valley volunteers abandoned the barricades and rode off for home. By dawn, the officer found he was left with less than eighty men all told: soldiers, civilians, and Charlot's Flathead, too.

Two hours after getting the report that the Nez Perce were packing up for the trail, those men behind the barricades spotted the first warriors leading the women and children up the narrow ridgeline until they disappeared behind a tall, conical hill, completely hidden from view.

By 11:30 A.M., the captain ordered a mix of forty-five soldiers and civilians to accompany Lieutenant Tom Andrews on a mission downstream, where they were to guard the trail below the barricades and arrest any stragglers they could.

No more than a half hour later, the last of the Nez Perce rear guard had disappeared from sight behind the high timbered ridge north of the barricades.

"Captain Rawn!" came the shout from the rifle pit nearest the steep slope to the north. "The Injuns coming our way! Coming for us!"

With a loud clatter of metal and wood, the squeak of leather, and the pounding of hundreds of feet, the soldiers, civilians, and Flathead warriors streamed toward that section of the barricades. As the men hunkered down in the dapple of overcast sunlight broken by the tall evergreens that towered over the canyon floor, the breastworks bristled with weapons trained on that small group of Nez Perce slowly advancing on the white men.

A civilian announced, "They got women with 'em, too."

"What the hell they doing?" someone asked as the group halted two hundred yards from the muzzles of those rifles.

Before anyone could venture a guess, one of the riders at the front of that group of men, women, and children advanced a few more yards, then stopped before he shouted something in bad English.

"Pierre!" Rawn ordered. "Tell 'im to talk Nez Perce so we can understand him!"

After a brief exchange, the Flathead declared, "Old man's name Amos. Friend of mine. Live for some winters near Missoula with his people. Eight lodges—men and women, children, too. They come surrender to you."

"Surrender?" Rawn asked dubiously. "What the blazes were they doing up here with the hostiles if they've been living friendly near Missoula City?"

Pierre shrugged. "Amos says he heard the Looking Glass people were coming. He was once a Looking Glass Injun. So he took his families up the Lolo to visit old friends. But when he saw there gonna be trouble, Amos want no part of it. Want to come in and give up to you. But Looking Glass and White Bird, they keep warriors close by Amos people so they don't surrender."

"But they're surrendering now?"

"Looking Glass let them go this morning because the village go on by your log soldier fort."

"All right. Captain Logan, go out there with Pierre and a squad of men. Quickly disarm those warriors."

"You want us to dismount them, Captain?" William Logan asked.

"No. Just take their weapons for the time being." Rawn turned to gaze down the valley where the Nez Perce camp was migrating at a leisurely pace. "We'll find out if they're all that friendly soon enough."

Fifteen minutes later the captain was leading out the rest of his force, turning east down Lolo Creek. Instead of hurrying to catch up to the tail of the Indians' march, Rawn had his men cautiously probing forward in a military formation, with flankers to the sides and a number of civilian skirmishers arrayed in advance of the main body.

It wasn't long before those volunteers grew increasingly bold and eased up much too close on the end of the column—where the Nez Perce fighting men suddenly whirled about on their ponies and stopped in their tracks, bringing their weapons up, ready to fire on the white men. For a moment there was an anxious clamor as the civilians skidded to a halt there on the banks of Lolo Creek and turned around, bumping into one another to be the first out of danger and rifle range.

"What the devil's going on?" Rawn bawled at the first of those retreating volunteers galloping back to the main group. "I didn't hear any damn shots—have you been fired on? Did you take any casualties?"

Alfred Cave, a settler from the Bitterroot valley, yanked back on his reins and stopped near the officer, breathlessly explaining, "They made a show to shoot us then and there! Bastards gotta be setting up an ambush for us right ahead, Captain! They was drawing us in closer and closer, just the way they would afore they'd close the trap!"

"Trap?" Rawn echoed skeptically. "How the blazes can those Indians lay a trap for us when we know right where they are?"

Without a word of reply, Cave sheepishly turned aside, rejoining the rest of those who had fled from the advance without uttering a word.

"Mr. Matte!" he called over to the older, French-blood half-breed from the valley.

Alexander Matte moved up on his horse, followed by a half-dozen Flatheads, all of whom wore strips of white cloth around their heads, another strip tied around one upper arm so that, should a fight erupt, soldier and civilian alike would know who was a friendly, who was not.

"Take your trackers and go up the line," Rawn ordered. "Keep your head down and find out if the Nez Perce are laying an ambush for the rest of us."

Chapter Forty-Three

Khoy-Tsahl, 1877

With brazen bravado, the soldier chief had yelled angrily at *Ollokot*'s warriors as the horsemen drifted down into the valley of Lolo Creek, ordering the *Nee-Me-Poo* fighting men to dismount, to give up their horses and weapons.

"Is the man crazy with whiskey?" Yellow Wolf asked some of his fellow riders.

Many of them laughed at such Shadow arrogance now that the village had made it all the way around the north side of the *suapies*' log-and-burrow fortress.

Ollokot asserted, "Does this little chief honestly think the *Nee-Me-Poo* would go on to the buffalo country without our horses and rifles?"

"How foolish he is to be a chief for the *suapies* at all!" snarled Shore Crossing. "That one is not even smart enough to be a horse holder for a *Nee-Me-Poo* war party!"

"Even if he had returned our weapons to us after we left the Bitterroot valley as he promised he would do," Yellow Wolf said, fixing his eye on those white men keeping their distance back in the trees, "how can any man actually think we would let him keep our cartridges?"

"Because that's what Looking Glass told the little chief we would do," *Ollokot* argued sourly.

"But Looking Glass said that only to buy us a little time while the women made ready for our trip down to the valley," Red Moccasin Tops spoke up.

Yellow Wolf thought that was a good idea to fool the soldier chief. Any soldier chief.

Like Looking Glass had just done with the little soldier, so, too, *Zya Timenna* had made a prank on Cut-Off Arm back at the Clearwater many suns ago. It was good to laugh after all . . . but—he stopped to think for the first time. Now the *Nee-Me-Poo* had hurt Cut-Off Arm's pride. When you hurt a man's pride, you make him angry.

To fight a stupid soldier was one thing. But to fight a stupid soldier you have made angry was a pony of an entirely different color. Stupidity made a soldier merely a nuisance. But anger could now make Cut-Off Arm a real danger. Yellow Wolf found himself hoping that Howard and his soldiers would indeed remain in Idaho country.

"Perhaps you are right," he said to Red Moccasin Tops. "None of our leaders want us to fight the soldiers in this country, to fight these settlers in the Bitterroot."

"So we let them fire a few shots at us?" Shore Crossing snapped. "To let the Shadows feel some pride in fighting our warriors? I think our chiefs shame us when they even talk of giving up our cartridges to the *suapies!* When they keep us from shooting back at the white men!"

There had been a little gunfire from the fighting men after the *suapies* and Shadows let go with a few arrogant shots. Yellow Wolf knew the white men had aimed their bullets high, none of them made to land anywhere near the column of women and children. Those silly whites fired only to make themselves feel better since they were being made to look the fools!

"Yes—why should we start a little war here in Montana?" Yellow Wolf declared, watching a change come over *Ollokot*'s face of a sudden. "Now that we are safe and getting that much closer to the buffalo country."

This part of his argument made the most sense to Yellow Wolf. After all, why had most of the Shadows chosen to slip away in the dark last night if it wasn't because of the Lolo treaty Looking Glass had struck with the soldier chief? All those white men abandoning their barricades and heading back to their homes just went to prove that the *Nee-Me-Poo* had indeed left the war behind in Idaho country. It was clear the Montana whites did not want to see the army make war on their *Nee-Me-Poo* friends.

Turning his gaze to his war chief, Yellow Wolf continued, "The trek over the Lolo Trail was the hardest part of our journey—but it is behind us now! Why should we start a war, even if it means a little lying to that soldier chief?"

His eyes narrowing with distrust, *Ollokot* declared, "I think Looking Glass will say or do anything—even if it is not the truth—to get this village through to the buffalo country without trouble. His reputation, his very honor, is at stake now."

Yellow Wolf watched *Ollokot* rein away, kicking his pony into a lope, sweeping toward the front of the long column as it neared the mouth of Lolo Creek, where its waters tumbled into the Bitterroot River flowing north through the last miles of that long, narrow valley. Shoulders squared, *Ollokot* was a fighting man by any definition, Yellow Wolf thought. Yet, this *Wallowa* war chief had been forced into a new role of late. Because his older brother had been shamed and shoved aside time after time in the council meetings of the chiefs, *Ollokot* had been compelled to step forward and take up more and more of the duties for the *Wallamwatkin* as the silenced Joseph slipped further and further into the background. Ever since Looking Glass had consolidated his control over the warrior bands, even Joseph's stature among his own people had been compromised.

Especially when Joseph had lobbied to have the Non-Treaties turn around for the Salmon, where they would make a stand in their own country rather than risking everything they had ever known on a life none of them knew anything about . . . the rest of the fighting men voted to leave the traditional *Nee-Me-Poo* homelands under Looking Glass's leadership, to abandon the bones of their ancestors, to leave behind the good memories their children and grandchildren would never share.

But last night a few of the fighting chiefs had begun to mutter among themselves that Looking Glass was wrong to even talk to the little chief about giving up their ponies and guns. When the headmen met to discuss those talks held with the soldiers, Red Moccasin Tops shouted at them.

"I will not lay down my gun! We will not quit fighting! Blood of my people has been shed and I will kill many of the white men before I die! My hands will be stained with the enemy's blood—only then will I die!"

Looking Glass defended himself, "I never meant to let the little chief think we would lay down our guns—"

At the edge of the council Rainbow sat upon his war pony, his rifle braced against his thigh as he declared, "Do not tell me to lay down my gun, Looking Glass! We did not want this war. Cut-Off Arm started it when he showed us the gun at the Lapwai peace talks. We answered his rifle and that answer still stands for me. Some of my people have been killed and I will kill some more of our enemies—then I shall die in battle!"

"Never again will there be any talk of giving up a thing to the white man," Looking Glass had vowed.

Early this morning, Looking Glass and White Bird had ordered their warriors into position along the front of their march, placing their ponies and their bodies between the soldier guns and their own women and children. It took only moments for Joseph to have that camp of women and children, the old, and the wounded ready to turn aside for the sharp ridge where scouts had located a narrow path only mountain goats must have used to cling to the back side of a tall peak.*

Once the fighting men had guided the column back to the Lolo Trail itself, they discovered how the soldier chief had ordered some of his men and the Shadows to press in upon the rear of the *Nee-Me-Poo* march. A few of the older warriors who had been to the buffalo country before recognized some familiar faces among the valley settlers and called out greetings to those they knew, even cracking some jokes back and forth with those Shadows trailing them at a distance while the entire procession slowly paraded toward the mouth of the Lolo. Why, Looking Glass even turned about and rode back to the settlers, doffing his tall beaver-

---

*This angling, northward movement took them out of Lolo Canyon, over to Sleeman Creek, which they followed until joining Lolo Creek again about two and a half miles west of its junction with the Bitterroot River.

felt top hat with its plume, smiling hugely as he shook a few white hands—reminding the Shadows that his people did not mean to cause trouble as they passed through the valley.

Only one time that morning were the white men foolish enough to get too close upon the column's rear, forcing *Ollokot* to order his young men to wheel about and level their rifles at their pursuers—ready to knock down the first ranks. The warriors all had a good laugh watching those Shadows rein up with surprise, stumbling over one another, barely clinging to their frightened horses, as they turned about in total terror.

Frightened white settlers such at these posed little threat. Twice already in this war, the *Nee-Me-Poo* had witnessed the Shadows' fighting resolve—once at White Bird Canyon, the second time at Water Passing.* Shadows could make a lot of noise and bluster, but there was little danger when it came down to making a fight of it.

"Perhaps the Shadows needed a little reminding that we do not want to fight them," Yellow Wolf stated to the warrior beside him as they laughed together, watching the white men scurry in retreat, "but that we will fight if pushed to it!"

"The little soldier chief realized we would fight. That's why he made his treaty with Looking Glass," *Wottolen* reminded grimly. "He knew it was far better to let us ride past with our promise not to make trouble than to have a lot of angry warriors turned loose on the Bitterroot valley."

The Non-Treaty bands had successfully scooted around the soldier barricade in a maneuver that had made the *suapie* chief look as much like a fool for failing to hold the *Nee-Me-Poo* back as he was a fool to erect a barricade in the Lolo Canyon to hold them back in the first place.**

—

*McConville's volunteers at Misery Hill.

**Because of this very public fiasco, in the local press Rawn's abandoned log-and-rifle-pit fortress immediately became known as "Fort Fizzle," its army and civilian defenders regarded as cowards afraid to fight, much less die, to halt the Nez Perce invasion of Montana Territory.

With Cut-Off Arm, the Book of Heaven chief, still far, far back in Idaho country and the little soldier chief turning aside now so that he no longer followed the camp, from this point on the journey couldn't look brighter!

Now that they had reached the Bitterroot valley, the sun finally came out behind the dissipating clouds, bright and hot, drying the muddy, mucky road so that the traveling was easier on the ponies and those who plodded on foot. In every direction Yellow Wolf chose to look, the sky was big and blue, barely a cloud marring the aching immensity of it. Here they were that much closer to the *E-sue-gha*, longtime friends and allies who would join them not only in the buffalo hunt but also against the army—should those *suapies* ever want to start another war on the *Nee-Me-Poo*.

Once they had climbed the road out of this long, narrow valley and made their way across the heights to the Place of the Ground Squirrels,* they would be within hailing distance of the buffalo country!

Eeh-yeh! Already Yellow Wolf could feel the joy of that realization spreading through him like the warmth of the sun, replacing the cold, bone-chilling despair and despondency he had suffered for having to put his *Aihits Palojami*, his fair Fair Land at his back.

He could not remember a finer day than this! Looking Glass had made his Lolo treaty with the little chief and those valley settlers, an agreement that guaranteed the *Nee-Me-Poo* passage up the Bitterroot without either side having to fear attack. And now the *suapies* had marched out of sight to the north, away from the noisy, joyous village that began to celebrate even before they started to make camp.** The women were trilling, jabbering, laughing—their high voices like happy birds on the wing. The children

---

*The Big Hole.

**That first evening out of the Lolo Canyon, the Nez Perce erected their camp on the McClain ranch, about five miles south of the Lolo's mouth, on Carlton Creek.

immediately picked up on the mood: running and shouting and laughing with such great abandon. Which meant the men, like Yellow Wolf, could congratulate themselves on how well they had fought the soldiers in Idaho country, how hard they had worked to get their families over the Lolo, how steadfast they had remained in their pledge not to fight the Shadows in Montana Territory.

Imene kaisi yeu yeu! With the Creator's blessing, there would be no fighting now!

Give great praise to *Hunyewat!* The war was over!

"SHIT! Them's the goddamn Nez Perceys!" exclaimed Henry Buck as he and more than two dozen civilians suddenly found themselves stumbling into the Indian camp after dark that Saturday night after the Indians had slipped around the Lolo barricade.

These twenty-six valley settlers and shopkeepers, who had answered the alarm to bolster Captain Rawn's small detachment of regulars from Missoula City, had remained with Rawn to the last. While most of their compatriots had turned back for their homes in the steady drizzle that fell the night before, most of Buck's friends had stuck it out, even as the Non-Treaty bands scooted right around them slick as a gob of wagon-hub grease.

For most of the day the civilians knew they were some distance behind the slow-moving village, but little had they realized that, when they turned south to ride up the valley of the Bitterroot for their homes near Stevensville, they would end up running right into the Nez Perce camp! Of a sudden these startled white men found themselves among the lodges and willow shelters before they had time to rein up and retreat.

"Shadows!" a Nez Perce voice called out from the hubbub and clamor as the civilians milled about and clattered together, not really knowing which way to turn now that they had stuck their foot right in it.

Voices were calling out to one another, many warriors

running up on foot, some racing up on horseback, until what seemed like more than a hundred of them had streamed out of the darkness—converging on the frightened whites from every direction.

"Stop, white men!"

More shouting arose as a handful of faces approached out of what starry light illuminated the valley floor. Closer and closer those new arrivals came, followed by a crowd of warriors, until their red noose came to a halt no more than six feet from the civilians' nervous horses.

"Hello, Boston Men!"

The speaker stepped forward, a figure sporting his famous tall top hat decorated by a showy bird plume attached to the very front, sticking straight up.

It was Looking Glass. Henry didn't know if he should be relieved or even more scared.

"W-we're lost." Buck could think of nothing more to say than the truth. The eyes of all those warriors gleamed in the starshine, measuring him and the rest of the citizens caught in this tightening snare.

The top hat walked closer to Buck's horse, held up his hand as if to shake. Grinned, too. "Me Looking Glass. You?"

"B-buck. Henry Buck," and he held down his hand, thinking it quite odd that this Nez Perce chief would practice such a custom—to shake hands with a white man when the chief should realize that earlier this day these very white men had attempted to bar the Indians' entry into the valley.

"Looking Glass?" Myron Lockwood echoed, sitting on the horse next to Henry's. "Why, I didn't know this was Looking Glass. This here's the chief hisself—the one who come back and shook hands with a few of us this mornin'!"

"I guess he puts great stock in this hand-shaking thing," John Buckhouse said, nervousness cracking in his voice.

"This ol' buck even had his eyes checked up to Missoula

City on his way back from the buffalo plains just this past spring," explained Wilson B. Harlan. "Doctor fit him for a pair of glasses, too, Henry."

"We're going home," Buck explained to the chief, speaking his words slowly. He pointed on south up the valley. "Home, there, tonight."

For a long moment Looking Glass turned to peer up the valley, too. "Yes, home." Eventually, he brought his eyes back to Buck and smiled when he said, "You home, no hurt you home now. No war with white valley man here. No war come to Montana buffalo land. No war. You go home all now, too. All white man go home. No war now."

He held up his hand to Buck and they shook again; then the chief moved among the civilians, eagerly shaking every white man's hand. When Looking Glass had greeted all the stunned horsemen he stepped back against that tight ring of warriors.

"No war now, white mans!" he cheered, doffing his tall hat, sweeping it to the south in a grand gesture. "Go home—you no fight. No war for you. No war for us."

"Y-yes. We go home," Buck repeated the chief's broken English, nodding as he urged his horse into motion. "No war. We'll go home because there ain't gonna be no war now."

More than a hundred warriors slowly parted, gradually forming a very long and narrow gauntlet as the white men started away, every one of the Nez Perce silent, glaring.

It wasn't until they were three miles farther south up the Bitterroot that Henry realized how tense his muscles had been, feeling just how tight his ass had been clenched from the moment he realized they had moseyed into that village by mistake. Even though he and his brothers had seen quite a few Nez Perce coming and going through the valley across the years and some had even visited their store in Stevensville on every journey through the Bitterroot, Henry Buck had never seen that many Nez Perce warriors in one place . . . nor that many so goddamned *close*—all of them glaring at him and the others. It was enough to make a man's scalp itch.

Henry Buck decided every fella was granted at least one second chance in life to make up for some stupid, lunkhead blunder. He figured he'd just used up his.

Chapter Forty-Four

July 29, 1877

Kamiah Indian Territory
July 29, 1877

My Precious Darling Wife,

Got here today at 10 A.M. without adventure of any sort. It seems a month or longer since I left you. Yet . . . I have, after a fashion, enjoyed this nomad's existence of two days and nights . . .

The troops to go (and with whom my lot is cast) are all across the river, and stores are being crossed over. It looks like a war picture, indeed quite an army, and among them, I am glad to see about 25 Indian scouts who were brought through by Colonel Sanford. By the by, I go with Colonel Sanford . . . 1st Cavalry . . .

I shall mess with Colonel Sanford—

U.S. ARMY SURGEON JOHN FITZGERALD PAUSED, PENSIVELY chewing on the wooden stem of his ink pen as he studiously gazed out upon the noisy clamor of that camp readying itself to follow General Oliver Otis Howard over the Lolo Trail into Montana Territory in pursuit of the escaping Nez Perce murderers and outlaws.

This might well be the last chance FitzGerald had for a long, long time to write Emily from the campaign trail—and know with any certainty that she would get his letter. Why, she might well be reading it by tomorrow afternoon. Each of the many officers had tossed a little something into a pool to entice one of the Christian Indians to ride off to Lapwai with their final messages before embarking on what they knew had to be a short campaign.

The Indian scouts will be in the advance. It is said and believed here that Joseph's Indians are all over in Montana and peacefully disposed among the settlers in that region. Doctor Alexander says that I will be back at my post in 30 days. I hope so, Darling, for I feel that I have been away from you for an age already. I don't see how I can stand it for 30 days. You may rest assured, Darling, that absence for that time, or maybe a week or so longer, is all you have to fear on my account.

Oh, how to tell her all that he sensed was ready to gush out of him here and now . . . yet how to keep from telling her what he must not let slip in there, even between the lines. He thought at first of somehow preparing her for the eventuality that he might not make it back home, then thought better of that idea and decided not to write anything morose or melancholy—exactly the way a man felt in those hours before riding into battle or setting off on an uncertain campaign.

. . . I forgot to tell you our Indians all wear soldier's uniforms with a kind of blue sash of stripes and stars. It looks, in fact, like a piece of old garrison flag. They belong to the Bannock tribe of Indians farther to the south, and they can be depended on . . .

I hardly know, Darling, what else to tell you. I suppose we will reach Missoula in a week at farthest. I was going to say you might write me there, but that would not do, as I suppose it would take two weeks for a letter to reach that place via San Francisco. There will be one or more opportunities for you to write me by courier from Lapwai. Take care of yourself and the babies, and wait for me as patiently as you can . . .

John FitzGerald quickly looked up to see if anyone might be approaching.

Furtively he dabbed his thumb at that errant teardrop soaking into the writing paper, then dragged the back of his hand beneath the end of his nose. This surgeon, husband, and father did not want another man to misread his reluctance to leave his family behind. After all was said and done, this was his calling. He was a soldier. A doctor yes, but a soldier above all.

Jenkins FitzGerald had been an army doctor since the outbreak of rebellion among the Southern states. And this was what a soldier did: go off to war against his nation's enemies.

I keep thinking of the long absence from you, my dear wife, but it must be. I suppose there are 30 to 40 more gentlemen in this command who have left their wives and babies, and who, in case of more fighting, will be in far greater danger than your man can possibly be in, but, honestly, I don't think we shall see an Indian hostile. I said to Colonel Miller, "Colonel, what are we all going to do over there?" He replied, "Oh, we will have a big mountain picnic with no Indians to trouble us."

. . . We will have some hard marching only, with no fighting of any kind—

"Dr. John!"

He looked up of a sudden, finding the Indian leading his horse, walking easily toward the cluster of hospital tents and baggage where FitzGerald sat. The dark-skinned Kamiah courier wore a large leather pouch over his left hip, the wide strap looped over his right shoulder. Already there were two other, younger, officers hurrying their envelopes up to the rider. Chances were neither one of them had a wife or children at home, FitzGerald thought as his eyes connected with the Nez Perce courier.

"Dr. John," the Treaty Indian said as he stopped a respectful distance away. "I go soon. Take mail to Lapwai. I go with your letter, yes? Take to Mrs. Doctor."

"Yes," he sighed sadly, then went back to chewing on the wooden stem of his pen, looking over those young men bringing their mail to the courier.

Such young, eager officers would have written home to mothers, perhaps even a sweetheart to whom they had pledged their hearts, planning a distant betrothal when affairs with the Nez Perce were settled.

So . . . until he got back from the far side of the Lolo . . . perhaps the far, far side of the world itself, this last letter to her might well have to be it for a long, long time—

Be patient, darling, sensible wife, as you always have been, and 'ere long I will be with you again. My ink is getting low, so goodbye, my honey, and believe me.

Ever your faithful,
John

"And I am especially glad to see you again, *Wa-wook-ke-ya Was Sauw!*" Looking Glass exclaimed as he moved among the small party of men, women, and children, touching hands, pounding backs.

The newcomers had just approached the large *Nee-Me-Poo* camp with their leader, Eagle-from-the-Light, being hailed by many of the Non-Treaty headmen who had come out to greet the new arrivals—six lodges of them, accounting for ten warriors. *Wa-wook-ke-ya Was Sauw*, this man called Lean Elk, was one of those fighting men who for the last few winters had paid his allegiance to the Eagle.

Weeks ago when the first flames were fanned in Idaho country, the men of their band had gone together to petition Flathead agent Peter Ronan at the Jocko agency for permission to camp on the reservation north of Missoula City, where they would be far from the danger of being swept up in a war should the Non-Treaty bands cross over the Lolo Trail, as everyone knew they would. For generations the Flathead people had been good friends of the *Nee-Me-Poo*, crossing over the Lolo each year to harvest those salmon doggedly fighting their way from the distant ocean to the high streams that fed the Clearwater River. When Ronan had refused their request, Eagle-from-the-Light kept his small band near Charlot's Flathead, who themselves had steadfastly refused government orders to move north from the Bitterroot valley onto their own reservation.

Then just a few days ago Charlot and some of his fighting men had ridden off to join those soldiers who planned to block the trail—so Eagle and his men decided to find another place to lay back out of sight, somewhere they might let events on the Lolo take their own course. But when the *Nee-Me-Poo* managed to slip around the foolish soldier chief, Eagle's band figured they could no longer ride the fence. Agent Ronan had plainly shown that he did not care to have Eagle's allegiance, so . . . Eagle-from-the-Light, Lean Elk, and the others figured they would feel out the mood of things in that Non-Treaty camp.

This first morning after the debacle up the Lolo Canyon, those ten warriors led their women and children down the Bitterroot valley to find the Non-Treaty village.

"Last time I saw you was in your camp at *Pitayíwahwih* on the Clearwater, Looking Glass," Lean Elk confided to the garrulous chief.

"Yes—just after you cut your leg carving the wood to make another one of your fine saddle frames," Looking Glass replied to the short, stocky half-breed. "Do you still limp like you did when you left to ride back to Montana?"

"I do," Lean Elk explained, patting his thigh. "But the wound is getting better."

Looking Glass snorted with laughter, "I hope you are getting better using a knife, too!"

"It is a good thing he cut his leg," Bird Alighting said with a smile as he came through the crowd. "He cannot race his horse against us until his wound heals!"

Their good-natured ribbing carried the weight of truth to it. Named Joe Hale by the Shadows over in Idaho country, Lean Elk was widely known for his love of gambling, betting on everything from horse races—this past spring he had beaten all the best ponies the Flathead could bring against him—to his favorite card game, poker. In fact, the white man had given Lean Elk a nickname, too, one that stuck to him much better than Joe Hale. *Poker Joe*, it was.

Considered a subchief among Eagle's band—his wife's people—this mixed-blood French-Canadian *métis** of Nez Perce descent was a good Shadow talker, too, able to keep up with most any white man in the white man's difficult tongue. Still, even that did not help Lean Elk when he returned from Idaho to the Bitterroot not long after he had cut his leg while visiting Looking Glass's people on the Clearwater. The deep, nasty gash gave him a decided limp—leading most Shadows to believe that he had been wounded in the fighting between the *Nee-Me-Poo* and the soldiers west of the Bitterroot.

Truth was, Poker Joe had cleared out of that camp, eager to recross the mountains with his family and rejoin Eagle-from-the-Light's band, just two days before the *suapies* attacked Looking Glass's village, driving the *Asotin* people right into the ranks of those disaffected warriors already creating havoc up and down the Salmon and boiling across the Camas Prairie. Over here in the Bitterroot, Poker Joe and his friends heard delayed reports of all the fighting on the Cottonwood, as well as that long two-day battle on the Clearwater. While a few of Eagle's young men thought they would like to be a part of the fighting, Lean Elk and most of the others had decided it best they stay out of the troubles and keep their relations with the valley settlers good.

But now that the Non-Treaty bands had come to the banks of the Bitterroot River, Eagle-from-the-Light's people decided they might do well to join up. If all the Shadows in this part of Montana Territory were in an uproar over the Idaho bands, it might be wisest for Eagle's small outgunned group to join up with the hundreds for the safety of their numbers. And if the fighting truly had ended and the war was left behind them back in Idaho—so much the better! Since he, better than most any other *Nee-Me-Poo*, carried in

---

*His father was said to be a Canadian voyageur, once employed by the Hudson's Bay Company of Adventurers.

his head all that terrain and geography of the buffalo country, it might just be time for Poker Joe to suggest another hunt on the plains.

Late the following afternoon three more newcomers showed up about the time the village was going into camp, having marched no more than a leisurely handful of the white man's miles that day. That trio of *Nee-Me-Poo* warriors rode among the lodges and celebrants, many of the bands noisily calling out their greetings to the new arrivals who were just returning from the country of the *E-sue-gha*.* For more than a year now, Grizzly Bear Youth and his two companions—*Tepsus*, called Horn Hide Dresser, and a Yakima scout named *Owhi*—had been scouting for the Bear Coat,** the soldier chief who was waging a very telling war on the Lakota from his log fort raised at the mouth of the Tongue River.

That evening, the chiefs called on the three to meet with them in council, seeking to learn more about the best path to take to the buffalo.

"The Bear Coat's fort lies east of the Bighorn," Grizzly Bear Youth explained. "He is the best *suapie* chief I know in tracking down an enemy, no matter how bad the weather."

"Not like Cut-Off Arm, still sitting way back there in Idaho country!" White Bird snorted with a wry laugh. "I think we should rename him Never Going to Fight Until Tomorrow!"

"If you go to *E-sue-gha* country," Grizzly Bear Youth warned grimly as the laughter died, "I think the army will tell the Bear Coat to stop you. I recommend you stay away from that soldier chief at all costs."

Now it was Looking Glass's face that turned grave with

—

*The Crow.

**Colonel Nelson A. Miles, Fifth U. S. Infantry, stationed on the Yellowstone River in Montana Territory, serving under Lieutenant G. C. Doane. See *Wolf Mountain Moon*, vol. 12, and *Ashes of Heaven*, vol. 13, the *Plainsmen* series.

worry. "You are warning us we should not go to the land of the *E-sue-gha*?"

Grizzly Bear Youth shook his head. "Go there if you must, but just stay as far away from the Bear Coat as you can. Indeed, we must now stay as far away as we can from any soldiers."

"So where would you have us go?" White Bird demanded impatiently. "If we have been driven out of our own homeland and we are not welcome to stay here in the Bitterroot valley—if we can't go to live and hunt with the *E-sue-gha*—where are the free *Nee-Me-Poo* to go?"

"To the Old Woman's Country," Grizzly Bear Youth declared with enthusiasm.

"To join up with the Buffalo Bull Who Rests on the Ground?" Looking Glass asked skeptically. "He is an enemy of ours. You yourself have just returned from fighting the Lakota for this Bear Coat. All of you know that I have fought the Lakota more than once. So how can I ever go to the Old Woman's Country to live with such a fierce Lakota leader?"

"He has run away from the army, too!" Grizzly Bear Youth argued. "No different from any of you leaders—even Joseph there. You are running away to the east, leaving the army behind. Buffalo Bull Who Rests on the Ground ran north to get away from the army, just like you have."*

White Bird wagged his head, appearing confused. "Why should we go north like they have?"

"With my own eyes I have seen what the soldiers can do to the mighty Lakota," Grizzly Bear Youth explained. "So I

---

*When the Lakota warrior bands considered waging their last great fight against the U. S. Army, they went so far as to invite all of their traditional enemies to a great council that was held in eastern Montana Territory, during the summer of 1875. It is indicative of the esteem the Lakota held for the Nez Perce that the Non-Treaty bands were invited to this council. In the buffalo country at that time, Looking Glass and Eagle-from-the-Light both attended. Even Joseph came from the *Wallowa* to listen to the Lakota proposal of a strategic alliance.

think it is folly to consider that we can continue to fight against the government and its army. For the sake of our families, we should just turn aside and go north as quickly as we can."

"How would we get to this Old Woman's Country from here?" *Toohoolhoolzote* asked.

Grizzly Bear Youth explained, "The shortest way is to turn directly north. March past Missoula City; continue across the Flatheads' reservation. Just beyond it lies the country where the army can bother us no more."

There was some downhearted muttering in the group, men murmuring among themselves in low tones—yanking on the question this way, tugging on it that way, like a woman would stretch a wet piece of rawhide. Poker Joe thought he liked the idea of going north through the Flathead reservation. The Flathead owned many good horses. This past spring he had raced against some of the finest. Perhaps on their way north to the Old Woman's Country, he could adopt some of those Flathead horses for his own, taking them across the Medicine Line to race against the Lakota!

That's when he cleared his throat. The chiefs looked in his direction. Poker Joe was not an important leader like the rest of them, not even as big as Eagle-from-the-Light. But he had something significant that needed saying.

"If you will think about it: These days we have more in *common* with Buffalo Bull Who Rests on the Ground than we have differences with the Lakota."

No one spoke for several minutes. The large fire crackled. Moccasins shuffled. Some bystanders coughed nervously. And women standing in the ring around the seated men hushed the noisy play of small children.

Toohoolhoolzote turned to White Bird. "Who wants to go to the Old Woman's Country?"

Old White Bird immediately raised both his spindly arms in a most dramatic fashion. "I believe it is time to consider a vote."

"To vote on what?" Looking Glass snapped uncertainly, his eyes darting over the others.

"Who agrees with Grizzly Bear Youth that we should march north through the Flathead's reservation?" White Bird proposed. "Start north from here to the Old Woman's Country?"

Poker Joe looked over the six chiefs who were present. White Bird had his arm up even as he asked for the vote. Then Red Echo raised his hand, too. For a long moment, the elderly, white-headed leader of the Salmon River band waited for more to join the two of them, but they were the only votes for turning north.

Looking Glass leaped to his feet and swaggered over to stand behind White Bird's shoulder, looking smug as a sparrow hawk with a fat deer mouse clamped in its beak. "I think these other leaders remember so well how Chief Charlot and his Flathead warriors joined the *suapies* in that silly attempt to bar our way into this valley. Since the Flathead are no longer our friends, to march north through their country now would be very, very dangerous."

"Charlot's Flathead are no danger to us!" Red Echo protested vigorously. "Without many guns and much ammunition, the Flathead need the white men to protect them. They are no threat to us by themselves!"

Looking Glass strenuously shook his head. "I will never trust the Flathead again!"

"So what do you propose?" Rainbow asked.

"Yes," Sun Necklace demanded. "Which way do we go to avoid the soldiers?"

"For many summers I always took the shortest way," Looking Glass explained. "From here we ride north and east, up the Big Blackfoot River, over the pass, and down to the plains at the Sun River."

"But that way is blocked by a *suapie* post,"* Five Wounds argued.

"Or we could go a more southerly route to the Three Forks country and on to the Yellowstone," Looking Glass proposed.

---

*Fort Shaw.

"And that is blocked by the *suapies* at another post,"* protested Rainbow.

"So where would you have us end up, Looking Glass?" Sun Necklace growled. "Right in the jaws of more soldiers?"

"Lean Elk, who knows the way, tells me we are less than five or six easy marches from the head of the Bitterroot valley," Looking Glass explained as Poker Joe nodded. The heads were turning to look at him in a different light now. "Once we get there, we drop over the mountains and are but a few more days from the buffalo country."

Five Wounds exclaimed, "It's a good way, Lean Elk! Maybe go through the Land of Smokes, out along the Stinking Water River. The road that way is open, with plenty of grass and not many whites, all the way!"

"Yes," Rainbow echoed. "That route avoids the soldier forts and the big mining camps, too!"

Wheeling an arm across the entire assembly, courting not only the handful of other chiefs but more so the audience of hundreds, Looking Glass moved the question, "Who votes for going on to the *E-sue-gha* country with me to hunt buffalo?"

As the *Asotin* chief's own arm shot into the air, his eyes raked over the group. Rainbow and his spirit brother, Five Wounds, immediately added their illustrious reputations to the vote in favor of the buffalo country.

Now Looking Glass slowly turned to the only chief who had not spoken out his wishes. "Joseph?"

"As before, there is nothing for me to vote on, Looking Glass," the *Wallamwatkin* chief said.

"Speak your mind, Joseph," White Bird prodded.

"When we were fighting in our homeland, there was a reason for us to fight, and for our men to die," Joseph declared. "But since we have left our country behind, it matters little to me. I am not in favor of taking my people far away to the Old Woman's Country . . . but neither am I in

---

*Fort Ellis.

favor of taking my people far away to the land of the *E-sue-gha* to live. We already have a home. We have a country of our own."

"If we go to the land of the *E-sue-gha*, we must all go united," White Bird warned.

"I agree with Joseph," Pile of Clouds suddenly spoke, surprising many in the council. "Why go to the land of the Sparrow Hawk people when we have a home of our own already? The land of the *E-sue-gha* is too open for good fighting—and we will have to fight the Bear Coat's *suapies* there, sooner or later."

"You want us to march back over the Lolo now that we have just arrived here?" Looking Glass asked with a trembling fury, clearly angry with the testing by this young *tewat*.

Pile of Clouds shook his head. "No, we go by the southern pass,* move quickly back to the Salmon River country where we will have the mountains and timber. That is the country good for fighting the soldiers."

Joseph nodded. Many of the others were looking at the *Wallowa* chief now. However; Poker Joe turned to Looking Glass, realizing what the angry *Asotin* chief must be thinking. Joseph was leader of the largest Non-Treaty band. His reluctance to come east had become like a sharp thorn in the *Asotin* chief's side.

Looking Glass suddenly loomed over Joseph, asking, "Did you, or did you not, with these other chiefs, elect me for leader through this country?"

"Because you knew this country and the people here," Joseph agreed.

"And did you not promise me that I should have the whole command to do with as I thought best?"

"Perhaps the *E-sue-gha* will help us as you say, Looking Glass. But in these two choices that you and White Bird have given us, I have no words," Joseph admitted to that

---

*Today's Lost Trail Pass.

hushed audience. "You know the country and I do not. So I can make no vote—"

Triumphant once more, Looking Glass whirled away from Joseph without even waiting respectfully for the man's words to drift away into silence. His voice thundered over them all.

"To the buffalo country!"

Chapter Forty-Five

July 30–August 1, 1877

Fort Lapwai
July 30, 1877

Mamma Dear,

. . . John left on Friday and I am lonely without him, but I would not be any place else than here for anything, as here I can hear from him every time anything goes in or out to General Howard. I heard this morning from Kamiah, and I will enclose John's letter . . .

The Indians, it is supposed, have gone off over that Lolo Trail to Montana. A dispatch from the Governor of Montana says a great number of ponies, women, and children, with a lot of wounded men, had come over the Lolo Trail, and he had not force to stop them. No one knows whether Joseph and his warriors have gone over there too, or whether they just got rid of their families and helpless men so they could make the better fight themselves. General Howard is determined to find them and has formed two columns. The one he commands himself will follow over the trail the Indians took into Montana. The other goes north through the Spokane country and joins General Howard's column sometime in September over at Missoula where General Sherman will meet them. Then, if the trouble is not over, a winter campaign will be organized, but we hope it will be over even before that . . .

Mrs. Hurlbut, the poor little laundress I have mentioned in several of my letters, the one who lost her husband in that first terrible fight, was here staying in my house at nights all that first month. She is expecting daily to have another baby, and she was afraid, in case of an alarm at night, she would not be able to get across the parade to the breastworks. So she asked me if she could bring her children and sleep up with our servant girl, Jennie, which she did until lately, since our fear for the post is over. She is a nice little woman, and her children are as nice as I know. She is left destitute. After her sickness, we will all help her. A purse will be raised to take her back to her friends . . .

Doctor, I expect, is marching up the mountains today, farther and farther away from us. How I hate the army and wish he was out of it! I hope they won't find any Indians, and I hope he will come back to me safe and sound . . . I don't see what they do want with John on that Lolo Trail . . . Sometimes when I think what might happen out there, I get half distracted, but I fight against it and keep my mind occupied with other things, and I plan for John's coming home . . .

All the Indian prisoners are here, some 60 in all. They are horrid looking things, and I wish they would send them away . . . Don't feel anxious about us. I am only anxious for the Doctor. Write soon. Lots of love to all.

Your affectionate daughter,
E.L.F.

BY TELEGRAPH

—

The Strike Virtually but not
Actually Ended.

—

Chicago and St. Louis Quiet.

—

Late Washington and Indian
Intelligence.

—

MONTANA.

—

Looking Glass Marching On.

DEER LODGE, July 30.—Governor Potts returned from Missoula this morning. On Saturday Looking Glass, with three hundred Indians and squaws and some Palouses, passed up a fork around Deep Bitter Root. Some settlers have been in the Indian camp and the Indians assured them that they would pass through the country without destroying property. The citizens therefore did not attempt to fight, and Rawn declined to open fire with his small command of regulars, and there was no pursuit made. On the Governor's arrival he ordered the volunteers who had gone to Bighole to return, the force being insufficient. There will be a party left in Bighole valley to observe and report the actions of the Indians.

TWO DAYS BACK, WITH THE FIRST SHRILL ANNOUNCEMENT that the Nez Perce caravan was coming their way, Henry Buck ran outside and clambered up on the old fort's fifteen-foot-high sod wall and watched to the west in the direction of the Bitterroot Mountains as the vanguard of the Non-Treaty bands hoved into sight on the flat of the river, just opposite the town of Stevensville. He thought to look down at his pocket watch, making a mental note of the time that warm summer morning, 30 July. Ten A.M.

For years now Henry and his two older brothers, Amos and Fred, had owned and operated the Buck Brothers' General Store in the thriving settlement of Stevensville, several miles south of Missoula City. When the alarm first came that the warrior bands were turning away from McClain's place near the mouth of Lolo Creek, headed their way, panic spread like a prairie fire igniting the Bitterroot valley. Most everyone up and down the river, Henry included, had herded their families into old Fort Owen,* a long-abandoned fur-trading post erected more than twenty years

---

*Partly reconstructed, between Highway 93 and the present-day community of Stevensville in Ravalli County, twenty-seven miles south of Mis-

earlier north of the little town—often used in the past as a bastion of safety during raids by the once-troublesome Blackfeet. More recently, the walls had been patched up by valley citizens, who now renamed the place Fort Brave because of the courage its high walls gave those who flocked within its protection during this current Indian scare.

After decades of weathering, the two-foot-thick walls were generally in good shape, except for sections on the north and west walls where the adobe was crumbling. At one time there had been four square bastions, complete with rifle ports, but now there were only two, both at corners of the south wall. As soon as the first alarm was raised weeks ago, the local citizenry promptly went about cutting green sod and repairing the gaps in the aging walls. Benjamin F. Potts's territorial government had seen to it the settlers were armed with a few weapons: obsolete Civil War–vintage muzzleloaders.

Three miles southwest of the fort where more than 260 people had taken refuge when their men marched off to aid Rawn's outmanned soldiers—almost within sight of the sod walls—the Nez Perce went into camp for the night on Silverthorne Creek. Within hailing distance of Charlot's home.

After tossing around how peaceful the Indians appeared to be, Henry and his brothers decided to reload the trade goods in a pair of wagons and return to their store in Stevensville. The threat appeared to be over. The Nez Perce were making good on their promise not to make a lick of trouble while passing up the valley.

Early on the morning of the thirty-first, as the three were restocking their shelves, a handful of Nez Perce women showed up at the doorway to make known their wants

—

soula, Montana. John Owen arrived in the valley in 1850, later buying the place from some Jesuit priests who were giving up their missionary work after witnessing nine years of constant warfare between the Flathead and Blackfeet. By the time of the Nez Perce War, Owen had lost his Shoshone wife, Nancy, drunken himself into madness, and been sent back to his family in Pennsylvania, where he slipped into obscurity.

through sign and a little halting English. To pay for those desired items, the women made it clear they had government money or gold dust.

"Henry, you tell them we'd prefer not to sell to 'em," his older brother Amos instructed from the back of the store.

A few minutes after the youngest Buck brother had declined to sell anything to those squaws, the women were back at the open doorway—this time with three middle-aged, dour-faced warriors. While two of the men stepped inside the store, their rifles cradled across their arms, to look about the place as if to ascertain just how many white men were about, the third came up to the counter where the three brothers nervously awaited trouble.

"Women, have gold for trade, you," he started, his English better than any from the squaws. "Take supplies. Pay gold now."

He patted the front of his cloth shirt, then stuffed a hand down the neck of the garment and pulled out three small leather pouches. One of them clanked with coins, while the other two must certainly be filled with dust.

"We don't want no trouble," Fred, the eldest Buck, declared confidently. "But you go take your business somewheres else."

The warrior measured him for a moment without a change coming over his stoic countenance; then the Indian gazed around the store shelves stocked with goods and said, "We need supplies. Supplies for our trail journey. You have supplies. We have gold. Trade now. If you don't let us buy supplies . . . we take what we need. You decide. Want our gold? Or you want us to take supplies for no gold?"

When the warriors put it that way, the Buck brothers felt they had little choice but to open up a limited trade with the migrating bands. The afternoon the Nez Perce arrived, small-time merchant Jerry Fahy had loaded up a creaky wagon with some sacks of flour and a few other items and rumbled across the river to do a brisk business with the Non-Treaty bands. Flour turned out to be the one item the women wanted most. Shame of it was, the Buck brothers had none on hand at the time. By the next morning the Indians had repaired to a mill near Fort Owen where they traded for all the flour they wanted.

Although Henry and his brothers decided they would trade for cloth and other staples, they steadfastly refused to barter away any powder or ammunition. Word spread quickly among the Non-Treaties, and by that afternoon the Nez Perce were showing up at the store from their nearby camp in clusters of eager shoppers. Still, it wasn't until the morning of 1 August when things got scary, as more than a hundred-fifteen warriors rode into Stevensville together under the leadership of the aging White Bird, all of them bristling with weapons. Henry rushed to the front of the store with his brothers to watch their colorful, noisy arrival. Even though they had spent those anxious minutes passing through the village coming back to Stevensville the night after the Lolo fiasco, Buck doubted he would ever forget the sight of so many fierce young warriors clotting the town's main street.

Wouldn't be able to ever forget their formidable appearance, their stern looks, their sheer swaggering aggressiveness and brazen actions—which all together put the white shopkeepers in town immediately on their guard. Riding their finest ponies—some of which wore the brands of their white Idaho ranchers—wearing their brightest blankets and showiest buckskins encrusted with beads and quillwork, all of the warriors strutted around with Henry repeating rifles or soldier carbines. In every store they entered, it was clear they had more than enough money to make their purchases as they shuffled through the few shops open that day in Stevensville.

While they came and went from the Buck Brothers' Store, Henry found the men an open and talkative bunch—willing, if not eager, to tell about their tribulations back in Idaho, what tragic events and wrongs had led up to the outbreak on the Salmon River, explaining in honest but graphic terms what depredations and murders they themselves had committed against innocent civilians before the army rode against them in White Bird Canyon. And most all of them spoke in bright and upbeat tones of their current condition, even disclosing where they were headed to make a new life for themselves now that they had left Cut-Off Arm and his army back in Idaho.

From time to time, old White Bird would yell something at one warrior or another from the middle of the street, where the chief maintained a wary vigil atop his pony. But his instructions were always in their native tongue, so it remained a mystery to Henry. White Bird and other older warriors were on guard and at the ready, keeping a watchful eye on some two dozen of Charlot's friendly Flathead, who had slipped into town once word was spread that the Nez Perce had shown up in great numbers. Their chief had ordered them into Stevensville to protect the tribe's white friends from the noisy, bellicose invaders.

Early that Wednesday afternoon, another merchant in town came huffing in the door, announcing that an unscrupulous trader down the street had opened up a whiskey keg and was selling it for a dollar a cup in gold dust or coin.

"Already there's a few of 'em getting real mean-faced and growling like dogs down at Jerry Fahy's place," the man explained to the Buck brothers.

"Fahy can't sell that whiskey to these here Injuns!" yelped Amos. "Henry, you go with him and put a stop to this. Hammer a bung back in that keg and make Fahy see the light!"

By the time young Henry had unknotted the apron from his waist and was stepping out the door, five more citizens were scurrying across the street, streaming right past White Bird himself. On the boardwalk a few yards to the north, about a dozen young warriors were clearly enjoying themselves, weaving side to side and lurching back and forth across the dusty street.

"Henry!" cried Reverend W. T. Flowers, the local Methodist minister, as his group of concerned citizens lumbered to a halt like a flock of chicks around a black-feathered hen. "You know the bartender down at the saloon?"

"Dave Spooner?"

"That's him," the preacher said. "We've just convinced Brother Spooner how wise he would be to cease selling bilious spirits to the redskins."

Henry asked, "Or?"

"Or he might feel the coarse rub of a hemp rope tighten around his neck!" Flowers warned, pantomiming with both hands clasped at his throat. "Now I've heard Fahy is doing a land-office business with a keg of his own. You're coming with us to see an end is made of that liquid evil?"

"I am, Reverend."

Stomping right down the middle of the street, the six of them crammed through Jerry Fahy's open doorway and demanded his whiskey barrel be turned over to them. Inches away, more than a dozen warriors stood in line clutching newly purchased pint tin cups, impatiently waiting their turn at the spigot.

"Why you want my whiskey?" Fahy demanded from behind the counter where he was dispensing the potent amber liquid.

"We're acting before any of these Injuns gets drunk and ready to raise some hair!" the gray-headed minister thundered, sweeping back the long tails of his black wool morning coat.

"You ain't got a leg to stand on, Reverend," the merchant chimed back with a gritty smile. "Begging God's pardon, but I'm just a shopkeeper doing an honest day's business, and I ain't breaking no Sabbath. . . . So I don't reckon it's a damn lick of your business."

"For sure it's my business, too," added one of the other merchants.

Fahy snorted, "By what authority do you fellas think you can come an' take my whiskey?"

Quick as a blink, Preacher Flowers yanked out a single-action army Colt .45-caliber revolver and immediately dragged back the hammer with a click made loud in the sudden silence of that room. Without the slightest hesitation, he shoved the muzzle against the whiskey seller's forehead, pressing it to that spot just above and between the eyes.

The right reverend announced gravely, "By *this* authority!"

"W-what you gonna do with my whiskey, if I give it to you?" Fahy asked, his eyes crossing each time he stared up at the long barrel. "You gonna pay me for it?"

"Not on your life," Flowers sneered. "We're gonna take your keg of evil concoction to Fort Owen for safekeeping until these Indians have departed from our valley."

"You're stealing my business from me!" Fahy squawked.

That's when an emboldened Henry Buck spoke up: "We could just knock a hole in that keg right here, 'stead of keeping it safe for you out at the fort."

"Take it, goddammit!" the merchant spit, unrepentant and taking the Lord's name in vain even before the fire-and-brimstone preacher. "Maybe one of these days the Nez Perce will come to pay a call on you and take what they want without payin'!"

"We're not stealing your whiskey," Henry said as the resealed keg was rolled out the door to a waiting wagon. "We're just borrowing it until this trouble all blows over."

When one of the concerned merchants and the reverend were on their way out to the fort with the trader's keg in the rear of a prairie wagon, Henry started back for the Buck Brothers' Store—only to find even more of the drunken warriors congregating in the street, their voices growing loud enough to wake up the dead. He had to zigzag to make his way across the rutted street, then shove past several inebriated Nez Perce clustered just outside the store's open doors. Henry stepped inside just as his two older brothers reached out from either side of the door and hoisted him toward a rack of hemp rope.

"Get in here so we can lock up!" Amos ordered.

"We're closing?" Henry asked his brothers.

"You see'd it yourself out there," Fred, the eldest, explained. "Better off not dealing with 'em while so many's got a snootful of that whiskey."

Henry proposed, "Maybe we'll wait till the whiskey wears off, then we can open up again—"

His voice dropped off just as he caught a flash of motion out the front window. One of the belligerent warriors he had pushed past at the doorway was dragging his wobbly rifle up, pointing it right through the large plate-glass window at Henry, beginning to clumsily drag back the hammer on his weapon.

In a blur of color, one of the Flathead suddenly rushed in from the right, his arm sweeping up, shoving the rifle away from its mark, wrenching the weapon from the Nez Perce.

At least ten of the warrior's friends immediately descended on the scene, along with a half-dozen of Charlot's Flathead. All appeared destined to die in a hail of angry gunfire . . . when White Bird appeared out of nowhere, still mounted on his pony, swinging his elkhorn quirt. Whipping his tribesmen with the long knotted rawhide straps, the chief drove his warriors back.

In a heartbeat the old chief dropped to the street, lunging at the youngster who had prepared to fire at Henry Buck. White Bird cocked his arm into the air. Eight, nine, ten times he savagely lashed the quirt across the offender's face and shoulders, back and arms, raising angry red welts wherever it landed, while the warrior pitifully cried out for his friends to pull the old man off.

When the youngster finally collapsed against the storefront, shielding his face behind a pair of bleeding forearms, White Bird ceased his furious attack, took a step back, and dropped his arm to his side. Then he called out in a loud, sure voice.

Two of the older men pushed their way through the cordon of young warriors, grabbed the offender by his wounded arms, and heaved him onto a nearby pony. Bellowing like a bull, White Bird motioned them in the direction of their camp.

Once the two guards were on the way with their young prisoner, the old chief turned to the rest of the drunken crowd, berating them, waving his quirt in the air threateningly.

As his brothers shoved the bolt through its lock on the double doors, Henry watched the old chief disperse the drunken rowdies and young troublemakers, driving them off toward their ponies.

Only as the noise died down and the hard-eyed, sullen young men drifted away from the front of the store and out of town* did Henry realize he was trembling like a leaf in a spring gale. Listening to his heart pound in his ears. Remembering how that whiskeyed-up warrior had pointed his rifle at him through the window.

Henry never wanted to be that close to death again, not for a long, long time.

---

*The older men managed to evacuate Stevensville about 3:00 p.m., having spent more than three thousand dollars in gold coin, dust, and paper currency. Out at the Silverthorne camp that night, unscrupulous traders arrived with ammunition and powder to sell to the Non-Treaty bands.

CHAPTER FORTY-SIX

WA-WA-MAI-KHAL, 1877

BY TELEGRAPH

—

ILLINOIS.

—

**Remains of General Custer at Chicago—
Other News Items.**

CHICAGO, July 31.—The remains of General Custer arrived here to-day from Fort Lincoln, and were forwarded at 5:15 p.m. by the Michigan Southern railroad, to West Point, where they will be interred in the receiving vault until the funeral in October. The remains of Colonel Cooke, Lieutenant Reilly, and Dr. DeWolf arrived on the same train . . .

IT WAS THOSE MEAN BOYS WHO WERE FOLLOWERS OF OLD *Toohoolhoolzote*—they were the troublemakers.

They were the ones lapping up a lot of the whiskey and making bold talk about what they would do if Cut-Off Arm and his soldiers ever caught up. These bad ones wanted to have another big fight with the army, even though most of the people believed the fighting was over now that they were in Montana, now that Looking Glass and White Bird had made a pact with the little chief and Shadows in Lolo Canyon, now that they were on the way to a new life in the buffalo country.

So when some hot-blooded young men got together and started talking tough with noplace to go where they could prove just how tough they were, Bird Alighting realized those bad-tempered ones were likely to cause some trouble. With no other way to get the fighting steam out of their systems, the mean boys rode away from the Non-Treaty camp,* itching for something that would break the boredom of camping and marching, camping and marching a little farther each day. Bird Alighting knew that bunch was up to no good the moment they thundered out of camp, most of them red to the gills with some whiskey brought into camp on a trader's wagon come out of Stevensville.

He was certain the swaggering youngsters had let the wolf out to howl by the time they came roaring back late that afternoon, leading seven stolen horses.

"Did you kill any Shadows while you were away disobeying me?" Looking Glass shrieked at *Toohoolhoolzote*'s young hotbloods the moment he had them stopped at the southern edge of the village.

"No," one of them replied in a surly manner as their ponies pranced around the chief and some of the older men. "Everyone is gone—so we weren't lucky enough to find any Shadows we could torture and kill!"

The rest in the party laughed along with their brassy leader, then stopped abruptly when Looking Glass hauled the arrogant leader to the ground. He stood over the youth, glaring down at him, trembling as he pointed at the stolen horses.

"Where did you get these Shadow ponies?"

"How do you know they are not my horses?" retorted the leader as he slowly got to his feet, rubbing a scuffed-up shoulder.

Grabbing hold of the callow youth's elbow and wrenching him around, Looking Glass pointed a finger at the picture scar on one horse's rear flank. "Is that a Shadow brand?"

"I-I—"

"Then this is a Shadow horse you stole!" the chief snapped.

"There was no one there to watch over them," the leader explained, turning with an impish grin to the rest of his friends, "so we took them."

—

*By now past Sweathouse Creek, farther up the Bitterroot valley.

Slamming the heel of his palm against the big youngster's chest, Looking Glass knocked the horse thief backward two steps as he thundered, "You have broken my promise to the Shadows!"

"The white men have no need of knowing," *Toohoolhoolzote* said as he stepped up beside the young man.

Looking Glass glared at them both. "It was *my* word," he snarled. "These stupid boys have broken my word not to cause any trouble as we pass through the Bitterroot!"

Taking a meaningful step toward the top-hat chief, the shaman said, "They are only horses—"

"*Toohoolhoolzote*, these are yours," Looking Glass chided, shoving the youngster toward the squat medicine man. "If they were my people, I would lay their backs open with a whip."

That old, square-jawed *tewat* began to speak: "But—"

"But," Looking Glass interrupted, "they are yours to discipline. If this happens again—if any man disobeys my orders against causing trouble—then I will see that he is severely punished and left behind."

Again the old shaman began to speak, but before he could, Looking Glass purposefully turned his back on *Toohoolhoolzote* and stuck his face right in that of the young leader.

"On second thought . . . I will discipline these stupid boys," he growled.

The young horse thief's eyes quickly snapped at *Toohoolhoolzote*, then back to Looking Glass.

"I want all of you to pick out one of your own horses from those you own," Looking Glass ordered, "and if you don't own another, then you will give me the one you are riding at this moment."

"W-what do you want our horses for?" the leader asked.

"You will take me back to where you stole the Shadow horses," Looking Glass declared sharply. "There you will leave your horses in place of the ones you stole."

Bird Alighting and others rode with Looking Glass when the horse thieves led them to the white man's ranch house and corral. The poles the young warriors had removed from a section of the corral lay scattered on the ground; the door to the cabin hung open. Inside they found how the young troublemakers had rooted through it all, breaking and destroying everything they did not want to carry away with them.*

"Build a fire over there," Looking Glass ordered the young thieves.

"Are you going to burn some of this?" the leader demanded, grinning, some haughtiness returning to his voice.

"No, I'm going to find this Shadow's iron marker and you are going to burn his brand into the horses you are giving him," the chief said sourly. "Go build that fire for me, now."

Proof of their raids back in Idaho became evident as some of the Non-Treaty warriors traded off a few horses to ranchers and merchants as they moseyed up the valley at a leisurely, unconcerned pace—animals that bore the brand scars of their Idaho owners. Here as they neared the head of the Bitterroot, Bird Alighting realized why Looking Glass was doing right by this individual settler: Maintaining the goodwill of these Montana Shadows was crucial to the success of a new life outside their ancient homeland.

In fact, if they were to be sure that relations with the white people of Montana did not disintegrate as they had in Idaho country, Looking Glass and the older men had to be constantly vigilant, assuring that the young men did not ride off and do something stupid to reignite the flames of war. In this case, the chiefs were clearly as anxious as the Bitterroot Shadows to avoid trouble.

Every time one of the white men had appeared with a wagonload of trade goods near the camp as the People slowly migrated up the Bitterroot valley, the older men remained close to the visitor so they could assure that the

---

*Myron Lockwood later put in a claim for $1,600 for the loss of not only some horses and a few cattle but also a supply of flour, all his busted furniture, some harness chopped up, and three of his favorite shirts.

young hotbloods fomented no trouble while the women purchased flour and cloth, and even some cartridges for the guns, although a few of the white men charged as high as one dollar a bullet.

But the *Nee-Me-Poo* had money! Lots of it: the Shadows' paper currency, silver and gold coins from Idaho, and sacks of gold dust earned in trade or taken in those first raids. A dollar a cartridge? That was no problem! After all, each of those bullets would kill a buffalo, making meat and providing another winter robe for the women to tan once they reached the land of their friends the *E-sue-gha*.

Far up the Bitterroot, where the terrain no longer lay flat, the valley narrowed and the slopes of the Bitterroot and the Sapphires closed in as the village began its ascent toward the nearby passes. But first, the *Nee-Me-Poo* temporarily halted their migration to pay homage at the Medicine Tree,* an ancient and hallowed site for them and the area's Flathead. For generations beyond remembrance the Non-Treaty bands had been coming and going by this spot, migrating between their homes and the buffalo country. Even before the arrival of the first pale-skinned Boston men, they had stopped to make offerings and pray at the base of this tree.

More than eight feet off the ground, embedded at the base of a large branch, hung the bleached skull and horns of a mountain sheep—those bony remains more encircled with every season as the ancient yellow ponderosa pine inexorably grew around that timeworn skull.**

Pausing briefly here in this region cloaked with heavy

---

*This colossal tree dating back to the 1700s still stands east of U. S. Highway 93 a few miles south of present-day Darby, Montana.

**For many years the local settlers protected this revered religious icon. Some time after the Nez Perce war, the skull was chopped out of the tree by a local lumberjack, roaring drunk at the time. After hearing that irate locals were planning to lynch him for his desecration of this sacred object, the man fled for safer parts. As the tale is told, he had only meant to adorn the wall of his favorite saloon in nearby Skalkaho (present-day Hamilton, Montana).

mystery and sure signs of the supernatural at work, the women came up, dragging young children they hushed as the People crowded around the tree's enormous base. With murmurs of prayers and praise, men and women alike tied offerings of cloth or ribbon, tobacco or strips of buckskin, even some copper-cased cartridges, to the branches and limbs, each item attendant with a special and heartfelt prayer . . . for this was known to the *Nee-Me-Poo* as the wishing tree.

Found along many Indian trails, these renowned "wishing" sites offered a traveler the opportunity to make his or her prayers for success in some current undertaking, be it as innocent as a new love affair or a hunting trip or as serious as a deadly foray against a powerful enemy. Far, far back into the days of the ancient ones, the Non-Treaty bands had believed this sacred tree itself would not only grant the wishes of those women who made their prayers at its base but also give their men the power of mastering horses and killing game for the survival of their people. There were powerful forces at work in this place of great mystery. Now that they were closing on the buffalo country, their prayers to such spirits would be vital to the survival of the bands—

"*Kapsisniyut!*" Lone Bird exclaimed. "This is a bad and evil thing I see!"

Everyone suddenly turned the man's way as he stumbled in approaching the base of the tree, collapsing to his knees—eyes rolling back in their sockets—a long moment while the crowd grew hushed.

Bird Alighting rushed to the man's elbow, supporting this warrior known as *Peopeo Ipsewahk*. As the frightened women pulled their children against their legs, everyone inching back to give Lone Bird a broad circle, the warrior's eyes slowly focused on the Medicine Tree's highest branches and he began to explain in a trembling voice.

"I have just had a dream given me while I was awake!" he spoke in a loud voice. "A dream of what is to come," he said a little quieter but even more emphatically. "A great heartbreak, a terrible tragedy, is about to befall us if we tarry too long in making our way into the land of the buffalo! *Koiimzi!* Hurry! We cannot wait; we cannot linger!"

Never before had Bird Alighting heard the slightest fear enter Lone Bird's voice. An icy-cold fingernail scraped itself down his spine.

All too true: They were moving slowly—taking as much as nine days to march the one hundred Shadow miles it would take to get from the mouth of the Lolo Canyon to reach the Big Hole Prairie.

"We are going, Lone Bird," consoled Looking Glass as he stepped to the man's side. "We are marching to the land of the *E-sue-gha*."

Lone Bird reached up to grab the front of Looking Glass's shirt as he leaped to his feet again. "No! I feel the breath of *hattia tinukin*, the death wind, on my neck," he pleaded. "We are taking too long, too long!"

White Bird himself shouldered his way through the fringe of the murmuring crowd and confronted the two men, glaring at Looking Glass with worry graying his wrinkled face. "See, Looking Glass? For the past two days I myself have told you we should leave the lodgepoles behind and hurry, hurry! The women can cut more another place."

"The war is far behind us!" Looking Glass argued, shrugging, his palms to the sky.

"Dragging our lodgepoles is making us too slow!" White Bird snapped.

"But we have children and women, a big herd of horses," the head chief explained.

"Yes!" Lone Bird warned, turning from Looking Glass, his frightened eyes searching out others in the front ranks of that hushed crowd shrinking back from his nightmare vision. "My dream showed me how we are moving too slow. Far too slow . . . on this trail that will bring us death—"

"Just on the other side of these heights is the *Iskumtse-*

lakik,"* Looking Glass scoffed. "And Cut-Off Arm is far, far behind us. Besides, the Shadows of Montana have shown themselves to be our friends. They trade with us; they sell us what we need for our travels. We have left the war far behind us—"

"No! Even as we stand here, the death wind is already coming up behind us!" Lone Bird whirled, pointing down the valley in the direction they had come.

Past the little settlement of Corvallis. On past Stevensville and their big earthen fort. Perhaps even past the mouth of Lolo Creek toward the community of Missoula City itself.

"I have seen the face of death," Lone Bird whispered in the stillness of that hushed assembly, "the death that is already stalking our trail!"

Bitter Root Mountains
Camp Spurgin in the Field
August 1, 1877

Darling Wife,

Last night we had rather an unpleasant time, but I was somewhat comforted with your letter of the Saturday after my departure, and was made happy in your saying that you are all well, or were so when I left. I said we had a rather unpleasant night of it, for we went to bed without our tents, and it began to rain about midnight. So I had to get up and make a shelter with a tent fly which I had laid on the ground as a sort of mattress. Doctor Newlands and I were bunking together. However, we finally made it comfortable and rain proof, and then slept on till morning.

Got up at 5 A.M. but did not march until 11 A.M., and then only went 8 miles and made the nicest camp we have yet had in among partially wooded hills, or rather,

---

*What the *Nee-Me-Poo* called the Place of the Ground Squirrels, the valley of the Big Hole.

mountains. We had some fine mountain views yesterday and today. We were so high up that the whole extent of mountainous country was spread around us. Tomorrow we are to march about 18 miles and make camp on the Clearwater River, the same river that runs by the Agency, only we shall find it a mere mountain brook that can be easily forded by the men and horses. I shall think then of my darlings, and make the stream a little mental address about going down to the Lapwai and leaving a message from me to those I so love.

Captain Spurgin, 21st Infantry, caught up with our army last night, and today some beef cattle arrived to serve as food for us all, poor things. We find for the last 3 nights hardly any grass for our horses and pack mules. It is very poor, indeed, and we shall not get any better for 3 or 4 days to come. We are still some 50 miles from the summit of the Bitter Root range of mountains which, you know, is the dividing line between Idaho and Montana Territory. Then we shall have 60 miles more to Missoula. No Indians have been heard of yet, and I suspect that our mountain climbing this week and next will not accomplish any substantial result. The life we lead on such a campaign is very rough, and it would puzzle many to account for the fact that it is, to some extent, enjoyable. Only when the elements frown upon us does it seem discouraging. Last evening and night, and also this morning, everyone looked disgusted with everything, but we made an early and very pleasant camp after a short day's march, and presto, everybody is changed, and a generally cheerful aspect prevails.

I hope, Darling, that this scribble will find you all well. Tell Bert that Papa is coming back to his place at the table and home just as soon as he can. Tell him that when I was riding along in the big woods today, I came upon a poor little Indian pony which had been left behind, and it followed us into camp. If I was only going towards home, I would try and bring it in for him. Tell Bessie, my girl, that Papa yesterday saw a great many beautiful flowers along the way, and they made me think of my little girl. I wish I could send her some fresh ones. As it is, I will put it in for you, Dear, and a sprig of heather in bloom which is all about our camp tonight. I gathered an armful of it to spread my blankets on for my bed tonight. I wish, Darling, you would write—every chance you get. I will endeavor to do the same.

Your loving,
John

Remember me to the Sternbergs and the Boyles.

Chapter Forty-Seven

August 2–7, 1877

BY TELEGRAPH

MONTANA.

Progress of the Indian War.

PORTLAND, July 30.—General Howard is at present at Kamia, awaiting the arrival of Major Sanford, and as soon as that officer joins him, Howard will take all the available forces and push vigorously on after Joseph and White Bird, who have already crossed Bitter Root mountains by way of the Lolo trail. He will go to Missoula as rapidly as his command can move. He will have in the neighborhood of five hundred men. Another force, under command of General Wheaton, will leave Fort Lapwai and pass through the Spokane country over into Montana, through Sahon pass. After crossing the mountains the troops will push down to Missoula, where they will join General Howard. It is expected that Howard's and Wheeler's detachments will reach that point simultaneously.

He had been the first white man to view the stripped, bloated, mutilated bodies of more than 220 dead soldiers offered up on that hot, grassy ridge beside the Little Bighorn River as if in sacrifice to some heathen deity.

First Lieutenant James H. Bradley was his name. Seventh U. S. Infantry; serving under Colonel John Gibbon out of Fort Shaw on the Sun River in north central Montana Territory.

This past May Bradley had celebrated his thirty-third birthday. Uneventful his life had been until April 1861, when seventeen-year-old Jim left his place of birth—Sandusky County, Ohio—and marched off to war with the Fourteenth Ohio Volunteers. Taken prisoner and held for half a year by the Confederates, he was released in time to serve during the siege of Atlanta. By the time he was discharged at the end of the war he had risen to the rank of sergeant with the Forty-fifth Ohio Volunteers.

The remembrance of those long, deadly days on the outskirts of Atlanta always made the young soldier smile at the ironic twists his life had taken. With Reconstruction under way across the Confederated states, he fell in love with and married a daughter of the Old South, her father, an Atlanta physician—his Miss Mary Beech.

Knowing what little opportunity he had to return home to at the end of the war, Bradley enlisted in the regular army, serving with the Eighteenth U. S. Infantry—which engaged against the Lakota at Crazy Woman's Fork in Dakota Territory during the early days of the Bozeman Road—before he was transferred to the Seventh U. S. Infantry in 1871, along with a promotion to first lieutenant.

The young lieutenant and his wife were soon blessed with the first of two daughters—Bradley called all three his houseful of ladies.

Those who served with him vouchsafed that he was a man absolutely without fear, a true warrior in whom the fighting spirit was aroused in battle. While not as large as many infantrymen of the day, Bradley was lithe and sinewy, ever active and energetic.

Ever since his arrival in Montana Territory, he had endeared himself to many of its earliest pioneers as he tirelessly collected their reminiscences for the possible publication of a book at some future date. In particular, he was fascinated with the early fur trade of the Far West. His collection of narratives was one of the earliest to record the history of Fort Benton and the American Fur Company on the Upper Missouri River. With an insatiable appetite for the history and ethnography of the region, this budding scholar—who was just now joining the ranks of other inquisitive frontier army officers like John G. Bourke and

Charles King—hoped his studies would one day provide a comfortable life for him and his Miss Mary and give both their daughters the grand weddings every girl dreams she will have.

But war would remain his chosen profession.

On the evening of 26 June 1876, as he was leading a few Crow scouts and the small advance up the valley where they would eventually discover the grotesque, dismembered bodies of the Custer dead, in some way the lieutenant already sensed what he was about to stumble across. Only a day earlier, he had confided to his journal: "There is not much glory in Indian wars, but it will be worthwhile to have been present at such an affair as this."

He hoped the Seventh Infantry would now have a chance to make a little history—instead of merely witnessing it.

Their colonel commanding had mobilized the Seventh from Camp Baker, Forts Ellis and Shaw, and even out at a tiny way camp pitched beside Dauphin Rapids on the Missouri River to pull together this skimpy force of eight officers and eighty-one* enlisted men.

Gibbon had wired Governor Benjamin F. Potts concerning two possible eventualities, depending upon where the Nez Perce turned once they debouched from the Lolo. If the Non-Treaty bands turned north at the end of the Lolo Trail for the Blackfoot River, Gibbon wanted Potts to have his local militia assist Captain Rawn, who would be forced to follow the Indians until the colonel met them somewhere west of Cadotte Pass. But if the hostiles turned south, Potts was to send his volunteers to guard those passes leading into the Big Hole basin, with orders to delay the Non-Treaty bands until Gibbon could catch them from the rear and give a fight.

"Please give instructions," the colonel told the governor, ". . . to have no negotiations whatever with the Indians, and the men should have no hesitancy in shooting down any

*Historians have concluded that Colonel Gibbon was incorrect when he listed seventy-six soldiers on his duty roster for that day.

armed Indians they meet not known to belong to one of the peaceful tribes."

Rendezvousing just west of Cadotte Pass with eight troopers from the Second U. S. Cavalry out of Fort Ellis, they soon met wagons loaded with families and their meager belongings, civilians escaping the western sections of the state. Near New Chicago, several small parties of militia from Pioneer and Deer Lodge, already on the way to the Bitterroot, joined Gibbon's men.

Accompanied by the eight cavalrymen, the colonel himself had pressed ahead of his column for Missoula City with all possible dispatch, reaching the community on 2 August. There he commandeered some wagons to be sent back for his foot soldiers and pack-master Hugh Kirkendall's mule train from Fort Shaw.

Bradley himself reached Captain Rawn's post the next afternoon with the rest of Gibbon's undermanned column. At this early stage of the pursuit, the colonel maintained the optimism that he could overtake the slow-moving village within two days by making long, forced marches.

"I speculated the same thing you did, General," Charles Rawn disclosed to Gibbon, using the colonel's highest brevet rank awarded for gallantry in the Civil War. "Utilizing locals and some of my own men as spies, I've managed to keep an eye on the hostiles, charting their movements every day. We should be able to overhaul them in a matter of days and bring them to a fight."

"They're headed over the mountains by their normal route, Captain?" Bradley asked Rawn.

"They'll have to go through Big Hole Prairie. Two days ago when I wasn't proof certain of when you'd arrive, I wired Governor Potts that I would lead some fifty or sixty regulars in pursuit, knowing full well I'd have to temporize my march so that you or General Howard could catch up before I overtook the rear of the hostile village."

"What do your sources tell you the bands are doing, Captain?" Bradley asked. "Are they moving any faster the closer they get to the head of the valley?"

"No, Lieutenant," Rawn said. "If anything, they appear to dawdle a little more each of the last few days. I've become pretty well satisfied that they will not hurry out of the Bitterroot until they know that one army or the other has arrived to give them chase. Not surprisingly, they have been keeping a watch on us, too, and therefore know everything that's going on with us."

"How many warriors do you estimate are with them at this point?" inquired Bradley, who would be in charge of a small detail of scouts.

Rawn turned to the lieutenant and said, "At least two hundred and fifty."

His eyes squinting with determination and a heap of keen anticipation, Bradley looked at Colonel Gibbon and declared, "That ought to make for a damn good scrap of it, sir."

BY TELEGRAPH

—

KANSAS.

—

An Imposing Military Funeral at Fort Leavenworth.

LEAVENWORTH, Ks., August 3.—Yesterday evening the Chicago, Rock Island and Pacific brought the remains of Captains Yates and Custer, Liets. McIntosh, Smith, Calhoun and Worth. The bodies were placed in the Post chapel, and a guard of honor was stationed and remained during the night. This morning a large number of people visited the chapel and viewed the caskets containing the remains of the honored dead . . . The procession was formed, and the remains taken to the cemetery, about one mile distant, upon artillery caissons. Each caisson was drawn by two bay horses. Following each caisson was a horse caparisoned in mourning, and led by a cavalry soldier, according to the custom of the funeral ceremonies for officers in the cavalry service. During the march to the cemetery, minute guns were fired and flags lowered to half-mast . . . Arriving at the Post cemetery, the Episcopal service was read and a salute of three volleys was fired over the graves. The ceremonies were very imposing. All the arrangements were complete and carried out in perfect order. It was estimated that there were nearly three hundred carriages in the procession . . . The fact that the lamented dead had lived at that garrison and were well known and honored by our people created an intense feeling of sympathy among the entire community. Five of the brave soldiers in the army have thus been tenderly placed in their final resting place in the beautiful Leavenworth cemetery with all the honors due to men of noble and daring deeds, and their memory will be cherished by every patriot in the land.

Fort Lapwai
Sunday August 5, 1877

Dear Mamma,

It is doleful living alone this way without John and not knowing when he will come home. I don't know how much longer I can get along . . . We are four ladies at the post now. Dr. Sternberg sent for his wife, and she has arrived.

Yesterday the Indian prisoners were taken away from here down to Vancouver. The squaws seemed to feel awfully about being taken away. Some of them moaned and groaned over it at a great rate. I did feel sort of sorry for them, as parts of all their families are still up here. One poor woman moaned and cried and really looked distressed. Just before she left, she took some ornaments of beads and gave them to the interpreter to give to her little girl who is up somewhere near Kamiah. One old man cut the bead ornaments off his moccasins and left them for his wife.

We have not heard anything from General Howard's command up in the Lolo Trail for a week. I wish we could hear! We have had all sorts of rumors about the

Indians, but we don't know anything. I had a note from John written Monday night at their first camp on the Trail. He said it was a hard mountain trail. They had been all day going 15 miles. It is a zigzag, winding, steep trail, in many places impossible for two to walk abreast, with either rocks or a dense pine forest close on all sides.

There are several companies of troops over on the other side in Montana, and we have heard that the Indians were allowed to pass, but we don't think it possible. We also hear the Indians have gotten back on General Howard's rear . . .

Your loving daughter,
Emily F.

Rationed for twenty days, General O. O. Howard's seven-hundred-thirty-man column struck out for the western terminus of the Lolo Trail beneath a steady, cold, depressing rain early that Monday morning, 30 July.

It had taken more than a day to repair the wire cable across the Clearwater, then two more days to slog the entire command across to the north bank. That final day of preparation, the twenty-ninth, was a Sunday. Howard attended a Presbyterian service conducted in both Nez Perce and English by Archie Lawyer, son of the great treaty chief. It was a chance to offer prayers to the Almighty. And that night, their last beside the Kamiah crossing, the general committed his innermost doubts to paper:

There is a stern reality in going from all that you love into the dread uncertainty of Indian fighting, where the worst form of torture and death might await you. It is very wise and proper to ask God's blessing when about to plunge into the dark clouds of warfare.

In the advance by four o'clock that Monday morning rode twenty-four members of a tribe that was an ancient enemy of the Nez Perce, Bannock scouts, who had arrived on the twenty-eighth from Fort Boise with Major George B. Sanford of the First U. S. Cavalry. Major John Wesley Green, also of the First, would be along soon, temporarily delayed with two infantry companies at the nearby mining community of Florence. Above their traditional leggings of buckskin or antelope hide the Bannock wore army tunics of dark blue, gaily set off with bright sashes of stars and stripes fashioned from old garrison flags. They were led by Buffalo Horn, who, just two days before departing Fort Boise, had returned to his people after serving Colonel Nelson A. Miles during the last skirmishes of the Great Sioux War.* Despite the rain that fell in sheets, Buffalo Horn and his fellow trackers were eager to hunt down the fleeing village filled with their longtime enemies. With the arrival of these Indian scouts, the general dismissed McConville's volunteers mustered from the rural settlements of eastern Washington.

The quartermaster had seen to it the column was supplied with rations for twenty days, along with additional beeves on the hoof. Howard designated Lewiston as the main depot for his army in the field, leaving orders that the general staff was to keep the depot well furnished with at least three months' supplies on hand. Forage would not be carried along, because the general and his officers believed they could obtain what they needed for their stock along the way.

The column's supplies would be transported on the backs of a long train of more than 350 mules, in addition to what mules were needed to carry the dismantled Coehorn mortar** and drag the two Gatling guns and a pair of mountain howitzers over the rugged Lolo Trail. This march would prove itself to be like no other since Hannibal himself had crossed the Alps.

**Wolf Mountain Moon*, vol. 12, and *Ashes of Heaven*, vol. 13, the *Plainsmen* series.

**A small bronze, twenty-four-pounder, Model 1841, used primarily as a seige or garrison mortar, mounted on a sturdy wooden bed. With a maximum range of 1,200 yards, this fieldpiece, including its bed, weighed

From the Kamiah crossing of the Clearwater, the rain-soaked, slippery trail was an ordeal Howard likened to a monkey climbing a greased rope, as it angled northeast for sixteen miles toward the *Weippe* Prairie—where the soldiers found that the Nez Perce women had dug up much of the lush camas meadows—then would extend almost due east into the Bitterroot Mountains for more than a hundred miles of narrow ridges and harrowing precipices, not to mention boggy mires where man and beast sank to their knees and slapped at blood-devouring mosquitoes or that fallen timber so thick an exasperated Howard believed a man could cross from one side of the Lolo to the other stepping only on downed trees, without his feet once touching the ground.

Eleven years before, at the time of both the Idaho and Montana gold rushes, Congress had funded a party of axmen and former Civil War engineers under Wellington Bird and Sewell Truax to survey and build a road over the Bitterroot. It was, by and large, this narrow, primitive "wagon road" that the Nez Perce had started out on a full two weeks before General Howard ever got under way, his column following the same exhausting path toward Montana Territory—fighting their way over and around trees felled by high winds and heavy, wet snowfall, over and across the remnants of once-massive snowdrifts. On either side of the plodding column arose peaks rising more than seven thousand feet high, all still blanketed with a thick mantle of white that day by day became moisture draining into the Middle Fork of the Clearwater on the west, into the Bitterroot River to the east.

So slow was their pace that it did not take long every morning for the entire command to find itself strung out for more than five, sometimes as many as six, miles in length.

—

about 296 pounds, and was easily transported by a mule. This particular gun had not been used in the Battle of the Clearwater, so I have to presume it arrived with the fresh batteries of the Fourth Artillery from San Francisco.

"How far ahead of us do you think Joseph's village is now?" Howard once asked Ad Chapman near the end of a day's march.

The civilian had shrugged, clearly unsure of how to answer. "Far enough I fear we won't catch 'em less'n they stay put for a time, General. No man can get so much out of a horse as an Indian can."

Almost from the first day they began to come upon remnants of the Indians' passage: horses abandoned with serious wounds and broken limbs, other ponies already dead and stiffening upon the trail. At many of the tightest switchbacks and where the Nez Perce had forced themselves through tight stands of trees, the soldiers found streaks of blood and bits of horsehide still clinging from the busted branches.

Just behind the Bannock scouts, who ranged far in the lead, a unit of fifty skilled civilian "pioneers" hired by Jack Carleton, a Lewiston timberman, all of whom served under Captain William F. Spurgin of the Twenty-first Infantry, labored day after day after day with their axes and two-man crosscuts to chop down and saw their way through that knotty maze of timber slowing the army's progress. When there was time, Spurgin's "skillets," as they were affectionately called by the soldiers, built bridges across rocky chasms and improved portions of the dangerous trail by corduroying with timber or shoring up muddy walls with fragments of rock.

Up every morning with reveille at four. Breakfast by five. On the march no later than six. One long, arduous afternoon as they plodded toward the pass, correspondent Thomas Sutherland reined to the side of the trail to let others pass by while he let his horse catch its breath.

He called out, "General!"

"Yes, Mr. Sutherland?" Howard asked as his horse slowly carried him past the newsman.

"I was wondering if you intended to kill all your men by these hard marches, rather than waiting for them to have the chance to kill Joseph!"

It rained every afternoon, long enough to soak through their woolen garments and make the trail a slippery, mucky, sticky obstacle to be endured. Many evenings when they finally limped into bivouac after 6:00 P.M., the men were mud-caked from chin to toe. But a cheery fire and a little sunshine as that bright orb fell from the undergut of those dark clouds to the west did much to raise any flagging spirits, despite a monotonous diet of salt pork, hardbread, an occasional dollop of potatoes while they lasted, and plenty of coffee to wash it down.

The column ended up losing a little of its crackers and some of its bacon the fourth day out, abandoned along the way with the injured and broken-down mules carrying those packs up the torturous loops of the Lolo Trail.

Not only did the unbelievably rugged terrain hamper the speed of the march, but so did the fact that the men could water only a few of their horses and mules at a time when they ran across those infrequent springs and freshets on their climb toward the Continental Divide. In addition, at one stop after another, the soldiers failed to find enough forage to fill their weakening stock. The Nez Perce herd had grazed nearly all of the coarse, non-nutritious wire grass down to its roots.

That, and the cocky defiance of the hostiles, infuriated Howard to no end. On the fourth day, the Bannocks located a beautifully executed carving of an Indian bow, whittled out of the bark of a dark pine tree growing alongside the trail. The bow and its arrow were pointed to the rear—clearly meant to strike Howard and those soldiers who were following.

That same afternoon the general's advance heard the dim rattle of gunfire up the trail. He and others hurried ahead, fearing the Bannock had been ambushed by a rear guard, but found instead his trackers, scouts, and some of Spurgin's pioneers standing knee-deep in the headwaters of a gushing creek, shooting salmon with their carbines. That night, most of the column had a brief change in diet.

Then on 4 August as the head of the column entered a

pretty mountain glade dotted with swampy ponds and the lushest green grass, disappointing news arrived with James Cearly and Joseph Baker, those two Mount Idaho couriers he had sent south over the Old Nez Perce Trail with dispatches for Captain Rawn. They rode up to Howard that Saturday afternoon, accompanied by Wesley Little, who had run across the couriers on the Elk City Road and ended up accompanying the pair all the way to Missoula City.

Rawn, he learned, along with his small force of soldiers and a large contingent of civilian volunteers, had somehow allowed the Nez Perce to get around them and exit the canyon into the Bitterroot valley. In fact, they were reportedly camped near the small community of Corvallis and were likely to move toward Big Hole Prairie on the Elk City Trail. And according to the dispatch brought him from Captain Charles Rawn, Colonel John Gibbon was momentarily expected from Fort Shaw, along with a small force of his Seventh U. S. Infantry.

The captain addressed his note to Howard:

> *Start tomorrow to try to delay them, as per your letter and Gen'l. Gibbon's order. Will get volunteers if I can. Have sent word to Gov. Potts, that it appears from information gained from men who know the country, that the Indians intend to go through Big Hole or Elk City trail. By sending his 300 Militia ordered mustered in, direct from Deer Lodge to Big Hole Prairie, can head them off.*

The only bright spot these revelations brought Howard was that, at the very least, now he no longer had to fear that Joseph's warriors would lay an ambush for his column somewhere along the Lolo Trail or fear that the village would double around and sneak back to the Camas Prairie, where they would recommence their deviltry, destruction, and murderous rampage.

Dropped right in his lap at that moment was the justification for splitting his force and attempting a junction with Gibbon. Hope rekindled, the glimmer of victory sprang eternal in his breast. Howard was about to put the frustratingly slow pace of the climb up the west side of the pass behind him.

On the following morning of 5 August, after they had awakened to ice in their water buckets, the general impatiently pushed ahead with his staff, the "skillets," and part of his pack train. Riding out at dawn with them and seventeen of the trackers were Major George B. Sanford's cavalry and Captain Marcus P. Miller's artillery battalion—who were serving as mounted infantrymen—leaving the foot soldiers and most of the pack train to follow behind at its slower pace. With this detached advance of some 192 cavalrymen, thirteen officers, and twenty of the Bannock scouts, in addition to one officer and fifteen artillerymen given charge of both mountain howitzers and that Coehorn mortar, Howard hurried for the summit of the pass, hoping to reach the Bitterroot valley in time to form a junction with Gibbon's undermanned infantry as quickly as possible.

While Joe Baker would continue as a guide for Howard, the general sent Cearly and Little on west to Lapwai, carrying messages for McDowell and Sherman.

The following day, 6 August, this fast-moving advance nooned at Summit Prairie,* where they finally gazed down into Montana Territory. They had crossed from McDowell's Division of the Pacific and entered General Alfred H. Terry's Department of Dakota, part of Philip Sheridan's Division of the Missouri. From here on out Howard was acting upon the direct orders of the commander of the army himself, William Tecumseh Sherman, ordered to forsake all administrative boundaries in running down the Nez Perce to their surrender or to the death.

From there Howard pressed on until they reached the lush meadows that surrounded the numerous hot springs. It was this afternoon of the sixth that Joe Pardee, one of Gibbon's civilian couriers, reached the Idaho column, explaining that the colonel's men had struck south from Missoula

---

*Present-day Packer Meadows.

City two days before, pressing up the Bitterroot with all possible dispatch. Gibbon was requesting a hundred of Howard's cavalry. That electrifying news, and this beautiful spot with its magically recuperative powers, went far to lifting the spirits of every officer and enlisted man, newly cheered to learn they were closing on the Nez Perce.

That following morning, the general composed a message for Gibbon that he himself was hurrying ahead with 200 horsemen:

> I shall join you in the shortest possible time. I would not advise you to wait for me before you get to the Indians, then if you can create delay by skirmishing, by parleying, or maneuvering in any way, so that they shall not get away from you, do so by all means if you think best till I can give you the necessary reinforcements. I think however that the Indians are very short of ammunition, and that you can smash them in pieces if you can get an engagement out of them. Your judgment on the spot will be better than mine. I will push forward with all my might.

This same morning he would send his quartermaster, First Lieutenant Robert H. Fletcher, ahead to the Missoula post with frontiersman Pardee, asking that rations and forage for his stock be waiting for him at the mouth of Lolo Creek.

If he hadn't felt McDowell's spur before, General Oliver Otis Howard sensed it cruelly raking his ribs at this moment. He found himself in another commander's department.

Joseph's hostiles were almost within reach.

Now the race was on.

CHAPTER FORTY-EIGHT

AUGUST 4–7, 1877

BY TELEGRAPH

—

News from the Indian War.

—

WASHINGTON.

—

General Sherman's Report: Pittsburgh Wants a Garrison.

WASHINGTON, August 4.—General Sherman, in a letter to the secretary of war, says: "With the new post at the fork of Big and Little Horn rivers and that at the mouth of the Tongue river, occupied by enterprising garrisons, the Sioux Indians can never regain that country, and they can be forced to remain at their agency or take refuge in the British possessions. The country west of the new post has good country and will rapidly fill up with emigrants, who will, in the next ten years, build up a country as strong and as capable of self defense as Colorado. The weather has been as intensely hot as is Texas. I am favorably impressed with the balance of this country on the upper Yellowstone . . .

"IF YOU CAN DO WITHOUT THE SLEEP, SERGEANT," THE GENeral said as he peered up at the veteran noncommissioned officer, "it will be a feather in your cap to reach General Gibbon that much earlier."

First Sergeant Oliver Sutherland saluted, his backbone snapping rigid there in the saddle as he gazed down at General O. O. Howard. "Sir, I'll do my damnedest to stay bolted to this saddle until I have delivered your dispatch to General Gibbon."

Howard took two steps back, joining the ranks of his headquarters staff and a gaggle of more than a hundred curious soldiers and civilians as Sutherland jabbed the heels of his cavalry boots behind the ribs of that well-fed and -watered cavalry mount he would ride on down Lolo Creek, reaching the Bitterroot valley, where he was to chase after the rear of Colonel John Gibbon's pursuit of the fleeing Nez Perce camp.

The general and his advance had been the first to reach the hot springs on the downhill side of the pass, with the rest of the command not trudging in till late that afternoon. Sutherland was amazed at just how fast the men could get shed off their clothing, flinging off their boots and stripping out of greasy sweat-caked trousers to ease themselves down into the steamy pools. After that initial plunge, the soldiers dragged their clothing into the steamy water with them as the sun sank behind the Bitterroot Mountains, doing what they could to scrub weeks of campaigning from their shirts, stockings, and britches, not to mention the frayed and graying underwear. Soon it had all the makings of a laundresses' camp, what with all the wet clothing airing on every bush, hanging from every limb.

It was as Sutherland was dragging his limp, but renewed, body out of the sulphurous waters that a civilian and a Flathead warrior rode into camp. The tall, lanky frontiersman dropped to the ground, announcing that he was carrying a message from Gibbon for the general.

"The Seventh Infantry departed Missoula City on the fourth," Howard told those hundreds who crowded around the two riders from the valley. "He's requested one hundred men to overtake his column before he pitches into the hostiles. I believe I alone can drive my troops more miles in a day than an officer less spurred by a sense of responsibility than myself. Therefore, I resolve to start in the morning with this advance force intact, marching as fast as possible with those two hundred men in hopes of reaching Gibbon before he reaches Joseph's camp."

Suddenly it appeared Howard was struck by a thought

that caused a crease of intensity to furrow his brow. The general turned round, spotted the officer he sought in the front ranks of the crowd, and called out, "Captain Jackson, select your best rider! A steady man, one enured to hardship—one who can make the ride without faltering."

"The ride, General?" asked James B. Jackson.

"I want a man I can depend on—no, a man General Gibbon can depend on—to get my message through."

Without a flicker of hesitation, Jackson turned on his heel and quickly located the half-naked Sutherland in the crowd.

"Sergeant Sutherland?"

"I'll be back with my horse inside twenty minutes, Cap'n," he had answered. "No sir, Gen'ral Howard. Beggin' your pardon—I'll be ready to ride in *ten* minutes, sir."

Now he was loping through the gathering darkness, speeding toward the mouth of Lolo Creek beside that taciturn Flathead who had accompanied civilian Joe Pardee to Howard's camp.

The sergeant's real name was Sean Dennis Georghegan. Wasn't all that odd a happenstance for a man to have his name changed once he set foot on the shores of Amerikay. Not long after reaching his adopted homeland, Sutherland had volunteered for the Union Army, rising in rank to serve as a noncom in the Eighteenth Infantry, regulars. Later in that war against the rebellious Southern states, Sutherland was transferred to the Tenth Infantry, where he distinguished himself in battle and rose to become a second lieutenant by the time the cease-fire was called at Appomattox. Rather than return back to the Northeast, Sutherland itched for more travel and adventure. He scratched his itch by enlisting in the postwar First Cavalry and coming west.

An arduous ride awaited the sergeant as both a gathering darkness and an intermittent rain descended upon the two horsemen. But this was just the sort of adventure a hardened boyo like himself had prepared for. Trouble was, the adventure awaiting Oliver Sutherland was not anything like the Irishman had planned.

Upon reaching the mouth of Lolo Creek and the Bitterroot River as first light embraced the western slopes, the Flathead did his best to shrug and gesture, attempting to communicate that he was not going any farther with the soldier. He pointed off to the north, in the direction of Missoula City, and tapped his chest. Then he signed that the Nez Perce and the other soldiers would be found moving off to the south, somewhere *up* the valley.

It was up to Sutherland alone from here on out.

The sun was refusing to blink its one dull eye through the sullen gray clouds overhead, suspended near midsky, when Sutherland realized his horse had been pushed to its limit and was all but done in from the punishment he had given it over the last eighteen grueling hours. Limping along on that exhausted animal with its bloody, spur-riven sides, the sergeant reined up in the yard of the next ranch he came across, hallooing with a voice disused for the better part of a day.

"I'm bearing dispatches from General Howard to General Gibbon," Sutherland croaked.

"Gibbon, you say? Yes, yes—you'll have to ride right smart to catch Gibbon's bunch."

"How long ago they come by?"

The settler considered that at the door of his small barn. "He streamed it by with his men in their wagons day before yestiddy . . . yes, yes. They've got three days on you now."

"Howard's give me authority to get a remount," Sutherland sighed, his body already aching for that hard road yet to come. "Back down the road, I was told this place might have a horse I could ride. Need to swap you a played-out cavalry mount for one what's fresh, mister," he explained while the settler stepped from the double doors of his small barn, shovel in hand, his britches stuffed down in gum boots, busy at mucking out the horse stalls.

After bounding over to quickly inspect the strong but lathered army horse, the civilian looked up and said, "I ain't got but two sorts. One is big and strong, but a mite slow—there's two of 'em pull my plows and wagon. Only other horse I can swap you is a green colt, half-broke by a neighbor cross the valley. I ain't had time to gentle it to the saddle yet. But by damn if you don't look like a spunky feller."

Sutherland ground his teeth on the dilemma, then hurried his decision. Hundreds of men were counting on him. Bringing a rapid conclusion to this Nez Perce war would depend upon his finishing this ride.

"Bring out that green-broke colt. Howard's quartermaster will settle with you when they come through. While you fetch up the colt I'll take my saddle off this'un here," he grumbled, his brogue thick as blood soup. Then as the settler turned away for the paddock behind the barn, the sergeant asked, "You got a saddle blanket I could swap you? This'un's near soaked through."

The two of them managed to drape a dry saddlepad on the back of that wild-eyed colt they had snubbed up to a fencepost, then laid the McClellan saddle across its spine, drawing up the cinch to tighten it down as the horse sidestepped this way, then that, forcing the two men to scurry left, then right, as they finished the job of securing the snaffle-bit over the animal's muzzle.

He tugged the brim of his shapeless rain-soaked campaign hat down on his brow, then stuffed his hand between the buttons of his shirt, fingertips brushing the folded message he had taken from General Howard's own hand—as if to remind him that he alone had been hand-picked for this duty. Shifting his pistol belt nervously as he glanced one last time at the colt's wide, terror-filled eye, Sutherland seized the reins in hand, then slowly poked his foot into the left stirrup.

"When I'm nested down into this here God-blasted army rockin' chair," he told the grim-faced settler, "you free up that knot and step back, real quick."

"You a good horseman, soldier?"

His puckered ass ground down into the saddle and he heeled up the stirrups, tight as he could. Then swallowed. "I'm a horse soldier, mister. Ain't a horse gonna throw this boyo. Now," and he paused, ". . . let 'im go."

And go that horse did let go. Like lightning uncorked.

Screwing up its back, head tucked south and tail tucked north, nearly folding itself in half, that green-broke colt compressed all its energy on a spot centered just beneath that man stuck on its back. The pony flung itself into the air just starting to rain once more with a fine, soaking mist. As it slammed down hard on all four hooves, Sutherland felt his teeth jar, the side of his tongue grazed painfully, some of the pasty hardtack still digesting in his stomach brutally shoved up against his tonsils.

The sting of bile and the pain beneath his ribs robbed him of breath. As he wheezed in shock, the pony beneath him twisted itself in half again, but sideways this time, attempting to hurl the rider off to the left. From the corner of his eye he saw the fence coming up in a blur as the pony's rear flank wheeled round. Suddenly wondering how in Hades he would get the general's message through with a broken leg, on instinct Sutherland hammered the pony's ribs with his boot heels.

Just inches from that crude lodgepole fence, the colt shot away toward the middle of the corral, racing with its head down for three mad leaps, then twisted sideways again, preparing to uncork itself once more. This time the pony shuffled left, then suddenly right, bounding up and down on its forelegs—each jarring descent to the rain-soaked ground hammering his breakfast against the floor of his tonsils, tasting stomach gall each time he landed with a smack in that damned McClellan saddle.

The wind gusted of a sudden, driving a sheet of the fine mist right into his face. Blinking his eyes that fraction of an instant, he opened them to find the colt tucking its head down as it careened toward the lodgepole fence anew but suddenly planted all four hooves, skidding in the drying mud, jerking to a halt as it flung its rear flanks into the air, catapulting the man ass over teakettle like a cork exploding from a bottle of fermented wine.

For a heartbeat Sutherland found himself suspended upside down, peering at the horse through wondering eyes, unable to make out the fence coming up behind him as he completed that graceful arc out of the gray, rainy sky, but having no time at all to realize anything before he collided with the top rail and a rough-hewn post of that paddock fence.

With a shrill wheeze, the air was driven out of his lungs . . . but it wasn't until after he had landed in a heap at the bottom of the fencepost that he realized he was lying in a shallow puddle. Dragging the side of his face out of the caking mud, Sutherland immediately sensed he had broken something deep inside him. The pain was faint-giving, hot and cold at the same time. Starting cold in his lower spine, as it radiated outward through his gut and lower chest, the agony flared with a white-hot fury.

"You hurt, soldier?" the settler asked as he came over and bent at the waist to stare down at the sergeant.

"Get that g-goddamned horse . . . ," he rasped, then gritted his teeth together and clenched his eyes shut while the pain exploded through him, "tied off again afore I shoot it an' you both."

A whitish look of fear crossed the settler's face as he tore his eyes from the old soldier and straightened, shuffling off toward the pony standing motionless, but for its head bobbing, near the barn doors.

Slowly, gingerly, Sutherland dragged an elbow under him, pushing himself up. The toughest part was the searing pain he caused his body as he attempted to rise. But once he was upright, the waves of nausea slowly dissipated. Only when he tried to twist round or slightly rocked side to side did he have to clench his teeth together to swallow down the bitter taste of gall as his stomach sought to hurl itself against the back of his acid-laced tongue.

Just the sort of motion his body would suffer on the back of a horse, any horse—even a plodding plow horse. But . . . Sergeant Oliver Sutherland, Sean Dennis Georghegan, did not have the luxury of time to find a gentle draft horse—

"Your saddle's broke."

He blinked at the settler. Then glared at the pony with a

look of pure hate. The McClellan lay across the muddy, hoof-pocked corral, its cinch broken. "Get me one of yours."

"I ain't got but the one—"

"Get me your goddamned saddle!" he snarled. "General Howard will damn well make it right for you when he comes through in a day or so."

"Day or so? You sure the quartermaster gonna make it right by me? Like I said, them other soldiers is three days ahead—"

Sutherland gripped his holster menacingly. "Get that saddle on, or I'll have to shoot you right after I kill the horse."

The frightened settler's Adam's apple bobbed nervously when he turned away from the old soldier, scurrying into the small barn.

In minutes the civilian had that colt snubbed to another post, the blanket dragged out of the mud and draped across the pony's back before he looped the cinch through its ring.

Sutherland moved slowly, each step its own agony, reaching the horse as the settler pulled up on the strap. "Kick the son of a bitch in the belly."

"What?"

"Said: Kick the goddamned horse in the belly," he wheezed. " 'Cause I can't do it my own self. An' when you do kick it, the bastard's gonna take a deep breath—that's when you pull like the devil to get that cinch tight as it'll go."

He watched the doubtful man do exactly as he had ordered—and, sure enough, the pony was forced to exhale, allowing the civilian to yank the cinch even tighter.

"Now, help me up . . . for I fear I might black out to do it my own self."

"You're hurt," the settler said, suddenly realizing what might be the extent of the soldier's injuries. "Maybe you'd be better off to wait out a few hours to see—"

"I ain't got a few hours," Sutherland cut him off. " 'Sides, my muscles only gonna get tighter every minute we stand here jawing. Get me in the goddamned saddle."

They both grunted as together they raised Sutherland into the old saddle. The sergeant's head swam with an inky blackness, and behind his eyelids swirled a cascade of shooting stars. But he managed to push through the faintness—tasting the bile over the extent of his tongue.

"I got a message to take to General Gibbon," Sutherland explained when his eyes opened at last. "Gotta get to him . . . afore he gets to the Nez Perce."

Sergeant Oliver Sutherland . . . once known as Sean Dennis Georghegan, now studied that length of rope as the knot came untied and the settler stepped back against the fence.

But—for some reason this time the pony did not fling itself about wildly. It fought the bit as he yanked its head to the left but it obediently lurched into motion when the sergeant gently tapped his brass spurs into its flanks.

"I was chose for this mission," Sutherland proudly declared to the civilian as he rode out of the yard for the Bitterroot Trail. "So . . . it's up to me."

He grimaced in pain as every hammering step felt like a cold blast of agony from his tailbone all the way up to the crown of his skull. Yanking up a generous dose of double-riveted courage from some secret well, the sergeant pushed on up the valley, the Bitterroot and Sapphire mountain ranges looming higher and higher, closer, too.

And him sittin' on busted j'ints, blackened with a Welsh miner's crop of bruises, perched on top of the most unlikely of trail horses he'd ever dared to ride!

From time to time, Sutherland clenched his eyes shut and reminded himself, muttering under his breath, "It . . . it's up to me. G-gotta find Gibbon's men afore they lay into that camp of murderin' hostiles."

Chapter Forty-Nine

August 6–7, 1877

Monday, August 6, 1877

Dear Mamma,

It always does seem as if everything goes wrong when the Doctor is away. Both children are just a little sick, just enough to make them fretful and worry me. I was awake with them many times last night. They seem better this morning and are playing, but my one wish is that the war was over and John home again.

Afternoon

Dr. Sternberg just came in to see the children. They are not well, either of them, and it is so hard to have them get this way when John is away . . .

You should see some of the Indian garments that were taken from the camp the day of the battle when the Indians left in such a hurry. They are made of beautifully tanned skin, soft as chamois skin, and cut something like we used to cut our paper dollie dresses. The bottom is fringed, and the body part down to the waist is heavily beaded. You never saw such bead work, and the beads make them so heavy. These, of course, are the costumes for grand occasions. One of them I could not lift. Then they have leggings to match, and if it is a chief or big man, they have an outfit for his horse of the same style. Doctor Sternberg is an enthusiast on the subject of collecting curiosities, and he purchased from the men who had gotten them four or five of these garments. For one he gave ten dollars in coin, and for another with a horse fixing, 25 dollars. So you can see, they must be handsome . . .

Your affectionate daughter,
E. L. FitzGerald

BY TELEGRAPH

—

THE INDIANS.

—

Late News from Joseph and His Brethren: They Will Fight.

SAN FRANCISCO, August 4.—A press dispatch from Lewiston, August 1st says: Yesterday Indians Joseph and his family, who have been with the people at Slate Creek all through the Indian troubles, and proved true and faithful to the whites, returned from Kamiah, where they had been sent to ascertain the movements of the hostiles. His squaw says the hostiles at Kamiah told her they were going across the mountains by the Lolo trail, with their stock and families and when they got there in a secure place they would return and fight the soldiers. She also states that before leaving Kamiah they went to a friendly Indian camp and drove off all the young squaws, beat them with clubs and forced them along, and many cattle also. They came back and robbed them of everything they could find, including all their horses of any value. She further states that the hostiles are to be reinforced by other Indians from the other side of the mountains when they return. Her statements are considered reliable by those who have known her. This morning Lieut. Wilmot with thirty men started to go across Salmon river to ascertain if any hostiles remain there. It has been reported for several days that a few had been seen in that direction, and the object is to hunt them out and destroy all their supplies. It is now believed by old acquaintances of Joseph, that he will put away in safety his stores and extra horses, and return to Comas prairie, returning by Elk City over the Pietee trails, which are much more easily traveled. The march will be made in about seven days. He has asserted his determination to burn the grain on the Comas prairie, and then arrange his plans to go to Willowa, and the opinion is prevalent that he will attack, before they break camp. Couriers say the hostiles have Mrs. Manuel with them as the property of a petty chief called Cucasenilo. Her sad story is familiar.

Camp on the East Lolo
20 miles from Missoula
August 7, 1877

Darling,

The last two days we have been in rather a handsome country, i.e., since we struck the eastern Lolo River, which is a tributary of the Bitter Root River. Last night we had the most picturesque camp I have ever seen—a very remarkable spot where there are 4 hot springs. The steam from them this morning rose up as if from a number of steam mills. I bathed my feet in one of them last night and found it as hot as I could bear comfortably. There was good trout fishing in the Lolo nearby, and Colonel Sanford and I got quite a fine string and had them for breakfast. Today we had a long hard march over the hill and got down on the Lolo again this evening for camp—and in a pretty place. Colonel Sanford and I again had some trout fishing.

We are 20 miles from Missoula, but we learn tonight that the Indians are about 60 miles off, and that General Gibbon is after them with about 200 infantry in wagons, and is within 30 miles of them. We are to push on tomorrow with the cavalry, with a view to overtake him.

The Indians were allowed to pass through this valley by the scalawag population that bought their stolen horses. And it is said some of them traded ammunition, powder, etc., to the redskins for their stolen property, gold dust, etc. We hear that several watches have been traded for by citizens of Missoula, and it is possible that Mr. Theller's watch may be recovered. Mr. Fletcher went into Missoula this morning, and Mr. Ebstein is to go in tomorrow, but our command, the cavalry, is to turn off in another direction about 10 miles this side of Missoula tomorrow. The artillery and infantry are nearly two days behind us, but General Howard and staff are now with the cavalry commands. It seems to me that things look as if we should have an end of it all in a few days or weeks, as the Indians will either be whipped or driven across the line into British possessions. The rumor is that Joseph has left White Bird and Looking Glass and is somewhere in the mountains by himself with his band.

Our poor animals are tired and considerably run down. Old Bill is but a shadow of what he was when I left Lapwai.

Well, Darling wife, how are my precious ones? What a happy hub you will have when his "footsteps homeward he hath turned." I hope you are well. I am and have been, and a large part of the time have rather enjoyed this nomadic life. Do you know, or rather, can you realize, that for nearly every morning of this month we have found ice in our wash basins and buckets? It is rather rough on us to be roused out of our warm beds at 3, 4, or 5 A.M. It almost "takes the hair off," as they say.

Your old husband,
John

AT TWO O'CLOCK ON THE AFTERNOON OF 4 AUGUST, Colonel John Gibbon had finally started his column away from the Missoula City post, his infantry rumbling south in those commandeered wagons, hurrying up the valley of the Bitterroot River in pursuit of the Nez Perce village. After pushing hard for more than twenty-five miles, at nine o'clock that night they went into bivouac opposite the community of Stevensville, camping on the southern outskirts of town located on the east side of the river. It was here that he and most of his officers were disgusted to learn for the first time how the civilians of the valley had bartered and traded with the hostiles as the overconfident Nez Perce moseyed south.

No matter, Gibbon thought. His men would put things right.

Including Sergeant Edward Page and those seven Fort Ellis troopers from the Second Cavalry who had joined G Company in its march over from the Gallatin Valley, Gibbon was now at the lead of fifteen officers and 146 enlisted men, in addition to a twelve-pound mountain howitzer mounted on a prairie carriage he managed to run across and commandeer at Fort Owen.

At dark that first evening of the pursuit, Gibbon rode over to the Flathead camp to have an audience with Charlot. The chief did not even give the officer the courtesy of inviting him into his lodge, much less offering to take part in the normal amenities of the pipe. And when the colonel asked for some Flathead to help H. S. Bostwick scout for his column, Charlot flatly refused.

"The Nez Perce have kept their promise," the chief's interpreter translated Charlot's words. "They did not start trouble in the valley. So I will honor my pledge to stay neutral."

Before departing their bivouac the morning of the fifth, Gibbon received word from Missoula City that as many as 150 civilians were already en route from Bannack City, Montana's first territorial capital, intending to head off the Nez Perce from the east. In addition, he took this opportunity to speak with Father Anthony Ravalli, a Catholic priest who had spent the last forty years ministering to those Flathead in the Bitterroot valley at St. Mary's Mission, erected just outside Stevensville.

"The Nez Perce are a very dangerous lot, Colonel," Ravalli declared dourly.

"That's why I intend to catch them just as soon as we can," Gibbon replied.

"How many soldiers are there with you?" the missionary asked.

Instantly suspicious that the priest might leak word concerning just how few soldiers he did have with him at present, Gibbon considered a small lie the most expedient route to take: "I have just over two hundred, Father."

Ravalli considered that, his brow creasing with worry. "Not enough," he remarked, grim lines crowfooting the corners of his eyes. "The Nez Perce boast of at least two hundred and sixty warriors, Colonel. They enjoy a reputation as splendid shots, besides being well armed and possessing plenty of ammunition."

So much for the priest's blessing.

That Sunday the colonel sent Howard his plea for 200 horsemen with civilian Joe Pardee and one of Charlot's Flathead, clearly not intending to await the reinforcements of that big column then somewhere in the Bitterroot Mountains. After turning those two couriers back for the Lolo, instead of delaying any longer Gibbon pushed his men up the valley, eventually encountering more than seventy-five volunteers from the Bitterroot settlements: a company of thirty-four who had ridden down from Stevensville under the leadership of "Captain" John B. Catlin and another forty-some who had come north from Corvallis under John L. Humble.

Upon catching up to Gibbon's column, Humble spared no effort to explain how he was personally opposed to chasing down the fleeing Nez Perce after reaching a peaceful accord with the Non-Treaty bands at Rawn's barricade. Catlin explained that although he was in favor of giving the Non-Treaty bands a fight, many of his men had their doubts about making war on those Indians who had kept their end of the Lolo agreement, passing peacefully through the Bitterroot.

Not only did many of the volunteers' Southern drawls*

---

*In his *Tough Trip Through Paradise*, frontiersman Andrew Garcia explained Gibbon's uneasiness: "One side of the Bitter Root valley was settled mostly by Missourians. The other side . . . mostly by Georgeians. So in all this bunch of Jeff Davis's Orphans, it could not be expected that their Civil War record, from a union man's point of view, was good."

make Yankee Gibbon a bit uncomfortable, but the colonel was taken aback, thinking it odd, even a bit amusing, that these men should vacillate in their loyalties the way they had over the past few days: Enthusiastically answering Rawn's call for volunteers when his soldiers headed up the Lolo to erect their barricade at the onset of troubles, those same citizens soon drifting off for their homes—Gibbon now bluntly told these seventy-five-some volunteers they had committed nothing less than outright desertion at the Lolo barricades—when it appeared the Nez Perce had given them a way to avoid a fight; later a few of the more enterprising civilians even pursuing the Nez Perce camp in wagons weighed down with trade goods so they could continue the profitable barter all the way up the Bitterroot valley.

Upon reaching Gibbon's troops, both companies of civilians had begun to grumble and argue with their elected "captains," Catlin, a steady-handed Civil War veteran who himself wanted to throw in with Gibbon's column while his volunteers were something less than enthusiastic, and John Humble, the leader who had openly argued with Captain Rawn's actions just before he and others abandoned the Lolo barricades.

It gave the colonel reason to question the volunteers' steadfastness. He was exasperated to see how these citizens ran hot and cold. Here, a matter of days after the barricade desertions and the scandal of trading with the enemy, these brave civilians were again offering their services to the army?

The colonel was dubious of the Missourians' intentions at best, if not outright scornful of their offer. So when Catlin and Humble formally presented themselves and their men, offering to join Gibbon's column, the colonel wagged his head.

"I prefer not to be encumbered with your company of volunteers," the colonel explained bluntly.

That chilly reception made no difference for the moment. Catlin, Humble, and their companies clung to the fringe of the column, refusing to be dissuaded and forced to turn around.

That afternoon of the fifth, the column rumbled past the small community of Corvallis, another fifteen miles up the valley, which boasted about one hundred inhabitants in 1877. When news of the Nez Perce escape from Idaho reached the Bitterroot, valley settlers had hastily built a fortress surrounded by twelve-foot-high sod walls, one hundred feet square, with interior rooms constructed of tents and canvas wagon covers, partially partitioned with rough-milled lumber. They named it Fort Skidaddle, since many of its occupants were settlers who had "skidaddled" from their native Missouri after suffering repeated attacks at the hands of Southern partisans before the bombardment of Fort Sumter, as well as harassment from Confederate soldiers during the Civil War.

Not much farther south, Gibbon's forces passed the much tinier settlement of Skalkaho,* where the eighty-some locals had constructed a small, crude stockade of rough timbers and sloping sod walls no more than five feet high. They christened the shabby affair Fort Run, because that's where their women and children would run in time of an Indian scare. But its sloping sod walls were so short that when the Nez Perce village marched past, more than two dozen warriors reined their ponies up to the top and peered down at the frightened families.

That night of the sixth they camped on Sleeping Child Creek, within hailing distance of the fort's walls.

Near noon of the following day, 6 August, after successively passing the ransacked houses belonging to a settler named Landrum, that of Alex Stewart, and even the cabin belonging to valley pioneer Joe Blodgett—who had enlisted at Corvallis as a volunteer and offered Gibbon his trail-scouting skills—the column discovered that volunteer Myron Lockwood's ranch house near the mouth of Rye

*"Sleeping Child" in Flathead.

Creek* had been vandalized worst of all. The structure itself had been gutted, every piece of furniture and china thrown into the yard, where it was broken, every tick, curtain, and pillow slashed with a knife. Lockwood wasn't the only civilian along who furiously gnashed his teeth at the wanton destruction, cussing the Nez Perce raiders in no uncertain terms now—especially when Lockwood discovered the warriors had left seven poor Indian ponies in his pasture to replace seven of his finest horses.

"That bunch of spavined cayuses are all sick and sore-mouthed, just plain used-up comin' over the Lolo!" the civilian yelped to Gibbon.

"I recommend that you file a complaint with Captain Rawn once the two of you return to the valley after we have subdued these predators, Mr. Lockwood." Gibbon brushed aside the vandalism he saw as a minor irritant when compared to the larger goal of stopping murderers, rapists, and thieves. "State the dollar amount of your loss, and I'm sure the Indian Bureau will consider your motion for recompense."

It was here that the volunteers held a heated argument among themselves on whether to go on or not, because they were low on provisions and many thought it better to return to their homes.

"Gather your volunteers," the colonel told Catlin and Humble. "I'll speak to them myself."

Minutes later when he stepped before the civilians, Gibbon said, "I want to assure you men that my soldiers will share their supplies with you, down to the last ration."

That got some of the heads nodding, a little of the gray worry draining from the faces. Gibbon continued, "And another thing I know I can assure you: We can give you a fight with these Nez Perces."

That singular remark elicited the first cheers and boisterous displays of the march, arising not only among the civilians but from all his soldiers as well.

---

*Approximately four miles south of present-day Darby, Montana.

"I plan to put these Nez Perces afoot," Gibbon explained as the crowd quieted. "So one last thing I can promise you civilians—you'll have all of the hostiles' ponies you can capture."

Setting off from that brief halt, Fort Shaw post guide H. S. Bostwick and local Joe Blodgett led them up toward the low saddle that would eventually carry them over to Ross's Hole.* On their rumbling journey up the twisting, torturous switchbacks in those wagons Gibbon and Kirkendall had commandeered from Missoula City civilians, the colonel and his men were suddenly struck with how the Nez Perce trail up the mountainside lacked a lot of those scars made by travois poles. Indeed, what they had been seeing at each of the enemy's camping grounds over the past two days was that the women weren't pulling along many drags burdened with heavy loads. Instead, the wide areas stripped of trees surrounding each new campground showed that the squaws were cutting down saplings and some lodgepole pine, leaving those temporary poles standing when they moved on come morning.

In the Hole, the colonel called "Captain" John Humble aside, asking him to take some of his locals and scout ahead.

"Scout how far ahead?" Humble sounded dubious.

"As far as is necessary to locate the enemy," Gibbon explained. "When you find them, engage and delay the village until I can catch up with my men."

Humble didn't give it much consideration. He wagged his head. "Don't think it's a good idea, General. Too damned risky."

"You're refusing to go?"

Humble hemmed and hawed, then said, "I'll supply four or five men, and you can furnish the same number of your soldiers. We can scout for the village, then send back a man to tell you where we've found them."

---

*Named for Alexander Ross (of the British Hudson's Bay Company of Adventurers), who first came here to trade with the Indians in the early days of the fur trade.

Gibbon was startled. "But you won't engage them, won't hold them till I can catch up with the rest of this command?"

"No, General," Humble eventually admitted. "I refuse to imperil my men on any such risky adventure."

Fuming, the colonel asked, "Do all your men feel the way you do, Mr. Humble?"

"They elected me as their leader, so I'm speaking for 'em—"

"Let's go have a talk with your . . . your outfit," Gibbon interrupted, turning aside.

He stomped over to the seventy-plus civilians who all got to their feet as the officer approached. Quickly he told the citizens of the conversation he just had about the scouting mission.

"I've been told you men would refuse to be part of such an important scout to find and hold down the enemy."

"General?" Myron Lockwood, the rancher whose house had been looted and stock stolen from his pastures, took a step forward, his eyes glowing with a fierce anger. It was clear he had undergone a change of heart. "I demand to see the color of the feller's hair who refused to go."

Before Gibbon had a chance to speak, John Humble stepped out from behind the colonel to say, "Mr. Lockwood, you better look at my hair. I am that man! If you choose to get into a scrap with those Indians, you will damn well know you have been somewhere!"

"It was you, Humble?" Lockwood took another step toward the man, his hands clenching.

Gibbon quickly moved in front of Humble. "Now's the time for all you men to decide on your own, or together, if you will continue with this army until we run the Nez Perce into the ground."

Those first moments were deathly quiet. Then Humble shuffled off to his horse tied nearby. Slowly, close to forty more civilians wordlessly went to their animals, too.

"Mr. Humble?"

The civilian leader turned before he climbed into the

stirrup. "This is as far as I propose to go with your army, General. I am not out to fight women and children." Immediately turning and rising to the saddle, Humble snubbed up his reins and concluded, "I am going home now. Any of you who want to come with me are welcome on the ride back to the Bitterroot. And those of my company who want to go on can throw in with Captain Catlin there."

For a few moments Gibbon watched Humble nervously shift in his saddle. When the man was sure no one else was about to join him, he turned and rode away, leading those forty-some for home.

The colonel waited a minute more, then turned to the thirty-five volunteers who would forge on. He sighed, "Let's get on the move."

As twilight deepened that evening of the seventh, making the narrow trail even more difficult to follow, the colonel ordered that camp be made there and then, just short of the summit of the divide. The site offered the men and stock no water to speak of.

"From the odometer I attached to a wheel on one of the wagons," Gibbon confided to Lieutenant James Bradley and the other officers, "it appears the hostiles are moving at a leisurely pace: no more than twelve to fourteen miles each day at the most."

"It won't take us long to overhaul them at the rate we're covering ground, sir," Bradley declared.

Gibbon looked at his most trusted lieutenant. "I intend to have this column march at least twice that distance every day from here on out until we catch up to the village. If my calculations are correct, we should accomplish that in as many as four days, perhaps no more than three at the most."

"From the summit of the pass ahead," Bradley explained, "we should be able to determine if the Nez Perce have turned south and are making for their homeland beyond the Salmon River Mountains in Idaho—or if they've turned east to the buffalo plains, where they repeatedly told the settlers they were headed."

Gibbon asked, "What's your instincts tell you they're going to do, Mr. Bradley?"

The lieutenant pointed toward the top of the divide. "Colonel—I'll bank a month's pay that Joseph and White Bird will take their families south and skedaddle for those mountains, where we'll have to pay the devil to ever get them out."

Chapter Fifty

Wa-Wa-Mai-Khal, 1877

It infuriated Looking Glass that these other chiefs should argue with him!

Who were they to carp and snipe at him anyway?

Hadn't they stirred up a hornets' nest all on their own—not listening to him from the very beginning of the troubles? Hadn't he told them they should do as he always had done: Simply stay out of the white man's way?

But when they went ahead with their foolish war, it had been like a kettle of bone soup suspended over a fire grown too hot—it boiled over, scalding Looking Glass's people, too, even though they had done everything they could to stay out of a war started by those who had no experience with war.

Looking Glass knew about war.

But these other chiefs who criticized him? Why, not one of them had fought against the mighty Blackfeet, or the Lakota on the plains of Montana Territory! Not like him, Rainbow, and Five Wounds—experienced war chiefs who regularly traveled to the buffalo country, where they would find themselves squarely in a disputed land, that country where the *E-sue-gha* held forth against stronger, more numerous tribes. No, none of these petty men arguing with him now knew anything of war!

But for some reason they prattled on like they knew everything better than Looking Glass.

Meopkowit! They are fools, he thought as he listened. Wasn't he the one who had led them to that victory after two days on the Clearwater? Wasn't he the one who had held forth and convinced the Non-Treaty bands they should leave Idaho country until the troubles cooled down? Wasn't he the chief who had ordered the raids on Kamiah and that scouting party along their back trail to delay the Treaty band traitors who were scouting for the *suapies*?

And wasn't Looking Glass the supreme chief who had toyed with the little soldier chief at the log barricades while they made ready to slip around the soldiers and Shadows in a maneuver of such genius that tribal historians would be singing his praises for generations to come?

In the end, wasn't it Looking Glass alone who was responsible for bringing the *Nee-Me-Poo* to the *Iskumtselalik Pah*, this Place of the Ground Squirrels,* this afternoon, a beautiful campsite where the People could rest themselves and their horses for a few days,** cut lodgepoles, and refresh their spirits before moving on to the buffalo country?

Why did these men of so little courage suddenly screw up enough bravery to dare ask that scouts be sent on their back trail now that they were nearing the western edge of buffalo country? To send back a party of young men simply to assure they were not being followed might well open the way for more stupid, foolish depredations against the settlers in the Bitterroot valley—perhaps even the thoughtless killing of any Shadows those scouts might run across. No, Looking Glass was still fuming at *Toohoolhoolzote*'s young vandals for what they had done to break his word to the white men. He refused to send back any scouts.

"Here we are safe!" he roared back at the *tewat*, Pile of Clouds. "That little chief and his few walking soldiers up at Missoula City are not foolish enough to follow us and make trouble now!"

Looking Glass knew only too well how this respected shaman's premonitions were valued. Pile of Clouds might

---

*In naming this place after a ground squirrel, the Nez Perce more specifically made reference to a smaller animal called a picket pin, due to the fact that when the tiny, thin animal stands at watchful attention beside its burrow, it looked just like the wooden picket pin a man would use to anchor his horse.

**The Non-Treaty bands arrived in the valley of the Big Hole on the afternoon of August 7, and would stay again the night of the eighth—relaxed and celebratory up to the fateful morning of August 9.

well start a mindless stampede; then nothing would stop them. So he sneered a little at the taller, younger man. "Maybe you are afraid of those fools we cowered and shamed at the log-and-hole fort?"*

"I am not afraid of any Shadow we passed to reach this place," Pile of Clouds answered defensively. "I am only afraid of . . . of—"

"Of *what?*" Looking Glass demanded, smelling the scent of blood from his adversary.

The *tewat* sighed. "I am only afraid of those white men I *cannot* see."

Looking Glass glanced around the crowd, quickly studying the faces of the other leaders; then his eyes narrowed on Pile of Clouds once more. "If you are so frightened, perhaps you should make a *tewat* or chief out of one of your brave fighting men. Then I would have no doubts that I am supported as we take our families into the land of the *E-sue-gha*."

Pile of Clouds blanched at the chief's slur on his courage. "When did you start turning your nose up at another man's medicine?"

Looking Glass scoffed at that transparent boast, "M-medicine?"

"My medicine has told me—not once, but twice!" the shaman asserted, waving his arm back up the hillside they had just descended. "Death is behind us! I am certain of that. We must hurry—there is no time to cut lodgepoles here. We must hurry away!"

Before Looking Glass could respond, even the elderly White Bird spoke of his doubts. "Why do you allow the women time here so they can drag lodgepoles from this place, Looking Glass? We should be hurrying away without lodgepoles!"

"We have only arrived at this place," Looking Glass's tone softened, became more fatherly. Better that the Non-Treaty bands see him as a benevolent leader rather than

---

*Rawn's Fort Fizzle in the Lolo Canyon.

despotic over the other chiefs. "Can't you see that we have left behind the war and the soldiers? Far behind us are the Shadows who wanted to do us great harm. All of that—left behind in Idaho country. There is no cause for alarm. Cut-Off Arm sits on his rump and does nothing. The white men who wished us evil are back there in Idaho country with his army, too."

"We can't wait!" Pile of Clouds repeated. "We must hurry away—"

"No," Looking Glass snapped. "We will stay here so the women can cut poles for the lodges. I will not have us arrive in the land of the *E-sue-gha* looking as if we are some poor relations without lodges!"

Many of the older women murmured their agreement with that on the fringes of that crowd gathering around the headmen.

"Here we will begin to regain our greatness." Looking Glass warmed to his oratory and the support of his people. "Here we will eat from the fat of the land and drink this good water. And here tomorrow night we will celebrate, dance and sing . . . for we have left the war far, far behind us."

Both upstream and down-, the slopes west of camp were thickly timbered. Only the hillside immediately across from the village stood barren of evergreens, covered only by sage and tall grass—except for a pair of immense fir trees that seemed to stand as sentinels near the base of the hillside. It was there the boys herded most of the more than two thousand horses.

Stopping at this traditional camping ground located in the southwestern edge of a narrow valley nestled between high mountain ranges, they did indeed have here everything they needed in a camp while they laid over for a few days to rest and recruit themselves before continuing on to the *E-sue-gha* country. Besides sweet, cool water of both the creek they had followed from the pass down to the valley,*

---

*Today's Trail Creek.

as well as the bigger stream it joined at the bottom of the hillside,* both of which were lined with dense thickets of head-high willow, the People had an abundance of good grass for the horses they had harried through the rigors of that mountain passage. What with the short marches they had been making ever since leaving those recuperative hot springs on this side of the pass, the spirit of every man, woman, and child had been soaring. Couldn't the other chiefs and *tewats* see what the leisurely pace had accomplished? Everyone but those complainers realized in their bones that they had left the fighting behind in Idaho country.

Sensing no threat from those Shadows and *suapies* they had tricked on Lolo Creek, Looking Glass and his leaders did not feel as if they should ring sentries around their camp, especially at night. Oh, they did know that the little soldier chief had spies following them and that some of the Bitterroot settlers were surely keeping an eye on the People's movements from site to site. But no one would be sneaking up on them, because the only Shadows who had worked for the *Nee-Me-Poo*'s destruction were a long, long way behind, back over a tall string of rugged mountains!

Not that they hadn't spotted a white man or two lurking on the hillside, and even the outskirts, of this new camp—spying on the *Nee-Me-Poo*, keeping the little soldier chief informed of everything. Those men seen prowling the fringes of the hills were of little consequence, Looking Glass told the other chiefs. The very fact that there were spies keeping an eye on their village was as good an argument as any that the Shadows did not intend to attack. Only to follow and watch.

So the camp making continued with renewed enthusiasm. Spread out along the east bank of the little river, eighty-nine lodges were eventually raised, their brown cones stark against the blue of that late-summer sky, arrayed in an irregular V formation, its apex pointed down-

---

*Today's Ruby Creek, which, with Trail Creek, forms the North Fork of the Big Hole River.

stream, toward the north. Between the camp and the base of that timbered mountainside flowed the wide, deep, gurgling creek where the children went to play, where the women bathed the tiny infants newly born during this difficult passage out of a troubled land, on to a life that now held nothing but promise for the *Nee-Me-Poo*.

With a breast-swelling pride, Looking Glass realized that as the women cut and dried new poles from those forests on the surrounding slopes, this would be one of the largest, happiest gatherings the Non-Treaty bands had experienced in the recent past. As a shaft of bright light suddenly burst upon the meadow, he was forced to squint. The high, thin rain clouds were breaking up. Then he remembered: Over here on this eastern side of the mountains, the sun always shone a little more strongly. There were fewer clouds to mar its intensity than there were on the west side of the Bitterroot range. It gave his heart a strong feeling to look over these seventy-seven lodges who had followed him over from Idaho country, good, too, in gazing upon those twelve lodges under Eagle-from-the-Light who had joined up in the Bitterroot valley.

Besides the women and children who waded across the stream and started up the slopes with their axes to chop down new lodgepoles, other women walked east from camp toward a half-mile of open ground fringed on the east by a low plateau, carrying their fire-hardened digging sticks—there to jab into the earth for the tasty camas roots in that *tegpeem*, an open meadow the *Nee-Me-Poo* called "a flat place of good grass." Riding north and south from camp, small hunting parties of men went in search of deer, elk, and especially antelope that would sizzle over the fires this first night at *Iskumtselalik Pah*. The People did not find antelope west in their old homeland.

Yes—Looking Glass thought—he would have to announce the dance he would hold tomorrow evening after everyone was settled in at this peaceful place. Such festivities would make his people even happier because it would be the first celebration of any kind since the war began and they started on their flight away from their old homeland.

It was about time that the Non-Treaty bands began their new life here in the buffalo country with a grand feast, Looking Glass decided—singing and dancing into the night!

It was here that the *Nee-Me-Poo* could begin to celebrate their victory over the white man!

BY TELEGRAPH

—

A Thrilling Chapter of Secret
Political History.

—

A Chicago Free Love Murderer Acquitted.

—

No more Arms to be Sold to
the Indians.

—

MONTANA.

—

Latest from the Indian War.

HELENA, August 7.—Advices from Missoula, up to August 6, say General Gibbon, with 200 regulars*— infantry, in wagons—left Missoula post to follow the hostiles at 1 p.m. Saturday. He designed making thirty-five miles a day. The hostiles were at Doolittle's ranch on [Sunday] night, seventy-five miles from Missoula and within ten miles of the trail to Ross Hole. Charlos declined to lend his warriors to General Gibbon, but will find the Nez Perces on his own account. The hostiles were moving with more celerity Friday. Stevensville had

—

*Do you remember this figure? It did not come from the actual number of soldiers Gibbon had along. Instead, this was the exact number he had told Father Anthony Ravalli he had with him back on August 5. The priest must have been the source for this news story!

> advices Saturday that 100 or 150 men were coming from Bannock to intercept the Indians. Howard has not heard from Lent, the courier. He had not returned on Sunday and anxiety was felt for him, as two Nez Perces had come over the trail. A considerable number of Missoula county volunteers are prepared to advance, but are independent of the regulars.

"I respectfully request the honor of leading this scout, sir," asked Lieutenant James H. Bradley, the officer who moments ago had suggested just such a reconnaissance to catch up to the hostile village.

"It is yours to lead, without question," Colonel John Gibbon replied that twilight of 7 August. "Mounted, of course. Take Lieutenant Jacobs with you, along with sixty picked men—soldiers and volunteers both—and do your best to overhaul the Nez Perce before dawn."

"Once we've made contact, what are your orders?" Bradley inquired.

"Send word back as quickly as possible."

"Am I to engage the Nez Perce, Colonel?"

"By all means. Stampede their horses. Impede their escape." Gibbon ground a fist into an open palm. "Immobilize their village and hinder their retreat until I can come up with the rest of the outfit."

Everything they had seen and heard as they hurried up the Bitterroot valley confirmed that the Nez Perce could boast somewhere in the neighborhood of 250 fighting men.* In addition, Gibbon's men had come to realize the village was moving slowly, unconcerned and perhaps completely unaware that the army was on their back trail . . .

---

*John Deschamps, a valley volunteer now with Gibbon, had counted 250 guns among the Non-Treaty bands and two-thousand-plus horses in their herd, some of which were fine "American" horses bearing their brands. One of the Nez Perce had tried to interest Deschamps in buying a gold watch with the former owner's name engraved inside, for the paltry sum of thirty dollars!

and closing fast. The distance from campsite to campsite was extremely short, indicating the village was making only brief migrations each day—perhaps only to find new forage for their horse herd. Gibbon and his officers determined that they could cover twice as much ground as the Nez Perce were each day—perhaps three times more. In that way, the Seventh Infantry and those few Second Cavalry troopers along would catch up to and surprise the enemy in less than half a week.

In fact, right now it appeared the hostiles were no more than a day and a half away! Perhaps as little as one long day's march to bring them to battle.

So now was clearly the time to go in search of the enemy. To account for Joseph's position and his strengths. To determine how best to attack the Non-Treaty stronghold—and send back word to Gibbon once contact had been made.

One thing was for sure as Bradley and First Lieutenant Joshua W. Jacobs led their sixty men into the dim light of dusk, clambering over a maze of downed timber for that two miles up to the summit: the Nez Perce hadn't turned aside with designs on doubling back for Idaho and their old haunts in the Salmon River country. They had clearly bypassed the route they would have taken if they had intended to return to their homeland.* It was abundantly clear that Joseph's warriors and their families had no intention of reclaiming their ancient homes. If Gibbon didn't stop them here and now, the Nez Perce could well be free to scatter, roaming and pillaging at will across Montana Territory—igniting a much farther-reaching war than General O. O. Howard had failed to put out back in Idaho.

Through the night of the seventh and into dawn's earliest light on the eighth of August, Bradley and Jacobs struggled ahead on horseback, a little quicker now that their scouting force could begin to see just where it was going. From the summit of the divide the trail angled down a gentle incline

---

*Through present-day Nez Perce Pass, in the extreme southwestern corner of Montana.

for about a mile, where it finally reached the headwaters of Trail Creek. From there trail guide Blodgett led them through some increasingly rough country, staying with the banks of that stream, forced to slog through boggy mires where Trail Creek meandered and cross from bank to bank more than fifty times in their descent.

Down, down, down now, accompanied by the first telltale indication of a coming sunrise—descending toward that high mountain valley a few of the Bitterroot civilians along were calling the Big Hole. Still no sign of the village. Not a sound or a smell, much less a sighting of fire smoke or smudge of trail dust rising from the plain below.

"They aren't where we figured we'd discover them," Bradley grumbled in dismay as he threw up his arm and ordered a halt to those soldiers and Catlin's civilians following the two of them.

"We've got to press on till we find them," Jacobs suggested.

"There never was any question of that!" Bradley replied peevishly, then instantly felt bad for snapping. "I figured we'd spot their camp right down there, where you can see the head of that valley. But," and he sighed, "their trail leads around the brow of these heights, angling left instead of dropping directly onto the valley floor. Damn, Jacobs—if we don't find that village soon, it's going to take even longer than we calculated for the rest of Colonel Gibbon's forces to catch up."

Jacobs spoke softly, "Do you think we should give the mounts a brief rest here?"

"No," and Bradley shook his head emphatically. "They'll have plenty of time to rest after we've caught up to the village and run off their horses—"

"L-Lieutenant! Lieutenant Bradley!"

He whirled on his heels, finding John B. Catlin, Joe Blodgett, and a handful of Bitterroot volunteers weaving their horses through the timber in their direction. Bradley brought up his long Springfield rifle, half-expecting there to be bullets accompanying the harried civilians, what with the dire expressions on their flushed and mottled faces.

"The hostiles?" he asked Catlin, lunging out to grab the bridle on the leader's horse.

Catlin gulped breathlessly, "We saw 'em."

A lump of apprehension rose in Bradley's throat. "They see you?"

"Don't think so," Catlin said too quickly. Then his eyes flicked away. "I . . . I dunno. Maybeso."

Letting go of Catlin's bridle, Bradley asked, "You were shot at?"

"No."

"They follow you?"

With a shake of his head, the civilian again answered, "No. If they saw us, they let us go 'thout any trouble."

"How far are they?"

"Not far at all, Lieutenant," Catlin replied with a swallow. Then the Civil War veteran said, "On round the gentle side of this hill, you'll hear voices, laughing, too. And the sound of chopping wood."

"Sergeant Wilson, you and Mr. Catlin see the men have their breakfast now."

"Yes, sir."

Then Bradley looked at Jacobs and Corporal Socrates Drummond. "The two of you, come with me on foot. We'll go see for ourselves."

When they reached the last of the thick timber, the lieutenant halted the pair. Quickly his eyes searched the trees at the edge of the grassy slope.

"Wait right here with our horses and guns, Corporal. The lieutenant and I are going for a climb."

Stripping off his blue wool tunic, the lieutenant then rebuckled his gun belt around his waist, and they started up the tree, hand and foot, slowly working this way and that around the thick trunk until their heads popped above the uppermost branches. It provided a perfect view, placing them atop the emerald evergreen canopy—giving the lieutenants a chance to gaze unimpeded over the entire vista as the narrow valley of the Big Hole stretched away from them some ten miles to the east.

"Jesus," Jacobs whispered.

Not only did the telltale sounds of chopping and women's voices drift up to him from below and far to the left, but he could also see the smudge of smoke from their many fires, the dust from the hooves of the ponies the young men were racing on the flat beyond the village, along with hearing the chatter of those small boys he spotted chasing one another through the horse-high willow growing along the creek that gurgled at the base of the slope right below him. Other youngsters sat atop their ponies, watching over the horse herd. More than a hundred warriors lazed about in the sunny camp. Women pitched tepees here or there; others dragged poles across the creek or prepared a midday meal over their fires.

His mind quickly turning like a steam-driven flywheel, Bradley began calculating the distance he had covered since separating from Gibbon, working over the hours it would take those foot soldiers in their wagons, pulled by the weary teams laboring up the divide, to reach the headwaters of Trail Creek before they could ever begin to work their way down to this spot. Only if those foot soldiers left the wagons behind . . .

"Come on," he whispered to Jacobs.

They scrambled down the limbs like a pair of schoolboys, exuberantly leaping the last five feet to the ground before trudging uphill to Drummond, waving for him to remount and follow rather than chancing any more words on the hillside. Surprise was of the utmost concern now. Surprise—that most fragile of military commodities.

Bradley threaded his way in and out of the trees, climbing slightly, following his own back trail to where he had left Blodgett, Catlin, and his sixty men. And as his horse huffed across the grassy hillside, he began to formulate the terse note he would send back to the colonel somewhere far above them this morning—perhaps still on the other side of the pass as the sun came up bold and brassy, striking the western slopes of the Big Hole. His heart sank as he recognized that it was too late for his small detachment to run off the horse herd and harry the village this day. The others were too far in the rear for that.

They would have to wait now, he would write Gibbon. Wait for the general to bring up his entire column before they would jump the enemy.

When that dispatch was written and the courier on his way, the lieutenant decided he would lead his advance detachment down this trail, to the very edge of that stand of timber where he had spied on the Nez Perce camp.

And there they would lie in wait for the arrival of Colonel John Gibbon—who would lead the rest of the Seventh Infantry when he unleashed all bloody thunder on that unsuspecting village.

CHAPTER FIFTY-ONE

AUGUST 7–8, 1877

AN HOUR BEFORE DAWN ON THE MORNING OF 7 AUGUST, their ninth day since departing Kamiah Crossing, General Oliver O. Howard had asked the tall frontiersman Joe Pardee to guide his aide-de-camp, First Lieutenant Robert H. Fletcher, and correspondent Thomas Sutherland down the Lolo to the valley below, from there to escort them north to Missoula City as quickly as they could ride without endangering their mounts. Fletcher, acting quartermaster for the column, carried writs to purchase what additional supplies were needed to see Howard's column through to the end of the chase.

At this point, they all had a feeling—admittedly something more than a mere hope—that the campaign was nearing its end.

By 9:00 A.M. when the command reached those log breastworks erected by Captain Charles Rawn's regulars and volunteers, Howard felt unduly disgusted, believing the Nez Perce War should have bloody well ended right there.*

"Over there, General," explained Joe Baker, one of the few citizens who rode at the head of the column, "you can see where Joseph's hostiles turned off to the north and circled around the barricades by going up that ridge."

"Joseph was too smart for them," commented Lieutenant C. E. S. Wood.

"Maybe they believed they could trust Looking Glass,"

---

*Even at this early date, the inaction of Rawn's soldiers and the wholesale desertions from the barricades by the valley citizens, along with the fact that the Non-Treaty bands were able to slip around the barricade without so much as an attempt made to stop them, were proving to be fodder for vehement editorials across the region. Rawn's log-and-rifle-pit structure erected across that narrow part of the Lolo Canyon was becoming known as Fort Fizzle.

Baker voiced the civilian point of view. "From what I hear, he's always been a good Indian when he's in the Bitterroot country."

Howard squinted beneath the high, intense sunlight, his eyes tracing that narrowing trail as it disappeared up the grassy hillside, looping behind the rounded hills far above Rawn's fortress, beyond the effective range of an army Springfield. *Joseph never should have gotten around them. How in blazes did he do this?* the general brooded, ruminating on just how many times the wily chieftain had outwitted him. Surely that *Wallowa* leader had to be one of the most talented military strategists Oliver Otis Howard had ever confronted on any battlefield.

"How far to the Bitterroot valley itself?" he asked of those who had joined him during this brief halt at the barricades.

Baker, who had made the crossing between Montana and Idaho territories many times, answered, "Not far, General. A few more miles is all."

Later that afternoon, when they did reach the mouth of Lolo Creek, Howard called for a halt to rest the men and graze the animals while he composed a short dispatch to Colonel Frank Wheaton, to be carried north to the Mullan Road, thence west, by two civilians from Idaho. He ordered the campaign's left column to shorten its daily marches until Wheaton would next hear from Howard about the possibility of returning to Lewiston, Idaho. "You may not be obliged to come through to Montana,"* the general wrote.

Because Division Commander McDowell in Portland had ordered Captain Cushing's and Captain Edward Field's batteries of the Fourth U. S. Artillery back to their stations days before Howard got around to starting east on the Lolo Trail and since Oliver could no longer justify needing the batteries because he was now *behind* the action, he separated those two units from his command at this point in the

---

*In fact, Wheaton's left column did not reach Spokane Falls in Washington Territory until August 10.

chase, ordering them on to Deer Lodge, from whence they would march south to reach the railhead at Corrine, Utah. From there they would travel in boxcars back to San Francisco. At the moment, however, both batteries were more than two days behind Howard, along with the infantry still negotiating the Lolo Trail.

Before he was finished composing his dispatch, Quartermaster Fletcher and Sutherland showed up at the head of a string of wagons the lieutenant had commandeered in Missoula City. Howard now had the supplies he hoped would allow him to catch Gibbon, who must surely be closing the gap on the Nez Perce.

"AWAKE! Awake! All the People must listen to the contents of my shaking heart!"

At the old warrior's cry Yellow Wolf sat upright, the single blanket sliding off his bare shoulder in the dim gray light of dawn. He squinted, blinked, then rubbed his gritty eyes with the heels of both hands. Last night, he and other young men and women had stayed up, dancing, singing, talking of sweet things in their future around the fire until well past the setting of the moon. He had been asleep no more than two hours at the most—

"Awake!" Lone Bird's voice crackled even closer as the old warrior emerged through the nearby lodges, his pony slowly carrying him toward that scattering of blanket bowers where many of the young men slept away from their families now that they were of an age to marry . . . of the age to become fighters.

Kicking the blanket from his legs, Yellow Wolf stood and darted unsteadily toward the brave warrior. Many others were emerging from their bowers now to listen to the warrior who had first given them warning at the Medicine Tree.

"I am awake, Lone Bird," Yellow Wolf muttered as he approached the horseman. "What say you now so early on a quiet morning?"

"This quiet will not last, Yellow Wolf!" Lone Bird announced as he eased back on the single buffalo-hair rein tied around his pony's lower jaw. The animal stopped.

More and more people gathered, still half-asleep, a murmur growing like an autumn brook as they emerged from their blankets and robes into the misty morning air, so damp and chill it penetrated to the bone.

Looking Glass suddenly appeared scurrying around the side of a lodge, looking perturbed. "Lone Bird—"

"My shaking heart tells me something, Chief Looking Glass," Lone Bird interrupted. "Listen again to my warning, for my words do not come easy."

"What warning?" demanded *Ollokot* as he pushed through the forming crowd and laid his hand on the older warrior's knee.

"Again I have been told, as I was at the Medicine Tree: The eyes in this heart of mine say trouble and death will overtake us if we make no hurry through this land," Lone Bird pronounced.

Looking Glass snorted a mirthless laugh. "We've heard your foolish talk before!"

"My heart does not regard it as foolish!" Lone Bird snapped. "I have never been one to talk of things that never came true." His eyes turned, glaring into the face of the *Wallowa* war chief. "You know that, *Ollokot*."

"Yes, I trust the eye of your heart, trust what it can see," *Ollokot* replied, his hand sliding from Lone Bird's knee.

"I cannot smother, I cannot hide, what my heart sees!" Lone Bird announced, his deep voice rattling over them all as if by the same thunder of the white man's throaty cannon. "I am commanded to speak what is revealed to me."

"What would you have us do?" White Bird asked, the crowd parting as he stepped into that tight circle gathered round Lone Bird.

"Let us be gone to the buffalo country, if that is where we are bound, you chiefs," Lone Bird demanded as he tapped his bare heels into the sides of his pony and moved into the crowd. "Let us be gone from this place. As quickly as the women can take down the lodges and pack the travois, let us be gone from the trouble and death that is already nipping at our heels."

For long moments Yellow Wolf watched the old warrior's back as Lone Bird's pony carried him away. That's when he recognized the face of Burning Coals, known as *Semu*, a man rich in horses. "Come," he said, tapping the arm of his friend *Seeyakoon Ilppilp*, the one called Red Spy.

Trotting over to the wealthy man, Yellow Wolf begged, "Burning Coals, please let me and my friend borrow two of your fastest horses—"

"You have horses of your own," Burning Coals responded, gazing down his expansive nose at the young warriors. "Why would I loan you two of mine?"

"Everyone knows you have the finest—the fastest—horses in all the bands," Yellow Wolf praised, hoping the compliment would seal the loan. "I grow concerned by these warnings from Lone Bird's lips."

"He is just a man given to unfounded fears," Burning Coals sneered, waving off argument.

"We should see for ourselves," Red Spy admitted. "Your horses are best for a hard scout up our back trail."

"Scout? Up our back trail?" echoed Burning Coals. "No. I will not let you use up my horses for that. They are too fine for the likes of you and your friends, Yellow Wolf. Go somewhere else to get horses to carry you on your fool's errand!"

"Even *Wottolen*, a man with strong powers, dreamed yesterday of soldiers!" Yellow Wolf argued in disbelief. "Surely you cannot dispute the medicine of *Wottolen!*"

Burning Coals turned away without a word, no more than a smug arrogance on his face as he waddled off.

"Go hunting, Yellow Wolf. There won't be any more fighting. I have seen it."

He twisted suddenly, finding the eyes of White Bull staring into his like two-day-old embers.

"You have seen this in a vision of your own?" Yellow Wolf asked. "A vision as powerful as that of *Wottolen* or Lone Bird?"

This loyal supporter of Looking Glass shook his head. "Fighting is over, young man. The war is done—war is far, far behind us now. Go hunting and think no more of war."

Many of the young men did just that. Quickly their thoughts shifted from making that scout to hunting the swift antelope. Children shuffled off in giddy play. Some of the women went back to their knees, digging the big, shallow pits they would line with heated rocks and grass, before covering the camas roots with more grass and letting them steam overnight. To be good, camas had to bake in the heated ground until the following morning.

As the crowd dispersed, their feet and lower legs kicking up swirls of ground fog here in the bottoms near the twisting creek, Yellow Wolf's gaze was drawn up the hillside, there to the south and west—across the stream, to the patches of dark timber . . . then back along the trail they had followed down from the high pass to reach this campground.

Place of the Ground Squirrels.

Realizing his own heart was sorely troubled. This was not a place of peace any longer. Too many upsetting visions already. As much as he tried to squeeze the dark, somber thoughts out of his mind, one question repeatedly floated to the surface.

If they had actually left the war behind them . . . then what trouble and death could be racing up on their back trail?

AT 5:00 A.M., just as soon as it was light enough to travel that dawn of the eighth, Colonel John Gibbon had stirred his men from their blankets and pushed ahead. Word was they had a little over two miles before reaching the pass. One way or the other—with mountain travel or the possibility of battle—they had a long day ahead of them. But as they put hour after hour behind them, Gibbon's hope that they would be able to launch an attack on the hostile camp this Wednesday faded.

During the first two hours it took to cover no more than a half-mile, the ordeal of wrestling the wagons and their teams over the downed timber, fighting their way up the ungraded slope, was excruciatingly slow. After that, the struggle up the next mile and a half of rugged slope to the top became all but unendurable. His civilian volunteers and soldiers alike stripped off tunics and coats in the high-altitude August heat, sweating as they double-hitched the teams and attached draglines to each of the wagons, so the men themselves could assist the draft animals in yanking one heavy vehicle at a time toward the pass, managing each foot of elevation only under the most extreme exertion. Grunting, sweating, cursing, they purchased another yard of the trail, rarely looking back down the slope to where they had started their climb . . . never, never looking up the hill to where they needed to will these wagons.

It would be small wonder, Gibbon brooded from atop his gray charger, that the Nez Perce didn't hear his army coming—what with all the cussing and pained yelps from both men and draft teams alike.

Just before one o'clock, as the hot sun sulled overhead like a stubborn mule and they reached the high, grassy divide* that meant the trail was all downhill from there on out, one of the advance men hollered that a rider was coming in. Gibbon's heart leaped, wanting to hope—not daring to let that hope show on his face—as he watched the horseman in blue rein up before him, salute, then reach inside his sweat-stained fatigue blouse.

"With Lieutenant Bradley's compliments, sir!"

Snatching the folded paper from the corporal's hand, Gibbon exclaimed, "He's spotted the Indians—this has to mean he's found their camp!"

"Yes, sir," the soldier answered as Gibbon tore open the dispatch and his eyes eagerly raced over Bradley's scrawl.

> Camp . . . horse herd . . . valley . . . will remain in hiding and await your arrival with the command.

---

*Today's aptly named Gibbon Pass.

His heart rising to his throat, the colonel's eyes misted. He would be the commander in at the kill. Howard was far behind. If any civilians from Bannack or Virginia City were coming west, they were still too damned far away to play any role in the coming fight. Gibbon squinted into the bright sun a moment, measuring what they had left of daylight.

Then he turned back to his company commanders, the half-circle of them like expectant actors awaiting their cue offstage. "We will leave the wagon train here to continue at its own speed."

"You want us to follow your trail, General?" Hugh Kirkendall asked.

Gibbon's eyes found his wagon master. "Yes, you must redouble your efforts to follow along as quickly as the animals and conditions will allow. The rest of us will push forward on foot with all possible dispatch. Bradley's found the village in the valley below us. We must . . . no, we *will* do everything in our power to reach his scouts before dusk."

"An attack at dawn, Colonel?" asked Captain James M. W. Sanno, commander of G Company.

"Yes, Captain," Gibbon said as he stuffed Bradley's note inside his own damp tunic. "We engage Joseph's warriors at first light."

"*TANANISA*!"

Shore Crossing bolted upright as he cursed, shaking like a leaf, sweating as if he had been lying out in the sun instead of sleeping in the shade of his wife's lodge, a gentle breeze wafting beneath the sides of the lodgeskins she had rolled up earlier that morning.

"What is it, my husband?" she asked, settling beside him on the robes.

For a moment he looked at her face, his eyes falling to glance at her swelling breasts, then staring at that rounded mound of a belly beneath her buckskin overshirt. She carried his child inside. In four more moons, no more than that, she would give him his first child.

And for that he resented her. When her time came he would not only be her husband, but he would be a father. He was not old enough to settle down with one woman and to make a family. He wanted other women—especially the sloe-eyed girl who watched him whenever he paraded about the camp or rode up and down the flank of their march coming out of Idaho country. He resented his wife for being here now, for carrying his child, for standing in his way of happiness.

"Leave me be!" he snarled, pushing her aside roughly as he kicked his way off the heavy wool blanket.

He heard her grunt in shock as she tumbled aside and he rose there beside the low fire. Like a quick flare of lightning he whirled on her, pointing his finger at her with an outstretched arm.

"You will be happy one day very soon, woman!" he growled. "I will be dead and you will have all this to yourself!"

"You are all that makes me happy!" she cried to him, both hands held up, imploring him as he escaped through the open doorway.

As he stood there, his eyes adjusting to the bright afternoon light, he looked this way and that, seeing how many cones of lodgepoles stood drying without any hide covers. Then he heard her begin to sob. Shore Crossing stopped, took a deep breath, then steeled his heart. He simply must not let her touch him there. His days were numbered. Perhaps no more than hours now. His dream foretold the coming of the end.

Holding his arms to the sky, Shore Crossing raised his voice to those at the middle of the village.

"My brothers! My sisters! Listen to my dream! Listen to the vision in my heart when I awakened moments ago!"

He waited a few breaths as the murmur grew into a loud cacophony, as footsteps and hoofbeats drew near. Men, women, and children came—like the young babe he would never hold on his lap or bounce on his knee. He resented his wife for getting herself with child . . . because now he would never know if she carried a boy or a girl. If it would survive the coming horror.

An old woman's voice called from the crowd, "What do you have to tell us, *Wahlitits*?"

"Yes, you are a brave fighter," White Bird said as he stepped to the fore of the crowd. "You were one of the Red Coats who started this war, one of the Red Coats who made the bravery runs past the soldiers who came to attack us at Lahmotta in the first battle. Tell us of your dream."

He took a breath. "In the dream that awakened me now, I saw myself killed!"

The crowd went to talking among themselves, a dull roar that seemed to crash about his ears. Some of the chiefs raised their arms, demanding silence from the hundreds.

White Bird prodded, "Continue, Shore Crossing."

"I will be killed soon—I saw this in my dream. For this I do not care. I am willing to die. But, before I am killed, I will kill some soldiers!"

"I will kill some soldiers, too!" cried Red Moccasin Tops, Shore Crossing's best friend, as he lunged through the fringes of the crowd.

Wahlitits laid his hand on his friend's shoulder. Together they had started this war against the Shadows, killing four white men on the Salmon River. Together they had raced back and forth across the front of *suapies* at the White Bird fight.

"I shall not turn back from the death that is coming my way!" Shore Crossing announced in a firm voice, finding that this knowledge that death was coming gave him a peace he had never known before.

"And I shall be at your side when the soldiers come to kill you!" Red Moccasin Tops roared.

As he slowly swept his arm across the gathered hundreds, Shore Crossing's eyes touched one warrior after another, one woman after another . . . until he found his wife's face, her eyes swollen and red from crying.

With his agonized heart swelling in his breast, *Wahlitits* warned, "I tell you this from my dream—there will be tears in many, many eyes . . . for most of us are going to *die!*"

Chapter Fifty-Two

August 8–9, 1877

How colonel John Gibbon wished Bradley had reached the Nez Perce camp before dawn that eighth day of August so the lieutenant could have initiated his preemptory attack and driven off the horse herd.

But from Bradley's report he had found the village situated a bit farther than where they had expected to locate it. Throughout the rest of that afternoon as his column was forced to cross and recross the twisting creek a half a hundred times, struggling through those boggy glades created by the meandering stream, Gibbon formulated his plan of attack—what companies would stand where on the line, who to put in the center with him as they stabbed into the heart of the hostile camp.

No matter what demands the terrain might compel him to make in the way of minor adjustments to his battle plan, the colonel was determined to hold fast to his original strategy. By attacking the very moment there was enough light to make out the lodges and horses he hoped to catch the warriors completely by surprise. Theoretically speaking, his men should be in the village before the enemy could mount any resistance. With their horses driven off and the camp surrounded, the warriors would have no choice but to surrender—rather than risk a slaughter of the innocents.

Gibbon knew those twenty men he left behind with Hugh Kirkendall and the wagons had their work cut out for them. When the iron-tired wheels weren't sinking to the hubs at every swampy crossing, the soldiers were having to muscle those wagons up every grade by double-hitching the teams and utilizing draglines as the twenty assisted the struggling mules. It made him all the more unnerved that the mule-drawn Fort Owen howitzer he had brought along with his advance was encountering the same frustrating delays every step of the way.

Then, near sunset, he caught sight of one of Bradley's men, stationed to watch over the back trail. Not that far on down the slope, the lieutenant's soldiers and civilians lay waiting in the timber.

"How far to the camp?" he asked, his voice breathless with excitement as the lieutenant loped up on foot.

"Five miles, maybe four," Bradley answered. "No more than five, sir."

"Then we'll await the wagon train here," Gibbon explained to the rest of his officers. "Take our supper, then advance within striking distance in the dark. That way we'll be in position come first light."

Just past dark, Kirkendall's wagon train rattled in. Hardtack was distributed among the men and raw bacon for those who wanted it, the soldiers washing their cold supper down with creek water from their canteens because the colonel had forbidden any fires for coffee—no fires for the lighting of pipes. With orders to sleep for the next few hours, the men wrapped themselves in their blankets and settled on the cold ground. John Gibbon was an old warhorse, the affectionate nickname his men of the Iron Brigade had first called him. Because he could sleep on the eve of battle, he was the envy of those who were a bundle of exposed nerves, unable to drift off.

He had graduated from West Point in 1847, a year after the war with Mexico had made heroes of, and bright futures for, the many. Instead, Gibbon tromped off to fight the Seminoles in Florida before he was selected as an instructor of artillery tactics at the military academy. In fact, he had authored the school's new *Artillerist's Manual*, which was finally published in 1863, about the time he was getting himself wounded at Gettysburg—his second of four wounds for that war.

Leaving orders with First Lieutenant Charles A. Woodruff to awaken him at 10:30 P.M., the colonel laid his cheek upon an elbow and for some reason thought back to the final miles on that journey from Fort Shaw to Missoula City. The Nez Perce had gotten around Rawn; Governor Potts was headed home saying the soldiers may no longer be needed; it appeared the crisis in the Bitterroot was over.

That's when the starch had seemed to go out of his men. They had endured a long, hot campaign the previous summer and ended the Great Sioux War a bridesmaid—without firing a shot at the enemy! Ever since they had received word they were moving out, Gibbon's men had known they were going to get in their licks against the Nez Perce. But over the past five days the colonel had kept their minds on the pursuit, put their vision on the horizon—and convinced them the enemy was within reach.

Pretty soon, it reminded him of a pack of hunting dogs howling down a hot trail the way his men were showing their eagerness for this fight.

By blazes—the Seventh wasn't going to be denied *this* fight!

Gibbon was snoring within minutes of closing his eyes.

ARISING in the dark, Gibbon gave the command to awaken the men and distribute ninety rounds of ammunition to each soldier for his Long-Tom Springfield rifle—fifty rounds stuffed into the loops of their prairie belts and twenty each in their two leather belt pouches, ofttimes called sewing kits.

"Bring the howitzer and fifteen shots forward at dawn," Gibbon gave the order to the gun crew under sergeants Patrick C. Daly and John W. H. Frederick. "Along with a pack mule carrying those two thousand rounds of extra ammunition for the men."

Everything else—rations, blankets, shelter halves, and more cartridges—would remain behind with Kirkendall's wagons.

Except for the horses of Gibbon and three other men, the animals were left behind with the wagon master, placed in a rope corral beside Placer Creek, a small guard to watch over them until the column's return or Gibbon ordered them forward. When all was in readiness, the colonel gave the command for the heavy wool greatcoats to be left behind at the corral; they would impede a man's movement not only on the nighttime trail ahead but also in the coming battle.

The civilians and those foot soldiers of the Seventh U. S. Infantry stood shivering slightly with the cold in that hour before midnight, 8 August, 18 and 77.

"Lieutenant Bradley," Gibbon said as those around them fell to a hushed silence beneath that starry sky and the nervous soldiers shuffled from foot to foot, "take us to the enemy's doorstep."

They moved out on foot, single-file behind Bradley, Blodgett, Bostwick, and Catlin's thirty-four civilian volunteers from the Bitterroot valley. A total of seventeen officers and 132 enlisted bringing up the rear.

Over the next three miles of sharp-sided ravines and washouts, swampy marshlands of saw grass—where they sank up to their ankles in cold mud and muck—alternating with thick stands of timber, where they stumbled and tripped over fallen and uprooted trees in the dark, broken up by patches of rocky ground strewn with sharp-edged boulders, Gibbon grew more and more anxious. Initially certain the Nez Perce would have sentries posted along their back trail, as his men marched farther without encountering any sign of guards, he became more and more convinced that he was being lured right into a trap.

His eyes straining into the moonless night, ears attuned for any sound that would mean they had been discovered, they crept toward the sleeping camp. On two occasions some of the men at the rear of the column got separated in the dark and mazelike forest, requiring the rest of Gibbon's men to stop and wait for the lost and the laggards to catch up before pressing ahead once more.

Of a sudden the whole sky seemed to open up to them as they emerged from the thick evergreen canopy, finding themselves on a gentle slope overgrown with sage, jack pine, and a fragrant mountain laurel. The heavens ablaze with stars, it was easy for a man to gaze across the full extent of the Big Hole and recognize where the distant, seamless mountains raised their black bulk against the paling horizon.

The grassy hillside where they found themselves was cluttered with little more than a few sagebrush, here above the confluence of two creeks.

"We're very close, Colonel," Bradley whispered, then pointed ahead to the left. "Around the brow of the hill. That's where you should get your first look at the enemy camp."

"You have a staging area in mind, Lieutenant?"

Bradley nodded. "From there we can watch the whole village until it's time to move into position for the attack."

"Show me."

The lieutenant and Fort Shaw post guide H. S. Bostwick led off now, angling left, heading northeast around the sweeping brow of the hill, at the base of which the stream they had just descended joined with Ruby Creek to form the North Fork of the Big Hole. It wasn't but minutes before Bradley and Bostwick suddenly stopped in their tracks.

In a whisper, the lieutenant said, "There they are, sir—look!"

The breath caught in the back of Gibbon's throat as he got his first glimpse of the Nez Perce camp in the valley below: Some of the lodges glowed faintly from within, even more the dull-red reflection of the embers in those abandoned fires still flickering in the open spaces among the lodges.

Gibbon swallowed. "How many are there, Lieutenant?"

Bostwick wagged his head as a dog yapped its warning below. "We never got close enough to count the tepees, Colonel."

Another dog bayed this time, and the faint wail of an infant drifted up the barren hillside to the expectant soldiers.

"Is your staging area close, Lieutenant?" Gibbon asked Bradley.

"On past that point of timber that extends almost down

to the edge of the water, Colonel," Bradley explained, pointing.

Gibbon nodded with approval. That dark patch of hogback timber narrowed from a wide V to a point just above the creek. It could well cover most any approach to the village. "What's on the other side of the timber?"

Bostwick said, "If my guess is right, it'll be the ponies."

With a smile, the colonel whispered, "Let's find out if your hunch is good."

Minutes later as they stepped out of the dimly lit timber, Gibbon was startled by the movement of forms on the starlit hillside at their front—fearing they were enemy warriors. After some anxious heartbeats while he sorted out what to do, the colonel realized they had bumped into the Nez Perce herd, right where Lieutenant Bradley had stated it would be.

Which meant that now Gibbon had a new worry, alarmed that the horses would make a great racket, maybe even bolt and stampede, before his men had a chance to direct their movement. But, to his utter surprise, the Nez Perce animals did little more than quietly snuffle and mill about when they winded the approaching white men. Meanwhile, down at the base of the hill, a few of the dogs in camp seemed to understand that warning inherent in the muted whinny of those ponies . . . but while Gibbon and his men held their breath—awaiting some shrill alarm from a camp guard—the dogs below quit barking and the nervous horses shuffled up the hillside, away from the soldiers.

"Bostwick!" he whispered for his post guide, a half-blood Montana Scotsman.

"Colonel?"

"Pick three or four of the citizens, men you can trust," Gibbon ordered. "Start driving this herd back on our trail toward the wagons. I want you to get the ponies out of here before—"

"Not a good idea, sir," Bostwick interrupted grimly, shaking his head in the starlight. "Could be, your surprise will be ruined."

"How?"

"These Nez Perce, they surely got 'em some guards on this hillside," Bostwick explained, "if they don't have guards down watchin' the camp. We go driving off the ponies—we'll be discovered and there'll be trouble, shots fired."

"Which will bring out the whole camp," Gibbon concluded, realizing the man's intuition had to be right. After all, Bostwick had spent his entire life in Indian country.

"Time come soon enough," Bostwick whispered. "We'll have them horses run off for you. But this close to having that camp in your hand, Colonel—you don't want to be discovered now."

"No," and Gibbon wagged his head. "We'll wait out the dawn right here."

"For a man to go on foot is one thing, General," Bostwick whispered. "But you lend me your big gray saddler there, I'll ride down, have a look at the camp."

Gibbon was dubious. "But you just said they'd have camp guards about."

"I'll wrap myself in a blanket," Bostwick explained. "If there's a picket about they won't think nothing of a horseman. A man on foot makes a noise that draws attention—but not a man riding a horse."

"All right," and the colonel passed his post guide the reins to his iron-gray gelding. And watched Bostwick disappear into the dim light.

So it was on that grassy sage-covered hillside that Gibbon would halt and hold his men in the dark and the cold.

"Canteens stacked by company," he told his officers.

They would have the tendency to bang and clank against rifle and belt pouch. No worry leaving them here: Soon enough, his men would be in control of that village nestled by a cold, clear gurgling stream.

With this task done, the colonel had his men settle on the cold ground no more than thirty yards directly above the sluggish twisting creek bordered by bristling stands of willow. As the shivering men collapsed around him on the hillside to await the coming of predawn light, the colonel dragged out his big turnip watch from a pocket, remembering he hadn't wound it since the previous morning when they started the wagons up those last two miles to the pass. Turning it just so in the faint starlight, he read that it was a little past 2:00 A.M. Here in this startling quiet, the softest of sounds emerged from the camp below: a horse's snuffle, a babe's cry quickly silenced by a mother's breast, the growl of a dog answering the howl of a coyote somewhere on the mountainside.

In minutes he had his officers together, issuing their orders. Bradley would take Catlin and the volunteers to the extreme left. Logan and Browning positioned on the extreme right flank. With Williams and Rawn serving as reserves right behind them, Captain Richard Comba and Captain Sanno would be in the middle, spearheading the dawn attack.

Once he issued the command to move out, the company commanders would spread their formation roughly as wide as the village itself—which appeared to be a distance of some twelve hundred yards. With his men deployed, the front ranks would ease down to water's edge. The signal to attack would be a single rifleshot, whereupon the men would quickly advance, fire three volleys into the camp, then immediately charge their entire line across the shallow river, certain to enter the village uncontested.

At that moment Gibbon's attention was drawn again to the horse herd. It had been of crucial importance to his plan all along to capture the ponies . . . but—it might be a stupid blunder to awaken the guards who surely must be watching over the horses. Better that they await the moment of attack before moving on the herd, he decided. Then he could seize the ponies at the same time he launched into the village—

"Put out that light!" a voice snapped sharply.

Gibbon wasn't sure who was involved, but there was a scuffle to his left as a few of the shadows quickly lunged toward the man who had just illuminated his face with the flare of a sulphur-headed match. One of the noncoms swung with the back of his hand, knocking both match and the stub of a pipe from the thoughtless soldier's mouth.

As the infantryman shrank back, holding up both hands before him protectively, he muttered, "I fergot, just fergot."

"Just like one of them blokes with Colonel Perry forgot when them horse soldiers was marchin' down White Bird Canyon," the gruff voice of a sergeant growled as he leaned right over the offending soldier, finger jabbing, those gold chevrons shimmering on his arm in the starshine.

"Lemme get my pipe, Sarge," the infantryman begged. "I'll put it in me haversack, straightaway."

"Just be glad I don't tuck you away in me own haversack," the sergeant grumbled. "One li'l slip now—an' our attack won't be no secret no longer."

As the line quieted once more and the forest resumed its night sounds, Gibbon sighed, damp, chill breath smoke slipping from his mouth. Across a deep and willow-choked slough where the meandering creek was backed up, the lodges were arrayed on a line running roughly southwest to northeast. The greater number of the poles were standing near the western end of the camp, off to Gibbon's right. The sky was starting to lighten as post guide Bostwick slid up beside Gibbon and settled to his haunches beside the colonel.

"Won't be long now and you'll see those tepees start to glow like Fourth of July lanterns," Bostwick explained. "That means them squaws are laying firewood on the fires."

"Why is that important to us?" Gibbon asked.

"It means the women are starting to build their breakfast fires, General. Which tells me we ain't been discovered."

"So when the fires flare up, that's a good sign."

Bostwick turned away to gaze into the valley. "It means that village down there will be yours."

A man snored nearby.

Running over the order of battle in his mind once more, Gibbon realized he had done just that hundreds of times since leaving the wagons and horses five miles behind.

Everything was ready, he told himself. A flawless plan that would end this Nez Perce war here and now.

All Colonel John Gibbon had to wait on now was the coming of this glorious day.

Chapter Fifty-three

Wa-Wa-Mai-Khal, 1877

BY TELEGRAPH

—

Indian News—Very Serious
Trouble in Texas.

—

THE INDIANS.

—

Shooting Match at Fort Hall.

FORT HALL INDIAN AGENCY, August 2.—A band of Indians shot two teamsters at this agency this morning, one seriously and the other slightly, but neither mortally. The shooting was done under the excitement caused by a rumor that hostile Indians were approaching the agency. The shooting was an individual act and condemned by all the Indians in the agency. Agent Donaldson immediately called together the head Indians in council, who condemned the act and sent men in pursuit of the Indians who had fled. They have assured the agent that they shall be caught and brought back and they will guard against any recurrence of the kind. Everything is quiet and peaceful now.

"BE CAREFUL, OLD MAN," SHE WHISPERED TO HIM.

Natalekin leaned over in the dark, his cold, stiff joints paining him, and touched her wrinkled face with his fingertips. He could not really see her for the darkness and their fire all but dead now. But he would know the feel of her face anywhere. This would be their fifty-first winter together. Although his rheumy eyes had been growing more and more dim with every summer, *Natalekin* had no doubt he could pick her out of a lodge filled with women.

She patted the back of his hand as she rolled onto her

side. He rocked back, slivers of ice stabbing his joints. The damp cold of this Place of the Ground Squirrels had seeped clear down to his marrow. Dragging on the worn, greasy capote, *Natalekin* shuffled around the firepit for that tall, graying triangle that indicated the doorway of their darkened lodge.

Outside at the edge of the brush where he quickly watered the ground, he found that the mist was no longer gray beneath the cover of night. Already that dense fog rising off the creek, clinging to the tall willow, and scudding along the ground between the lodges was beginning to shine with a whitish hue, announcing the coming of first light far to the east behind that barren plateau beyond the camp.

Natalekin heard the old pony snuffle in recognition as he approached, even before he spotted the animal tied there to the fourth stake left of the doorway or it saw him. One cold, throbbing hand followed the picket rope from its jaw down to the stake, untied it clumsily, then took a deep breath. It always hurt to climb atop this steady, old horse. He caught his breath again when he was on its back, letting the waves of cold pain wash through him and out again. A little colder every morning, this agony of growing old became like icy lances stabbing through his joints.

Wiping the hot tears from his eyes at that diminishing pain, *Natalekin* pulled the single rein about and nudged the old pony into motion. He blinked to help clear his foggy eyes of everything that prevented him from seeing what little his old eyes could still see while the animal led him past an old woman trudging between the lodges with her loads of firewood. Three others were already hunched over, starting life anew in cooking pits dug outside their lodges. On down to the shallow creek his old horse led him among the buffalo-hide covers and a few of those tall, bare cones of freshly peeled lodgepoles, stacked in their timeless hourglass shape, drying for their journey to the buffalo country.

At the creek's edge, the horse did not falter as it stepped into the water with a shocking splash to his bare legs. Together they parted the thick, drifting fog bank that seeped along the low, cold, damp places near this north end of the camp, clinging tenaciously to the head-high willow as the pony carried him into the north end of that boggy slough tucked against the base of the nearby hillside where he would find the herd.

Natalekin did not have to awaken so early of a morning just to bring his handful of horses down to water. Chances were they would wander down to the creek on their own, if they hadn't already. But he was an old man and couldn't sleep very well, or very much, anymore. Restless especially when the dark and the damp penetrated his bones with all the more bite. Better to be up and moving about, sensing a little warmth creep back into his body with his spare and economical movements—

Dragging back on that single rein, *Natalekin* halted the horse, letting the quiet, cold water settle around his bare ankles as he stared into the darkness. Then rubbed his dimly seeing, watery eyes with his fingertips. How far away was that?

He squinted, then shifted his head slowly from side to side, attempting to make out the dim forms. These were not horses he saw.

Quickly glancing up the grassy hillside, he could make out no more than the dark squirming of the herd on the slope above. His eyes came back down to the willows ahead. Had some of the horses wandered down into the creek bottom to water or graze on the tall, lush grasses sheltered by the thick banks of willow?

Or was it a prowling coyote? For the past two nights they had bayed and yipped from the hillsides at the camp dogs—

There! Now that was a sound he knew did not belong to a horse. Or a scavaging coyote, either. That breathy rasp, something just sort of a cough. These were not horses. After rubbing his eyes again, he nudged the pony forward another few steps. Ten horse lengths away, no—less than that now. He could see the first three of them. Gradually he made out even more of them, nothing but shapes. Dim figures, man-sized and -shaped, slowly taking form out of the swirling fog snagged above this boggy mire where the creek slowed down and backed itself against the side of the hill.

Perhaps these strangers were those spies the chiefs said were keeping an eye on their camp yesterday. Shadows from the Bitterroot valley who had traded with the Non-Treaty bands, everything from whiskey to bullets. Belief was that such white men had followed the village over the mountains and down to this place—perhaps to do even more trading.

But he did not want them bothering the horses, did not want the strangers to even make an attempt to cut out a few of the *Nee-Me-Poo* ponies they would take back to their towns and ranches in the Bitterroot because the *Nee-Me-Poo* had so many—

Natalekin heard the low voices. Unable to understand any of the words, he could nonetheless understand the harsh tone—like a knife blade grating across a stone—and thereby understood the meaning. These were not spies. Nor were they here to strike up some trading. These Shadows had indeed come to steal.

"Go away!" he called to them as he leaned forward on his pony.

Fuzzy and dreamlike—how he watched the yellow tongues of fire spew from the muzzles of those guns, puffs of gray, gauzy smoke drifting up from the mouths of each one, even before his weakened, arthritic body snapped back, back . . . back again with the terrible impact of each lead bullet.

His eyes were open as he spilled off the back of the pony, feeling the animal twist to the side, rising slightly on its hind legs as its rider tumbled into the waist-deep creek. Flat on his back on the stream bottom, staring up through the dark water. Eyes frozen, staring at the way the fog skimmed along the creek's surface just above him. Hearing the hollow, muted reverberations of those many guns that quickly answered the ones that had killed him. Watching the dark, shadowy figures move past, legs lunging, the water churning with their hurried passage as they advanced on the village. But from here he could do nothing.

Realizing, too, he had no worry about smothering here at the bottom of the creek as the gentle current nudged him slowly around, easing his body downstream. A body that no longer ached.

Natalekin realized he had already begun the journey of death.

FIRST Lieutenant James H. Bradley had brought his left wing of the attack into these tall willows at the bottom of the hill. He commanded no company of his own here; instead, he was the only officer leading both the cavalrymen and Catlin's thirty-four volunteers from the Bitterroot valley. Stepping off the low cutbank, he had quietly plunged into the frigid water that nearly rose to his crotch, so shockingly cold it robbed him of breath for a moment.

The rest came off the bank behind him, stretched out to right and left.

Since witnessing the Custer dead last summer, the lieutenant had been compiling his memoirs of that Great Sioux War. In fact, the day before departing Fort Shaw for the Bitterroot valley, he had completed his remembrances of 26 June 1876—the day before that terrible Tuesday when he had been the first to discover that gruesome field of death.*

But what jarred him now was that he had intended to write another letter to his sweet Miss Mary waiting back at Fort Shaw, some word before he found himself caught up in finding this village. The last he had sent her was written at twilight back on the third of August, from Missoula City

*Lieutenant James H. Bradley would not live to complete this vivid chronicle of that war on the northern plains. Ever since, Custer scholars have regretted not having his recollections of the twenty-seventh and the subsequent days of burials, along with the discoveries his advance detail made in the Cheyenne-Sioux village.

before Gibbon decided to march after the Nez Perce with an undermanned force.

It has not yet transpired what we are to do, but it is probable we will remain inactive for a few days till Howard comes up from the west side of the mountains and the 2nd Cavalry battalion from the Yellowstone, and then we will push for the Indians.

Events had a way of catching up a man and hurtling him along with them. Maybe Gibbon was smarting at all the criticism Rawn was taking for his lack of action up the Lolo. That reflected on the Seventh Infantry. Or maybe the colonel was simply tired of all the rumors of his overcaution during the campaign of 1876. For the last year that had reflected on John Gibbon himself.

Bradley was a soldier. A good soldier. Yet the husband and father in him now made him regret not sending a letter back from Stevensville or Corvallis, some word sent with a civilian courier, just a note to tell her where they were going and what they were about.

As James Bradley stepped off the edge of the bank into the cold water, he had a remembrance of how he had ended that letter already on its way to his Miss Mary.

Kisses for the babies and love for yourself.

Most of Catlin's civilians were gathered right behind him at his elbow as they slowly waded toward that last stand of willow shielding them from a certain view of the lodges. Across no more than a half-dozen steps, the water slowly rose past his waist, deeper, too, eventually drenching some of the shorter men clear up to their armpits. They slogged forward at an uneven gait, boots frequently slipping on the uneven creek bottom, shuddering with their cold soaking, parting the stringy mist with each step.

"Hold up!" one of the civilians whispered harshly, and a little too loudly, too, down to his right.

Everyone froze.

"One of 'em comin'!" another voice announced.

"How many?"

"See only one," a different voice asserted. "On a horse."

Of a sudden, there he was, taking form behind the gauzy fog. The warrior's pony eased off the far bank into the creek, gingerly picking its way across the rocky bottom, slowly, slowly without the clatter of iron horseshoes. The figure and his horse were swallowed by the dancing mist, then reemerged once more, a few yards closer.

Bradley heard low whispers murmured to his right among the civilians and wanted desperately to call out to them, to order silence. Nothing must spoil their surprise. Catlin's men must goddamn well wait until they heard Gibbon fire that shot announcing their charge into the enemy camp.

Maybe the lone warrior would somehow manage to pass on by them, if the civilians just stayed quiet enough, hunkered down in the willows—let that horseman ease past on his way to the pony herd on the slopes behind them. Then Bradley saw the rider wasn't going to bypass them unawares. The warrior stopped, cocking his head this way, then that.

He'd heard those goddamned volunteers whispering!

Leaning forward, Bradley looked harder than ever, studying the horseman—figuring he really wasn't a warrior at all. Not sitting his pony lithe and agile. It was an old man, nearly white-headed, wrapped in a blanket, maybe a blanket coat.

It surprised the lieutenant when the figure drew one of his legs up, bracing the knee atop the pony's spine, rising and rocking forward as if to have himself a better look at something. Some*thing*? Hell, the old bugger was trying to get a good look at their line! How could he disable the old man without firing a gun—

Suddenly the old man spoke a sharp question, deciding it.

His words were instantly answered, without orders, from

the right side of that line Bradley had been leading toward the north end of the village.

Four, five, maybe more guns rattled in volley—their low boom muffled slightly by the sodden air. More than one bullet caught the old man, driving him off his horse as it reared slightly—probably hit by bullets, too. The rider sank beneath the surface of the water as the pony wheeled about in fright, scrambling back for the creek bank.

On down to their right, the other units opened up: Logan, Browning, Comba, Sanno. Damn, that old man had robbed Colonel Gibbon of his chance to make the first shot!

"Forrad!" Bradley bellowed to the ranks.

Remembering how the colonel himself had quietly admonished him in the dark that morning, warning him to use great caution going into the tall brush on this far left flank of the line. "Stay with the riverbank as much as possible—where they can't see you so well," Gibbon had asked of him.

The men were starting to talk now, the way a man always would to work himself into the fighting lather.

"Remember your orders!"

They stepped on out of the thick willows, onto some spongy ground there in the slough, seeing how fires instantly brightened in a few of the lodges, shrill voices calling wildly from beyond the gray, swirling mist.

"Hold for my command!"

Another volley roared to their right, from those units positioned farther south along the line of attack.

Screams from the village now. Women's and children's voices—

Quickly interrupted by the ordered third volley from the other companies.

"That's our cue, men!" Bradley bellowed. "Charge!"

With that third wave of rifle fire fading from his ears, Bradley turned to his left slightly as a half-dozen naked figures flitted between the northernmost lodges and those bare skeletons of poles erected on the bank ahead. He raised his right arm, waving to all those around him as their wide front burst from a thick pocket of fog.

"Shoot low!" he hollered a reminder at them as he poked the muzzle of his rifle into some tall brush, taking his first step through the patch of willow. "Shoot low and pay heed to women and children!"

"Hold on, sir!" a voice cried behind him. "Don't go in there—it's sure death!"

The muzzles of those weapons in the village jetted bright flame—

Bradley instantly sensed it like a steam piston slamming into the left side of his chest. No wonder. Here in this brush he was so close to the bank he could make out the fury in the eye of the man who had shot him.

Sitting down in the water as the strength went out of his legs like the gush of a river over a busted dam, the lieutenant found it none too cold now. The creek lapped around his chest, swirled under his armpits, as he sat there, weaving slightly and wondering what had happened to his Springfield. Did he forget it back . . .

He blinked, staring now at the surface of the stream, not sure if the water around him was turning a different color here just before the coming of the sun. Maybe even warming slightly with his flowing blood. But his chest was becoming so heavy he wanted to lie back and sleep. Even right here in the water. After all, it wasn't cold anymore.

The water sucked at him, drawing him back, back so he could sleep just a little.

Eyes closing, he suddenly recognized the top of the timbered hill from his boyhood in Ohio. A few more desperate steps and he found himself on its crest, looking down into a beautiful valley, a wide, beckoning meadow ringed with green, leafy trees barely rustling at the tug of a warm breeze.

The water surrounding him like summer air was cold no longer.

And he heard voices, the chatter of men who hadn't been able to speak for more than a year now. He recognized faces, even though he had never served with any of them. Cavalrymen all. Off to the side somewhere, his ears brought him the music of a fiddle. Some man playing a mighty fine fiddle.

He started to turn that way—then Bradley realized why he heard such music. Knew why he recognized these faces . . . they were Custer's dead, one soldier after another.

The very first time, and the very last, too, he had seen these men, they had been lying upon a bare, stark field of death—bodies stripped of clothing, heads completely scalped, nearly every one of the horse soldiers mutilated: hands, feet, arms, privates hacked off, heads smashed to jelly.

No matter how much he stared at the soldiers now, Bradley could see no signs of mutilation as they turned in his direction and started walking toward him; the first of those two hundred called out to Bradley, welcoming him to Fiddler's Green.

He had made it. Thank God he had made it.

So this was how it was for a soldier to die, he remembered thinking as the first of these heroes came up and put their arms around his shoulders, others pounded him on the back—bringing him along to that green and leafy meadow.

So this . . . is how it feels for a good, good soldier to die.

CHAPTER FIFTY-FOUR

WA-WA-MAI-KHAL, 1877

SHE WAS THE WIFE OF A GREAT WARRIOR, *WAHLITITS*. THE one called Shore Crossing.

After enduring many winters of ridicule and sniping, he had started this war to wash himself clean of the shame of that vow he had made to his father not to take vengeance upon the Shadows. After all the *Nee-me-poo* had endured over the years . . . not to take vengeance?

For some time now she had struggled to understand what made him flirt with other, younger women. Perhaps it was only the pain he tried so hard to hide from everyone but her. Seeking the approval of the younger women to somehow make up for the lack of respect from the older men—warriors they were.

With Red Moccasin Tops her husband had started this war. Swan Necklace came along as their horse holder. Every war party needed at least one horse holder. And when the trio returned to the traditional camp at *Tepahlewam*, they were instantly covered in glory. Shore Crossing was a changed man. No longer did he make courting eyes at the women younger, prettier, than she. Women who still had their flat bellies while hers had begun to swell big and round with Shore Crossing's child.

She had long prayed it would be a son. Not just for her husband, the child's father . . . but for all *Nee-Me-Poo* people. To carry on the bloodline of a great warrior of the People.

From that season of *Hillal*, when Shore Crossing had started the war that would finally throw off that yoke the white man had put upon the *Nee-Me-Poo*, down through *Khoy-Tsahl* and now into the time of *Wa-Wa-Mai-Khal*, these three summer seasons, at long last the People had risen up against an enemy much stronger, far more numerous. Yet their warriors had been victorious in one fight after another against greater foes.

Although the People had been compelled to leave their traditional homelands in Idaho country, she knew they could make a new home with their allies the *E-sue-gha* in the buffalo country. While it would not be the high, green hills she had known since her birth, that new land was where their son would be born in freedom. Perhaps she would name him Buffalo Calf, or Little Buffalo, or something of that sort, to commemorate their coming to the land of the buffalo to escape the war and white men of Idaho country.

The people of Montana country were not angry with them. They had allowed the *Nee-Me-Poo* passage through the Bitterroot valley and over the mountain pass without trouble, once the village had skirted around the small band of soldiers hiding behind their log barricades.

But that next night, Shore Crossing awoke her for the first time with his disturbing dream, seeing himself killed by a soldier's bullet. He was unable to sleep for the rest of the night and told no one else of his frightening vision the next day.

When he finally fell into a troubled sleep the following night, his terrible dream returned. And for every one of the last few nights as the village slowly made its way up the Bitterroot River and down to this Place of the Ground Squirrels.

Here, for the first time in many nights, *Wahlitits* wasn't troubled by the nightmare! Instead, they celebrated with the others their arrival in this country where they could take the time to cut, peel, and cure lodgepoles in the timber above their camp. Last night there had been a lot of gambling by stick or bone around the fires. Dancing, singing, drumming, and laughter. Much, much laughter. They had left the war behind.

Even more important to her, Shore Crossing had finally left his terrifying dream behind. No more would he jerk awake with that vision of a soldier aiming his rifle at him, a powerful bullet taking his life—

That first quick burst of shots awoke her with a start.

She quickly turned to him beneath the buffalo robe beside her. Shore Crossing lay on his back, eyes open and unblinking, staring at the place where the lodgepoles were lashed together with loops of thick rope. She knew he had heard those gunshots, too.

Deliberate in his actions, *Wahlitits* threw back the robe, exposing her, as he reached for his breechclout and leggings.

"No!" she wailed.

He flung her hand off his arm without a word and belted on the breechclout.

Gritting her teeth stoically, she sat up. Over the past few weeks of travel from camp to camp, her once-small breasts had grown heavy atop the swelling mound of her belly. She reached up on the liner rope and took down the cloth skirt and overshirt, quickly pulling them on as Shore Crossing finished tying his leggings to his belt, then quickly knelt to pick up his cartridge belt. Looping it over his forearm, he grabbed his moccasins in hand and took up the carbine he had stolen from the first Shadow he had killed.*

"I want to go with you, *Wahlitits*."

"Yes," he said softly after pausing a moment for reflection at the doorway in the gray light of predawn spreading upon the valley. More gunfire crackled outside, loud, booming volleys of soldier guns. "I want you to come watch a brave man die this morning."

She stifled a wounded cry that fought to free itself from her throat.

He buckled the cartridge belt around his waist, then chambered a cartridge with the gun's lever and quickly ducked from the door.

The instant she followed on his heels, she realized there

---

*Englishman Richard Devine.

weren't many husbands and fathers stepping forward to meet the attack. Downstream and up, she heard the soldiers, saw so many of them—more than Shore Crossing could ever stop by himself.

But she knew he had to do what he could.

At the first crackle of gunfire off to their right, her husband seemed to come alive, animated now of a sudden, hearing some other man, another warrior, young or old, crying out his war song, making his stand against the first of those *suapies* in blue slipping out of the whitish mist so cottony it clung to the twisting stream. A lot more soldiers emerged from the brush and willows to their left, wading waist-deep in places as they splashed toward the nearby bank.

"Go with the people to hiding!" he ordered.

"No!" she shrieked, her sob lost in the terrifying racket falling around them.

Bullets began to slap against the new lodgepoles, to thunk through the thick, dampened buffalo hides stretched upon some of the hourglass cones. Lead ricocheted, clanging off iron skillets and brass pots. Favorite war ponies whinnied and cried out humanlike as the bullets struck them, become as thick as wasps on a late-summer day.

"Woman!" Shore Crossing cried out, ripping her attention from the rest of camp and riveting it to him. "See how a brave man dies!"

He fired the carbine at those soldiers no more than twenty feet away now. Striking one of them, driving the white man back into the water.

Quickly levering, Shore Crossing aimed again, fired a second time, and hit another *suapie*.

"Make yourself smaller!" she begged him from the doorway of their lodge.

Ejecting a hot copper cartridge, Shore Crossing did not answer but continued to stand at his full height, turning slightly as he selected another target—

She watched the bullet slam under his chin, driving him off his feet, but as quickly she twisted aside to locate the soldier who had shot him. Wanting so badly to be able to tell her husband who needed killing next.

But when she turned back to her husband, *Wahlitits* was flat on his back, sprawled there near the log he could have taken cover behind, right in front of their lodge.*

Her heart froze a moment as she gazed down at him—struck with the fact that he looked so much the way she had seen him just moments ago: lying so still and unmoving on his back, eyes wide open and staring right up at the sky. . . .

Moving on instinct, she lunged across his body, snatching up the carbine he had dropped. Without thinking of what to do, she pressed the weapon against her shoulder, laying her cheek along the stock as she had always seen him do—then found the soldier at the end of the barrel.

The same *suapie* who had killed Shore Crossing.

She pulled the trigger, surprised with the force of the kick against her shoulder as the carbine bucked upward in the air.

Knowing she had to lever another fresh cartridge into the weapon for it to fire another time, she shoved the lever downward, watching the hot, empty casing come spinning out of the action—immediately feeling a tongue of fire course through her upper chest.

Making her feel so heavy she didn't think she could breathe.

Struggling to draw in a breath as she lurched to the side, she felt a second bullet smack into her body, just below her left breast. A third, at the base of her throat. It spun her around violently, flinging her off her feet.

Where she landed, she could almost reach out and touch *Wahlitits* with her fingertips.

It was the greatest struggle of her life—but one that the wife of a great warrior had to make, she told herself with every inch she dragged herself across the grass grown soggy with their blood.

Until she found herself at his side, peered into his wide,

---

*Stake No. 10, Big Hole National Battlefield.

staring, glassy eyes one last time—then collapsed across his body . . . her final thought that the bloodline of Eagle Robe and *Wahlitits* was no more.

"GET under that buffalo robe and stay there!"

He could tell by the look in his father's eyes that he meant for his son to obey. All little Red Wolf could do was nod his head. No words would come out, he was so frightened.

Although he was tall for his age, this was only his sixth summer. And he was scared to his core. Never had Red Wolf heard such a clatter of gunfire, all the screaming of the women, so much yelling from the men as they darted here and there past his family's small lodge.

"*Suapies!* They have come to kill us!" a voice screamed.

Another warned, "*Suapies* in the river!"

From those first loud shots that brought the whole family awake, Red Wolf looked to others to tell him what to do. First to his mother—but she was busy dragging his younger sister out of the blankets, where the girl had been sleeping beside Red Wolf after the late night of dancing and singing that had followed a long summer day of swimming and watching the young men race their ponies on the bench near camp. His little sister clung to their mother like a plump deer tick not yet ready to drop off its host.

"What of Red Wolf?" his father had asked as he reached the door of their lodge and stopped.

"I cannot take him, too," his mother said. "He would have to hold my hand."

That's when his father dived back into the lodge, knelt, and dragged up the buffalo robe over his six-year-old son. "Stay here until one of us comes back for you. No matter what. Stay under that robe!"

It went dark. He listened as his father dashed away, swallowed by the screams, the gunfire, the terror that had struck their village in the gray light of dawn.

"Do as your father says," his mother's voice came to him

muffled by the robe. "One of us will be back for you very soon."

"Good-bye, Red Wolf," his little sister said through the robe.

He did not answer her as he carefully raised the edge of the buffalo hide and peered out at his mother's face one more time before she turned away and squatted through the doorway, that little girl clinging to her back.

The moment they disappeared from view, Red Wolf disobeyed his father and rolled toward the side of the lodge, raising up the edge of the sleeping robe, then tugging at the side of the buffalo hide so he could watch his family make their escape. He did not see his father at all but quickly found his mother racing toward the eastern plateau that stood several short arrow flights from the cluster of lodges.

Strange voices—unfamiliar words—snagged his attention, suddenly yanking his eyes to the left. Red Wolf spotted the first of the strangers standing in the creek: working their rifles, moving forward a few steps, aiming and shooting, then working at their rifles again before they would advance a few more steps.

That one clearly had to be aiming at his mother.

Quickly Red Wolf twisted his head to the right there beneath the edge of the lodgeskins—watching the bullet strike his sister in the back. Watching her spin away and fall, unable to hold onto their mother any longer.

Then he saw the red patch on his mother's bare back as well, the same blood-smeared hole she scratched at with her arm as she stumbled forward a few more steps after losing his sister. Watching his mother pitch onto her face—arms spread wide, legs tangled in each other. She did not move—

A lodgepole just above his head splintered.

On instinct he dropped the edge of the lodgeskins and quickly ducked back under the buffalo robe as his father and mother had instructed. He lay there in the deafening darkness, the suffocating sounds of death all around him—

screams of horses, cries of other children he had played with in the creek now possessed by the soldiers, the grunts of those struck by the white man bullets. Crackle of fractured lodgepoles above him as the bullets splintered new wood. Hot lead whining through the air, hissing through one side of the lodgeskins and hissing on out the other side.

He trembled in the darkness. Drawing his legs up fetally. Covering up both ears with his arms, Red Wolf began to cry. Silent sobs as he realized his mother and sister would never come back for him, even though they had promised. Knowing somehow that his father would never return, either. That he was already dead somewhere on that bank of the creek where a few of the first warriors had stepped out to confront the *suapies* emerging from the willows and fog still hugging the ground the way his sister had clung to their mother's back.

No one would be coming back for him now. Little Red Wolf's agonized sobs were drowned out in the darkness that embraced and cradled him.

Chapter Fifty-Five

August 9, 1877

As things turned out when they inched down to the creek, the soldiers of William Logan's Company A had the farthest to go in reaching the village the moment those shots rang out.

They had been moving forward in perfect silence. A silence suddenly shattered.

For a heartbeat, the Irish-born captain wasn't certain what to do. He had heard Gibbon's aide-de-camp say the colonel would fire one shot—*one* shot would be his order to commence their three volleys followed by the rush into the enemy village.

But that had been more than one solitary shot.

Nonetheless, Logan could not deny that the battle had been enjoined. Not with that loud, unmistakable roar of voices all the way down the line that extended far to their left, a raucous cheer clear over to where Bradley led his horse soldiers and volunteers, too. Comba and Sanno were bellowing in the thick of it now. It seemed the whole line on their left had taken to yelling as they started forward.

"Volley-fire!" he reminded his company. "Three volleys—low! Fire low into the tepees! Ready . . . aim . . . fire!"

Although some men had instinctively jumped the gun and started for the village, with his loud bellow Logan yanked them to a halt. He ordered the second volley after a few seconds, watching the men palm down the trapdoors on their Springfields and thumb the heavy hammers back into position.

"Aim low! Ready!"

Ahead of them the Nez Percé were breaking from their lodges.

"Aim!"

They'd been caught by surprise. Ripped out of their beds at those first shots, half-clothed. Dazed and terrified, they scattered in half a thousand directions.

"Fire!"

More than fifteen rifles roared again.

"Reload for the third volley!" cried this solid, unflappable twenty-seven-year veteran of both the Mexican War and the rebellion of the Southern states, realizing his voice had risen in pitch. Probably in excitement, knowing that after the third volley his fourteen men and three officers would be pitching into the village.

This warmhearted Irishman well known for his rollicking sense of humor turned and peered momentarily into the camp. Amazed to see so many of the warriors already massing, appearing among the lodges, guns in their hands as they came forward to blunt Logan's attack. A few of the Nez Perce had already begun to kneel or drop to their bellies, carefully aiming their weapons at the fifteen men of Logan's A Company, Seventh U. S. Infantry.

He had to get his men into that camp, drive back those warriors, and put the Indians on the defensive—before the Nez Perce could muster enough fighting men to mount a counterattack.

"Ready!"

Suddenly he thought about his son-in-law, D Company's captain, Richard Comba, another good Irish-born soldier somewhere down the line to his right at this very moment. Regretting how just this past spring they'd both suffered the unexpected death of Logan's daughter, Anna, Comba's wife. And the baby, too. She was the captain's granddaughter, Anna's first child. Born sickly, the little thing hadn't lasted much longer than her mother after a hard and terrible labor.

Logan quickly stuffed his left hand in his pants pocket and fingered the rosary beads that had been his mainstay during those first tragic hours at Fort Shaw this past March. He gripped them tightly in his palm, the crucifix digging into his flesh—

"Aim . . ."

And as he said a prayer for his son-in-law, begging God to remember Comba now in battle before these screaming warriors—

"*Fire!*"

Captain William Logan turned right, then left, peering down his line. Some of the warriors had jumped over the bank into the creek at the extreme southern end of the village, attempting to take cover and return his company's fire from there. He wasn't sure, but he thought he saw a few women taking refuge there among the fighting men. Logan knew he would have to remind the men to watch for the women.

His company was out in the open now. They had the farthest to go before they punched to the far side of the creek and into the village. The farthest, by bloody damn.

But that was the sort of job the generals always gave to the Irish in this man's army. Cross the open ground where lesser men might shrink from duty. Close on the enemy no matter how they're throwing lead at you. Then seal the damned village tight.

"Reload, goddammit!" he hollered above the racket as they started taking a heavy fire. "Reload!"

On the bank just ahead of them a few young boys appeared with only knives in their hands—dashing headlong into his fifteen. The youngsters slashed, screaming, mouths open like deadly *O*s as the infantrymen clubbed them this way and that instead of wasting bullets on such small defenders.

"Don't shoot the women and the young!" he bawled. "Don't shoot the noncombatants!"

When most of his men had flipped open their trapdoors and the hot, smoking copper cases came spinning out of the chambers to land in the creek, only to stuff fat new shiny cartridges back down into the breeches, their captain knew the time had come to take the village.

He dragged the back of his hand beneath one end of his

grand, sweeping, gray-flecked mustache and gave his men their final order.

"Charge, you soldiers! Char—"

The bullet drove him off his feet with a deafening echo in his head.*

Logan lay there on the damp grass, boots tangled in the willow, listening to all their feet pounding on the rocky cutbank as his men carried out the last command he would ever give them.

Ah, now, he thought as he opened his eyes slightly. *This truly is peace.*

Tears slowly drained from Captain William Logan's eyes. There before him swam the face of his beloved Anna. Cradled in one arm was the newborn babe, every bit as lovely as Anna had been on her birthing day.

"Here," Anna said in a whisper as she floated above him, stretching out her empty arm to him while brilliant light tunneled into eternity behind her, "let me help you along, Papa."

HUSIS Owyeen, called Wounded Head, was not thinking clearly as he burst from the door of his family's small lodge at the southern end of the encampment.

With those first shots he was on his feet, shouting to his wife, *Penahwenonmi,* to get their son out of the lodge to safety. But he himself did not catch up his rifle so that he could fight these attackers. He forgot that soldier gun he had taken from one of the *suapies* who had raided their *Lahmotta* camp. With that gun and the cartridge belt he had taken off the dead soldier, Wounded Head had defended his family and his people in every skirmish that summer.

But this was the first time the soldiers had ever gotten this close to the women and children! To find them almost at their lodge doors, crossing the creek.

---

*Stake No. 36, Big Hole National Battlefield—although Nez Perce testimony after the battle place the death of an officer wearing "braid and ornaments" at the nearby Stake No. 13.

"Father!"

He wheeled suddenly, finding his two-year-old son staggering toward him, arms outstretched. Behind the child at the darkened doorway, his wife's frightened face suddenly appeared. Helping Another was screaming for their child—

As he was slammed forward, Wounded Head thought how the feel of that bullet striking the top of his skull, how the very sound of it, must be the same noise a *kopluts*, the short *Nee-Me-Poo* war club, would make in colliding against a man's head. From his first experience, he knew he had been struck a second time in his life by a soldier bullet not strong enough to penetrate his skull.

Stunned, knocked senseless, he lay there, strangely remembering the morning he had taken the soldier rifle in battle—the same day he had saved the life of a white woman on that battlefield,* back in the season of *Hillal*.

Ho! How foolish were those white men to bring along their women merely to warm their blankets when taking to the war trail! But there she was, left completely alone, abandoned in the wake of the soldier retreat up White Bird Hill. Even though neither one could speak the other's language, he convinced her she would be safer with him than on the side of that grassy slope with the many enraged warriors chasing after the fleeing *suapies*.

He started back to the village with his prisoner mounted behind him—no telling how much she might be worth if the *Nee-Me-Poo* had to barter for the return of prisoners when making peace with the Shadows following this fierce and bloody fight. That frightened, blood-splattered, mud-coated white woman might be worth something after all. Besides, he was anxious to show her off to his wife and others. Not only had he taken himself a rifle and bullets, but he had captured himself a prisoner, too!

Then five women had appeared and scolded him for wanting to keep her. That was something the white men did. *Nee-Me-Poo* did not take captives! Besides, she would only

---

*Isabella Benedict in *Cries from the Earth*, vol. 14, the *Plainsmen* series.

bring them trouble if Wounded Head kept her. Finally he was convinced that he should let her go back to the soldiers so the white men wouldn't be angry with the *Nee-Me-Poo* for keeping their woman.

He let her go so the soldiers wouldn't come following the Non-Treaty bands to get their woman back . . . although one of the mean little chiefs had kept his white woman prisoner ever since he stole her from a house on the *Tahmonah*,* that woman with hair the color of honey.

Wounded Head had held out his hand to the woman he was freeing, and they had shaken before she turned to disappear in what brush dotted a crease in the grassy slope. At the time he figured that was what he must do in saving his people from another soldier attack. Give back the woman so the white men won't come looking for her.

As he lay there this morning, unable to move, it was abundantly clear to him that the soldiers had come looking for that honey-haired prisoner they had dragged along with them ever since the first troubles. The *suapies* were here to take her back and exact their revenge on the *Nee-Me-Poo* for stealing her from Idaho country, from her man, from her people.

"Wounded Head!"

Blinking his eyes groggily, he forced them to focus momentarily on his wife, who crouched at the lodge door, pointing frantically.

Helping Another screamed again, "The boy!"

His youngest child was staggering toward the line of soldiers less than an arrow flight away. More than two-times-ten of them, just dropping to their knees, drawing their rifles to their shoulders to fire into the lodges.

No-o-o! his stunned mind cried out, even if his tongue could not make a sound.

But words never did stop a bullet. Lead whined overhead, slapped the lodgepoles, tore through the hide cover,

---

*The Salmon River, where Jennet Manuel and her infant son were kidnapped in the outbreak of the Nez Perce War.

and made his wife scream in terror. Yet in the midst of all that thundering noise, Wounded Head still heard the startled grunt escape his boy's throat as the child was pitched onto the ground no more than three pony lengths away from him. Rolling onto his back, the boy dragged a right hand over one wound, now covered with blood. Then a left hand over another wound. The bullet had gone in one hip, out the other, passing completely through the child's body.

With a shriek Wounded Head had never heard her make, Helping Another sprang to her feet, sprinting for the boy even though she was running toward the soldier guns. Smoke and fog clung low to the ground in riven shreds as she raced into danger, scooped up the child, and turned in retreat, hunched protectively over the boy she cradled in her arms. No more than four steps when a bullet caught her low in the back.

Wounded Head watched how the impact made her stumble as the bullet blew out the front of her chest, just below one breast. She dropped the child, their boy rolling across the trampled grass, crying piteously as he tumbled toward his father.

His wife lay on her belly, barely moving, lips trembling. Wounded Head knew she must be dying.

Their son lay on his back, arms flailing, unable to stand, even to roll over—in great pain.

Still Wounded Head could not move. It was as if the bullet that had struck him just above the brow had taken away all movement from his chin down to his toes. Wounded Head wore the front of his hair in the traditional upsweep of a Dreamer. But what made his different was that it was much longer than Joseph's or *Ollokot*'s. With a thin strip of *hemene*, a piece of hide from a wolf he had used ever since he was a boy, Wounded Head tied up his hair in front—daring any enemy to take it. The wolf had always been his spirit animal.

But now it was only a matter of time until they all would be dead, he decided. Cursing the spirits for this terrible fate: forced to lie pinned to the spot, unable to move, watching as his wife and young son died before his eyes, just beyond his reach. Unable to respond to the boy's calls, to drag his wife to some safe place to die . . . unable to give back hurt for hurt against these soldiers who had come to retake their honey-haired woman and punish the *Nee-Me-Poo* once and for all.

A hard lesson, this pain of watching his family die right before his eyes.

"CLEAR that goddamn tepee, Private!"

Young Charles Alberts nodded and gulped his reply. "Yes, sir, Sergeant!"

Captain Logan's A Company was spreading out through the south end of the village now, having started to push the Nez Perce out of their lodges after a little trouble stabbing into the camp at first, seeing how the captain was knocked off his feet and killed. But Sergeants John Raferty and Patrick Rogan were taking a few of the men off the firing line as the resistance slowed, sending a few of the privates here and there to check the tepees for any of the enemy who might be hiding inside and capable of doing some sniping.

It was dangerous work, but this San Francisco–born soldier never had been one to shy away from anything that smacked of danger.

Flicking open the trapdoor on his Springfield, the private assured himself that he had a live round in the chamber before he clicked it shut again and pulled the hammer back to full-cock. With the weapon braced against his hip, ready to fire, Alberts stopped just to the side of the loose hide suspended over the tepee door. Using the muzzle of his rifle, the private pushed the door flap away from him, staying well to the side in case one of the occupants fired a weapon at him.

He counted slowly to ten, then snatched a quick peek inside before he jerked his head back again. Not good to give them a target to aim at, he thought. After another quick look into the darkened interior, he felt ready to dive inside himself. In a squat, Alberts stepped through the doorway, stopping immediately inside to let his eyes grow accustomed to the dim light—

Black shadows suddenly tore themselves out of the darkened interior, streaking his way. Two, then three, then more than five of them. Women and children all. His wide, frightened eyes instantly raked them to see if there was a warrior in their number, remembering that Colonel Gibbon had given orders to kill just warriors—women and children only when it was unavoidable. But later on in the dark as they had waited out those last hours before launching this attack, word quietly filtered through the units that Gibbon really had no use for any prisoners.

"You fellas know what to do," Sergeant John Raferty told A Company. "When the time comes, the general's counting on you boys all knowing what to do for captives."

Screaming, shrieking, making the hair rise at the back of his neck—the women and children clambered toward him in that heartbeat.

Alberts lurched back, his head and shoulders bumping against the low top of the doorway as he reversed the Springfield in his hands—intending to use it as a club. Even though he was a good soldier who obeyed orders and knew what to do when it came to taking women and children prisoner . . . the private nonetheless would do everything short of giving up his own life to keep from killing one of these innocents.

"None of 'em innocent," an older soldier had grumbled in the darkness just before it got gray enough to move into their final positions. "Squaws and nits—they'll all gut you soon as look at you. Taught that right from the day they was whelped. Ain't no different than the bucks that way. You watch out for 'em, sonny—or they'll slip a knife atween your ribs!"

Before Alberts knew it he was swinging that rifle left and right, back and forth, in a panic, smacking wrists and whacking elbows—knocking their knives and axes out of the way as he stumbled backward through the doorway with the ferocity of their attack.

Kicking out with one boot, he freed his leg from a child attempting to hold him while the women and other children finished his execution. A woman flopped backward, senseless, when his rifle butt collided against her skull. That only emboldened the other two women and the last three children.

Alberts spilled backward, tripping at the lodge door. Dragging up the Springfield where he lay on his back, he pointed it at the open doorway, ready to fire at the first one of them who came vaulting out with a weapon in her hand.

But for the first heartbeat no one burst from the darkness. Two, then three more heartbeats—not one of his attackers showed her face.

Quickly Private Charles Alberts elbowed his way backward, never taking the muzzle of his rifle from the doorway; then he swallowed hard. Realizing he'd stumbled into a nest of vipers but—for some reason—had just been spared.

"S-sergeant!" he bellowed for Patrick Rogan, managing to catch his breath. "Gimme a hand for God's sake! They amost killed me in there!"

Chapter Fifty-Six

Wa-Wa-Mai-Khal, 1877

Eelahweemah was called About Asleep. Now in his fifteenth summer, he was nearing the age when young men began thinking of those rituals that would lead to full manhood.

Never before in the history of the *Nee-Me-Poo* had the killing of Shadows and *suapies* been part of those rituals.

While part of him was racked with the fright and terror of a child watching the soldier attack on his sleeping camp, another part of him felt the fury of a young warrior throwing himself into battle against the white men who had slithered up on this village, intent upon killing the innocent women and little ones who had never hurt another person in anger.

"Bring your brother!" his mother had yelled at him just before the three of them squirted from their lodge right behind his father.

While the man of the family sprinted off to join *Ollokot*, who stood hollering for others to rally with him near the center of the long, irregular camp, About Asleep's mother pointed to a nearby group of four women, all nearly naked, who were huddled just beneath the creek's sharp cutbank, frantically waving at the others to join them.

"This way!" his mother ordered, unable to pull anything more about her in the instant panic than a leather skirt that she had knotted at her waist. Gripping her oldest son's elbow in one hand, she dragged About Asleep's younger brother along by the wrist while the tiny child sobbed in confusion and fear, bullets striking the lodges all about them, splintering poles.

Together now, the five women and two boys dashed right over the lip of the cutbank and into the shockingly cold water, the leap of each one dispersing a little more of that thick fog clinging to the rippled surface of the creek.

One of the older women pointed out a different direction, saying, "We must take cover beneath those willow!"

Without a word of argument, the seven began wading into the deeper part of the creek, struggling over the slippery rocks and hidden holes to reach the west bank where they could hide beneath the lush overhanging branches.

Just as they were reaching the leafy cover, strange voices speaking the Shadow tongue began crying out both up- and downstream from them. This close to cover, the women did not have a chance to get beneath the long, bobbing branches before three *suapies* appeared, suddenly parting the brush to stand almost directly above the seven cowering *Nee-Me-Poo*.

Unable to comprehend that what he was watching could actually be real, About Asleep saw the first bullet strike the woman beside his mother. She whimpered as if an infant, with that faint cheep of a newborn sage chick when she slipped beneath the water.

The other four women cried hideously at the sight, both in anger and in panic as they bent to scoop her from the water that swirled in this deep eddy, soaking those who wore any covering to their armpits.

A second of the soldier guns fired. About Asleep's own mother jerked, back arching violently; then she eased down into the water, slowly turning around on the surface, her eyes wide but already lifeless.

About Asleep shrieked in terror, his younger brother, too, their voices joining those of the three gray-headed women.

With another gunshot, About Asleep felt the burn along his upper arm, heard the big bullet *ploosh* into the water beside him.

"Come on!" he screamed to his brother, waving desperately for the women to follow before he grabbed the youngster with his other hand.

But the women were not as quick as the youngsters.

While About Asleep and his brother lunged out of the water to grab a soldier's ankle, vainly attempting to upset him, the women were paralyzed in fear.

The young soldier easily kicked himself free, then wheeled away into the brush, crying for his companions. About Asleep realized the two of them would never have a better chance of escape.

"Get out of the water!" he ordered his younger brother.

Dragging himself onto the grassy bank among the thickest growth of the willow, About Asleep reached out and pulled his brother into the brush.

Four soldiers suddenly burst through the thick vegetation, their rifles already pointing down at the older women in the creek. Even though those women waved their arms and pleaded for mercy, the bullets erupted from the guns in a fury—driving the victims back, back, back until they slipped lifeless beneath the surface turned white with angry foam, tinged red with the blood of their many wounds.

"Run!" About Asleep shouted at his brother, pushing the youth ahead of him into the leafy brush that whipped and cut and lashed their naked bodies.

Yet About Asleep did not feel the mere touch of a single branch or suffer the clawing of any of the sharp alder limbs.

To stay alive, they had to run far, far from this killing place.

CORPORAL Charles N. Loynes quickly looked left, then right. Every other soldier was too consumed with something else to notice what the young corporal had just witnessed, disbelieving. No one else saw it . . . so maybe those women weren't really there.

Loynes blinked his eyes, rubbed them with the heel of his left hand, and looked again.

But there they were, four Nez Perce squaws sliding that buffalo robe over their heads once they had slipped over the creek bank and all were in the water.

Moments ago he had breathlessly watched the four, admiring their courage and amazed at their audacity, as the side of a lodge was split open with a huge butcher knife and the women popped out of that long slit like peas from a crisp pod, dashing for the edge of the stream, one of them dragging a hairy buffalo hide behind her—the sort he knew these Nez Perce curled up in to sleep. Every few seconds Loynes had looked left and right to check if any other soldier in his I Company, even one of the civilians, had spotted what he was watching.

Somehow the four had managed to dash through the fog and gunsmoke unnoticed by anyone but the corporal, who found himself somehow separated from the rest of his unit at this moment—Captain Rawn's own company, men who had watched these same Nez Perce skip right around them on the Lolo. *They're a tricky bunch, these Injuns!*

He immediately scolded himself for not inspecting those women more closely. Since both the bucks and squaws wore their unbound hair long and loose, it was hard for him to remember if all of the four truly were women. Maybe there was a fighting man or two among them. Just fine that the women should make a run of it—but if one or more happened to be a warrior with blood on his hands, then Loynes wouldn't be doing his job as a soldier to clean up this village of rapists, thieves, and murderers. A warrior who would escape death today could well be a warrior who would kill more soldiers, pillage more settler homes, and shame more white women with his evil somewhere on down the line.

With their buffalo robe unfurled upon the surface of the creek he had lost all chance to tell buck from squaw. But he immediately knew how to get himself a good look at the four: Loynes figured he would shoot at the floating robe while the four started downstream past the middle part of the enemy camp.

"What the bloody hell you shootin' at down there, Cawpril?" a voice demanded just after Loynes had pulled the trigger for the first time, standing on the bank overlooking the hide.

"Look!" he exclaimed as Sergeant Michael Hogan

stomped over to his elbow and peered at the creek, too. "Watch that robe—there's four of 'em under it!"

"Four?" the sergeant boomed, bringing up his Long-Tom. "Warriors?"

"I think some of 'em are," Loynes answered with a swallow, noticing the edge of the robe rising slightly from the surface of the water as if one of the four were peeking out from under the hide. "Lookee there—them bucks is sneaking in a breath of air!"

"Lemme shoot one of them red bastards when he pops up for a breath," the sergeant growled, shoving his Springfield into the crook of his shoulder.

"I get another shot after you, Sarge."

One after the other, the two soldiers swapped shots at the floating buffalo hide, their bullets piercing the robe here, then there. One time Loynes caught a glimpse of a hand, another time a cheek, and once he saw an eye peer beneath the dark blot of shadow before the robe was dropped onto the surface again. Inching slowly along the brushy bank, both sergeant and corporal followed the floating robe, reloading while they kept a watchful eye locked on the hide—strangely oblivious to the terrible fight raging behind them in the Nez Perce camp.

One at a time, the bodies of the Indians they had killed rose to the surface at the edge of the robe, twisted and rolled gently in the current, then bobbed slowly downstream . . . until there were no more to shoot and the hide finally swerved about and became ensnared on some overhanging willow—now that no one controlled its movements.

"Four more bucks won't be cutting no shakes no more!" Sergeant Hogan exclaimed, immensely proud of himself.

Loynes smiled wanly. "Four . . . four more. That's right, Sarge."

"Won't be jumping no more white women now, Cawpril."

"No, the four bastards gonna feed the coyotes now," Loynes replied, remembering how that eye had peered out at him.

Hogan pounded him on the shoulder. "You helped me make 'em good Injuns!"

The corporal nodded. "Yeah, Sarge. We made all of 'em good Injuns!"

Chapter Fifty-Seven

Wa-Wa-Mai-Khal, 1877

STRUCK IN THE HEAD BY A *SUAPIE* BULLET, *HUSIS OWYEEN* had no idea how long he had lain there, stunned and unable to move, while more wayward bullets hit both his son and wife near their lodge at the southern end of the village.

His muscles not heeding his desperate cries, Wounded Head cursed the spirits for dealing him such an agonizing blow as this—not only having to watch his beloved family die right before his eyes but being unable to go help them. Forced to listen to the boy's whimpers as the child struggled again and again to rise, Wounded Head could see how his son couldn't roll this way or that because of his broken hips.

And Wounded Head was forced to watch the way his wife's hand clawed at the grass at her side for the longest time. It was the only part of her body that moved, all she could do, so badly wounded through the chest was she.

Slowly, with excruciating discomfort, he sensed feeling beginning to return to his body, an icy tingle eventually creeping down his legs, worming its way out through both arms, until all his limbs finally did as he willed them.

Wounded Head sat up in the midst of that yelling and gunfire, the hammer of running feet and the whine of bullets.

"Father!"

Instantly he knew what he must do.

Rocking onto his feet unsteadily, running in a lumbering crouch, Wounded Head clambered toward his son. He paused to scoop the boy's bloody body into his arms, then wheeled about and made for a patch of thick willow on the creekbank. Inside that modest cover, he laid his son upon the ground.

"I'm going back for your mother." And he touched his son's cheek, his fingertips wet with the boy's blood.

The moment he reached *Penahwenonmi*'s side, Wounded Head stretched out upon the ground beside her—the better to appear wounded or dead himself. Carefully he reached out and rolled Helping Another onto her back. A flood of relief washed through him when his wife's eyes fluttered open.

"Th-the boy?"

"He should live," Wounded Head whispered.

"Take good care of him . . . always," she said in a raspy voice pierced with much pain.

"I'm taking you to him now," he vowed.

"No!" she whimpered, tears bubbling from her clenched eyelids. "It hurts too much."

"If I leave you here, surely you will die," he said with a touch of anger at her refusal. "Or the soldiers will find and kill you, maybe even shame you with their lusts before they put a bullet in your head."

Only her eyes moved as she peered at him, each of them with a cheek resting on the ground, their faces only inches apart, noticing his head wound. "You are hurt, too."

"I'm taking you now," he said suddenly, scrambling up to a kneeling position, looping his hands beneath her shoulders, and gripping her armpits.

Whirling her around despite her shrill wail of pain, Wounded Head started backward in an ungainly wobble, making for the brush where he had secreted their son. All around them, on both sides of the creek, the booming of guns and the shouts of fighting men failed to drown out the screeching of those terrified women and children who were unable to escape the village before the soldiers were upon them.

Not far to his left stood the maternity lodge.

Wounded Head wondered if any young mother would still be in there, if one of the aged midwives remained with her. Forced by nature to be giving birth at this hour of travail and horror. It could not be a good omen for the child.

In heartbeats he got his wife inside the concealing brush with the boy. She held out an arm as he gently slid the boy across the blood-soaked grass, nestling their son against his mother.

"Stay here until I—"

"Don't go!" she whimpered in a gush.

"There is a fight," Wounded Head said as he bent over her and kissed her damp cheek. "If the Creator decides that I am to come back for you, I will return when the fighting is over."

"Father?"

"I brought you both here where you will be safe," he told the boy. "And when you cry, do not cry out loud so those soldiers will find you like hungry wolves sneaking through the willow. Bite down on your teeth so they do not hear you cry. I will come back for you when this fight is done."

In a matter of a few breaths he was back beside his lodge, stabbing a slit through the side of the spongy dew-soaked hides. Diving inside, he quickly gathered his soldier rifle and cartridge belt taken from the *suapie* he had killed at the *Lahmotta* fight back in the season of *Hillal*. While he was buckling the belt around his waist, he heard a familiar voice sing out a brave-heart song just beyond the lodge cover—the great warrior Rainbow, calling for the men to rally around him.

"I am here, Rainbow!" he shouted as he crouched from the lodge door and dashed around the side of his home.

Already more than ten warriors stood or knelt around Rainbow as Wounded Head ran up—all of them concentrating their fire on a cluster of soldiers they had pinned down at the edge of the village, on the cutbank where the white men could not gain any more ground. "A Shadow for every bullet!" Rainbow yelled.

Sliding up beside the great warrior, Wounded Head went to one knee and dragged back the hammer on his short soldier carbine. As he sighted along its barrel, Rainbow continued to shout encouragement above them all. His gallant, brave voice suddenly made Wounded Head remember the words known to so many of the *Nee-me-Poo*: this great fighting man's vow.

"*I have the promise given me by the spirits that in any battle I engage in after the sun rises*," Rainbow had told and retold of his powerful vision, that sacred *wyakin* or warrior's medicine, "*I cannot be killed. I can therefore walk among my enemies. I can even face the points of their guns. My body will be no thicker than a hair. The enemies can never hit me with their bullets. But . . . if I fight any battle before the sunrise—I will be killed.*"

The shock of that sudden remembrance shot through him like a bolt of summer lightning, Wounded Head immediately twisted around, peering over his shoulder at that low bench east of the village—terrified to find that, even though it had grown light enough to dispel all the dark, murky vestiges of night, the sun had not yet made its appearance over the edge of the earth.

"Rainbow!" he shrieked in panic, reaching up to seize the great warrior's forearm. "Look! The sun! It hasn't shown its face yet today!"

His cry of encouragement ceased in the middle of a sentence as the war chief turned suddenly, staring in panic over his shoulder at the eastern bench a long, long time. Then the fear faded from his face. Gone was the terror that had clouded his eyes only a moment before. He turned to gaze down at Wounded Head, laying his empty hand on the warrior's shoulder, the look upon his face one of deep calm now.

Rainbow said, "Tell my brother, Five Wounds—that this *is* a good day to die!"

Once more the war chief turned to face the assault, again raising his voice against those four-times-ten he and the few were holding back while the women and children made their escape from the village. Standing unafraid in the midst of the others who knelt or lay on their bellies to make themselves smaller, Rainbow refused to cower in the face of all those bullets.

Of a sudden, no more than four paces from them, a tall

soldier leaped from behind some brush. The much shorter Rainbow raised his weapon at the same instant and the two enemies fired together. But the great warrior's action clicked—his carbine was empty. The white man's bullet struck Rainbow squarely in the breast, knocking him backward a wobbly step.

The tall soldier immediately whirled on his heel and dived back into the bushes.

"Rainbow!" Wounded Head shouted, bolting off the ground for the war chief.

As Rainbow collapsed to his knees, then crumpled backward into the grass, that look of calm on his face seemed to grow all the more serene as he cried out to others, "Fight on! Remember always to fight on! You must fight—"

His last words were choked off by a gush of blood.

But before anyone could grieve Rainbow's death rattle, Grizzly Bear Youth shouted a warning. This warrior named *Hohots Elotoht* lunged to his feet and darted for the tall soldier who reappeared from the bushes with his rifle reloaded. As Grizzly Bear Youth leaped for him, the hammer on the soldier's gun snapped without firing—exactly as Rainbow's had done the instant before he was killed.

Now the two enemies brandished their empty weapons overhead as they raced toward each other—colliding with a crunch of bone, falling to the ground in a heap. It was immediately clear to Wounded Head how much smaller Grizzly Bear Youth was than the bigger white man. In moments the soldier had the warrior pinned to the ground.

As he struggled for his life, Grizzly Bear Youth cried out to his *wyakin* for power to defeat this big enemy!

The warrior was soon answered and managed to somehow drag himself out from under the soldier—yet the white man quickly gripped Grizzly Bear Youth around his neck and began to choke him. At that moment *Lakochets Kunnin* burst from some nearby willow, landing right beside the wrestlers, and fired his carbine into the *suapie*'s side.

It did not take long for the soldier to let go of Grizzly Bear Youth, stumbling backward before he collapsed against the brush and lay perfectly still. Nearby the smaller warrior sank to his knees, clutching his forearm. Blood oozed between his fingers.

"Your bullet broke my arm!" he cried out to *Lakochets Kunnin.*

"Maybe it did," said this warrior called Rattle on Blanket, "but I saved your life!"

While they argued, Wounded Head turned to stare down at the great warrior Rainbow, who had been offering encouragement and hope with his final words, in his last act of defiance . . . even though it was a battle waged before the coming of the sun, before the awakening of his powerful *wyakin*. He had refused to shrink from his duty to his people—

When Wounded Head looked up, none of the other fighters remained. He was alone with the body of Rainbow. The others were scattering this way and that as the soldiers finally began to gain ground, quickly advancing on the spot where Wounded Head knelt over the great warrior's lifeless body.

"If you can be killed," he whispered to Rainbow, starting to weep as he closed the man's blood-splattered eyelids, "then we all can be killed."

HE could not remember when his head had ever hurt this bad.

Nor could Private George Leher* recall just where he was, what day it might be, or what he was doing flat on his back—finding himself dragged along the wet, soggy grass by the older woman who took shape as he came to and his blurry eyes began to focus.

It took a few moments, this realization did, what with the bullet wound to the head that had knocked him senseless. Struggling to remember how he had come to find himself lying flat on his back, Leher recalled bits of things the way a man might tear up the whole sheet of a memory into tiny

*Variously spelled Lehr in some of the Big Hole battle literature.

pieces of confetti and toss them into the air. A panic gripped him, as he realized he never would get all those pieces back together again, not in the same order, nor with all the details intact. . . .

She gripped him by one heel, tugging him over the ground one yard at a time, his ankle pinned beneath her armpit as she struggled to drag him to the closest tepee, his rifle used as a crutch in her other hand while she lunged forward a few feet, replanted the weapon, and lugged him a little farther.

The numbness he felt radiating through his body from the head wound gave him such panic—just knowing that he was powerless to do a damned thing to save himself for the moment.

That's when he remembered that he had just come out of the water, cold and wet from his midchest down, hearing the enemy's rifles crack all across their front, seeing the enemy flitting here and there, watching a bullet hit Captain Logan himself—when lights suddenly exploded in his head.

Since the old shrew could have finished him off where she found his body if she'd had a knife or ax, she must be dragging him toward the lodge to kill him there.

Leher tried to twist his leg free of her grip.

The woman immediately stopped and peered back at him with an angry face, screeching at him in her strange talk that only made his head hurt even more. She shook his rifle at him menacingly, then turned around and started off again.

This time the private somehow willed his loose leg to coil up, cocking it near his body—then lashed out at her.

His water-soaked boot caught the older woman in the small of the back, sending her sprawling with a yelp of surprise.

His head swam as he slowly rolled onto his hip, spying the rifle lying between them. Rocking forward, he seized it by the butt and began to drag it toward him in his left hand just as she pounced forward and snagged hold of the muzzle.

Back and forth they tussled with it, she gripping the barrel in one hand and swinging her closed fist at his head like a club, forcing him to duck this way, then that, as his right hand crawled up the stock, farther and farther, reaching the wrist, then the trigger guard, finally to yank back the hammer—

When the weapon went off, it blew a bullet through the side of her face as she was leaning away, almost as if she had realized in that final moment what was about to happen to her. The close impact of that bullet striking her in the head drove the woman backward a few feet, her body flopping against the dew-dampened buffalo-hide lodge.

She slowly slid down the tepee, the pulpy side of her head smearing the hide cover with a wide, moist, red track until she came to a rest on the ground, staring at him—her eyes already glazing in death before her silent mouth moved one last time. Then she teetered to the side and fell on her shoulder to budge no more.

With his head still ringing from his own wound, Private George Leher felt along his prairie belt and pulled one of the long copper cartridges from its canvas loop. When he flung up the trapdoor, the extractor shot the empty cartridge from the smoking breech and he jammed home the fresh round.

Snapping down the trapdoor and dragging the hammer back to full-cock, he took a deep sigh and closed his eyes a minute more—relieved that he had possession of his rifle once more. No squaw was going to drag him anywhere. None of these screaming bucks was going to get close enough to finish him off.

He'd just lie there by the side of this lodge and wait until one of Logan's A Company came back to find him . . .

Act like he was dead till someone came along to help.

He clenched his eyes shut a moment longer, praying that next person would be a white man.

Chapter Fifty-Eight

Wa-Wa-Mai-Khal, 1877

BY TELEGRAPH

—

Indian News—Very Serious
Trouble in Texas.

—

THE INDIANS.

—

Sitting Bull Heard From.

WASHINGTON, August 8.—A letter from the United States consul at Winnipeg says: Near Sitting Bull's encampment a war party of twenty-seven Sioux robbed the traders of three kegs of powder and one bag of bullets. Besides Sitting Bull's band there is an equal number of Sioux refugees from the Minnesota massacres of '62 and '63, over whom Sitting Bull seems to exercise much influence.

ONE DAY HE ALONE WOULD CARRY HIS ELDERLY UNCLE'S name, but for the present, this ten-year-old was merely known as *Young* White Bird.*

Awakening with the first rattle of gunfire, the youngster was dragged from beneath his sleeping blanket by his mother as his father, Red Elk—a brother to Sun Necklace—dashed from their lodge. Bullets ripped through the lodge-skins, pattering like hailstones and splintering the new poles.

"Come with me, Son! Run, run!"

—

*Under tribal practice, he would not actually receive this name until he had reached manhood, at which time he began to tell his remembrances of this Big Hole fight. I was unable to locate any reference to what this child's name was *at the time* of the Nez Perce War.

He followed his mother outside, where they immediately started for the closest protection: a bunching of tall willow some of the charging soldiers had just abandoned as they thrust into the village. Here and there favorite ponies were hitched near the lodges, where they would be close when a man or youngster went to see to the herd. One by one, these animals were being killed on their tethers. As they neared the brush, his mother cried out, shaking her free hand. It dripped with blood as she held it up for her son to inspect. A bullet had clipped off a finger and the end of her thumb.

Young White Bird was just reaching out to cradle his mother's wounded hand when they both flinched the instant another bullet struck the hands they had joined. His left thumb was severed now, the splintered end of the whitish bone poking out of the raw, bloody stub on his hand.

"We can't stay here!" she cried. "To the water!"

They lunged toward the nearby creek, leaped in, and waded across a narrow tongue to reach a patch of overhanging willow, where they sank to their haunches in the cold water so only their heads would be showing to any soldiers on the riverbanks.

No sooner had they squatted among the branches than a young girl appeared on the bank opposite them. Naked, she jumped into the water and quickly swam toward the willow where Young White Bird and his mother were hiding.

"Come in here with us!" his mother sang out.

The young girl reached them just as three more children, all about Young White Bird's age, appeared at the same spot on the bank and hurtled themselves into the water without hesitation. They floundered and splashed, kicking their way across the languid stream to reach the willow and the three who waited under the branches.

Through the noisy din of battle Young White Bird recognized his uncle's voice, raised loud and strong above the racket of gunfire.

"Why are you young men retreating! Are we going to run to the mountains and let the white men kill our women and children? It is far better that we should be killed fighting!"

His uncle's words gave him a fierce pride.

A soldier suddenly stood on the bank, then disappeared as quickly. The next few minutes were filled with terrifying screams and the shouts of frightened white men, before a different soldier appeared on the opposite bank, looked across the water at that group huddled beneath the willow. He, too, disappeared without taking any action.

The moment he was gone, a young woman of no more than fifteen winters, naked to the waist, bolted over the edge of the bank at full speed as if she were being pursued. She hit the water flat on her belly with a painful smack, immediately churning her arms like wind-driven limbs on a high-mountain aspen during a strong gale.

Young White Bird and his mother reached out to offer their hands to her, pulling the young woman into their temporary shelter just as another girl about his own age crawled to the edge of the bank on her belly, flopped over the precipice, and landed in the water.

"Get her, Son!"

He swam out to retrieve the girl, dragging her back to rejoin his mother.

"See there, how she was wounded in the arm," his mother said, holding the young child's upper arm out of the cold water. The girl winced as he peered at the bullet wound. He could see all the way through the ragged bullet hole—

One of the youngest children shrieked in terror the instant a young woman—old enough to marry and have a child of her own—pitched off the bank into the stream but did not move much to save herself from the water.

"Bring that one to us!" his mother commanded.

Her body was limp as he dragged it, bobbing gently on the current, toward their hiding place.

"Help me place her head on the sandbar so she can breathe," his mother said.

The older girl helped them. She asked, "Will she live?"

Gravely Young White Bird's mother shook her head. "I don't think so. She has a big bullet wound in her chest. But we can help her breathe until she either wakes up or she dies."

He looked at the young woman as she lay in his mother's arms, finding her very pretty. Young White Bird did not remember ever seeing this unconscious one before. He thought she was one of the prettiest young women he had ever seen. Her blood colored the water around her body.

"Soldiers!" one of the children cried out before an older one could get her hand clamped over the child's mouth.

Young White Bird counted seven of the *suapies* spread out on the far bank, all of them training their rifles at the clump of overhanging willow. Just as he was about to yell in protest—to curse the white men for killing women and children—his mother shoved his head under the water.

Sputtering, he leaped back up for air, finding his mother had stepped from beneath the overhanging branches, both arms raised, waving them from side to side, yelling in the white man's tongue.

"Women! Only women and children here! Do not shoot! Only women and children!"

First one, then two more of the soldiers slowly lowered their rifles, talking among themselves. Finally the rest of them took their rifles from their shoulders and quickly backed away from the creek bank.

"You saved our lives," the young woman told his mother when the *suapies* were gone.

Young White Bird's mother wagged her head as she lifted the youngest children onto the grass bank opposite the village.

"Saved your lives only for a little while," she said grimly. "Let's do what we can to save you for good."

HE had to restrain himself to keep from cheering aloud!

Colonel John Gibbon had rarely been this elated before. His men had control of the village about twenty minutes after those first confusing shots rang out. The Nez Perce were on the run, driven from their lodges. And it appeared some of Catlin's civilians had a good chance to capture the horse herd and get it started on their back trail, depriving the warriors of mobility and escape.

Despite the blunder with those opening shots from the overeager volunteers and despite the momentary delays of some units charging across the creek and into the village . . . the surprise had nonetheless been sudden and utterly complete.

The only drawbacks were that their twelve-hundred-yard front had not been long enough to completely encompass the southern end of the village. That and the northern end, too—where the attack completely stalled.

Despite all these failures, the Nez Perce had been caught sleeping!

The men, women, and children, too—all came tumbling from their beds partially dressed, if not naked, ill-prepared to mount a momentary defense. Watching from the side of the hill across the creek, he waited until the bulk of his troops were across the slough before he gave his big gray charger the spur and moved toward the seat of the action. Gibbon hadn't been in the village very long when the first report arrived, accounting the high rate of casualties among his officers.

Lieutenant Bradley was dead almost from those first shots. Captain Logan had also fallen among his men, shot by a woman.

"A woman?" Gibbon had asked for clarification.

"Yes," replied Lieutenant Charles Woodruff, his aide-de-camp, who rode back and forth carrying messages in that first desperate hour. "Seems the women and young boys are fighting as hard as their men, General."

"It's difficult to tell the fighters from the innocents in this melee, Mr. Woodruff," he told the soldier. "Some accidents are unavoidable."

"The women—they're fighting like she-cats on the other end of the village, General."

That caused him to look at the far northern flank of their line, off to the left side of the assault. There on the hillside above Bradley's initial position he had hoped to find the Nez Perce herd under control of Catlin's civilians, perhaps even started away on their back trail already. Instead, some of the volunteers were trading shots with more than a dozen of the half-naked warriors crouched on the fringes of the herd while nervous ponies reared and jostled one another.

He had to find a way to drive off that small band of warriors and seize their herd. Those horses must not fall into the hands of the enemy, now that it was painfully clear his men had failed to seal the trap around the village.

WHEN Yellow Wolf saw his chief, Joseph of the *Wallowa*, for the first time that terrible morning, the leader was crossing the creek bare-legged with No Heart—both of them barefoot. Joseph had a shirt on, and breechclout, too, but instead of leggings Joseph wore half a blanket belted around his waist as he clambered out of the water, onto the bank, and lunged up the slope toward the horse herd. At first Yellow Wolf thought it might be *Ollokot*—the two looked so similar in many ways—but after a moment he was sure it was Joseph.

After all, going for the horse herd was something a camp chief was sure to do, while staying in the village to fight the soldiers was what a war chief would do. Joseph had gone to secure the herd so the People could make good their escape on this awful morning.

Before everything had come undone in a noisy instant, Yellow Wolf recalled awakening to the sound of a horse crossing the stream. After a long night of singing and dancing, he had gone to sleep in his parents' lodge erected right against the creek bank. At the time he heard the hoofbeats, Yellow Wolf wondered if the man was crossing to his horses on the west side. But later he came to think it must have been one of the white spies: riding his horse close to the sleeping village before the attack was ordered.

At the first shots he had bolted out of his blankets there in his parents' unfinished lodge. They hadn't put up the heavy lodge cover. Instead, they had roped together the cone of freshly peeled poles, then draped part of some old hides over the lower part of the framework to give them a little privacy when they all trudged off to bed after a late night of celebrating their escape from the war in Idaho country.

Sleeping in his parents' dwelling meant Yellow Wolf was caught away from his rifle, too. When the fight started, he had nothing more than a war club handy. Grabbing the *ko-pluts*, Yellow Wolf dashed into the fray.

A woman stood near the edge of the village, scolding in a shrill voice, "Why aren't you men ready to fight? You sing and dance all night—so you are slow to fight these attackers! Get up and do not run away from this battle!"

Her stinging words made a lot of sense as so many of the young men stumbled from the lodges, rubbing the sleep from their bleary eyes, shaking their groggy heads, ill-prepared to turn away this challenge from the soldiers.

"*Ukeize!*" a woman cursed at Yellow Wolf, reaching out to grab his arm and stop his dash. "Rainbow is dead! Rainbow is dead!"

This is unbelievable, his mind raced. The *Nee-Me-Poo* had three great warriors: *Ollokot*, Rainbow, and Five Wounds. Now one of the bravest was killed!

Sprinting as fast as he could through the first bullets, Yellow Wolf started for the far northern end of camp where Joseph's lodge was standing. Near the middle of camp he encountered *Jeekunkun*, called Dog. This older man was bleeding badly from his head and stumbling along, plainly unable to use the rifle he dragged along the ground.

"Give me your gun!" Yellow Wolf demanded. "You have plenty of bullets on your belt and I have nothing but this *ko-*

pluts. Trade me now so you can get away from danger and see to your wounds!"

"No!" Dog growled angrily, clumsily swinging the rifle's muzzle at Yellow Wolf, forcing the young warrior to back away. "I must keep my gun. I don't want to die with no way to fight back!"

Yellow Wolf pushed on. Close by he came across a younger warrior, this one wounded more severely than Dog. "Red Heart," he called out to *Temme Ilppilp*. "Trade me your carbine so I can fight the soldiers who have hurt you!"

But Red Heart would not let go of his gun even though he had a very serious stomach wound and could not straighten up, as he walked bent over in a crouch.

Of a sudden Yellow Wolf heard some Shadow cursing. A grin began to grow on his face. Creeping around the side of a lodge, he spotted a soldier crawling on his hands and knees, wobbling side to side like a man with too much whiskey in his belly, as he dragged a rifle along. The white man did not hear Yellow Wolf approaching until the last minute, when the soldier looked over his shoulder, eyes growing big as brass *conchos* to find the *kopluts* swinging down at his head. The white man's teeth loosened in his mouth as he fell.

Bending over the dead man, who had blood seeping from both his ear and the splintered bone on the side of his head, a curious Yellow Wolf pushed on the loose teeth with two fingers. All the teeth moved together. He pulled on them, finally freeing those at the upper part of the mouth, then those from the bottom. Now the white man had no teeth and Yellow Wolf had an extra set!

A bullet whined past his head. He scolded himself for being so heedless in his curiosity. Tossing the false teeth into the brush, he swept up the dead man's rifle.

Yellow Wolf now had a soldier gun and a cartridge belt, nearly every one of its loops filled with shiny bullets. He immediately turned to go in search of *Ollokot*.

With bitterness he recalled how the head chiefs had given orders to the bands not to harm any Shadows in Montana as they started away from the Idaho country.

"No white man must be bothered on the other side of the Lolo!" Looking Glass had commanded.

"We will only fight the enemies here in our old homeland," White Bird had emphasized. "Trouble no white people after passing over the mountains. Montana people are not our enemies. Only the Idaho people."

"Do not kill any cattle across the mountains," Looking Glass had warned. "Only if our women and children grow hungry will we take cattle or any food we need to feed our people."

Those were strong laws made by their leaders—laws that must not be broken for the sake of all the *Nee-Me-Poo*, since they were leaving the war behind by crossing the mountains.

Now it was clear the Montana whites did not think the same way as Yellow Wolf's people.

Even though the warriors had taken precautions not to injure any of the soldiers and Shadows at the log barricades, even though the People had been scrupulous in their dealings with the Bitterroot settlers . . . the *Nee-Me-Poo* had been betrayed. At first the angry warriors were confused, baffled how Cut-Off Arm could have gotten his slow-moving soldiers up the trail so fast as to catch them here at the Place of the Ground Squirrels.

Then *Ollokot* startled them all with his assertion right in the midst of the fighting.

"These are not Cut-Off Arm's Idaho soldiers!" the war chief declared. "They are Montana soldiers!"

"The *suapies* who tried to stop us with their log fort on the Lolo?" Yellow Wolf asked as he chambered another round into his soldier gun.

"Yes, those soldiers and settlers, too," *Ollokot* answered angrily as he shook his rifle in the air, leading his band of young men southward toward the brush where they would pitch themselves into a close, hot fight with the double-talking white men.

"And many, many more who have come from far away to catch us sleeping here," *Ollokot* explained. "These soldiers and settlers of Montana betray the trust we put in the people on this side of the mountains!"

Chapter Fifty-Nine

August 9, 1877

Henry Buck had been with Captain Rawn at that barricade the newspapers in the region had already christened Fort Fizzle. Later he and his two brothers had watched the great Nez Perce village drag its horse herd past Fort Owen and go into camp, then mosey into Stevensville the following day for some trading—flour and cloth were all the Buck brothers would sell at their store, even though other merchants had traded whiskey and cartridges.

Well, now them chickens was coming home to roost!

Following in the wake of the Nez Perce, this Colonel Gibbon had taken his pitifully small bunch of soldiers and licked out after the Indians. When the valley's leading citizens issued a call for volunteers, forming militia companies of their own, Henry Buck offered his services to John Catlin of Stevensville. Their bunch caught up with Gibbon's men just shy of Ross's Hole—more than half turning back for home with "Captain" Humble, while the rest ended up pushing over the divide in the advance with Lieutenant Bradley to find this enemy camp.

That march seemed so damned long ago now—thinking how them warriors drank up all that whiskey, every last one of them redskins wearing a full cartridge belt around his waist, the whole of this foolishness made possible by those traders . . . more correct to call them *traitors*, Henry Buck brooded the moment Lieutenant Bradley's charge faltered at the far northern end of the village, positioned at the extreme left of Gibbon's line.

Not one of the men, soldier or civilian, had been told to ask any mercy of, or to give any mercy to, this enemy that had blazed a wide swath of murderous destruction through central Idaho. Now the time had come for those Injuns to pay the piper, the officers had told their men in those last hours before the attack.

"When you get within firing range of the village," explained one of the cavalry sergeants who had crawled over from Bradley's company to relay the message to the volunteers, "fire low into the tepees. That'll scare the bejesus out of 'em, and kill a bunch, too." Then the trooper paused a moment before adding, "The general, Gibbon I mean—ain't said it right out . . . but we all been told he don't want no prisoners."

Some of Catlin's men laughed at that, buoyed up by bravado and feeling this would be a quick, easy fight as they waited restlessly to start the advance.

Then that old man had to show up on his horse and all hell busted loose. Catlin finally barked the order for a half-dozen of them to fire. The ball was opened and Bradley led the whole outfit toward the north end of the camp . . . where things stalled and turned ugly.

"Bradley's dead!"

Another claimed, "Shot in the head!"

And by then, there were a couple of dozen warriors with carbines—not just those old muzzleloaders but good repeaters probably bought off some low-minded trader, if not taken off some white man they'd killed. Those warriors had that north end of things snarled up and bogged down just across the creek. Even before the civilians and soldiers got anywhere close to the village.

Natural was it that those men around Henry Buck drifted to the right, making for the two companies already pressing against the village and having a hot time of it. Hell, so hot a time that Gibbon hadn't held any companies in reserve but ended up throwing every man right into the fray as soon as their advance stalled, his advance moving slower than he had a liking for.

"Give it to 'em!" shouted one of the officers in those companies at the center of the line, prodding his soldiers forward. "Push 'em! Push 'em hard now!"

A sergeant was bellowing, "Shoot low! Shoot low! Into the lodges, boys!"

Henry had levered another round into the chamber of his Winchester carbine and was preparing to fire at a group of warriors making from right to left, frog-hopping from lodge to lodge, when he suddenly realized they weren't warriors at all. A small knot of women and children, all of them running hunched over, arms looped protectively over the little ones.

He gulped a deep breath, glad he hadn't fired—then blinked his eyes, startled.

Right there in the midst of those women and children was a blond woman!* Her waist-length honey-colored hair whipped this way and that. There was no mistaking its color among those squaws and children. She glanced Henry's way, gazing at those soldiers and civilians they were racing past; then she was gone behind another lodge.

"Did you see that?" he asked, turning quickly to the man on his right.

Tom Sherrill was struggling over the action of his rifle, intent on the weapon he held in his hands. "See what, goddammit?"

"N-nothing," Henry murmured and looked back at those lodges where she had disappeared, the open ground between him and the camp littered with a clutter of fog and a little gunsmoke.

Suddenly he caught a glimpse of the group as it reappeared for an instant among more of the stacks of lodgepoles and the last few tepees at the far northern end of the village . . . but he never saw the honey-haired woman again.

Squeezing his eyes shut, then opening them quickly, Henry Buck wondered what the hell a white woman was doing with all them squaws—and dressed just like them, too.

"Give 'em hell, boys!" an officer bawled near his shoulder, moving up behind the volunteers.

---

*Was this the long-lost Jennet Manuel from the Salmon River valley?

"You heard 'im!" Catlin cheered. "Shoot anything what moves afore it shoots you!"

Henry Buck brought that carbine to his shoulder, sighting down the barrel, looking for a target as they continued for the creek bank.

Then he glanced one last time between those northernmost lodges where she had disappeared. Wondering if he really had seen her at all.

HIS uncle was Joseph, chief of the *Wallamwatkin* band from the *Wallowa* Valley. *Ollokot*, the great war chief of their people, was his other uncle.

But he wasn't old enough to talk in council or to become a fighting man—not yet he wasn't. Because *Suhm-Keen* was barely ten summers old. He lived with his parents and his father's parents in a small lodge after leaving their old homes west of the mountains to come to the buffalo country. Here at the Place of the Ground Squirrels, their lodge stood in the midst of those erected at the far southern end of camp.

As had been his grandfather's practice for many years now, early every morning, the old man would leave to go check on the horses or walk off by himself to watch the sun come up. That's when his grandmother, *Chee-Nah*, would softly whisper for *Suhm-Keen* to come join her beneath her buffalo robe, where he would drift back to sleep beside her warmth.

Many rifleshots had startled him just as he was drifting back to sleep that morning, curled against her soft bulk. Many horses tied outside the lodges were calling out, neighing in fear. His father grabbed up his rifle and dived out of the door, closely followed by his mother. Now the boy was alone with *Chee-Nah* in the shattered grayness of that dawn yet unborn.

"Grandmother!" he cried when she brushed by his shoulder and started for the door.

"I must see for myself," she said, then knelt at the opening and peered out as bullets came thick, like summer hail rattling on the taut hides.

Chee-Nah had no sooner settled to her haunches when she was driven back into the darkness near the firepit, a soft whimper escaping from her throat.

"You are hurt!" he cried, frightened, as he vaulted to her.

Although blood streamed from the wound in her left shoulder, the old woman firmly grabbed hold of his bare arm and pushed him toward the side of the lodge, where she quickly jabbed a knife through the pliant, fog-dampened buffalo hide.

"Get out, *Suhm-Keen!*" she ordered. "Run to the trees and hide! Run as fast as you can!"

As he stood frozen, staring at the blood oozing from her wound, his grandmother had to nudge him one more time before he turned and did as she instructed. Stretching apart the sides of that slit, he jumped free of the lodge and started running, barefoot and naked but for his little breechclout.

He dived to the left out of a horse's way, then scrambled to the right as two fighting men sprinted around a lodge, headed for the gunfire that was rising steadily, grown almost deafening . . . except for that pounding of his heart. Already there were other children, some younger than *Suhm-Keen*, some older, too, all dashing for the brush on the south where the low plateau bordered the valley. Bullets clipped the branches and rustled leaves on either side of him as he clawed his way up the slope—more frightened than he had ever been.

As the sun had gone down yesterday, he and some other boys had been playing the stick game near a large clump of brush beside the creek. With the coming of darkness, they lit a small fire for light and warmth and continued to play happily. That was when one of his friends noticed two men stepping out of the nearby brush. Both were wrapped in gray blankets up to their noses, not Indian blankets at all. *Suhm-Keen* looked close and could see the men were not Indian. Frightened, the boys ran away.

But rather than alarm the adults, one of the older youngsters said, "Leave it be. Our parents and the chiefs know we are being watched by spies. Leave it be."

"That's right," another boy said. "Awhile ago I saw a Shadow on horseback cross the canyon on the other side of the creek. No one was excited when they talked about it. Some of the adults think he must be a spy. But other men think he is a miner, working his mine somewhere close by. He might have quarreled with other miners and be looking for a new place to stay away from the other Shadows."

When the group came back to their little fire later, the strangers were gone—as if they never had been there. The boys returned to their play, and those two spies were quickly and completely forgotten.

Until now. What if they had reported their news to the chiefs? he wondered. Would it have made any difference? Would the headmen have put out guards to watch for soldiers?

As he fled, *Suhm-Keen* found a depression in the ground not too far from the lodges and sank to his belly in it. Peering over the edge, the boy had watched the madness for the longest time when his attention was caught by one of the *suapies* who limped behind one of the lodges and settled against the buffalo-hide cover with a loud grunt. He took something large and flat from inside his blue shirt, then removed a small twig from somewhere else in his shirt. The youngster was mesmerized, watching the small soldier scratch on the thin, flat object with that twig* while the battle raged on around him.

Not a lot of time passed before the *suapie* was hit by a

---

*It was not until some years later, when *Suhm-Keen* was able to understand that the white man wrote his language down, using a pen and paper, that he was able to explain to others what he had watched the soldier doing in the village that morning. So who was this soldier? Whom was he writing to? Because *Suhm-Keen*'s testimony states that the soldier was already wounded when he got behind the lodge, did the white man sense he was about to die, and was he attempting to write down some last words for his loved ones back home?

bullet. His hands flew up—the flat white object flying one way, the small twig sailing in another. *Suhm-Keen* was even more astounded as he watched the white object slowly become many, all of them gradually scudding across the ground like the dance of swirling feathers with each gust of breeze.

Suddenly he heard a man's loud voice booming nearby.

"Soldiers are right on us! They are now in our camp! Get away somewhere or you will be killed!"

Breathless, but afraid to stop until he had scrambled to the top, *Suhm-Keen* raced to the base of the plateau and started climbing to the rim. Only then did he turn to glance over his shoulder, surprised to find so many other children right behind him, scratching up the side of the ridge to join him. Then he peered back at the village. Hard as he looked, he could not find his parent's lodge at first, what with the gunsmoke, people scrambling here and there, and the dense ground fog.

He squatted on the rim of the plateau with the other children, watching, listening to the battle as the white-skinned *suapies* entered the village, spreading out to search the lodges. . . .

He managed not to cry until he saw the soldiers start to burn the first of those lodges. That's when *Suhm-Keen* buried his face in his arms, realizing that first one had started to smoke, a greasy black tendril stretching to the sky.

It was the lodge where his grandmother lay bleeding.

AT this side of camp where the fiercest fight was raging, Yellow Wolf watched many things that he was certain would stay burned in his memory for as long as he lived.

Somehow through the noisy din of battle he nonetheless heard the cries of a small infant. Turning in a squat to peer over his shoulder, he spotted the tiny child sobbing next to the body of its mother. The woman lay sprawled, blood on her leg and belly—unmoving and clearly dead. Then there was a rush of blurred motion, and a knot of soldiers appeared around the side of a lodge, yelling very loudly. Out of the lodge crouched an old woman, her hands held out in supplication. Yellow Wolf was afraid she was about to be shot. . . .

But instead, one of the *suapies* bent over the bawling infant and picked it up as if he was quite used to holding a baby. He patted its back a few moments, then passed the child to the startled woman and motioned for her to go. She stood there a breathless heartbeat longer, plainly baffled. He motioned again, yelling at her this time, pantomiming for her to run off. The soldiers watched her lunge away, then turned aside to another lodge, their rifles pointed and ready.

This confused Yellow Wolf. Maybe not all Shadows were brutal and without feelings for people they did not understand.

But minutes later, not far away at that same end of camp, he and two others came to the birthing lodge . . . where they discovered the wife of Sun Tied had been shot in her bed. Beside her lay the body of the older midwife, a woman named Granite Crystal, who had helped the young mother deliver a child. She, like the young mother, had been shot.

Clutched in the birth nurse's arms lay the still form of the newborn, its tiny skull brutally crushed with either a boot heel or a rifle butt. In Sun Tied's lodge nearby, Yellow Wolf and his friends found the woman's two older children, both of them shot with soldier bullets.

Looking at those little bodies, he felt the sting of gall rise from his belly, and with it a deep and unsettling anger. While there might well be a few Shadows who could commit acts of kindness and generosity that might come close to rivaling the humanity of the *Nee-Me-Poo*, most white people were simply a dark-hearted race intent upon taking everything they coveted, killing everyone who stood in their way. A black and shadowy race.

Then he remembered *Ollokot*'s words spoken to his warriors after they fled the fight on the Clearwater.

"Fear can be a potent killer in battle—paralyzing those it strikes—but anger is the greatest killer of all," the war chief had declared. "Anger always assures that the warrior consumed with rage will not be thinking clear enough to be wary of every danger."

Sucking in a deep breath as he stared at the bodies of these children, Yellow Wolf vowed he would not let anger eat away at his common sense. No, he vowed to see this day out, alive.

"My brothers—see how they set the first lodge on fire!" he heard *Kowtoliks** shouting, "Make a good resistance! We are here today for that reason!"

Around the young *Kowtoliks*—no more than sixteen summers old—rallied some warriors, their guns firing. They were all whooping together as Yellow Wolf spotted movement from the corner of his eye. He whirled, ready to shoot, when he saw it was an older man emerging from his lodge pitched upriver toward the south end of camp. He had a white King George blanket belted around his waist, covering only his legs, while his upper chest and shoulders were bare.

It was *Pahka Pahtahank*, who was called Five Fogs—a man of middle age who had never learned a thing of the white man's firearms. He was one of the very best among Yellow Wolf's people at using a bow.

Five Fogs held his short, sinew-backed bow at the end of his outstretched arm, firing steadily at the wave of soldiers near the riverbank. Not running away from his home, the warrior stood his ground, methodically shooting one arrow after another at the white men who were aiming their rifles at him. He moved slightly from side to side after every shot, then aimed and freed another arrow. A volley of bullets clattered against the lodge behind him, then a second burst of gunfire. Then a third time after he shifted and loosed two more arrows at the advancing soldiers.

But a fourth, massive volley struck Five Fogs and the

---

*This name has no definitive translation but refers to the hair and bones of human dead that are scattered by wild predators.

brave *Nee-Me-Poo* bowman fell beside the door to his home.*

Uttering a quick prayer to *Hunyewat* for the spirit of Five Fogs, Yellow Wolf had just started around a lodge, ready to make for the far end of camp, when he suddenly slid to a halt, unable to believe his eyes!

Not far away a very, very old man sat outside his lodge** apparently calm in the midst of the frantic fighting, warriors and soldiers running here and there, horses rearing and racing about, smoke and fog roiling along the ground. Yet this ancient one sat and smoked his pipe as if it were a quiet autumn morning in an abandoned camp.

Wahnistas Aswetesk sat upon a small rug cut from a buffalo robe, his tobacco pouch beside his knee, puffing calmly on his pipe as the first bullets began to fall about him.

Yellow Wolf started for the old one—to drag him to safety—but the fury of the soldier guns drove him back. Instead, he had to take cover beside a lodge, where Yellow Wolf could only watch what he was sure would be a quick and terrible end for the pipe smoker.

The first time a bullet hit the ancient one, his body jerked, but still he did not topple to the side. Two and then a third struck him. He simply did not move to safety or collapse from his terrible wounds. More bullets rattled the lodge cover and poles around him. To Yellow Wolf it sounded like the battering of hailstones—but the ancient one did not budge. As if the bullets were nothing more than harmless drops of rain!

Twenty bullets—a full two-times-ten—must have entered his body as Yellow Wolf counted, amazed.

Then as suddenly as the shooting had converged on the old man, the soldiers moved on past, running into camp, ei-

---

*Stake No. 50 designates where his lodge stood, and Stake No. 49 shows where this bowman died. His quiver and bow are in the Big Hole National Battlefield collections.

**Stake No. 24, Big Hole National Battlefield.

ther satisfied they had killed the ancient one or deciding they never would.

When Yellow Wolf slid up beside him and crouched over the wrinkled face, he was surprised to find *Wahnistas* breathing. "Are you alive?"

The creased eyelids fluttered open. "You go fight, young man. Do not worry about an old man like me. I have seen many days and if this is to be my last—then I have had my smoke to the new sun. Go now, and fight for those you can save."

The young warrior said, "You are brave to look at the face of death so calmly—"

"*Eeh-heh*, Yellow Wolf!"

The young man turned to look over his shoulder and spotted *Seeskoomkee* propped against a nearby lodge. This one called No Feet was leaning against some poles to hold himself and his soldier rifle in place while he fired with the one hand left him.

"Do you need my help?" Yellow Wolf yelled at the former slave, who had brought the warning of soldiers advancing the morning the *Nee-Me-Poo* had their first battle with the *suapies* at *Lahmotta*.

"Do you have any bullets for my gun?"

Yellow Wolf saw No Feet was using a lever-action repeater. "I don't have any bullets that will fit your carbine!" he replied.

Seeskoomkee laughed boldly as he pointed at Yellow Wolf's rifle. "I will see what I can do to kill a soldier so you can have more bullets to use!"

"I will kill some soldiers myself."

"There, young man," the old one said, tapping Yellow Wolf on the forearm. "Look there."

When he turned around to see where *Wahnistas* pointed, Yellow Wolf spotted his chief again. Joseph had returned from the horse herd where Yellow Wolf had first sighted him and No Heart early that morning at the beginning of the fight. Now the chief stood in the midst of some warriors at the center of camp, cradling his two-month-old daughter within one arm while directing action with the other arm.

When he had spotted Joseph on the hillside in those first moments of battle and now, too—neither time was the chief holding a gun. He was not a fighting man, not a fighting chief like his younger brother. Instead, Joseph was assisting the flight of the innocent women and children caught sleeping in the village.

"There, you see, young man?" *Wahnistas* asked. "Do not waste your time here with me! I am old and will die soon. So go give a good fight like our chiefs—save the little ones, and our people, for tomorrow!"

Chapter Sixty

August 9, 1877

By 8:00 a.m. John Gibbon wondered if he should have ordered his men to set fire to the lodges or not.

That simple command ended up taking a good number of his men off the firing line and prevented them from keeping the pressure on the Nez Perce fighting men. But he had already committed his manpower, so he would follow through with his original battle plan . . . even though some doubt still nagged at him—causing him more than a little concern that perhaps he should have pursued the warriors until they were completely driven off, away from the lodges, far enough from his perimeter that they could not cause his lines any real worry.

He had remained on the hillside across the stream from the camp for some time, watching from that elevated vantage point that soon showed him that the attack on the left side of his line had faltered under Bradley. It wasn't until Lieutenant Woodruff galloped up carrying the news that the lieutenant had been killed that Gibbon suffered his first apprehensions, misgivings that he might have blundered in his planning, if not in his plan's execution.

Not until the Nez Perce launched a fierce counterattack, lodge by lodge near the center of the village, did he decide to venture across the boggy slough to get a closer look for himself. No sooner had he emerged near the south end of the camp among the units attempting to set fire to a seventh and eighth lodge than Gibbon realized he made a pretty target of himself perched high upon this nervous horse he was repeatedly having to rein up, as it clearly wanted to bound away, what with all the gunfire and yelling going on around them.

"Horseback's not the healthiest position for a man in

battle," he said to his aide-de-camp as he landed on the ground and snubbed up the reins of the nervous animal.

Lieutenant Woodruff turned to say, "While an officer might stay mounted to rally his troops, sir, you can look around you and see your men already have reason enough to fight off the hellions who are trying to make a counterattack of it—"

"General Gibbon!"

He wheeled at the call, finding a sergeant hurrying over.

"General, sir—did you know that your horse is wounded?"

"N-no," he muttered as he went to his knee beside the sergeant, immediately finding the animal's front leg broken. It wobbled nervously on the other three, unable to put any weight on that bleeding leg. "A stray bullet, damn," Gibbon muttered. "Must've happened just now when I entered the village—"

"You're bleeding, too, sir!" Charles Woodruff announced with a little fear in his voice. "My God!"

Peering down at his calf, just above the top of his boot, Gibbon saw how the sky blue of his wool britches was generously stained with a circle of blood surrounding a small black hole. Curiously detached, he bent over to study the wound, amazed that he felt no pain from it.

"The bullet came out the back, sir," the sergeant offered.

Woodruff wagged his head. "Maybe even the same bullet hit you somehow came out to break your horse's leg."

"I doubt that," Gibbon replied. "Been a tough angle."

"We don't have a surgeon along," the sergeant said.

"I don't need a doctor, Sergeant," the colonel argued. "I'll walk down here to the stream to wash it out myself, then tend to it better later on in the day when we've tied up everything here."

Waving off Woodruff's offer to help him clamber down the short, but steep, cutbank, Gibbon stood a moment, watching how the sergeants and their details were working over the lodges.

To expose any possible snipers who could be hiding

within a lodge, several of the soldiers tore at the buffalo-hide covers while others stood back at the ready, prepared to shoot anyone who might be flushed from within. Now that Gibbon's men were discovering how difficult it was to torch a dew-damp buffalo hide, they were content to throw lariats over the uppermost lodgepoles, toppling the cones with the power of a horse or with a squad of men all pulling together.

Gibbon turned away for the creek bank, even more amazed that the double wounds did not give him any complaint at all. Squatting on the grassy bench next to the stream, he pulled off his boot and stocking, then tugged at the leg of his britches until he could begin to bathe the wounds with the cold water. Some movement at the corner of his eye caught his attention and he looked up—

To find a large number of warriors having crossed the stream opposite the village to the west side, where they were making their way through the brush toward the horses and the timber. Several of the Nez Perce were already skirmishing with a few of Gibbon's men, those warriors succeeding in driving off the herd by waving pieces of blanket at the animals, shooing them north along the grassy hillside, eventually sloping back into the valley once they were away from the soldiers and the fighting.

But even more of the warriors streamed into the trees on the hillside directly above the enemy camp, taking positions above his men at work in the village.

It was not only as clear as the coming sun that his men had just lost any crack at those horses Bostwick hadn't wanted to drive off in the early-morning darkness because of possible horse guards . . . but also clear that some troublesome warriors were about to flank his men—securing the hill behind and above his line, where they could do a lot of damage.

Of a sudden he became aware of a growing clamor—voices and gunshots quickly and steadily rolling his way from the village he thought his men had secured. Gibbon scrambled up the bank to find the Nez Perce darting this way and that on both sides of his men. Try as they might, his companies hadn't been able to hold the warriors off those units assigned to torch the lodges.

Here and there soldiers were already dragging their wounded comrades back from the firing lines to a safer place. Trouble was, Gibbon was coming to realize, there wasn't much of anyplace safe here in the village now. Not with Joseph's hellions throwing everything they had back against his lines in a fierce concerted counterattack.

It hit the colonel like a bucket of cold water dashed in his face: He had committed a blunder in not pursuing the enemy on out of the valley, driving them far from their homes.

From everything he had ever learned of the Sioux and Cheyenne on the northern plains, once soldiers had them on the run from their camp, once the warriors had their women and children on the way, the fighting men would dissolve and disappear.

Not so these damned Nez Perce. They weren't about to merely cover the retreat of their families, then pull back and disappear themselves. These warriors appeared determined to snatch victory from the jaws of defeat, which Colonel John Gibbon had planned to snap shut on them at dawn. Measured by every axiom and theory taught at the U. S. Military Academy, these unlettered stone-age warriors had turned the tables and were now getting the best of his classically trained officers.

Where was that damned howitzer?

He whirled to the left in frustration and anger, looking most longingly toward the side of the hill where the path out of the timber had carried his units down to this valley. That gun crew should have had the howitzer here by now!

"Lieutenant!" he cried.

Woodruff trotted over to the edge of the cutbank. "General—your leg, it's better?"

"Forget the damned leg," he growled. "Pass the word among the officers. We've got to begin a retreat. Get me Captain Rawn—"

"R-retreat, sir?"

"To that point of timber, across the creek—there!" he said as he pointed. "Rawn's company will lead the file. I tried to hold them in reserve as long as possible, so I Company will form a skirmish line they will hold long enough to get the rest of us through to the hillside. Remind every one of the officers that all dead and wounded must go with us."

"Of course, sir! All dead and wounded."

"Let's make this orderly, Mr. Woodruff. Impress that upon Captain Rawn and the other officers. Orderly. We don't want this to become a . . . ," and Gibbon paused, having started to say the word *rout*, but instead he finished by declaring, "We want to assure we hold on to our victory we've won here."

FOR as long as they could, the young men around Yellow Wolf and *Kowtoliks* made a furious struggle of it, throwing themselves against the soldiers who were attempting to tear down and burn the lodges.

A woman screamed behind the warriors, a terrified mother—shrieking that she had left her five children beneath buffalo robes in that lodge the *suapies* had just set on fire. Her little ones were being consumed by the flames and there was no way for the men to drive back the soldiers, to get anywhere close to that lodge as the smoke turned black and curled upward in the heavy, damp air. From inside that lodge Yellow Wolf heard the pitiful screams of the helpless ones over the rattle of gunfire.

He vowed to kill as many of these monsters as he could this day, to avenge this terrible, tragic war being made on the women and children.

First one soldier, then a second, and finally a third went down before Yellow Wolf's accuracy with that rifle. Each time he pulled the trigger, he saw a white enemy fall. And when he could, he hurried in to seize the dead man's gun, freeing the cartridge belt from his waist. He passed them and the soldier weapons on to warriors who had no firearms of their own. One by one, those rifles were turned against the Shadows and soldiers. It was for the lives of the women and children that the warriors were fighting, throwing the battle back into the faces of the enemy.

If the *Nee-Me-Poo* were whipped in this fight, it was better to die in the struggle than live on in bondage with freedom gone.

"Look at them now!" Five Wounds roared.

"They are running away from us!" Yellow Wolf shouted in glee as they all leaped to their feet and started rushing after the escaping soldiers.

Many of the white men stumbled in the brush, bumping into each other, tripping over their own feet as they rushed out of the village, down into the creek, then slogged up the other side into the bogs and mire of the slough, desperate to reach that point of timber angling down from the western slope. It was as if the whites refused to put up much resistance—all of them become creatures to be herded by the Nez Perce rushing up from behind.

Upon reaching an open space among the tall willows, Yellow Wolf spotted a lone soldier no more than a few steps away. No one else had spotted that soldier who was moving almost too cautiously, perhaps slowed down by the thick brush or the muddy, foot-sucking mire of the slough.

The *suapie* was so intent on escape that he had not noticed Yellow Wolf, so the warrior decided he would touch this soldier while he lived—a great feat of battle courage.

But suddenly—the soldier must have somehow *felt* Yellow Wolf directly behind him, because the white man whirled without warning, hoisting his gun up to fire. But Yellow Wolf fired first, knocking the soldier down. He did not move as Yellow Wolf came up to stand over him, reloading.

After waiting a moment for any sign of life, he knelt to take the soldier's gun, his belt filled with bullets, and a strange knife, too.* Giving the rifle and most of the ammunition away to a warrior who had none, Yellow Wolf fol-

---

*Later determined to be the soldier's Rice or trowel bayonet, which hung from the belt in a leather scabbard.

lowed after the others who were pursuing those fleeing soldiers. But as he came to the creekbank where the stream made a hard turn to the west, he immediately stopped, jerking up his rifle, pointing it at the soldier who stood at the steep bank, staring directly at him.

But the white man did not fire. He made no movement. No sound of any kind. Ready to pull the trigger, Yellow Wolf advanced cautiously—eventually to realize the soldier was already dead, somehow propped against the bank, standing rigid in death!

"We have them surrounded in the trees!" *Ollokot* hollered from above as Yellow Wolf reached the bottom of the hill.

"They cannot escape?" he asked.

Red Moccasin Tops shook his head. "Warriors stopped them from above—no way for them to get away now!"

Yellow Wolf took a deep sigh, then looked across at the village. He said, "I want to go back to the camp for a while—to see what they did to our homes."

"This is a good thing," Five Wounds said, a grim sadness surrounding him. "When you come back, you tell me what the soldiers have done to our village."

Halfway down to the camp, Yellow Wolf had just emerged from a thick stand of willow when he happened upon the body of a soldier sprawled in the damp grass near the creek bank. Here was another rifle and more cartridges, too!

But as he knelt down to retrieve the weapon off the ground, the soldier came back to life—jerking up an arm, swiping the point of a knife just past the end of Yellow Wolf's nose. As the warrior lunged backward, out of the way of the blade, he dropped his carbine and instinctively lashed out with the *kopluts* that hung from his wrist. In a loud, resounding crack, he connected against the man's head—sending his soldier hat sailing.

Pouncing on the *suapie*, Yellow Wolf finished him off with the man's own knife, the blade that had almost taken off his nose. As he caught his breath there beside the dead man, the warrior noticed another soldier lying in some brush nearby. His eyes were closed—so Yellow Wolf was concerned that this one was also feigning death.

The warrior poked and prodded the body with the muzzle of his rifle to assure himself the soldier was fully unconscious. After digging around in the man's pockets, the warrior opened a leather pouch strapped over the white man's shoulder, finding inside a little of the hard, crunchy bread and some greasy bacon, too. He would take it to eat for his lunch later on that morning. While he thought he should finish off the wounded soldier, Yellow Wolf nonetheless left the man alone and continued on into camp. It was plain from the chest wounds that the soldier couldn't live for much longer.

"Kill him!" came the shouts from a chorus of throats just beyond a cluster of lodges as Yellow Wolf approached.

He hurried to the scene, where many angry people shoved tightly around Looking Glass and Rattle on Blanket, who together held the arms of a captured Shadow, who, from his clothing, was certainly one of the Bitterroot valley settlers.*

"No!" Looking Glass snapped at the angry crowd as Yellow Wolf shouldered his way to the front of the ring. "Stay back and he will tell us some news!"

"This one was playing dead so he could sneak away!" a woman cried out in anger.

Looking Glass shouted back, "So for being a coward he should die?"

All around them in that smoky village arose the wails of grief mingled with cries of horror, fury, and revenge. It was clear why most in that group wanted to kill this prisoner, now that they had time to extract some exquisite torture from their victim.

"Get him to tell us some news from the army," Looking

*As best as historians can ascertain, this was Campbell Mitchell, civilian volunteer from Corvallis, Montana.

Glass demanded of Rattle on Blanket. "These soldiers who have followed us here from Idaho country."

After exchanging some Shadow words back and forth, the warrior turned to Looking Glass and said, "This one says these are not Cut-Off Arm's soldiers."

"Who are they?"

"They came from this Montana country, like *Ollokot* believed," Rattle on Blanket explained. "This Shadow tells me news of Cut-Off Arm: that he is following behind us very swiftly. Perhaps even to be here by this afternoon so his soldiers can continue the attack on our camp."

That brought a great and anguished wail from the crowd of women and old men, every person fearful of even more destruction and death.

"We must leave in a hurry!" a woman yelled. "Get away before Cut-Off Arm's soldiers catch us again."

"Looking Glass!" someone accused bitterly. "I thought you told us we would be safe when we left Cut-Off Arm and his soldiers back in Idaho!"

Another angry woman snarled, "Yes, Looking Glass—you said the war was over when we came here to Montana!"

"Look at us now!" screamed a third. "You said we would be safe here—the war over for us—so you forced us to stay in this camp when so many of us wanted to hurry away!"

An old man shrieked at Looking Glass, "Yes—many of us wanted to hurry away, but you would not let us!"

"We still can go to the buffalo country," Looking Glass proposed. "We must gather up all that we have and start out today—"

"This Shadow says there are more Montana settlers waiting for us between here and the buffalo country," Rattle on Blanket interrupted suddenly. "He says the settlers from the mining towns are coming to attack us before we can reach the land of the *E-sue-gha*."

"So we will reach the land of the buffalo by another trail," Looking Glass promised, his eyes darting about anxiously like those of a man distrustful of those pressing in around him. "Make another trail of our own if the Shadows try to block us from joining up with our friends."

Rattle on Blanket asked, "What do we do with this one when we leave this camp?"

"Take this Shadow to my lodge," Looking Glass ordered. "I'll keep him there until I want to dig more news out of him."

With both of the prisoner's arms pinned behind him, Rattle on Blanket started the Shadow across the middle of camp. They hadn't gone but a few steps when out of the crowd lunged a woman who stopped them, raising her loud, shrill voice to Looking Glass in complaint.

"Why do you let this Shadow live anymore?" she demanded, jabbing a finger at the chief. "He's told you all he is worth! My brother is already dead by the hands of these strangers. And I watched my children die when the white men set fire to my lodge! Let me kill him myself!"

With that last word of hers, the woman reached up and slapped the Shadow across the face, so hard it immediately raised a bright red mark on his cheek, clearly visible even though the man had not shaved in several days.

His lip curled in instant fury. With his arms pinned behind him, the Shadow lashed out at that woman the only way he could, kicking her savagely in the leg with his muddy boot. She crumpled to the ground, clutching her shin and crying in pain as a warrior jumped from the crowd, shoving his gun against the white man's chest, and pulled the trigger. It was Yellow Wolf's cousin *Otskai*.

"Why did you kill him?" Rattle on Blanket shrieked as his prisoner crumpled to the ground at his feet.

"We can't waste time—we must kill him," *Otskai* sneered, a big and powerfully muscular man. "No use to keep him alive. The difference is, had he been a woman, we would have saved him. Sent him home unhurt. Are not warriors to be fought and killed? Look around you! These babies, our children are killed! Were *they* warriors? These young girls, these young women you see dead all around you. Were these young boys, these old men, were they warriors?"

"They were not warriors," Rattle on Blanket replied. "But does it make you brave to kill an unarmed man?"

"*We* are the warriors!" *Otskai* snorted with scorn. "But these Shadows are not brave men—coming on us while we slept in our beds! And once we had a few rifles in our hands, these cowardly Shadows ran away to the hillside!"

"So must we become as evil as these white men?" Yellow Wolf demanded of his taller cousin.

Whereupon *Otskai* whirled on him, snarling, "My brother, tell me if these Shadows who came with the soldiers are our good friends from the Bitterroot? See how they traded with us for our gold—then sneaked behind us with the soldiers to rub us out. Our promise given in the Bitterroot was good and honorable . . . while their Lolo treaty was a lie made with two tongues! Why should any of us waste time saving this Shadow's life?"

The more Yellow Wolf thought about it, the more he found he could not argue with his cousin. Even though *Otskai* was impulsive and was well known to do the wrong thing at the wrong time, he could never be faulted for his bravery. He never hid from a fight.

At first Yellow Wolf had believed *Otskai*'s act one of crude and bloody impulsiveness, thinking Looking Glass was right—that the Shadow might have told them a little more news about how that "day after tomorrow soldier chief," Cut-Off Arm, was following closely on their heels now.

But the more Yellow Wolf considered it . . . maybe they had already heard everything they needed to know to save themselves.

Chapter Sixty-One

August 9, 1877

BY TELEGRAPH

—

THE INDIANS.

—

More About the Indians.

HELENA, August 8.—W. J. McCormick, of Missoula, writes to Governor Potts on the 6th, as follows: A courier arrived from Howard at 6 o'clock this evening. He left Howard Saturday morning last; thinks Howard will camp near the summit between the Lolo and Clearwater to-night. He is distant about fifty miles from the mouth of the Lolo. The courier reports that Joseph, with over one-half of the fighting force has gone to the head of the Bitter-Root valley by the Elk City trail, and will form a junction with Looking Glass and White Bird near Ross Hole. He says Howard has 750 men, and 450 pack mules, and is moving forward as rapidly as possible. Advices from the upper Bitter-Root say the Indians will camp to-night in Ross Hole. Gibbon is following rapidly. Other advices say the Indians were still at Doolittle's sixteen miles above Corvallis, and Gibbon expects to strike them on the morning of the 7th, before they break camp. Couriers say the hostiles have Mrs. Manuel with them as the property of a petty chief called Cucasenilo. Her sad story is familiar.

JOINING THOSE FIRST SOLDIERS AND CATLIN'S VOLUNTEERS in flight, Henry Buck scrambled toward the point of timber that stretched down from the western slopes in a narrowing V, a small flat-topped promontory that jutted out from the mountainside, terminating just above the boggy slough they had struggled across in their retreat.

The Nez Perce horse herd was already gone—successfully driven off by a few mounted warriors. Which meant Gibbon had failed to put the hostiles afoot.

And now it looked damned good the army wouldn't end up destroying the village, either. While many of the lodgepole cones had been pulled over, only eight of the damp covers smoldered back there in the enemy camp.

Neither of those failures would have caused a man great consternation, at least to Buck's way of thinking. Henry was certain there wasn't a soldier or a civilian who would fault Gibbon for failing to capture the herd or to hold onto the village long enough to destroy the hostiles' homes and possessions. Not with the way the Nez Perce had surprised every last one of them by striking back with such fury.

So what stuck in Henry's craw so bad was the fact that Gibbon didn't make sure the warriors would give up when they were attacked.

As bullets hissed and whined about the retreating white men like acorns falling on a shake roof in autumn winds—smacking tree limbs and knocking leaves off the surrounding willow, even digging furrows into the ground at their feet or where they planted their hands whenever they stumbled in their race—it was plain as the sun rising at their backs that the Nez Perce had no intention of scooping up their survivors and fleeing the valley.

Isn't that what Indians are supposed to do? his mind burned with the question. *To run away when attacked?*

These . . . these *red bastards aren't about to give up!*

There was a good number of the warriors already on the slope, positioned in the timber, by the time the soldiers started clearing out of the village. That meant the whole of Gibbon's command suddenly found itself caught in a hot little cross fire, strung out in the bottomground between those warriors pushing out of the encampment itself and those warriors tidily ensconced on the western slope above the creek.

No men had a hotter time of it than Captain Charles C. Rawn's I Company, detailed to lead the retreat—which as quickly became both confusing and terrifying to boot, with a little eye-to-eye and hand-to-hand fighting in the brush and tall willows as they vacated the village itself. Skirmishing for the contested ground with their firearms was so close that a few of the men were powder-burned by their enemy's weapons; a warrior's shirt was set on fire with a muzzle blast. Men on both sides fell noisily, calling out, beseeching their friends to help as the tide of battle moved past.

Then men who had started their retreat in two lines, back-to-back, quickly began to drift apart as the fighting grew intense. Ordered to bring out their dead and wounded, many of the soldiers merely stopped long enough to pick up a fallen comrade's rifle so it could be pitched into the deep water in their retreat and kept from falling into the enemy's hands.

With the death of A Company's Captain William Logan, command had fallen to First Lieutenant Charles A. Coolidge, who had begun this Nez Perce War by scouting part of the Lolo Trail. In Gibbon's retreat, Coolidge's men were assigned to close the file.

But just short of the boggy slough, Coolidge dropped before Rawn's advance had even reached the bottom of the hill—wounded through both thighs in the nose-to-nose skirmishing the embattled A Company encountered in covering the rear of the retreat. Once more the command of A Company and responsibility for covering their retreat to the timber was transferred, this time to Second Lieutenant Francis Woodbridge, newly turned twenty-four years old.

Under Gibbon's orders, once the base of the timbered point of land was reached by Rawn's advance, Woodbridge wheeled his men about and anchored them just above the creek—where they were to cover the retreat of the rest of the command scrambling up behind them. Spread out some three to five yards apart, wherever they could find a little cover on the hillside, Rawn's foot soldiers watched the other infantrymen and civilians stream through the wide gaps in their line while they continued to lay down a hot covering fire, until the last man moving out of the slough had been accounted for. Only then did Captain Rawn cry out his order to about-face.

Needing no more prodding than that, I Company bolted to their feet and resumed their retreat up the slope behind the rest.

Henry Buck turned his head quickly, glancing over his shoulder as he made his climb into the timber, hand over foot, slipping and falling, then crabbing back into motion again. He thanked his lucky stars he wasn't one of the stragglers slow in getting out of the village when the red sonsabitches came flooding back in. By that time the aim of those warriors had become deadly. At every crack of a rifle, it seemed, one of the white men fell somewhere in the retreat. Most of the wounded, and even a few of the dead, were promptly scooped up by the wrists or ankles and dragged along—those bleeding and unable to get out on their own begged not to be left behind, terrified those warriors and squaws would get their hands on them.

Just inside the point of timber the first of the soldiers staggered to a breathless halt and started to regroup, many of Catlin's civilians among them. They still were far from being safe. Bullets snarled through the trees, smacking trunks and branches, whining in ricochet as the lead hornets slammed against exposed rocks protruding from the loose soil. Henry's eyes darted about. This spot was about as good as they were going to find on the side of this mountain.

He sucked in a breath and flopped to his belly, clutching his carbine like life itself. Although it seemed like no more than mere minutes to the attackers, Gibbon's assault on, and temporary possession of, the village had lasted a little less than two and a half hours.

In bemused exhaustion, Buck watched several weary soldiers lunge right on past him and the others, running still farther up the slope—either terrified of the snipers already at work from the timber around them or frightened of those warriors herding the white men into this surround.

"Don't run, men!" Gibbon shouted as he limped into the timber, dragging his wounded leg, and started to collapse. "If you run away . . . I will be forced to stay right here alone!"

Through their midst sprinted a young corporal, head down and legs churning, huffing up the slope in full panic. "To the top of the hill!" he screamed as he ran. "To the top of the hill or we're lost!"

"Corporal!" Gibbon shouted above the tumult. "By bloody damn, your commanding officer is still alive!"

Henry watched that yank the corporal to a halt, wheeling around, his face flushed as he said, "General! We gotta get these men to the top of the hill! Only safe place—"

"As you were, Corporal!" Gibbon snapped, then turned to the rest, balancing on his one good leg. "This is the place, men. Take cover and dig in!"

From where Gibbon had sunk to the ground in utter exhaustion and pain, the south end of that enemy camp where the colonel had been wounded was no more than a half-mile away.

"Is this our last horse, General?" shrieked Adjutant Woodruff as he lunged up through the timber leading his mount.

"Get on the ground!" Gibbon hollered.

A spray of bullets spit through that stand of timber. The lieutenant instantly flopped to the ground with no more urging. For a few heartbeats it seemed all those men hugging the forest floor were staring at that lone horse among them. It tugged and pulled at the young lieutenant lying on the ground gripping its reins, nearly stepping on several men as it pranced about in fright.

"Sh-should I let go, General?"

"No!" Gibbon replied sternly. "Long as it's alive, we've got a chance to send a courier out on horseback."

After no more than the space of another heartbeat, Captain Rawn lunged into the grove, surrounded by what he had left of his skirmishers, dragging four of their wounded and one dead man slung between a pair of soldiers, the casualty's boots bouncing loosely over the rough ground.

"General Gibbon!" Rawn yelled. "Lieutenant English* is down, sir!"

"Get in here, man! Get in here!" Gibbon hollered in a crimson frustration. "Keep your heads down! Company commanders, spread your men out! Firing lines, dammit! Form a skirmish formation and give them back what they're giving us!"

With agonizing slowness, the soldiers and most of Catlin's volunteers did as Gibbon ordered—what good sense itself dictated. With the soldiers and volunteers bunched up the way they were, the warriors could slip in all the closer on them. So they began to spread out, forming a long irregular corral running, for the most part, up and down the slope, from east to west.

"Dig in!" came the call from one of the captains as the men began moving apart.

"You heard 'im!" a frog-throated sergeant bellowed. "Entrench, you goddamned buckos! Entrench afore they blow your bleeming brains out!"

Those infantrymen equipped with the Rice bayonets tore them out of the leather scabbards hung from their prairie belts and put the small trowels to work. Those cavalrymen and volunteers who did not have the luxury of such a tool went to work with tin cups, belt knives, even folding pocketknives—anything they could use to scrape away at the loose, flaky surface of the forest floor. A few of the men slashed the wool covers off their canteens and started whittling at the thin bead of solder welding the two halves together. When finally pried apart, a half a canteen made an admirable entrenching tool. Around Henry it appeared about half of the men had started digging, while the other half worked to keep the warriors back from their lines. Looking around at their ragged oval, he thought that those

---

*William L. English, I Company, Seventh U. S. Infantry.

who had been lucky enough to end up behind some downed timber or a tree stump were rich men by any measure.

"You dig," said the soldier beside him. "I'll spell you later."

Buck snapped his pocketknife open and started digging. After a few scrapes with the blade, he pushed the loosened soil away from the hole he had started. More digging, followed by moving another handful of dirt, slowly beginning to build up a low mound in front of the long, shallow trench he was gouging out of the ground. Copying the work of the soldiers who seemed to know what they were doing, no questions asked.

A few of the soldiers and volunteers returned the enemy's fire from time to time—if for no other reason than to keep the warriors honest, holding the enemy back from their ragged perimeter—while the rest continued to dig in for themselves and those wounded who could do nothing as the sun rose higher and the air got hotter. Shafts of hot, steamy light burned through the thick canopy of tree branches.

"What you think of that, Henry Buck?" Luther Johnson called out a few yards away. He was consumed with scratching at a trench using his big belt knife. "You know I dug for gold on this very hillside back in the sixties, the angels' truth it is. Never, Henry Buck, never did I figger I'd be back on this spot one day—not digging a shaft to find some gold . . . but digging a hole to save me life!"

Henry saw how much soil those soldiers moved with their bayonets and realized how pitifully slow he was getting the same job done with his folding knife. But as long as he could dig for a while, then shoot every now and then, Henry Buck figured it would keep his mind off the fact that Gibbon's attackers were now surrounded . . . maybe sixty or more miles from any assistance . . . without food or water . . . cut off from resupplying their ammunition.

"Where's that howitzer?" Gibbon wondered aloud. He slammed a fist into an open palm angrily.

"The gun crew should have had that twelve-pounder here by now," Rawn complained.

"Not just the howitzer," Gibbon muttered with a barely bottled frustration. "We're damn well gonna need those two thousand extra cartridges they were bringing us, too."

WITH Looking Glass slinking back from the front lines, aware of the new anger and undisguised contempt most of the *Nee-Me-Poo* now held for him, White Bird—oldest chief among the Non-Treaty bands—now assumed the ascendancy. Hard as he was on all the fighting men, he was even more brutal on his own young warriors.

"Ho—Red Moccasin Tops! And you there, Swan Necklace! See how your friend Shore Crossing is already dead!"

Yellow Wolf, like many of the other fighting men, turned his attention away from those soldiers retreating from the village, curious to watch White Bird scold the two surviving members of those first raids along the Salmon River that had ignited this wholesale war.

"Look at these *suapies* and Shadows, Red Moccasin Tops!" the old chief chided the two young men. "Swan Necklace—see how these enemies are not asleep like those you murdered back in Idaho country!"

Lumbering up to the front lines in the village, old White Bird shrieked right into the face of Red Moccasin Tops, "This is battle against an enemy who can defend themselves! Now is the time to show your courage and fight!"

Without a word, but plainly smarting from the chief's public rebuke, both of the young warriors led the charge into the willow, sprinting ahead along the path the retreating soldiers were taking—beginning to lay down a deadly fire into the white men as the soldiers scattered through the brush, racing madly for the hillside across the stream.

"I would like to ride them down on horseback!" Old Yellow Wolf suggested as he came up to grab his nephew's elbow. "Come with me!"

Yellow Wolf agreed. He spotted a brave warrior coming

toward the village from the willow. It was *Weyatnahtoo Latat*, the one called Sun Tied. Yellow Wolf's eyes immediately darted to the birthing lodge as he sadly remembered the brutal death he had seen inside earlier that morning, the man's wife and newborn daughter savagely killed.

"Sun Tied!" he called out. "Catch up a horse and come with us to kill the stragglers running for the hillside!"

The warrior looked over the uncle and nephew quickly and agreed with a harsh grin. "A fine idea! We can shoot them like ducks on a pond!"

Three more* joined the trio, and all six sprinted away to locate any ponies still tied to lodges, horses that hadn't been killed or hadn't bolted off with the noise, gunfire, and confusion.

Once they were mounted, the small war party raced their ponies south, to the upper end of camp, heading for a shallow crossing, where they would double back on the other side of the creek and launch their mounted attack on the last of the retreating soldiers—

Yellow Wolf and the other fighters jerked with the loud, shrill whistle as the cannonball hissed overhead on its way toward the village. They waited, watching the last of its flight—fully expecting the ball to explode the way such singing balls had at the Clearwater fight when Cut-Off Arm's soldiers used just such a cannon. As their eyes followed the descent of the black ball, it landed just beyond the easternmost lodges but failed to detonate.

Sun Tied turned, a smile widening on his powder-grimed face. "Yellow Wolf—I would like to see these soldiers who have brought this big gun that shoots twice. Maybe we can capture it for ourselves."

"*Eeh-heh!*" Yellow Wolf exclaimed, spotting the puff of powdersmoke clinging to the hillside. "We must do everything we can to keep any more of the big bullets from reaching our village!"

**Tenahtahkal Weyun* (Dropping from a Cliff), *Pitpillooheen* (Calf of Leg), and *Ketalkpoosmin* (Stripes Turned Down).

The six set off at a gallop, their horses splashing across the shallow ford and onto the grassy slope, angling southwest as they climbed toward that place where he had seen the curl of gray gunsmoke.

A second roar belched from the wide throat of that cannon on the hill as the horsemen entered the timber just north of the big gun's position. Ahead through the labyrinth of trees, Yellow Wolf spied the six mules and the big gun's wagon those mules were hitched to. He and Sun Tied immediately reined to the right, moving uphill through the trees to come around on the soldiers, when a single shot rang out from the forest, followed by a rattle of gunfire from those huddled around the cannon.

Someone was shooting at the *suapies* from above, and the soldiers were firing back.

Then Yellow Wolf heard gunfire coming from the direction his uncle had taken to launch his attack. That meant they had the soldiers wrapped up on three sides now! As he and Sun Tied reined their horses to the left and started downhill toward the gun crew, Yellow Wolf watched two of the *suapies* bolt from the ground and take off at a dead run into the trees. He fired his rifle at the pair, the exact moment one of the frightened mules reared in its harness—a soldier clinging to its back. The bullet struck the mule and it crumpled on all fours, crying out almost humanlike in its noisy bawl.

As the animal fell, it caught the soldier beneath it, pinning the man's legs beneath its heavy bulk while the mule shuddered, dying slowly.

Quickly dismounting so that he would do better with his aim, Yellow Bird sighted another warrior on the far side of the white men. *Seeyakoon Ilppilp*, known as Red Spy, was the one making things hot for the *suapies* from above. The moment one of the cannon men popped up to make a shot, Red Spy was already aiming and fired his gun. His bullet struck the soldier in the back and he crumpled over the gun's wagon, then slumped to the ground.

In the next heartbeat, Dropping from a Cliff fired at the

other lead mule. The animal kicked twice, then went down in a heap. That's when Stripes Turned Down stepped from the edge of the trees and bravely aimed his rifle at the last of the handful of soldiers still huddled around their gun. His bullet struck one of them, causing the rest to suddenly bolt, turning tail and dashing into the timber, heading up the hill, away from their back trail.

Earth Blanket, the one named *Wattes Kunnin*, surprised Yellow Wolf by bursting into the clearing from the southwestern side of the hill, his face flushed with excitement. He did not carry a firearm in his hands.

"Where is your rifle, Earth Blanket?" Yellow Wolf asked.

"I have none!"

"You do now," and Yellow Wolf pointed to those rifles abandoned by the fleeing soldiers.

With a big gulp of air, the breathless Earth Blanket nodded, saying, "I came to tell you of more soldiers coming!"

Sun Tied looked at Yellow Wolf and asked, "Could it be Cut-Off Arm and his *suapies*?"

"No," and Earth Blanket wagged his head. He was a half-*Umatilla* who had been born on White Bird Creek but had nonetheless joined Joseph's *Wallowa* band. "Only the fingers on my two hands, maybe less. All but one riding horses. That black-painted Shadow man walking on foot is leading a mule—and it carries a heavy load: four boxes on its back."

"Four boxes?" Old Yellow Wolf repeated. "Those boxes must hold something very, very important for that mule to have so many soldiers to tend to it!"

"Come with me to see what surprise we can make of this!" Sun Tied suggested.

"Horses and guns!" shouted Dropping from a Cliff in excitement.

At the same time they sighted the oncoming riders and the black-skinned man on foot with his single pack mule, Yellow Wolf also spotted his mother's brother, *Espowyes*, called Light in the Mountain, another relation of Joseph of the *Wallamwatkin* band. He was without a horse, crouched near the side of the trail where he was about to ambush the *suapies*.

Light in the Mountain stood and fired at the lead soldier who held the rope to the pack mule in his hand. When the bullet whistled past him, the soldier jerked backward, twisting to the side in his saddle, immediately freeing the rope as hc spurred his horse in the flanks and reined it back up the trail.

Instantly Yellow Wolf and the others kicked their horses into a gallop, every one of them yelling his loudest, their shrill war cries ricocheting off the side of the mountain. As that lead soldier wheeled and bolted his way back up the trail, the rest of the *suapies* scattered like a flock of frightened quail, turning to flee in a wild dash to safety.

"Cut those ropes!" Sun Tied ordered.

The four boxes clattered to the shady ground as Light in the Mountain crouched over the first one and hollered, "Bring me a rock for my hand!"

Slamming the rock down on the wooden crate again and again, he finally succeeded in busting it open about the time more of their number started work on the other three crates. Inside were small boxes made of hard paper. And inside each one stood as many bullets as Yellow Wolf had ever seen on a cartridge belt!

Old Yellow Wolf laid his hand on the young man's shoulder. "Nephew, come with me."

"You want the soldiers who got away from us?" he asked.

His uncle nodded. "I think we might find out where those soldiers are running to."

"Maybe they will have more bullets for our guns?" Yellow Wolf asked as they caught up their ponies and mounted.

With a grin, the uncle said, "And if the spirits are smiling on us . . . we will get ourselves a look at Cut-Off Arm's soldiers coming up the other side of this mountain."

Chapter Sixty-Two

August 9, 1877

He could hear the muffled hoofbeats coming in that ear pressed against the forest floor. Even more of the red buggers come to join in the god-blamed slaughter.

In panic, Private John O. Bennett took another deep breath and heaved with his free leg, giving all he had to shove it against the ribs of the dying mule, desperate to pull the pinned leg free before those horsemen, or those working in on foot, got close enough to finish him off. Grunting again, straining harder this time, Bennett threw every bit of his dwindling reserves into his task—heart thumping, breathing short and ragged, his eyes ever darting about, ears attuned to every little sound that thundered out of the shadowy timber.

It wasn't as if John O. Bennett were a stranger to fighting; no stranger to tough scrapes was he. Why, he'd even be celebrating his fifty-seventh birthday this fall if he ever got his leg out from under this damned mule. If, that is, the critter hadn't broken any of his bones when it collapsed with him under it.

Bennett clenched his eyes shut, of a sudden praying that God with His limitless grace would move the damned mule so he could make a run of it, just to have a chance . . . rather than be trapped here when the red bastards showed up.

He'd marched into Mexico with Kearney's frontier army back in '46, no mere lad at twenty-five. Dragoons, they were called in those days. Then he had served out another entire war in Union Blue. While there were some who craved the stripes of corporal or sergeant—Bennett had tried them both—private had a much nicer ring to it these days of what he had figured would be his last enlistment. B Company, Seventh U. S. Infantry.

Last summer he'd been with his captain, James H. Bradley, that hot afternoon they spyglassed the carcasses of man and beast on the distant hillside overlooking what few burial lodges the Sioux and Cheyenne had left behind at the Little Bighorn.

Old enough to be the lieutenant's father, how Bennett had wanted to march into battle with Bradley again that morning—good man that the lieutenant was and all—but Bradley had other ideas for the aging private who vividly personified "an Old Army soldier."

"You know how General Gibbon feels about you, Private."

He had smiled at Bradley. "You always did know how to make this old man blush now, sir."

"Gibbon calls you his 'brave old John Bennett,' " Bradley had repeated. "So we want you to stay and give the two sergeants a steady hand."

"They ain't young whips, are they, Lieutenant?"

Bradley had shaken his head. "No. Daly and Frederick. Both old salts."

"Not near as old as me."

The lieutenant had grinned. "No man's a fighting man like you, Private Bennett. With you along, we know the gun will get down there when we need it to open up on 'em come morning."

Minutes later Bradley was leading the rest of Gibbon's boys away, leaving that mountain howitzer and its six-man gun crew to nurse the balky six-mule team down the trail behind a civilian who would scout ahead and pick a way down to some spot overlooking the village, where they could put the fieldpiece into action. Wouldn't that make them Nez Perce scamper and prance!

At the wagon train in those final minutes before Joe Blodgett started them down the creek, Lieutenant Jacobs's Negro manservant, William Woodcock, decided he'd come along, too, rather than waiting back with the train guard on the mountainside.* Woodcock figured he would carry his master's double-barreled shotgun along for some proper protection since he was going on foot, leading a packhorse burdened with a quarter of a ton of rifle ammunition.

Bennett climbed up on the off-hand lead mule and they rumbled out of the wagon camp, the twelve-pounder on its prairie carriage, its long, wheeled caisson attached, following Sergeant John W. H. Frederick, a thirty-year veteran of both the Civil War and the Seventh Infantry with a record marked "*most exceptional*"—the only man in the crew with any artillery experience—and Sergeant Patrick C. Daly, a forty-four-year-old emigrant from county Limerick, Ireland. After three long enlistments in the Seventh Infantry, his was an excellent duty record as well.

The rest of the detail consisted of Corporal Robert E. Sale, a twenty-nine-year-old recruit with an extreme devotion to duty; Private Malcolm McGregor, a thirty-one-year-old emigrant from Glasgow, Scotland; and Private John H. Goale, a twenty-six-year-old recruit from Cincinnati.

"I hear you know where you're going, Blodgett," Bennett said as they rumbled across the slope.

"I been down this way more'n once," the civilian said. "We'll be there in no time."

Fact was, Blodgett had been in and through this part of Montana Territory before it even was Montana Territory. The first time was back in 1859, when the entire Bitterroot valley had no more than twenty-nine white settlers! Three years later he had guided supply wagons over from the bustling mining settlement of Bannack, by way of the Big Hole and this very same Trail Creek. His road was used two years later in '64 by a party of emigrants and again in '69 by another train of settlers bound for the Bitterroot. Using that path he knew so well, Blodgett got the gun crew down

—

*Such relationships between officers and slaves were not unheard of in the Indian-fighting army of the West. It was more often than not a relationship that was ignored by the higher echelons of the army, just as it was with Surgeon John FitzGerald's Negro cook and house servant, Jennie.

to the bluff overlooking the village just past daylight, after they had been hearing the gunfire for some time.

Bennett had glanced over his shoulder, just barely seeing Woodcock back up the trail, patiently leading that lone pack mule on foot.

Upon reaching the clearing Blodgett had picked out, the old private remained atop that howitzer's lead mule, coaxing that beast the best he could to get the team turned so the howitzer could be put into action. That's when the sergeants got the rest of the crew to unhitch the caisson and muscle it to the side, chocking the wheels, then throwing back the tops of both chests to expose the eight rounds held by each box.

"Give it to 'em down there where all them warriors are!" Sergeant Frederick ordered. "Bring its ass round this way!"

Their breath puffing in the cold morning air, the four others laid their shoulders into the wheels.

"Gimme some elevation," Frederick growled at them. "We gotta make it reach, boys."

"Which of these charges do you want?" Sergeant Daly asked as Corporal Sales went to work dropping the elevation screw.

"One of them spherical cases to start!" Frederick ordered. "This gun won't reach much more'n a thousand yards. But that spherical case'll give them warriors something to reckon with anyway, I'd wager."

Bennett kept a tight rein on the mule team when the howitzer belched that first time, jolting the piece as Frederick and the others scrambled to swab out the bore and reload, this time using one of the shells.

"Two pounds lighter!" Frederick was explaining when Blodgett suddenly gave the warning.

"We're gonna have company soon!" the civilian barked.

They all peered down the slope for but a moment, seeing how some of the Nez Perce horsemen were starting from the south end of the village toward their position.

"How sharp's that slope?" Frederick grumbled as he turned his back on the valley below. "Thirty degrees?

Maybe more? Crank down that screw and gimme all the elevation you can by rolling the bloody gun up on these chocks! This'un's gotta reach farther for us to do any good for our men down below!"

"You damn well better hurry, boys!" Bennett roared about the time Blodgett leaped atop his horse and shot right on past him without a word of fare-thee-well, lunging up the back trail.

While Bennett had been concentrating his attention on those warriors streaming out of the village for a notch of timber north of their gun placement, he hadn't been at all aware of the Nez Perce dashing toward them *along* the slope just above their position—horsemen who had already fled the camp below and were well along in the process of flanking Gibbon's attack force. The first shot stung the lead mule low in the neck, not far from where the private gripped the harness straps. It whipped its head from side to side, then started kicking as a second shot struck it low in the belly—doing everything it could to pitch its rider off.

He cursed himself many times for blindly doing his best to stay on that wounded mule, even as it keeled to the side and crashed down on his right leg in a web of tangled harness, noisy, braying mules, and a maze of stomping, thrashing legs and hooves.

The first thing Bennett did when he caught his breath was try to pull himself free. No good. The second thing he thought to do was look around for what help he could call over.

"This is another Custer massacre!" one of the privates shrieked as he bounded away up the hill.

Bennett watched the backs of McGregor and Goale disappear up the hill through the shadows of the lodgepole pine. *Likely gonna run all the way to Fort Ellis—brave sons a bitches they are!*

He heard a loud slap of blood hitting flesh and bone—wondering if it were another one of these cantankerous mules as he brought up his arms to cover his face from their slashing hooves. Through the dancing legs he caught a glimpse of Corporal Sales sliding down against one of the caisson wheels, his Springfield still clutched in both hands, the front of his gray pullover dark with a shiny gravy stain. The corporal's chin slowly sank until it rested against his breastbone and he didn't move again.

"You hit, Bennett?"

"No, Sergeant Frederick!" he cried, recognizing the artilleryman's voice. "I can use your help gettin' my leg out—"

"I was hoping you could help me!" Frederick interrupted with a sputter. "I've took a bullet."

"Shit," Sergeant Daly grumbled aloud. "I s'pose neither of you's gonna be coming to help me get outta of me fix, are you now?"

"You wounded, too?" Frederick asked.

"Not so bad I can't make a run for it with you," Daly admitted.

Frederick said, "Get over here on this side of the gun and together we'll get up to them trees—"

"Sergeants!" Bennett cried.

"Shuddup and lay quiet!" Frederick ordered as he crabbed around the far side of the caisson in a crouch. "There ain't nothing we can do for you. Maybe they'll run right past you and come after us!"

Bennett listened as the two men shuffled away, half-dragging each other into the timber—the sound of their scuffing boots quickly drowned out by the chorus of victorious war cries headed his way.

"Shuddup and lay quiet, he says!" Bennett cursed. "Goddamn the sergeants of this world!"

He damn well wasn't going to take the chance those horsemen would rush on past him when they found a white man pinned down—prime pickings for some delicious torture. He thrashed to one side, pushing with his free leg again, then turned himself onto the other side, ready to thump the heaving animal on the back of the head—

When he felt the knot under his right thigh. His bloody folding knife!

Twisting slightly to drag it out of the front pocket of his britches, the private snapped it open as he stretched his body for all it was worth, struggling to get close enough to the mule's neck to do some good. Spitting out a mouthful of pine needles and dirt, Bennett jabbed the knife's tip into the mule's hide. The animal barely moved. Again he stabbed. And the beast moved a little more.

Finally he jabbed and jabbed, all the harder—heaving back on his leg at the same time.

It popped free!

Quickly looking around, he saw his Springfield was under the same damned mule, but he had that knife. The leg was coming alive with agonizing stabs of pain as blood surged back through the crushed, thirsty tissue. Bennett thought he should give it a try and shifted a little weight onto it—nearly falling—then whirled around suddenly at that war cry.

Across the clearing a warrior was charging him on foot.

Lunging on that half-asleep leg, Bennett scooped up Corporal Sales's rifle and immediately dropped to his knee. Firing off a shot that made the Nez Perce skid to a halt and duck for cover, Bennett clambered to his feet and started up the trail behind everyone else.

He wasn't sure how long that wooden leg of his would stay under him, what with the strain of his run, or how long his lungs would hold out, burning the way they were with such exertion at this high altitude—but Private Bennett wasn't about to turn belly-up now!

Not after the greasers down in Mexico and the Rebs down south had both tried to kill him more times than he cared to count . . . this was one soldier who wasn't about to turn his scalp over to these red bastards!

Chapter Sixty-Three

August 9, 1877

"Kill that goddamn horse, will you, sir!"

Lieutenant Charles Woodruff had listened to many of those pleas over the last few minutes . . . then reluctantly decided he had but one thing he could do.

His was the only horse that had reached the siege area alive. Colonel John Gibbon had abandoned his big gray down in the village with its broken leg, and by the time the retreat began none of the other handful of mounts a few of the civilians rode down from the wagon train ever managed to get out of the village alive.

Just as soon as they were completely surrounded, the Nez Perce began sighting in on Woodruff's animal—certainly the biggest target, easiest, too, since the men were religiously hugging the ground and digging in.

At first Woodruff had resisted the notion of killing the animal himself. If the Indians ended up doing it, he could accept that. But to kill such a magnificent horse himself?

For a long time as he brooded on it the lieutenant kept waiting to hear a third shot from that howitzer, knowing that the arrival of the fieldpiece was sure to drive off the warriors who had them surrounded, forcing them to flee on out of the village, raising their seige before his horse was wounded beyond any hope of recovery. But they heard no more than those two cannonshots—his hopes fading as quickly as had the hissing boom of that second, and final, blast from the mountain howitzer.

"Just shoot your horse and be done with it, Mr. Woodruff!" Gibbon finally growled himself, grown exasperated as the lieutenant's mount kicked and thrashed against the hold the lieutenant had on it, its wild gyrations endangering any of the men entrenching nearby as it danced this way and that.

"Yes, sir."

One of the civilians shouted, "We're gonna need them horse steaks for lunch, Lieutenant!"

Without paying the brittle laughter any heed, Woodruff grabbed hold of the stirrup, quickly dragged himself to his feet, then lunged alongside the nervous animal to its head. Before he had time to reconsider what he was doing he fired a pistol bullet into the horse's brain.

It dropped like a sack of buckshot, kicked a few times, then lay still with a final shudder as a bullet scuffed into the dirt beside his left foot. For an instant, that foot went numb; then his heel began to burn. Sinking to his knee as bullets whined through the trees, he twisted around to inspect his boot. A bullet had sliced through the back of the leather, making for an oozy flesh wound.

"Very good, Mr. Woodruff," Gibbon said. "Come with me and the others."

Woodruff rose to a crouch, slowly putting pressure on the wounded heel, finding that it didn't hurt nearly as bad as it looked. He stretched out on his belly, following the colonel and a handful of officers as they crawled to the end of their crude one-acre fortress, right to the very last of the skinny lodgepole pines, where they found themselves at the edge of a sharp embankment that fell away some twenty feet to the creek and willows below.

"Look there, General," Woodruff announced. "Warriors working their way at us."

"Should we fire at them?" Captain Rawn asked.

Gibbon wagged his head. "No. I came here only to have us a look at the village, reconnoiter the enemy's retaking of their camp."

Those warriors and the Nez Perce who had already closed in around them on the hillside, had Gibbon's command surrounded. It was clear from the discussion the officers held there at the edge of the embankment that there was no way to break out of the lines and rush the encampment in some desperate bid to locate more ammunition among the lodges. That became the overriding concern there and then: the fact that they were separated from their wagon train carrying a reserve of ammunition.

"But what if the Nez Perce ride back on our trail and find our wagon corral?" asked Captain Richard Comba.

Gibbon's face turned a solemn gray. "The train guard isn't big enough to hold off a stiff attack."

"I respectfully submit we've got to have our company commanders stop their men from throwing away their ammunition," Woodruff suggested.

Gibbon agreed as they heard an unearthly scream from one of the wounded men left in the creek bottom—those agonized cries from below filling the quiet pauses between gunshots on this hillside. "All of you, we must conserve our cartridges. Put a stop to rapid firing at the enemy. Shoot only when you are assured of a target."

As Woodruff was just starting to rock onto a knee to follow the others crabbing back to rejoin the men in that corral of rifle pits, a volley of shots persuaded the lieutenant to pitch himself onto the ground with the rest. He lay there a few moments, catching his breath, then realized his legs hurt like hell—probably from that excruciating climb up the slope.

But when he attempted to drag the legs under him preparing to get back onto his feet, Woodruff realized it was more than mere muscle fatigue. The pale sky blue of his wool britches was spotted with glistening blood. Both legs. Just above the knees.

Mortally scared, he immediately grabbed both burning wounds and squeezed, hopeful it would relieve the rising pain, then quickly felt along the big bones for any fractures.

"Thank you, God," he whispered.

Woodruff's head sagged back in his shoulders as he closed his eyes, grateful the bullet that had sliced through both legs had missed the bones. Otherwise, he would have lost both legs.

Oh, Louie, he thought of his wife as he opened his stinging eyes, smearing a tear across a powder-grimed cheek with the back of his bloody hand.

At least I can still dance with you on our next anniversary!

WHILE most of the warriors who had taken part in the capture of the big wagon gun now went back to fight the soldiers who were hiding down in their hollows, Yellow Wolf and his mother's brother, Light in the Mountain, rode off up the slope, leading a small scouting party to search for more soldiers who must surely be coming their way.

Not far up the trail, the scouts divided, most continuing right on up the mountainside to put themselves above the soldiers who had escaped the village and taken refuge in the trees, while Yellow Wolf and Light in the Mountain stayed with the route the wagon gun soldiers had taken when they turned around and fled during the capture of their weapon. Farther and farther the two rode, without seeing any sign of the white men.

"These soldiers have run very fast," sighed Light in the Mountain as they finally brought their ponies to a halt.

"Do you think they have run all the way back to the settlers' valley?"* Yellow Wolf wondered.

"I hoped we could see Cut-Off Arm and his soldiers coming over the mountains," said his uncle. "At least to run across some of their big wagons filled with supplies and more ammunition."

"Listen, you can even hear the guns of *Ollokot*'s warriors firing from so far away," he told his uncle. "Since we did not find the soldiers, or their wagons, let's go back and see if we can help the families."

"Maybe there is something for us to do in the village, to help the wounded," Light in the Mountain suggested.

As they backtracked down that trail both the village and the soldiers had used to reach the Place of the Ground Squirrels, Yellow Wolf began to hear the first faint wails of grief rising from those in the encampment. As the pair reached the bottom and were beginning to angle left to see

---

*The Bitterroot valley.

how the fight was going at the siege area, both riders heard a loud scream—one clearly made by a man.

Thinking one of their own might be in danger, they immediately kicked their ponies into a lope for the tall willows in the boggy bottom. It was there they came upon a scene of three older women hunched over a figure wearing the muddy pale blue britches of a soldier.* His legs kicked and flailed as two of the old women pinned him down and a third squatted over him, straddling her victim. She had a bloodied knife clutched in both of her hands, poised with it over her head, preparing to plunge it into the soldier a second time.

The wounded man screamed even louder this time, kicking with his legs as the two warriors came upon the brutal scene.

Down slashed the knife as the soldier attempted to twist out of the way. Just when he turned his head to the side, the woman jammed the big blade into the side of his neck, blood squirting from a ruptured vessel, spraying her in the face and across her breasts.

His back arched in agony, his legs thrashing. On and on the white man begged and pleaded, fighting from side to side as his clothing and the ground beneath him grew soggy with blood. For a brief instant his eyes caught and held on Yellow Wolf's, then rolled back in his head a little as the old woman plunged her knife into his neck a third time. The soldier went limp and stopped fighting.

The other two women slowly dragged themselves to their feet, wiping their blood-splattered hands and arms on the white man's britches. That's when the three noticed the two warriors.

"He was already wounded," the knife holder explained as she wiped off the man's blood on her torn and soot-smudged dress. "I wanted to help him die faster. Even

---

*Historical testimony reveals that this soldier was in all likelihood Private Michael Gallagher, musician, attached to D Company of the Seventh U. S. Infantry.

though my son did not die fast this morning when one of these soldiers shot him. So I think this *suapie* got better than he deserved."

"Does he have any bullets on him?" Light in the Mountain asked.

The woman shook her head. "There was no gun or bullets near him. He must have lost them running from the village."

"Or," Yellow Wolf commented as he looked up the hillside to where the gunfire was sporadic, "the other soldiers took his gun and bullets for themselves when they left him behind to die a hard way."

"Let's go see these soldiers who would leave one of their own behind in battle," his uncle suggested.

"Yes—I want to see what sort of creature would leave his friends behind to die at the hands of women."*

Now that he and the other men had rallied and taken back their camp here in the river bottom, Lean Elk's curiosity was drawn by that loud roar of a wagon gun. He knew a little something about such weapons. The half-breed Frenchman galloped uphill to lead in the dismantling of the soldier cannon.

Showing the others how to use the white man's tools found in the wagon boxes, Poker Joe directed the loosening of each hub and the removal of the wheels. The warriors had great fun starting these heavy wheels spinning and

*Big Hole battle historians have documented that as many as eight of Gibbon's soldiers and Catlin's volunteers were indeed left behind in the retreat, eight white men still alive to one degree or another at that point when the rest made their mad dash to the hillside point of timber. These men were discovered by the women, old men, and boys who eagerly scoured through the brush to find any such white enemies still breathing. After *Ollokot*'s warriors had pulled back the following day and Howard's men had reached the scene a day after that, upon a search of the creek-bottom battlefield these eight bodies were discovered—not one of those wounded still alive after the Nez Perce had finished them off in a most horrific manner.

bounding down the hillside toward the creek bottom. With the gun eventually removed from its wagon, several of the stronger men worked hard to pitch the shiny brass barrel down the slope, watching it tumble and bound through the saplings trees and over the soft ground until it came to a stop just two short arrow flights below them.

That's when Bird Alighting took over the destruction, pulling his skinning knife from his belt and showing the others how they were going to dig a hole in which to bury the cannon.

"It's a great pity you destroyed this gun."

Turning at the words, Bird Alighting, Poker Joe, and the others looked up at the older horseman who had stopped above them. Of this warrior Joe did not know, he asked, "Why such a pity?"

"I know how to use this kind of gun."

Very dubious of such a claim, Poker Joe got to his feet and walked over to the horseman. He asked, "How would you know such a thing?"

"I learned when I was with the soldier chief named Wright."

That almost sounded convincing to Joe. "You fought alongside the soldiers in that war with Wright?"

"Yes," the horseman answered. "Against the Cayuse and Yakima. That's where I learned."

"Did you ever fire the gun yourself?" Bird Alighting challenged.

"No, but I watched them load and fire it over and over again, so I know how the white men do it."

Poker Joe looked down at the half-buried fieldpiece and shrugged. "Too late."

"Yes," the horseman said as he eased away. "And too bad. We could have used it to dislodge those soldiers from their rabbit hollows over in the trees."

Chapter Sixty-Four

August 9, 1877

Lieutenant Charles Woodruff flinched at that next dull thud—more lead slamming into human flesh.

The distinctive slap made his own wounds ache all the more, his soul whimpering as the men around him were hit, one after another.

Sometimes he could tell when a bullet struck bone. Other times it was no more than a moist slap as lead penetrated soft tissue. Woodruff couldn't help cringing when he heard a man cry out in pain, begging for help from his bunkies.

One at a time, the wounded were adding up, not just the ones they had managed to drag up here with them in the retreat but also those wounded the snipers were accounting for as Nez Perce marksmen sighted in on the soldiers' perimeter. By now there wasn't a white man who still had his hat on—they made such fine targets of a fellow.

Without a surgeon along, they had no clean bandages for each new wound. Instead, the men did what they could, pulling free their long shirttails and using their dirty digging knives to hack off wide strips of greasy, soiled cloth. At first it had galled Woodruff to see how the old files and the civilians spit a little tobacco juice into the wounds of their comrades before knotting a bandage over the puckered hole, but it didn't take long for him to accept that this was the way of things with these veteran frontiersmen.

Still, for a few of the worst cases, mere tobacco juice wrapped up with a piece of shirttail wasn't nearly enough to stop the bleeding of a blood vessel nicked by a Nez Perce bullet.

An old sergeant was the first to crab over to a rifle pit to help two young soldiers with their seriously wounded comrade. Quickly fingering a rifle cartridge from a loop on his prairie belt, he snapped open his pocketknife and deftly pried the lead bullet loose from its copper casing.

"Hol' 'im down, boys," he grumbled as he positioned the open cartridge right over the oozy leg wound.

As the two soldiers rocked their weight on top of their reluctant comrade, the old file reached in one of his belt pouches and pulled out a sulphur-headed lucifer he stuffed between his front teeth. Now with the fingers of his left hand, the old sergeant gently spread apart the ragged edges of the gaping wound and up-ended the cartridge before tamping the last of the black powder grains into the hole with a dirty fingertip. He quickly brushed away the excess powder, then leaned back.

As the sergeant pulled the match from between his teeth, the wounded soldier on the ground quit thrashing a moment, gazing up at the old file, and said, "H-hell, that wasn't so bad, Sarge."

But when the old soldier dragged his thumbnail across the head of the match, the young soldier went cross-eyed staring at the sudden flare as the whitish-blue flame inched closer and closer to his wounded leg. "Wh-what you gonna do with that—"

His question was instantly answered as the sergeant laid the burning lucifer down against the pocket of black powder with a sudden fiery *phfffft*. Spitting a momentary tongue of flame, a narrow tendril of greasy smoke rising from the wound, the fire had done its work, cauterizing the injured blood vessel.

"Looks like he'll be out for a while," the sergeant said, inspecting the soldier by gently raising the unconscious man's eyelids. He rolled back onto his knees and crabbed away, passing the young lieutenant on the way to his rifle pit.

The sergeant nodded at Woodruff and said, "How your bullet holes, sir?"

"T-they aren't bleeding like his was, Sergeant."

The old file grinned, his eyes crinkling. "Call me if you need me, Lieutenant."

Woodruff gulped, knowing exactly what the soldier was referring to. "A fine job over there, Sergeant. Man won't bleed to death now."

"Thankee, sir," he said, a little embarrassed as he started to move on. "Jus' a li'l something I picked up many a year ago during the Great War."

WHEN Yellow Wolf and his uncle reached the point of timber on the hillside overlooking the camp, a sporadic rattle of gunfire was still continuing as *Ollokot*'s warriors settled into the siege around the *suapies*. Many of the men on all sides were continuing to sing or chant their war and victory songs—each warrior calling on his *wyakin*, his individual spiritual power.

Yellow Wolf rode up to a knot of men surrounding Five Wounds, the famous warrior called *Pahkatos Owyeen*.

The grieving warrior stood in the middle, talking in low tones to the rest as Yellow Wolf slid off his pony, tied it to a nearby sapling, and stepped over to listen to their quiet discussion. He recognized the grave expressions on all the faces . . . but most especially that ghostly look on Five Wounds's face. His skin had taken on a gray pallor that only served to accentuate the reddened eyes, swollen from much crying.

That's when Yellow Wolf remembered the courageous death of Five Wounds's best friend, Rainbow, earlier that morning in the village fight.

"This sun, this time," Five Wounds was saying as he stared down at his repeater, "I am going to die."

"You are going to make a bravery run against the *suapies*?" asked *Ollokot*.

"No, this is not a run against them," Five Wounds explained. "I am going to charge right into their burrows and have them kill me when I reach them. Kill me when I am so close I can see the fear in their eyes."

His words, perhaps more the tone of Five Wounds's voice, immediately tugged at Yellow Wolf's heart. He knew the story—every *Nee-Me-Poo* knew that tale by heart—how these two had begun their friendship as small boys, a kinship that would be nurtured over more than two decades as they traveled ancestral lands and journeyed many times to *Illahe* together—sometimes fighting enemies, side by side, in that buffalo country far to the east.

Theirs was a bond not of blood but of the heart, even of their very spirits. And now that Rainbow had been killed, every man gathered there knew it was Five Wounds's day to die as well. Everyone knew that years ago the two brothers-in-arms had taken a vow that they would die on the same day.

No one dared stand in his way as he sought to fulfill his vow to Rainbow.

Otskai rode up and dismounted, holding out a soldier canteen as he stepped toward the group. "Five Wounds—see what I have found in the village."

"I am not thirsty," Five Wounds said.

Removing the stopper, *Otskai* held the canteen under Five Wounds's nose. "This isn't water, my brother."

"Whiskey," Five Wounds said, taking the canteen. "Yes, I will have a drink now."

"The white men drank whiskey before they attacked us?" Yellow Wolf asked as Five Wounds passed him the canteen, but he passed it right on. He never touched liquor.

"My brother is killed today," Five Wounds reminded those who needed no reminding while each man took a sip from the fragrant canteen. "And I shall go with him . . . while the sun is in this sky. We will die together the way his father and my father died together in the buffalo country. They lay side by side where the battle was the strongest. And now I shall lie down beside my warmate. He is no more and I shall see that I follow him."

Yellow Wolf remembered how the two fathers had been killed in a fight with Lakota over on the eastern plains. "Do you want us to lay down some cover fire as you make your charge?"

The dark, red-rimmed eyes in that tortured face turned to the younger man as Five Wounds said, "Yes. That would help me to get as close as I can to the white man's burrows before their bullets kill me."

Ollokot seized Five Wounds's forearm in his, and they shook, wrist to wrist. Several other men offered their arms, too, and Five Wounds took the forearm of each, to grasp in that manner of men who have suffered hardship together, men who have stood against powerful enemies together, men who have repeatedly placed their bodies between their families and the *suapies* . . . together in the brotherhood of warriors.

It made Yellow Wolf's eyes mist as Five Wounds turned away from him and the others, stepping to the edge of the shallow, narrow gulch that separated them from the soldiers.

Instead of immediately dashing for the white men's hollows, Five Wounds paused to look up at the sky, declaring, "Rainbow—may your spirit look over me now. I am coming! I am coming to join you!"

As those last words escaped his tongue, Five Wounds bolted away at a sprint, racing around the head of the ravine and dodging between trees as the first of the soldier bullets began to whine around him, some smacking the narrow trunks of lodgepole pines, others snapping off small branches.

They saw the first bullet hit Five Wounds, striking him in the shoulder, momentarily slowing his gait as the impact shoved him around to the side, knocking him off-stride but for an instant until he shrugged off the injury and ran even faster, half bent over, nearing the soldier burrows.

The others joined *Ollokot* as their war chief started singing his own war song in a loud, strong voice. Yellow Wolf raised his voice with the rest. In chanting their own medicine song, Five Wounds's warrior brothers were sending him on his way to meet his dearest friend—their songs his medicine songs at this fragile moment between life and death. Their combined strength would become his strength alone for as long as he needed theirs to accomplish this last great act of friendship.

A bullet ripped into Five Wounds's thigh, sending a shudder through his body, causing him to slow noticeably. He was limping—but still he plunged on, closer, ever closer, to the soldier burrows.

Now the white men were yelling, some of the men beginning to stand behind their rifle pits, shouting at one another and pointing their weapons at that lone oncoming warrior. It was as if all those rifles were suddenly trained on Five Wounds, fixed on him alone.

One of the bullets that snarled his way smacked into his chest, blowing out a large hole in his back—but it did nothing to stop the man now that he was nearing his goal. Five Wounds was almost close enough that he could throw his *kopluts* at the soldiers. . . .

Another bullet rocked him, striking him low in the other shoulder. He was so near the soldier hollows that the impact shoved him backward a faltering step. At that moment another bullet hit him low in the belly, knocking him sideways—before he visibly shook it off and bent over again, limping toward the hollows. But this time Five Wounds moved much, much slower.

Another bullet tore through his chest, leaving a second gaping hole in his back.

Yellow Wolf and many of the others stood there, every man openly weeping now as they watched this last selfless act of bravery for a friend.

"I am come this day to be with you, Rainbow!"

Though his body faltered, weaving and tottering very slowly toward the soldier burrows, Five Wounds's voice rang stronger than ever . . . even as another bullet rocked him, made him stumble and then collapse to his knees just short of the soldier lines.

Try as he might, he could not rise again, struggling to get his feet under him when two more bullets smacked into his body with the telltale breaking of bone as he was whirled one way, then the other, his weakened arms windmilling with the force of each impact. Still his head was held high as his undaunted will struggled to control his failing body.

Collapsing forward, he planted both hands in front of him. Five Wounds crawled on.

Three more bullets hit him: one in the leg, another in the chest, and the third in the hip, breaking the big bone that could no longer support his weight.

And as Five Wounds wobbled there on one knee, he looked up at the sky, opening his mouth to speak—

"Rainbow, I am come to join—"

A bullet slammed into his forehead, snapping it backward violently, driving him off that one knee and hand, pitching his body backward onto his side . . . just short of his goal.

But Yellow Wolf knew better than to think Five Wounds hadn't finished his quest. As he wiped a hand down his face and cleared his eyes, he knew Five Wounds had reached his goal. Even though he hadn't made it into the heart of the soldier hollows, he had nonetheless gotten close enough to gaze into the eyes of the men who would kill him.

By now, this brave man was already reunited with Rainbow.

"DAMN—will you lookit that down there!"

Turning painfully at that exclamation from a nearby soldier, Lieutenant Charles Woodruff slowly crawled over to have himself a look from the edge of the bluff.

A warrior was coming out from the village, mounted on a showy pony. He guided the animal into the willow as he headed for the base of the soldiers' hill.

"Five dollars to the man who knocks him down afore me," proposed Second Cavalry Sergeant Edward Page, lying off to Woodruff's left.

After only two shots from the warrior, who reappeared in the brush below to fire up the slope—Page's head flopped backward, a neat, black hole below his chin, the top of his head blown off.

"I'll get that son of a bitch for you, Sarge," vowed one of the cavalrymen near Page's body. "An' you won't owe me a goddamned fiver!"

When that horseman next appeared, he didn't even have the time to raise his rifle before the trooper's bullet knocked him off the back of his pony.

"Watch 'im," the marksman warned those around him. "If he moves while I'm reloading, hit him again to make sure he's a good Injun—"

Down below in the creek bottom, a horrendous cry interrupted him. The sort of sound that would make any man's blood curdle.

" 'Spect they found 'nother of our wounded, Lieutenant," a soldier said quietly.

"Goddamn 'em to Hell!" a corporal cursed as they all listened to the pitiful screams of that white man—soldier or volunteer—whose life was slowly snuffed out in a most horrible fashion.

One of the older men ground his hands together, his words slipping out between clenched teeth: "If I just could get my hands on one of them monsters right now!"

Woodruff reclined back against a small mound of dirt thrown up by a long-fallen tree's roots. Swallowing down the rising pain in his left heel and both thighs, he wondered if they all would have that chance to get their hands on the Nez Perce soon enough . . . when the red bastards made one final charge.

Chapter Sixty-Five

Wa-Wa-Mai-Khal, 1877

While the sun rose higher and hotter through that long morning, Yellow Wolf had watched how Red Moccasin Tops had done such effective work with his soldier carbine against the *suapies*. This warrior, who was called *Sarpsis Ilppilp*, crouched behind a small boulder close to the hollows, where he undeniably had accounted for several of the soldiers who had fallen, either killed or badly wounded.

When his bullets struck a victim, Red Moccasin Tops celebrated and roared loudly, chanting his own strong-heart song while he reloaded and adjusted the white wolfskin cape he had tied around the shoulders of the red flannel shirt he had on—one of the powerful talismans he wore to ward off the death spirit. No other fighting man had dared crawl as close to the white enemies as Red Moccasin Tops.

"Where is White Bird now?" he shouted to the other warriors every time he hit one of the white men.

"He is not here!" a voice answered.

Someone else said, "Maybe still in the village."

Each time, the exchange was the same. Red Moccasin Tops told those who had the soldiers surrounded, "Don't you see that I am here and he is not! But this morning White Bird accused me of being a coward. *Wahlitits* and I were the only men brave enough to start this war. Who is this White Bird to call *us* cowards when Shore Crossing lies dead in the village—killed defending his home and family? He was a patriot killed defending his people and their freedom!"

Over time Yellow Wolf thought Red Moccasin Tops grew a little bolder as he popped out from the protection of his rock, quickly aimed, and fired a shot at the soldiers huddled like scared voles in their rifle pits.

"Who is White Bird to accuse me of being a coward because I started this war with my friend?" he shouted as he reloaded another cartridge into his soldier carbine. "See the soldiers cower from me in their hollows! Let no man question my courage now—"

At the instant he crept around the side of the boulder in a crouch, his rifle already at his shoulder, a bullet struck Red Moccasin Tops in the side of his throat, not only slashing open a massive blood vessel but also cutting the leather strand of his sacred dentalium-shell necklace, which he tied choker-style around his neck. For some weeks now *Sarpsis Ilppilp* had believed this necklace held *hattia tinukin*, the death spirit, at bay.

His body was hurtled to the side, landing in a heap, where he gurgled for a few moments, trying to speak, his legs pumping in anguish while blood spurted onto his sacred wolfskin cape.

For some time the others were stunned into complete silence.

"Who will bring Red Moccasin Tops out to safety?" someone finally cried from the late-morning shadows.

"Who among you is bravest?" immediately echoed a familiar voice. It belonged to the young warrior's father, Sun Necklace.

"Perhaps I am brave enough!" another voice called out.

His voice cracking with deep emotion, Sun Necklace hollered, "We do not want to leave Red Moccasin Tops there! We cannot leave him for the crazy white people to cut him up in pieces to make a fool of this brave warrior! Who will bring his body away, and carry him to me?"

"I am his good friend—I will bring *Sarpsis Ilppilp* away!" sang Strong Eagle. "Come along, all those who want to save the body of a hero."

Yellow Wolf and six others hollered their agreement and hurried to follow Strong Eagle, the cousin of Red Moccasin Tops. Running and dodging in a crouch, they used the narrow trees the best they could to cover their intent. Inside their ring of rifle pits, the soldiers yelled their warnings at one another, becoming very animated. Yellow Wolf decided that, with Five Wounds having made his suicide charge not long ago, the white men believed that the rest of the warriors were now coming in for a massive assault.

The *suapies* laid down a murderous fire, knocking over the man beside Yellow Wolf. A bullet struck *Weweetsa*, called Log, in the collarbone and came out the opposite shoulder. The warriors left the wounded man where he lay and continued to sneak toward the boulder.

The remaining seven didn't get much closer when *Quiloishkish* had his right elbow shattered by a soldier bullet. He twisted to the ground, writhing in pain, groaning through clenched teeth.

"We should go back," Strong Eagle said regretfully.

Yellow Wolf reminded, "It is yours to decide: he is your cousin."

"His body is too close to the soldiers!" Strong Eagle snapped. "We will go back."

The six retreated, gathering up their two wounded on the way out.

It wasn't very long before Strong Eagle resentfully worked himself into a frenzy once more, desiring to retrieve the body of his cousin. "I will go again," he announced. "Come with me if you want to save his body."

For this attempt there were only five, since one of the warriors dropped out. And this time Strong Eagle led them in a different direction, staying at the bottom of a shallow draw that led down beneath the rifle pits to a spot not far from where Red Moccasin Tops lay.

"Wait here for me," Strong Eagle instructed the others. "I will bring his body back to this ravine."

Vaulting over the top of the shallow gully and surprising the *suapies*, the warrior scrambled on all fours to reach the boulder as bullets slammed against trees and plowed into the ground all around him. A moment after he reached the body, Strong Eagle shouted back to the others.

"My cousin is not dead! He still breathes!"

That was momentous news to Yellow Wolf as he

watched Strong Eagle start away from the boulder, slowly standing with Red Moccasin Tops draped across his shoulder. He managed to lunge toward the ravine only a matter of steps before a soldier bullet found its mark, hitting Strong Eagle in the side. He pitched forward into the dirt and pine needles, dropping his cousin with a grunt.

Gasping in pain, Strong Eagle caught his breath, glancing down at the two wounds along his lower ribs. Then he crawled over to his cousin's body, grabbed hold of the belt, and started to pull Red Moccasin Tops onto his shoulder once more. Wobbly, Strong Eagle struggled to rise and eventually managed another half-dozen steps toward the ravine, when he collapsed under the weight, too weak from his loss of blood.

"My cousin, now he breathes no more," Strong Eagle announced some time later after he had rested on the ground.

"Come out by yourself!" Yellow Wolf shouted.

With a weak voice, Strong Eagle whimpered, "My heart feels small and cold that I cannot bring out the hero!"

His very soul aching for all the loss he had witnessed this day, Yellow Wolf said, "If your cousin is dead, he is beyond your help now."

"LIEUTENANT? I wan'cha lookit this bullet hole in me."

Charles Woodruff turned slightly as the enlisted man twisted about in his shallow rifle pit when the lieutenant was dragging himself past, sent by Gibbon to have someone check on the men and count the number of cartridges each of them still had available in the event of a rush by more than one warrior—the likes of which they had experienced a little while before.

"It can't be too bad now, can it?" he asked as the private inched toward him, pushing himself along with one hand, sliding on his hip. "If you can move that well—"

Charles Alberts* pulled his other bloody hand away from the damp, dark patch on his chest as the lieutenant

---

*See chapter 55.

bent forward to look. That's when Woodruff's words caught in his throat.

Moist blood not only continued to seep from the bullet hole the soldier had been pressing his hand over, but there were frothy bubbles escaping from the wound as well. From what little the lieutenant remembered of his basic human anatomy, the Nez Perce bullet had gone through the man's lungs. Woodruff took a deep breath, unsure what he would say to the soldier, since those bubbles did not bode well for the man surviving a lengthy siege.

"I near got myself killed by some women in a tepee this morning," Alberts confessed quietly. "Was ordered to search the tepees—them squaws tried to kill me, but I didn't hit till just a little while ago."

Woodruff could only stare at that dark, bubbling hole.

"I'm asking you, Lieutenant," the private said, a slight quiver in the voice he consciously attempted to keep from wavering, " 'cause we don't have no surgeon along."

"You sure picked a poor substitute," Woodruff eventually replied, remembering to keep the gravity from showing in his eyes and his voice. "Here, let me take a look at your back. See the exit wound."

But when he looked at the soldier's shirt, then pulled up the blouse and peered at the back of the man's gray fatigue pullover, there was no hole. That meant no exit wound.

"Seems the bullet didn't come out, Private."

Alberts asked, "Wha-what's that mean, Lieutenant?"

"Means it's a serious wound, soldier."

Alberts swallowed hard, then coughed a little as he pressed his sticky fingers against the hole all the more firmly. "What you think of my chances, sir?"

Woodruff sighed, ruminating on what to say. It didn't make sense to tell the private just how bad things were, but . . . his conscience wouldn't let him lie to a man in that condition, either.

"Alberts, you have a serious wound—but there is no need of your dying . . . if you've got the nerve."

"The n-nerve, Lieutenant?"

"The nerve to hang on until relief comes and a surgeon gets here. You've already shown you had the nerve to see it through our difficult march and this hellish battle. If you've got the nerve to make it through this siege, you'll come out just fine on the other side."

It took a moment, but Private Charles Alberts finally grinned wanly. He said, "Thank you, Lieutenant. I promise I'll keep my nerve up."

Woodruff watched the soldier slide sideways around in his shallow rifle pit, lean back against the dirt breastwork, then close his eyes as another round came whining through their position—

"The red sonsabitches gonna burn us out!" came the pained yelp just as Woodruff's nose registered that peculiar stench of burning grass.

"Where's that coming from?" an officer called.

"Up the hill!"

"There—to the west!"

The first smudge of pale, whitish smoke wafted through the stand of lodgepole, assaulting their noses. The wounded began crying out all the more piteously with a new danger that only intensified their suffering from the heat and want of water. Now the very air around them was becoming a suffocating blanket too heavy to breathe.

"This can only mean the warriors are going to charge us!" Gibbon shouted from his place near the southern edge of the scene. "They're gonna rush in under cover of the smoke!"

Alberts reached out to snag Woodruff's arm. He pleaded, "Promise you'll kill me with your revolver afore they get their hands on me, Lieutenant."

"I don't want one more of our wounded to fall into their bloody hands," Woodruff vowed, instantly recalling the cries of those they had left in the creek bottom when they retreated to this little plateau. "This pistol is our last resort, soldier."

"Lieutenant Woodruff!"

"Yes, sir, General Gibbon?"

"Do you remember last year about this time, up at Fort Shaw, when Looking Glass himself and some of his warriors were on their way back home from the buffalo plains?"

Woodruff swallowed, the war cries and chants behind the smoke becoming louder still. The recollection was clear as rain-rinsed crystal.

"Yes, sir. Looking Glass held a sham battle for you on the broad plain near the stables—divided his warriors in two for the show."

"One band lit a grass fire," Gibbon recalled. "Made a charge in beneath all the smoke, driving the other side from the field."

"You heard the general, men!" Woodruff roared now with the certainty they had only moments to live. "This is a tactic the Nez Perce love to use in battle. Be prepared for a final charge. Make every one of your last cartridges count!"

As their throats became raw with coughing and their eyes stung with tears, attempting to peer through the billowing waves of grass smoke, Woodruff listened to the increasing amplitude of the war cries. They swelled in a seeming crescendo over several minutes as the breathless soldiers waited for the charge to come—a charge that meant the very real possibility of defeat and death . . . perhaps even worse.

"The smoke! My God—it's dyin' off!"

Sure as sun, the wind had suddenly shifted and blew the fire right back on the scorched hillside. Starved for fuel, the flames were swiftly snuffed out. No longer did the afternoon breeze carry the thick, stifling clouds of gray right into the soldier lines.

With his eyes tearing now that he could actually begin to see some distance beyond their ragged rectangle of rifle pits, Woodruff whispered a silent prayer, the first he had said in many a year.

He vowed to the Almighty that he would pray a little more often from here on out.

Chapter Sixty-Six

Wa-Wa-Mai-Khal, 1877

In their third attempt to retrieve the body of Red Moccasin Tops, a group of warriors led by Old Yellow Wolf managed to lay down enough harassing fire that Bighorn Bow, called *Tahwis Takaitat*, crawled under a barrage of soldier bullets and pulled *Sarpsis Ilppilp* away from the soldier hollows.

"You have done what I wanted!" roared Sun Necklace in relief.

By the time they carried the body out of the timber to the mouth of the ravine, a small crowd of old women had gathered in the creek bottom, patiently waiting to assist the family with the burial. It was not the first such ceremony those women had helped with that day. Yellow Wolf and his mother's brother stood by while the women cleaned the warrior's body, then wrapped it in a new blanket. After laying the body on a travois, they began walking their pony into the timbered hills, planning to leave Red Moccasin Tops in a secret place.

When the oldest among the women determined the spot, she signaled the others to halt. There they quickly went to work scraping at the soft forest floor, gouging out a final resting place for this hero's body.

"I remember a time early this summer, when he showed me his shell necklace," the dead man's father said quietly, standing to the side with Yellow Wolf and his uncle, joined by the oldest woman in charge of the burial party. "He said his medicine would be strong when he wore it into battle."

"He was right," the matriarch added, a slight lisp to her words due to the loss of so many of her front teeth. "Red Moccasin Tops *was* bullet-proof from the neck down when he wore it around his throat."

"Did you see how strong his medicine worked at that first battle against the soldiers?" Sun Necklace asked the woman proudly. "When the *suapies* attacked us in *Lahmotta*?"

"I did see with my own eyes," she replied, her old eyes filled with wonder. "After the fight was over and the soldiers all ran away . . . Red Moccasin Tops came back to the village and leaped off his horse in front of a big crowd of us who were singing the fighters' praises. I noticed how many bullet holes punctured his red flannel shirt and the blanket around his neck, but not a single bullet wound in his flesh!"

"After I gave him a hug of congratulation," Sun Necklace explained, "he took off the gun belt he had strapped around his waist—"

"Everyone standing there saw how many flattened, misshapen bullets fell from his shirt then," the old woman concluded. "Because they were trapped beneath his shirt and spilled out when he finally took off his belt."

"The *suapie* bullet hit him many times that day, yet not a one of them penetrated his flesh," his proud father remarked.

Then Sun Necklace fell silent for some time as the women laid the shroud into the long, shallow hole and started to scoop dirt back into it with their hands. "Some soldier made a lucky shot this day, to kill my son with a bullet that struck him above his medicine necklace."

"And what of your promise, Sun Necklace?" Old Yellow Wolf asked the father.

"Promise?"

"To give the wolf hide away to the man who rescued your son's body."

He nodded once. "Yes. I forgot about that. I will have to think about that—and talk to his mother, too."

"But that was a vow you made to those young warriors!"

Sun Necklace's face hardened like flint, his eyes glaring at Old Yellow Wolf and his nephew. "Why should I be held to a promise made in the heat of emotion—at the death of my son? His mother is a medicine woman. She made him that wolf-hide cape. It is she who should decide what becomes of her son's talisman."

"But *you* offered it—"

"That makes little difference," Sun Necklace interrupted. "It was never mine to offer."

Yellow Wolf watched the father turn his back on them as he stared down at the last of the burial process. The old women laid some rocks and several logs on the site before they stood and dusted their hands on their clothing.

This is not good, Yellow Wolf thought to himself. *First we had Looking Glass denying the strong medicine of several warriors who had bad visions about this Place of the Ground Squirrels . . . and now this revered war chief, Sun Necklace—who led so many of the first attacks on the Shadows in the early days of this war—he is breaking a blood oath made in battle, when death hovers near every man.*

Even though the *suapies* were huddled in their burrows and Cut-Off Arm was still far away, Yellow Wolf shuddered with a chill of defeat.

The white man had already defeated them.

While the *Nee-Me-Poo* might run to the buffalo country, they would never be the same people they had been before these troubles. No longer were the chiefs listening to quiet voices of the spirits around them. No longer would those spirits guide the actions of chiefs who broke their vows to the people.

How could such men of little honor ever hope to protect, much less lead, the *Nee-Me-Poo* . . . now that the People were running for their lives?

HENRY Buck wondered if there would be anyone to bury him with such care and affection when he died.

Watching a few knots of women and old men as they went about their grim business of burying their dead in the creek bottom brush or dragging the bodies away toward the eastern plateau on travois, the civilian wondered if he would be missed nearly as much when his name was called from the great beyond.

As he sat alone with his thoughts, he brooded on how many of those victims were women and children—realizing now in the fading light of dusk that Gibbon had unleashed pent-up men on a sleeping village where shadowy figures darted from lodges in all directions, where every Nez Perce was a potential enemy. In the heat of that sort of warfare and battle, chances were more than good that many of those half-naked, blanket-wrapped forms hadn't been warriors at all.

But then . . . was anyone in that village entirely innocent of what outrages of murder and rape, theft and arson had been committed back in Idaho?

They were all guilty to one degree or another, he decided. Man, woman, child.

Henry tried to convince himself that the reason he suffered such gloomy thoughts was only because he had gone without sleep for so long. Because he was sitting here, pinned down without any food or water, surrounded by an enemy that might well kill him before sunrise, now that dark had come to bring an end to that bloody day.

Every time he tried to convince himself that Gibbon and the others were right in punishing these Nez Perce, some tiny hairline fractures began to splinter his certainty. All he had to do was watch the women, little ones, and old men go about their grim burials on the outskirts of that village for Henry Buck to finally realize this never had been a war of warriors. Right from the beginning of the troubles over on the Salmon River and the Camas Prairie, too, this hadn't been a story of men making war on men.

No, right from the first spasm of violence this had been a drama that swept up the women and children, a tragedy that made all the innocents not only unwitting victims but unwilling participants, too. The Nez Perce had started this tragedy by making war on *all* whites—not only men. So to Henry, it stood to reason that the army and its civilian volunteers made war on *all* Nez Perce . . . wherever they could find them.

The Indians gave the first hurt, attacking homes and families. The white man struck back, attacking homes and families.

Why had he ever thought that war was an honorable profession practiced between warriors? To consider it a noble art—practiced by fighting men, by those who truly understood its deadly risks? With this bloody day everything he had once believed had been turned on its head, his whole world yanked out from under him.

As the hours of siege had dragged by that afternoon, he kept reminding himself that once their families had cleared out of the village, the warriors would in all likelihood end their sniping and pull back. And once that red noose was loosened, the soldiers and Catlin's civilians could slip down to the creek to fill what few canteens they had among them, splash some cold water on the backs of their necks, and . . . and hell—he didn't know what the blazes any of them would do next.

But he watched those last three women attack a lodge cover together in the half-light of dusk, tearing it down, then tying all the belongings onto a travois suspended behind one of the ponies, many other pony drags already bearing what Henry took to be the wounded, slowly angling up the side of that plateau east of camp. At the top they struck out across the prairie.

South, he thought. Back for Idaho. Perhaps they were making for their homeland after this battle had proved so disastrous for both sides.

Home. It sounded damn good right then.

Then his heart clutched as he realized those Nez Perce never would have their old homes again—no matter how long they fought or where they ran. That was all a matter of long ago now. There could never be any heading *home* for them.

As the sun sank behind the mountains and threw an immediate darkness on the Big Hole, the night sounds began softly, slipping out of the forest around them, the slough somewhere below. Not just the chatter of the animals out there in the night, not only the frightening war cries and death oaths of the warriors who still made their presence known from time to time . . . but the whimpering sobs of a few of the soldiers and civilians as the cold black blanket of night settled over the hillside and a man felt much more anonymous, far more alone.

Many of the wounded begged for water. Some pleaded for a doctor. A few anguished for a bite of food when all any of them had to chew on was some raw, stringy horse that had been lying out in the sun all day, bloating and flyblown. To Henry's way of thinking, there were a thousand good reasons for any of them to cry.

No food but raw, rancid horse. No water, neither.

And precious little hope for what the new dawn would bring.

IT seemed as if daylight never would come to Lieutenant Charles Woodruff. Nights in the mountains were always cold, even at the height of summer.

Before dawn that morning the men had abandoned their heavy coats, leaving them behind with the bedding and supplies back in Kirkendall's wagons. Woodruff wondered once or twice about those seventeen soldiers and three civilians left up the trail at the wagon camp. Had the same warriors who overran the howitzer grown curious and back-trailed to overwhelm the wagon guard?

Most, if not all, of the men in the compound began shivering as the night deepened and temperatures slid lower and lower. More than twelve hours ago they had all waded through that creek below, some of the men forced to make a crossing in water that lapped up to their armpits. In a wild retreat, they had splashed and slogged their way back through that deep creek and boggy slough to reach this hillside. So once the sun's relentless heat dissipated with the coming of night, the men began to tremble and quake in their damp clothing.

He did not want his thoughts to drift to his three wounds. So Woodruff willed his mind to busy itself with other things as the darkness deepened and some of the more than forty wounded men whimpered, sobbed, or outright cried for water, food, and a merciful relief. He knew that several of the men even suffered from more than one wound.

The rest of Gibbon's command put their anger, frustration, and fears into work: doing what they could in the dark to make their breastworks a bit higher, digging their rifle pits a little deeper. As the stars came out and a sliver of moon arose from the far horizon, he could hear soft scraping sounds of rocks being piled one on the other and the scratch of bayonet and knife where earth was slowly separated from itself at this corner or that of their little corral.

Charles wondered if these men who were still whole in body were soldiers and citizens who had never claimed to be totally without fear—merely men who struggled to keep their fear from paralyzing them as he did.

Of those one-hundred-eighty-three men who had pitched into the Nez Perce at dawn that morning, seven of Gibbon's seventeen officers were either dead or wounded . . . twenty-nine of the rank and file were dead, and forty more had suffered wounds—two of them mortal.

From time to time when the quiet of that night grew heavy, Woodruff even heard a man digging his fingernails across the bottom of his haversack, doing his best to peel free every last pasty residue of the hardtack he had packed into battle, his ration of tasteless crackers having suffered two unavoidable soakings. It was that or the flesh of the lieutenant's horse. Without the benefit of fire to roast a stringy strip he hacked from a rear flank, the lieutenant found he couldn't choke down the raw meat. One of the old files suggested they pry the bullets off their cartridges, the way some had done to cauterize a few of the most terrible wounds, using the powder now to season the uncooked raw meat . . . but Gibbon promptly issued an order against the wasting of even one of those precious cartridges.

Shortly before midnight three of the men, all recruits from G Company, came to the colonel and declared their willingness to make an attempt at bringing back some water from the creek below their plateau. As soon as they began to crawl out from the lines, each of them dragging four canteens strapped over his shoulders, the Nez Perce hollered their warnings to one another. Gibbon ordered a half-dozen volleys fired in the direction of the stream, in hopes of clearing a way for the water carriers. As the echo of those army guns faded, a few random Nez Perce carbines began to make some scattered noise. For those left behind in the compound to wait and wonder, intent upon every distinct sound the darkness brought to them, it was an eternity until they heard a lone white man cry out to the others that he was hit, but could still crawl.

By the time all three had slithered back in with one minor wound and their canteens refilled, one of the astonished trio announced that he had been so scared he forgot to get himself a drink at the stream while he was filling the canteens hung around his neck!

"I know it was only a hunnert yards, Lieutenant," exclaimed Private Homer Coon, "but it sure as hell seemed like a hunnert miles to me! An' lemme tell you—I never had no idea how much a canteen can hold while you're waiting on ever' one. Why, I thought them four'd never fill up!"

Woodruff figured it would have been a merciful death if any of the Nez Perce had caught those water carriers down by the stream in the dark: a bullet ending things quickly—before the warriors, or their squaws, scrounged through the brush to find him where he lay wounded and helpless. Better to go fast without any pain . . .

Not the way First Lieutenant William L. English was suffering with increasing agony from his numerous wounds to the wrist, the ear, the scalp, and a major penetration of his bowel. He was the worst of any, and Woodruff feared his fellow officer would not last out the night.

Not long after the water carriers returned, Gibbon called his officers together to assess their situation. Accounting for the expenditure or loss of more than nine thousand rounds, their desperate need for ammunition rested alone at the top of the list.

"One of the civilians, a half-breed named Matte," the

colonel explained, "came up to report he knows the enemy's language. Said he overheard some of the Nez Perce talking out there in the dark. One of the chiefs was urging their men to be ready for a morning attack—because the white man's ammunition had to be nearly done for."

"We don't get more cartridges soon," Captain Rawn said, "they'll overrun us in one swift rush, sir. What can we do to assure the survival of the command?"

Reminding his officers that this very day, the ninth of August, commemorated his thirtieth year in the army, the colonel prepared to dispatch a runner, who would slip off through the dark, ordered to find the supply train and bring through the much-needed cartridges before their tiny compound ran out, making them helpless before a concerted charge by the Nez Perce come morning. Once he had started the train on its way, that courier was to continue on his way to next find General Oliver O. Howard—likely somewhere between them and the end of the Lolo Trail.

By pale starlight Gibbon wrote a brief message to Howard, penciling his words on a square piece of paper no bigger than a calling card:

> *GENERAL: We surprised the Nez Perce camp at daylight this morning, whipped them out of it, killing a considerable number. But they turned on us, forced us out of it, and compelled us to take the defensive. We are here near the mouth of Big Hole pass, with a number of wounded, and need medical assistance and assistance of all kinds, and hope you will hurry to our relief.*
>
> *GIBBON,*
> *COMM'DG*
> *Aug. 9, '77*

In addition, the colonel readied another two men—civilians both—to sneak off for the settlements, striking out to the east for Deer Lodge via Frenchman's Gulch, both to carry messages requesting food, ammunition, and medical supplies.

"My boots ain't worth a damn no more, Lieutenant,"

grumped William H. Edwards as he prepared to slip away in the darkness.

Woodruff looked down at the man's footwear. "You think we're about the same size?"

Edwards nodded. "Worth a try, Officer. If you don't mind, I got more'n sixty miles to walk to French Gulch, and these ol' boots of mine won't make it all that way."

"A noble donation to the cause," Woodruff announced, painfully dragging off one boot at a time to make the exchange with the civilian. "Besides, with these holes in my legs, I'm not fit to do much walking for the next few days anyway. Part of that leather heel got shot off."

Peering closely at the back of the fractured heel, Edwards said, "There's still enough here to hold me up till I get to Deer Lodge."

The civilian had stood, working his toes around in the unfamiliar boots, when Gibbon came up to stop in front of Edwards.

"I want you to remember, we need an escort sufficient to protect the wagons they'll send to relieve us," the colonel impressed upon his messenger. "Load the wagons as light as possible—for speed, you understand. Tell them how the Indians have cut us off from our own supply train. And take this message with you." He handed Edwards a folded paper.

The civilian said, "General?"

"At the first telegraph key you reach, it's to be wired to my commander, General Alfred Terry, headquarters in Minneapolis."

Big Hole Pass, August ninth

Surprised the Nez Perces camp here this morning, got possession of it after a hard fight in which both myself, Captain Williams and Lieuts Coolidge, Woodruff and English wounded, the last severely.

Gibbon,
Comm'dg
Aug 9, '77

For a long time after the two couriers melted away into the dark, each taking his separate direction, those left behind listened to the night for some idea as to the success of their escape. Only an occasional shot whined into their dark compound. Just enough gunfire to keep Woodruff rattled, even more jealous of a civilian who continued to sleep nearby. The young volunteer lay on his back, hip-to-hip beside another citizen in their shallow rifle pit. His mouth had gone slack, and he began snoring loud enough that it eventually attracted the attention of an Indian sniper.

Just about the time Woodruff was finding himself in awe that anyone could sleep in such conditions, a bullet smacked the dirt piled up beside the rifle pit, filling the snoring man's mouth with soil and pine needles. Sputtering and choking, he flopped awake, spit, and wiped his tongue clean, then promptly rolled onto his side and fell right to sleep again.

Sometime in the middle of the night he heard two of the civilians whispering in a nearby rifle pit.*

"You wanna get out of this, Tom?"

"Why, what the hell do you mean?"

"Well, there's several of us going tonight."

Tom asked, "All of you?"

"No, just a few, it appears."

Then Tom prodded in a softer whisper, "What about the wounded? What's to become of them?"

After a long pause, grave with silence, the other man answered, "We'll just have to let them go, Tom."

"That don't set right with me. Them wounded have to be took care of. I ain't going unless ever'body's pulling out together."

"Suit yourself, Tom. I just wanted you to know we was goin'."

Later that dark night, Woodruff overheard the scuffing of

---

*This documented conversation took place at marker No. 7, hillside siege site.

boots as the unnamed civilian crawled out of his rifle pit to join the half-dozen who were intending to make their escape through the Nez Perce lines. For a time after they had gone, he was jealous of them and their freedom to make the attempt—while his would be a soldier's fate.

Woodruff would wait for dawn and see what the morrow held in store for the stalwart and steadfast who had remained behind.

Chapter Sixty-Seven

August 9, 1877

"Rider! Lookee—it's a goddamned rider comin' in!"

Henry Buck shook himself out of a fitful sleep with that yelp, instantly awake with the horseman's whooping and hoofbeats, accompanied by a few scattered shots from the Nez Perce who still had them surrounded this gray morning.

Buck got his knuckles out of his gritty eyes in time to watch the civilian's horse skidding to a halt in the middle of their rectangle of rifle pits. Dawn was coming.

"By God—is that you, McGilliam?" John Catlin roared as he leaped up to the side of the barely restrained horse.

Around them, the survivors in the compound were cheering lustily, many of them barking their own questions at the newcomer.

In the hubbub that lone rider held his hand down to Catlin and said, "Good to see you still standing on your pins, Cap'n Catlin. Where's your general?"

"Right over here," Gibbon announced from the spot where he was dragging his good leg under him and struggling onto his feet. "Where the hell did you come from and just how in blazes did you get through?"

"This is Nelse McGilliam, General," Catlin introduced the civilian who had just dropped to the ground.

"You come from Howard?"

"Yes, General—"

"So what do you know of our wagon train?"

McGilliam shrugged. "Nothing. Never saw it comin' through on my own."

"You're alone?"

"Yep."

"How do you come to be here?" Gibbon prodded.

"I slept back up the trail last night, in my saddle blanket—no more'n a mile from here, out in the black of night," the civilian explained as he swung out of the saddle. "I heard shooting now and again, so I didn't dare come any closer till I had enough light to see my way on in here."

"Can't believe the Injuns let you waltz on through 'em the way you did!" Catlin cheered, slapping McGilliam on the shoulder.

"I didn't see a damned Injun. Not one!"

"But they're out there," Catlin argued. "You heard 'em shooting as you rode in?"

"But I didn't see a one—"

"What's Howard got to say?" Gibbon demanded the courier's attention again. "When's he going to be here?"

"He's on his way behind me, bringing more'n two dozen riders on their best horses."

"T-two dozen?" Gibbon echoed. "That's all?"

"There's more coming up behind him, General," McGilliam explained. "With them first soldiers Howard's got some Bannock scouts, too. All of 'em riding hard. Should be here afore tomorrow morning."

It was easy for Henry Buck to see the disappointment from that register on Gibbon's face.

"Very well. We don't have much to offer you in the way of anything to eat—except for some half-rancid horse." Gibbon pointed out Woodruff's partially skinned horse, the flies not yet buzzing in the chill dawn air. The decomposing carcass had stewed and bloated with gases to a point where all four of its legs stuck straight out grotesquely.

"N-no thanks, General," McGilliam responded with a shake of his head. "I'll be fine—"

A sudden volley exploded outside their lines, bullets smacking the trees and whining through the men. Luckily, no one was hit as they dived in all directions, flopping to their bellies. McGilliam struggled to hold onto the reins from where he lay, his horse fighting to break free.

"May be some fresh horse meat soon, General!" the courier hollered.

"Do what you can to protect that animal, mister!" Gibbon ordered. "We're damn well gonna need it to ride out on before the day is out."

As that short summer night had worn on, more and more of *Ollokot*'s warriors had slipped away. But . . . their leaving was not a reflection upon their bravery.

By the time the light turned gray and foretold of dawn-coming, perhaps no more than the fingers on both hands still remained with the war chief and Yellow Wolf. Nowhere near enough to try rushing the *suapies*. No, the white men were safely corralled in their dirt hollows.

Besides, the families were a good distance away by now.

There had simply been too many dead to try carrying them all away from the battlefield for burial. Instead, the women and old men had done the best they could with the bodies of those who would be left behind at this tragic place. Many of the dead were carried to the edge of the creek, where they were laid beneath an overhanging cut-bank before the earth was caved in over the bodies in a simple, but effective, grave.

A few families nonetheless chose to drag a loved one from the scene on a travois as the village started south toward Horse Prairie and on to the far pass over the mountains.

Whatever the sheer numbers of the dead—men, women, and children—Yellow Wolf realized that the loss of so many of their greatest warriors in this one fight was something that could never be measured in any terms.

At this Place of the Ground Squirrels, the *Nee-Me-Poo* had lost the flower of its young manhood. Their finest had fallen.

Rainbow.
Shore Crossing.
Five Wounds.
Red Moccasin Tops.
Five Fogs.
Red-Headed Woodpecker.

Black Owl.

No Heart—

And the list went on.

No matter trying to put a count to them. The loss was great by any measure. From here on out, the People would never be as strong, never be as capable of defending their families, as they had been when they had marched over the pass to this peaceful valley where the women had time to cut lodgepoles and the children to laugh. The *Nee-Me-Poo* hadn't had much of either lodgepoles or laughter since the war began.

Perhaps the most tragic death was that of No Heart.

In the very first moments of the fighting, Yellow Wolf had spotted Joseph and No Heart fording the stream and racing up the hillside opposite camp, making for the horse herd. How brave they were to assure that the white men could not steal the ponies. But because of a terrible rumor that the Flathead had come to steal the horses, one of *Toohoolhoolzote*'s men rushed across the creek and shot No Heart by mistake!

Late in the afternoon when Yellow Wolf heard about the death of this good warrior, he crept around to the hillside where the herd had been grazing, to see for himself this spot where No Heart was killed. To grieve where his friend had fallen. But he did not find the body where others said they had seen it during the fighting. For a long time while the last light remained in the evening sky Yellow Wolf had searched and searched, unable to find No Heart's body or the warrior's horse.

"Perhaps he came back to life after the others left," Yellow Wolf confided to *Ollokot* this gray morning.

"Maybe he got on his horse and went somewhere else to die,"* the chief replied.

---

*Two years after the Battle of the Big Hole, when frontiersman Andrew Garcia and his Nez Perce wife, who had herself survived the battle, visited the Place of the Ground Squirrels, he stated in *A Tough Trip Through Par-*

Yellow Wolf shook his head sadly. "I think No Heart might still be alive—"

He jerked up at the sound of a horse's running hooves. Through the trees he saw a blur of movement, then heard cheering from the white man's corral of rifle pits.

Yellow Wolf thought that must mean it was a messenger coming in, breaking through their skimpy surround of the soldiers. With the sounds of those soldiers celebrating the man's arrival, Yellow Wolf remembered how he had heard a Shadow voice in the dark of last night. A man apparently lost, calling for someone to answer. But no one responded and the voice eventually was heard no more. Had likely been this messenger, a rider who halted where he was until it was light enough to charge on in.

"It is better that he go on in, anyway," declared *Ollokot* as he turned to his horse. "Now we will have some good idea what news he brought the other Shadows."

Such loud cheering that accompanied the messenger's arrival could only mean one of two things. Either the man carried some more ammunition for the soldiers—which Yellow Wolf doubted; after all, how many cartridges could one man carry on one horse?

Or the Shadow was bringing word of another army coming to their rescue.

"I think more soldiers are coming," *Ollokot* commiserated as he got on the back of his pony.

"Perhaps we should look on their back trail to find those soldiers who are coming, maybe find their supplies to steal," Yellow Wolf suggested.

His chief agreed and that morning a handful of them moved up the trail, attempting to locate some sign of an advancing army. Hard as they scoured the hills on both sides of the creek, they discovered no sign, no wagons or horses, and no sighting of an army coming.

—

adise, they located the grave of an Indian on the hillside where his wife reported No Heart was killed.

But later that second afternoon of the fight, there wasn't a man gathered around *Ollokot* near the south gulch who didn't feel in his marrow that more soldiers were already on their way. Cut-Off Arm would be there eventually. Even if he and his men were the "day after tomorrow army," they would get there soon.

"I want to see to my wife," *Ollokot* confessed to those faithful warriors who had remained with him even as their families had packed up and marched away a day ago. "Our people are buried, and our wounded are gone with the rest of the village. There is nothing more that we can do to these soldiers now."

"Do you want some of us to stay in the hills to watch for Cut-Off Arm and his soldiers?" Yellow Wolf asked. "To stay till we know the army is coming?"

Ollokot's eyes were as sad as any of them had ever seen the man. "Stay and spy if you want. As for me, I want to see my wife one more time before she dies."

BY now General Oliver Otis Howard was brutally aware that he should have pressed ahead more than a day earlier than he had when setting off from the Lolo hot springs.

Instead of starting out at dawn on 7 August when he dispatched Sergeant Oliver Sutherland with his message for Colonel Gibbon as originally planned, the general chose to leisurely lead his entire command down the Lolo Trail another nineteen miles to Woodman's Prairie, where they went into camp. It wasn't until the following day that he finally set off at a rapid gait with his advance unit of 200 horsemen, yet he and his staff took time out from their pursuit for a lengthy inspection of Rawn's barricades and rifle pits at "Fort Fizzle" before continuing down to the mouth of the canyon, where Howard again halted, this time for more than two hours, while he dictated several more dispatches he wanted carried north to Missoula City. It had proven to be a good road that eighth day of August—his advance group of 200 horsemen made at least thirty-four miles before sundown.

But on the morning of the ninth, the strenuous pace of the previous day had told on the weakening horses. Howard's advance made less than twenty miles that Thursday—the first day of Gibbon's fight in the Big Hole. The following dawn, 10 August, Howard finally made the decision he should have back on the night of the sixth when Joe Pardee rode up the Lolo to the hot springs with the message that Colonel Gibbon was in pursuit of the fleeing Non-Treaty bands.

That morning the general selected twenty of the best troopers, mounting them on the best of his horses, and prepared to push ahead with all possible dispatch, accompanied by seventeen of "Captain" Orlando "Rube" Robbins's twenty Bannock scouts. Howard left the rest under the command of Major Edwin C. Mason of the First Cavalry to come along at all possible dispatch. With his twenty handpicked men under First Lieutenant George R. Bacon, and aide-de-camp Wood, Howard set off, accompanied by correspondent Thomas Sutherland and a rival journalist, Mr. Bonny, who was also serving the column as Quartermaster Ebstein's clerk.

They moved out in a trot, column of twos. After they kept that pace for fifty minutes, a ten-minute halt was called every hour. Ride hard, then rest the horses, and ride hard for another fifty minutes. They took a brief midday rest at Ross's Hole; then both men and horses toiled up the steep, winding six-mile ascent to the top of the divide.

Despite their efforts at speed, these forty-some men managed to cover no more than twenty-five miles that day, beginning their climb over the divide to the Big Hole.

As grueling as the climb had been and as weary as the horses had become, they went into camp that Friday evening—10 August—far up on the eastern slope at the head of Trail Creek, where Howard sent frontiersman Robbins ahead, along with his Bannocks, to do some scouting while a little light remained in the sky. Just past dark a dozen of the Bannocks came back at a trot, escorting seven dismounted civilians.

"My God—you men are on foot!" Howard exclaimed as the Indians brought the exhausted volunteers huffing up to the general. "Where are your horses?"

"S-shot, most of 'em."

Another citizen confessed, "Rest of 'em got run off by the Injuns."

Howard tingled with the old excitement, mixed with a little envy. "Then Gibbon's had a fight."

"Oh, we had a fight, we did!" another one grumbled.

"What have you got to tell us?" the general prodded.

"General Gibbon pitched into them Injuns yesterday morning," began one. Said another, "Lost half his men by the time the sun come up."

"They was having a hard go of it when we left."

Concern crossed the general's face. He asked, "You—you ran off and left the rest behind?"

The man looked at Howard as if the general were daft. " 'Course we did. We was gettin' whipped something terrible—gone with no sleep and nothing to eat in two days now. . . . You got something to eat here, don'cha, General?"

Howard looked aside at his aide, saying, "Lieutenant Wood, see that these men are given some bacon and hardbread. Bring them some cups for coffee, too." Then he turned back to the civilians warming their hands over the headquarters fire as the temperature dropped and the light drained from the sky.

"Your supper is coming," the general explained while Robbins and the last of the Bannock rode into camp. "Now, tell me everything."

They did, slowly, a bit here and a fragment there—at least what the seven had seen from their vantage point of things. After giving a graphic account of the early-morning assault and the capture of the village, they told of how the chiefs and their warriors had rallied to regain the camp and driven the white men to the hillside siege area. One of the seven, a civilian from the Bitterroot valley settlement of

Corvallis, even had a brother* who had been wounded and forced to go into hiding near the boggy marsh when the rest failed to take him along with them in their retreat to the hillside.

Howard found himself repulsed that this volunteer had abandoned his brother in that escape to the timber, and again when he fled Gibbon's siege, apparently without suffering any shame or disgrace whatsoever. And now at the fire, the general discovered that no amount of money, not even the attraction of a brother wounded and sorely in need of rescue, could induce one of these seven brave citizens to guide Robbins and the Bannock to the battlefield!

Brave citizen militia indeed!

After they had wolfed down their dinner, even to licking the grease from the tin plates, the seven continued with their tales of Gibbon's fight up to the night they had slipped away through the warrior lines, enumerating the casualties and repeatedly expressing how gallantly the colonel and his soldiers had given back a struggle in their desperate fight, even though heavily outnumbered by the Nez Perce.

"How far do you figure you've come from where you left General Gibbon?" Howard asked as the stars came out.

One of the civilians dragged the back of his hand across his greasy lips and said, "Fifteen, no more'n twenty miles, General. But them are hard, hard miles gettin' down there from here."

Oliver Otis stood at last, his back kinked with knots from the hard riding along with sleeping on the cold ground. He knew the exhausted horses would not last another league that night.

"Lieutenant Bacon, have your men start and feed several fires here; scatter them across this clearing. Then barricade the best you can with what we have for saddles and baggage," Howard explained. "In case Joseph has his spies out

---

*Campbell Mitchell, chapter 59.

in these hills, I want it to appear we are a much larger force than we are."

Bacon asked, "We'll push on at first light, General?"

"We'll move out as soon as we have enough light to see the trail ahead," he told his soldiers gathered close. "By the Almighty—we'll lift that siege and drive the warriors off."

As he turned aside to drag a trail-worn Bible from his haversack, Howard's mind began to turn upon an offer he now made to God: praying they would find some of Gibbon's soldiers alive.

EPILOGUE

AUGUST 10–11, 1877

AT SUNDOWN THAT NIGHT OF 10 AUGUST, HUGH KIRKENdall's wagon train rattled into the siege compound without any interference from the Nez Perce everyone believed were still in the area.

It was accompanied by Captain George L. Browning and Second Lieutenant Francis Woodbridge, who, earlier that afternoon, had been directed by John Gibbon to lead twenty-five men up the mountainside and escort the wagons on down Trail Creek. Hours before at daybreak, the colonel had dispatched Sergeant Mildon H. Wilson of I Company and six men from K Company to reach the wagon corral and bring in the train. But as midday came and went Gibbon grew more apprehensive that Mildon's small squad had been ambushed; he had dispatched Browning's detail.

Those wagons arrived about 6:00 P.M., carrying all the coffee and hardtack the ravenous men could eat, along with their wool blankets. At least this night would be a shade more comfortable for the survivors.

"Wish we had some more of that bacon those two civilians brought in this morning," said the colonel.

"It didn't last long, did it, sir?" asked Lieutenant Charles Woodruff.

"A few bites for each man sure didn't go far." Gibbon sounded regretful.

"There will be more coming when General Howard arrives."

The lieutenant prayed his words would come true.

Earlier that morning Sergeant Oliver Sutherland had himself come on down the trail after spending most of the previous day at Kirkendall's corral. He was carrying that message from Howard telling Gibbon how he was coming ahead with 200 horsemen and hoped to catch up to the infantry before Gibbon pitched into the Nez Perce.

"Why did you end up staying with the wagon train instead of riding on down here to deliver your message as ordered, Sergeant?" Woodruff asked the question he was sure Gibbon wanted to have answered.

"Made a try, sir," Sutherland admitted. "I started out with eight or nine of the wagon guard you left—but we was met on the trail by a big war party and drove back. A damn lucky thing they didn't follow us up the trail and find our wagons, Lieutenant."

That's when Gibbon had proposed, "I'm going to send an escort back right now—and bring those supplies in."

Minutes later two of Kirkendall's teamsters—Jerry Wallace and John Miller—rode in, having started down the trail right on the heels of Sergeant Sutherland. Hung from Wallace's saddle horn was a grease-stained canvas bag that contained a side of bacon. It was promptly divided up among the famished men, disappearing down their gullets with an amazing speed. After suffering some thirty-six hours without anything more to eat than the pasty remains of hardtack scraped off the bottom of their haversacks and a few strips of raw meat butchered from Woodruff's bloated horse, Gibbon's compound was next to famished.

While this one side of bacon had done little to fill their shrunken bellies that morning, it had nonetheless gone far to lifting their sagging spirits for the rest of that day.

Not long after Kirkendall's wagons rattled in, it began to grow dark on that lonely rectangle of rifle pits for a second night. Twilight was deepening when one of the civilians called out, asking the rest to look at the three dim, flickering lights he had spotted to the southeast. Woodruff saw them, all three slowly bobbing, wavering, either on or against the plateau rising beyond the flat where much of the Nez Perce village still stood.

"What you make of that?" Charles asked the colonel.

Gibbon shook his head. "Can't be torches. Maybe

they're small fires where their sharpshooters huddle to warm themselves."

"I didn't see any fires while they had us surrounded last night, General," Woodruff had replied. "Why would they light those three fires way off over there tonight, and nowhere close at all—"

Woodruff was interrupted with what he figured was the answer. A cluster of twelve distinct shots tore through their compound, some from each of the three sides. Then the echo of all that gunfire quickly faded, absorbed by the coal-cotton black of night.

Several discordant voices shouted at them from the river bottom—not in the manner of a war cry . . . but more so as a salutation.

"I think we've just been told they're leaving," Gibbon commented quietly.

Those mysterious lights, along with that final volley and farewell salutation, were just enough to keep Woodruff restless through that night. Despite his knotted belly finally being filled by hardbread and coffee and despite the warmth of a wool blanket to curl up inside, the lieutenant remained wary that the departure was all a ruse, right up till dawn on the eleventh of August.

"That lieutenant's in a bad way," confided Tom Sherrill, a civilian who had a rifle pit right beside Woodruff, the moment the lieutenant stirred.

First light was beginning to seep into the Big Hole.

"You mean English?"

Sherrill nodded, then whispered again. "Ain't a man here can't tell how bad he's suffering. That back wound of his is the worst I've ever seen."

"We'll have a surgeon here soon, Tom."

"The lieutenant, he asked me to take his boot off and rub his feet—saying they was getting stone-cold on him," Sherrill said in a hush. "But I couldn't get 'em off, everything was so wet. I ended up cutting the stitches on one of his boots with my folding knife, right down the back. Got it off that way. Started rubbing his foot. Wasn't long before he told me, 'It's no use; I'm done for this time.' "

Woodruff nodded knowingly. "I'd consider it a personal favor to me, if not to General Gibbon, if you'd do all in your power to make Lieutenant English as comfortable as you can until a surgeon arrives."

"How long you figure on that?" Sherrill asked. "Till Howard gets here with them reinforcements?"

"I'm praying they will show up tomorrow."

"It's Myron! My stars—it's Myron Lockwood!"

Lieutenant Woodruff looked up from an inspection of Private Edward D. Hunter's wound to his right forearm. Both bones had been shattered by a Nez Perce bullet, and without proper bandages the gaping hole—like the rotting horse carcass—had become flyblown. Try as Woodruff might to protect the wound with strips of the soldier's uniform these last two days, this morning it was a wriggling mass of maggots.

Getting to his feet, Charles thought he recognized that civilian slung between the two Sherrill brothers, Tom and his older brother, "Bunch."

"How bad is he?" John Gibbon asked as he rolled onto his hip and struggled to rise, dragging that wounded leg of his.

"He'll live!" Bunch Sherrill bellowed enthusiastically. "If those Nez Perce couldn't kill Lockwood in our attack and they never found 'im hiding in the bushes—by damn, this tough ol' nail ain't gonna die on us now, General!"

Just before daylight the brothers had slipped down to the mouth of the gulch* to look for their Bitterroot friend, the same Myron Lockwood who had horses stolen from him and his house looted as the Nez Perce meandered up the valley.

"I really 'spected to find 'im dead," Tom Sherrill confessed as they dragged Lockwood up to the fire and eased

---

*Today's "Battle Gulch."

him down between them, the trio hunkered close to the flames.

To Woodruff's way of thinking, for the moment Lockwood hovered a little closer to death than he clung tenaciously to life.

"Found 'im sitting with his back against a wall of rock,"*

Bunch Sherrill declared. "From the looks of 'im, he's lost considerable blood."

"How is it he's still alive and the Nez Perce killed every other one of our wounded they got their hands on?" Gibbon asked. "He tell you that?"

Tom Sherrill shrugged. "Myron's so damned cold and stiff after these last two days and nights—he ain't been able to say a thing to us yet."

"Fortunate he kept that coat with him," Woodruff commented as the damp wool of the man's heavy hip-length coat steamed so near the warmth radiating from their fire.

"This wasn't his," Bunch Sherrill admitted quietly. "We took the coat off Elliott."**

"He won't mind now, Elliott won't," Tom assured the others as he kneaded one of Lockwood's hands between his. "Man's been dead for two days now."

"That's a dead man's coat?" asked Captain James Sanno.

"Don't appear it's making a damn bit of difference to Myron that's he's wearing a dead man's coat," Tom grumbled. "After them red bastards run off with his horses a few days back, sacked his house, and stole everything of value from him. Then this poor son of a bitch almost died down there in our attack on that village. That should show you Myron's a hard piece of iron. He ain't the sort what's easy to kill."

After sunrise, Colonel Gibbon asked Woodruff to select one of their best riders and put him on the strongest horse. "I have a sinking feeling that Mr. Edwards didn't get

—

*Stake No. 50, Big Hole National Battlefield.

**Lynde C. Elliott, Stevensville volunteer.

through the Nez Perce gauntlet when they had their noose tightened around us the other night."

"You're afraid he could be dead, sir?"

"Or worse," Gibbon admitted in a whisper. "A captive, tortured like the rest we heard being butchered down in the river bottom the day of our fight."

Sergeant Mildon H. Wilson was again the man for the assignment: a ride of more than eighty miles. While Gibbon completed another set of dispatches, Woodruff had the courier select his mount and saddle from what had been brought down with Kirkendall's wagons the afternoon before. When Wilson began to knot two small leather satchels behind his saddle, each one carrying an extra pistol and some ammunition for his Springfield, the lieutenant was struck with a sudden impulse.

"Sergeant, I want you to wait a few minutes before you ride out of here."

"Sir?"

"I've got something to write," he explained in a hush. "A letter I want you to see gets started back to Fort Shaw from Deer Lodge for me."

The older man nodded, his eyes crinkling with warmth. "Of course, Lieutenant. Something for your missus."

At the edge of his rifle pit, Lieutenant Charles A. Woodruff propped his dispatch ledger on his knees and began to scratch out a heartfelt communication to his wife, hopeful it would reach her at Fort Shaw before word of their terrible fight reached the telegraph keys of the outside world. Hoping to reassure her that he was alive, and whole. . . .

Camp on Ruby Creek
Aug. 11th 1877

My darling Louie:

I wrote you a note day before yesterday and will write to-day as we send out a courier.
I am getting along well, our train came up last evening

and we expect Genl. Howard today. The Indians have all left

We had a hard fight lost 2 Officers Killed 10 Soldiers and 6 citizens, Wounded 5 officers 34 soldiers and 2 citizens. "K" Co., Şergt Stortz Private Kleis (the Carpenter) and Mus. Steinbacker were Killed.

I was shot in the heel of the left foot and in both legs above the knee, fortunately no bones broken. The Genl. and I were the only ones mounted, both our horses were shot, I got mine into camp and he was shot again, we ate some of him yesterday.

I left the gun back the night we struck the village it started up at daylight and was attacked, one of the horses was shot and fell on Bennett, lamed him some, and of the three men with the gun one was killed and two wounded.*

Our men charged the village in fine shape and the reason we didn't hold it was there was so much brush and high bluffs that we couldn't occupy all the places at once The Indians suffered severely, I think their loss cannot be less than seventy-five or a hundred. We killed them right and left. Hurlburt of "K" killed the Indian that shot Bradley. Jacobs Killed three. Rawn two Hardin & Woodbridge one each, I didn't get a chance to Kill any of them I was carrying orders &c. The General and I were all over the field and were lucky to come off as well as we did.

The officers and men behaved well and gave the Indians the worst handling they ever seed before.

Bradley and Logan were both Killed dead.

It looked blue for us here on Thursday afternoon, the Indians set fire to the forest and kept up a fire from the brush and the hills, their idea was to follow up the fire and charge us when it reached us, I began to fear I should never see you again, some of the wounded covered up their heads and expected to be killed, I got my

---

*Howitzer.

two revolvers said my prayers thought of you and Bertie and determined to kill a few Indians before I died, Our Heavenly Father was on our side and the wind changed and blew away from us.

I didn't know how much I loved you until I thought we would never see each other again.

We shall start this afternoon or tomorrow for Deer Lodge, I expect to get home in about ten-days . . .

Your loving husband,
Charles

AUTHOR'S AFTERWORD

As I began collecting my thoughts to write this wrap-up to *Lay the Mountains Low*, I discovered I had more than two dozen subjects I originally wanted to discuss here at the end of this second novel on the Nez Perce War. Trouble is, I feel compelled to pare away at that list of topics, because this has been the longest, most complex, book I've ever written.

While there are lots of interesting subjects I would like to tell my readers after researching and writing this dramatic, and ultimately tragic, story, *Lay the Mountains Low* is a big book to begin with. After muddling over every one of those two dozen topics I wanted to write about, I came to believe that while most are interesting at the very least, what I should do here in these next few pages is deal with only one of those subjects—a topic most compelling, downright intriguing. An unfinished story I promised you more about in the last book, *Cries from the Earth.*

Even though I am omitting the rest of those two dozen historical topics for now, I plan to eventually discuss the most important of them in a *final* author's afterword, the one I'll write at the conclusion of this trilogy on the Nez Perce War. For any of you who want to read about my ongoing research travels along this second segment of the Nez Perce Trail, I'll refer you to my annual news magazine, *WinterSong*, in every edition of which I recount my journey to go where this Indian Wars history actually happened. For more information on this publication, please see the "About the Author" section that follows this afterword.

Rather than reprinting the long list of titles I relied upon while researching and writing *Cries from the Earth* as well as the story you have just read, I will refer you back to the listing I gave in the Author's Afterword at the end of that previous book. Additional sources I have used for telling this second tragic tale in *Lay the Mountains Low* are:

An Elusive Victory—the Battle of the Big Hole, by Aubrey L. Haines

A Sharp Little Affair: The Archeology of the Big Hole Battlefield, by Douglas D. Scott

"Battle of the Big Hole," by General C. A. Woodruff, *Contributions to the Historical Society of Montana* 7 (1910)

"Chief Joseph's Flight Through Montana: 1877," by Verne Dusenberry, *The Montana Magazine of History* 2 (October, 1952)

Frontier Regulars: The United States Army and the Indian, 1866–1891, by Robert M. Utley

"Review of the Battle of the Big Hole," by Amos Buck, *Contributions to the Historical Society of Montana* 7 (1910)

Before jumping any further, I want to acknowledge the immeasurable help of two people, without whom this book could not have been written. The story you have just read is a chronicle, a rendering of the latest, most up-to-date research into the Nez Perce War.

I could not have researched this story over the past twenty-seven months without the assistance of my longtime friend Jerome A. Greene of the National Park Service's Rocky Mountain Regional Office. A few years ago Jerry began compiling his research for a soon-to-be-published volume on the *Nee-Me-Poo* Crisis, for the most part relying on primary accounts rather than secondary sources, along with his own intimate travels through Nez Perce country. His efforts serve as the framework for my three-book chronicle of the Nez Perce struggle: a trilogy of gut-wrenching novels that recount a five-month, fifteen-hundred-mile odyssey from tribal greatness to the "Hot Place" in Indian Territory. My hope is that Jerry's newest book, to be published by agreement between the National Park Service and the Montana Historical Society, will be available to the general reader sometime in the year 2000.

Since his work is not yet available to the public, I relied upon the kindness and generosity of both Jerry Greene himself and the research librarian at the Nez Perce National Historic Park in Spalding, Idaho, Rob Applegate. With Rob's timely assistance, I got my hands on a copy of Jerry Greene's monumental manuscript, which is undergoing a final copyedit at this time. After I met Rob on his first day at Spalding back in 1998, it wasn't long before I found him to be a real asset to the National Park Service—always cheerful and helpful with my obscure and ofttimes troublesome requests.

Again I want to emphasize that *Lay the Mountains Low* could not have been written without both Jerry and Rob being in the background to answer my questions and give me their support. If you find you've had some of your questions answered on this part of the Nez Perce War story or you simply enjoyed this captivating tale, then you must surely appreciate the efforts these two fine employees of the National Park Service gave to see this novel written.

Were you as tantalized as I was with the mystery of what became of Jennet Manuel and her infant son at the end of *Cries from the Earth*?

If you weren't as baffled or eager to find out as I was, you have no need of reading any further. The rest of this abbreviated afterword will deal with that little-known and heartrending tale of the Nez Perce War.

The shedding of blood is always answered. Almost two decades of assault, robbery, rape, and murder committed against the Non-Treaty *Nee-Me-Poo* brewed the foul-smelling recipe that boiled over along the Salmon River, then spilled across the Camas Prairie in mid-June 1877.

Blood cries out for blood. Following those outrages against innocent white women and children committed by drunken, revenge-seeking warriors from White Bird's and *Toohoolhoolzote*'s bands (and I use the term *warriors* very loosely, because I prefer to call them criminals, if not thugs), young men who felt very brave sweeping down upon unarmed or outnumbered civilians in overwhelming force, this mystery revolving around Jennet Manuel came to captivate an entire region of our country during that bloody summer. The speculation continues to this day.

Some of the contemporary testimony tells us that Mrs. Manuel, and perhaps her son, too, were taken along with the retreating warrior bands as they fled over the Lolo Trail to Montana Territory. Other reports have her being killed by a drunken and spiteful warrior just days after she was captured at her home (the former Ad Chapman homestead on White Bird Creek adjacent to the battlefield of 17 June). Some Nez Perce sources, who claim to have been at the scene, would have you believe mother and son were murdered and their bodies consumed in the fire that consumed the Manuel house—a few of the Indian stories admitting that Jennet Manuel was still alive and conscious when the drunken murderers set fire to the house—while other Nez Perce sources claim she was killed somewhere along the Lolo Trail.

Let's go back to chapter 18 in *Cries from the Earth*, when Maggie Manuel has crawled out of her house and into the timber, attempting to find either her maternal grandfather, George Popham, or a local miner, Patrick Brice. She finds the Irish prospector and relates her story of how she watched from hiding as Joseph (who was widely reputed to abstain from whiskey—a fact testified to by even his most ardent spiritual enemy, Kate McBeth, thc Christian schoolteacher at Kamiah, when she wrote: "Joseph had one good thing about him. He was a temperance man") and his drunken warriors clubbed both Maggie's mother and little brother before dragging them off to finish the murders. The story Maggie later told with consistency has her watching Joseph stab her mother in the breast, as she is nursing the infant, before Maggie herself is taken to another room, where she falls asleep.

This outrageous accusation that Joseph himself killed Mrs. Manuel simply refuses to die, especially among the Christian Nez Perce of today! Back in the summer of 1939, when Congress was considering a monument to Joseph, a Nez Perce from Lapwai, J. M. Parsons, wrote to U. S. Representative Usher L. Burdick to protest. Burdick had the Indian's letter read in the chamber and subsequently entered into the *Congressional Record*:

> Chief Joseph was not the man which history would place before the educational institutions as has been suggested along with the erection of the memorial. He is guilty of wantonly killing a white woman, Mrs. J. Manuel, while he was under the influence of liquor. On June 15, 1877, the chief and two companions, also under the influence of liquor, visited the home of the Manuels on White Bird Creek, where friendly Indians were keeping guard over the wounded Mrs. Manuel and baby with the understanding that the woman would be given aid in escaping to the white settlement. Joseph proceeded to wrangle over the succoring of the enemy white woman, and when the friendly Indians remonstrated, the chief reached out with a dagger and plunged it into her breast, killed her almost instantly . . . There is an old warrior living today who was present when the killing took place, and it has been generally known among the Nez Perce that Joseph committed the deed.

Upon learning of this claim, Nez Perce supporter and writer L.V. McWhorter wrote to Parsons, demanding he produce the "old warrior" and all evidence leading to Joseph's guilt. Parsons never answered any of McWhorter's entreaties.

In his book *Chief Joseph—the Biography of a Great Indian*, author Chester Anders Fee appears to have bought the whole of Maggie's story of how her mother was killed when he writes:

> . . . Mrs. Manuel, and her ten months old child fell injured when their horse stumbled. She with her baby and daughter, who had also broken her arm in the fall, were taken back to the ranch house by the Nez Perce, who then told her they would take no more lives if she gave them Mr. Manuel's rifle and ammunition. This she did, and the Indians left. But soon several others of the party returned and one plunged a knife into her breast, killing her, and later they also killed her baby.

A pretty convoluted explanation of how suddenly well mannered were that gang of murderers, while they were seizing everything and anything that suited them—including guns, ammunition, and white women. Mr. Fee simply can't have it both ways.

To continue with young Maggie's rendition of her story: When she awakens, the house is filled with an ominous silence. Opening the door to the main room, Maggie finds her mother's naked body lying in a pool of blood on the floor. That "blood oozed between my toes." Near her mother's head lay her baby brother, John. In her version of the story, when she located Brice outside in the woods, she took him back into the house to view the bodies before they both returned to the timber.

Although Brice would never confirm that part of the girl's story—he stated that when he went back to the house he found it empty—Maggie Manuel remained consistent with every other detail of that night, right on into her adulthood.

First of all, let's lay to rest her allegation that Joseph killed her mother. Aside from whether or not Maggie herself had ever seen Joseph, chief of the *Wallowa* band, and would be able to identify him, the simple fact is that he could not have been in the White Bird Canyon the night of 15 June 1877. He and his brother, *Ollokot*, along with their families and the rest of the *Wallamwatkin*, were far, far to the north, sleeping in their camp near Cottonwood Creek after fleeing *Tepahlewam* at news of the murders and outrages against the whites on the Salmon.

When Brice left the White Bird Creek area with Maggie, he said the house was still standing. Later when the Irish miner was reunited with George Popham in Grangeville, Popham told him the house was burned to the ground. There should have been charred bodies, if not human skeletons, among the ashes as forensic evidence. When two local frontiersmen, Ad Chapman and James Conely, raked through the cinders of the Manuel place, they found some bones—but both men remained convinced the charred bones they discovered belonged to an animal.

But there were those who disagreed with this assessment. Writing a letter to the editor of the Lewiston *Teller* on 19 July, local resident J. W. Poe stated: "It was currently believed that Mrs. Manuel and the child were still alive until I had examined the ruins and found positive evidence to the contrary." On his journey back to his own looted store along the Salmon River after Howard's army marched into the area, H. C. "Hurdy Gurdy" Brown visited the Manuel homestead and declared his certainty that Jennet and little John had perished in the fire. However, historian Jack McDermott could not locate what "evidence" led Poe and Brown to unwaveringly declare both mother and son had died in the flames.

Perhaps it was nothing more conclusive than the jewelry someone unearthed in raking through the ashes of the Manuel home . . . earrings Maggie stated unequivocally that her mother was wearing the day of the attack.

The certainty that mother and son had been killed at their home was further solidified when local trader Harry Cone recorded his reminiscences as one of the settlers who took shelter behind the stockade at Slate Creek (see chapter 46 in *Cries from the Earth*). Cone remembered how one of the Nez Perce horsemen who came to the stockade wall to settle accounts with trader John Wood disclosed to an old

Nez Perce woman, Tolo, who was in the stockade with the whites, how Mrs. Manuel was killed by a fellow warrior under the influence of whiskey: "She [Tolo] began to talk, upbraiding them for killing their friends and hers, and Mrs. Manuel, who, we learned from them, one of them had killed, who was full of bad whiskey."

Yet on 28 July, more than a month later, the Lewiston *Teller* stirred things up anew by announcing: "Squaws still report that Mrs. Manuel is living and a prisoner."

Additionally, here in *Lay the Mountains Low* we told you Henry Buck's story of seeing a blond-haired white woman among a small group of squaws he saw fleeing from the Nez Perce village at the time of Gibbon's attack at the Big Hole. But it wasn't until years later that a settler in the Bitterroot valley finally reported that he had spotted a blond-haired white woman with the Non-Treaty bands as they made their way to the Big Hole.

Two independent, and highly intriguing, sightings far, far from the charred remains of the Manuel house on White Bird Creek.

This story refused to take an entirely straight and uncompromising path, just as much of history itself refuses to do. A hint of something stuck its head up here, a rumor was reported there—and that's the way the mystery rested for almost a quarter of a century.

It wasn't until 1900 that the first Nez Perce account of the raid and abduction was given to a white man. Yellow Bull (who was called Sun Necklace at the time of the war) told his story to C. T. Stranahan—Nez Perce agent at the time—swearing the white man to keep his story secret until after Yellow Bull's death (which did not occur until July of 1919). According to the war chief, Mrs. Manuel was captured and kept a prisoner by an Indian Yellow Bull refused to name. Some time after the Non-Treaty bands had crossed the Lolo Pass into Montana Territory, Yellow Bull continued, her captor and another warrior began to quarrel over the white woman. The bickering escalated until friends had to keep the two apart.

As the village was preparing to march the morning after the heated argument, Yellow Bull and others discovered Mrs. Manuel missing. The war chief told Stranahan he believed she had been killed and her body hidden in the brush, somewhere off the Lolo Trail.

Around this same era on the reservation, one of L.V. McWhorter's informants said that Red Wolf (this is not the same "Josiah" Red Wolf who was but a young child at the time of the Big Hole fight so the Red Wolf referred to might well have been the child's father or an uncle) attempted to abduct Mrs. Manuel from her ranch, riding with her on horseback, "when she snatched the knife from his belt and attempted to kill him. He struck her, felling her to the ground, and she died from the fall."

To that testimony McWhorter adds: "Presumably she was carried back to her home and the house then set afire."

Which, at least to me, is a convenient and blameless way to deflect a certain guilt for the murder—after all, the woman was "threatening" her kidnapper with his own knife—as well as a means to conceal the fact that Mrs. Manuel had started over the Lolo Trail with the Non-Treaty bands. Why are there so many different stories if every one of McWhorter's informants is telling the truth? There are so many attempts to have Jennet Manuel killed in her own home and her body conveniently consumed to ashes so the hunt for her would end.

Including the journalist who rendered a questionable version of Patrick Brice's story in 1911. Charles S. Moody chronicled the miner's experiences in an article for *Century Magazine*, "The Bravest Deed I Ever Knew." Brice carried the wounded Maggie Manuel back to her home, Moody writes, which was "only a heap of smoldering ashes. Among the embers lay the charred body of a woman and her infant. The Indians had taken Mrs. Manuel and her baby back to the house, killed them, and then fired the house."

Trouble is, Brice had testified that when he left the White Bird Canyon the Manuel house had not been destroyed.

It took nearly fourteen years after that before there arose any corroboration for Yellow Bull's account to Nez Perce agent Stranahan. Enter a young Treaty or Christian Indian named Many Wounds, who had taken the white name of Sam Lott. He approached an old warrior, who was embittered by the decades of struggle as he had watched the *Nee-Me-Poo* lose their land to white gold seekers and settlers. *Peopeo Tholekt*, known as Bird Alighting, had survived the many battles the Looking Glass band suffered during the war—a struggle that many of their people considered both their finest hour and their worst calamity.

Arriving at Bird Alighting's poor shack at the appointed hour on the appointed day, Many Wounds decided to begin their discussions by having the old warrior talk about many of the relics and artifacts Bird Alighting had in sight there at his tiny cabin. One of the very first Many Wounds took in hand to ask about was a blond scalp lock.

"Hair of white woman," Bird Alighting explained. "Mrs. Manuel."

He went on to relate how the woman was taken prisoner in the first raids and was subsequently taken with them as they started toward Montana Territory. On the way she took sick and died. The men buried her under some rocks beside the Lolo Trail. Bird Alighting related how Joseph took the woman's scalp after she was dead.

"The hair was beautiful," Bird Alighting explained the chief's motivation.

Years later, Bird Alighting somehow had fallen heir to the blond scalp lock. To Many Wounds he explained how sorry he was, how sorry Joseph himself was, for the woman's capture, her plight, and her death far from loved ones.

Personally, I don't know how much credence to put into the second part of this story, concerning Joseph scalping a dead woman on the Lolo Trail because he wanted to keep her blond locks. With what I know of the band structure at that time, it doesn't seem feasible that Joseph, a leader of the *Wallowa* people, would pass down such an important memento to an unrelated person like Bird Alighting, who was a member of Looking Glass's *Alpowai* band—especially when they were living apart on different reservations (remember, Joseph never was allowed to return to his homeland, living out his final days at the Colville agency). Perhaps that second part represents a little embellishment, while the kernel of the story remains intact and truthful.

A year after the Nez Perce War, Duncan McDonald undertook a journey to visit White Bird and those Nez Perce who made it across the Canadian border at the time of the Bear's Paw fight. A half-breed (McDonald's mother was Nez Perce and his father a factor with the Hudson's Bay Company), he served as the agency trader for the Flathead tribe at Jocko. He wrote a series of articles that appeared in the Deer Lodge, Montana, newspaper, the *New North-West*, adding a colorful dimension to the entire story on the outbreak and war, including this confusing and controversial subject of Mrs. Manuel's disappearance.

McDonald muddied the waters about Joseph in specific, and this incident in general, even more than they already were when he wrote:

> It seems that at the earliest commencement of the Nez Perces war there were two white women murdered. One of them was murdered by an Indian who was drunk. The other white woman was burned in a house with her child. When her husband and others were murdered by the Nez Perces, she went upstairs. The Indians say they did not see her at the time of killing the men. When the Indians got possession of the house, Joseph, Jr. was present. He was sitting at one side of the place smoking his pipe. He was asked by the warriors what should be done—whether they should set fire to the house or leave without destroying it. All this time the woman and child were upstairs, but the Indians say they did not know it. Young Joseph answered, "You have done worse deeds than burning a house. You never asked our chiefs what was best to be done. You have murdered many men and not

asked advice of your chiefs. You can do as you please about the house."

Some of the young men lit a match and set fire to the building. They then went back a little and sat down to watch it burn. They were suddenly startled by the piercing screams of a woman in the second story of the house. Young Joseph ordered them to put out the fire. The young Indians ran down to the water, filled their hats, threw it on the flames, and tried every way they knew to extinguish the fire and to save the woman. But it was too late. She and her child perished.

The same young warriors who were with Joseph, Jr., at the time told me that when he left the place, Joseph held down his head for a long time and, at last looking up, he said they had done very wrong in burning the woman, that he was very sorry, that he had believed the house empty.

The burning of this poor, harmless woman looks very bad for the Indian side. Still there is some blame should attach to the white man. The white man does wrong in allowing the Indian to have whiskey. It is easy to reply that the Indians take the whiskey away from them by force, but there are many whites who are ready to sell whiskey to them in time of Indian Wars.

Both Duncan McDonald and L. V. McWhorter lived in and wrote about the final days of an intensely racist era in the American West. Since we know of their passionate support of the Nez Perce, is it reasonable to assume that they would do everything in their power to deflect blame from the raiders and murderers, but to place it instead on the white victims? Blaming them for bringing on themselves their own brutal deaths?

Neither George Popham (Jennet's father) nor Patrick Brice was a witness to what happened to Mrs. Manuel, so they can't be considered as anything resembling reliable witnesses. Nor was her husband, John, who had been left for dead out by the White Bird Road as told in *Cries from the Earth*; then we learned he had miraculously survived here in *Lay the Mountains Low*. John Manuel rarely, if ever, made any statements about the disappearance of his wife and son—but on one of the few occasions he ever talked about the tragedy, Manuel only said his family had been captured by the Nez Perce and "doubtless killed as they were never found afterwards."

As Jack McDermott sees it, John Manuel clearly harbored his own doubts about Maggie's and George Popham's cremation theory.

Friends and associates of the family throughout central Idaho refused to question Maggie's version of the story or her integrity. Everyone who ever talked to the child came away asserting, at the very least, that Maggie believed her own tale. Years later, some historians even purported that the girl must have suffered some traumatic hallucination—a reasonable assumption given the fact that she was a very young and impressionable child at the time of the brutal attack and had witnessed the killing of "Ol' man" James Baker, the murder of her father, and the long hours of terror that followed, culminating in what she claimed was Joseph's murder of her mother and brother before the warriors set fire to the house in an attempt to destroy evidence of their dastardly crime.

But . . . maybe there's a way to reconcile Maggie's account that does not rely on having to ignore her testimony or call her account a "post-traumatic stress" hallucination.

Clearly, Maggie saw some Nez Perce leader take a hand in the abduction of her mother. The fact that Joseph was the best known of the leaders in that locality and at that time must have played a major role in her testifying that Joseph was the murderer. Makes sense to me that a six- or seven-year-old girl could make such a claim and continue to believe it down to her dying day in Butte, Montana.

And perhaps she did actually see that Indian leader "stab" her mother and brother. Or perhaps the truth is as I chose to write it: that they were clubbed and dragged off, because Patrick Brice never saw the bodies, nor did he see the "pool of blood" Maggie claimed her mother and brother were lying in. The flow of Maggie's events is murky, but the truth may well be that the warrior who wanted Jennet Manuel for his own may have slashed her in a struggle over the infant she clutched in her arms. Then to subdue her, he or another of the attackers clubbed her over the head, as well as he or another warrior clubbing the child.

Here's where Maggie's story gets really muddied. It's entirely possible the drunken warriors left Jennet and baby John lying in a puddle of blood on the floor and departed, thinking them dead, when Maggie chanced to discover the bodies in the silent house—taking them for dead. As for me, I have a pretty good idea that Maggie found her baby brother in a pool of blood, but not her mother. Maggie concocted that part of the story.

Why kill one and not the other? Because the war chief wanted only Jennet Manuel and had killed the infant child so that she would not be dragging him along and tending to his needs. There are cases known to Western historians of such infanticides occurring during the Indian wars on the central and southern plains. White woman captured, her infant child has its brains dashed against the trunk of a nearby tree . . .

Perhaps some hours later when a little of the mind-numbing whiskey began to wear off, the raiding party returned for either or both of two purposes. First, to see about acquiring more whiskey. L.V. McWhorter, like many of the apologists, was well ahead of his time with what I will call "blame deflection." It's always good for someone who can't take personal responsibility for himself to blame his divorced parents, an alcoholic father, sexual abuse, or absentee parents. In the case of these first raids on the Salmon and Camas Prairie, McWhorter points his finger of blame not at the thugs and criminals who committed the murder and mayhem, rape and arson . . . but at the white man and his terrible whiskey!

> It is only fair to the Indians to call attention to the fact that the outrages against women and children did not oc-

cur until after the raiders became beastly drunk on whiskey found by the barrel at Benedict's store-saloon located on the lower reaches of White Bird Creek. That atrocities were committed by a few of the young Nez Perces, no one pretends to deny. But whiskey was at the bottom of all of them.

Or perhaps the raiding party returned for a second reason: As the murderer brooded long and hard on what he had done, perhaps he decided his best course would be to destroy the evidence of his crimes of kidnapping and murder. To his way of thinking, if he burned down the Manuel house, with the child's body therein, then the white man would think that both mother and child were burned—eliminating any need for the whites to pursue the war party to get the captive woman back.

I'm of the opinion that the whites at the Slate Creek stockade were told Jennet was dead because the Nez Perce warriors did not want the white men to know she was still alive and in the possession of one of their petty war chiefs. What Harry Cone and others heard doesn't serve as a discrepancy. I think it serves to prove that Jennet Manuel was still alive at the time.

And the presence of those earrings found among the ashes of the house is the flimsiest of circumstantial evidence. After all the time that had elapsed, and after what might have been the first stripping and rape of Mrs. Manuel there and then in her own house, the discovery of those earrings in the house proved one thing only—that some searcher found earrings belonging to Jennet Manuel in the ashes of the house where Jennet Manuel used to live. Nothing more.

When all is said and done, I believe that baby John was dead the night of 15 June. It was his bones discovered in the ashes by Ad Chapman and James Conely. Bones they said were those of an animal. Why would they say that? Because they were too small to be Jennet's? Could the bones have been those of baby John? But why weren't there enough bones found together for a savvy frontiersman to realize he was looking at a human skeleton?

And what of the stories left by Bird Alighting and Yellow Bull telling how Mrs. Manuel started the trip over the Lolo Trail with the Non-Treaty bands but either was killed in some sort of rage (according to Yellow Bull) or died of sickness, perhaps of exposure (according to *Peopeo Tholekt*)? It's hard to believe that either of them would have reason to lie at such a late date, what with the many years that had elapsed, not to mention that each man knew he was nearing the end of his life. I can't believe either man had anything to gain by concocting a bald-faced lie that many years after the crime. Especially after so many sources, down through the intervening years, had done their level best to convince journalists and writers that Jennet Manuel had died in her own house, where her body was consumed by the flames of revenge.

As I sit here on the hillside above the Big Hole Battlefield this cold, cold dawn in May of 1999, I ask myself again: Why am I so consumed by this mystery? Is it only because I sit here in the remnants of last night's crusty snow, staring down on the cones of skeletal lodgepoles erected where the Non-Treaty village once stood, thinking of that young blond-haired white woman Henry Buck glimpsed for two fleeting instants as she fled the pandemonium and terror in the camp, protectively surrounded by other squaws? If it was Jennet Manuel, and she did turn to look directly at the white civilian—why in hell didn't she cry out to him, yell something, anything, to beg for help?

Could it be that she had long ago decided she was already dead? Jennet had seen her husband fall from his horse, her young daughter, too. Although she would have known Maggie was going to survive her wounds, Jennet had to believe her husband dead. Then the young mother had watched the murder of her son, perhaps even witnessing the first flames starting their destruction of her home. After unimaginable abuse at the hands of some unnamed petty chief, could it be that Jennet believed nothing would ever be the same again, that she could never return home, that she was . . . as good as dead already?

Where did she go after the Big Hole? I brood on that simple mystery this subfreezing morning as the wind picks up and the sun finally emerges, briefly bubbling into that narrow ribbon of sky between the far mountains and the low gray hulking clouds that betray the reputation of this Big Sky Country.

There never was another report of the mysterious blond-haired woman spotted with the Non-Treaty bands. Did she live to make it to the Camas Meadow fight? And did she last out their perilous passage through Yellowstone National Park? The Canyon Creek fight? Cow Island? . . . And was Jennet Manuel still with the *Nee-Me-Poo* when they reached the cold, windswept hills at the foot of the Bears Paw Mountains when both a winter storm and Miles's Fifth Infantry caught them just short of the Medicine Line and the sanctuary of the Old Woman's Country?

Was Jennet Manuel still alive then?

Blood always answers blood.

This battlefield is like a lonely, hollow hole in the heart of the earth, especially now as I remember that all-too-quiet cemetery on a shady hillside back at Mount Idaho where stands a tall marble headstone erected for Jennet Manuel. I remember how I paused there, gazing down at that patch of ground, knowing hers was an empty grave . . . this silent haven adorned with a simple, beautiful piece of marble. If her body could not be laid to eternal rest, then I figure some of this war's survivors sought to put Jennet's soul at peace.

In a very real sense this morning, I feel a palpable connection between these two places—both sites are cemeteries. In both I sense the death of some innocence. You only have to walk among the tombstones and marble markers at the Mount Idaho cemetery to realize this was not a war between fighting men. In both places—the quiet cemetery and here at the hallowed Big Hole—lie the innocents: the women and children who gave a lie to the belief that this was a war between soldiers and warriors.

Right from the outbreak on the Salmon River, and on into Montana Territory, this was a dirty war that recognized no gender, nor youth.

The wind comes up as the sun disappears behind the low clouds, and I feel even colder than before. In chasing down the Nez Perce, Sherman and Sheridan once more had their "total war."

But blood will always demand more blood.

The great and deep wound Gibbon's men inflicted at this place of tears will now be answered in a frenzy of murder, an orgy of senseless killing that will mark with shame the return of the *Nee-Me-Poo* to Idaho and their migration through Yellowstone Park—pausing only when they discover that their old friends the Crow won't join them in a war against the soldiers.

I wipe the moisture from my eyes and stand, hoping I have what it will take to finish this sad story many months and many, many miles from here among the cold hills at the Bear's Paw. Blood always answers blood.

It has always been that way. I doubt anything man can ever do will change that.

Blood cries out for blood.

Terry C. Johnston
Big Hole National Battlefield
13 May 1999

About the Author

TERRY C. JOHNSTON was born on the first day of 1947 on the plains of Kansas and has lived all his life in the American West. His first novel, *Carry the Wind*, won the Medicine Pipe Bearer's Award from the Western Writers of America, and his subsequent books have appeared on best-seller lists throughout the country.